THE RING OF THE SEVEN WORLDS

GUALDONI
CLIMA
PIANA
& TUROTTI

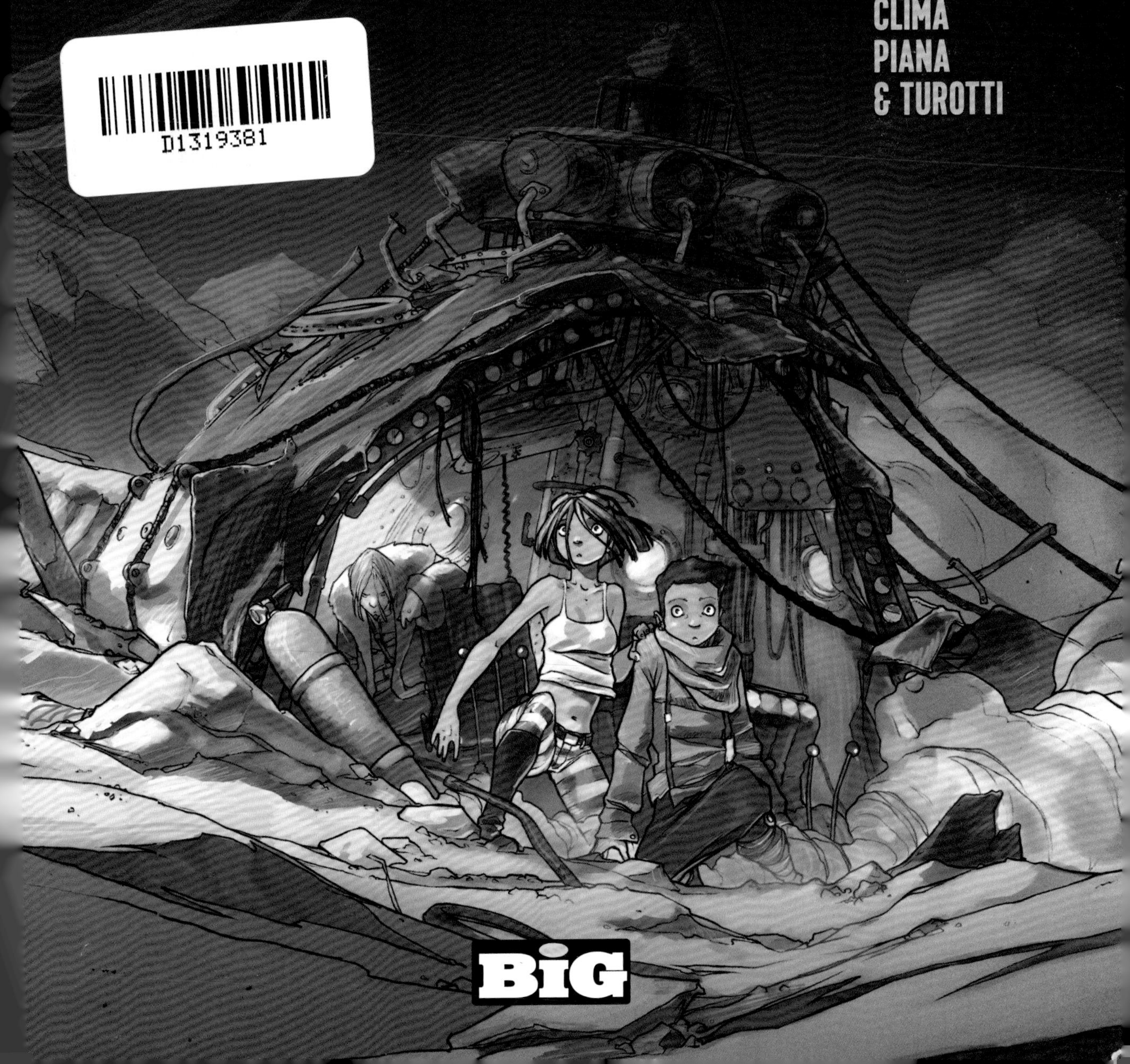

BiG

GIOVANNI GUALDONI & **GABRIELE CLIMA**
Writers

MATTEO PIANA
Artist

DAVIDE TUROTTI
Color Artist

•

BLASE A. PROVITOLA
Translator

•

ALEX DONOGHUE & **FABRICE SAPOLSKY**
US Edition Editors

AMANDA LUCIDO
Assistant Editor

MAXIMILIEN CHAILLEUX
Original Edition Editor

JERRY FRISSEN
Senior Art Director

FABRICE GIGER
Publisher

Rights and Licensing - licensing@humanoids.com
Press and Social Media - pr@humanoids.com

THE RING OF THE SEVEN WORLDS
This title is a publication of Humanoids, Inc. 8033 Sunset Blvd. #628, Los Angeles, CA 90046.
Copyright © 2016, 2019 Humanoids, Inc., Los Angeles (USA). All rights reserved.
Humanoids and its logos are ® and © 2019 Humanoids, Inc.

Library of Congress Control Number: 2018954844

BiG is an imprint of Humanoids, Inc.

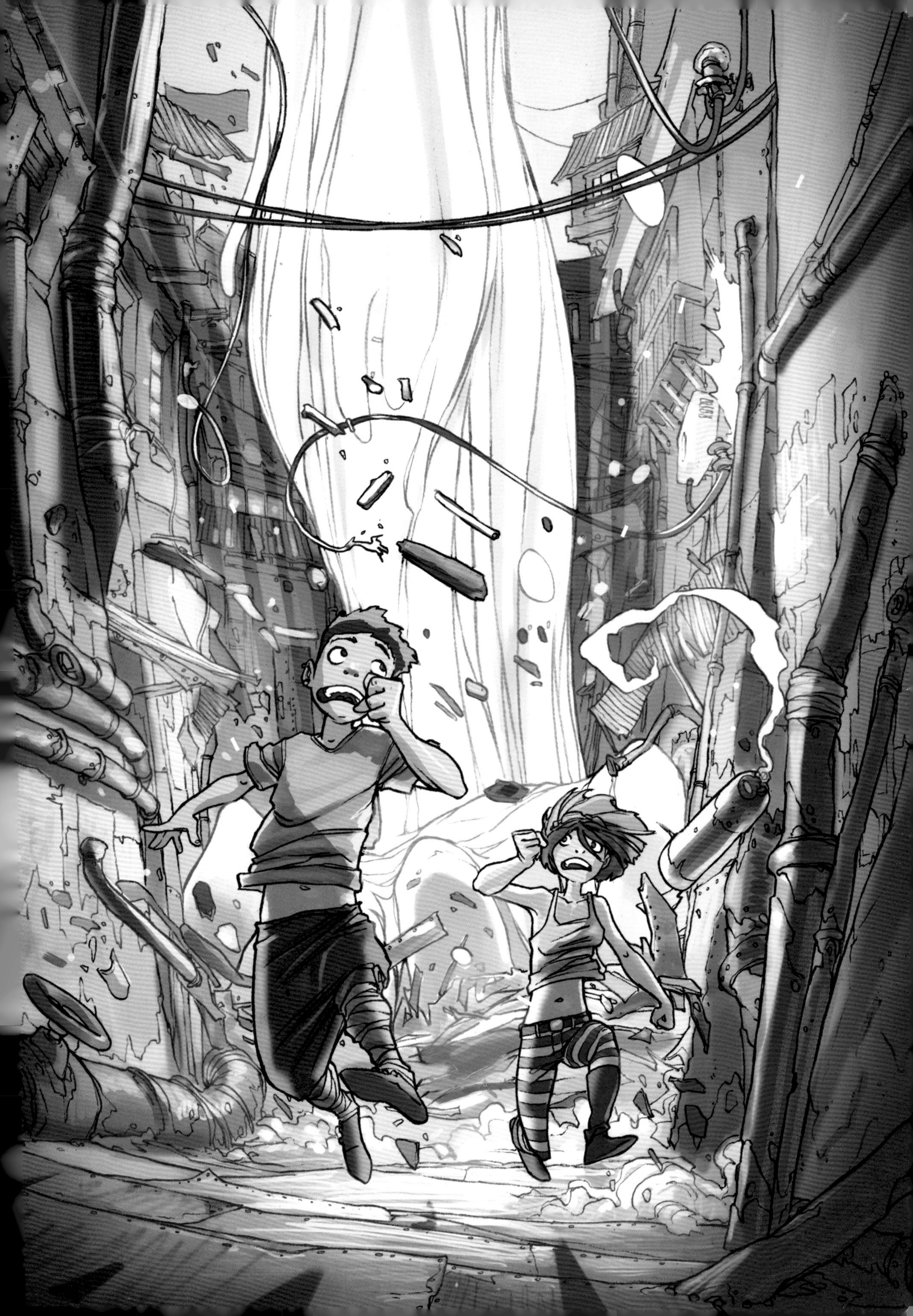

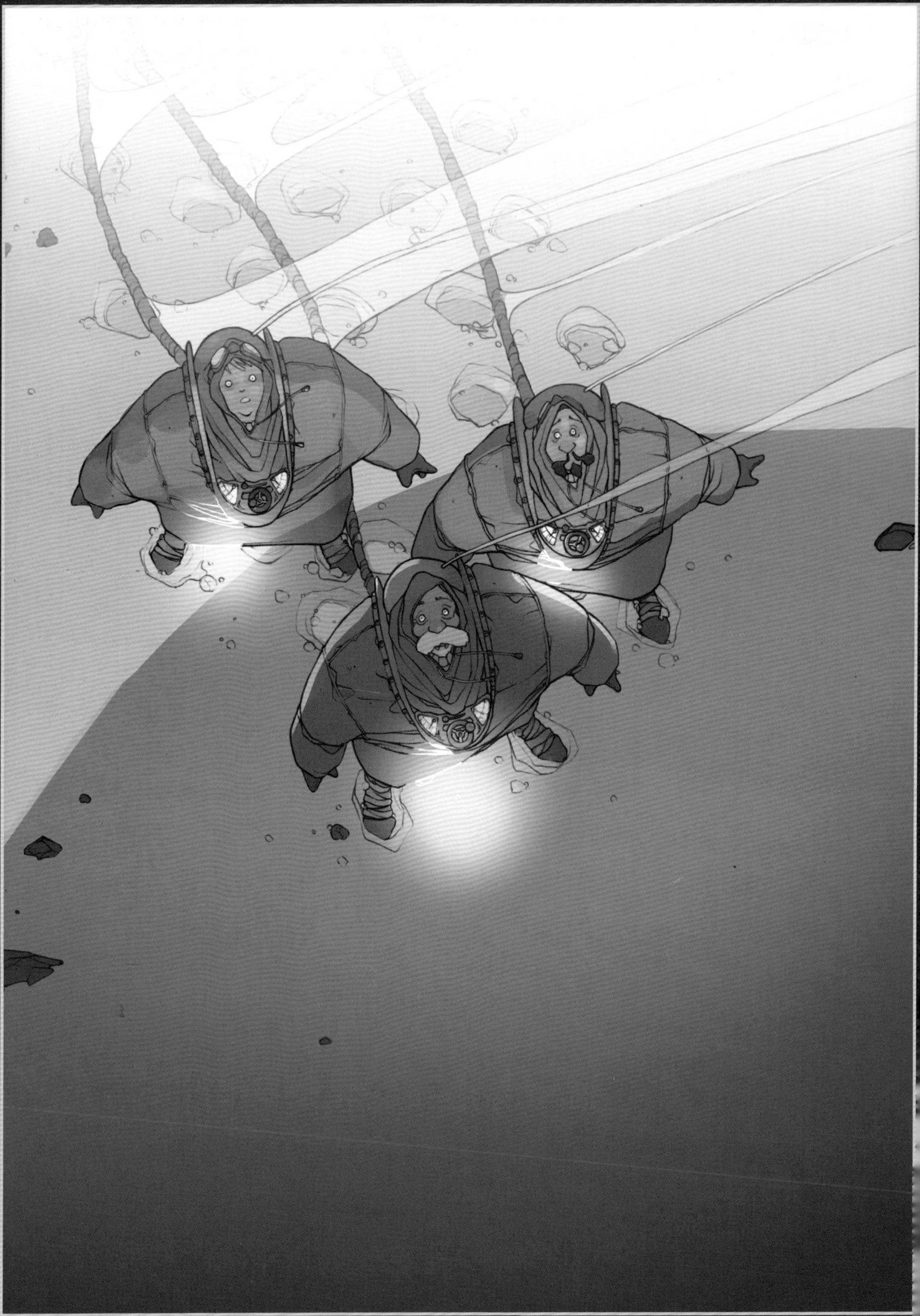

MOSE IS THE FIRST OF THE SEVEN PLANETS WHICH FORM THE EMPIRE OF THE SEVEN WORLDS.

SEVEN LANDS CONNECTED TO EACH OTHER THROUGH SEVEN RING-SHAPED DIMENSIONAL DOORS, A MASTERPIECE OF LONG-FORGOTTEN TECHNOLOGY.

THE SKY ABOVE THE SOUTH POLE OF MOSE IS NOW DARK. LONG AGO, IT WAS ILLUMINATED BY THE LIGHTS OF GREAT AIRSHIPS PREPARED FOR COMBAT.

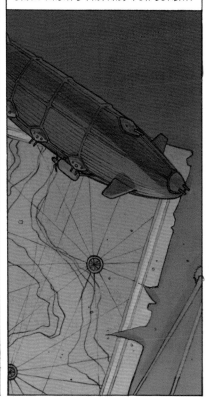

THE WAR WITH THE WORLD OF NEMO WAS SUPPOSED TO PREVENT THE DEMONS FROM THE LAST OF THE SEVEN WORLDS FROM INVADING THE REST OF THE EMPIRE. THREE CENTURIES AGO, VICTORY RESULTED IN THE DESTRUCTION OF THE RING OF THE SOUTH POLE. THE INVADERS WERE LEFT TO LIVE IN THEIR OWN HELL, CUT OFF FROM THE OTHER WORLDS. FOR MOSE, IT PROMISED PROTECTION AGAINST ANY FUTURE RISK OF INVASION...

...OR SO WE THOUGHT.

BE QUIET! I'M TELLING YOU, I SAW SOMETHING IN THE MIDDLE OF THE RING!

YOU'RE IMAGINING THINGS, ENO! THERE'S NOTHING HERE BUT US.

SERICKO'S RIGHT, TRY TO CALM DOWN! IT'S ONLY TWO WEEKS BEFORE THE CHANGING OF THE GUARD, AND--

NO, I WON'T CALM DOWN! I KNOW WHAT I SAW: *SOMETHING* IS MOVING INSIDE THE RING! YOU *HAVE* TO BELIEVE ME!

...

WHAT I *CAN'T* BELIEVE IS THAT YOU MANAGED TO DRAG US ALL THE WAY OUT HERE!

TAKE A LOOK FOR YOURSELF THEN!

...THERE'S ABSOLUTELY NOTHING THERE TO SEE! NOW *PLEASE*, ENO, LET'S GET BACK INSIDE!

I *SWEAR* I SAW TWO HUGE, ODDLY-SHAPED OBJECTS HEADED STRAIGHT FOR THE OUTPOST!

COME ON, ENO! IT'S JUST THE COLD, AND ALL THE CREEPY STORIES ABOUT THIS PLACE THAT ARE GETTING TO YOUR HEAD!

YOU'LL SEE, A NICE HOT SHOWER AND A BOWL OF SOUP AND YOU'LL BE FEELING BETTER IN NO TI--

!!!

VRRRRRRRRRRRRRRRRRRR

6

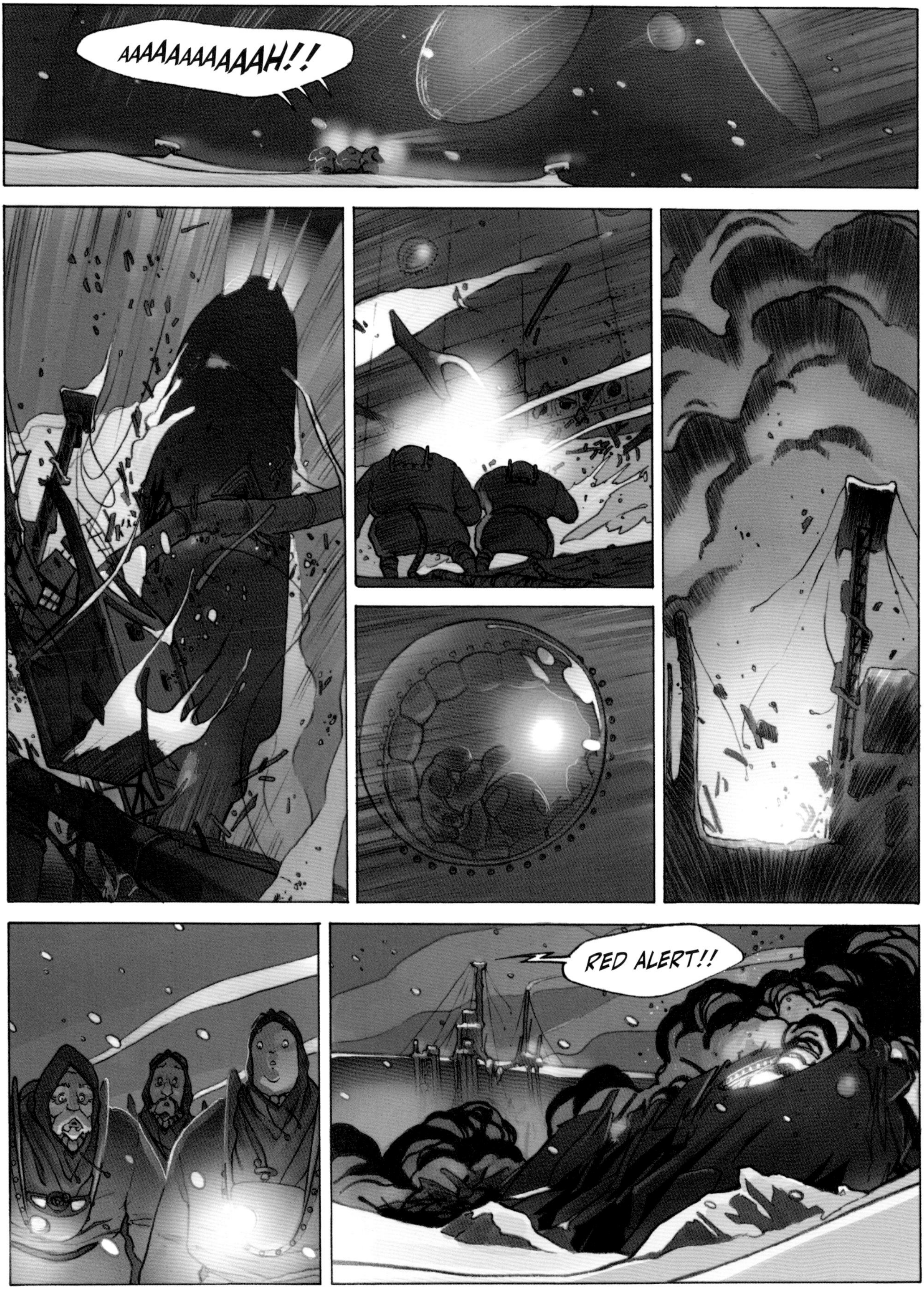
AAAAAAAAAAAH!!
RED ALERT!!

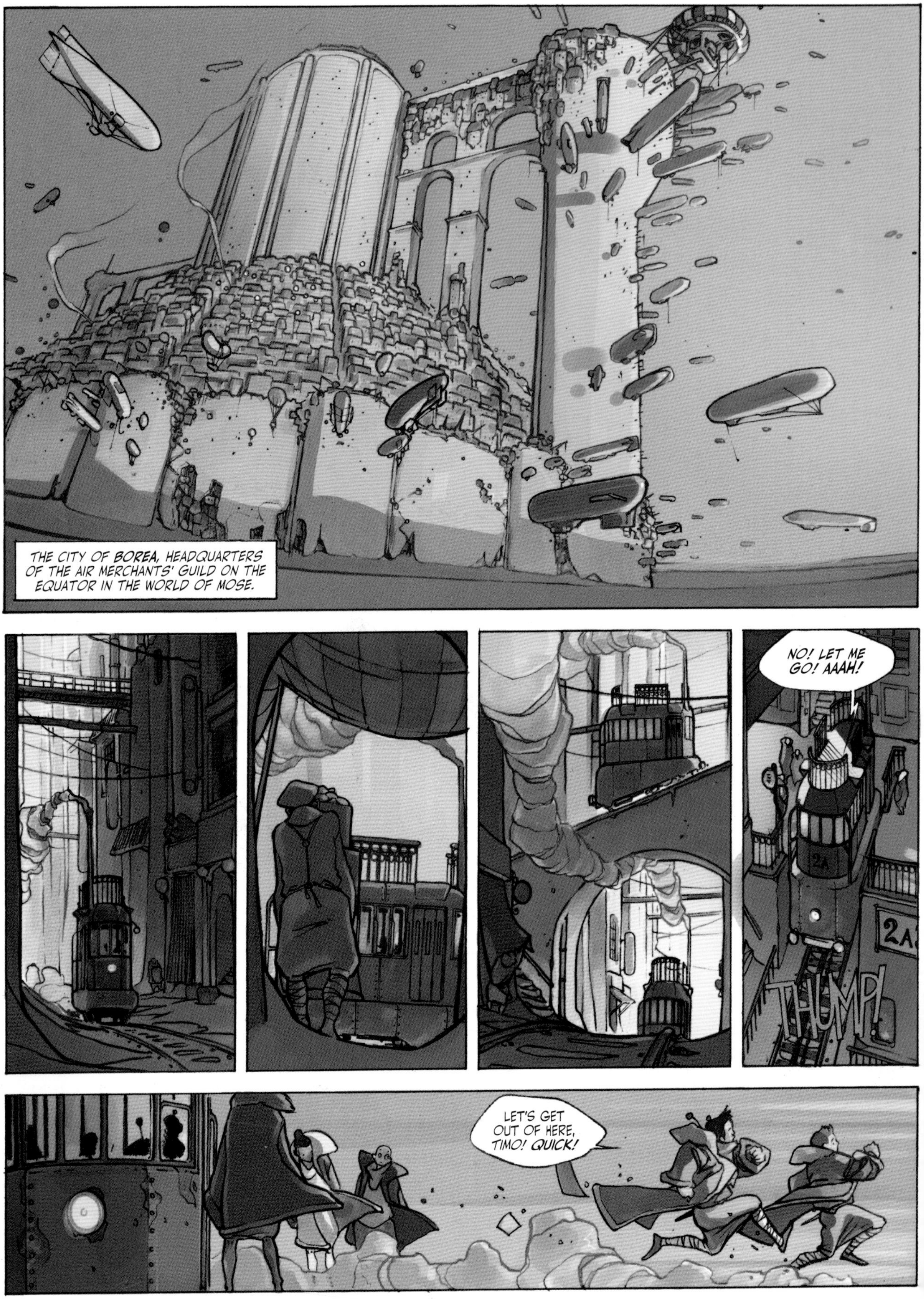
THE CITY OF BOREA, HEADQUARTERS OF THE AIR MERCHANTS' GUILD ON THE EQUATOR IN THE WORLD OF MOSE.
NO! LET ME GO! AAAH!
2A
THUMP!
LET'S GET OUT OF HERE, TIMO! QUICK!

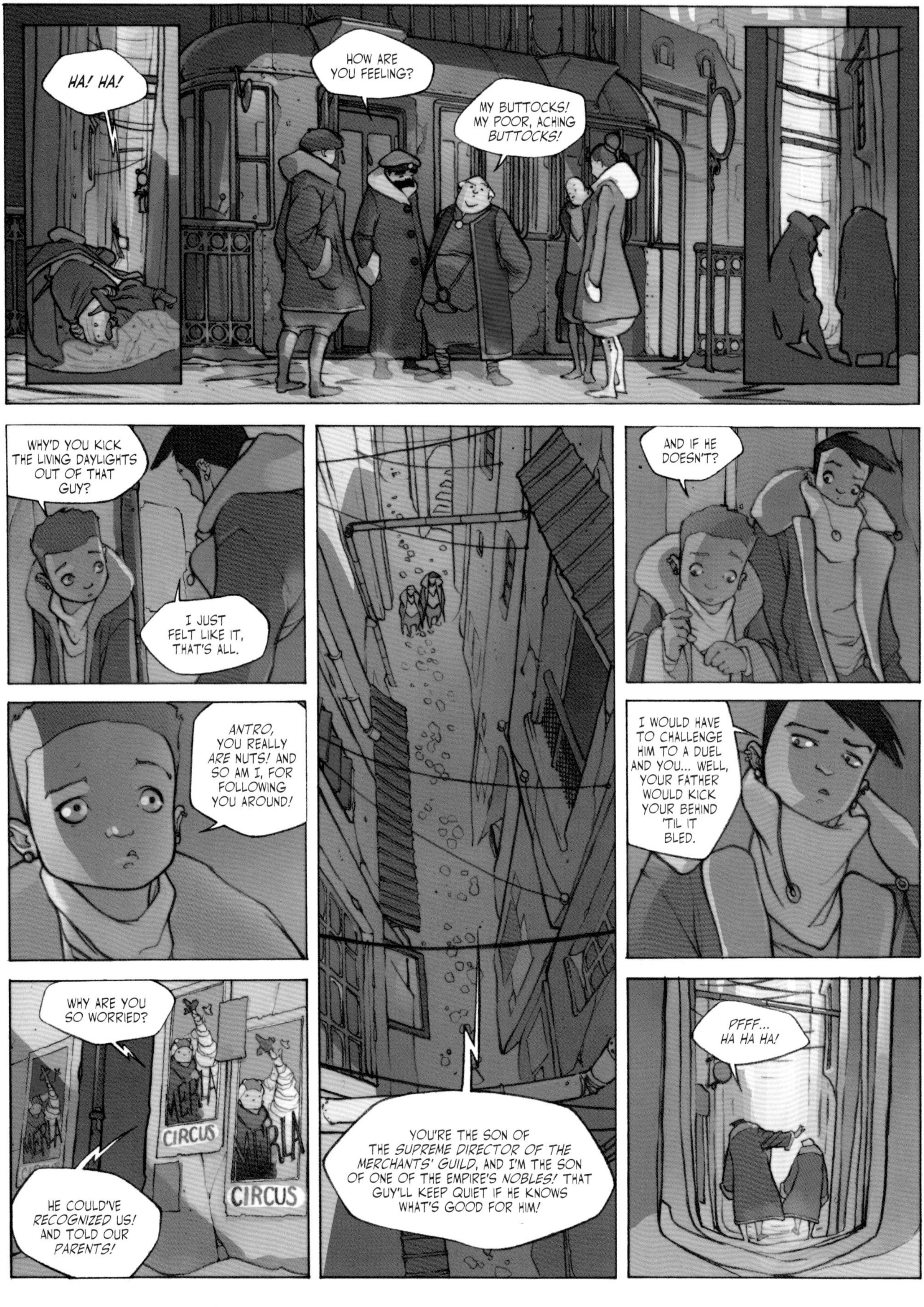
HA! HA!
HOW ARE YOU FEELING?
MY BUTTOCKS! MY POOR, ACHING *BUTTOCKS!*
WHY'D YOU KICK THE LIVING DAYLIGHTS OUT OF THAT GUY?
I JUST FELT LIKE IT, THAT'S ALL.
ANTRO, YOU REALLY ARE NUTS! AND SO AM I, FOR FOLLOWING YOU AROUND!
WHY ARE YOU SO WORRIED?
MERLA
CIRCUS
MERLA
CIRCUS
HE COULD'VE *RECOGNIZED* US! AND TOLD OUR *PARENTS!*
YOU'RE THE SON OF THE *SUPREME DIRECTOR OF THE MERCHANTS' GUILD*, AND I'M THE SON OF ONE OF THE EMPIRE'S *NOBLES!* THAT GUY'LL KEEP QUIET IF HE KNOWS WHAT'S GOOD FOR HIM!
AND IF HE DOESN'T?
I WOULD HAVE TO CHALLENGE HIM TO A DUEL AND YOU... WELL, YOUR FATHER WOULD KICK YOUR BEHIND 'TIL IT BLED.
PFFF... HA HA HA!

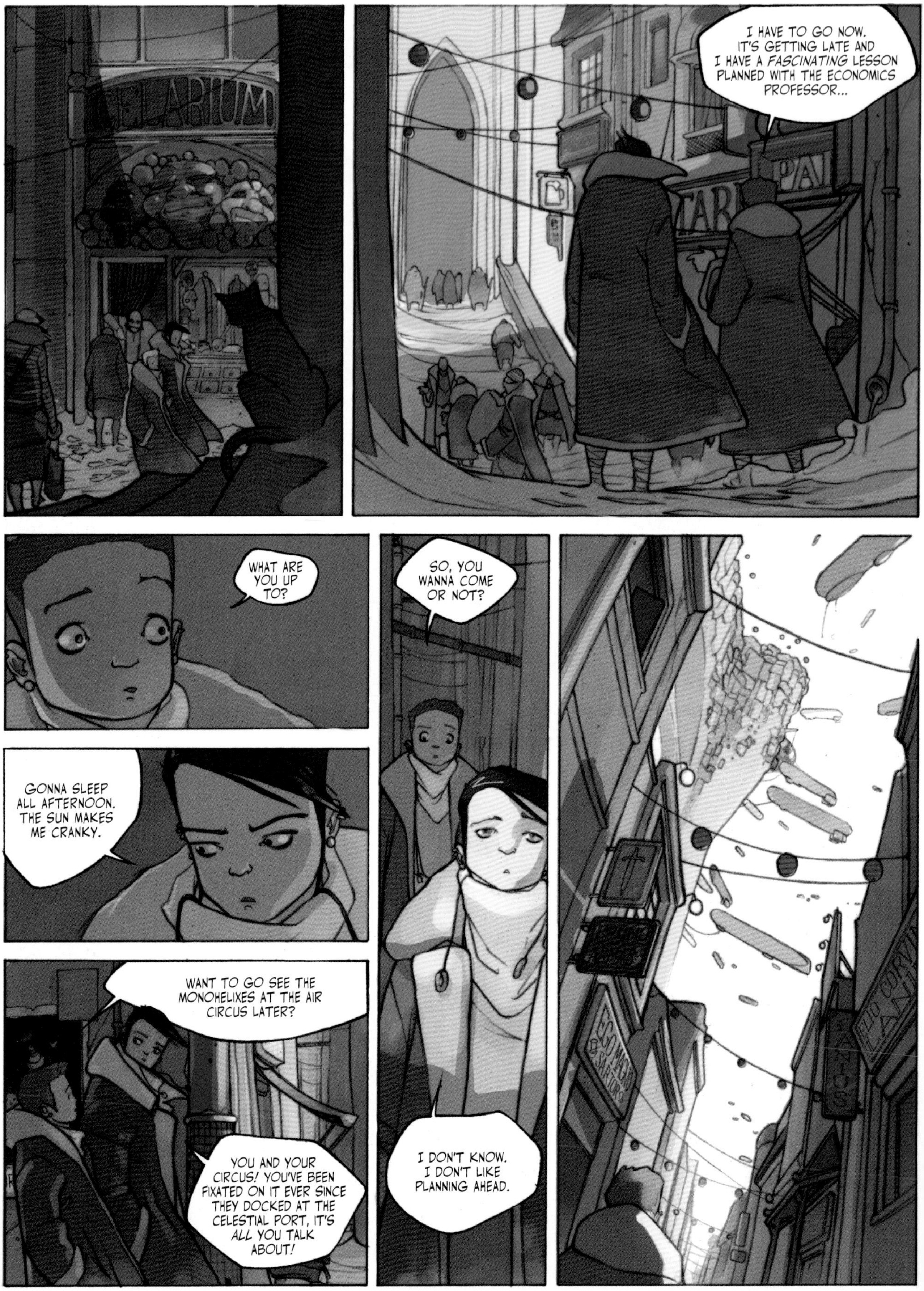

GELARIUM
I HAVE TO GO NOW. IT'S GETTING LATE AND I HAVE A *FASCINATING* LESSON PLANNED WITH THE ECONOMICS PROFESSOR...
WHAT ARE YOU UP TO?
GONNA SLEEP ALL AFTERNOON. THE SUN MAKES ME CRANKY.
WANT TO GO SEE THE MONOHELIXES AT THE AIR CIRCUS LATER?
YOU AND YOUR CIRCUS! YOU'VE BEEN FIXATED ON IT EVER SINCE THEY DOCKED AT THE CELESTIAL PORT, IT'S *ALL* YOU TALK ABOUT!
SO, YOU WANNA COME OR NOT?
I DON'T KNOW. I DON'T LIKE PLANNING AHEAD.

HMMPFF!

MUGO?!

ARE YOU IN LOVE, LUCE?

ARE YOU *STUPID* OR SOMETHING? WHAT KIND OF QUESTION IS *THAT*?

LEO SAYS THAT WHEN A GIRL STARES INTO SPACE AND SIGHS IT MEANS SHE'S IN LOVE.

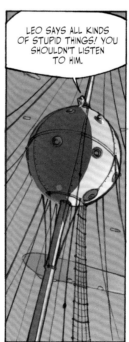

LEO SAYS ALL KINDS OF STUPID THINGS! YOU SHOULDN'T LISTEN TO HIM.

AND BESIDES, I WASN'T STARING INTO SPACE.

THERE'S NOTHIN' OVER THERE. NOTHIN' BUT ANOTHER CITY, SAME AS ALL THE OTHERS.

MAYBE ALL THE CITIES ONLY LOOK THE SAME TO US BECAUSE WE SEE THEM FROM SO FAR AWAY.

LEO SAID THAT *ALL* CITIES ARE THE SAME: NOT ENOUGH AIR, TOO MUCH SAND, AND NOBODY SMILING.

LEO ONLY WENT DOWN TO LAND *ONCE*, AND EVEN THEN IT WAS ONLY BECAUSE HE *FELL!*

STILL, THAT'S ONCE MORE THAN EITHER OF US. HE'S THE ONE WHO SENT ME TO FIND YOU BY THE WAY. HE SAID THAT, IF YOU WANT, YOU CAN START YOUR EXERCISES EARLIER TODAY.

NOW YOU TELL ME!

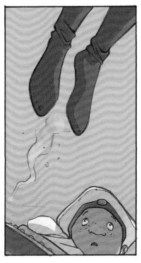

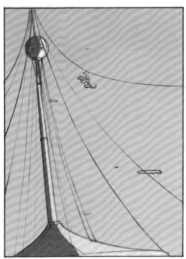

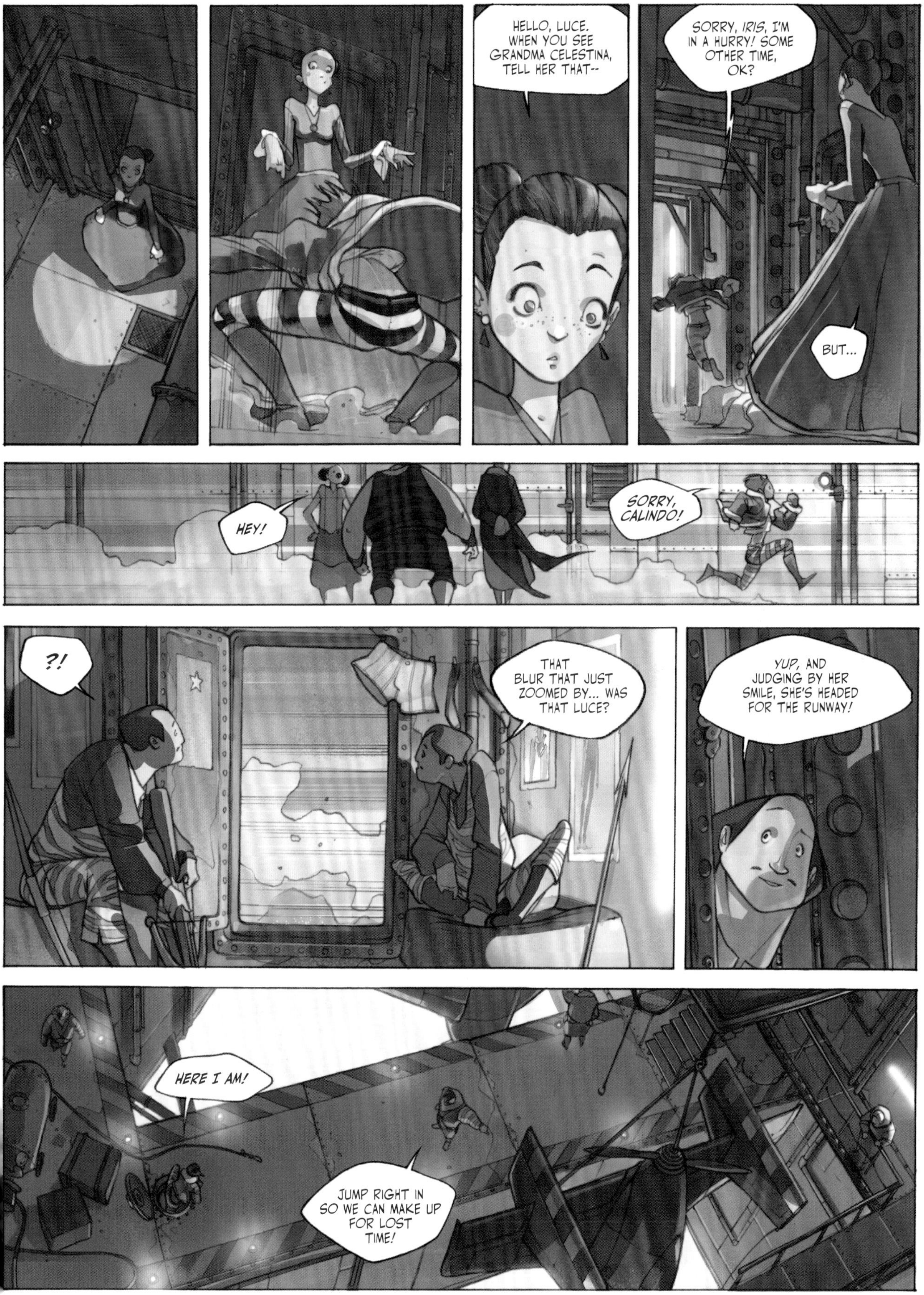
HELLO, LUCE. WHEN YOU SEE GRANDMA CELESTINA, TELL HER THAT--
SORRY, *IRIS*, I'M IN A HURRY! SOME OTHER TIME, OK?
BUT...
HEY!
SORRY, CALINDO!
?!
THAT BLUR THAT JUST ZOOMED BY... WAS THAT LUCE?
YUP, AND JUDGING BY HER SMILE, SHE'S HEADED FOR THE RUNWAY!
HERE I AM!
JUMP RIGHT IN SO WE CAN MAKE UP FOR LOST TIME!

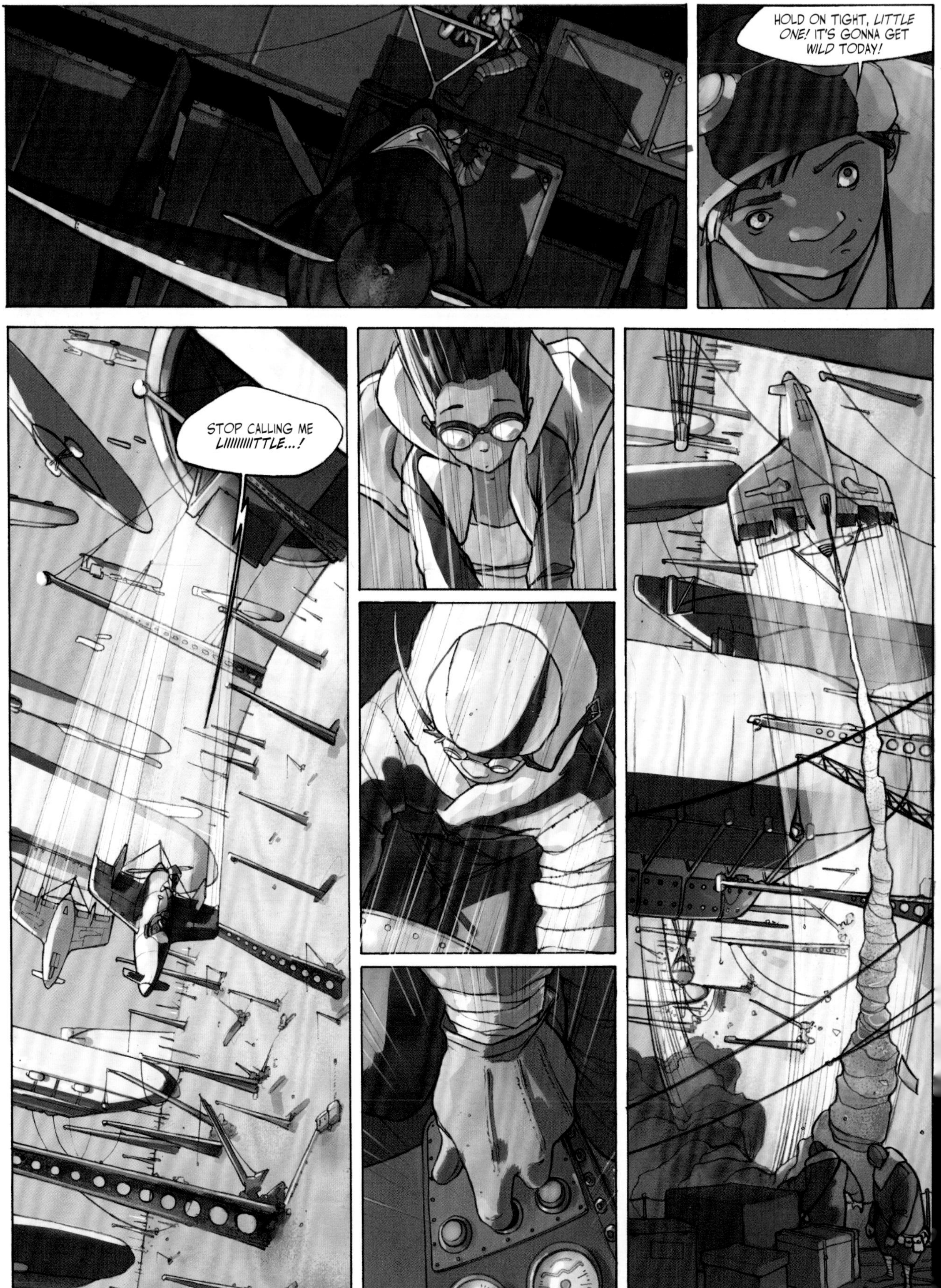
HOLD ON TIGHT, *LITTLE ONE!* IT'S GONNA GET *WILD* TODAY!
STOP CALLING ME *LIIIIIIIITTLE...!*

MR. SUPREME DIRECTOR?

EXCUSE ME, GENTLEMEN, I WAS JUST LOOKING AT THOSE MONOHELIXES. MY SON IS CRAZY ABOUT THEM... WHERE WERE WE?

I BELIEVE, MR. SUPREME DIRECTOR, THAT YOU WERE ABOUT TO DISCUSS YOUR RECENT DECISIONS WITH MR. PIROPA AND ME.

THAT'S RIGHT, LEPONTE. I'VE THOUGHT LONG AND HARD ABOUT YOUR INQUIRY, AND I'VE COME TO THE CONCLUSION...

...THAT IT WOULD BE VAIN AND IMPRUDENT TO DISMISS THE IMPORTANCE OF THE RUMORS SPREADING AMONGST OUR COMMANDERS. I AM THEREFORE AUTHORIZING YOU TO GO TO THE CAPITAL.

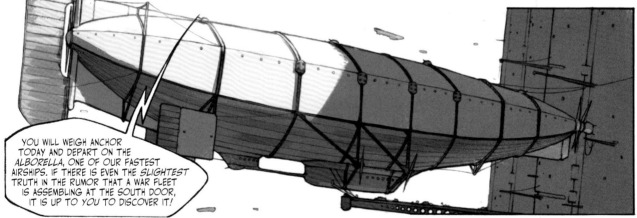

YOU WILL WEIGH ANCHOR TODAY AND DEPART ON THE *ALBORELLA,* ONE OF OUR FASTEST AIRSHIPS. IF THERE IS EVEN THE *SLIGHTEST* TRUTH IN THE RUMOR THAT A WAR FLEET IS ASSEMBLING AT THE SOUTH DOOR, IT IS UP TO *YOU* TO DISCOVER IT!

REST ASSURED THAT I SHALL FULLY DEVOTE MY SCIENTIFIC CAPABILITIES TO THE COURT'S SERVICE, MR. SUPREME DIRECTOR!

AS ALWAYS, YOU HAVE MADE A WISE DECISION, MR. SUPREME DIRECTOR. A *VERY WISE* DECISION!

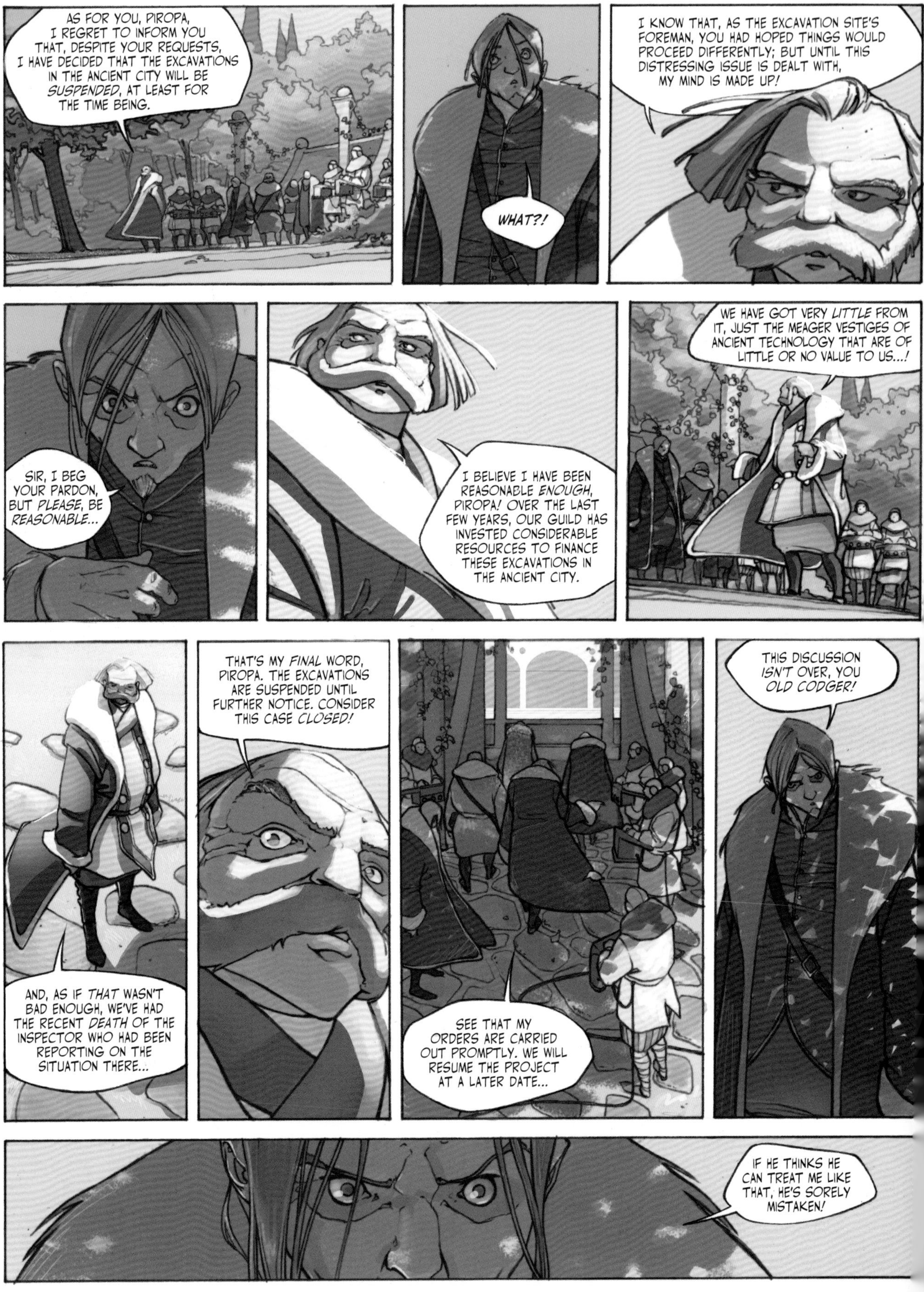
AS FOR YOU, PIROPA, I REGRET TO INFORM YOU THAT, DESPITE YOUR REQUESTS, I HAVE DECIDED THAT THE EXCAVATIONS IN THE ANCIENT CITY WILL BE *SUSPENDED*, AT LEAST FOR THE TIME BEING.
WHAT?!
I KNOW THAT, AS THE EXCAVATION SITE'S FOREMAN, YOU HAD HOPED THINGS WOULD PROCEED DIFFERENTLY; BUT UNTIL THIS DISTRESSING ISSUE IS DEALT WITH, MY MIND IS MADE UP!
SIR, I BEG YOUR PARDON, BUT *PLEASE*, BE *REASONABLE*...
I BELIEVE I HAVE BEEN REASONABLE *ENOUGH*, PIROPA! OVER THE LAST FEW YEARS, OUR GUILD HAS INVESTED CONSIDERABLE RESOURCES TO FINANCE THESE EXCAVATIONS IN THE ANCIENT CITY.
WE HAVE GOT VERY *LITTLE* FROM IT, JUST THE MEAGER VESTIGES OF ANCIENT TECHNOLOGY THAT ARE OF LITTLE OR NO VALUE TO US...!
AND, AS IF *THAT* WASN'T BAD ENOUGH, WE'VE HAD THE RECENT *DEATH* OF THE INSPECTOR WHO HAD BEEN REPORTING ON THE SITUATION THERE...
THAT'S MY *FINAL* WORD, PIROPA. THE EXCAVATIONS ARE SUSPENDED UNTIL FURTHER NOTICE. CONSIDER THIS CASE *CLOSED!*
SEE THAT MY ORDERS ARE CARRIED OUT PROMPTLY. WE WILL RESUME THE PROJECT AT A LATER DATE...
THIS DISCUSSION *ISN'T* OVER, YOU *OLD CODGER!*
IF HE THINKS HE CAN TREAT ME LIKE THAT, HE'S SORELY MISTAKEN!

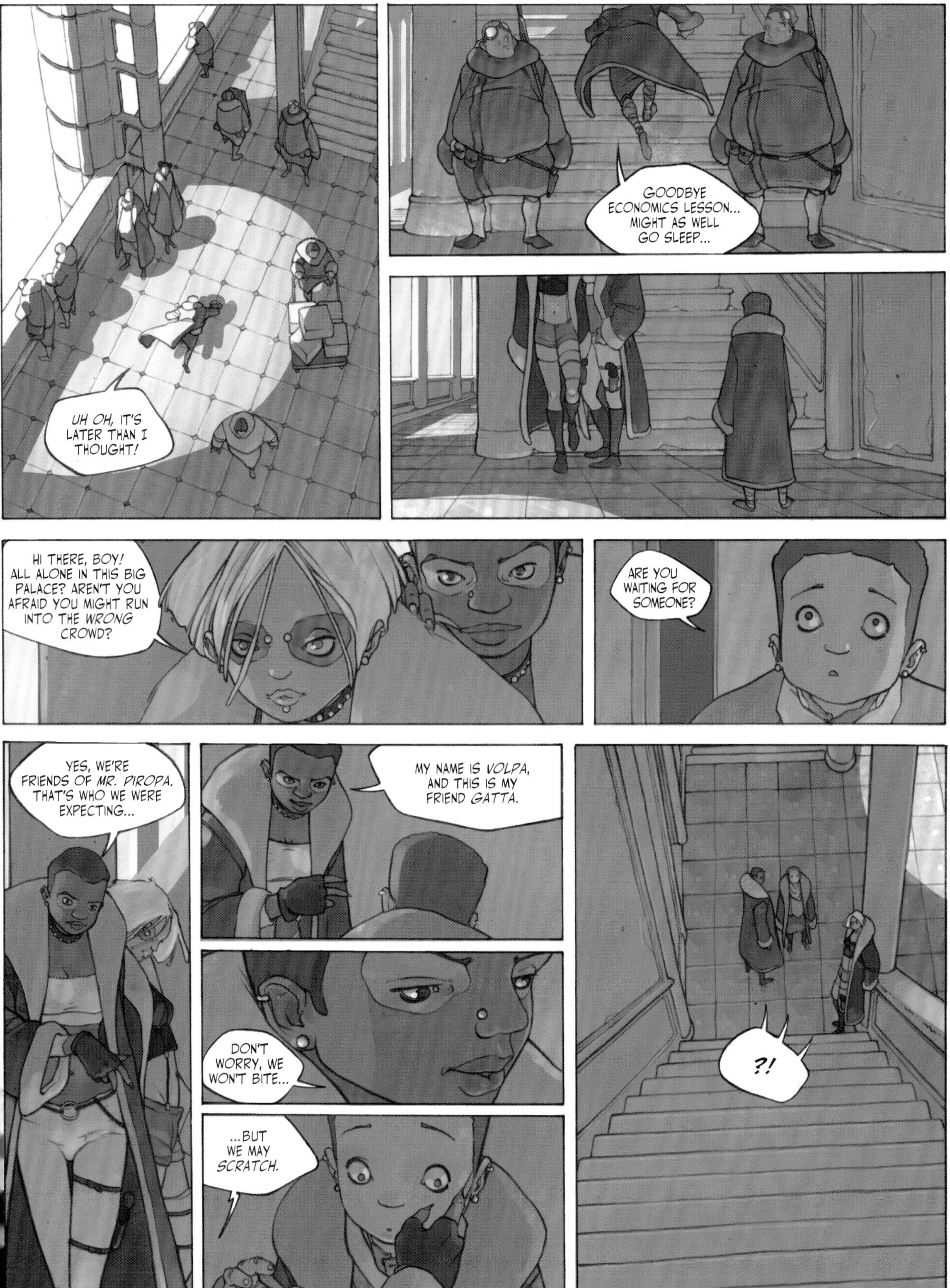
UH OH, IT'S LATER THAN I THOUGHT!
GOODBYE ECONOMICS LESSON... MIGHT AS WELL GO SLEEP...
HI THERE, BOY! ALL ALONE IN THIS BIG PALACE? AREN'T YOU AFRAID YOU MIGHT RUN INTO THE WRONG CROWD?
ARE YOU WAITING FOR SOMEONE?
YES, WE'RE FRIENDS OF MR. PIROPA. THAT'S WHO WE WERE EXPECTING...
MY NAME IS VOLPA, AND THIS IS MY FRIEND GATTA.
DON'T WORRY, WE WON'T BITE...
...BUT WE MAY SCRATCH.
?!

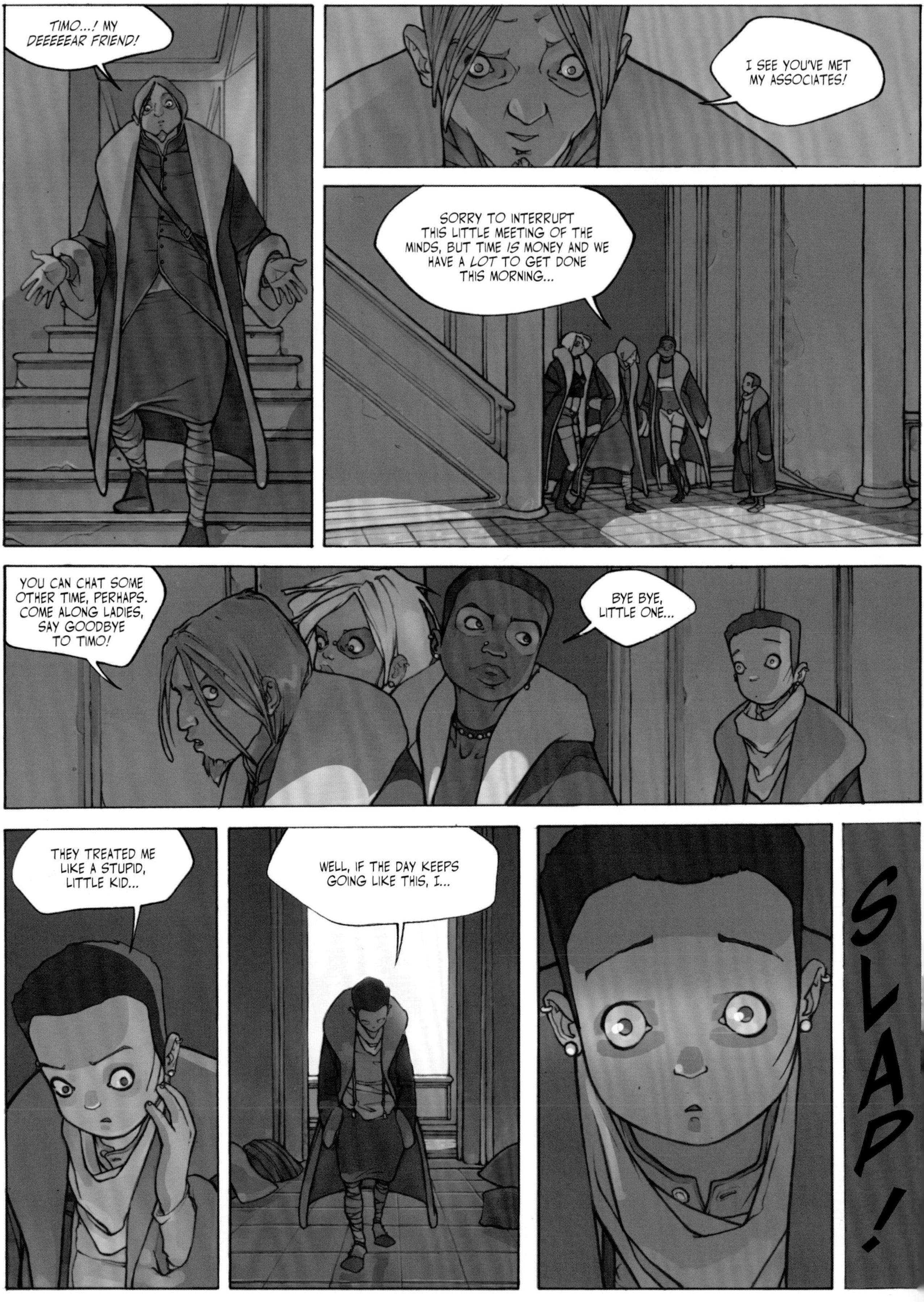
TIMO...! MY DEEEEEAR FRIEND!
I SEE YOU'VE MET MY ASSOCIATES!
SORRY TO INTERRUPT THIS LITTLE MEETING OF THE MINDS, BUT TIME *IS* MONEY AND WE HAVE A *LOT* TO GET DONE THIS MORNING...
YOU CAN CHAT SOME OTHER TIME, PERHAPS. COME ALONG LADIES, SAY GOODBYE TO TIMO!
BYE BYE, LITTLE ONE...
THEY TREATED ME LIKE A STUPID, LITTLE KID...
WELL, IF THE DAY KEEPS GOING LIKE THIS, I...
SLAP!

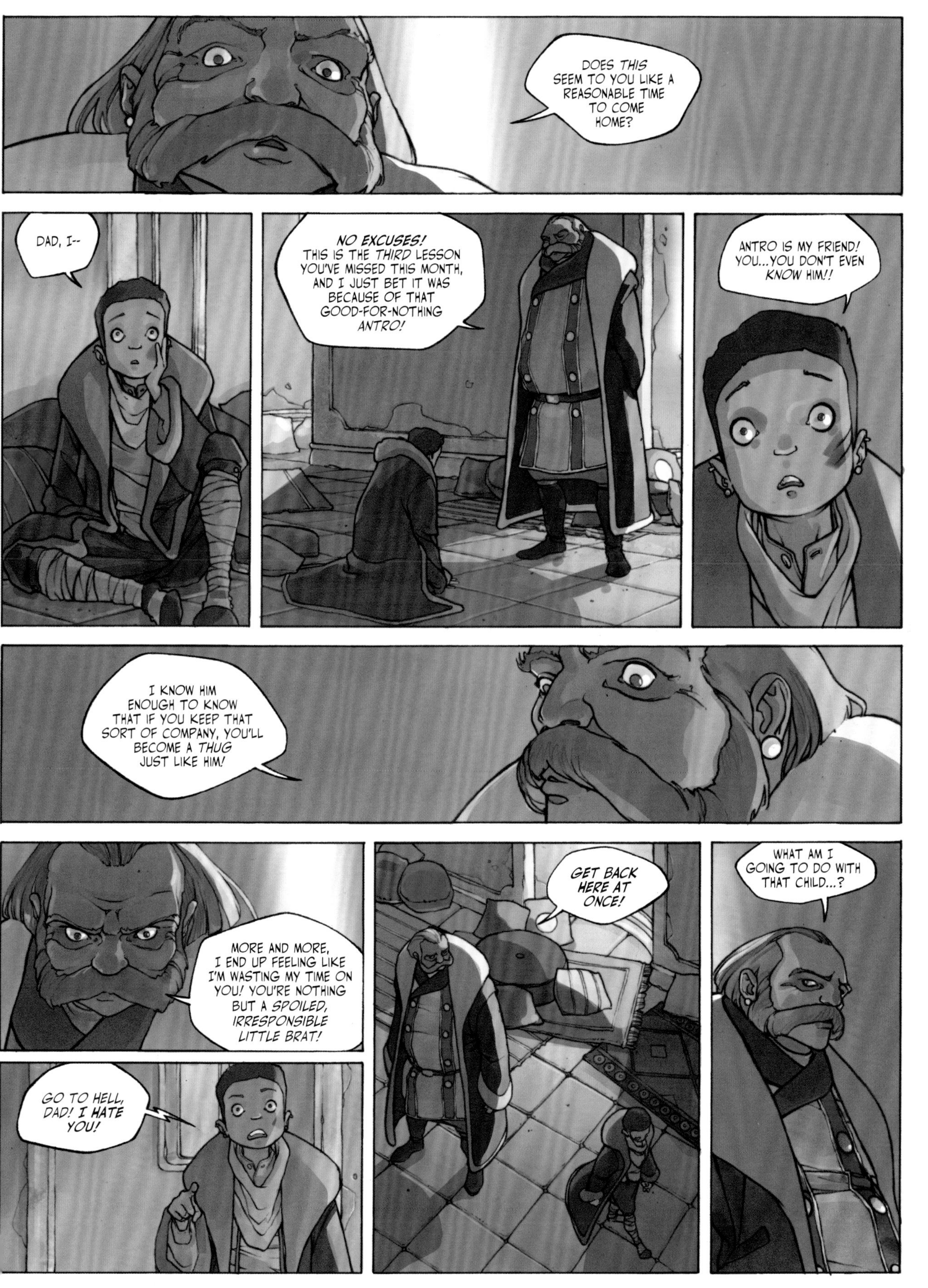
DOES THIS SEEM TO YOU LIKE A REASONABLE TIME TO COME HOME?
DAD, I--
NO EXCUSES! THIS IS THE THIRD LESSON YOU'VE MISSED THIS MONTH, AND I JUST BET IT WAS BECAUSE OF THAT GOOD-FOR-NOTHING ANTRO!
ANTRO IS MY FRIEND! YOU...YOU DON'T EVEN KNOW HIM!!
I KNOW HIM ENOUGH TO KNOW THAT IF YOU KEEP THAT SORT OF COMPANY, YOU'LL BECOME A THUG JUST LIKE HIM!
MORE AND MORE, I END UP FEELING LIKE I'M WASTING MY TIME ON YOU! YOU'RE NOTHING BUT A SPOILED, IRRESPONSIBLE LITTLE BRAT!
GO TO HELL, DAD! I HATE YOU!
GET BACK HERE AT ONCE!
WHAT AM I GOING TO DO WITH THAT CHILD...?

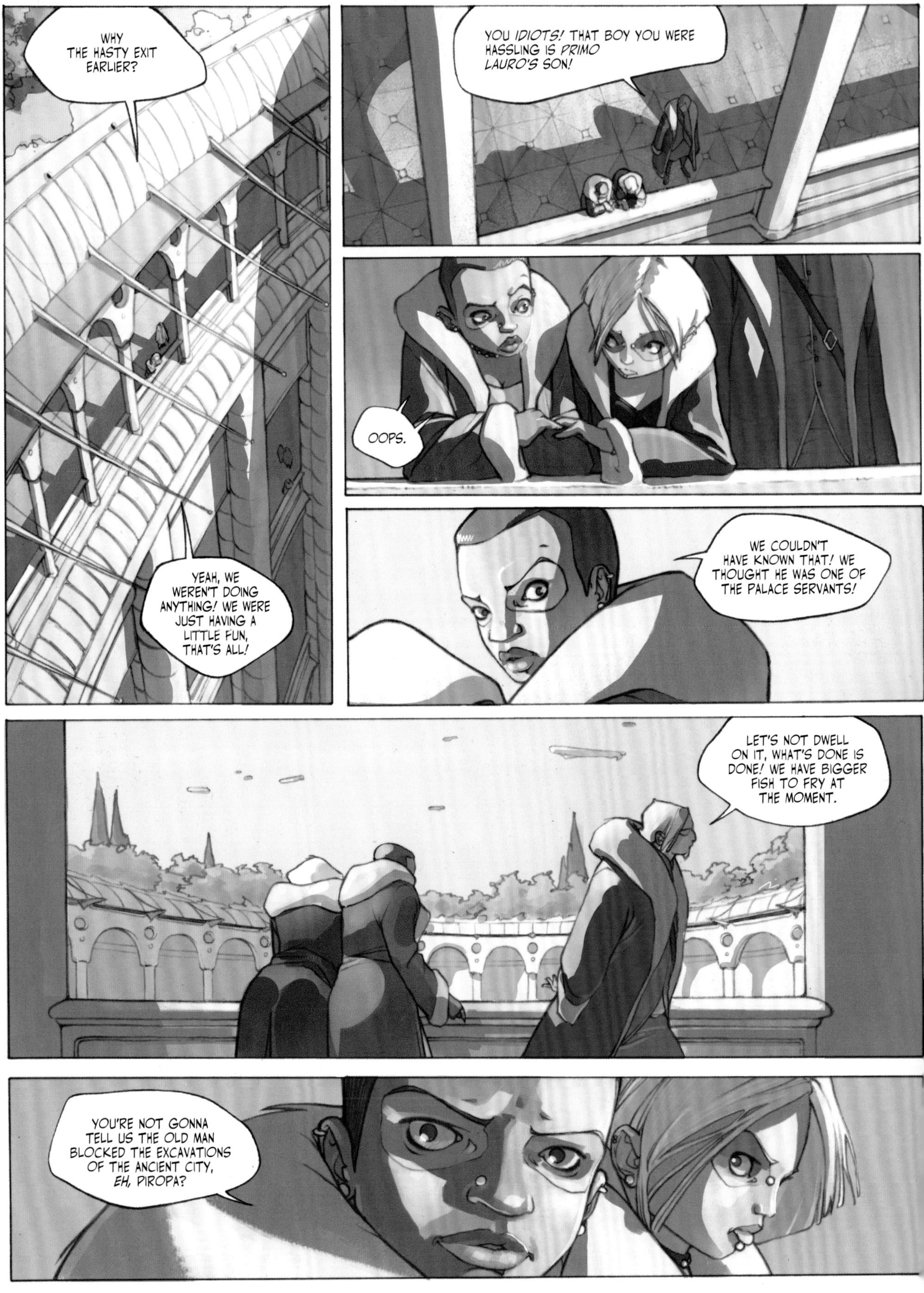
WHY THE HASTY EXIT EARLIER?
YOU IDIOTS! THAT BOY YOU WERE HASSLING IS PRIMO LAURO'S SON!
OOPS.
YEAH, WE WEREN'T DOING ANYTHING! WE WERE JUST HAVING A LITTLE FUN, THAT'S ALL!
WE COULDN'T HAVE KNOWN THAT! WE THOUGHT HE WAS ONE OF THE PALACE SERVANTS!
LET'S NOT DWELL ON IT, WHAT'S DONE IS DONE! WE HAVE BIGGER FISH TO FRY AT THE MOMENT.
YOU'RE NOT GONNA TELL US THE OLD MAN BLOCKED THE EXCAVATIONS OF THE ANCIENT CITY, EH, PIROPA?

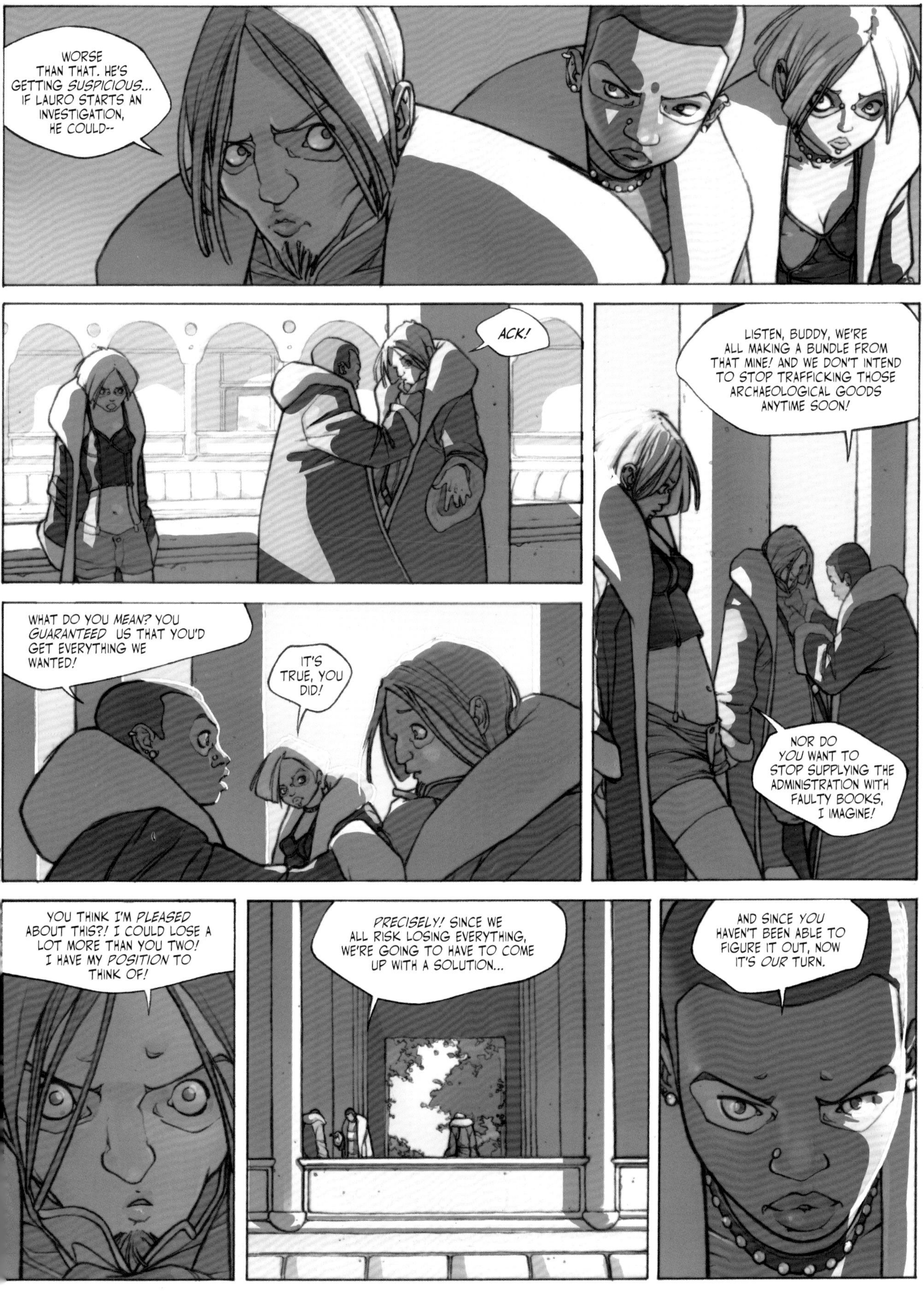

WORSE THAN THAT. HE'S GETTING SUSPICIOUS... IF LAURO STARTS AN INVESTIGATION, HE COULD--
ACK!
LISTEN, BUDDY, WE'RE ALL MAKING A BUNDLE FROM THAT MINE! AND WE DON'T INTEND TO STOP TRAFFICKING THOSE ARCHAEOLOGICAL GOODS ANYTIME SOON!
WHAT DO YOU MEAN? YOU GUARANTEED US THAT YOU'D GET EVERYTHING WE WANTED!
IT'S TRUE, YOU DID!
NOR DO YOU WANT TO STOP SUPPLYING THE ADMINISTRATION WITH FAULTY BOOKS, I IMAGINE!
YOU THINK I'M PLEASED ABOUT THIS?! I COULD LOSE A LOT MORE THAN YOU TWO! I HAVE MY POSITION TO THINK OF!
PRECISELY! SINCE WE ALL RISK LOSING EVERYTHING, WE'RE GOING TO HAVE TO COME UP WITH A SOLUTION...
AND SINCE YOU HAVEN'T BEEN ABLE TO FIGURE IT OUT, NOW IT'S OUR TURN.

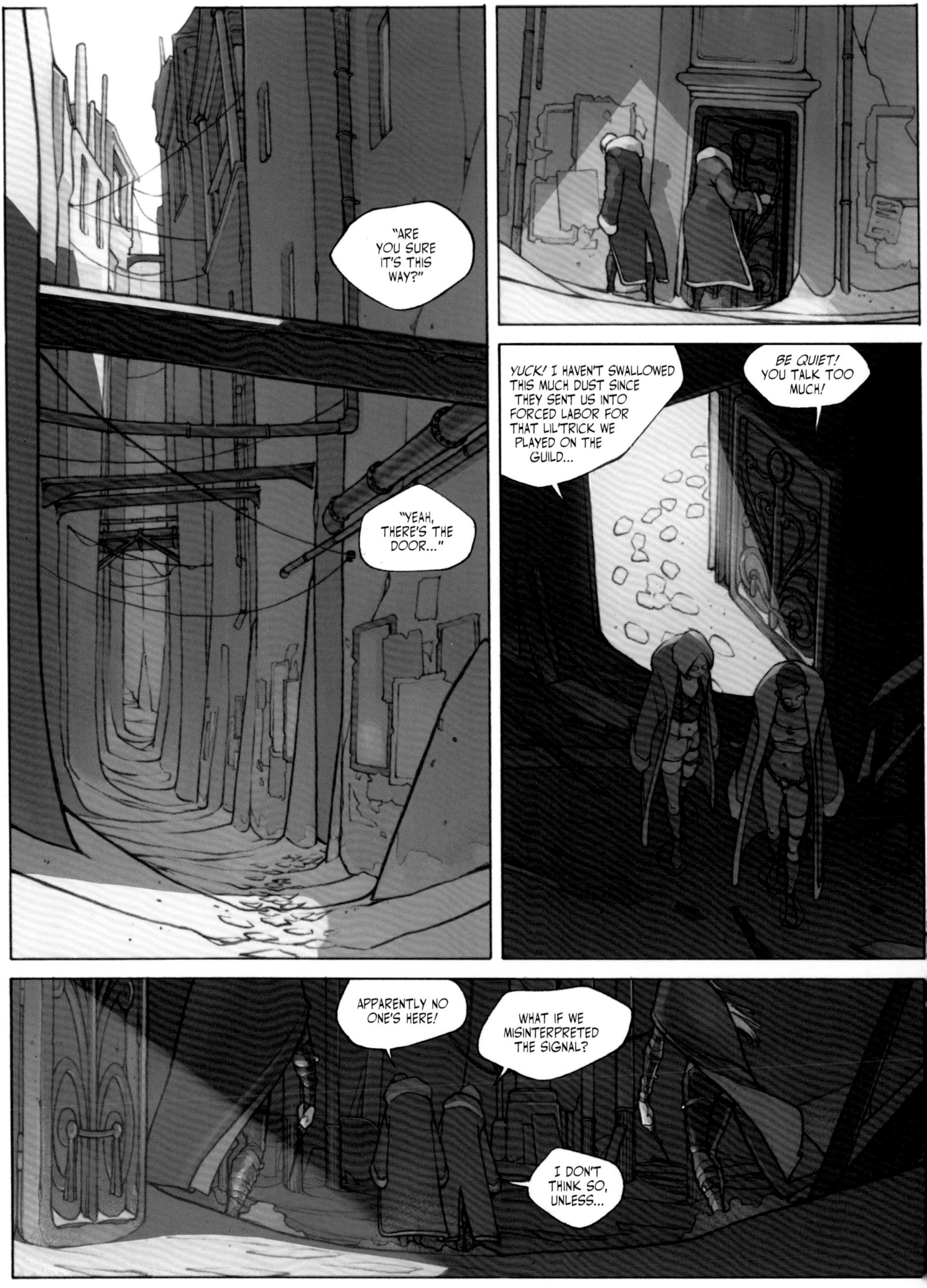
"ARE YOU SURE IT'S THIS WAY?"
"YEAH, THERE'S THE DOOR..."
YUCK! I HAVEN'T SWALLOWED THIS MUCH DUST SINCE THEY SENT US INTO FORCED LABOR FOR THAT LIL'TRICK WE PLAYED ON THE GUILD...
BE QUIET! YOU TALK TOO MUCH!
APPARENTLY NO ONE'S HERE!
WHAT IF WE MISINTERPRETED THE SIGNAL?
I DON'T THINK SO, UNLESS...

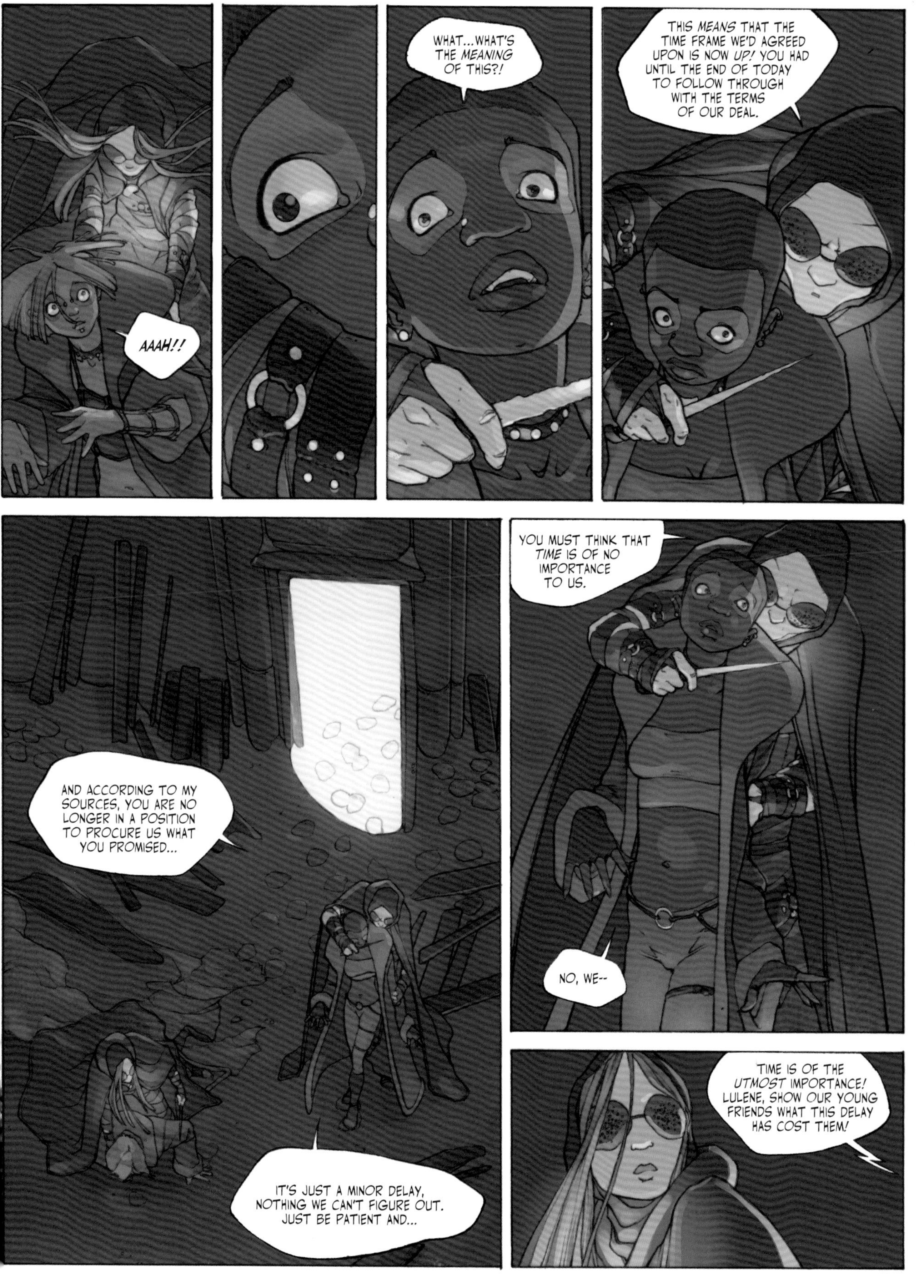
AAAH!!
WHAT...WHAT'S THE MEANING OF THIS?!
THIS MEANS THAT THE TIME FRAME WE'D AGREED UPON IS NOW UP! YOU HAD UNTIL THE END OF TODAY TO FOLLOW THROUGH WITH THE TERMS OF OUR DEAL.
AND ACCORDING TO MY SOURCES, YOU ARE NO LONGER IN A POSITION TO PROCURE US WHAT YOU PROMISED...
IT'S JUST A MINOR DELAY, NOTHING WE CAN'T FIGURE OUT. JUST BE PATIENT AND...
YOU MUST THINK THAT TIME IS OF NO IMPORTANCE TO US.
NO, WE--
TIME IS OF THE UTMOST IMPORTANCE! LULENE, SHOW OUR YOUNG FRIENDS WHAT THIS DELAY HAS COST THEM!

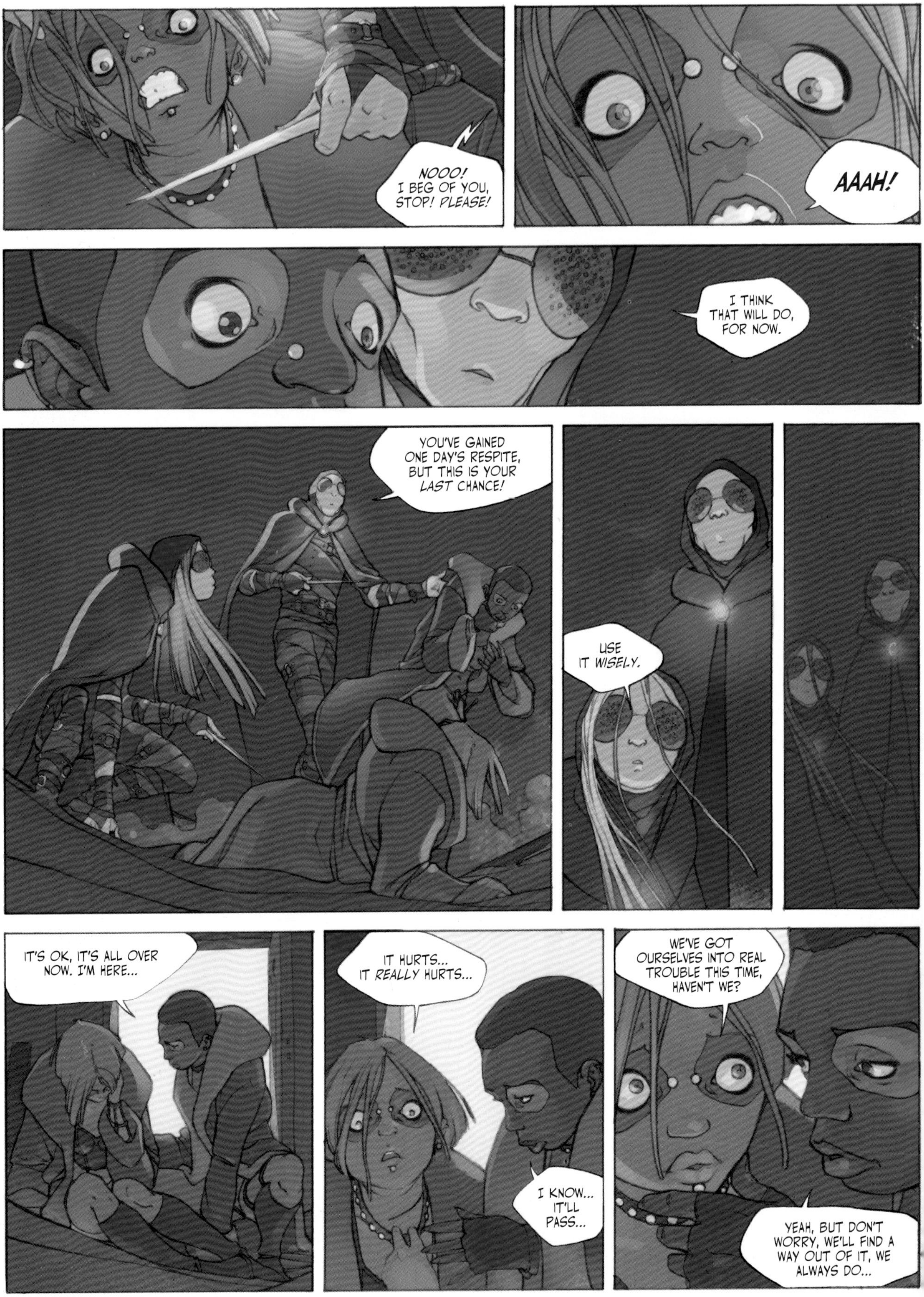
NOOO! I BEG OF YOU, STOP! PLEASE!
AAAH!
I THINK THAT WILL DO, FOR NOW.
YOU'VE GAINED ONE DAY'S RESPITE, BUT THIS IS YOUR LAST CHANCE!
USE IT WISELY.
IT'S OK, IT'S ALL OVER NOW. I'M HERE...
IT HURTS... IT REALLY HURTS...
I KNOW... IT'LL PASS...
WE'VE GOT OURSELVES INTO REAL TROUBLE THIS TIME, HAVEN'T WE?
YEAH, BUT DON'T WORRY, WE'LL FIND A WAY OUT OF IT, WE ALWAYS DO...

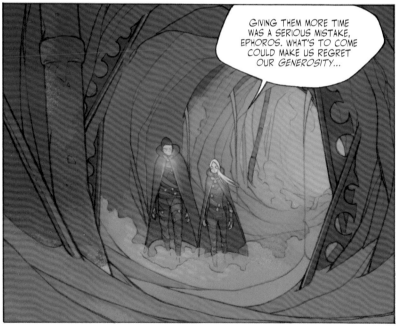

GIVING THEM MORE TIME WAS A SERIOUS MISTAKE, EPHOROS. WHAT'S TO COME COULD MAKE US REGRET OUR *GENEROSITY...*

THIS CITY'S HOURS ARE NUMBERED. IF WE WANT TO GET OUR HANDS ON THE OBJECT BEFORE THE OTHERS, WE MUST ACT QUICKLY AND *DIRECTLY!*

NO! YOU KNOW VERY WELL THAT IS *NOT* HOW WE *ENTOMBED* COMPORT OURSELVES!

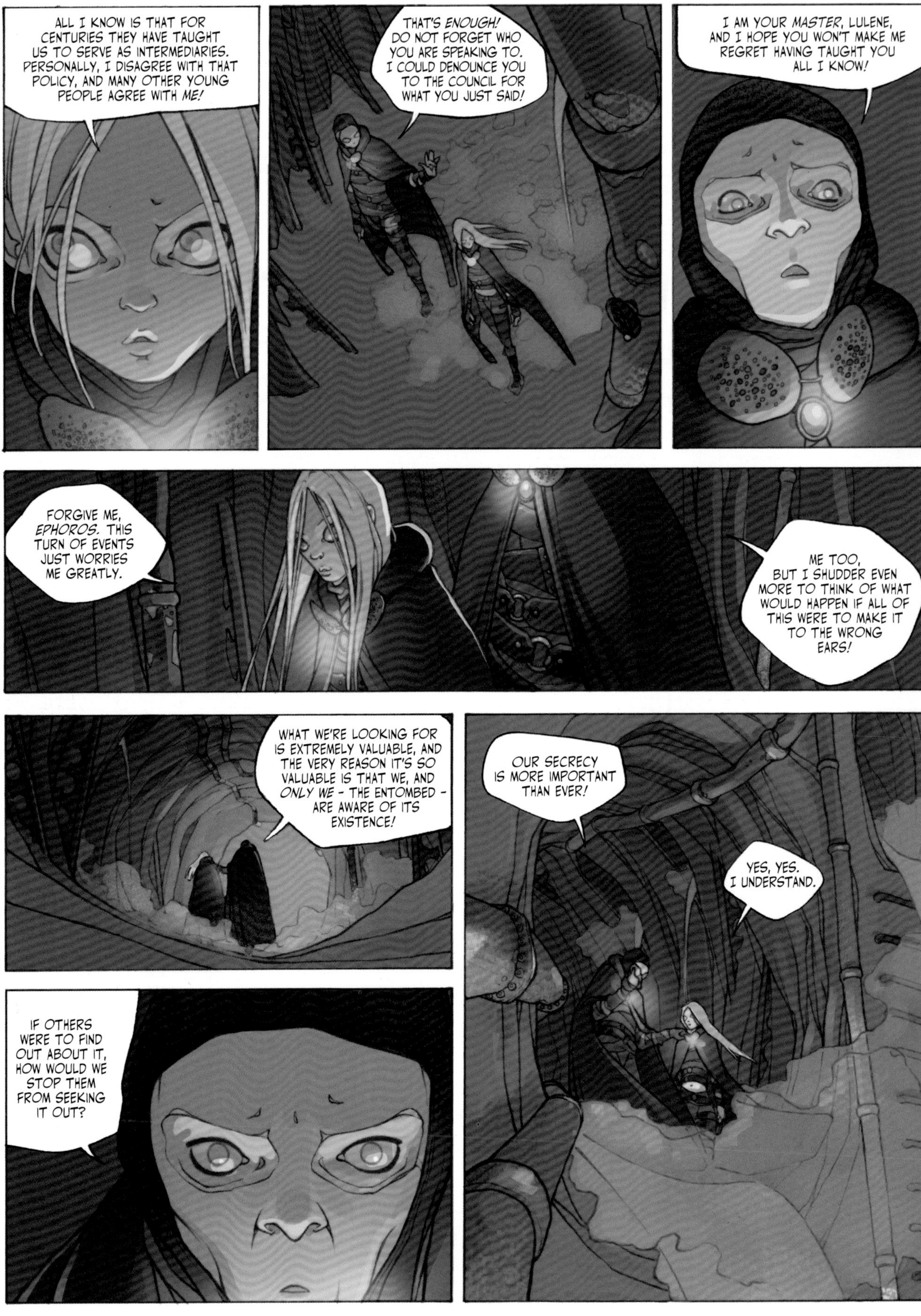
ALL I KNOW IS THAT FOR CENTURIES THEY HAVE TAUGHT US TO SERVE AS INTERMEDIARIES. PERSONALLY, I DISAGREE WITH THAT POLICY, AND MANY OTHER YOUNG PEOPLE AGREE WITH *ME!*
THAT'S *ENOUGH!* DO NOT FORGET WHO YOU ARE SPEAKING TO. I COULD DENOUNCE YOU TO THE COUNCIL FOR WHAT YOU JUST SAID!
I AM YOUR *MASTER*, LULENE, AND I HOPE YOU WON'T MAKE ME REGRET HAVING TAUGHT YOU ALL I KNOW!
FORGIVE ME, *EPHOROS.* THIS TURN OF EVENTS JUST WORRIES ME GREATLY.
ME TOO, BUT I SHUDDER EVEN MORE TO THINK OF WHAT WOULD HAPPEN IF ALL OF THIS WERE TO MAKE IT TO THE WRONG EARS!
WHAT WE'RE LOOKING FOR IS EXTREMELY VALUABLE, AND THE VERY REASON IT'S SO VALUABLE IS THAT WE, AND *ONLY WE* - THE ENTOMBED - ARE AWARE OF ITS EXISTENCE!
IF OTHERS WERE TO FIND OUT ABOUT IT, HOW WOULD WE STOP THEM FROM SEEKING IT OUT?
OUR SECRECY IS MORE IMPORTANT THAN EVER!
YES, YES. I UNDERSTAND.

GOOD. KEEP FOLLOWING THOSE GIRLS AND MAKE SURE THAT NOTHING TROUBLING HAPPENS TO THEM. MEANWHILE, I'LL WARN THE COUNCIL OF THE DELAY.

IF ALL GOES ACCORDING TO PLAN, I'LL BE BACK AT THE FIRST LIGHT OF DAWN...

BE CAREFUL. THE CREATURES OF THE ENTOMBED WORLD ARE BEGINNING TO STIR, AS IF THEY SUSPECT SOMETHING...

HAVE NO FEAR, IT WILL ALL BE OK...

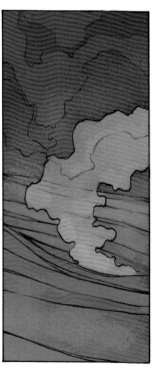

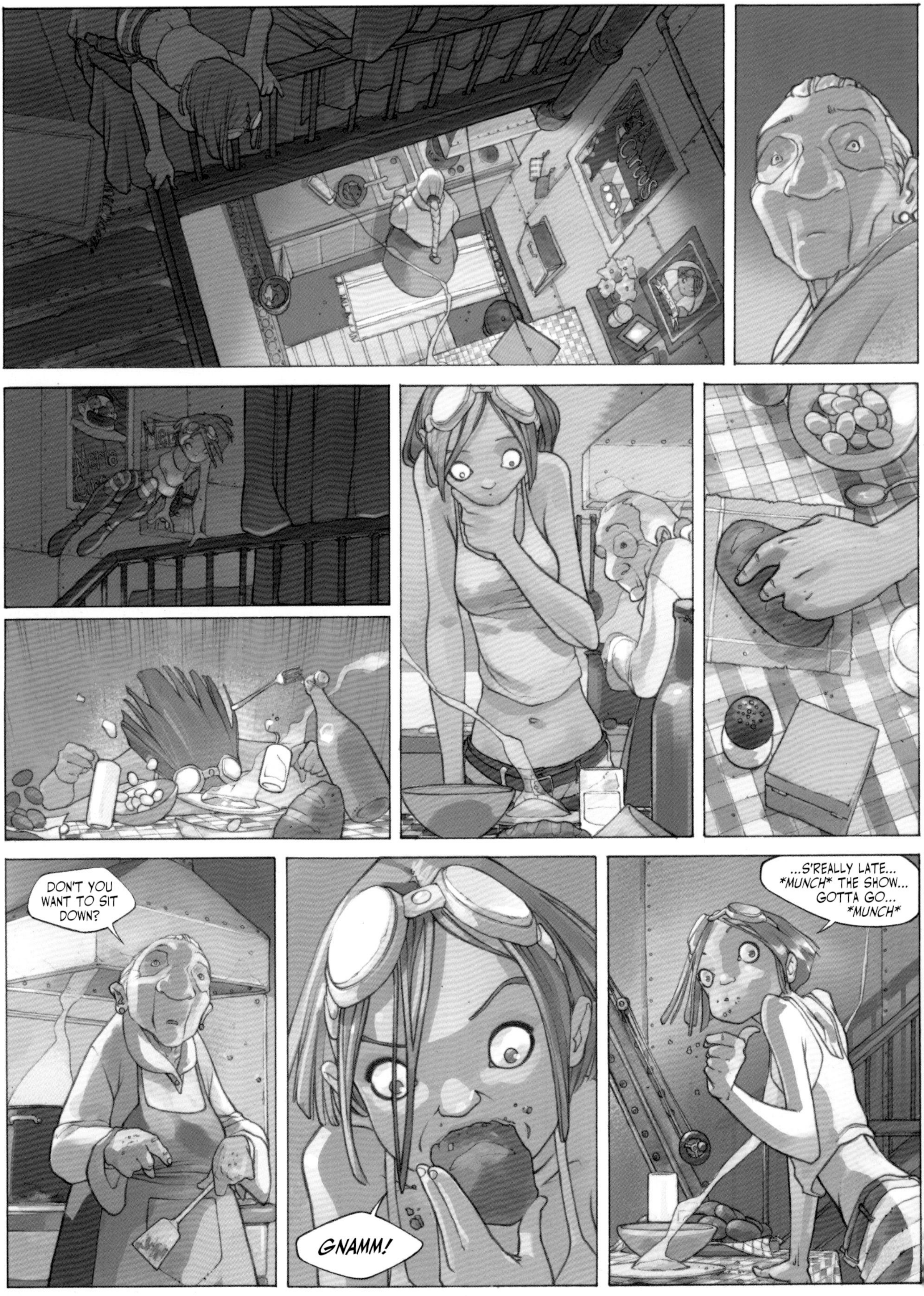
DON'T YOU WANT TO SIT DOWN?
GNAMM!
...S'REALLY LATE... *MUNCH* THE SHOW... GOTTA GO... *MUNCH*

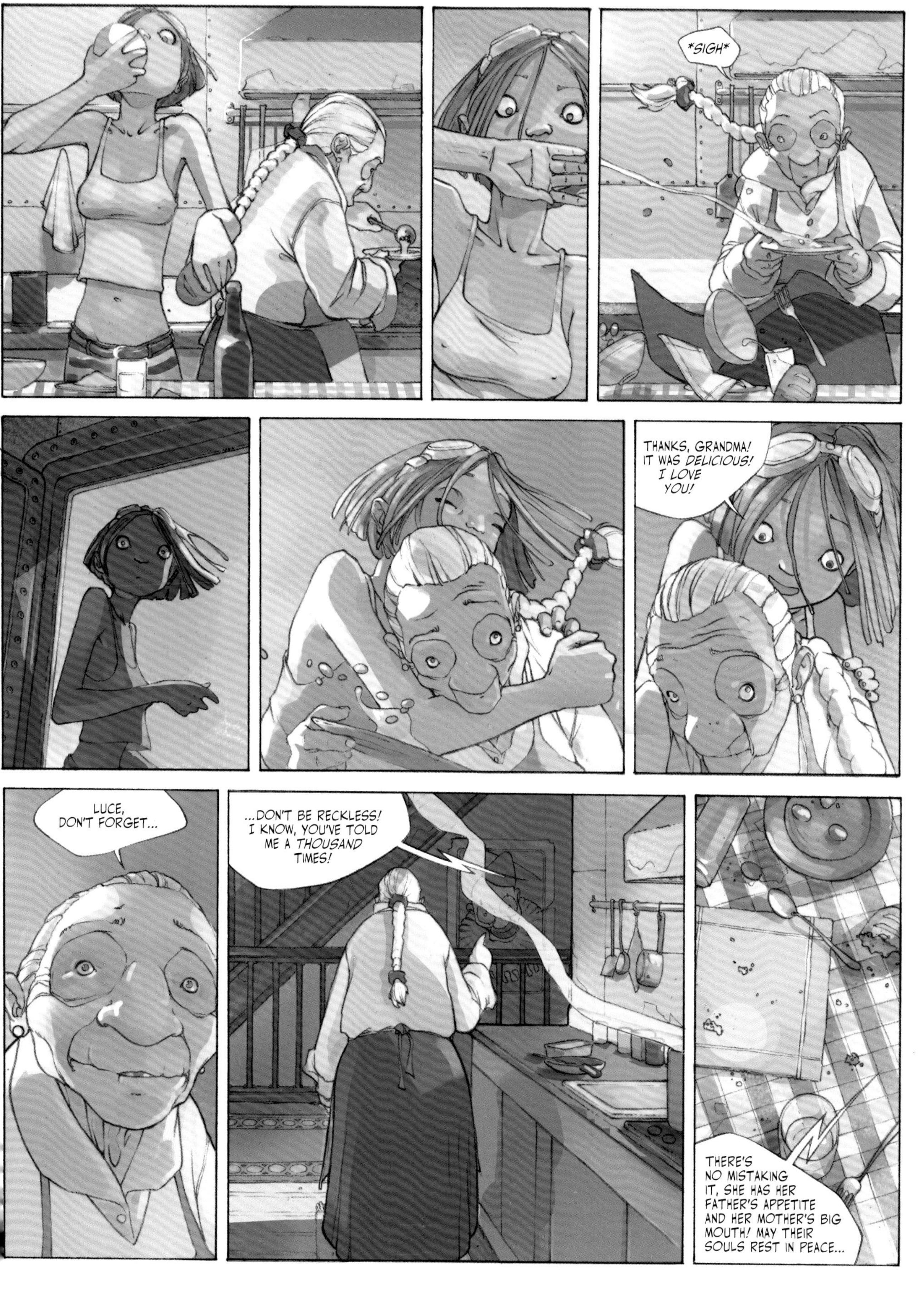
SIGH
THANKS, GRANDMA! IT WAS DELICIOUS! I LOVE YOU!
LUCE, DON'T FORGET...
...DON'T BE RECKLESS! I KNOW, YOU'VE TOLD ME A THOUSAND TIMES!
THERE'S NO MISTAKING IT, SHE HAS HER FATHER'S APPETITE AND HER MOTHER'S BIG MOUTH! MAY THEIR SOULS REST IN PEACE...

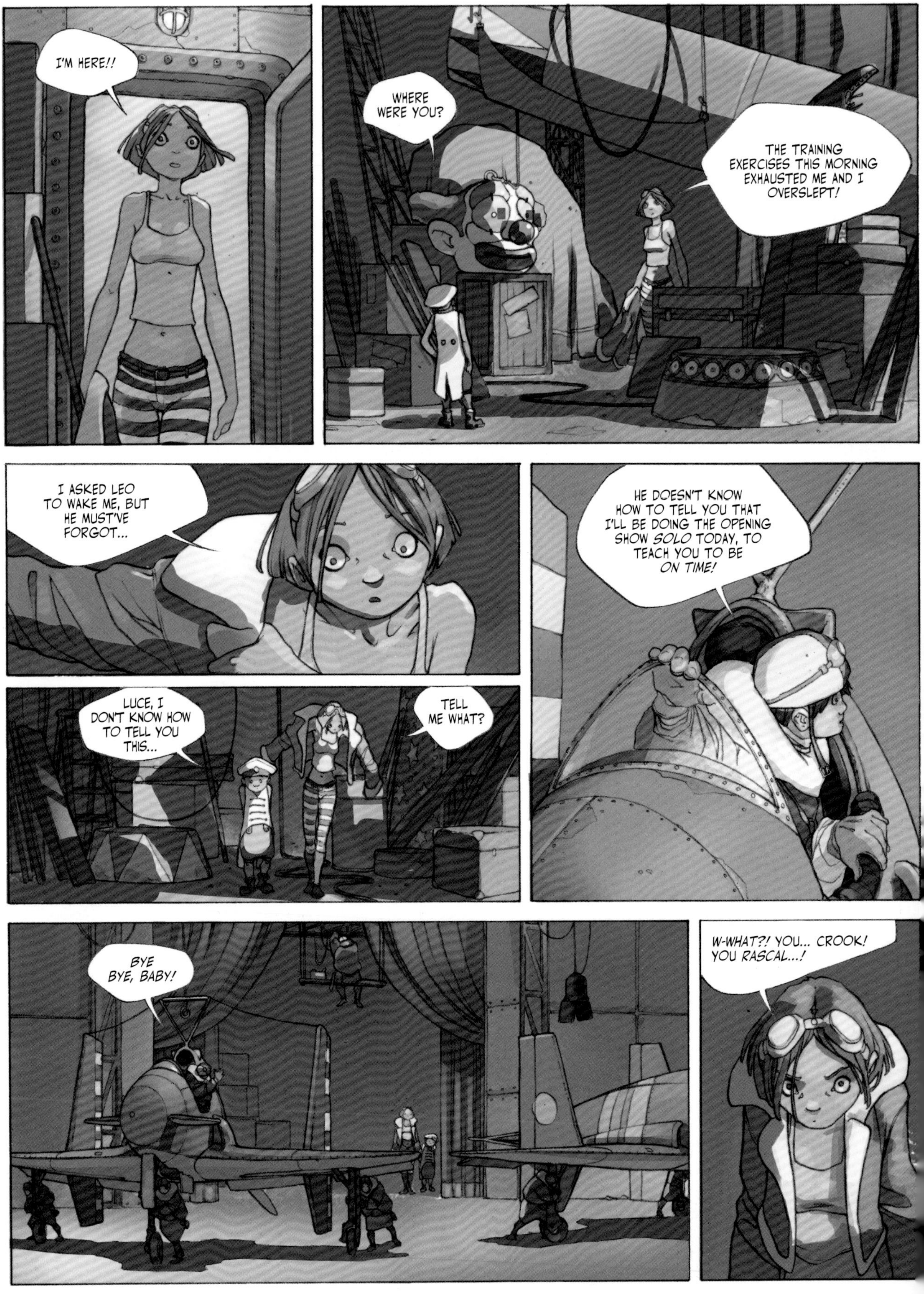

I'M HERE!!
WHERE WERE YOU?
THE TRAINING EXERCISES THIS MORNING EXHAUSTED ME AND I OVERSLEPT!
I ASKED LEO TO WAKE ME, BUT HE MUST'VE FORGOT...
LUCE, I DON'T KNOW HOW TO TELL YOU THIS...
TELL ME WHAT?
HE DOESN'T KNOW HOW TO TELL YOU THAT I'LL BE DOING THE OPENING SHOW *SOLO* TODAY, TO TEACH YOU TO BE *ON TIME!*
BYE BYE, BABY!
W-WHAT?! YOU... CROOK! YOU *RASCAL*...!

DEAR WONDERFUL FOLKS OF BOREA, WELCOME TO THE GREATEST AERIAL SPECTACLE EVER PRESENTED IN THE SKIES OF ALL THE WORLDS OF THE RING!

A SPECTACLE THAT WILL TAKE YOUR BREATH AWAY...

...STARTING WITH THE DAREDEVIL EXPLOITS OF THE MAGNIFICENT LEO!

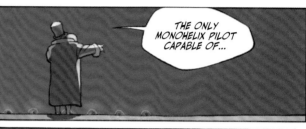

THE ONLY MONOHELIX PILOT CAPABLE OF...

LOOK!!

WHAT'S THAT GIRL DOING ON THE RUNWAY?!

SHE'S CHASING THE MONOHELIX!

?

!!

SHE'S RUNNING FULL SPEED AFTER HIM!

I BET YOU EVERYTHING IN MY POCKETS THAT SHE WON'T CATCH IT!

YOU'RE ON!

THE MONOHELIX IS GOING TOO FAST. HE'LL MAKE IT TO THE END OF THE RUNWAY LONG BEFORE SHE CAN...

YOU'LL SEE, HE'S GONNA STOP!

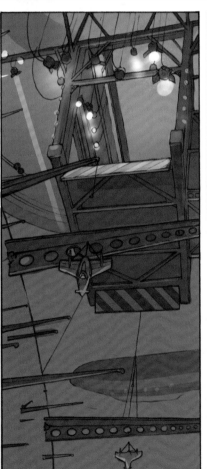

PFFF! WELL, LOOKS LIKE I LOST MY BET!

AS I WAS SAYING, IT'S IMPOSS--

HOT DAMN, LOOK!!

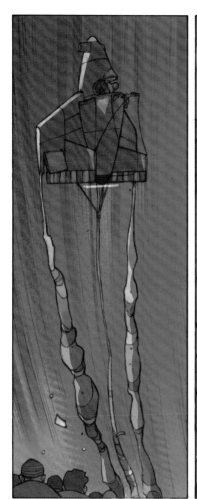

SHE *FELL!*

NO, SHE *JUMPED,* I SAW HER DO IT!

SHE MUST HAVE WIPED OUT...

I DIDN'T SEE HER FALL!

THEN WHERE *IS* SHE?

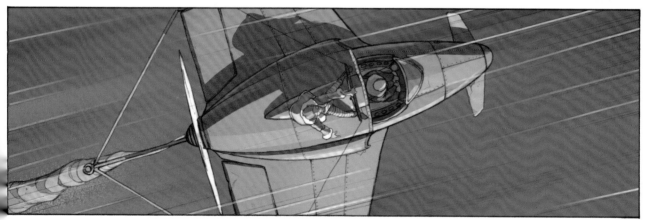

SHE'S ALIVE!

AMAZING, SHE GRABBED IT ON HER WAY DOWN!

IT MUST HAVE BEEN PART OF THE SHOW!

HURRAY!!

BRAVO!!!

ENCORE!!

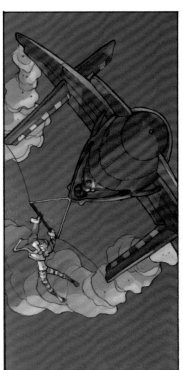

DID YOU SEE THAT, DAD? WHAT *ENTHUSIASM!* I HAD THEM FROM THE START! MAYBE I SHOULD START DOING SOLO NUMBERS FROM NOW ON, WHAT DO YOU THINK?

I THINK YOU'RE AN IDIOT!

AS FOR *YOU,* YOU FOOLHARDY GIRL, THIS LITTLE SHOW OF BRAVERY IS GOING TO *COST* YOU!

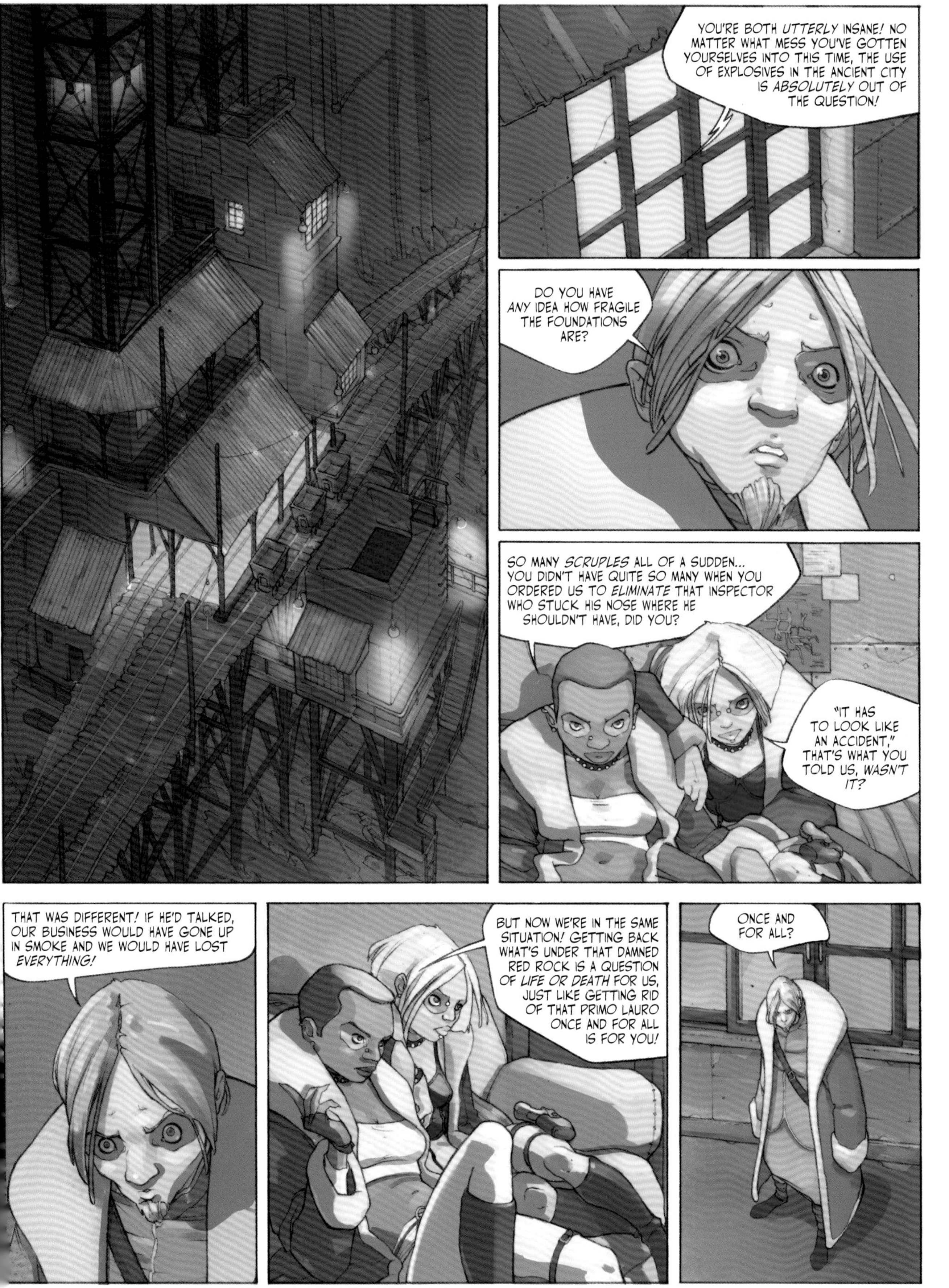
YOU'RE BOTH UTTERLY INSANE! NO MATTER WHAT MESS YOU'VE GOTTEN YOURSELVES INTO THIS TIME, THE USE OF EXPLOSIVES IN THE ANCIENT CITY IS ABSOLUTELY OUT OF THE QUESTION!
DO YOU HAVE ANY IDEA HOW FRAGILE THE FOUNDATIONS ARE?
SO MANY SCRUPLES ALL OF A SUDDEN... YOU DIDN'T HAVE QUITE SO MANY WHEN YOU ORDERED US TO ELIMINATE THAT INSPECTOR WHO STUCK HIS NOSE WHERE HE SHOULDN'T HAVE, DID YOU?
"IT HAS TO LOOK LIKE AN ACCIDENT," THAT'S WHAT YOU TOLD US, WASN'T IT?
THAT WAS DIFFERENT! IF HE'D TALKED, OUR BUSINESS WOULD HAVE GONE UP IN SMOKE AND WE WOULD HAVE LOST EVERYTHING!
BUT NOW WE'RE IN THE SAME SITUATION! GETTING BACK WHAT'S UNDER THAT DAMNED RED ROCK IS A QUESTION OF LIFE OR DEATH FOR US, JUST LIKE GETTING RID OF THAT PRIMO LAURO ONCE AND FOR ALL IS FOR YOU!
ONCE AND FOR ALL?

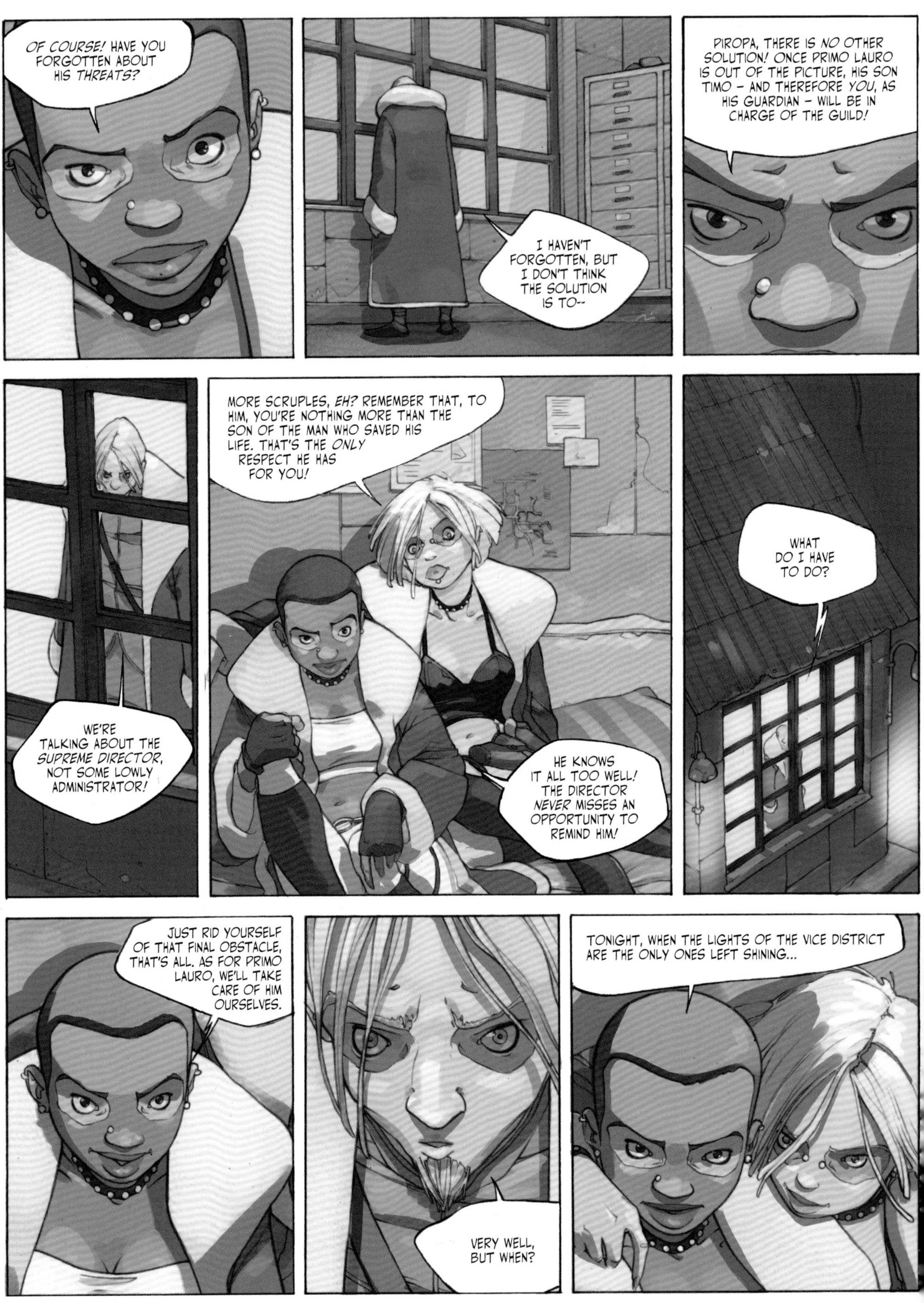
OF COURSE! HAVE YOU FORGOTTEN ABOUT HIS THREATS?
I HAVEN'T FORGOTTEN, BUT I DON'T THINK THE SOLUTION IS TO--
PIROPA, THERE IS NO OTHER SOLUTION! ONCE PRIMO LAURO IS OUT OF THE PICTURE, HIS SON TIMO – AND THEREFORE YOU, AS HIS GUARDIAN – WILL BE IN CHARGE OF THE GUILD!
WE'RE TALKING ABOUT THE SUPREME DIRECTOR, NOT SOME LOWLY ADMINISTRATOR!
MORE SCRUPLES, EH? REMEMBER THAT, TO HIM, YOU'RE NOTHING MORE THAN THE SON OF THE MAN WHO SAVED HIS LIFE. THAT'S THE ONLY RESPECT HE HAS FOR YOU!
HE KNOWS IT ALL TOO WELL! THE DIRECTOR NEVER MISSES AN OPPORTUNITY TO REMIND HIM!
WHAT DO I HAVE TO DO?
JUST RID YOURSELF OF THAT FINAL OBSTACLE, THAT'S ALL. AS FOR PRIMO LAURO, WE'LL TAKE CARE OF HIM OURSELVES.
VERY WELL, BUT WHEN?
TONIGHT, WHEN THE LIGHTS OF THE VICE DISTRICT ARE THE ONLY ONES LEFT SHINING...

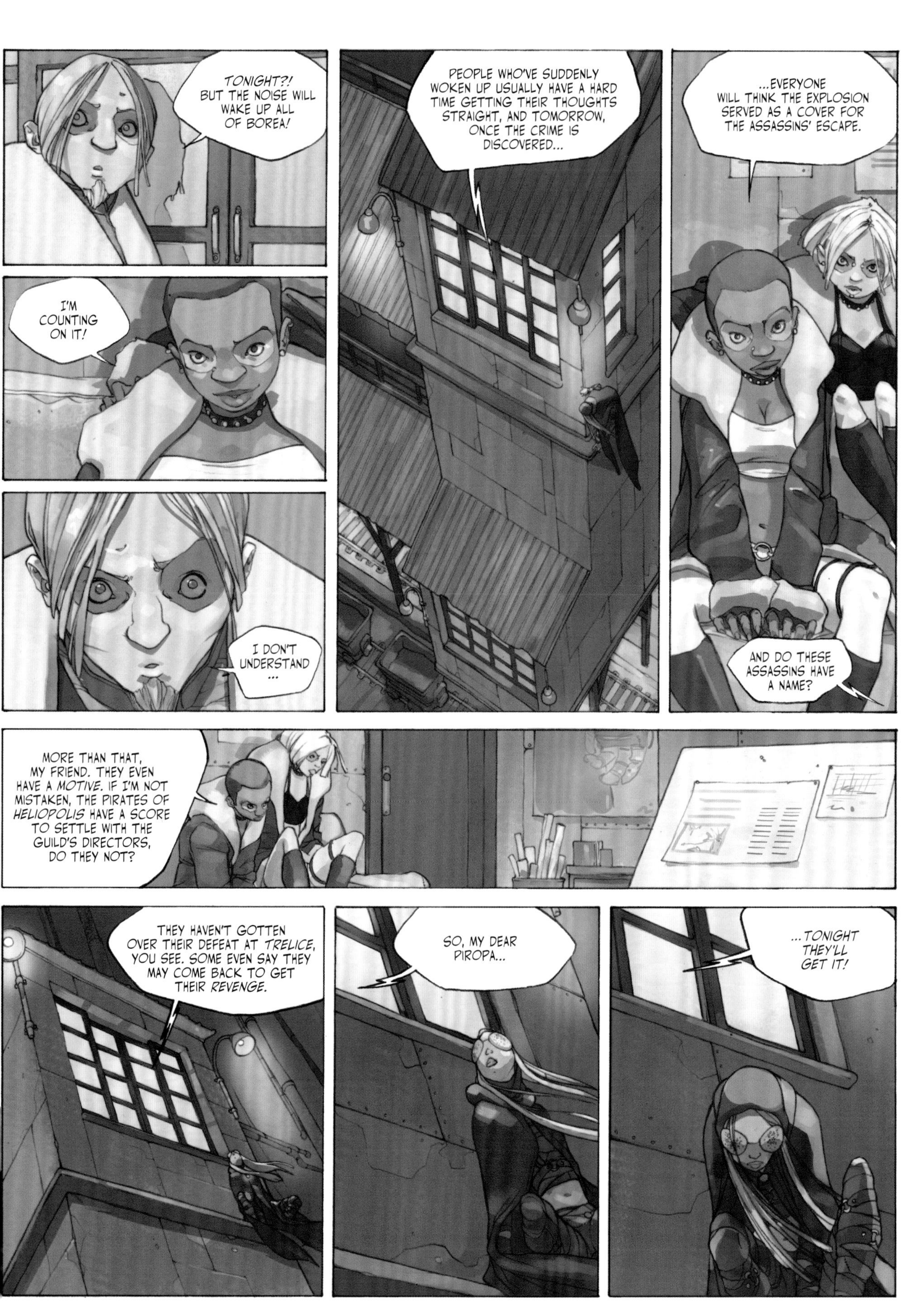
TONIGHT?! BUT THE NOISE WILL WAKE UP ALL OF BOREA!
I'M COUNTING ON IT!
I DON'T UNDERSTAND ...
PEOPLE WHO'VE SUDDENLY WOKEN UP USUALLY HAVE A HARD TIME GETTING THEIR THOUGHTS STRAIGHT, AND TOMORROW, ONCE THE CRIME IS DISCOVERED...
...EVERYONE WILL THINK THE EXPLOSION SERVED AS A COVER FOR THE ASSASSINS' ESCAPE.
AND DO THESE ASSASSINS HAVE A NAME?
MORE THAN THAT, MY FRIEND. THEY EVEN HAVE A MOTIVE. IF I'M NOT MISTAKEN, THE PIRATES OF HELIOPOLIS HAVE A SCORE TO SETTLE WITH THE GUILD'S DIRECTORS, DO THEY NOT?
THEY HAVEN'T GOTTEN OVER THEIR DEFEAT AT TRELICE, YOU SEE. SOME EVEN SAY THEY MAY COME BACK TO GET THEIR REVENGE.
SO, MY DEAR PIROPA...
...TONIGHT THEY'LL GET IT!

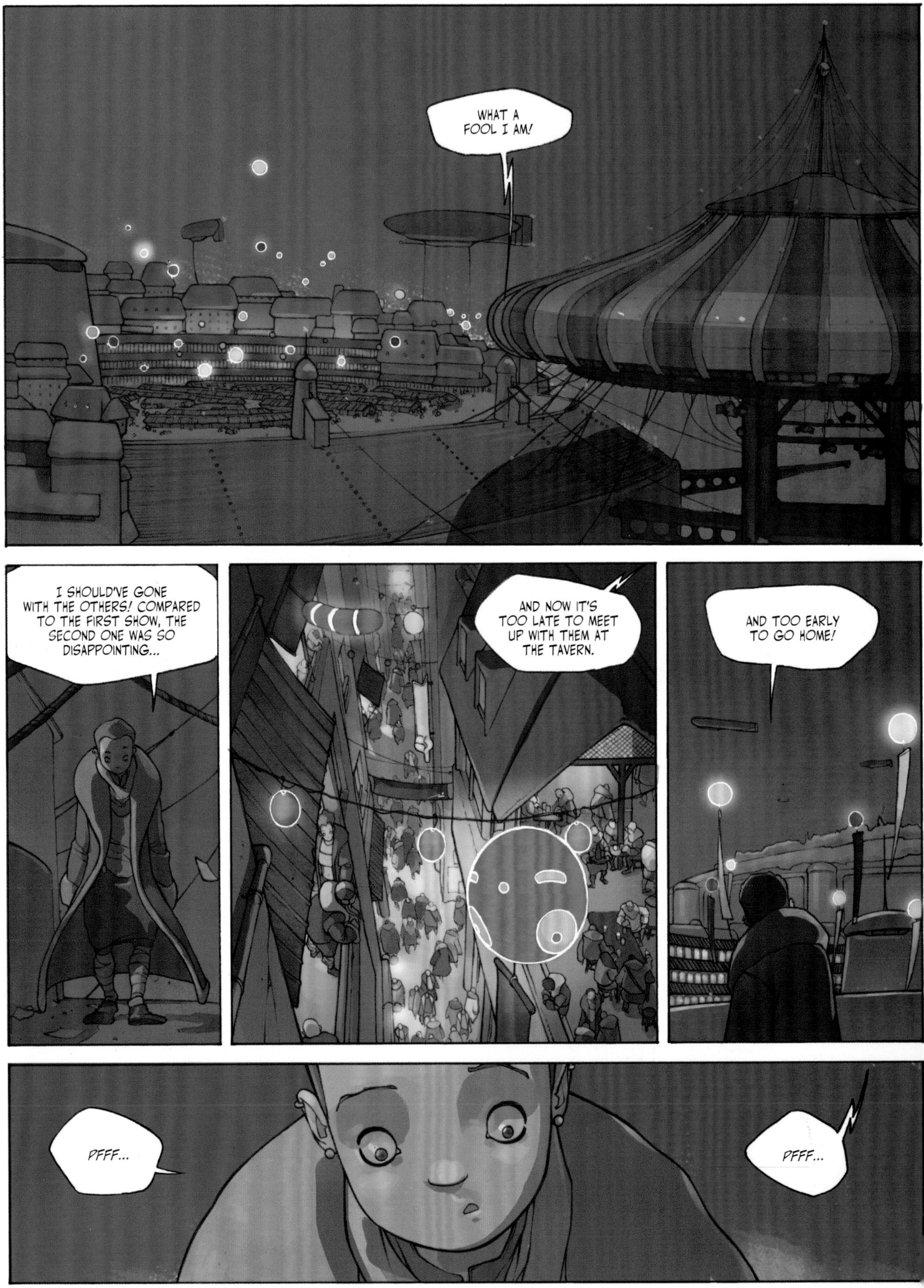
WHAT A FOOL I AM!
I SHOULD'VE GONE WITH THE OTHERS! COMPARED TO THE FIRST SHOW, THE SECOND ONE WAS SO DISAPPOINTING...
AND NOW IT'S TOO LATE TO MEET UP WITH THEM AT THE TAVERN.
AND TOO EARLY TO GO HOME!
PFFF...
PFFF...

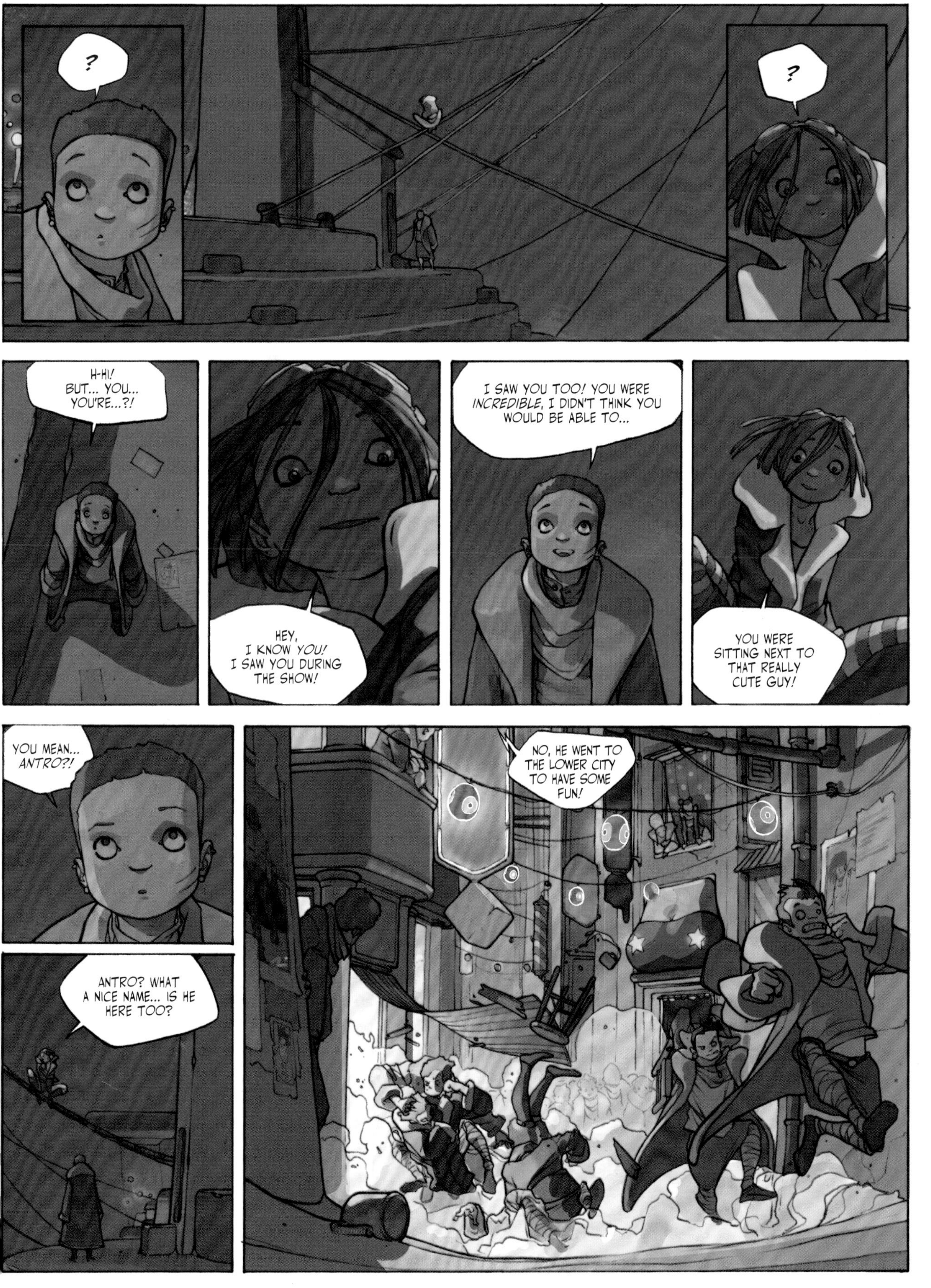
?
?
H-HI! BUT... YOU... YOU'RE...?!
HEY, I KNOW *YOU!* I SAW YOU DURING THE SHOW!
I SAW YOU *TOO!* YOU WERE *INCREDIBLE*, I DIDN'T THINK YOU WOULD BE ABLE TO...
YOU WERE SITTING NEXT TO THAT REALLY CUTE GUY!
YOU MEAN... *ANTRO?!*
ANTRO? WHAT A NICE NAME... IS HE HERE TOO?
NO, HE WENT TO THE LOWER CITY TO HAVE SOME FUN!

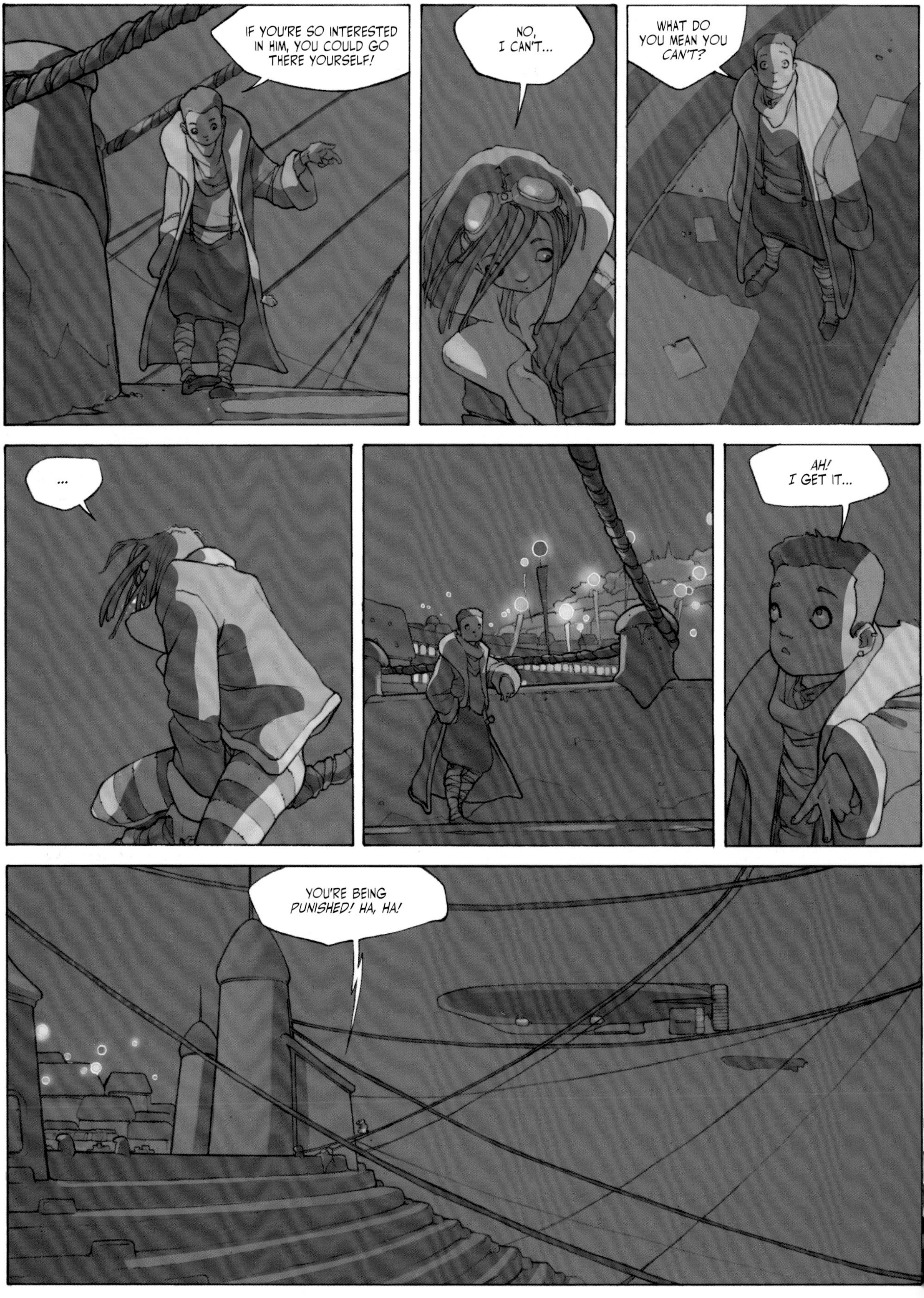
IF YOU'RE SO INTERESTED IN HIM, YOU COULD GO THERE YOURSELF!
NO, I CAN'T...
WHAT DO YOU MEAN YOU CAN'T?
...
AH! I GET IT...
YOU'RE BEING PUNISHED! HA, HA!

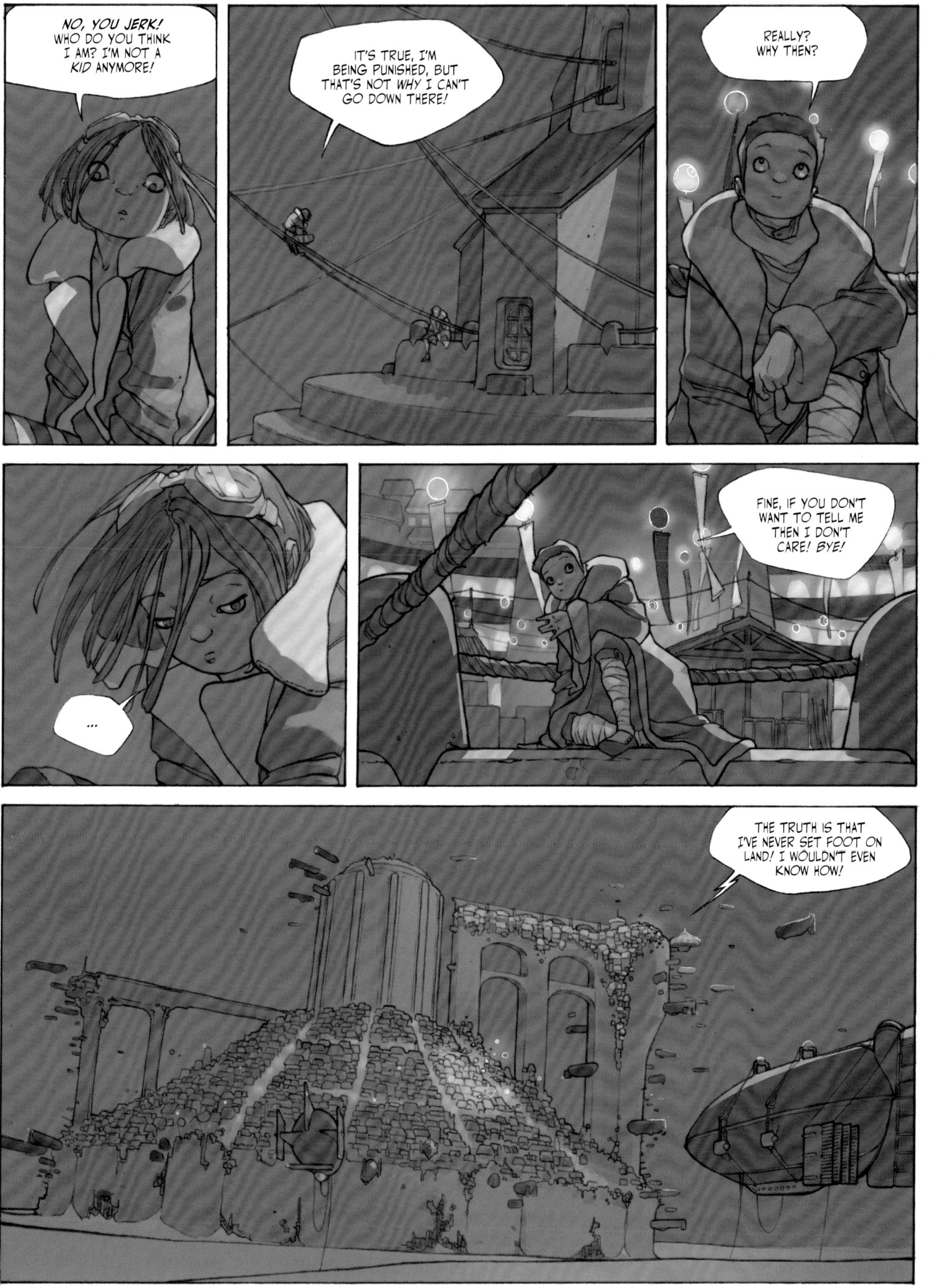
NO, YOU JERK! WHO DO YOU THINK I AM? I'M NOT A KID ANYMORE!
IT'S TRUE, I'M BEING PUNISHED, BUT THAT'S NOT WHY I CAN'T GO DOWN THERE!
REALLY? WHY THEN?
...
FINE, IF YOU DON'T WANT TO TELL ME THEN I DON'T CARE! BYE!
THE TRUTH IS THAT I'VE NEVER SET FOOT ON LAND! I WOULDN'T EVEN KNOW HOW!

ARE YOU KIDDING ME?

IT'S EASY! JUST A LITTLE JUMP, AND THAT'S IT!

HMMM...

I SWEAR, I'VE NEVER GOTTEN OFF AN AIRSHIP!

I GET IT, YOU NEED A LITTLE HELP! HOLD ON, BE RIGHT BACK!

BUT ...

WHERE ?!

AAAAAAAH!!

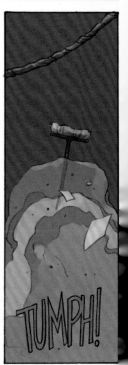

TUMPH!

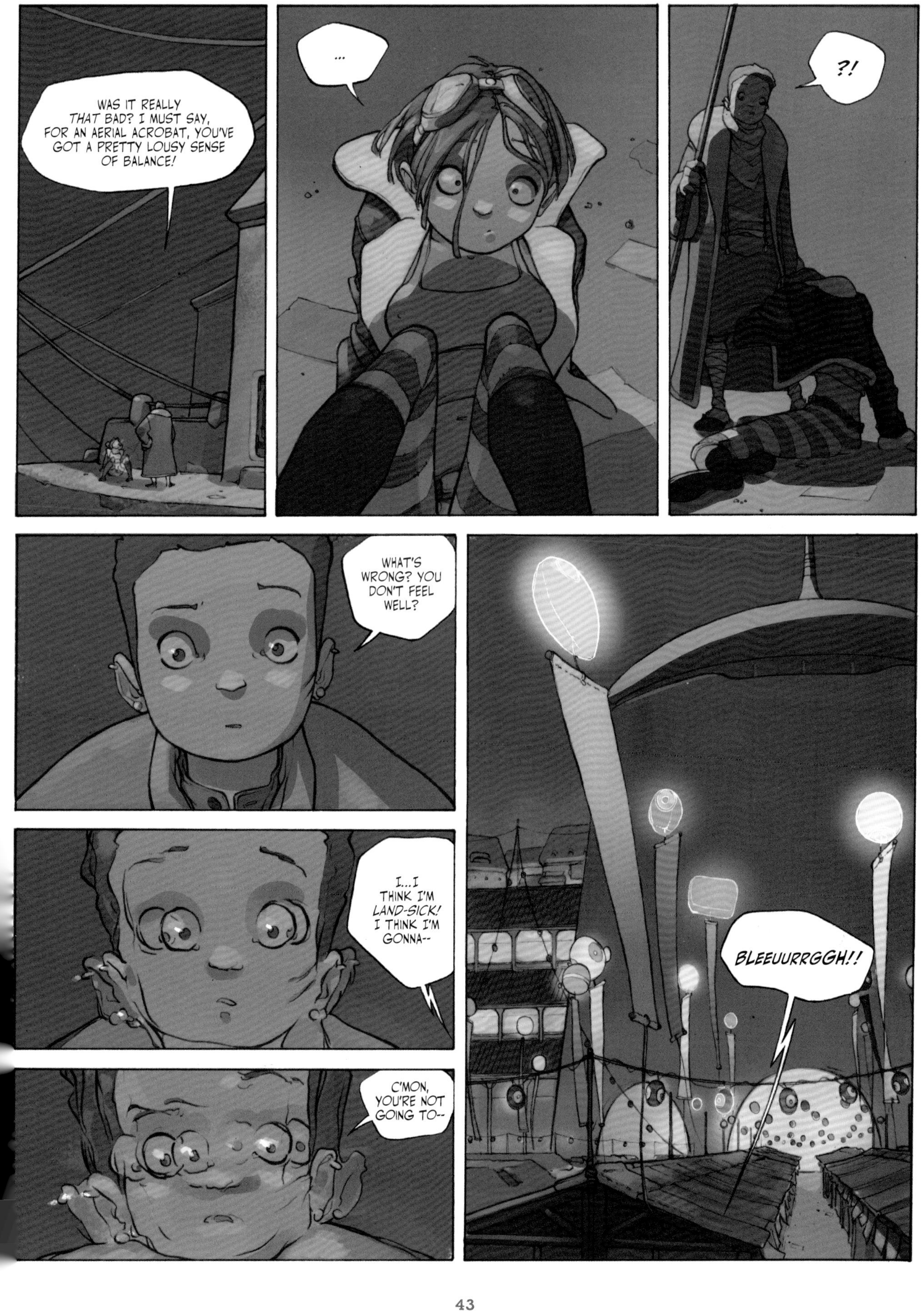
WAS IT REALLY *THAT* BAD? I MUST SAY, FOR AN AERIAL ACROBAT, YOU'VE GOT A PRETTY LOUSY SENSE OF BALANCE!
...
?!
WHAT'S WRONG? YOU DON'T FEEL WELL?
I...I THINK I'M *LAND-SICK!* I THINK I'M GONNA--
C'MON, YOU'RE NOT GOING TO--
BLEEUURRGGH!!

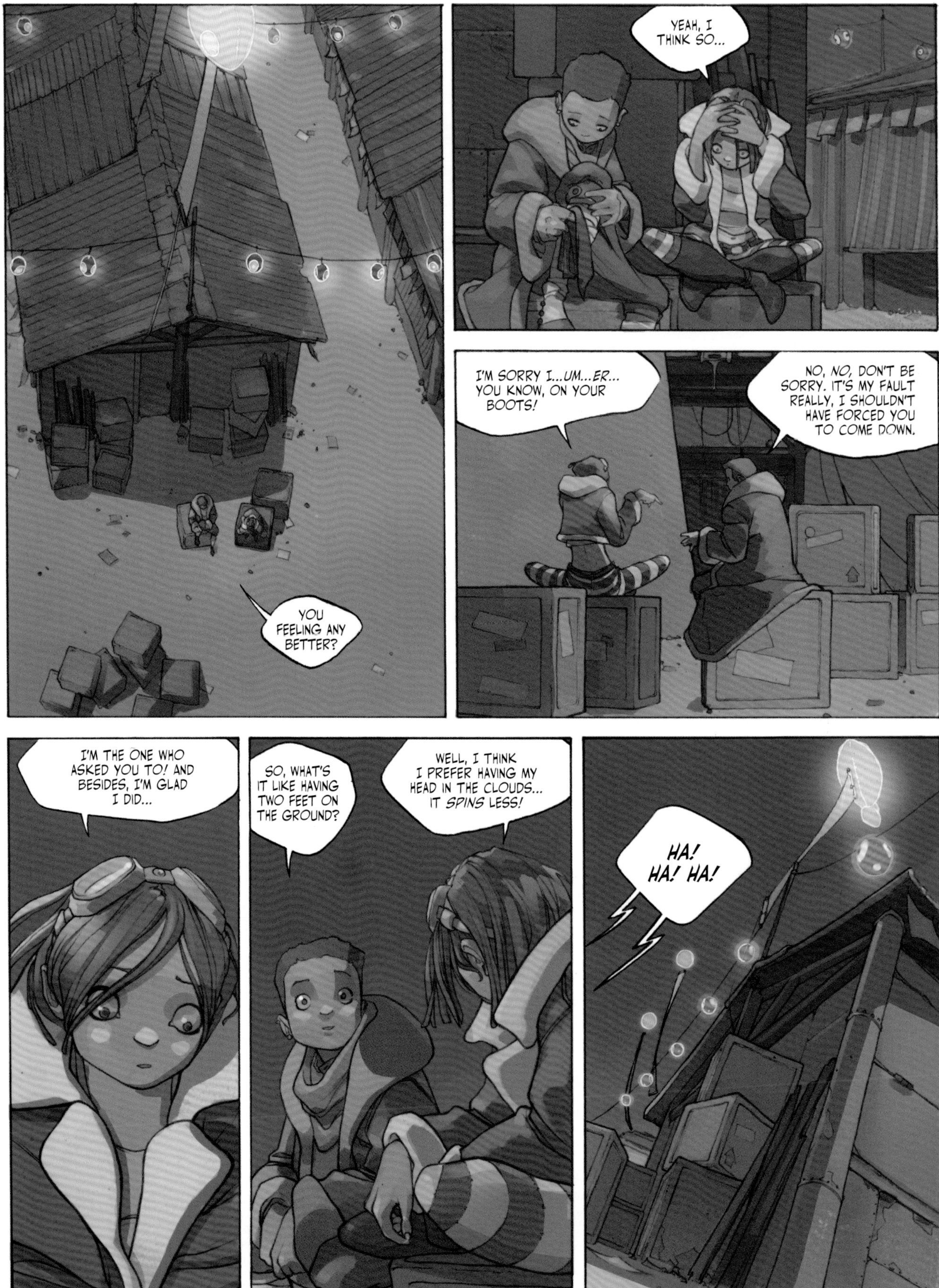
YOU FEELING ANY BETTER?
YEAH, I THINK SO...
I'M SORRY I...UM...ER... YOU KNOW, ON YOUR BOOTS!
NO, NO, DON'T BE SORRY. IT'S MY FAULT REALLY, I SHOULDN'T HAVE FORCED YOU TO COME DOWN.
I'M THE ONE WHO ASKED YOU TO! AND BESIDES, I'M GLAD I DID...
SO, WHAT'S IT LIKE HAVING TWO FEET ON THE GROUND?
WELL, I THINK I PREFER HAVING MY HEAD IN THE CLOUDS... IT SPINS LESS!
HA! HA! HA!

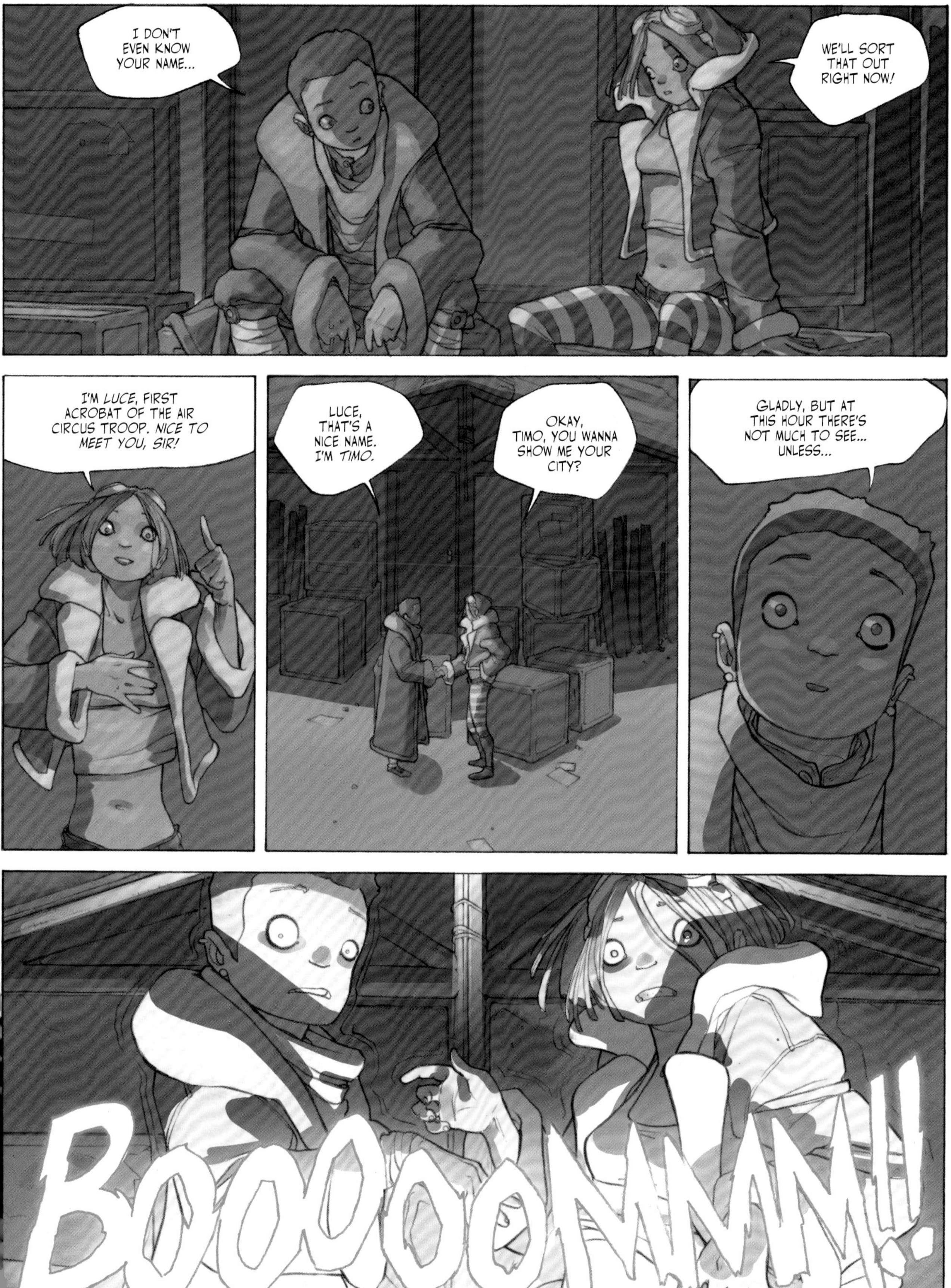
I DON'T EVEN KNOW YOUR NAME...
WE'LL SORT THAT OUT RIGHT NOW!
I'M LUCE, FIRST ACROBAT OF THE AIR CIRCUS TROOP. NICE TO MEET YOU, SIR!
LUCE, THAT'S A NICE NAME. I'M TIMO.
OKAY, TIMO, YOU WANNA SHOW ME YOUR CITY?
GLADLY, BUT AT THIS HOUR THERE'S NOT MUCH TO SEE... UNLESS...
BOOOOOMMM!!

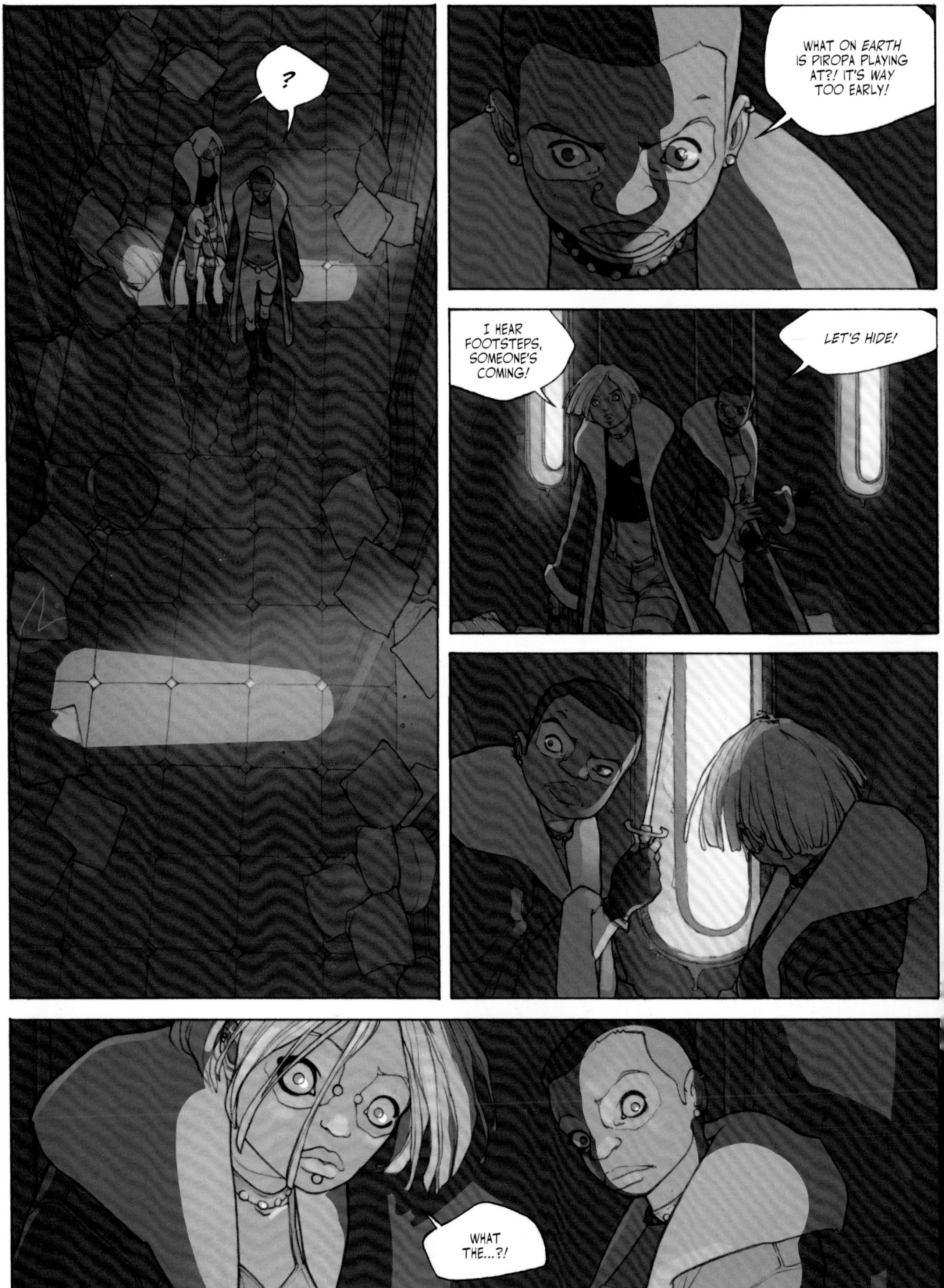
?
WHAT ON EARTH IS PIROPA PLAYING AT?! IT'S WAY TOO EARLY!
I HEAR FOOTSTEPS, SOMEONE'S COMING!
LET'S HIDE!
WHAT THE...?!

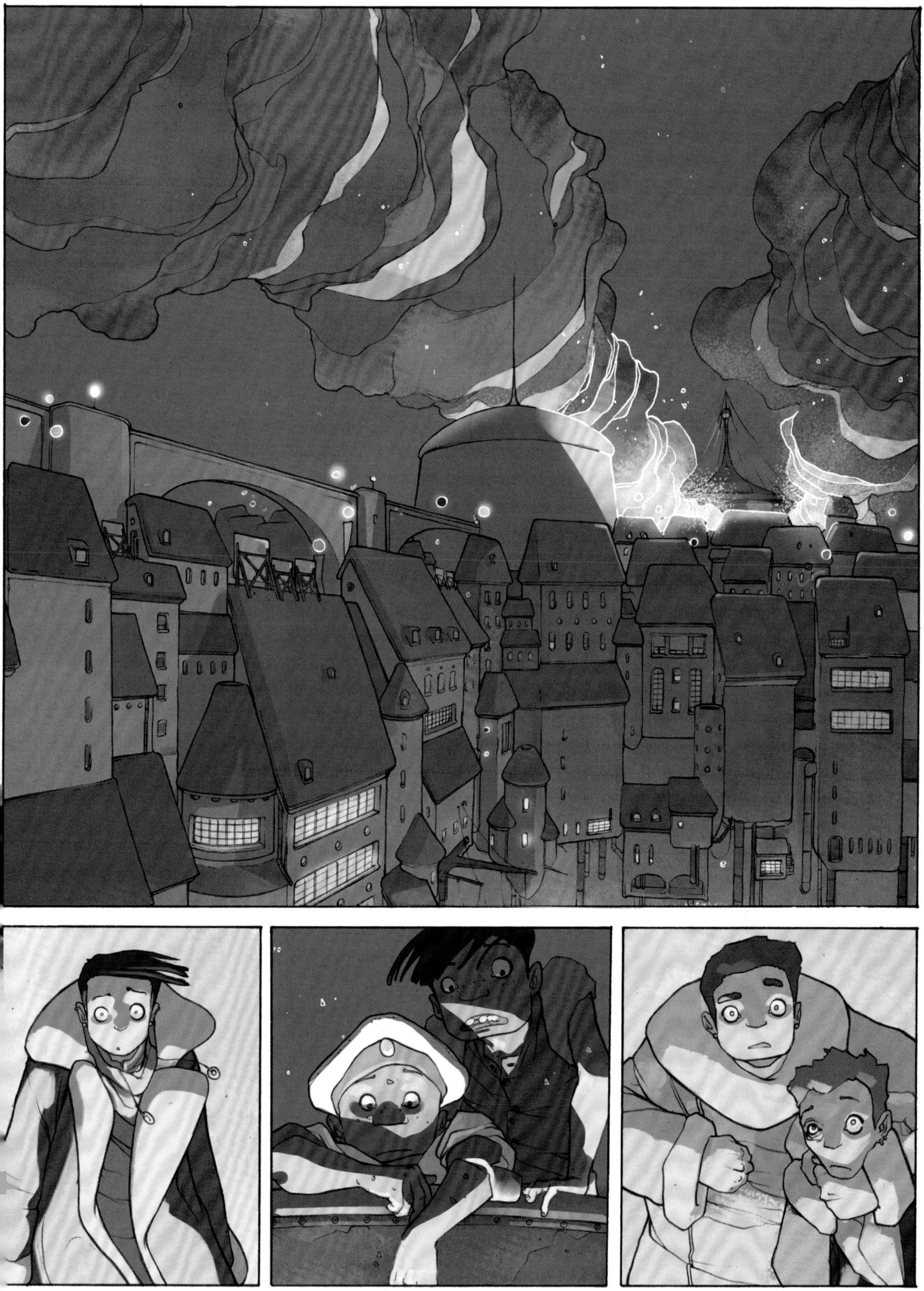

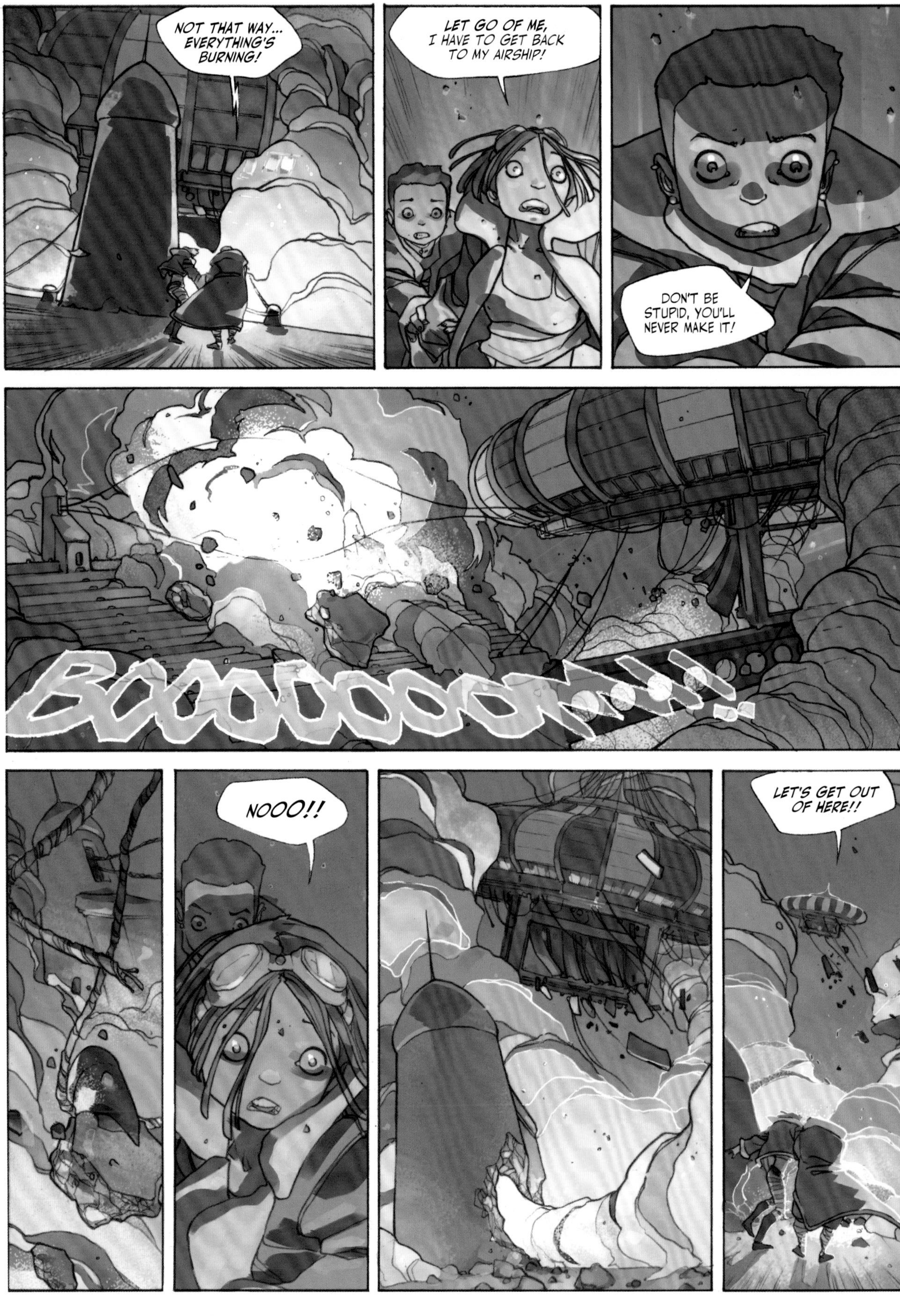
NOT THAT WAY... EVERYTHING'S BURNING!
LET GO OF ME, I HAVE TO GET BACK TO MY AIRSHIP!
DON'T BE STUPID, YOU'LL NEVER MAKE IT!
BOOOOOOOM!!!
NOOO!!
LET'S GET OUT OF HERE!!

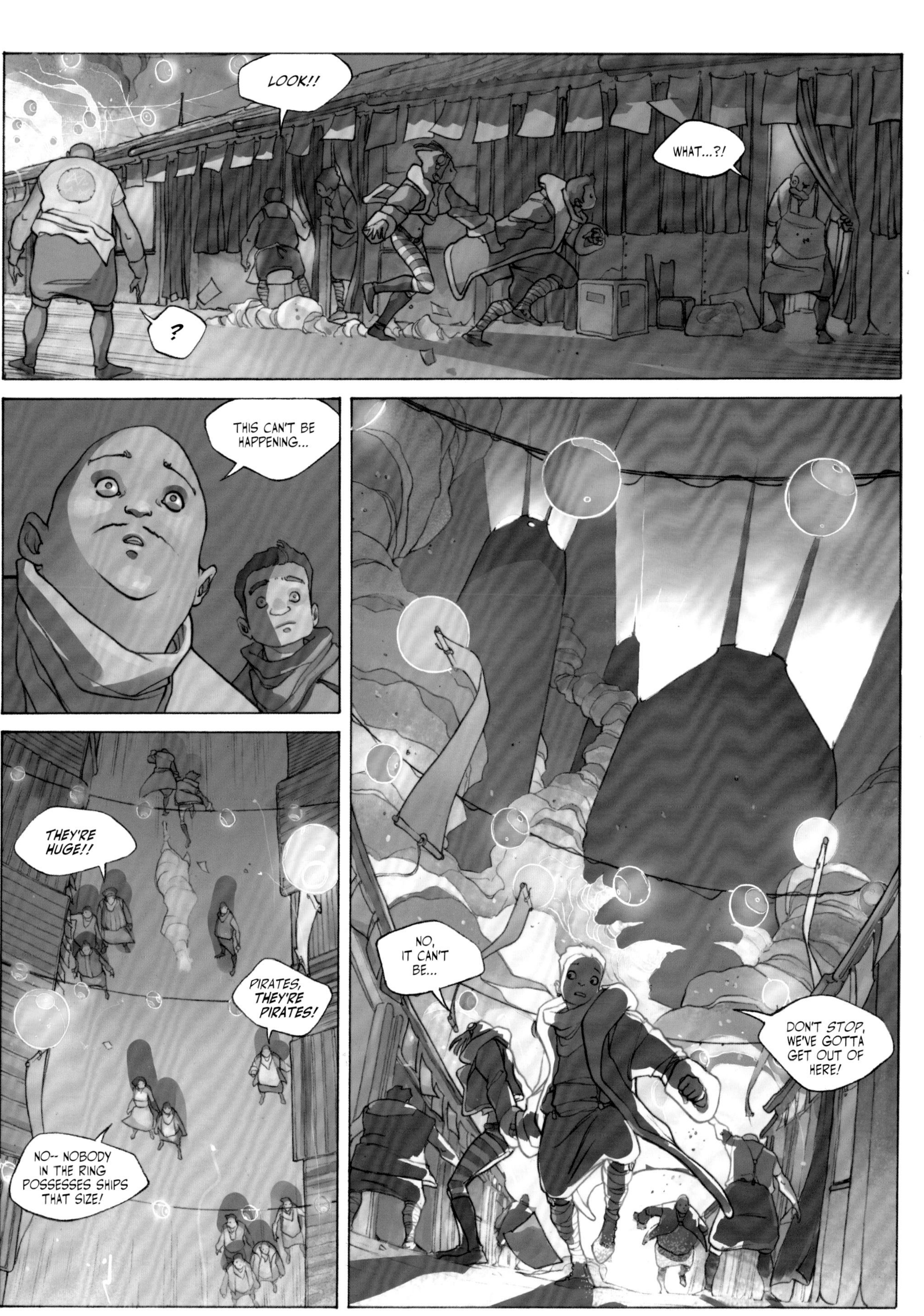
LOOK!!
WHAT...?!
?
THIS CAN'T BE HAPPENING...
THEY'RE HUGE!!
PIRATES, THEY'RE PIRATES!
NO-- NOBODY IN THE RING POSSESSES SHIPS THAT SIZE!
NO, IT CAN'T BE...
DON'T STOP, WE'VE GOTTA GET OUT OF HERE!

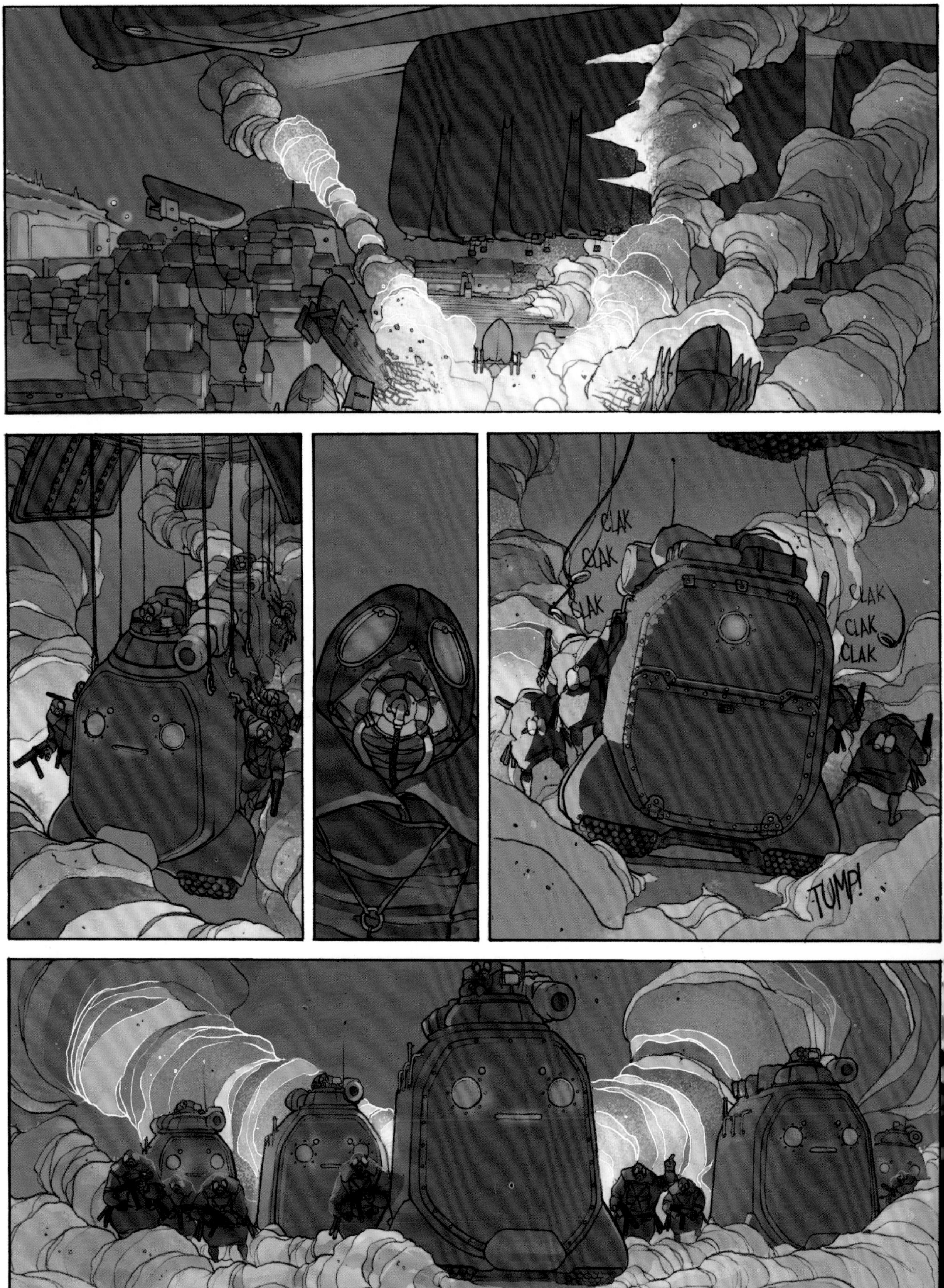
CLAK
CLAK
CLAK
CLAK
CLAK
CLAK
TUMP!

WHAT ARE THOSE?

I DON'T KNOW, I'VE NEVER SEEN ANYTHING LIKE THEM!

WE HAVE TO GET TO THE GUILD'S PALACE!

RRR-RRRRR-VRRR-VRRRRRR-V

CLANK CLANK   CLANK CLANK

CRAASH!!!

!!

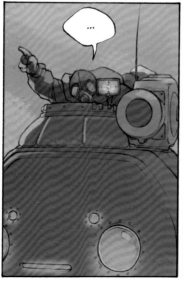

...

BOOOOMM!!

51

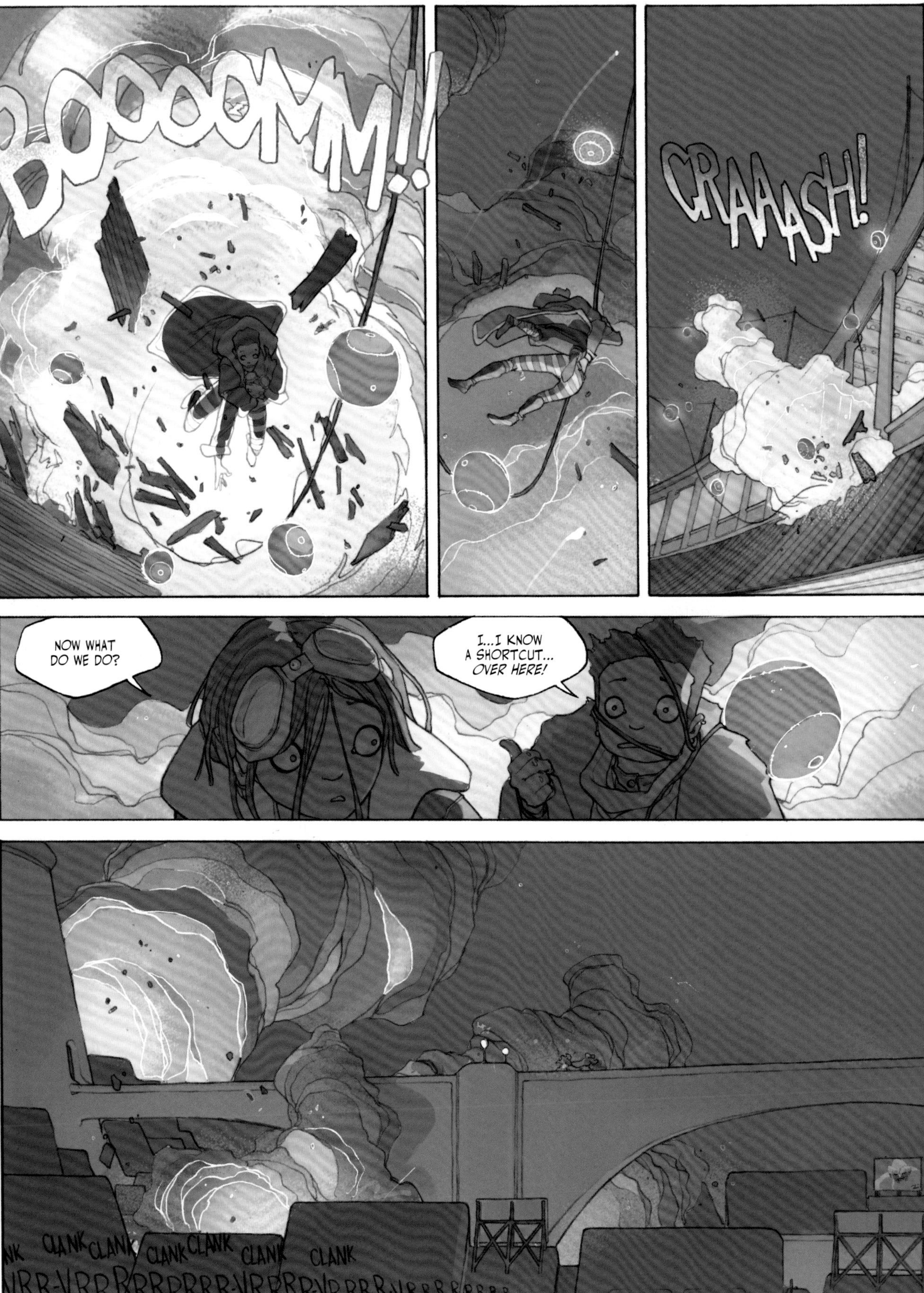
BOOOOMM!!
CRAAASH!
NOW WHAT DO WE DO?
I...I KNOW A SHORTCUT... OVER HERE!
NK CLANK CLANK CLANK CLANK CLANK CLANK
VRR-VRRRRRRRRR-VRRRR-VRRRR-VRRRRRRRRR

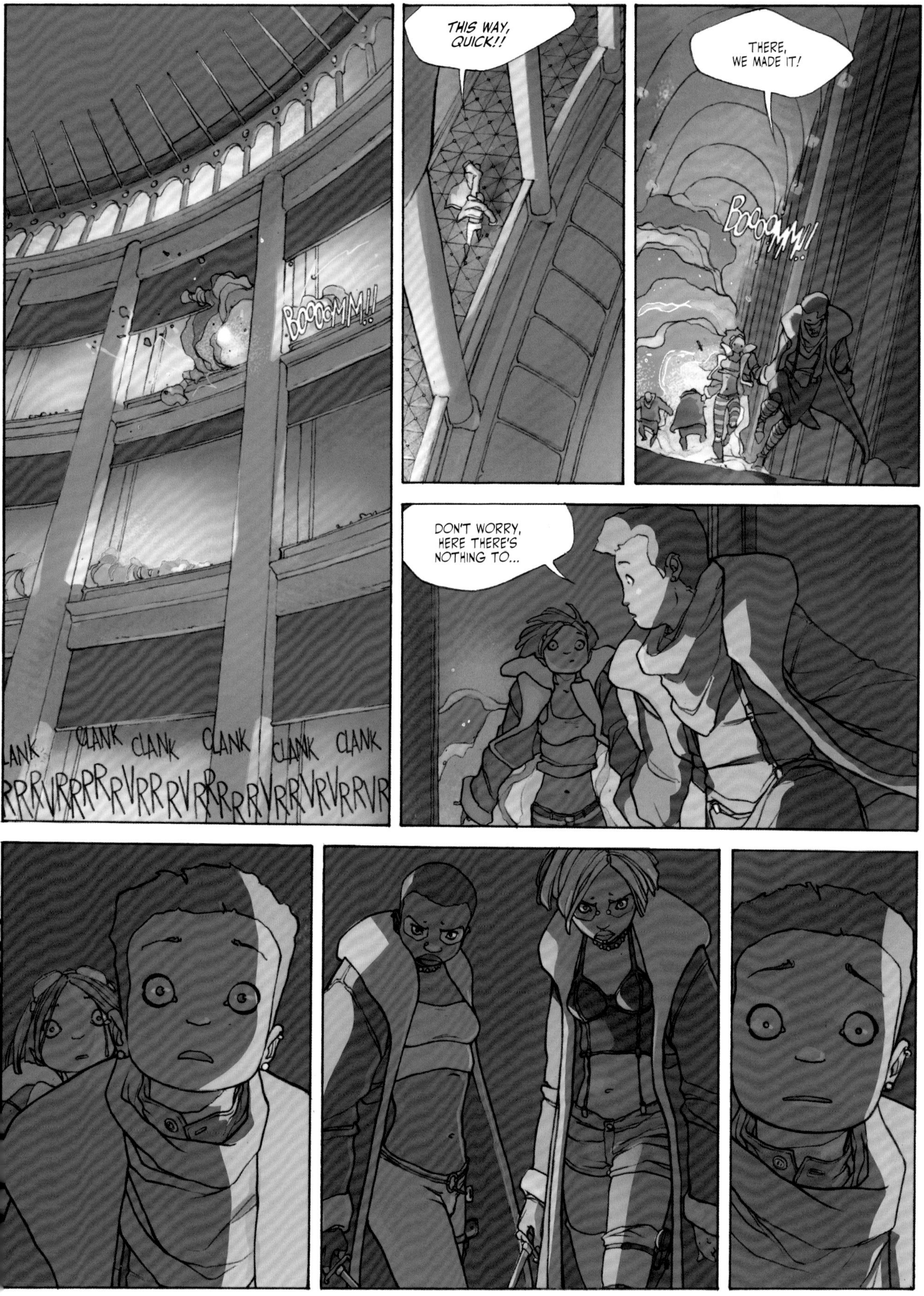
BOOOOMM!!
CLANK CLANK CLANK CLANK CLANK
THIS WAY, QUICK!!
THERE, WE MADE IT!
BOOOOMM!!
DON'T WORRY, HERE THERE'S NOTHING TO...

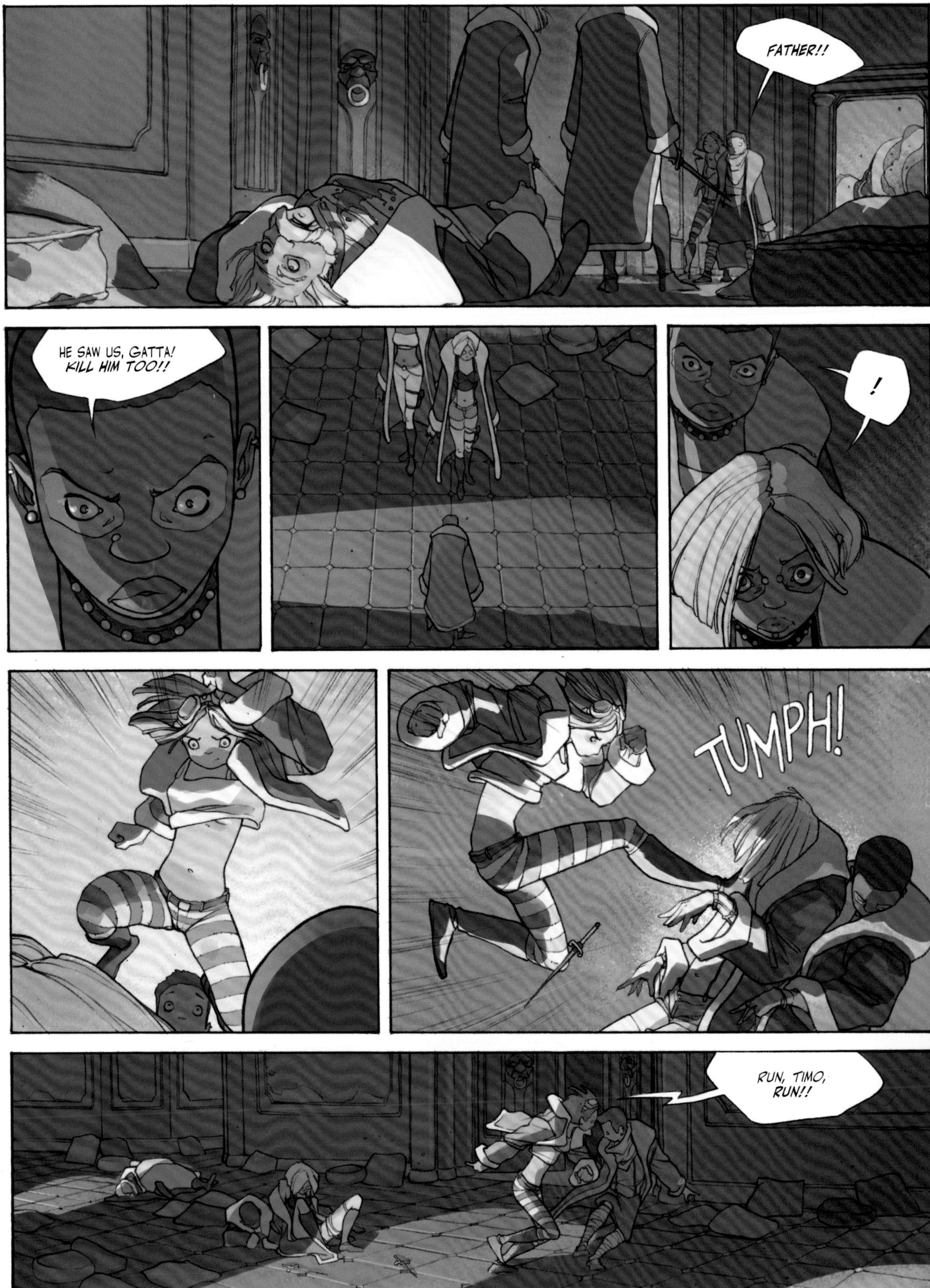
FATHER!!
HE SAW US, GATTA! KILL HIM TOO!!
!
TUMPH!
RUN, TIMO, RUN!!

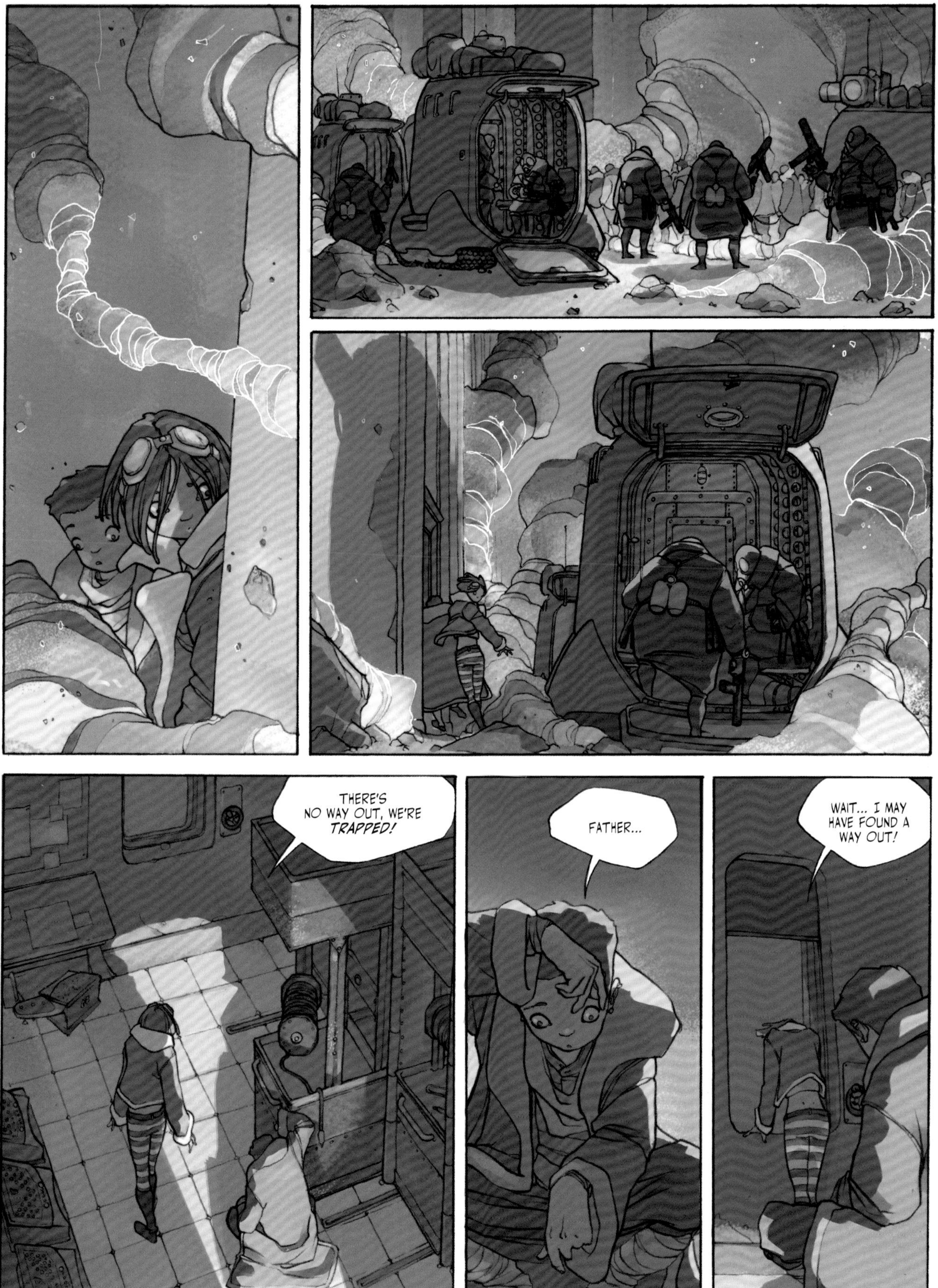
THERE'S NO WAY OUT, WE'RE *TRAPPED!*
FATHER...
WAIT... I MAY HAVE FOUND A WAY OUT!

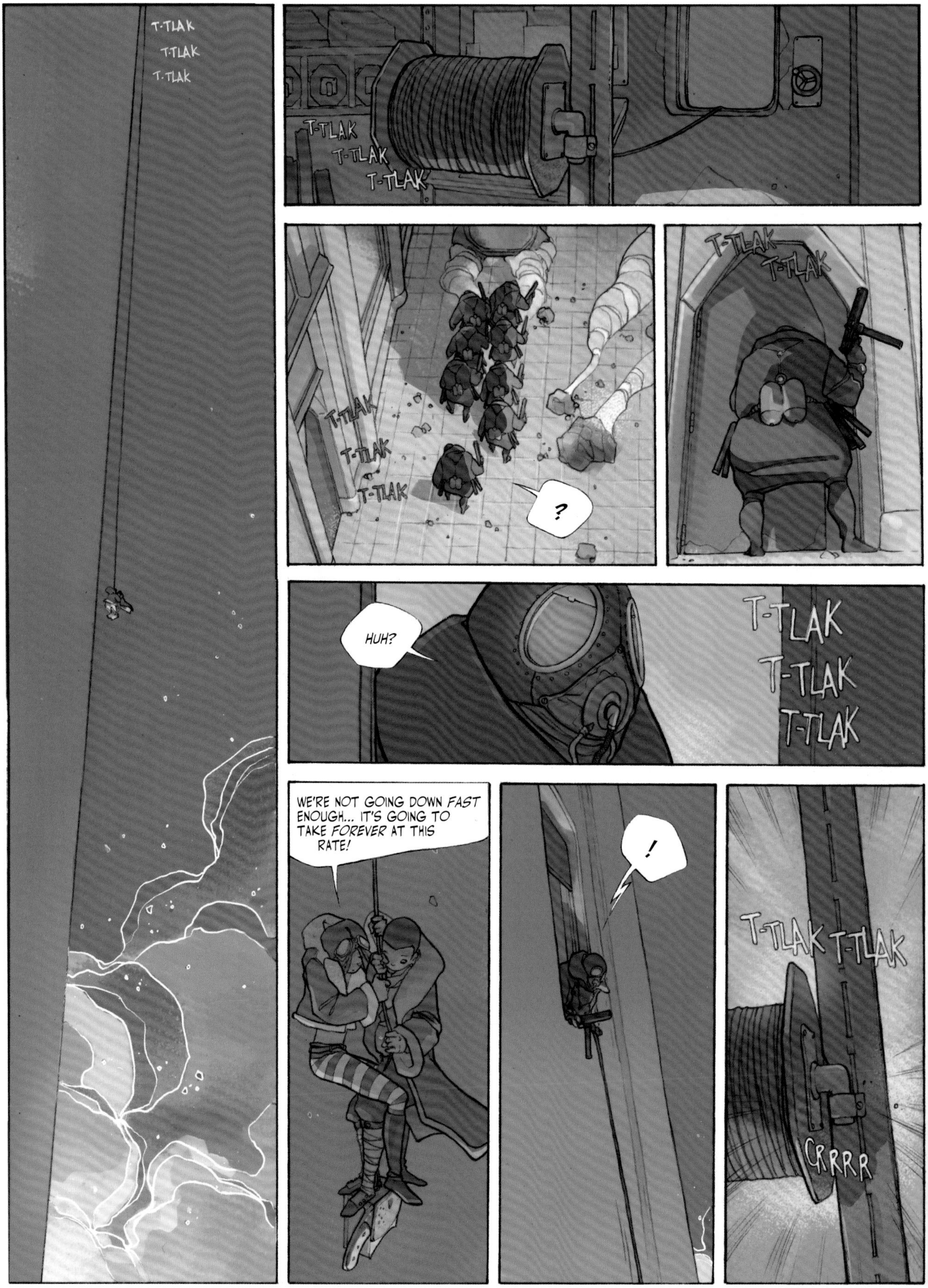
T-TLAK
T-TLAK
T-TLAK
T-TLAK
T-TLAK
T-TLAK
T-TLAK
T-TLAK
T-TLAK
T-TLAK
T-TLAK
?
T-TLAK
T-TLAK
HUH?
T-TLAK
T-TLAK
T-TLAK
WE'RE NOT GOING DOWN *FAST* ENOUGH... IT'S GOING TO TAKE *FOREVER* AT THIS RATE!
!
T-TLAK T-TLAK
CRRRR

C'RAAAAK!!

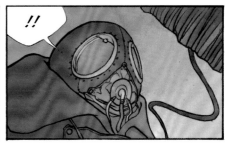

!!

TUMP!!

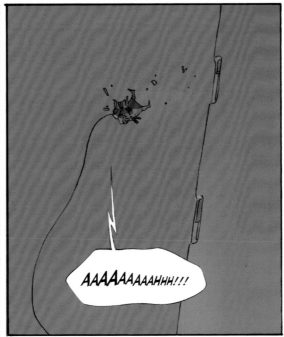

AAAAAAAAAAHHH!!!

AAAAAAAAAHHH!!!

CRAAASHH!!

AAAAAAAAAHHH!!

AAAAAAAAHHH!!

T·MM

AAH-H...

...H-HU-HU...

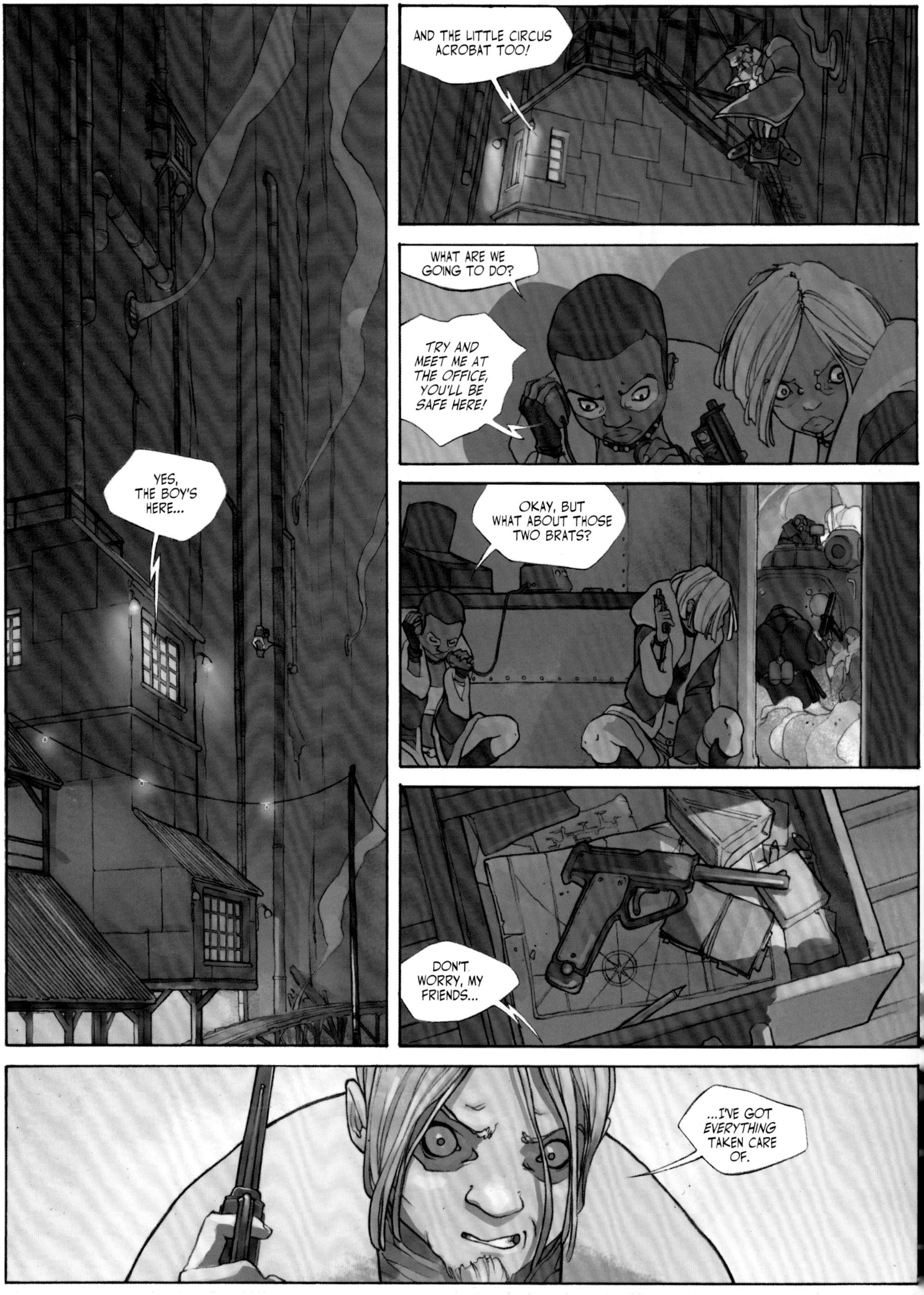
YES, THE BOY'S HERE...
AND THE LITTLE CIRCUS ACROBAT TOO!
WHAT ARE WE GOING TO DO?
TRY AND MEET ME AT THE OFFICE, YOU'LL BE SAFE HERE!
OKAY, BUT WHAT ABOUT THOSE TWO BRATS?
DON'T WORRY, MY FRIENDS...
...I'VE GOT EVERYTHING TAKEN CARE OF.

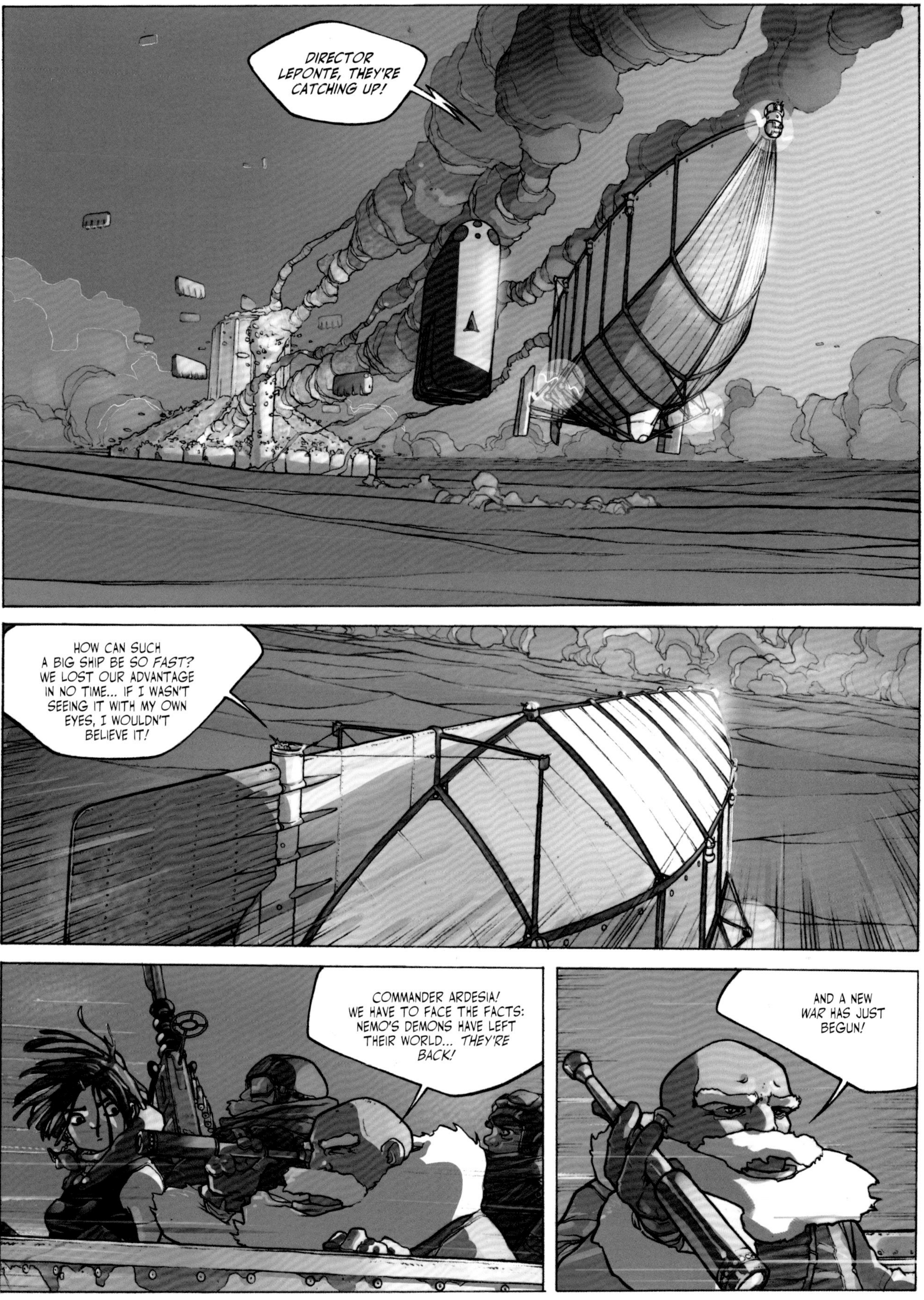
DIRECTOR LEPONTE, THEY'RE CATCHING UP!
HOW CAN SUCH A BIG SHIP BE SO FAST? WE LOST OUR ADVANTAGE IN NO TIME... IF I WASN'T SEEING IT WITH MY OWN EYES, I WOULDN'T BELIEVE IT!
COMMANDER ARDESIA! WE HAVE TO FACE THE FACTS: NEMO'S DEMONS HAVE LEFT THEIR WORLD... THEY'RE BACK!
AND A NEW WAR HAS JUST BEGUN!

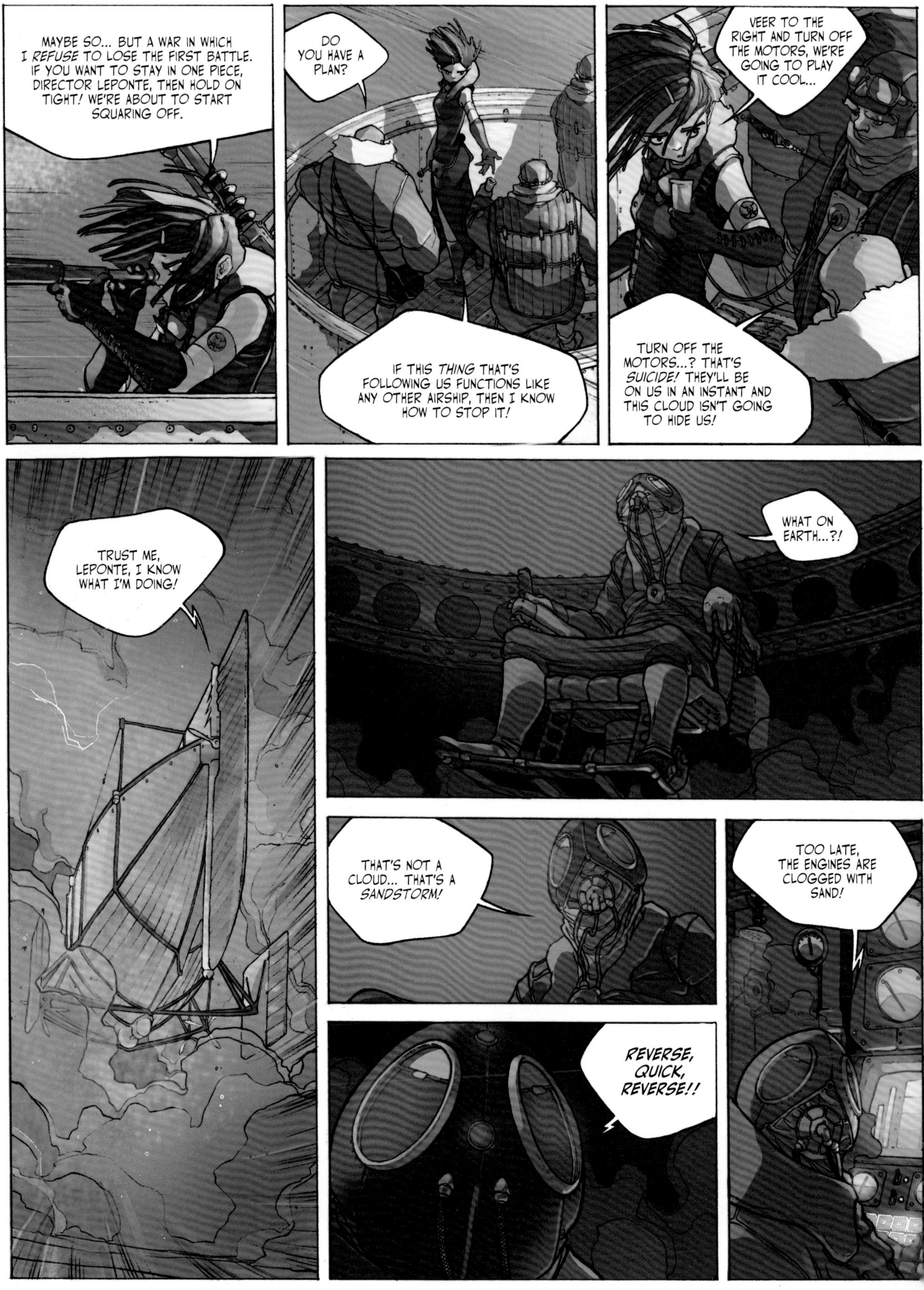
MAYBE SO... BUT A WAR IN WHICH I *REFUSE* TO LOSE THE FIRST BATTLE. IF YOU WANT TO STAY IN ONE PIECE, DIRECTOR LEPONTE, THEN HOLD ON TIGHT! WE'RE ABOUT TO START SQUARING OFF.
DO YOU HAVE A PLAN?
IF THIS *THING* THAT'S FOLLOWING US FUNCTIONS LIKE ANY OTHER AIRSHIP, THEN I KNOW HOW TO STOP IT!
VEER TO THE RIGHT AND TURN OFF THE MOTORS, WE'RE GOING TO PLAY IT COOL...
TURN OFF THE MOTORS...? THAT'S *SUICIDE!* THEY'LL BE ON US IN AN INSTANT AND THIS CLOUD ISN'T GOING TO HIDE US!
TRUST ME, LEPONTE, I KNOW WHAT I'M DOING!
WHAT ON EARTH...?!
THAT'S NOT A CLOUD... THAT'S A *SANDSTORM!*
REVERSE, QUICK, REVERSE!!
TOO LATE, THE ENGINES ARE CLOGGED WITH SAND!

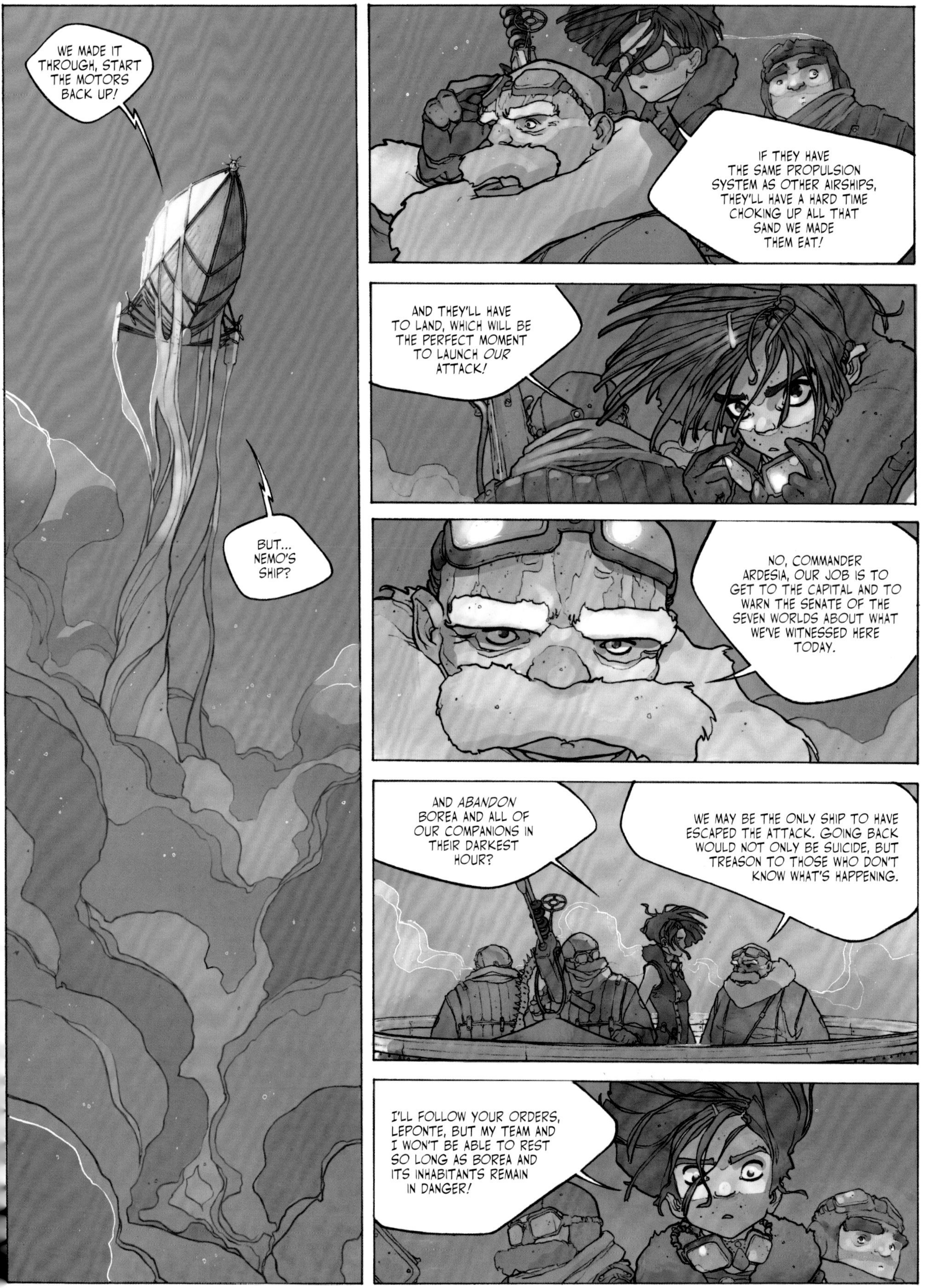

WE MADE IT THROUGH, START THE MOTORS BACK UP!
BUT... NEMO'S SHIP?
IF THEY HAVE THE SAME PROPULSION SYSTEM AS OTHER AIRSHIPS, THEY'LL HAVE A HARD TIME CHOKING UP ALL THAT SAND WE MADE THEM EAT!
AND THEY'LL HAVE TO LAND, WHICH WILL BE THE PERFECT MOMENT TO LAUNCH OUR ATTACK!
NO, COMMANDER ARDESIA, OUR JOB IS TO GET TO THE CAPITAL AND TO WARN THE SENATE OF THE SEVEN WORLDS ABOUT WHAT WE'VE WITNESSED HERE TODAY.
AND ABANDON BOREA AND ALL OF OUR COMPANIONS IN THEIR DARKEST HOUR?
WE MAY BE THE ONLY SHIP TO HAVE ESCAPED THE ATTACK. GOING BACK WOULD NOT ONLY BE SUICIDE, BUT TREASON TO THOSE WHO DON'T KNOW WHAT'S HAPPENING.
I'LL FOLLOW YOUR ORDERS, LEPONTE, BUT MY TEAM AND I WON'T BE ABLE TO REST SO LONG AS BOREA AND ITS INHABITANTS REMAIN IN DANGER!

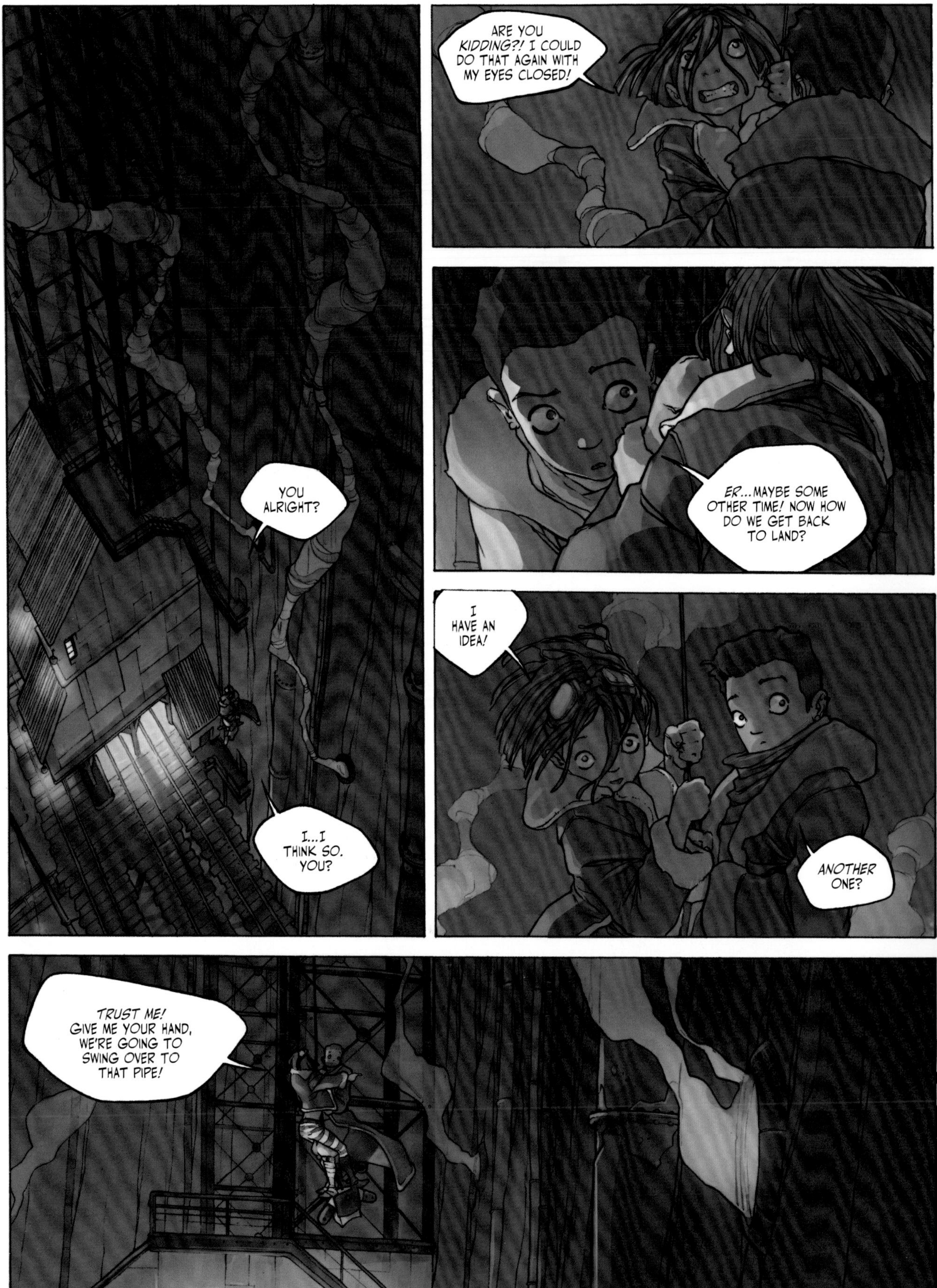
YOU ALRIGHT?
I...I THINK SO. YOU?
ARE YOU *KIDDING?!* I COULD DO THAT AGAIN WITH MY EYES CLOSED!
ER...MAYBE SOME OTHER TIME! NOW HOW DO WE GET BACK TO LAND?
I HAVE AN IDEA!
ANOTHER ONE?
TRUST ME! GIVE ME YOUR HAND, WE'RE GOING TO SWING OVER TO THAT PIPE!

THERE,
I GOT IT!

ARE YOU
SURE IT'LL HOLD
OUR WEIGHT?

ARE YOU
INSINUATING THAT
I'M FA--

GRRR-T-T-TAK!

AHHH...!!

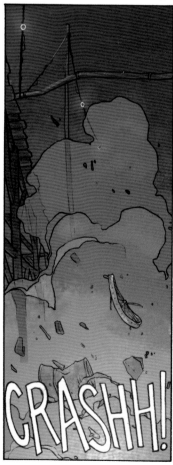

CRASHH!

63

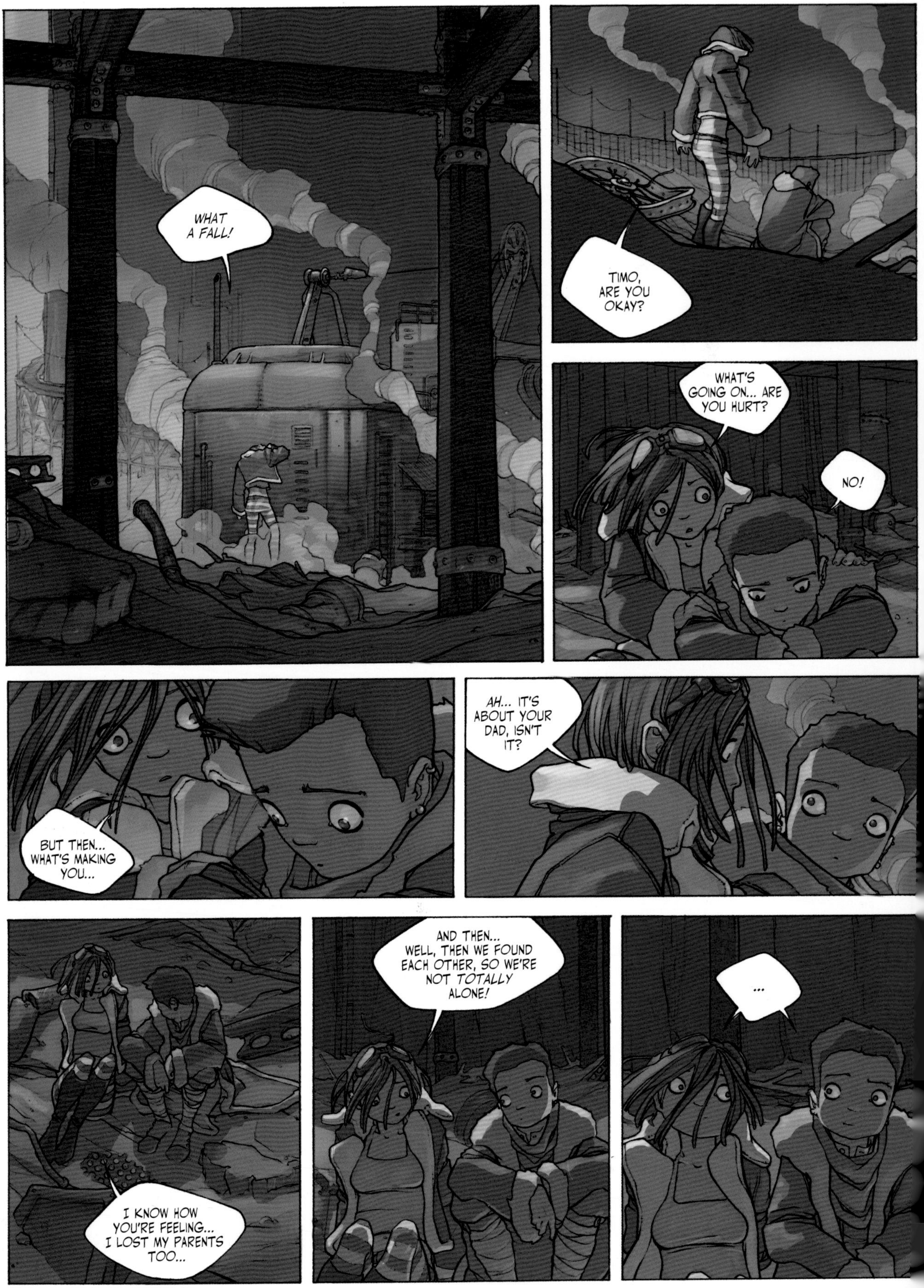
WHAT A FALL!
TIMO, ARE YOU OKAY?
WHAT'S GOING ON... ARE YOU HURT?
NO!
BUT THEN... WHAT'S MAKING YOU...
AH... IT'S ABOUT YOUR DAD, ISN'T IT?
I KNOW HOW YOU'RE FEELING... I LOST MY PARENTS TOO...
AND THEN... WELL, THEN WE FOUND EACH OTHER, SO WE'RE NOT TOTALLY ALONE!
...

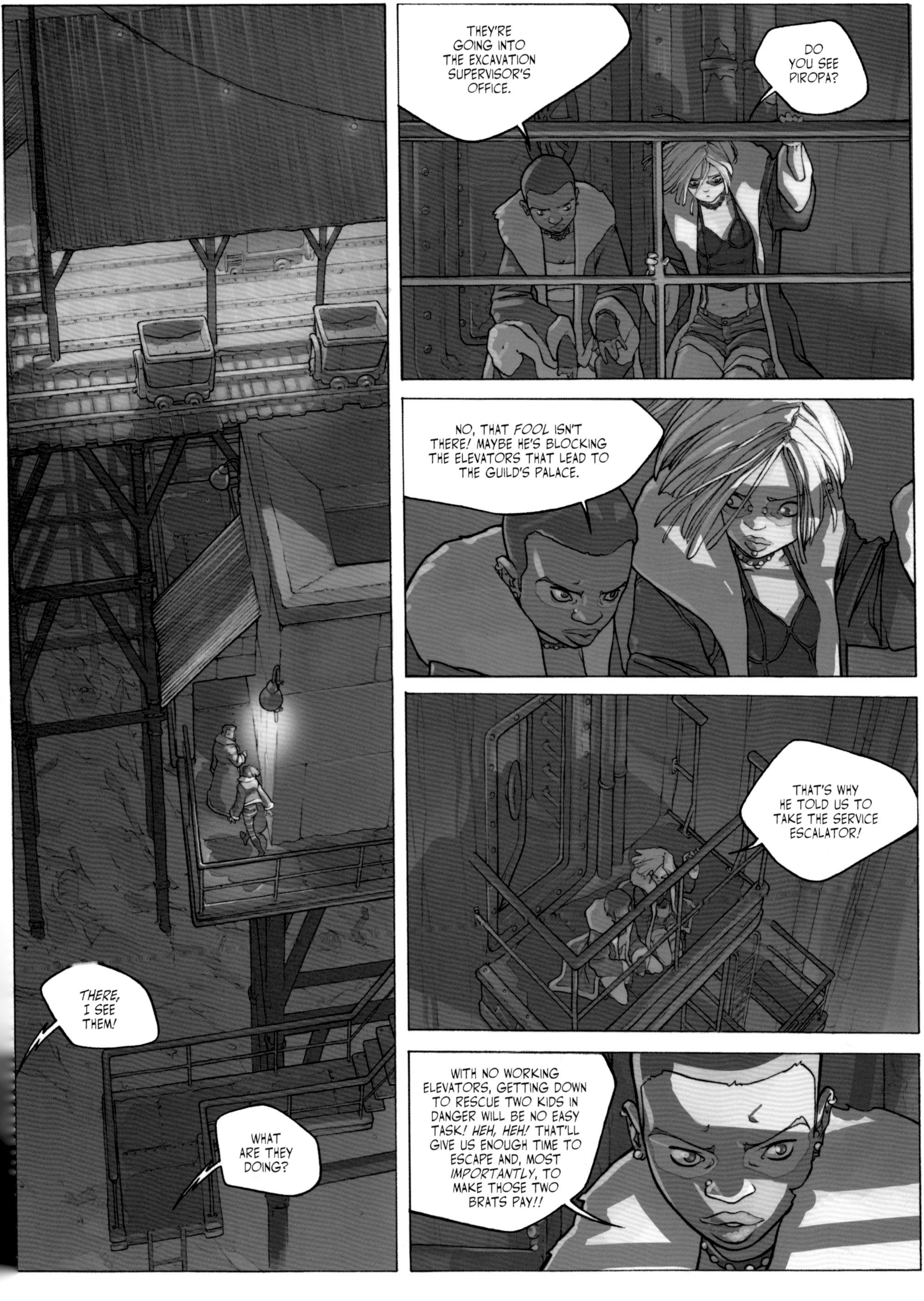
THERE, I SEE THEM!
WHAT ARE THEY DOING?
THEY'RE GOING INTO THE EXCAVATION SUPERVISOR'S OFFICE.
DO YOU SEE PIROPA?
NO, THAT *FOOL* ISN'T THERE! MAYBE HE'S BLOCKING THE ELEVATORS THAT LEAD TO THE GUILD'S PALACE.
THAT'S WHY HE TOLD US TO TAKE THE SERVICE ESCALATOR!
WITH NO WORKING ELEVATORS, GETTING DOWN TO RESCUE TWO KIDS IN DANGER WILL BE NO EASY TASK! *HEH, HEH!* THAT'LL GIVE US ENOUGH TIME TO ESCAPE AND, MOST *IMPORTANTLY*, TO MAKE THOSE TWO BRATS PAY!!

WHERE ARE WE?

MR. PIROPA'S OFFICE. HE'S THE EXCAVATION SUPERVISOR!

HE'S THE ONE MY FATHER DESIGNATED AS MY GUARDIAN, IN CASE SOMETHING EVER HAPPENED TO HIM...

WHAT EXCAVATIONS?

THE SCRAP HEAPS!

SCRAP HEAPS?

LOOK, I'LL SHOW YOU!

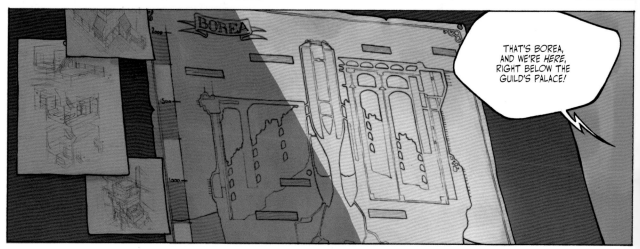

THAT'S BOREA, AND WE'RE HERE, RIGHT BELOW THE GUILD'S PALACE!

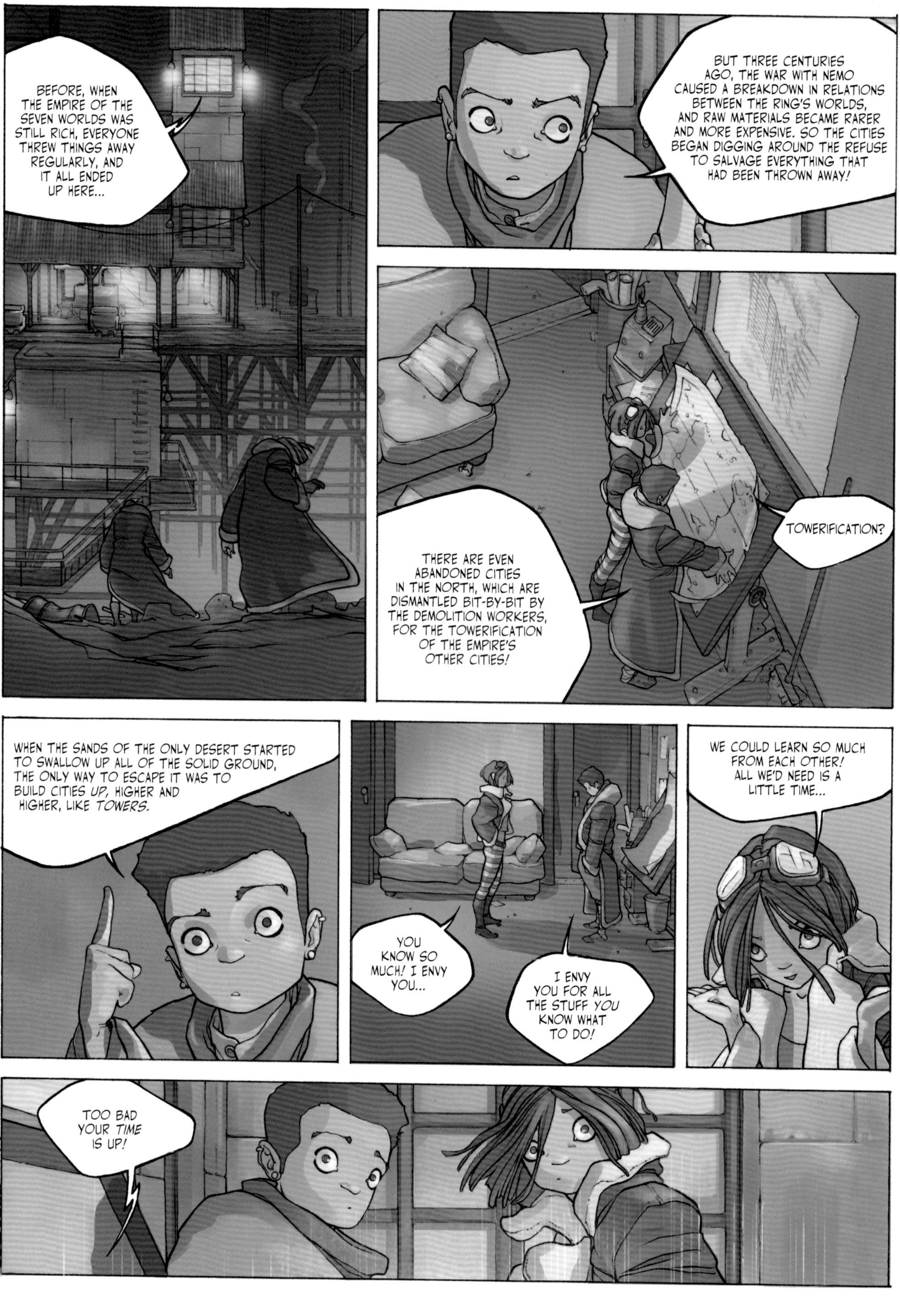
BEFORE, WHEN THE EMPIRE OF THE SEVEN WORLDS WAS STILL RICH, EVERYONE THREW THINGS AWAY REGULARLY, AND IT ALL ENDED UP HERE...
BUT THREE CENTURIES AGO, THE WAR WITH NEMO CAUSED A BREAKDOWN IN RELATIONS BETWEEN THE RING'S WORLDS, AND RAW MATERIALS BECAME RARER AND MORE EXPENSIVE. SO THE CITIES BEGAN DIGGING AROUND THE REFUSE TO SALVAGE EVERYTHING THAT HAD BEEN THROWN AWAY!
THERE ARE EVEN ABANDONED CITIES IN THE NORTH, WHICH ARE DISMANTLED BIT-BY-BIT BY THE DEMOLITION WORKERS, FOR THE TOWERIFICATION OF THE EMPIRE'S OTHER CITIES!
TOWERIFICATION?
WHEN THE SANDS OF THE ONLY DESERT STARTED TO SWALLOW UP ALL OF THE SOLID GROUND, THE ONLY WAY TO ESCAPE IT WAS TO BUILD CITIES UP, HIGHER AND HIGHER, LIKE TOWERS.
YOU KNOW SO MUCH! I ENVY YOU...
I ENVY YOU FOR ALL THE STUFF YOU KNOW WHAT TO DO!
WE COULD LEARN SO MUCH FROM EACH OTHER! ALL WE'D NEED IS A LITTLE TIME...
TOO BAD YOUR TIME IS UP!

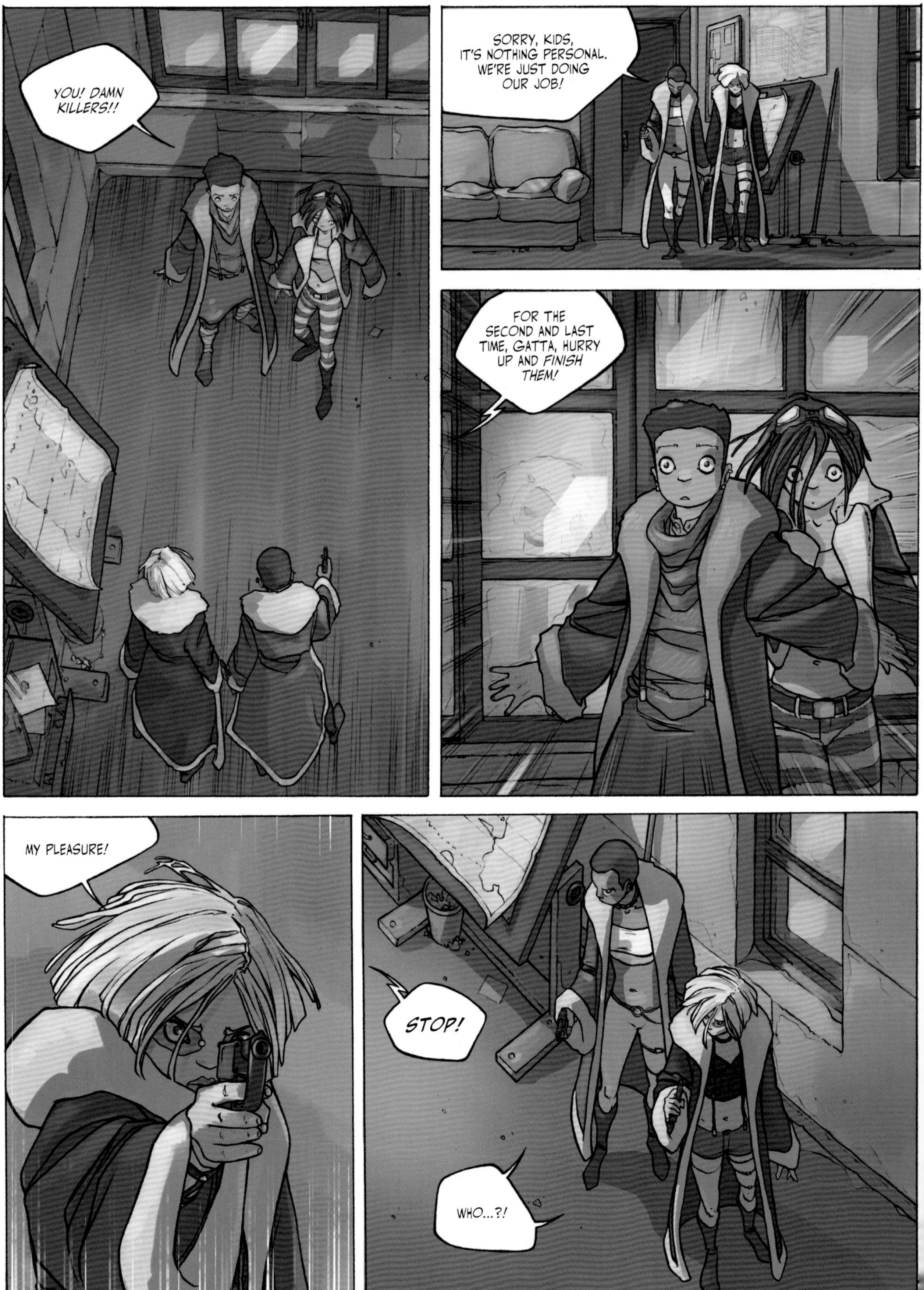
YOU! DAMN KILLERS!!
SORRY, KIDS, IT'S NOTHING PERSONAL. WE'RE JUST DOING OUR JOB!
FOR THE SECOND AND LAST TIME, GATTA, HURRY UP AND FINISH THEM!
MY PLEASURE!
STOP!
WHO...?!

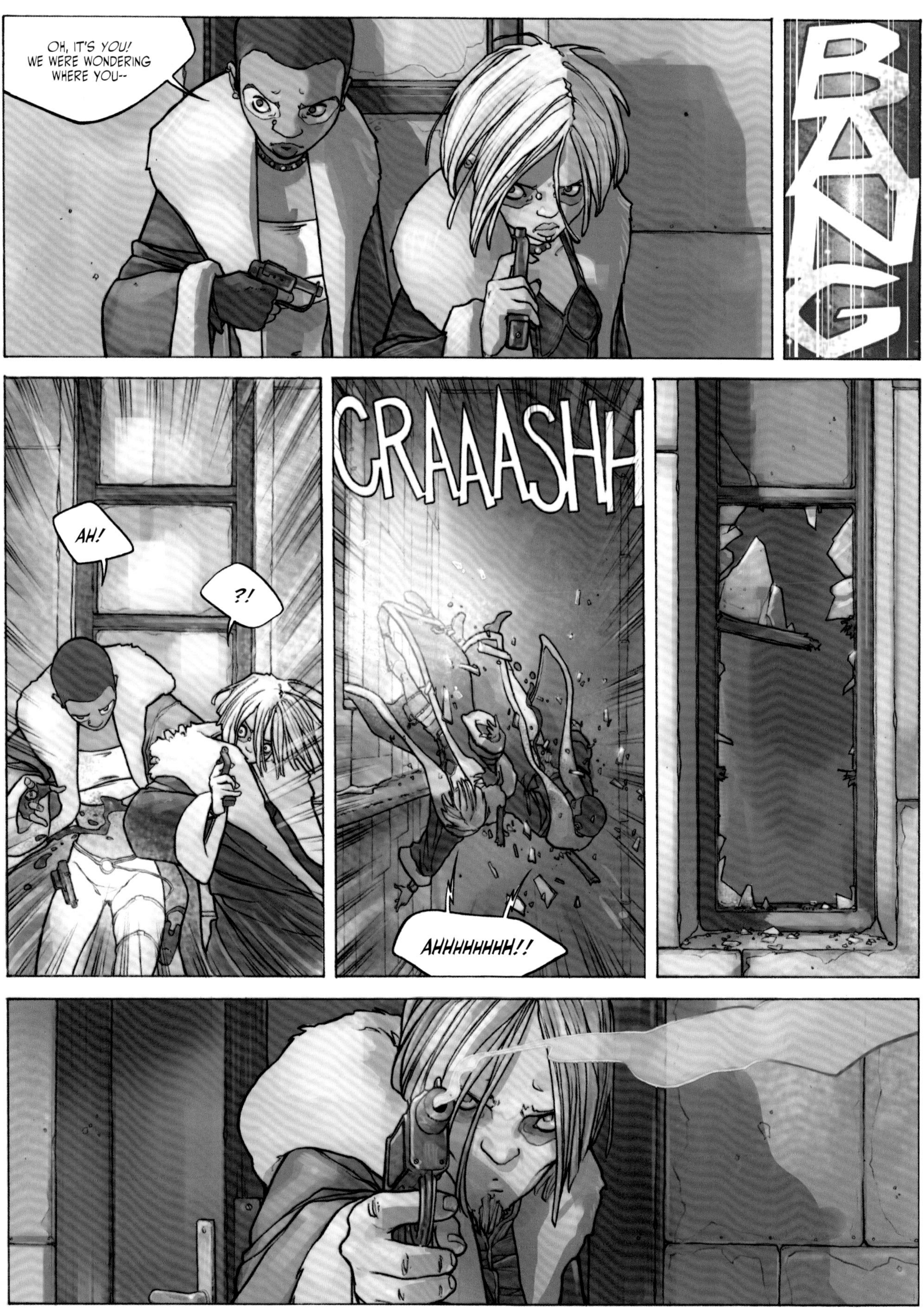
OH, IT'S YOU! WE WERE WONDERING WHERE YOU--
BANG
AH!
?!
CRAAASHH
AHHHHHHHH!!

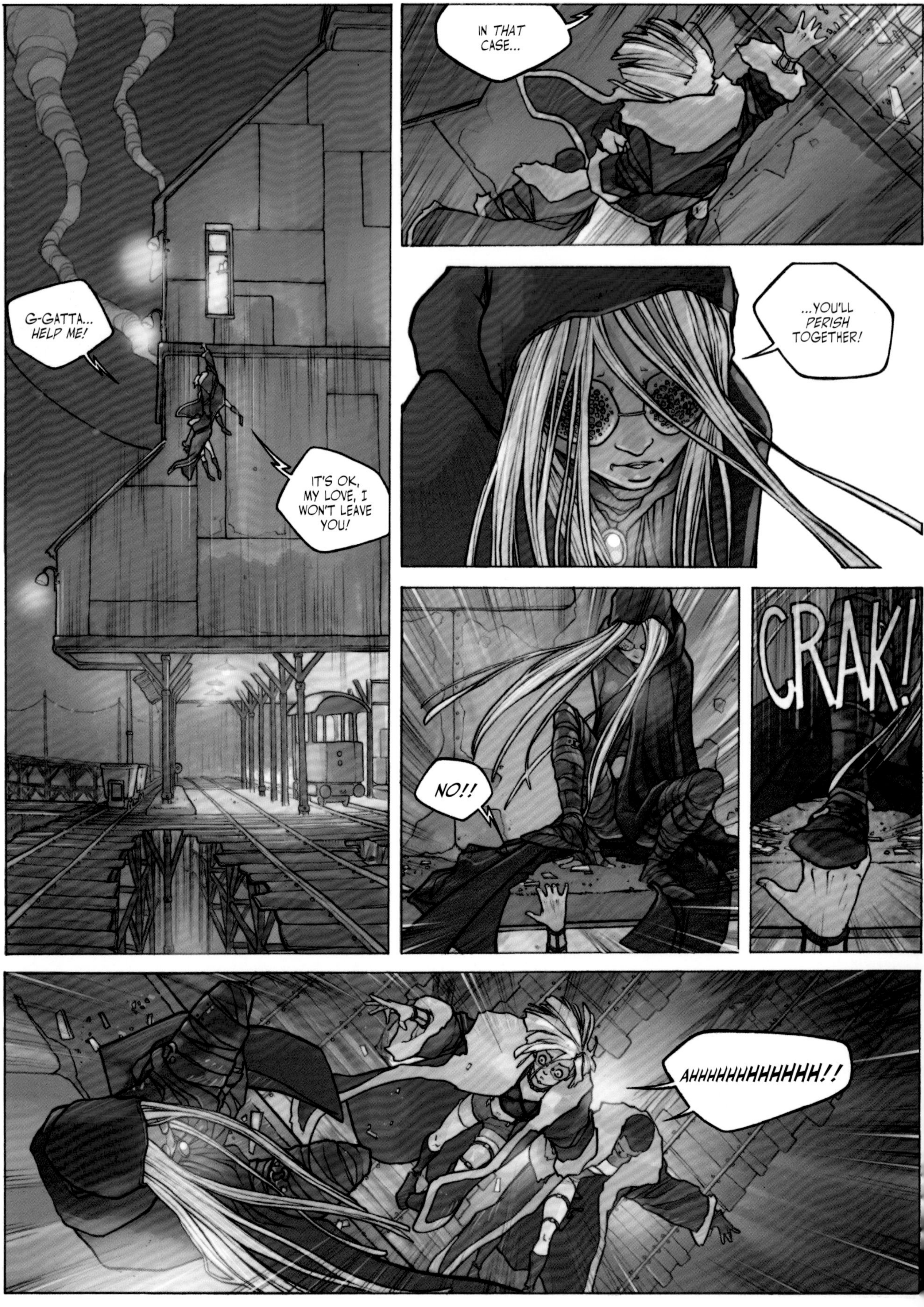
G-GATTA... HELP ME!
IT'S OK, MY LOVE, I WON'T LEAVE YOU!
IN THAT CASE...
...YOU'LL PERISH TOGETHER!
NO!!
CRAK!
AHHHHHHHHHHHH!!

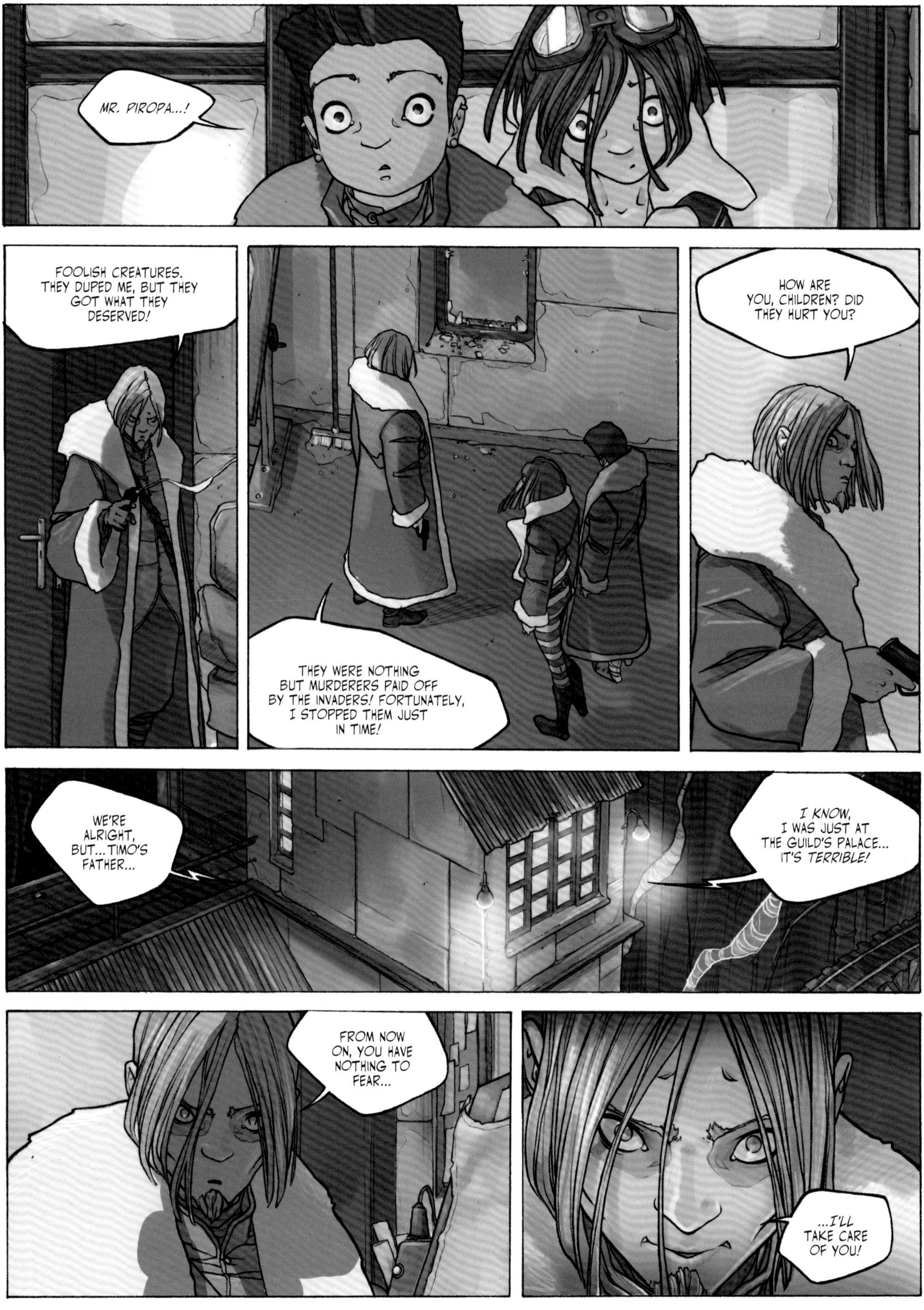
MR. PIROPA...!
FOOLISH CREATURES. THEY DUPED ME, BUT THEY GOT WHAT THEY DESERVED!
THEY WERE NOTHING BUT MURDERERS PAID OFF BY THE INVADERS! FORTUNATELY, I STOPPED THEM JUST IN TIME!
HOW ARE YOU, CHILDREN? DID THEY HURT YOU?
WE'RE ALRIGHT, BUT... TIMO'S FATHER...
I KNOW, I WAS JUST AT THE GUILD'S PALACE... IT'S TERRIBLE!
FROM NOW ON, YOU HAVE NOTHING TO FEAR...
...I'LL TAKE CARE OF YOU!

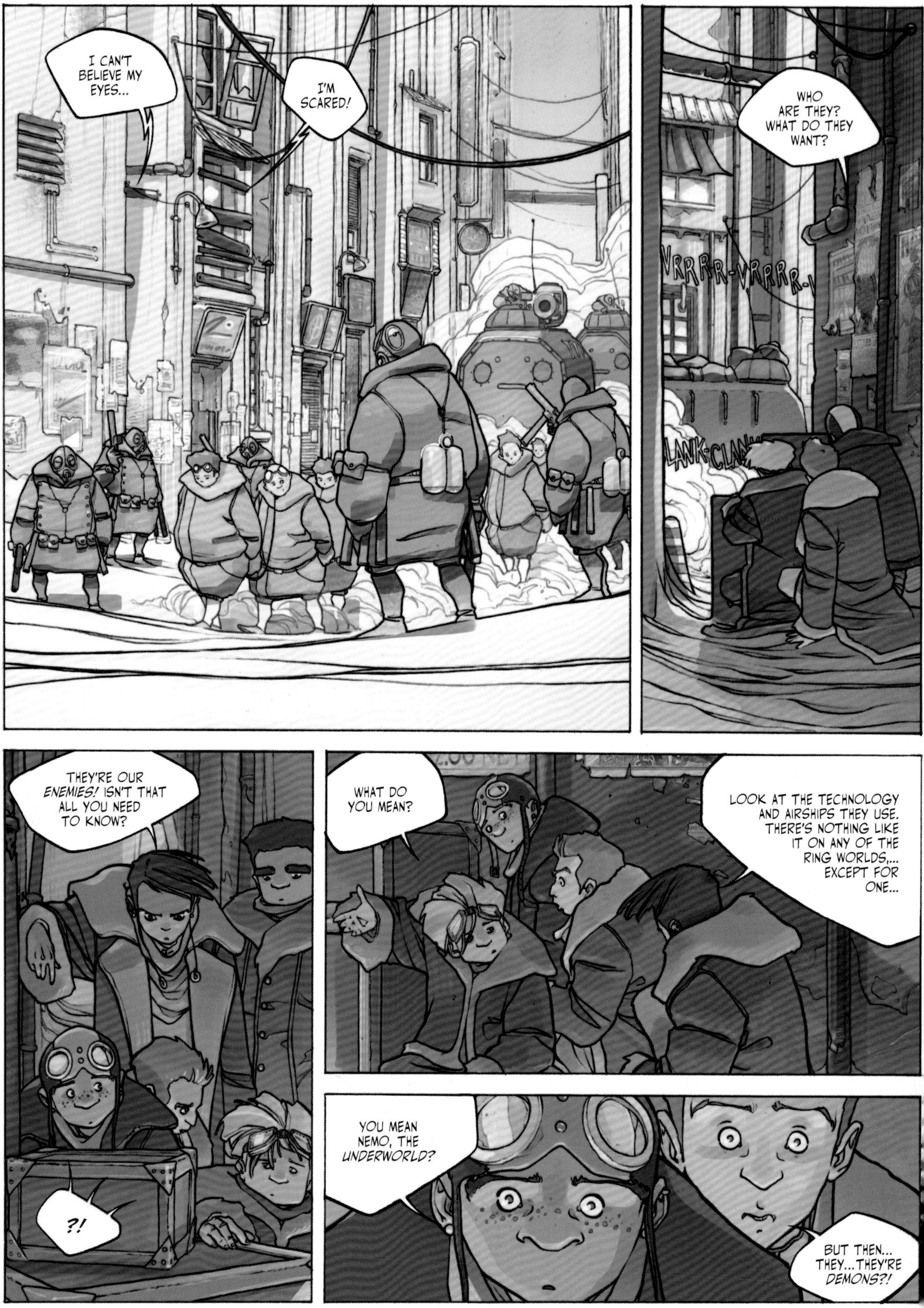
I CAN'T BELIEVE MY EYES...
I'M SCARED!
WHO ARE THEY? WHAT DO THEY WANT?
VRRRR-VRRRR-
LANK-CLAN
THEY'RE OUR *ENEMIES!* ISN'T THAT ALL YOU NEED TO KNOW?
?!
WHAT DO YOU MEAN?
LOOK AT THE TECHNOLOGY AND AIRSHIPS THEY USE. THERE'S NOTHING LIKE IT ON ANY OF THE RING WORLDS,... EXCEPT FOR ONE...
YOU MEAN NEMO, THE *UNDERWORLD?*
BUT THEN... THEY...THEY'RE *DEMONS?!*

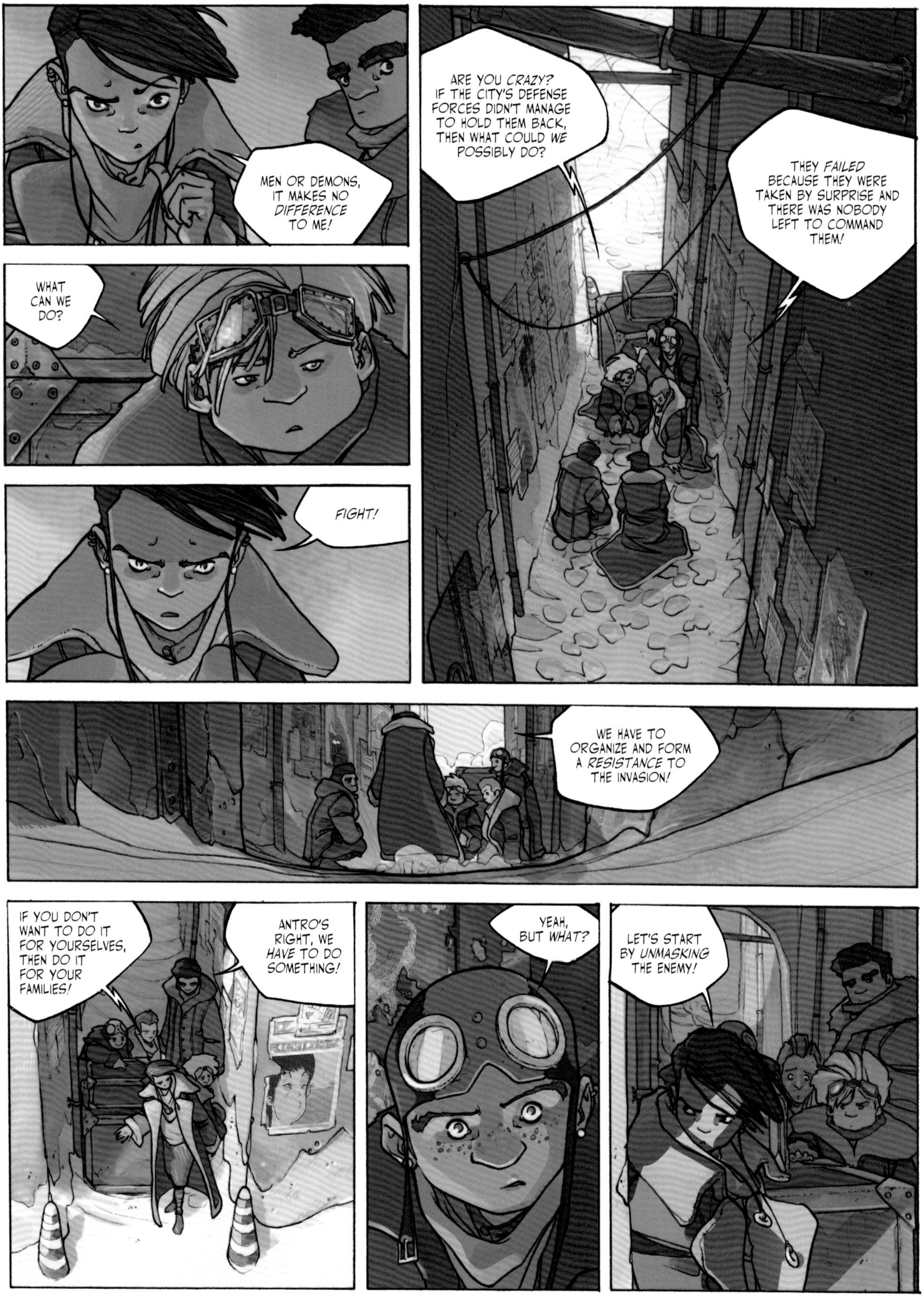
MEN OR DEMONS, IT MAKES NO *DIFFERENCE* TO ME!
WHAT CAN WE DO?
FIGHT!
ARE YOU *CRAZY?* IF THE CITY'S DEFENSE FORCES DIDN'T MANAGE TO HOLD THEM BACK, THEN WHAT COULD *WE* POSSIBLY DO?
THEY *FAILED* BECAUSE THEY WERE TAKEN BY SURPRISE AND THERE WAS NOBODY LEFT TO COMMAND THEM!
WE HAVE TO ORGANIZE AND FORM A *RESISTANCE* TO THE INVASION!
IF YOU DON'T WANT TO DO IT FOR YOURSELVES, THEN DO IT FOR YOUR FAMILIES!
ANTRO'S RIGHT, WE *HAVE* TO DO SOMETHING!
YEAH, BUT *WHAT?*
LET'S START BY *UNMASKING* THE ENEMY!

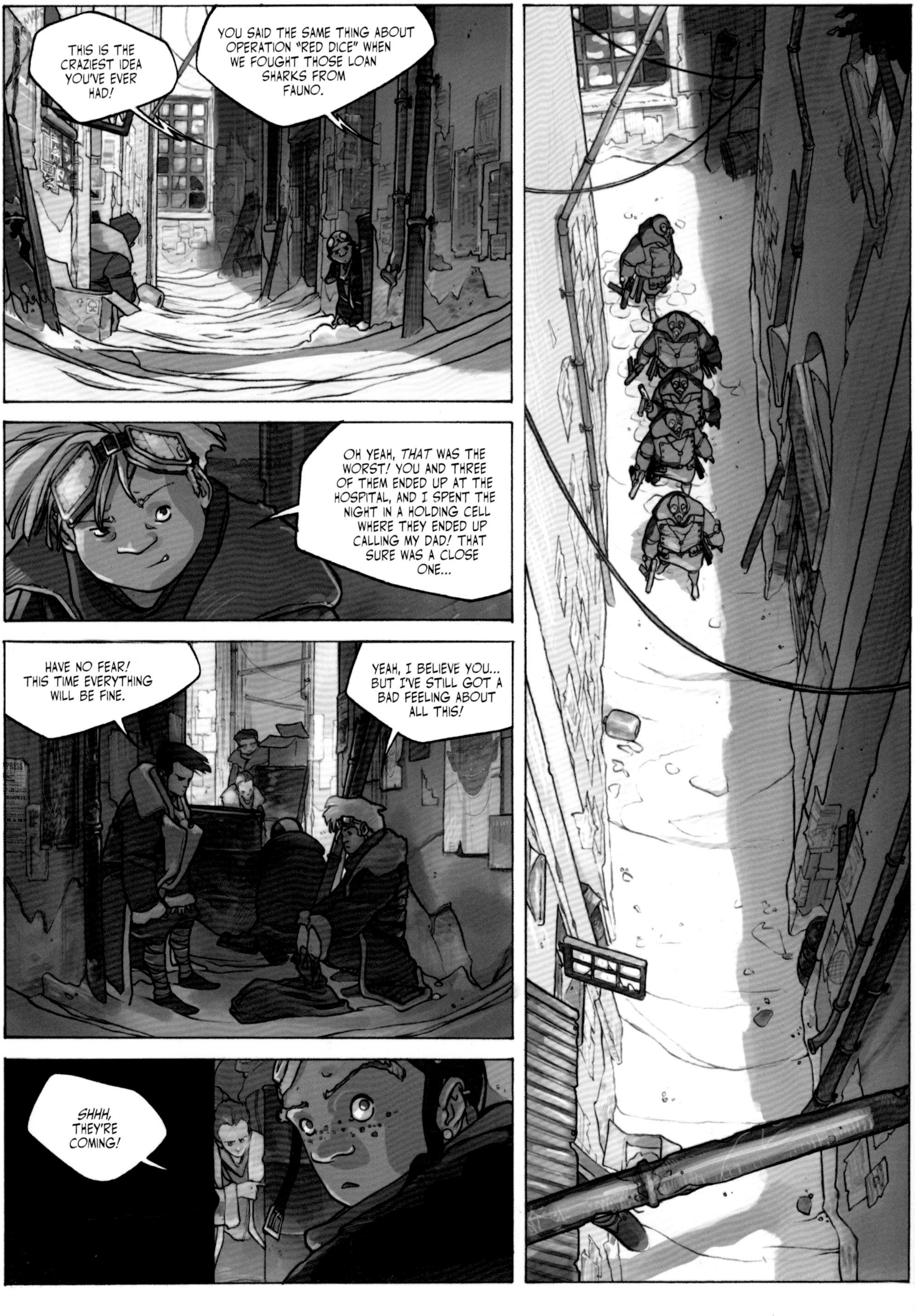
THIS IS THE CRAZIEST IDEA YOU'VE EVER HAD!
YOU SAID THE SAME THING ABOUT OPERATION "RED DICE" WHEN WE FOUGHT THOSE LOAN SHARKS FROM FAUNO.
OH YEAH, THAT WAS THE WORST! YOU AND THREE OF THEM ENDED UP AT THE HOSPITAL, AND I SPENT THE NIGHT IN A HOLDING CELL WHERE THEY ENDED UP CALLING MY DAD! THAT SURE WAS A CLOSE ONE...
HAVE NO FEAR! THIS TIME EVERYTHING WILL BE FINE.
YEAH, I BELIEVE YOU... BUT I'VE STILL GOT A BAD FEELING ABOUT ALL THIS!
SHHH, THEY'RE COMING!

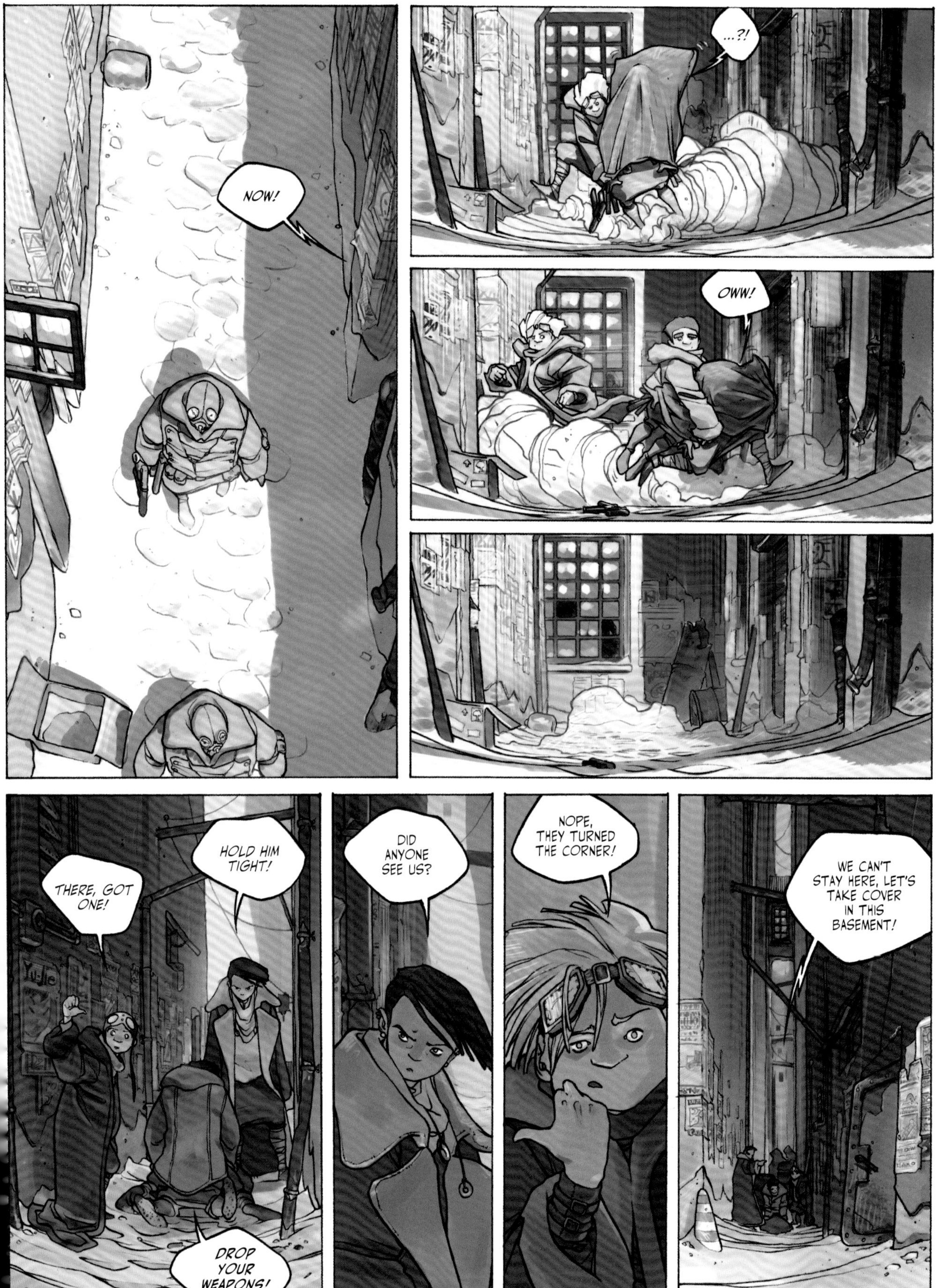
NOW!
...?!
OWW!
THERE, GOT ONE!
HOLD HIM TIGHT!
DROP YOUR WEAPONS!
DID ANYONE SEE US?
NOPE, THEY TURNED THE CORNER!
WE CAN'T STAY HERE, LET'S TAKE COVER IN THIS BASEMENT!

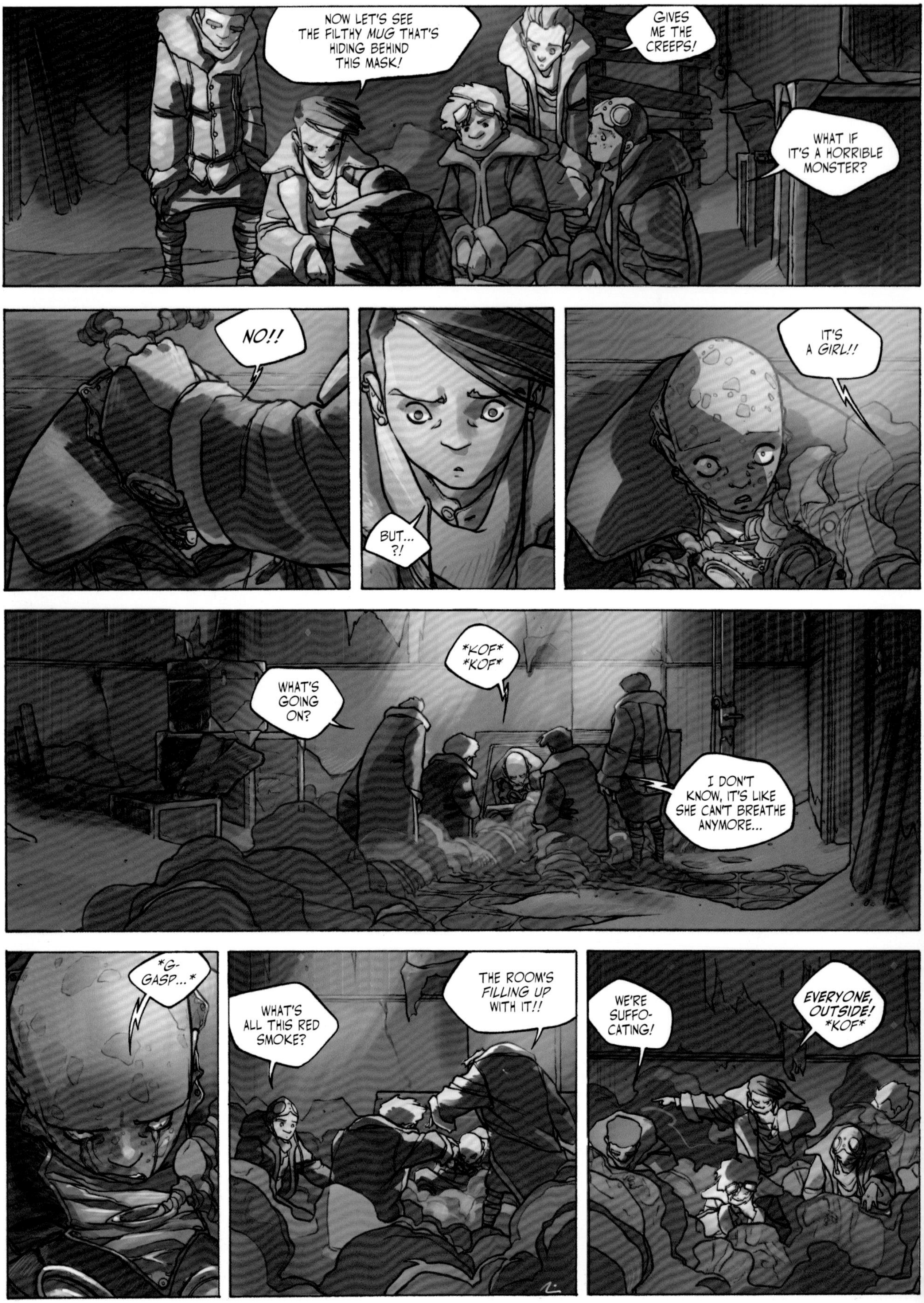
NOW LET'S SEE THE FILTHY MUG THAT'S HIDING BEHIND THIS MASK!
GIVES ME THE CREEPS!
WHAT IF IT'S A HORRIBLE MONSTER?
NO!!
BUT... ?!
IT'S A GIRL!!
WHAT'S GOING ON?
KOF *KOF*
I DON'T KNOW, IT'S LIKE SHE CAN'T BREATHE ANYMORE...
G-GASP...
WHAT'S ALL THIS RED SMOKE?
THE ROOM'S FILLING UP WITH IT!!
WE'RE SUFFO-CATING!
EVERYONE, OUTSIDE! *KOF*

UH-OH!

RUN FOR IT!

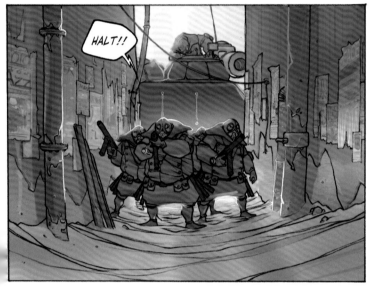

HALT!!

UH!

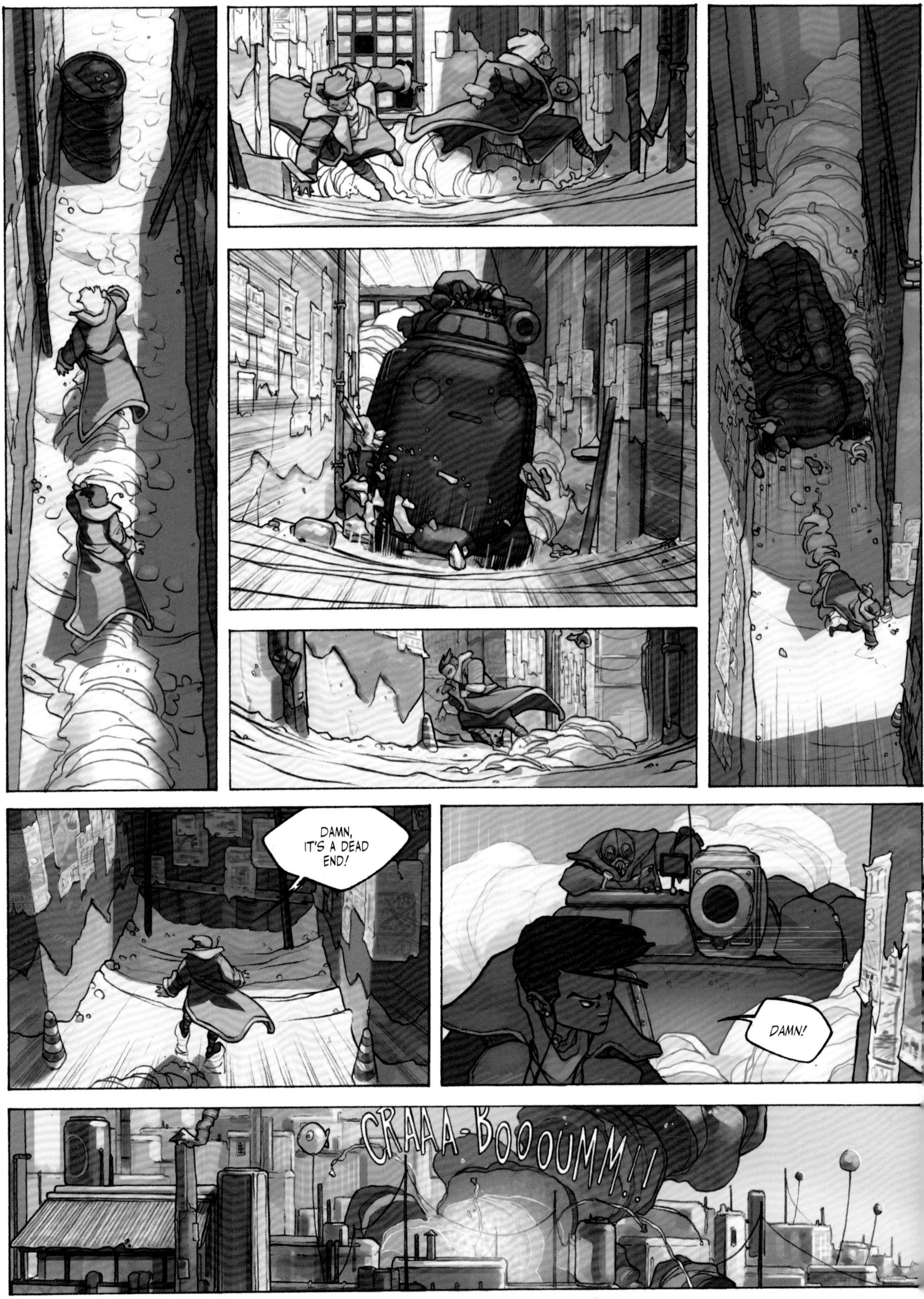
DAMN, IT'S A DEAD END!
DAMN!
CRAAA-BOOOUMM!!

NOTHING BUT THE ECHOES OF VAIN RESISTANCE, *ADMIRAL NYKTOS!*

THE BATTLE IS OVER. THE CITY IS UNDER *OUR CONTROL!*

THE MILITARY AIRPORT WAS, UNSURPRISINGLY, THE ONLY STRONG RESISTANCE. BUT THANKS TO OUR HEROIC CAPTAIN, THE ZONE HAS NOW BEEN PACIFIED!

WHAT IS YOUR NAME?

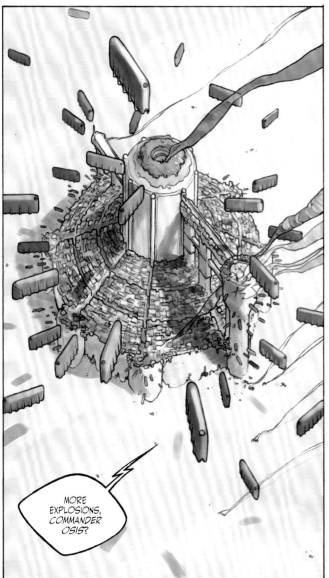

MORE EXPLOSIONS, *COMMANDER OSIS?*

CAPTAIN FERAXIS, ADMIRAL, AT YOUR SERVICE!

COMMANDER OSIS CERTAINLY DOESN'T HESITATE TO PRAISE YOUR ACHIEVEMENTS... DO YOU THINK YOU *DESERVE* IT?

I ONLY CARRIED OUT MY *DUTY*, ADMIRAL. I HAVE NO OTHER MISSION IN LIFE THAN TO SERVE *PRINCE GERARCA!*

IF THAT IS YOUR *SOLE* DESIRE, CAPTAIN, THEN IT SHALL BE GRANTED! AS OF THIS VERY MOMENT, YOU ARE BOREA'S NEW COMMANDING *GOVERNOR!* BE SURE TO NOT *BETRAY* THE TRUST THAT WE ARE PLACING IN YOU!

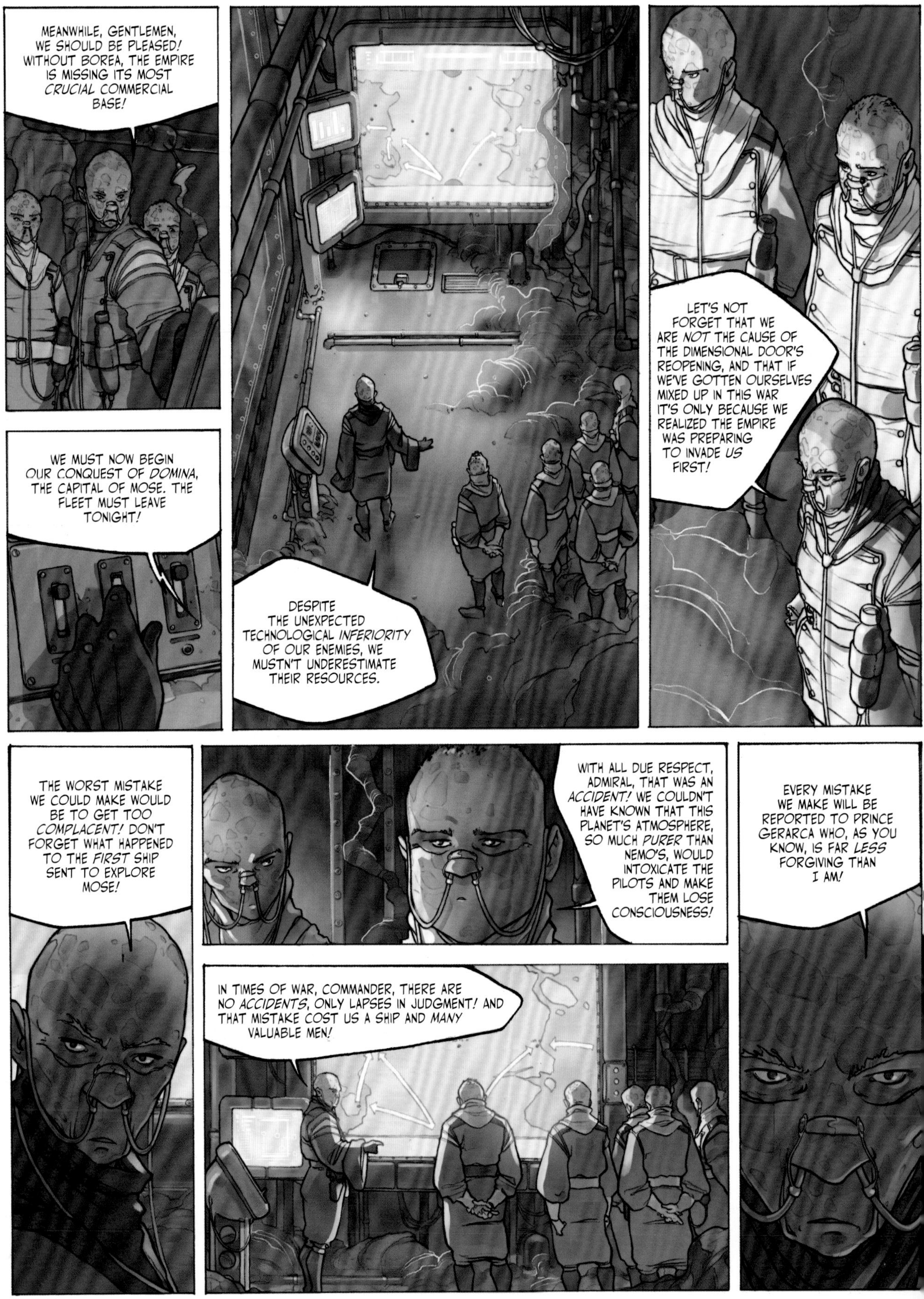

MEANWHILE, GENTLEMEN, WE SHOULD BE PLEASED! WITHOUT BOREA, THE EMPIRE IS MISSING ITS MOST *CRUCIAL* COMMERCIAL BASE!
WE MUST NOW BEGIN OUR CONQUEST OF *DOMINA*, THE CAPITAL OF MOSE. THE FLEET MUST LEAVE TONIGHT!
DESPITE THE UNEXPECTED TECHNOLOGICAL *INFERIORITY* OF OUR ENEMIES, WE MUSTN'T UNDERESTIMATE THEIR RESOURCES.
LET'S NOT FORGET THAT WE ARE *NOT* THE CAUSE OF THE DIMENSIONAL DOOR'S REOPENING, AND THAT IF WE'VE GOTTEN OURSELVES MIXED UP IN THIS WAR IT'S ONLY BECAUSE WE REALIZED THE EMPIRE WAS PREPARING TO INVADE *US* FIRST!
THE WORST MISTAKE WE COULD MAKE WOULD BE TO GET TOO *COMPLACENT!* DON'T FORGET WHAT HAPPENED TO THE *FIRST* SHIP SENT TO EXPLORE MOSE!
WITH ALL DUE RESPECT, ADMIRAL, THAT WAS AN *ACCIDENT!* WE COULDN'T HAVE KNOWN THAT THIS PLANET'S ATMOSPHERE, SO MUCH *PURER* THAN NEMO'S, WOULD INTOXICATE THE PILOTS AND MAKE THEM LOSE CONSCIOUSNESS!
IN TIMES OF WAR, COMMANDER, THERE ARE NO *ACCIDENTS*, ONLY LAPSES IN JUDGMENT! AND THAT MISTAKE COST US A SHIP AND *MANY* VALUABLE MEN!
EVERY MISTAKE WE MAKE WILL BE REPORTED TO PRINCE GERARCA WHO, AS YOU KNOW, IS FAR *LESS* FORGIVING THAN I AM!

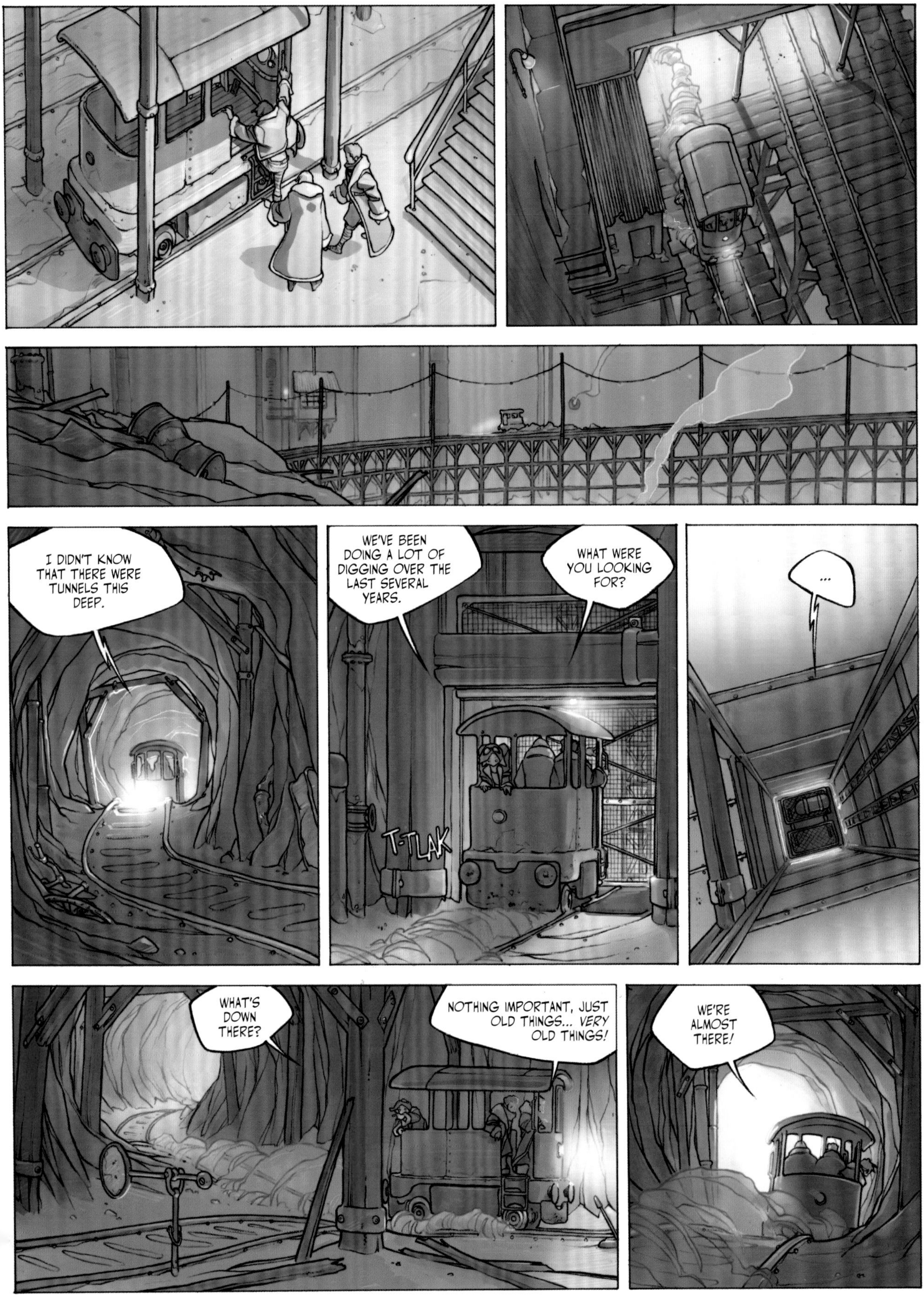
I DIDN'T KNOW THAT THERE WERE TUNNELS THIS DEEP.
WE'VE BEEN DOING A LOT OF DIGGING OVER THE LAST SEVERAL YEARS.
WHAT WERE YOU LOOKING FOR?
T-TLAK
...
WHAT'S DOWN THERE?
NOTHING IMPORTANT, JUST OLD THINGS... VERY OLD THINGS!
WE'RE ALMOST THERE!

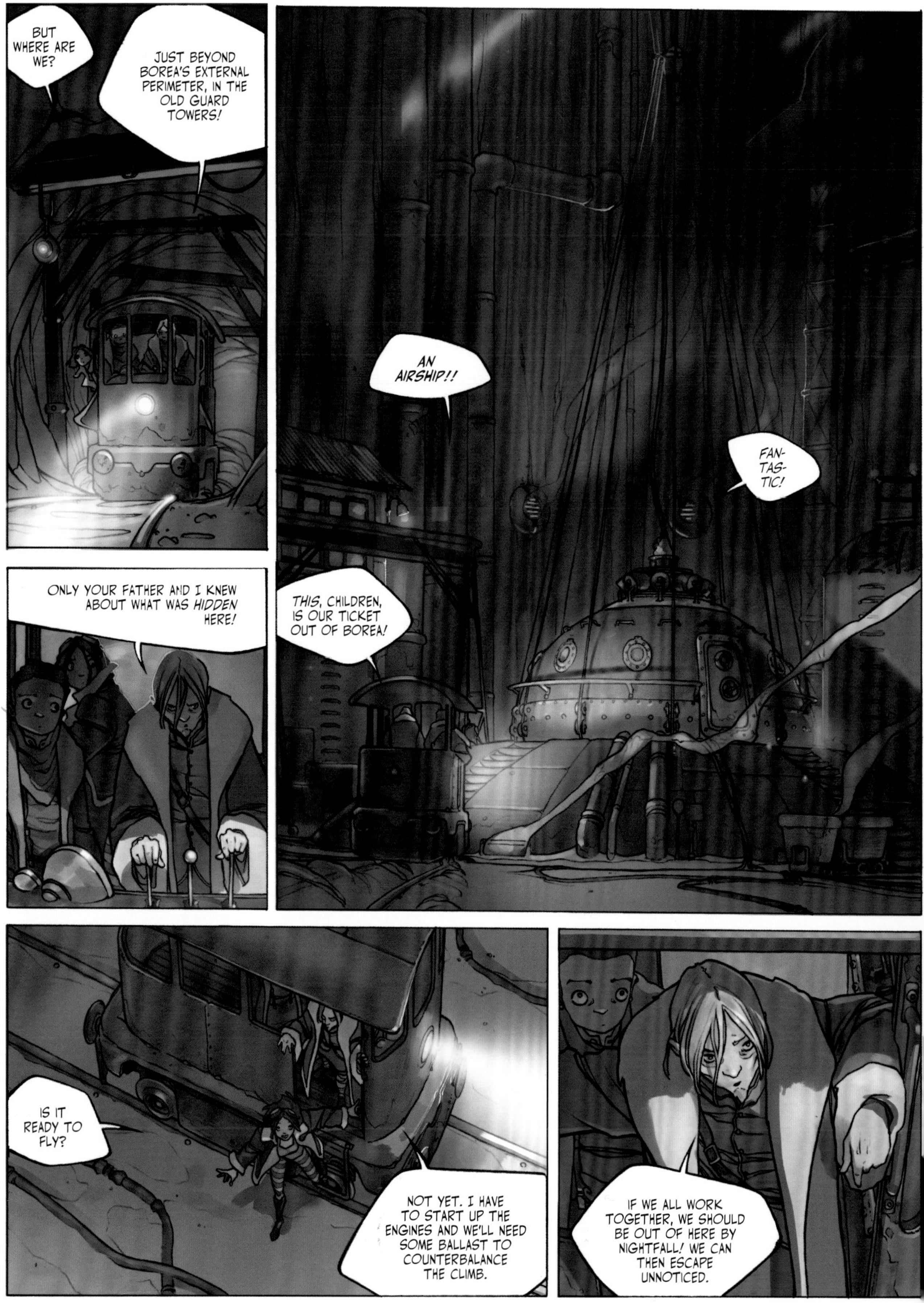
BUT WHERE ARE WE?
JUST BEYOND BOREA'S EXTERNAL PERIMETER, IN THE OLD GUARD TOWERS!
AN AIRSHIP!!
FAN-TAS-TIC!
ONLY YOUR FATHER AND I KNEW ABOUT WHAT WAS HIDDEN HERE!
THIS, CHILDREN, IS OUR TICKET OUT OF BOREA!
IS IT READY TO FLY?
NOT YET. I HAVE TO START UP THE ENGINES AND WE'LL NEED SOME BALLAST TO COUNTERBALANCE THE CLIMB.
IF WE ALL WORK TOGETHER, WE SHOULD BE OUT OF HERE BY NIGHTFALL! WE CAN THEN ESCAPE UNNOTICED.

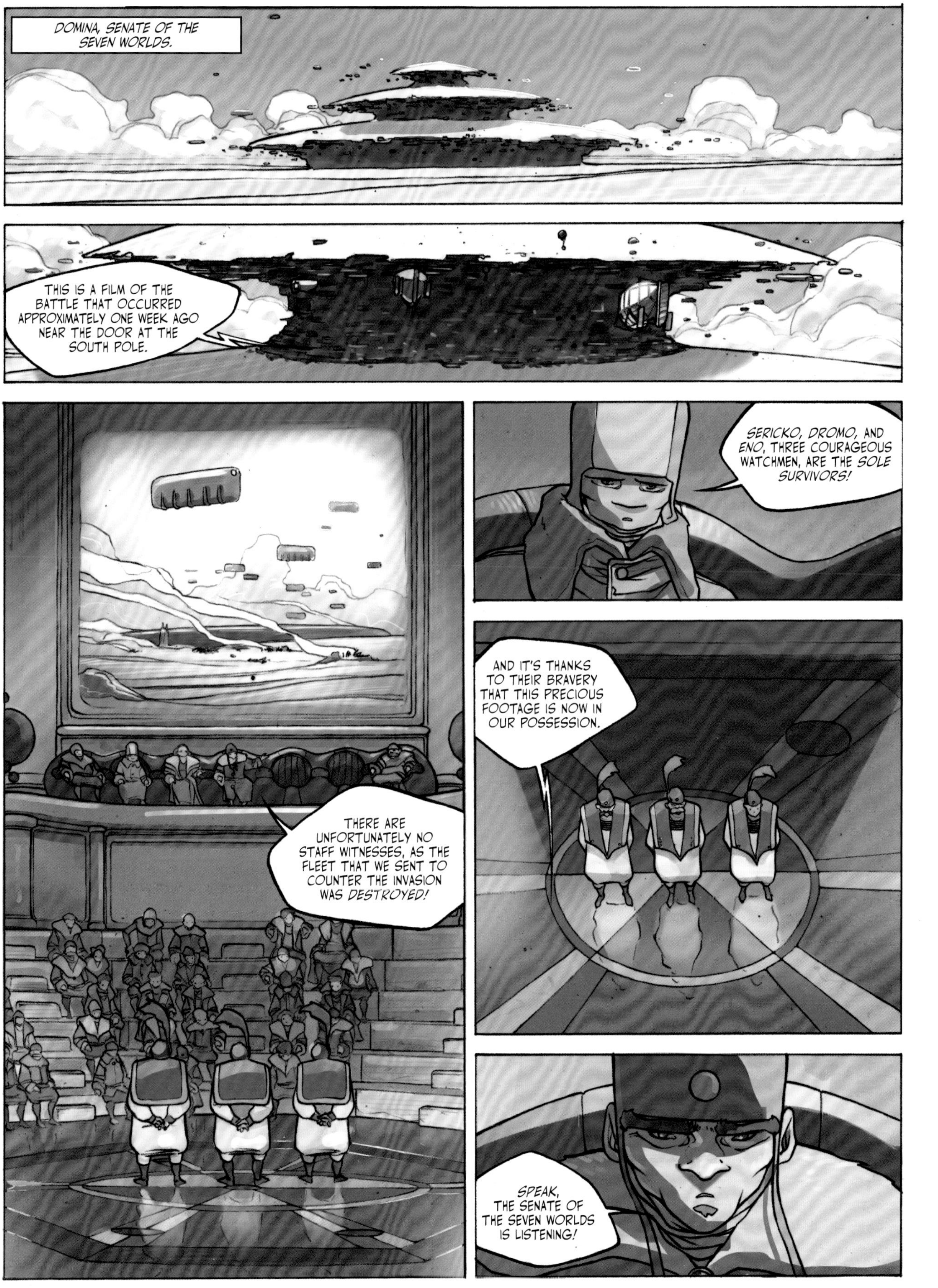
DOMINA, SENATE OF THE SEVEN WORLDS.
THIS IS A FILM OF THE BATTLE THAT OCCURRED APPROXIMATELY ONE WEEK AGO NEAR THE DOOR AT THE SOUTH POLE.
THERE ARE UNFORTUNATELY NO STAFF WITNESSES, AS THE FLEET THAT WE SENT TO COUNTER THE INVASION WAS DESTROYED!
SERICKO, DROMO, AND ENO, THREE COURAGEOUS WATCHMEN, ARE THE SOLE SURVIVORS!
AND IT'S THANKS TO THEIR BRAVERY THAT THIS PRECIOUS FOOTAGE IS NOW IN OUR POSSESSION.
SPEAK, THE SENATE OF THE SEVEN WORLDS IS LISTENING!

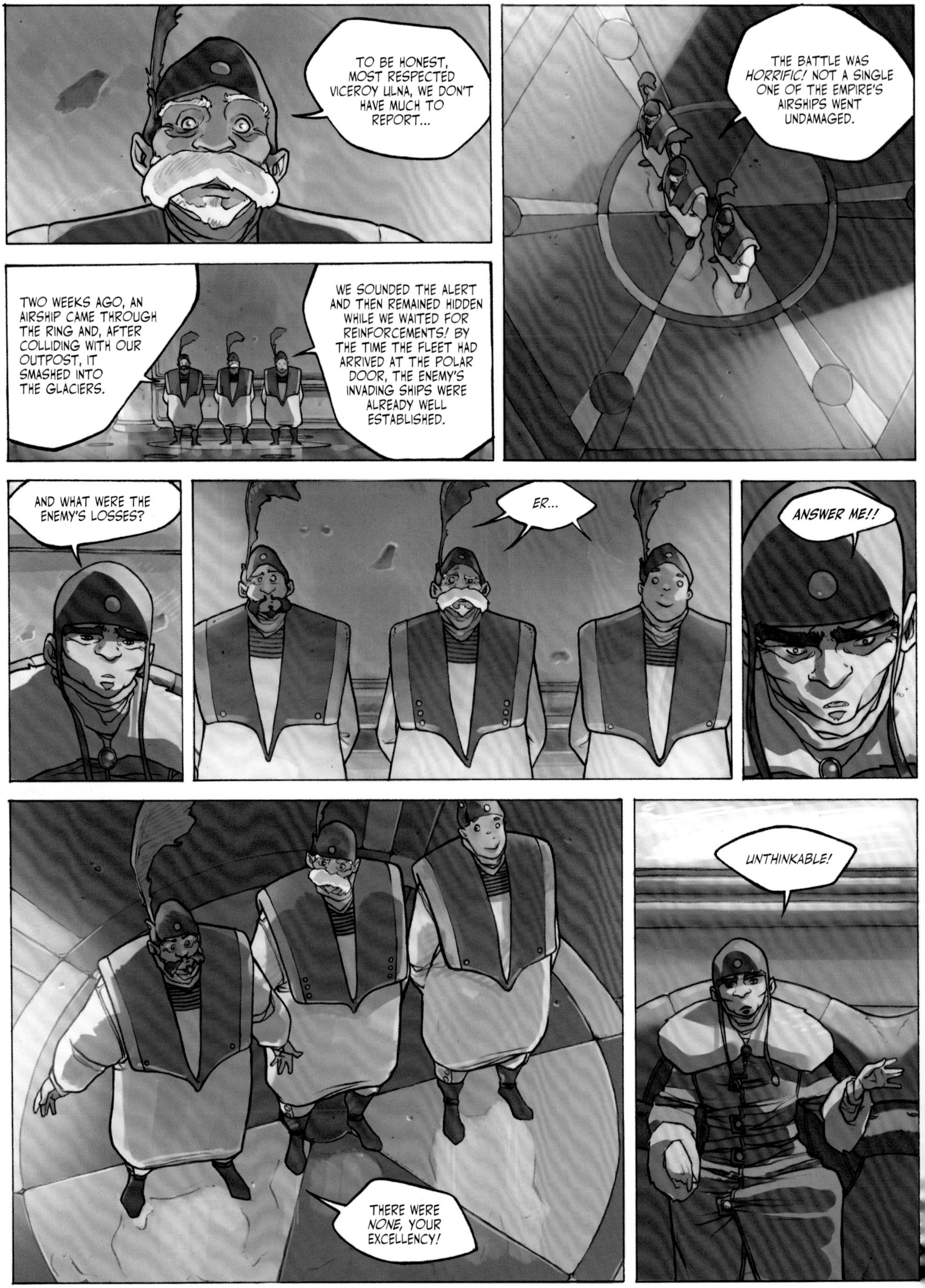

TO BE HONEST, MOST RESPECTED VICEROY ULNA, WE DON'T HAVE MUCH TO REPORT...
THE BATTLE WAS HORRIFIC! NOT A SINGLE ONE OF THE EMPIRE'S AIRSHIPS WENT UNDAMAGED.
TWO WEEKS AGO, AN AIRSHIP CAME THROUGH THE RING AND, AFTER COLLIDING WITH OUR OUTPOST, IT SMASHED INTO THE GLACIERS.
WE SOUNDED THE ALERT AND THEN REMAINED HIDDEN WHILE WE WAITED FOR REINFORCEMENTS! BY THE TIME THE FLEET HAD ARRIVED AT THE POLAR DOOR, THE ENEMY'S INVADING SHIPS WERE ALREADY WELL ESTABLISHED.
AND WHAT WERE THE ENEMY'S LOSSES?
ER...
ANSWER ME!!
THERE WERE NONE, YOUR EXCELLENCY!
UNTHINKABLE!

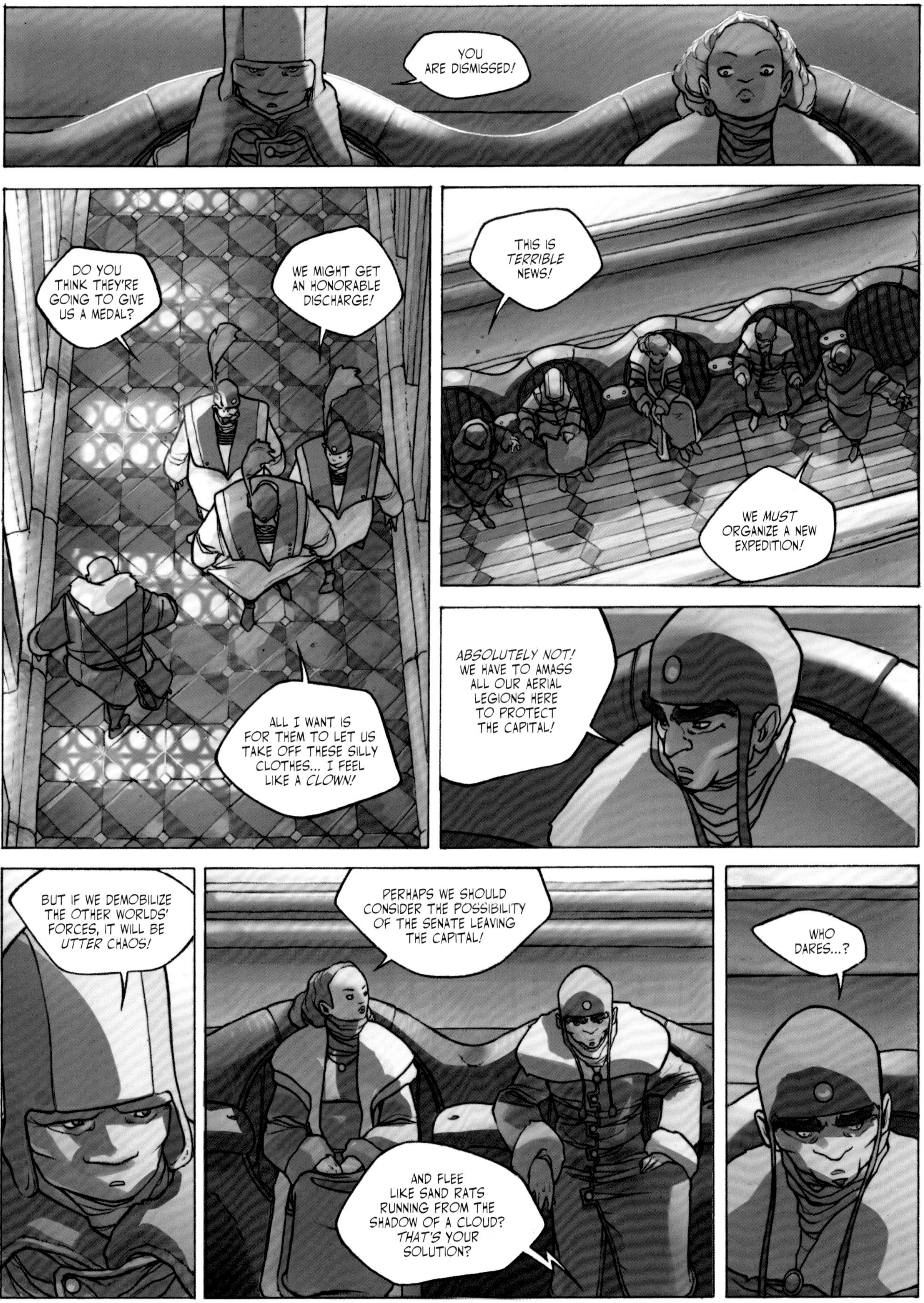
YOU ARE DISMISSED!
DO YOU THINK THEY'RE GOING TO GIVE US A MEDAL?
WE MIGHT GET AN HONORABLE DISCHARGE!
ALL I WANT IS FOR THEM TO LET US TAKE OFF THESE SILLY CLOTHES... I FEEL LIKE A CLOWN!
THIS IS TERRIBLE NEWS!
WE MUST ORGANIZE A NEW EXPEDITION!
ABSOLUTELY NOT! WE HAVE TO AMASS ALL OUR AERIAL LEGIONS HERE TO PROTECT THE CAPITAL!
BUT IF WE DEMOBILIZE THE OTHER WORLDS' FORCES, IT WILL BE UTTER CHAOS!
PERHAPS WE SHOULD CONSIDER THE POSSIBILITY OF THE SENATE LEAVING THE CAPITAL!
AND FLEE LIKE SAND RATS RUNNING FROM THE SHADOW OF A CLOUD? THAT'S YOUR SOLUTION?
WHO DARES...?

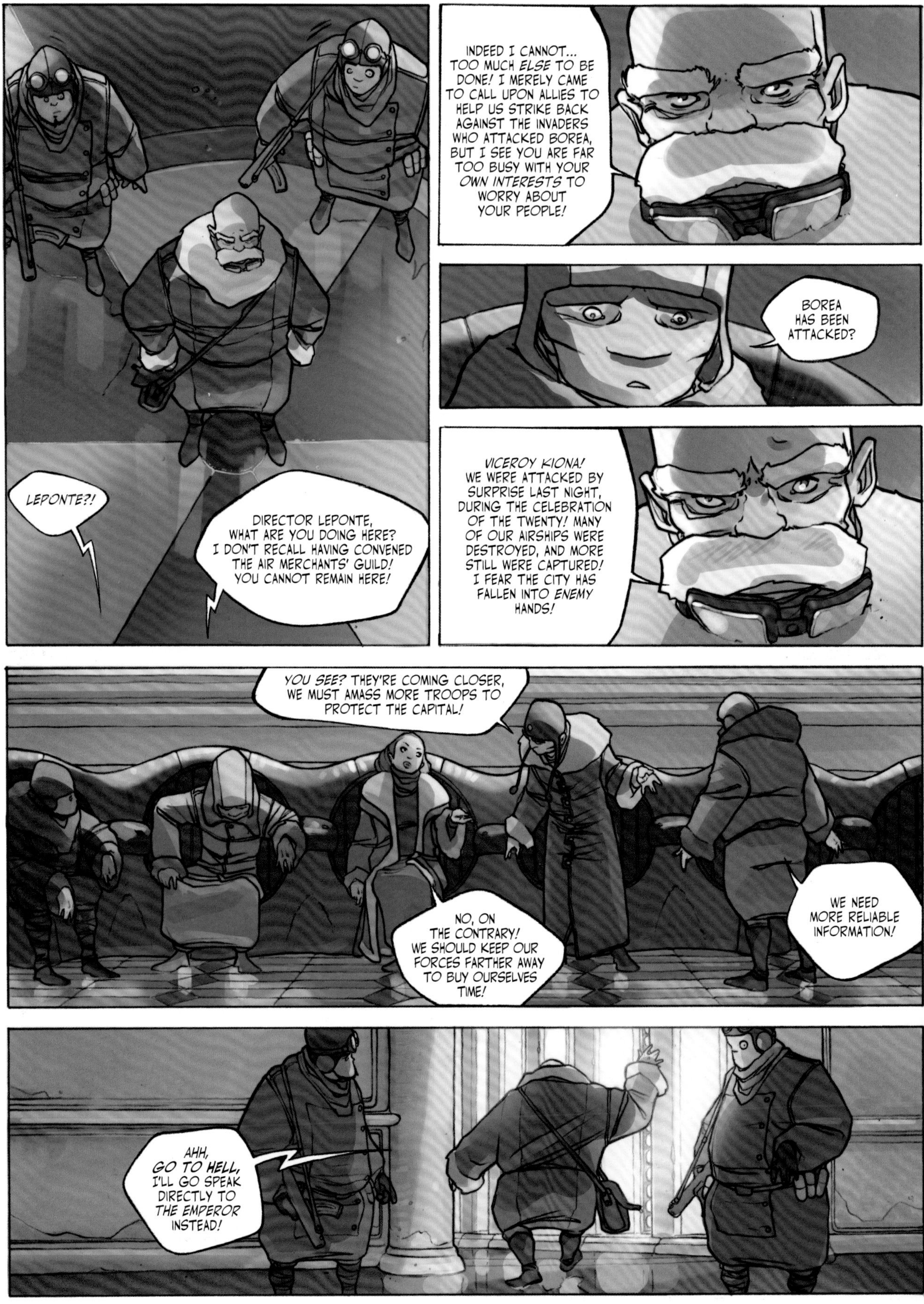
INDEED I CANNOT... TOO MUCH *ELSE* TO BE DONE! I MERELY CAME TO CALL UPON ALLIES TO HELP US STRIKE BACK AGAINST THE INVADERS WHO ATTACKED BOREA, BUT I SEE YOU ARE FAR TOO BUSY WITH YOUR *OWN INTERESTS* TO WORRY ABOUT YOUR PEOPLE!
BOREA HAS BEEN ATTACKED?
VICEROY KIONA! WE WERE ATTACKED BY SURPRISE LAST NIGHT, DURING THE CELEBRATION OF THE TWENTY! MANY OF OUR AIRSHIPS WERE DESTROYED, AND MORE STILL WERE CAPTURED! I FEAR THE CITY HAS FALLEN INTO *ENEMY* HANDS!
LEPONTE?!
DIRECTOR LEPONTE, WHAT ARE YOU DOING HERE? I DON'T RECALL HAVING CONVENED THE AIR MERCHANTS' GUILD! YOU CANNOT REMAIN HERE!
YOU SEE? THEY'RE COMING CLOSER, WE MUST AMASS MORE TROOPS TO PROTECT THE CAPITAL!
NO, ON THE CONTRARY! WE SHOULD KEEP OUR FORCES FARTHER AWAY TO BUY OURSELVES TIME!
WE NEED MORE RELIABLE INFORMATION!
AHH, ***GO TO HELL,*** I'LL GO SPEAK DIRECTLY TO *THE EMPEROR* INSTEAD!

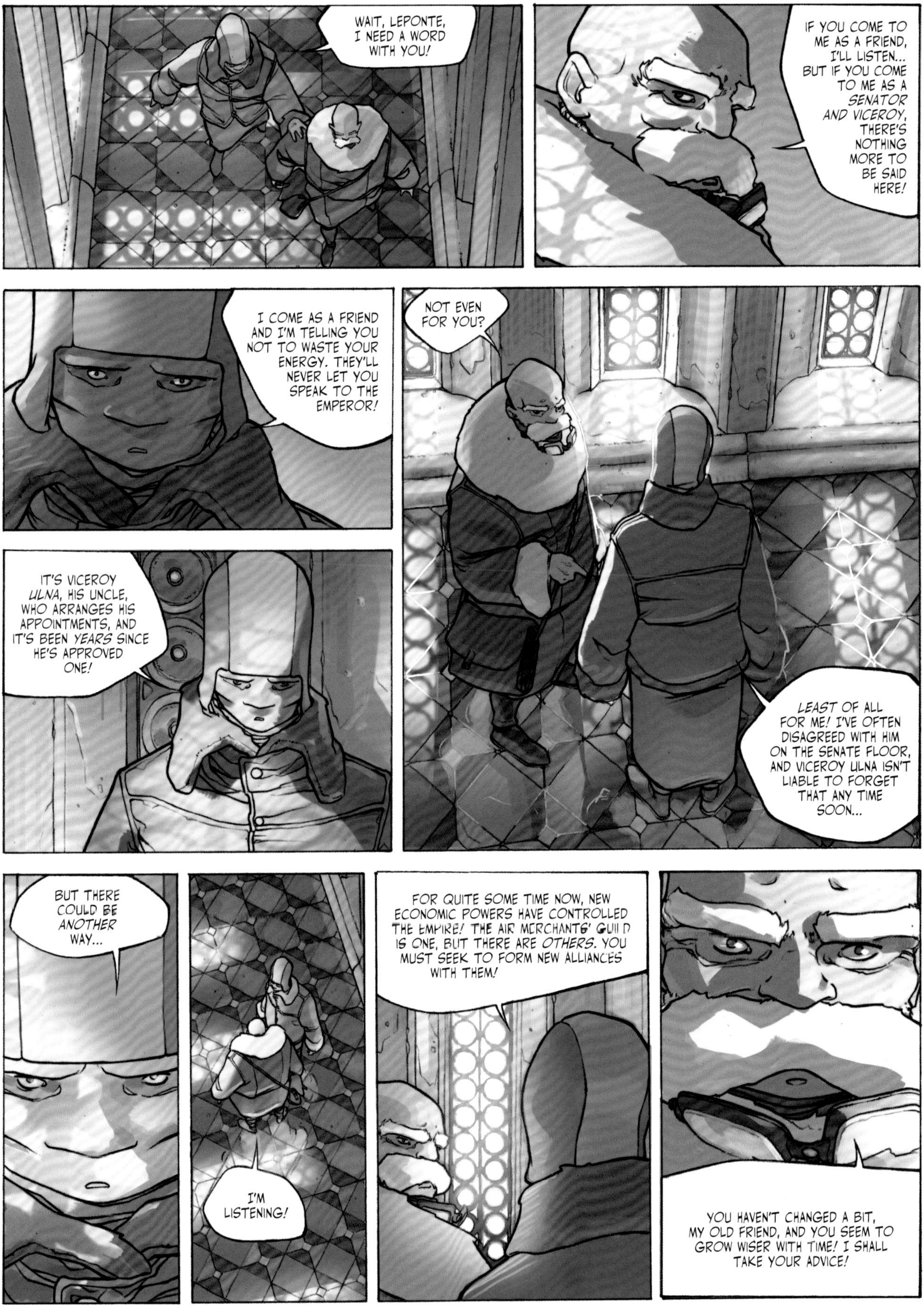
WAIT, LEPONTE, I NEED A WORD WITH YOU!
IF YOU COME TO ME AS A FRIEND, I'LL LISTEN... BUT IF YOU COME TO ME AS A *SENATOR AND VICEROY*, THERE'S NOTHING MORE TO BE SAID HERE!
I COME AS A FRIEND AND I'M TELLING YOU NOT TO WASTE YOUR ENERGY. THEY'LL NEVER LET YOU SPEAK TO THE EMPEROR!
NOT EVEN FOR YOU?
IT'S VICEROY *ULNA*, HIS UNCLE, WHO ARRANGES HIS APPOINTMENTS, AND IT'S BEEN *YEARS* SINCE HE'S APPROVED ONE!
LEAST OF ALL FOR ME! I'VE OFTEN DISAGREED WITH HIM ON THE SENATE FLOOR, AND VICEROY ULNA ISN'T LIABLE TO FORGET THAT ANY TIME SOON...
BUT THERE COULD BE *ANOTHER* WAY...
I'M LISTENING!
FOR QUITE SOME TIME NOW, NEW ECONOMIC POWERS HAVE CONTROLLED THE EMPIRE! THE AIR MERCHANTS' GUILD IS ONE, BUT THERE ARE *OTHERS*. YOU MUST SEEK TO FORM NEW ALLIANCES WITH THEM!
YOU HAVEN'T CHANGED A BIT, MY OLD FRIEND, AND YOU SEEM TO GROW WISER WITH TIME! I SHALL TAKE YOUR ADVICE!

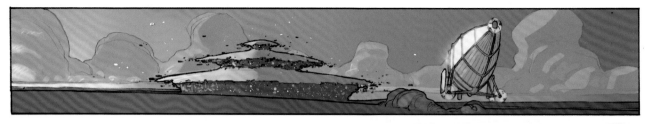

YOU'RE LATE, MARITO!

SORRY, *SEBA*, I HAD TO SPEAK WITH A FRIEND.

NO NEED TO EXPLAIN. WE WILL TRANSFER YOUR MOST RECENT MEMORIES DURING THE MEETING!

GOOD, WELL THEN LET'S BEGIN. MONITOR YOUR DOSE OF *EDON* CLOSELY. YOU'RE ALL WELL AWARE OF HOW HARD IT'S BECOMING TO FIND SOME.

THE ENTOMBED, WHO USED TO PROVIDE US WITH THIS SUBSTANCE FROM THE OLD TECHNOLOGY, HAVE INEXPLICABLY STOPPED ALL TRADE.

PERHAPS THEY'RE JUST RE-EXAMINING THEIR PRICES, OR PERHAPS THEY HAVE DISCOVERED SOMETHING ABOUT THE *TRUE* NATURE OF THESE ANCIENT OBJECTS THEY POSSESS...

ONLY TIME WILL TELL. FOR THE MOMENT, WE HAVE OTHER MORE *PRESSING* MATTERS AT HAND!

ESTABLISH THE CONNECTION!

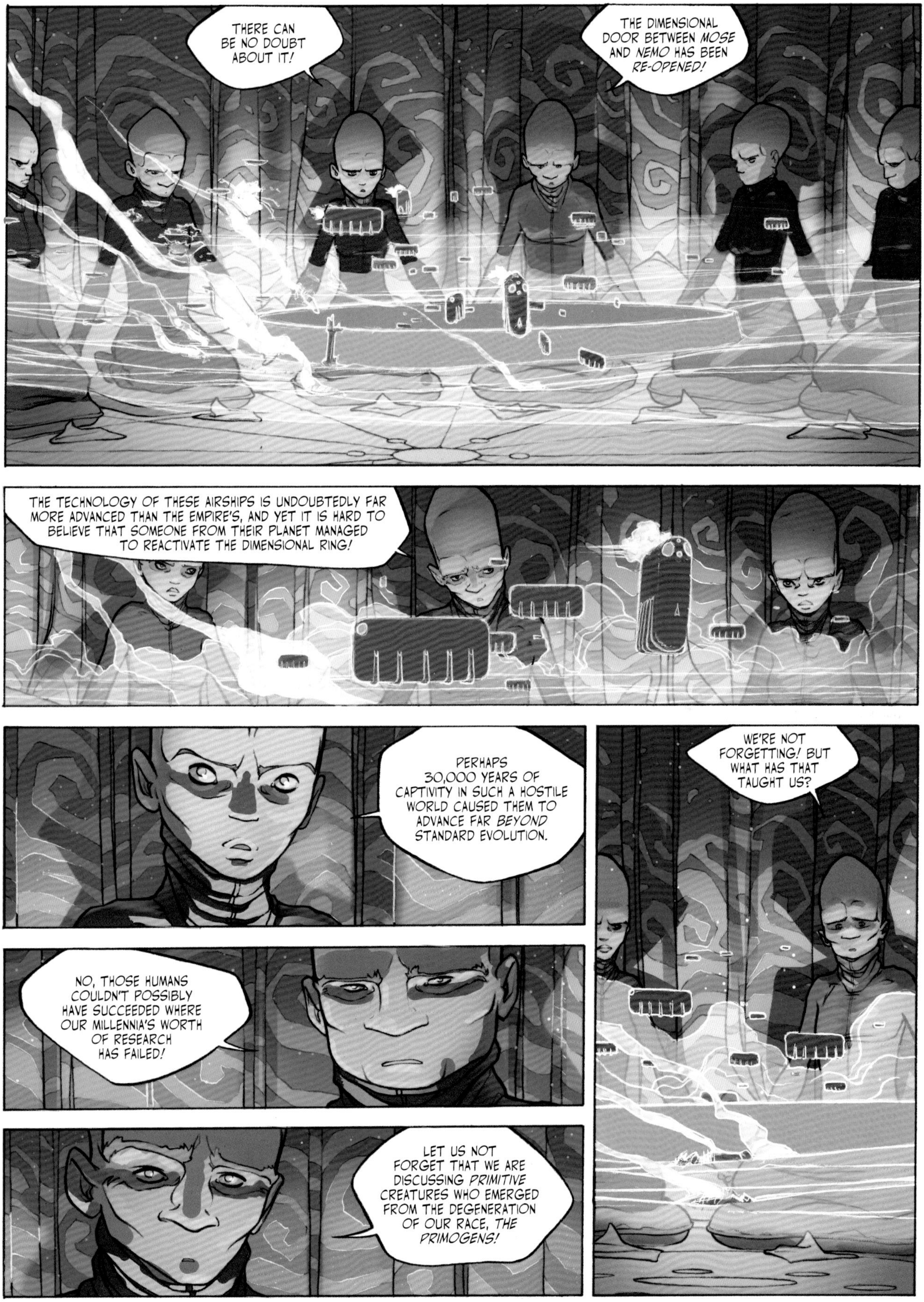
THERE CAN BE NO DOUBT ABOUT IT!
THE DIMENSIONAL DOOR BETWEEN *MOSE* AND *NEMO* HAS BEEN *RE-OPENED!*
THE TECHNOLOGY OF THESE AIRSHIPS IS UNDOUBTEDLY FAR MORE ADVANCED THAN THE EMPIRE'S, AND YET IT IS HARD TO BELIEVE THAT SOMEONE FROM THEIR PLANET MANAGED TO REACTIVATE THE DIMENSIONAL RING!
PERHAPS 30,000 YEARS OF CAPTIVITY IN SUCH A HOSTILE WORLD CAUSED THEM TO ADVANCE FAR *BEYOND* STANDARD EVOLUTION.
NO, THOSE HUMANS COULDN'T POSSIBLY HAVE SUCCEEDED WHERE OUR MILLENNIA'S WORTH OF RESEARCH HAS FAILED!
LET US NOT FORGET THAT WE ARE DISCUSSING *PRIMITIVE* CREATURES WHO EMERGED FROM THE DEGENERATION OF OUR RACE, *THE PRIMOGENS!*
WE'RE NOT FORGETTING! BUT WHAT HAS THAT TAUGHT US?

30,000 YEARS HAVE NOT ERASED MY MEMORIES OF A TIME WHEN OUR PEOPLE RULED THIS PLANET WITH UNPARALLELED SOCIAL AND TECHNOLOGICAL ADVANCEMENT.

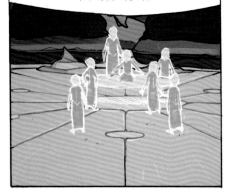

THE INVENTION OF EDON, THE SUBSTANCE THAT CAN TAKE ANY FORM AND ITS RESPECTIVE FUNCTION, WAS THE FRUIT OF MUCH LONG AND HARD LABOR.

THANKS TO EDON, WE BUILT IDEAL CITIES AND CREATED LOYAL SERVANTS WHO, ALL LINKED TO ONE ANOTHER, COULD SEAMLESSLY COMMUNICATE WITH EACH OTHER EVEN AT A DISTANCE AND ANTICIPATE OUR EVERY NEED AND DESIRE.

FREE OF THE CONSTRAINTS OF DAILY LIFE, WE DEDICATED OURSELVES ENTIRELY TO ART, RESEARCH, AND THE EXPLORATION OF OUR WORLD, WHICH WE KNEW SO LITTLE ABOUT.

AND WE DISCOVERED THE *RINGS*, THE TWO DIMENSIONAL DOORS SITUATED AT EACH PLANETARY POLE AND THROUGH WHICH WE COULD ACCESS THE SIX NEW WORLDS THAT NOW FORM OUR EMPIRE.

THESE DOORS WERE FORMED FROM A TECHNOLOGY SIMILAR TO OUR OWN BUT FAR MORE *DEVELOPED*. DESPITE OUR BEST EFFORTS, WE WERE NEVER ABLE TO UNDERSTAND OR REPLICATE IT.

IT WAS AN UNACCEPTABLE REALITY FOR MOST OF US, AS WE HAD FOUND THE DOOR THROUGH WHICH WE COULD FREELY TRAVEL THE UNIVERSE, BUT WE COULD *ONLY* FOLLOW THE PATHS THAT THOSE BEFORE US HAD ALREADY CREATED!

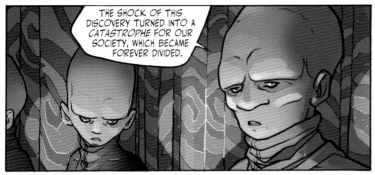

THE SHOCK OF THIS DISCOVERY TURNED INTO A *CATASTROPHE* FOR OUR SOCIETY, WHICH BECAME FOREVER DIVIDED.

ON ONE SIDE: THOSE WHO *REJECTED* TECHNOLOGY AND TRIED TO ERASE IT FROM THEIR MEMORIES. THEY WERE THE MOST NUMEROUS AND, IN TIME, BECAME THE HUMAN RACE.

AND ON THE *OTHER* SIDE: US, A SMALL GROUP OF VERY POWERFUL FOLLOWERS WHO, THANKS TO THE USE OF SMALL DOSES OF EDON, OVERCAME BOTH TIME AND SICKNESS. SINCE THEN, WE HAVE PURSUED OUR RESEARCH...

WE *KNOW* ALL THIS, *KIONA.* WHAT ARE YOU GETTING AT?

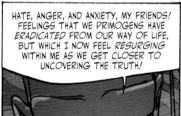

HATE, ANGER, AND ANXIETY, MY FRIENDS! FEELINGS THAT WE PRIMOGENS HAVE *ERADICATED* FROM OUR WAY OF LIFE, BUT WHICH I NOW FEEL *RESURGING* WITHIN ME AS WE GET CLOSER TO UNCOVERING THE TRUTH!

THEN BE SURE THAT THIS TIME, NO ONE WILL ESCAPE!

YOU'RE RIGHT, SEBA! THAT'S WHY WE MUST IMMEDIATELY TRANSFER OURSELVES TO NEMO!

WE'LL BE ABLE TO PURSUE OUR RESEARCH THERE BY INTEGRATING OURSELVES INTO THEIR SOCIETY, JUST AS WE DID WITH THE EMPIRE HERE!

AND THE HUMANS? WHAT WILL BECOME OF THEM?

SEBA AND I WILL STAY HERE TO TAKE CARE OF THAT! I'VE ALREADY DRAWN UP A SERIES OF EVENTS DESTINED TO LEAD THE EMPIRE TOWARDS AN ALL-OUT WAR THAT WILL ULTIMATELY RESULT IN THEIR *EXTINCTION!*

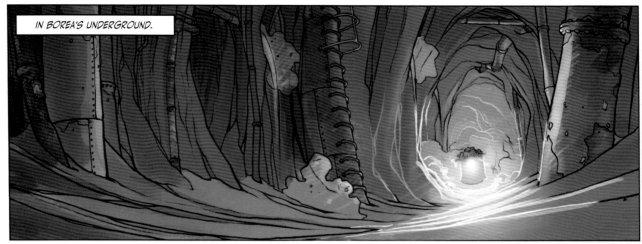

IN BOREA'S UNDERGROUND.

THIS CITY IS NOTHING BUT A DAMN PILE OF SAND! YOU CAN'T FIND *ANYTHING* DOWN HERE!

GOVERNOR FERAXIS' ORDERS WERE VERY CLEAR! WE MUST SIFT THROUGH THE UNDERGROUND TUNNELS AND DRIVE OUT ANY REBELS WHO HAVE ESCAPED US!

ALL WE'RE GOING TO DO IS GET LOST IN THIS SANDY LABYRINTH!

ZITTA, I HEARD SOMETHING!

WHAT THE...?!

STOP, DON'T MOVE!

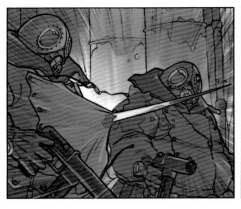

DIE, YOU
BEAST!!

WHERE'D
SHE G--

UHNN!!

NO, I DON'T
WANT TO DIE!
HELP!!

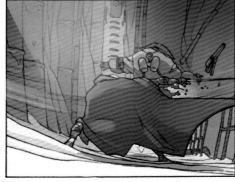

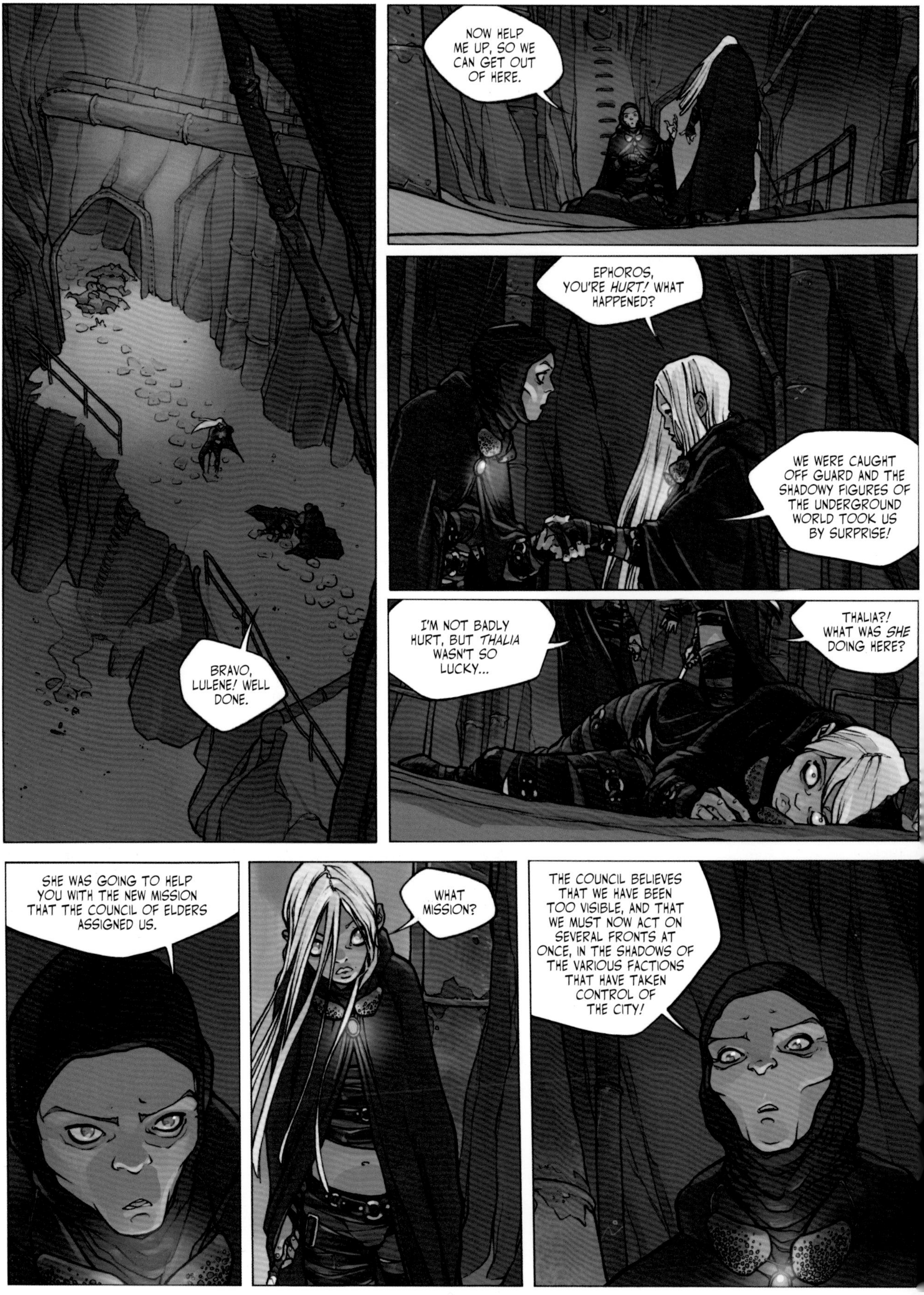
BRAVO, LULENE! WELL DONE.
NOW HELP ME UP, SO WE CAN GET OUT OF HERE.
EPHOROS, YOU'RE *HURT!* WHAT HAPPENED?
WE WERE CAUGHT OFF GUARD AND THE SHADOWY FIGURES OF THE UNDERGROUND WORLD TOOK US BY SURPRISE!
I'M NOT BADLY HURT, BUT *THALIA* WASN'T SO LUCKY...
THALIA?! WHAT WAS *SHE* DOING HERE?
SHE WAS GOING TO HELP YOU WITH THE NEW MISSION THAT THE COUNCIL OF ELDERS ASSIGNED US.
WHAT MISSION?
THE COUNCIL BELIEVES THAT WE HAVE BEEN TOO VISIBLE, AND THAT WE MUST NOW ACT ON SEVERAL FRONTS AT ONCE, IN THE SHADOWS OF THE VARIOUS FACTIONS THAT HAVE TAKEN CONTROL OF THE CITY!

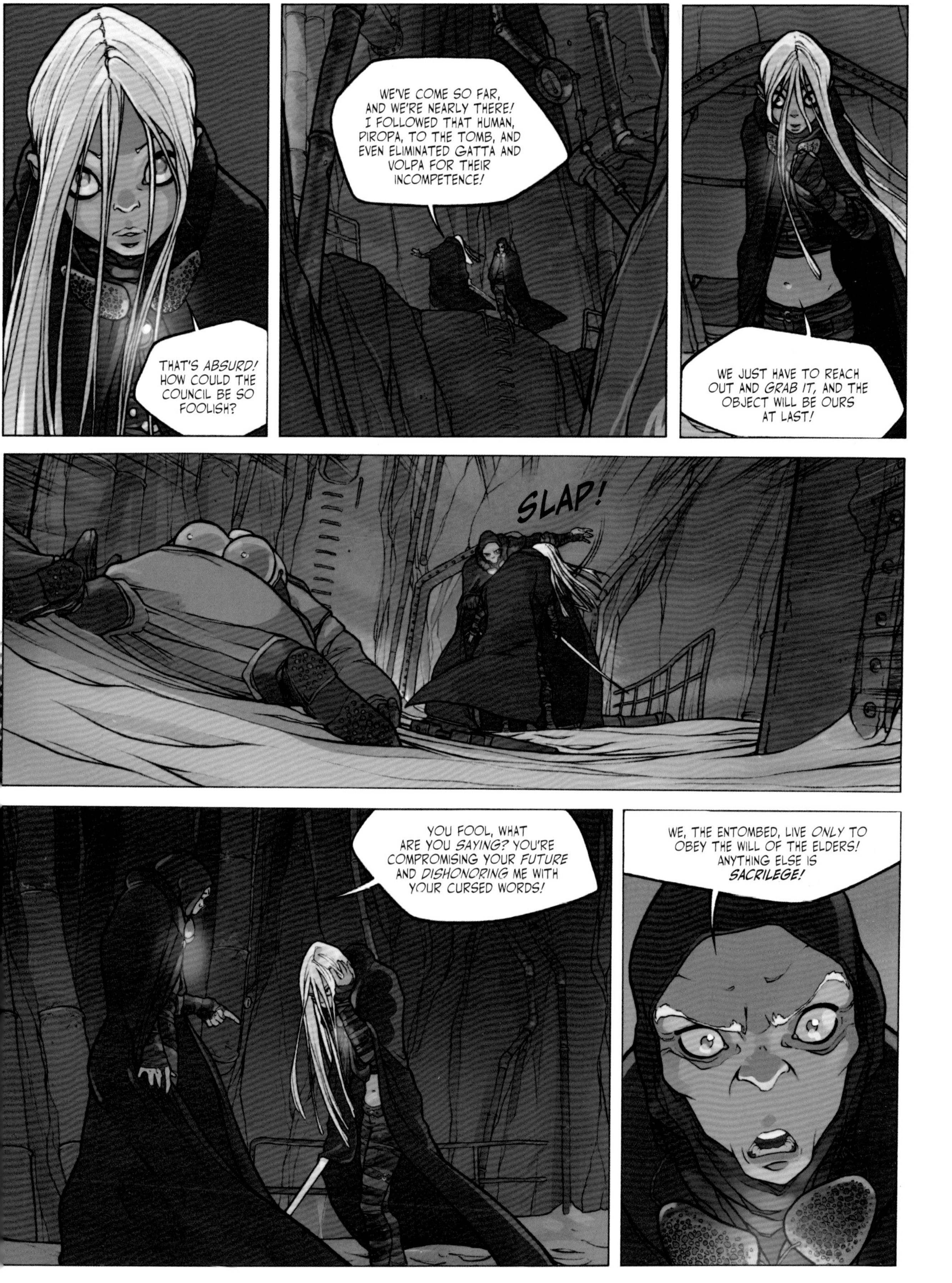
THAT'S ABSURD! HOW COULD THE COUNCIL BE SO FOOLISH?
WE'VE COME SO FAR, AND WE'RE NEARLY THERE! I FOLLOWED THAT HUMAN, PIROPA, TO THE TOMB, AND EVEN ELIMINATED GATTA AND VOLPA FOR THEIR INCOMPETENCE!
WE JUST HAVE TO REACH OUT AND GRAB IT, AND THE OBJECT WILL BE OURS AT LAST!
SLAP!
YOU FOOL, WHAT ARE YOU SAYING? YOU'RE COMPROMISING YOUR FUTURE AND DISHONORING ME WITH YOUR CURSED WORDS!
WE, THE ENTOMBED, LIVE ONLY TO OBEY THE WILL OF THE ELDERS! ANYTHING ELSE IS SACRILEGE!

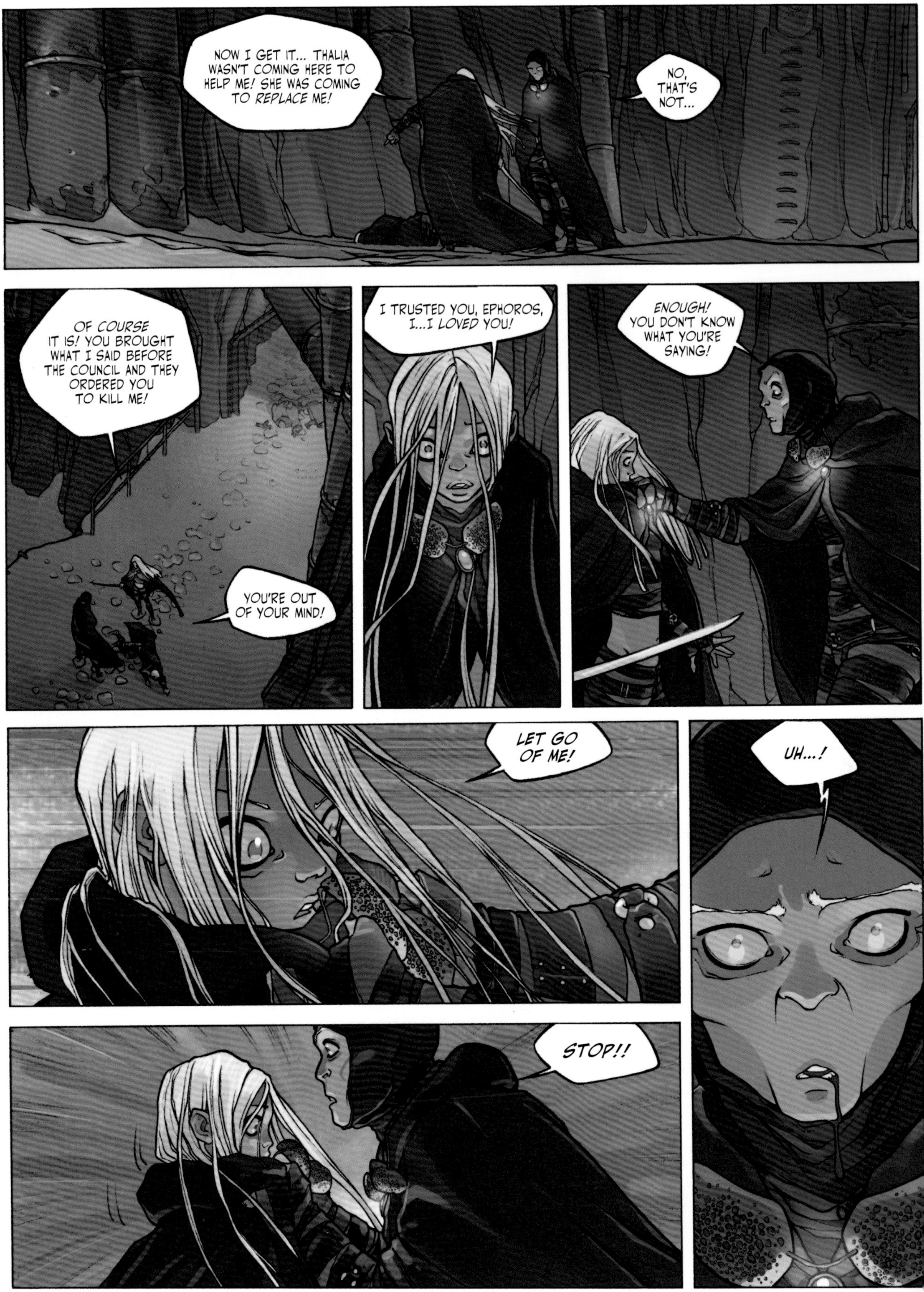
NOW I GET IT... THALIA WASN'T COMING HERE TO HELP ME! SHE WAS COMING TO *REPLACE* ME!
NO, THAT'S NOT...
OF *COURSE* IT IS! YOU BROUGHT WHAT I SAID BEFORE THE COUNCIL AND THEY ORDERED YOU TO KILL ME!
YOU'RE OUT OF YOUR MIND!
I TRUSTED YOU, EPHOROS, I...I *LOVED* YOU!
ENOUGH! YOU DON'T KNOW WHAT YOU'RE SAYING!
LET GO OF ME!
UH...!
STOP!!

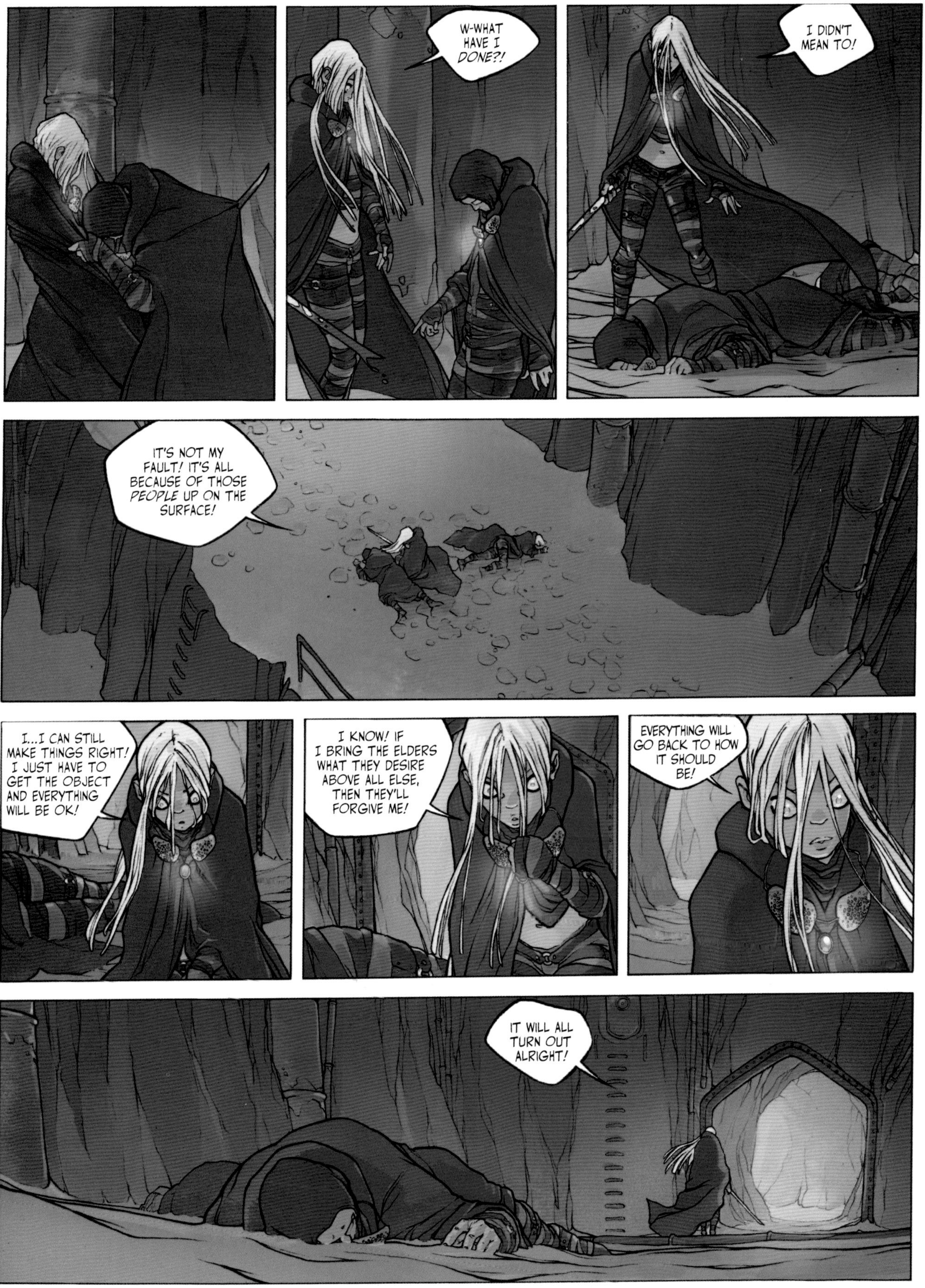
W-WHAT HAVE I DONE?!
I DIDN'T MEAN TO!
IT'S NOT MY FAULT! IT'S ALL BECAUSE OF THOSE PEOPLE UP ON THE SURFACE!
I...I CAN STILL MAKE THINGS RIGHT! I JUST HAVE TO GET THE OBJECT AND EVERYTHING WILL BE OK!
I KNOW! IF I BRING THE ELDERS WHAT THEY DESIRE ABOVE ALL ELSE, THEN THEY'LL FORGIVE ME!
EVERYTHING WILL GO BACK TO HOW IT SHOULD BE!
IT WILL ALL TURN OUT ALRIGHT!

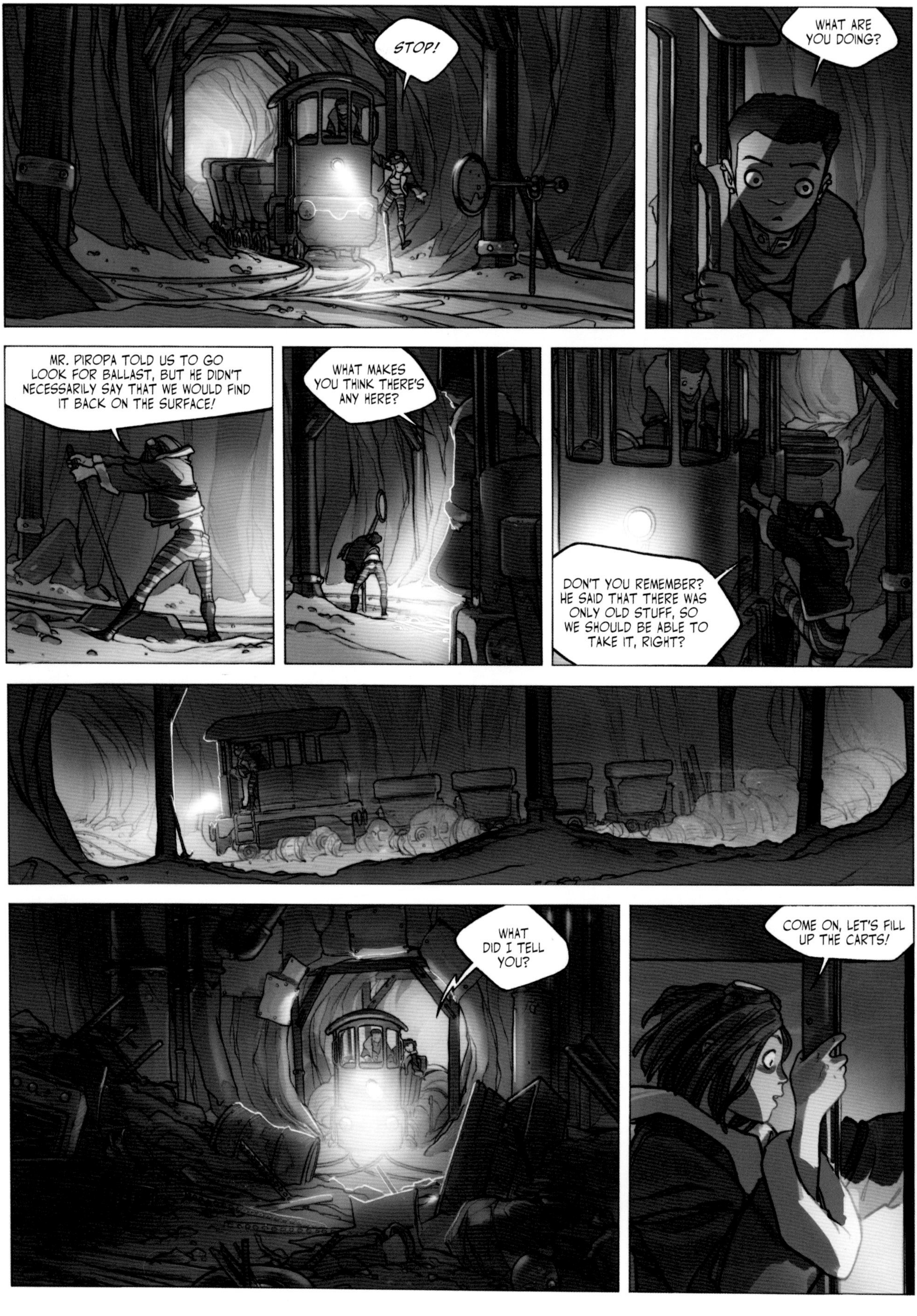
STOP!
WHAT ARE YOU DOING?
MR. PIROPA TOLD US TO GO LOOK FOR BALLAST, BUT HE DIDN'T NECESSARILY SAY THAT WE WOULD FIND IT BACK ON THE SURFACE!
WHAT MAKES YOU THINK THERE'S ANY HERE?
DON'T YOU REMEMBER? HE SAID THAT THERE WAS ONLY OLD STUFF, SO WE SHOULD BE ABLE TO TAKE IT, RIGHT?
WHAT DID I TELL YOU?
COME ON, LET'S FILL UP THE CARTS!

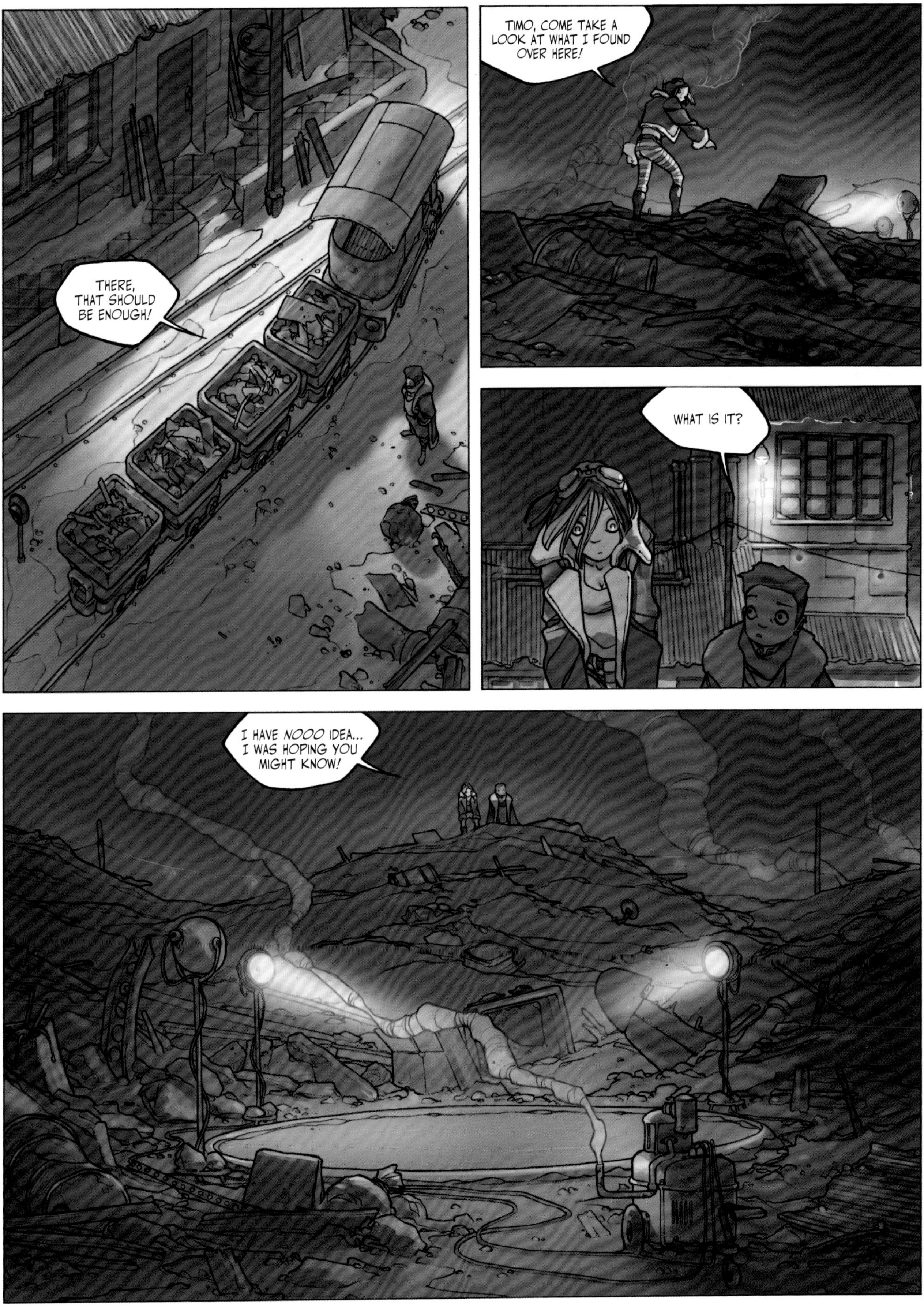
THERE, THAT SHOULD BE ENOUGH!
TIMO, COME TAKE A LOOK AT WHAT I FOUND OVER HERE!
WHAT IS IT?
I HAVE NOOO IDEA... I WAS HOPING YOU MIGHT KNOW!

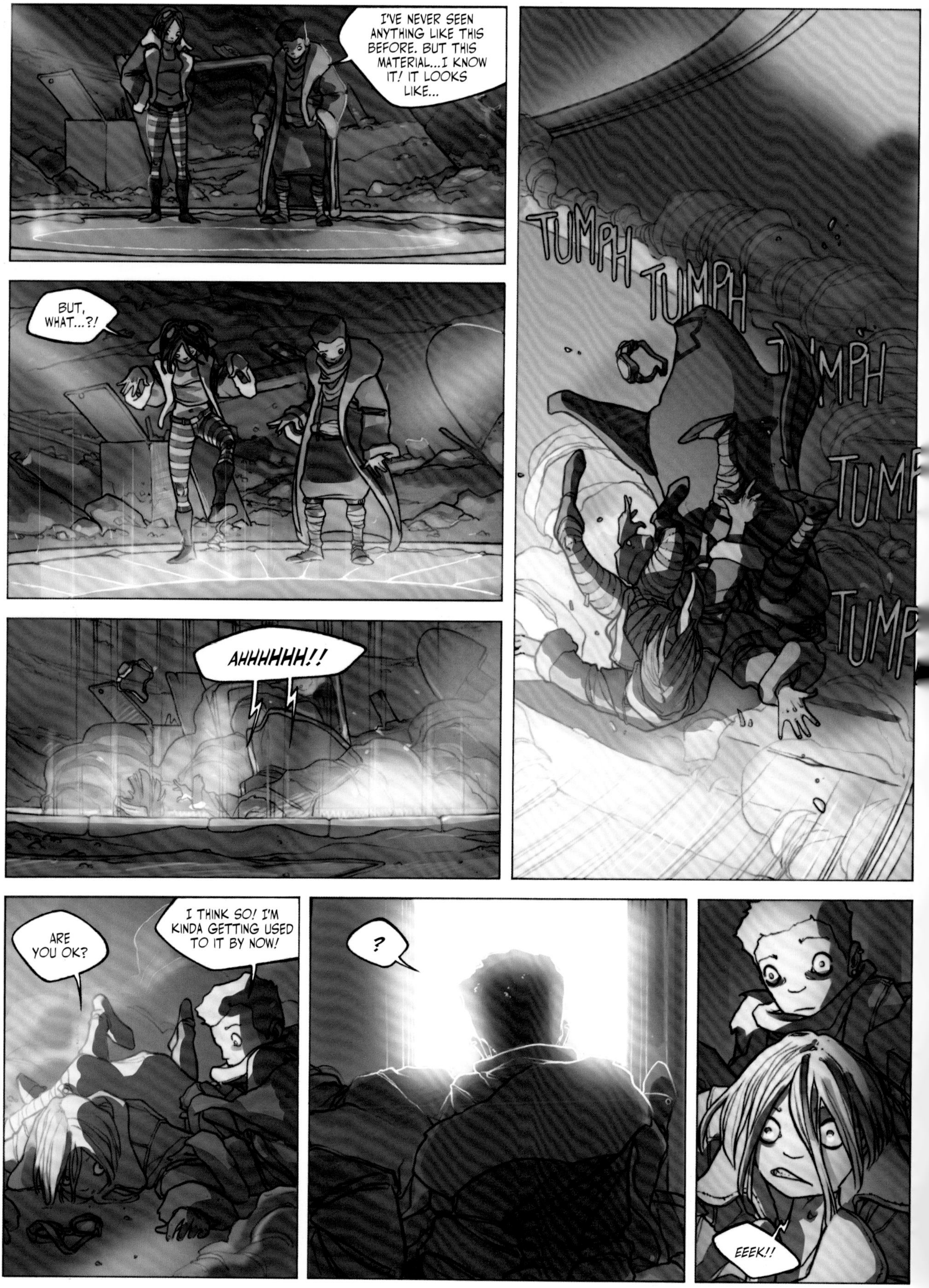

I'VE NEVER SEEN ANYTHING LIKE THIS BEFORE. BUT THIS MATERIAL...I KNOW IT! IT LOOKS LIKE...
BUT, WHAT...?!
AHHHHHH!!
TUMPH
TUMPH
TUMPH
TUMP
TUMP
ARE YOU OK?
I THINK SO! I'M KINDA GETTING USED TO IT BY NOW!
?
EEEK!!

IT LOOKS LIKE...A *CHILD!*

LOOK, ITS HEAD IS *HUGE!*

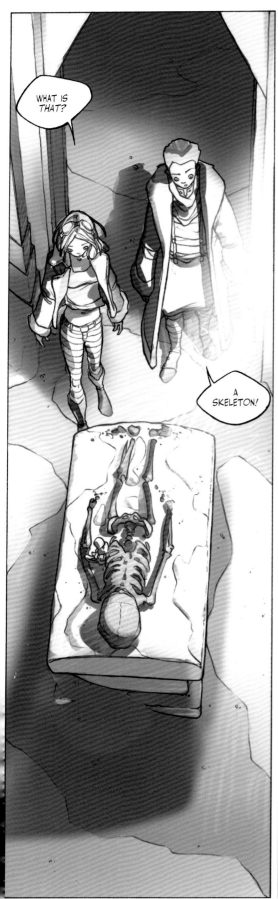

WHAT IS THAT?

A SKELETON!

COME ON, LET'S GO... THIS PLACE GIVES ME THE CREEPS!

OK, OK... I'LL BE THERE IN A SECOND.

?!

ARE YOU COMING?

NOT SO FAST!

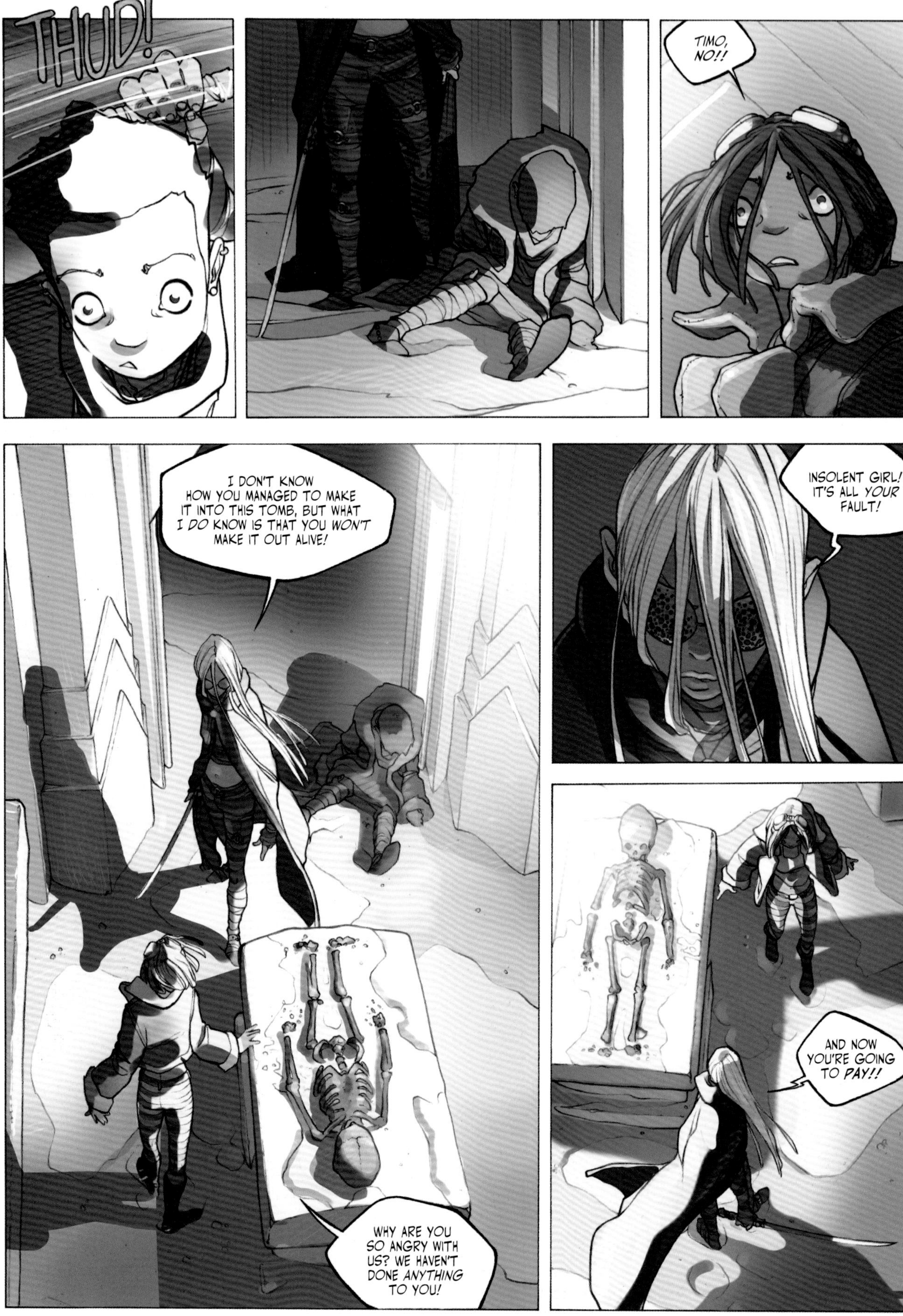
THUD!
TIMO, NO!!
I DON'T KNOW HOW YOU MANAGED TO MAKE IT INTO THIS TOMB, BUT WHAT I *DO* KNOW IS THAT YOU *WON'T* MAKE IT OUT ALIVE!
WHY ARE YOU SO ANGRY WITH US? WE HAVEN'T DONE *ANYTHING* TO YOU!
INSOLENT GIRL! IT'S ALL *YOUR* FAULT!
AND NOW YOU'RE GOING TO *PAY!!*

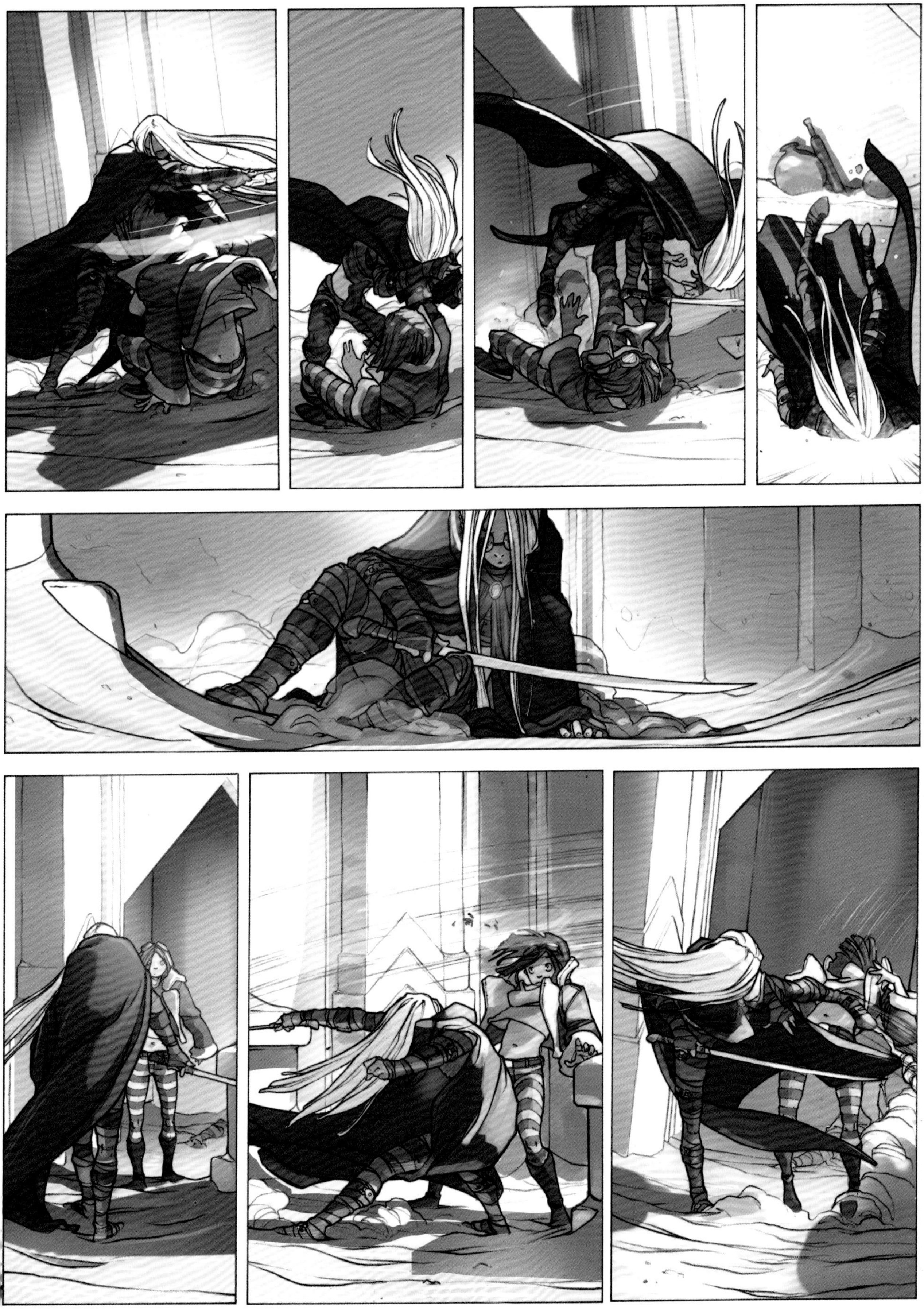

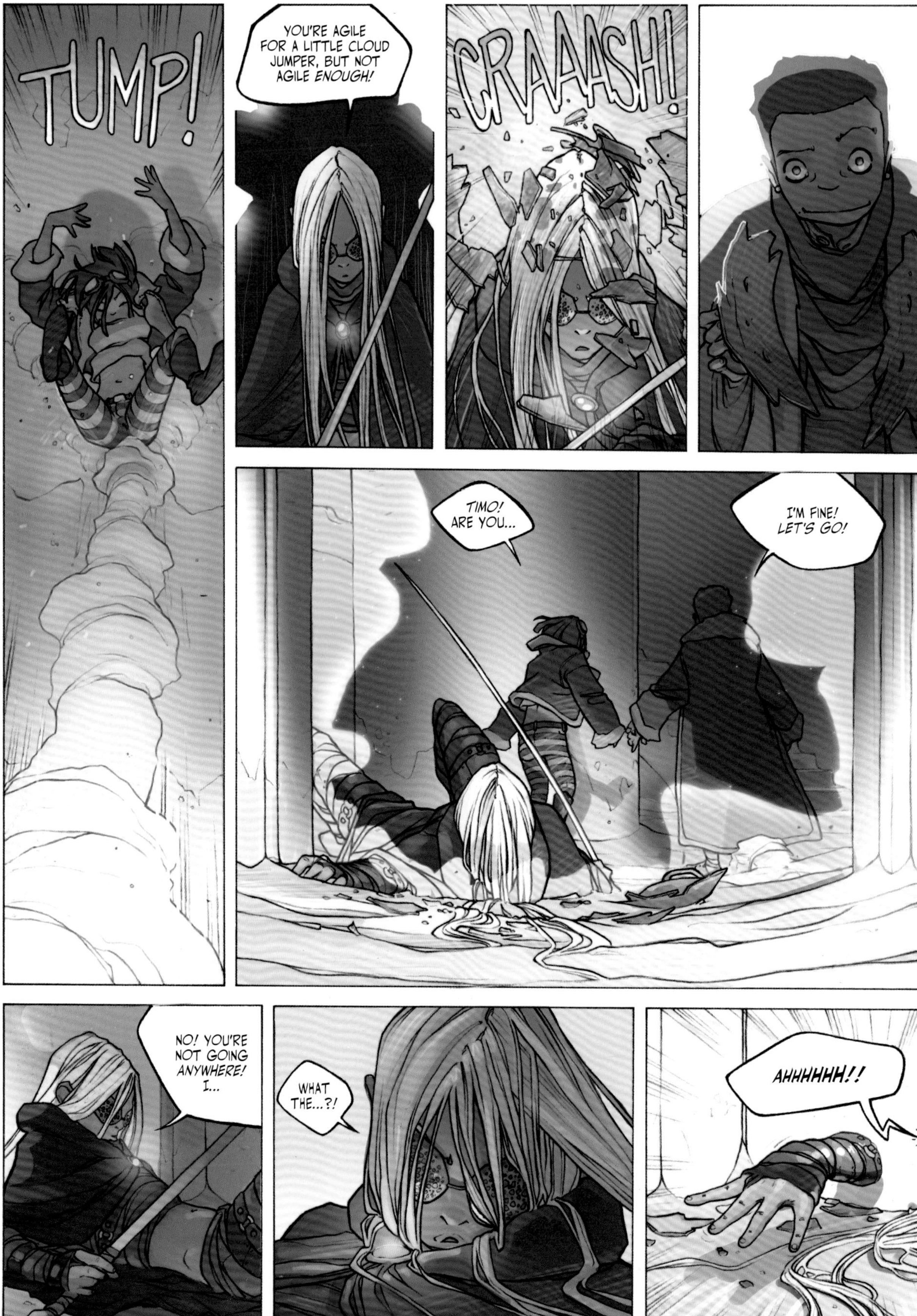
TUMP!
YOU'RE AGILE FOR A LITTLE CLOUD JUMPER, BUT NOT AGILE *ENOUGH!*
CRAAASH!
TIMO! ARE YOU...
I'M FINE! LET'S GO!
NO! YOU'RE NOT GOING *ANYWHERE!* I...
WHAT THE...?!
AHHHHHH!!

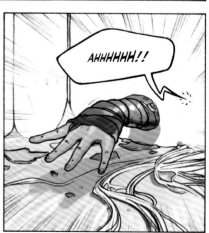

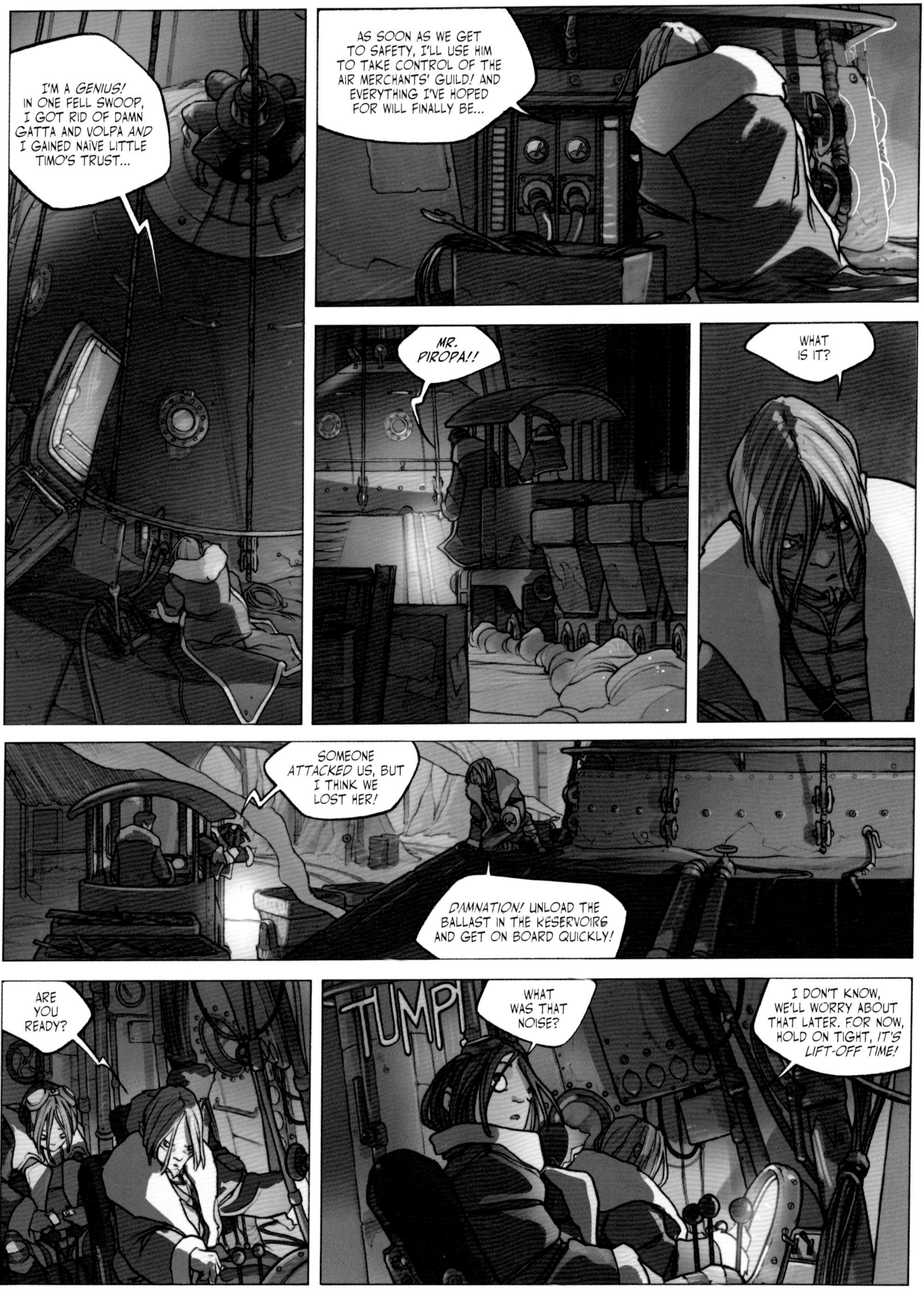
I'M A *GENIUS!* IN ONE FELL SWOOP, I GOT RID OF DAMN GATTA AND VOLPA *AND* I GAINED NAÏVE LITTLE TIMO'S TRUST...
AS SOON AS WE GET TO SAFETY, I'LL USE HIM TO TAKE CONTROL OF THE AIR MERCHANTS' GUILD! AND EVERYTHING I'VE HOPED FOR WILL FINALLY BE...
MR. PIROPA!!
WHAT IS IT?
SOMEONE *ATTACKED* US, BUT I THINK WE LOST HER!
DAMNATION! UNLOAD THE BALLAST IN THE RESERVOIRS AND GET ON BOARD QUICKLY!
ARE YOU READY?
TUMP!
WHAT WAS THAT NOISE?
I DON'T KNOW, WE'LL WORRY ABOUT THAT LATER. FOR NOW, HOLD ON TIGHT, *IT'S LIFT-OFF TIME!*

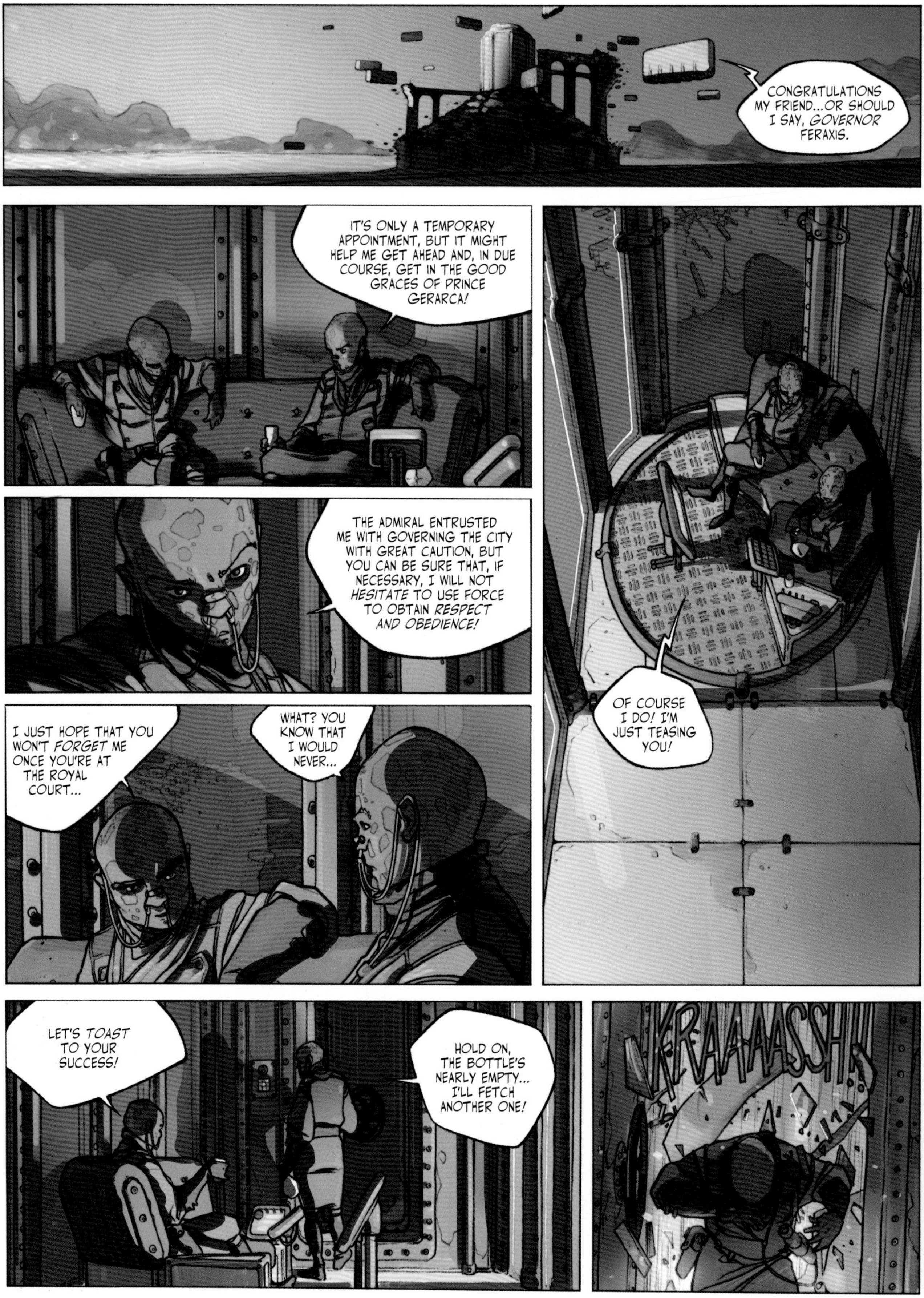

CONGRATULATIONS MY FRIEND...OR SHOULD I SAY, GOVERNOR FERAXIS.
IT'S ONLY A TEMPORARY APPOINTMENT, BUT IT MIGHT HELP ME GET AHEAD AND, IN DUE COURSE, GET IN THE GOOD GRACES OF PRINCE GERARCA!
THE ADMIRAL ENTRUSTED ME WITH GOVERNING THE CITY WITH GREAT CAUTION, BUT YOU CAN BE SURE THAT, IF NECESSARY, I WILL NOT HESITATE TO USE FORCE TO OBTAIN RESPECT AND OBEDIENCE!
I JUST HOPE THAT YOU WON'T FORGET ME ONCE YOU'RE AT THE ROYAL COURT...
WHAT? YOU KNOW THAT I WOULD NEVER...
OF COURSE I DO! I'M JUST TEASING YOU!
LET'S TOAST TO YOUR SUCCESS!
HOLD ON, THE BOTTLE'S NEARLY EMPTY... I'LL FETCH ANOTHER ONE!
KRAAAASSH!!

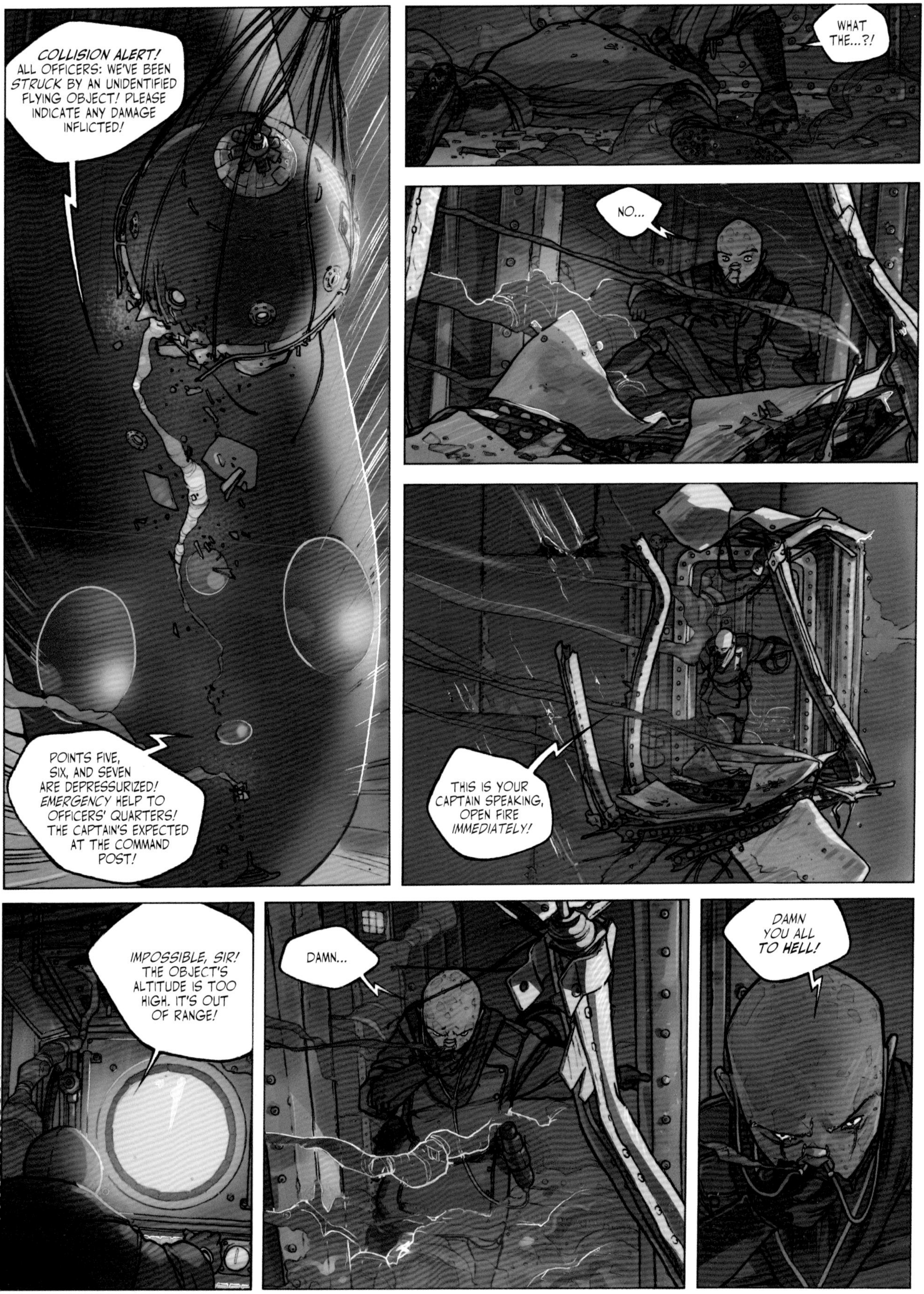
COLLISION ALERT! ALL OFFICERS: WE'VE BEEN STRUCK BY AN UNIDENTIFIED FLYING OBJECT! PLEASE INDICATE ANY DAMAGE INFLICTED!
POINTS FIVE, SIX, AND SEVEN ARE DEPRESSURIZED! EMERGENCY HELP TO OFFICERS' QUARTERS! THE CAPTAIN'S EXPECTED AT THE COMMAND POST!
WHAT THE...?!
NO...
THIS IS YOUR CAPTAIN SPEAKING, OPEN FIRE IMMEDIATELY!
IMPOSSIBLE, SIR! THE OBJECT'S ALTITUDE IS TOO HIGH. IT'S OUT OF RANGE!
DAMN...
DAMN YOU ALL TO HELL!

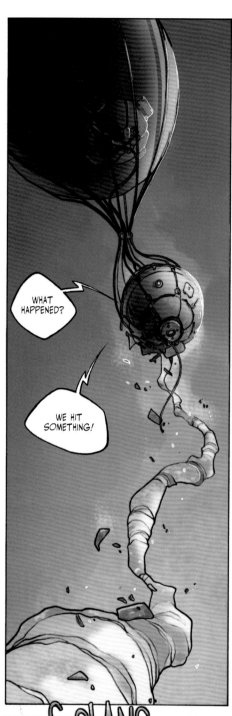

WHAT HAPPENED?

WE HIT SOMETHING!

THE BALLAST CRATES FELL OFF UPON IMPACT!

WE'RE RISING TOO RAPIDLY AND WE HAVE NO WAY TO COUNTERACT OUR MOMENTUM!

WHICH MEANS...?

WHICH *MEANS* WE'RE AT THE MERCY OF VIOLENT AIR CURRENTS IN THE STRATOSPHERE!

CLANG

WHAT WAS THAT NOISE?

OH NO! A BREACH! WE'RE LOSING OXYGEN!

I...I'M GETTING DIZZY...

DON'T LET GO OF THE CONTROLS!

TIMO, HELP ME...!

NO!

I HAVE TO REGAIN CONTROL... I HAVE TO...

I NEED...

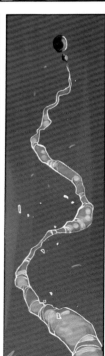

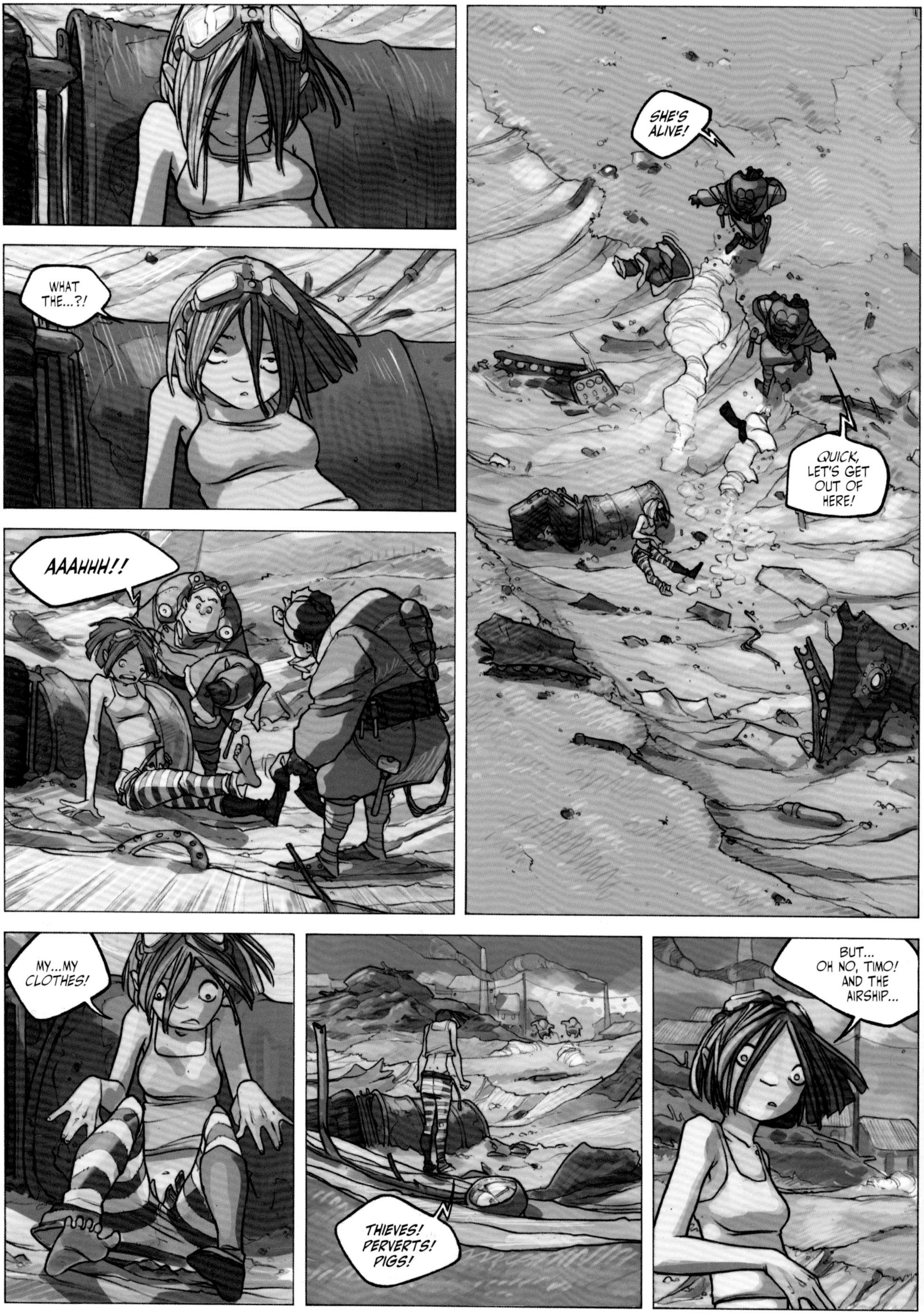
WHAT THE...?!
AAAHHH!!
SHE'S ALIVE!
QUICK, LET'S GET OUT OF HERE!
MY...MY CLOTHES!
THIEVES! PERVERTS! PIGS!
BUT... OH NO, TIMO! AND THE AIRSHIP...

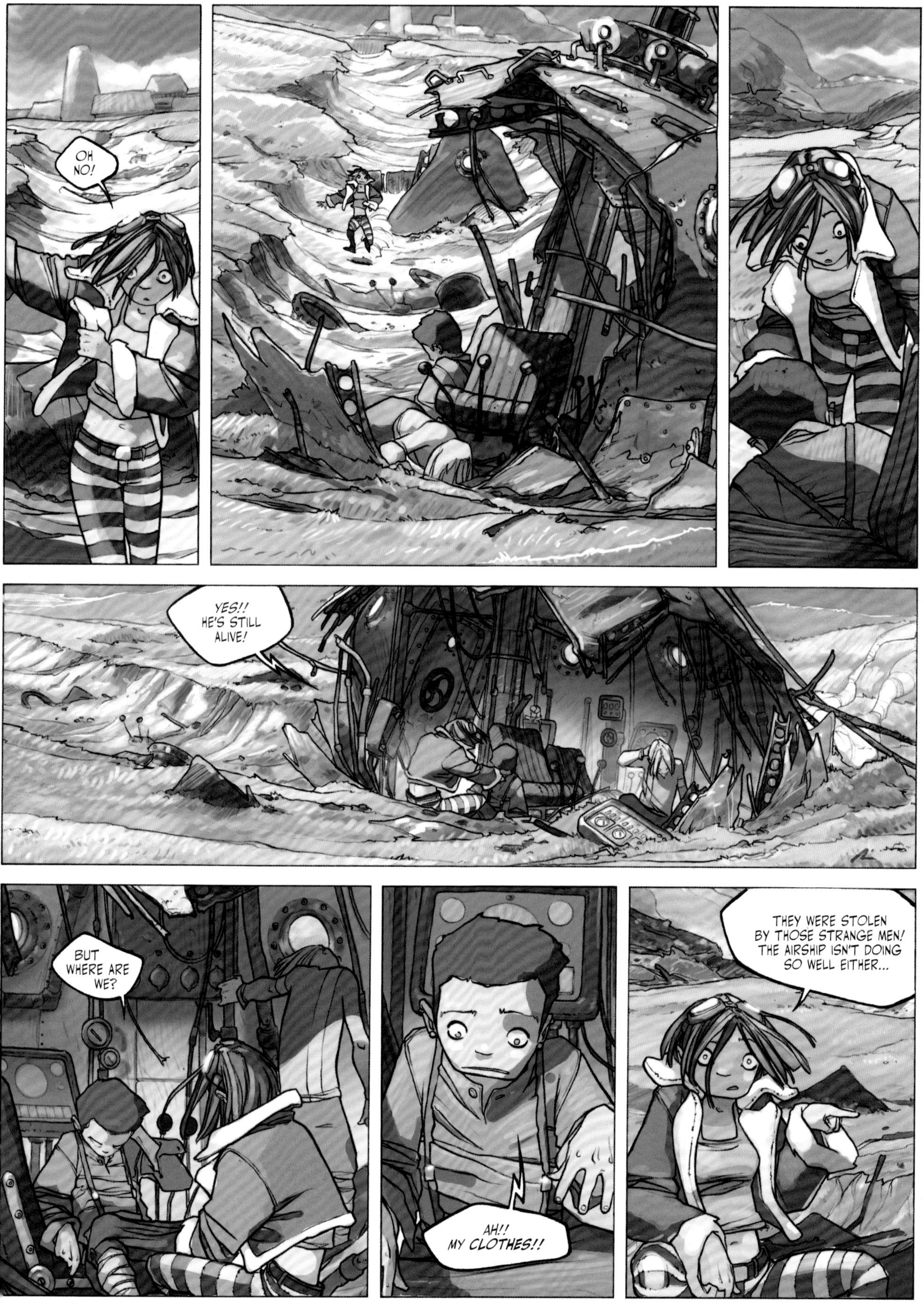
OH NO!
YES!! HE'S STILL ALIVE!
BUT WHERE ARE WE?
AH!! MY CLOTHES!!
THEY WERE STOLEN BY THOSE STRANGE MEN! THE AIRSHIP ISN'T DOING SO WELL EITHER...

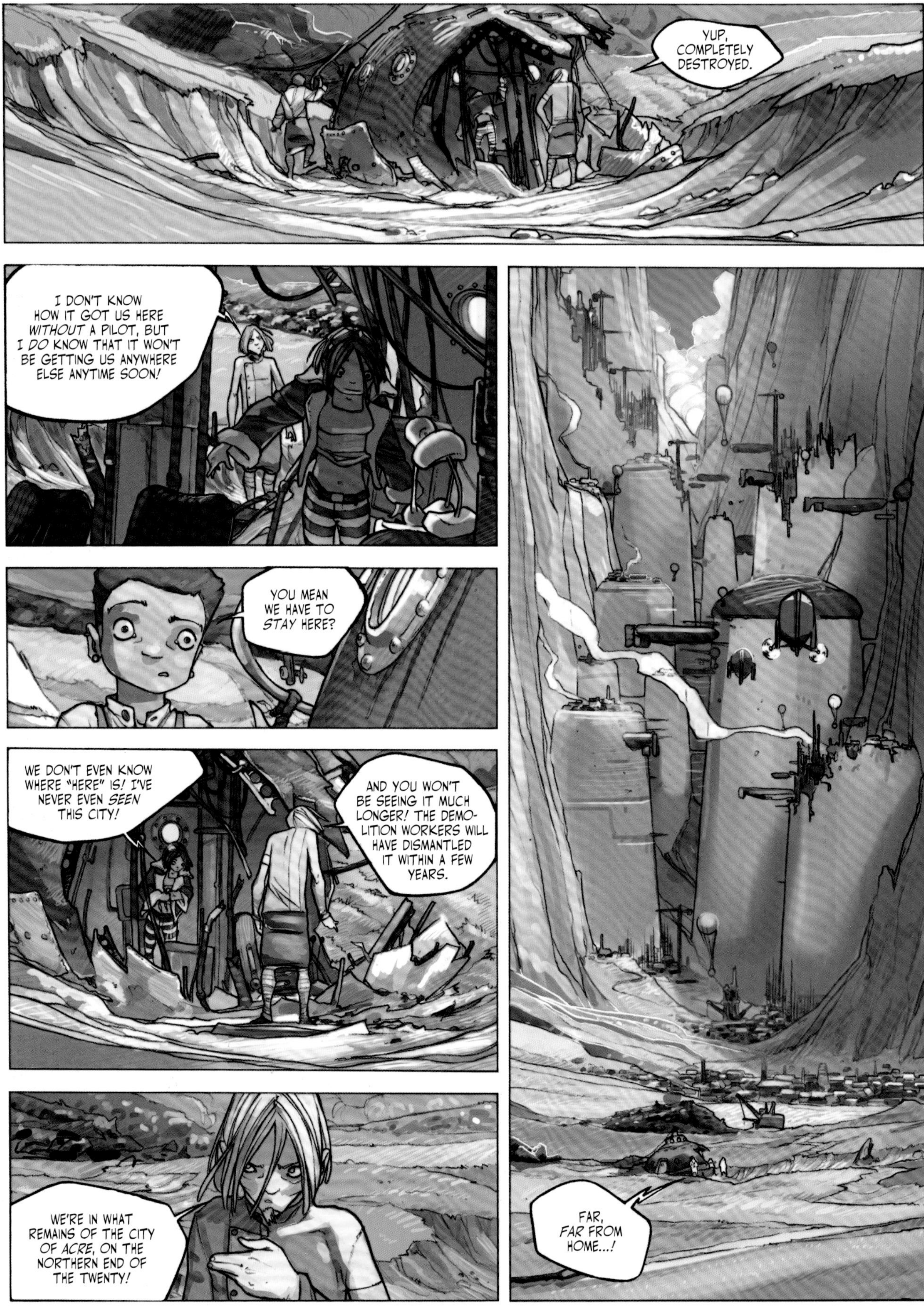
YUP, COMPLETELY DESTROYED.
I DON'T KNOW HOW IT GOT US HERE *WITHOUT* A PILOT, BUT I *DO* KNOW THAT IT WON'T BE GETTING US ANYWHERE ELSE ANYTIME SOON!
YOU MEAN WE HAVE TO *STAY* HERE?
WE DON'T EVEN KNOW WHERE "HERE" IS! I'VE NEVER EVEN *SEEN* THIS CITY!
AND YOU WON'T BE SEEING IT MUCH LONGER! THE DEMOLITION WORKERS WILL HAVE DISMANTLED IT WITHIN A FEW YEARS.
WE'RE IN WHAT REMAINS OF THE CITY OF *ACRE*, ON THE NORTHERN END OF THE TWENTY!
FAR, *FAR FROM* HOME...!

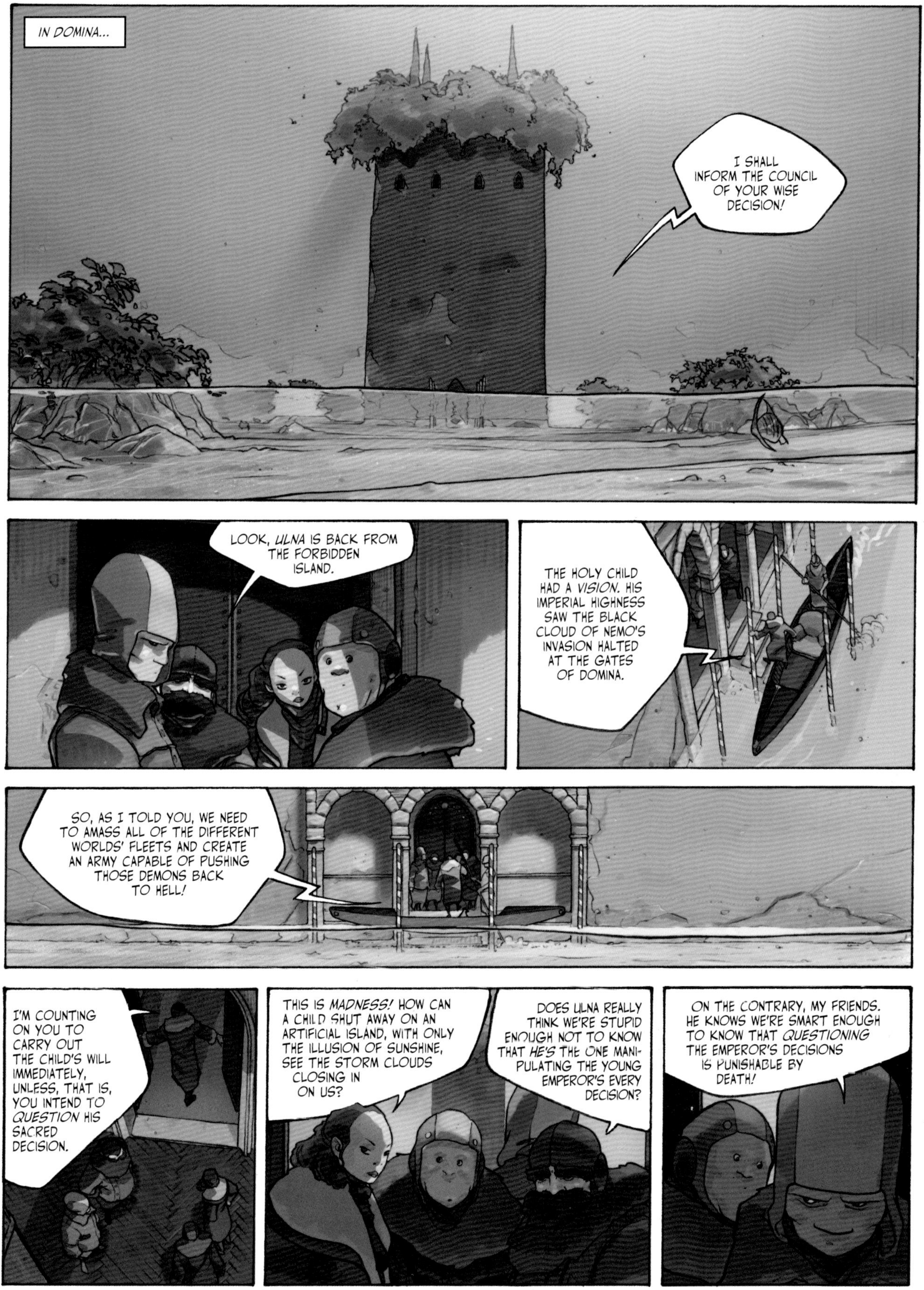
IN DOMINA...
I SHALL INFORM THE COUNCIL OF YOUR WISE DECISION!
LOOK, *ULNA* IS BACK FROM THE FORBIDDEN ISLAND.
THE HOLY CHILD HAD A *VISION*. HIS IMPERIAL HIGHNESS SAW THE BLACK CLOUD OF NEMO'S INVASION HALTED AT THE GATES OF DOMINA.
SO, AS I TOLD YOU, WE NEED TO AMASS ALL OF THE DIFFERENT WORLDS' FLEETS AND CREATE AN ARMY CAPABLE OF PUSHING THOSE DEMONS BACK TO HELL!
I'M COUNTING ON YOU TO CARRY OUT THE CHILD'S WILL IMMEDIATELY, UNLESS, THAT IS, YOU INTEND TO *QUESTION* HIS SACRED DECISION.
THIS IS *MADNESS!* HOW CAN A CHILD SHUT AWAY ON AN ARTIFICIAL ISLAND, WITH ONLY THE ILLUSION OF SUNSHINE, SEE THE STORM CLOUDS CLOSING IN ON US?
DOES ULNA REALLY THINK WE'RE STUPID ENOUGH NOT TO KNOW THAT *HE'S* THE ONE MANIPULATING THE YOUNG EMPEROR'S EVERY DECISION?
ON THE CONTRARY, MY FRIENDS. HE KNOWS WE'RE SMART ENOUGH TO KNOW THAT *QUESTIONING* THE EMPEROR'S DECISIONS IS PUNISHABLE BY DEATH!

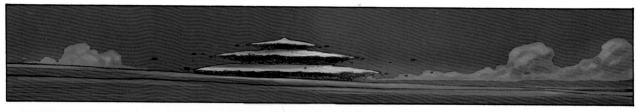

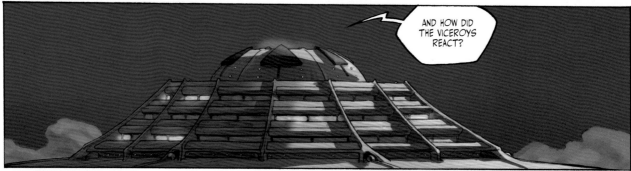

AND HOW DID THE VICEROYS REACT?

NOBODY WILL GO THROUGH WITH IT UNLESS THEY RECEIVE AN OFFICIAL ORDER. BRINGING ALL FLEETS BACK TO MOSE MEANS CONDEMNING THE REST OF THE RING TO CHAOS AND DESTRUCTION!

HOW *PREDICTABLE.* HUMANS ARE SELFISH ANIMALS BY NATURE. THEY'RE READY TO SACRIFICE THOSE AROUND THEM JUST TO SAVE THEMSELVES.

SEBA AND I WILL WAIT HERE UNTIL EVERYTHING HAS BEEN TAKEN CARE OF, AND THEN WE WILL COME MEET YOU.

BE CAREFUL, THIS DIVISION INTO TWO GROUPS WILL MAKE YOU MORE VULNERABLE THAN EVER TO THE CONTAGION OF HUMAN EMOTIONS. IF YOU GIVE IN TO THEM, IT WILL BE YOUR DOWNFALL.

WE'VE SAID ENOUGH. THE HUMANS' TIME IS COMING TO A CLOSE. IT'S TIME FOR *US,* THE PRIMOGENS, TO MOVE TOWARDS *OUR* FUTURE.

WE WILL PROTECT OURSELVES BY TAKING A STRONGER DOSE OF EDON, SO THAT OUR SENSES WILL BE AMPLIFIED AND WE WILL FEEL YOUR PRESENCE DESPITE THE DISTANCE BETWEEN US.

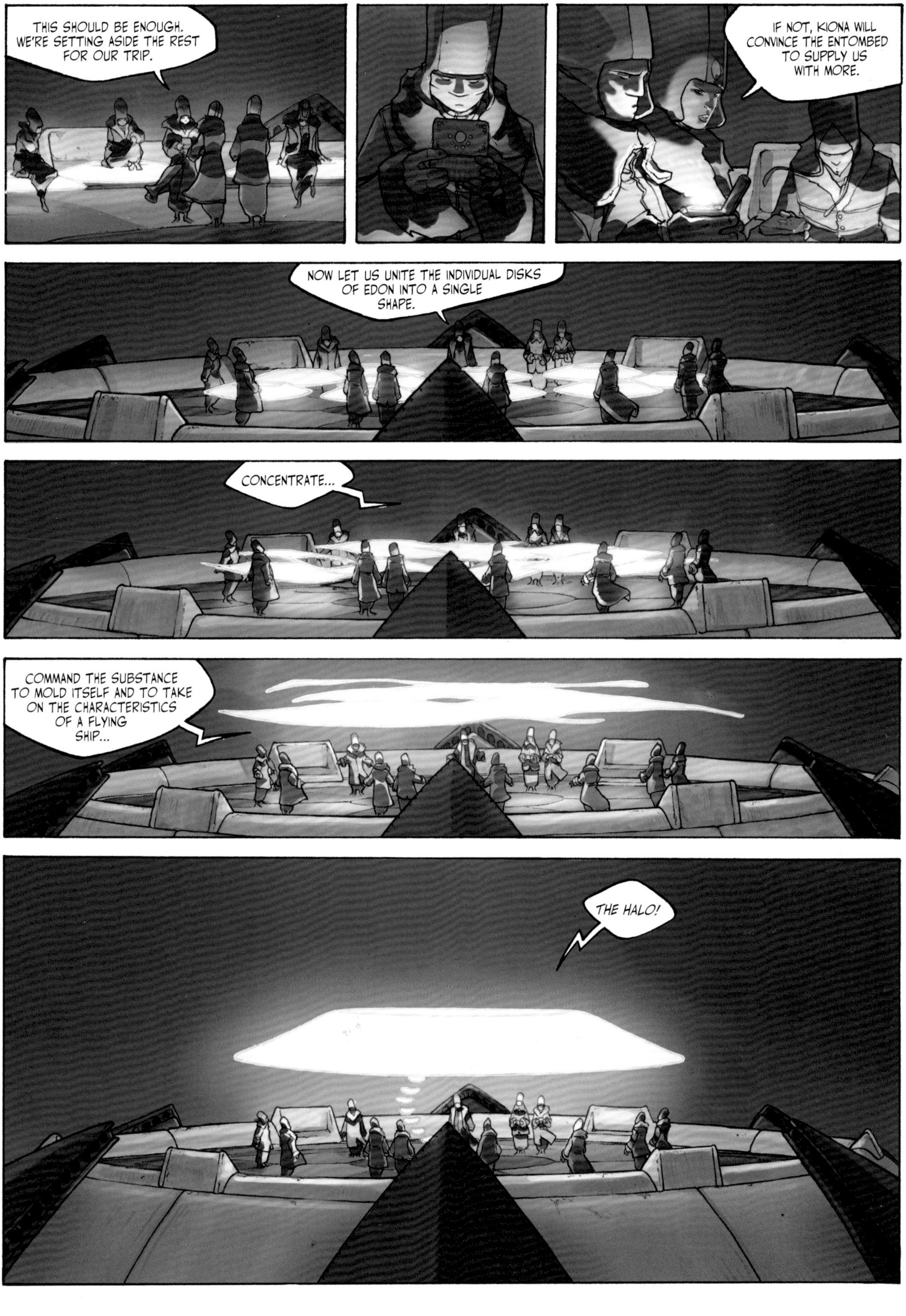
THIS SHOULD BE ENOUGH. WE'RE SETTING ASIDE THE REST FOR OUR TRIP.
IF NOT, KIONA WILL CONVINCE THE ENTOMBED TO SUPPLY US WITH MORE.
NOW LET US UNITE THE INDIVIDUAL DISKS OF EDON INTO A SINGLE SHAPE.
CONCENTRATE...
COMMAND THE SUBSTANCE TO MOLD ITSELF AND TO TAKE ON THE CHARACTERISTICS OF A FLYING SHIP...
THE HALO!

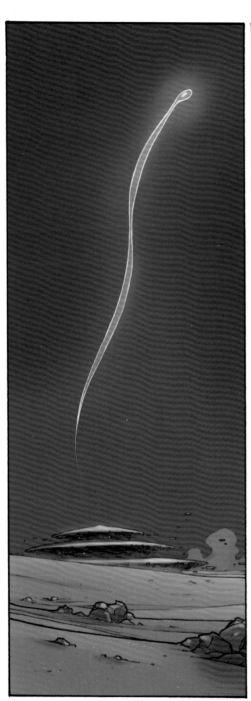

WHAT ARE YOU THINKING ABOUT?

HUMANS. WHEN THEY ARE SEPARATED FROM WHAT THEY LOVE, THEY EXPRESS IT BY CRYING.

EVEN IN THAT AREA, WE ARE FURTHER EVOLVED THAN THEM. THE EDON THAT CIRCULATES THROUGHOUT OUR BODIES HEALS BOTH PHYSICAL AND MENTAL WOUNDS, AND PROTECTS US FROM ANY VIOLENT EMOTIONS THAT COULD CLOUD OUR JUDGMENT!

YOU SPEAK OF THAT WITH SUCH PRIDE!

WHY WOULDN'T I?

SEBA, DO YOU REMEMBER THE LAST TIME WE CRIED?

NO...

WE CRIED WHEN HIS TOMB WAS BEING SEALED. DO YOU REMEMBER? DO YOU RECALL HOW AT THE LAST MOMENT HE GOT SCARED OF THE DARK AND WAS CLUTCHING HIS LITTLE TOY IN HIS ARMS?

I'D FORGOTTEN...

BUT CAN YOU BLAME ME FOR WANTING TO FORGET A MEMORY AS HORRIBLE AS LOSING A SON?

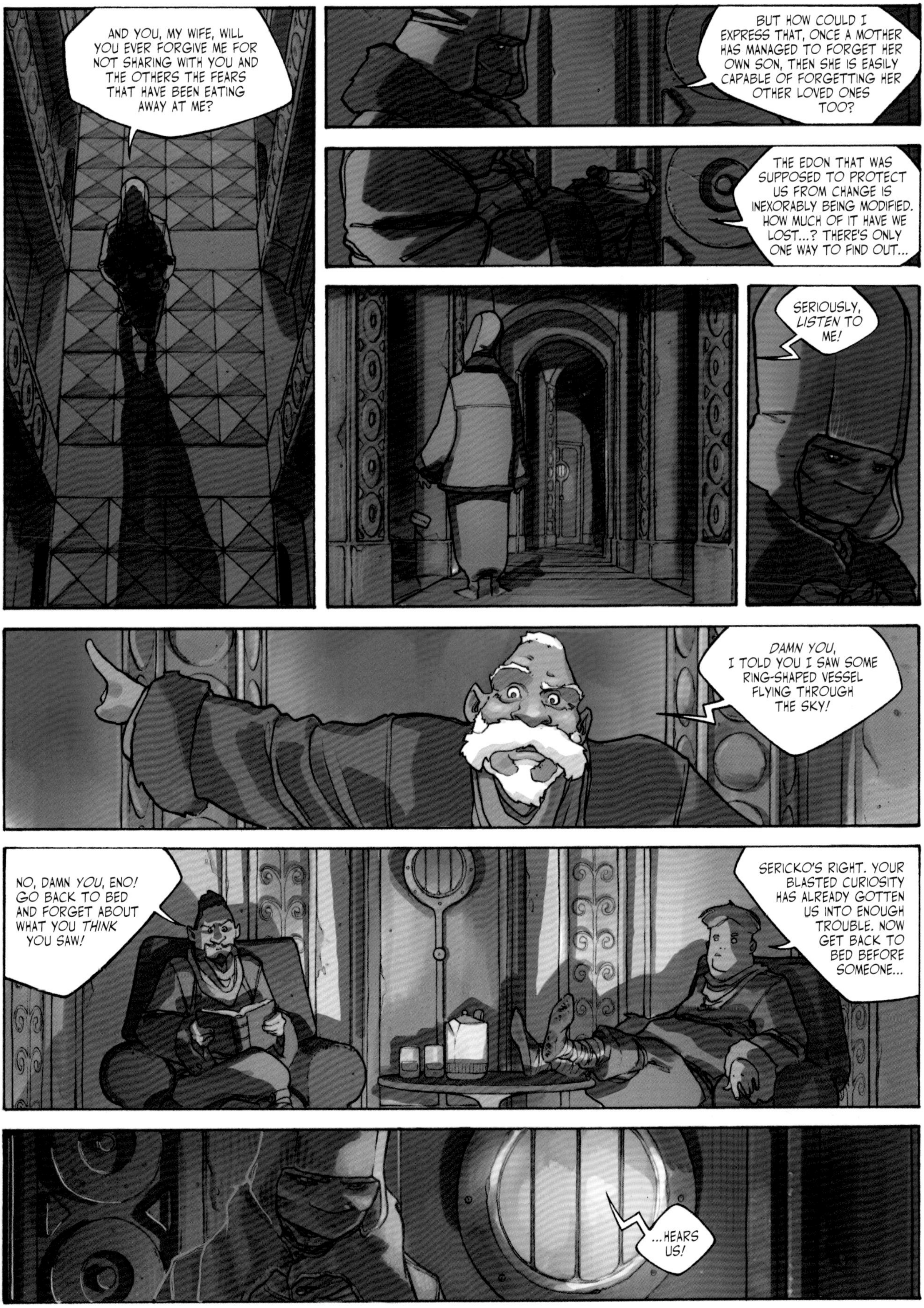
AND YOU, MY WIFE, WILL YOU EVER FORGIVE ME FOR NOT SHARING WITH YOU AND THE OTHERS THE FEARS THAT HAVE BEEN EATING AWAY AT ME?
BUT HOW COULD I EXPRESS THAT, ONCE A MOTHER HAS MANAGED TO FORGET HER OWN SON, THEN SHE IS EASILY CAPABLE OF FORGETTING HER OTHER LOVED ONES TOO?
THE EDON THAT WAS SUPPOSED TO PROTECT US FROM CHANGE IS INEXORABLY BEING MODIFIED. HOW MUCH OF IT HAVE WE LOST...? THERE'S ONLY ONE WAY TO FIND OUT...
SERIOUSLY, *LISTEN* TO ME!
DAMN YOU, I TOLD YOU I SAW SOME RING-SHAPED VESSEL FLYING THROUGH THE SKY!
NO, DAMN *YOU*, ENO! GO BACK TO BED AND FORGET ABOUT WHAT YOU *THINK* YOU SAW!
SERICKO'S RIGHT. YOUR BLASTED CURIOSITY HAS ALREADY GOTTEN US INTO ENOUGH TROUBLE. NOW GET BACK TO BED BEFORE SOMEONE...
...HEARS US!

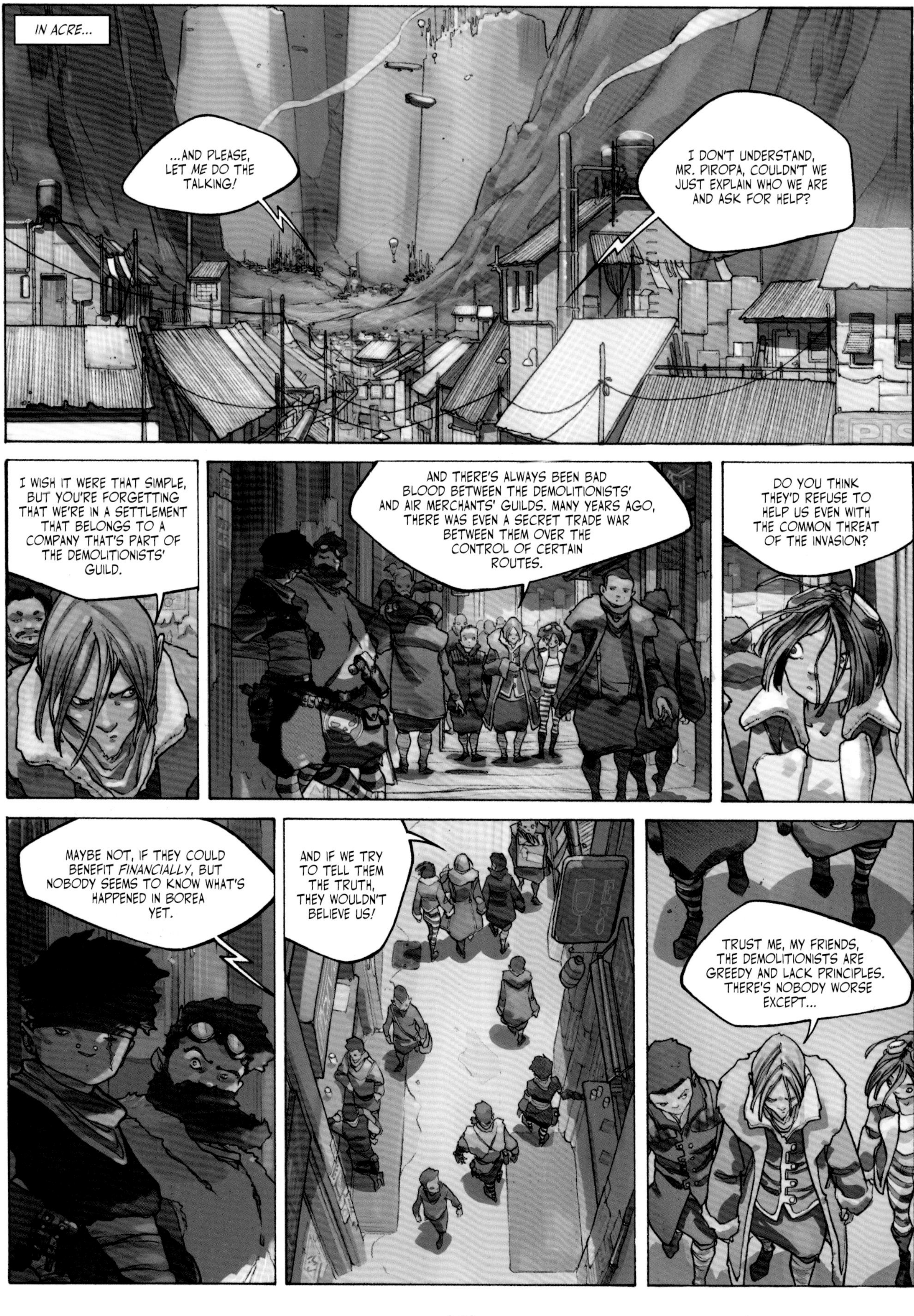
IN ACRE...
...AND PLEASE, LET *ME* DO THE TALKING!
I DON'T UNDERSTAND, MR. PIROPA, COULDN'T WE JUST EXPLAIN WHO WE ARE AND ASK FOR HELP?
I WISH IT WERE THAT SIMPLE, BUT YOU'RE FORGETTING THAT WE'RE IN A SETTLEMENT THAT BELONGS TO A COMPANY THAT'S PART OF THE DEMOLITIONISTS' GUILD.
AND THERE'S ALWAYS BEEN BAD BLOOD BETWEEN THE DEMOLITIONISTS' AND AIR MERCHANTS' GUILDS. MANY YEARS AGO, THERE WAS EVEN A SECRET TRADE WAR BETWEEN THEM OVER THE CONTROL OF CERTAIN ROUTES.
DO YOU THINK THEY'D REFUSE TO HELP US EVEN WITH THE COMMON THREAT OF THE INVASION?
MAYBE NOT, IF THEY COULD BENEFIT *FINANCIALLY*, BUT NOBODY SEEMS TO KNOW WHAT'S HAPPENED IN BOREA YET.
AND IF WE TRY TO TELL THEM THE TRUTH, THEY WOULDN'T BELIEVE US!
TRUST ME, MY FRIENDS, THE DEMOLITIONISTS ARE GREEDY AND LACK PRINCIPLES. THERE'S NOBODY WORSE EXCEPT...

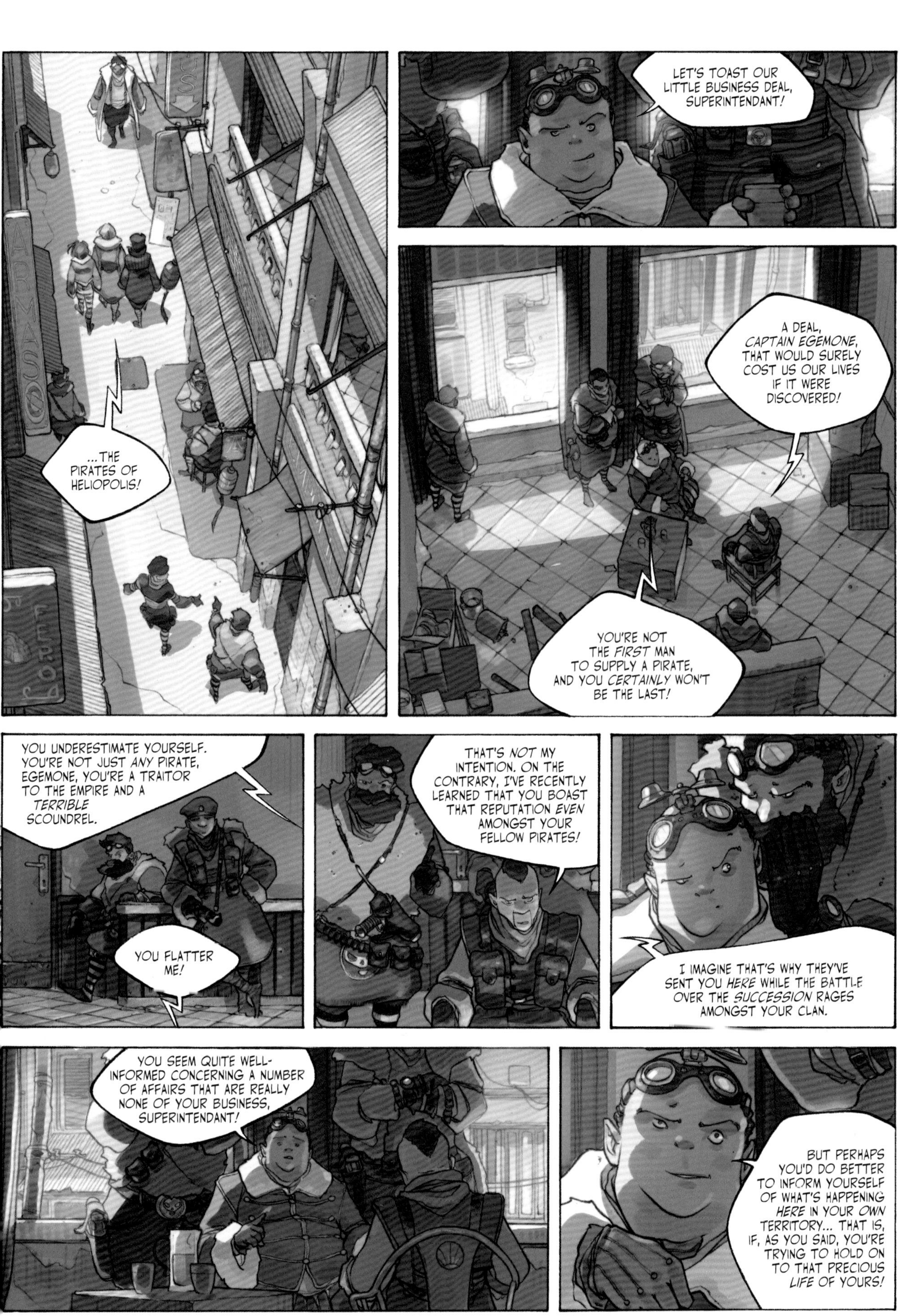
...THE PIRATES OF HELIOPOLIS!
LET'S TOAST OUR LITTLE BUSINESS DEAL, SUPERINTENDANT!
A DEAL, CAPTAIN EGEMONE, THAT WOULD SURELY COST US OUR LIVES IF IT WERE DISCOVERED!
YOU'RE NOT THE FIRST MAN TO SUPPLY A PIRATE, AND YOU CERTAINLY WON'T BE THE LAST!
YOU UNDERESTIMATE YOURSELF. YOU'RE NOT JUST ANY PIRATE, EGEMONE, YOU'RE A TRAITOR TO THE EMPIRE AND A TERRIBLE SCOUNDREL.
YOU FLATTER ME!
THAT'S NOT MY INTENTION. ON THE CONTRARY, I'VE RECENTLY LEARNED THAT YOU BOAST THAT REPUTATION EVEN AMONGST YOUR FELLOW PIRATES!
I IMAGINE THAT'S WHY THEY'VE SENT YOU HERE WHILE THE BATTLE OVER THE SUCCESSION RAGES AMONGST YOUR CLAN.
YOU SEEM QUITE WELL-INFORMED CONCERNING A NUMBER OF AFFAIRS THAT ARE REALLY NONE OF YOUR BUSINESS, SUPERINTENDANT!
BUT PERHAPS YOU'D DO BETTER TO INFORM YOURSELF OF WHAT'S HAPPENING HERE IN YOUR OWN TERRITORY... THAT IS, IF, AS YOU SAID, YOU'RE TRYING TO HOLD ON TO THAT PRECIOUS LIFE OF YOURS!

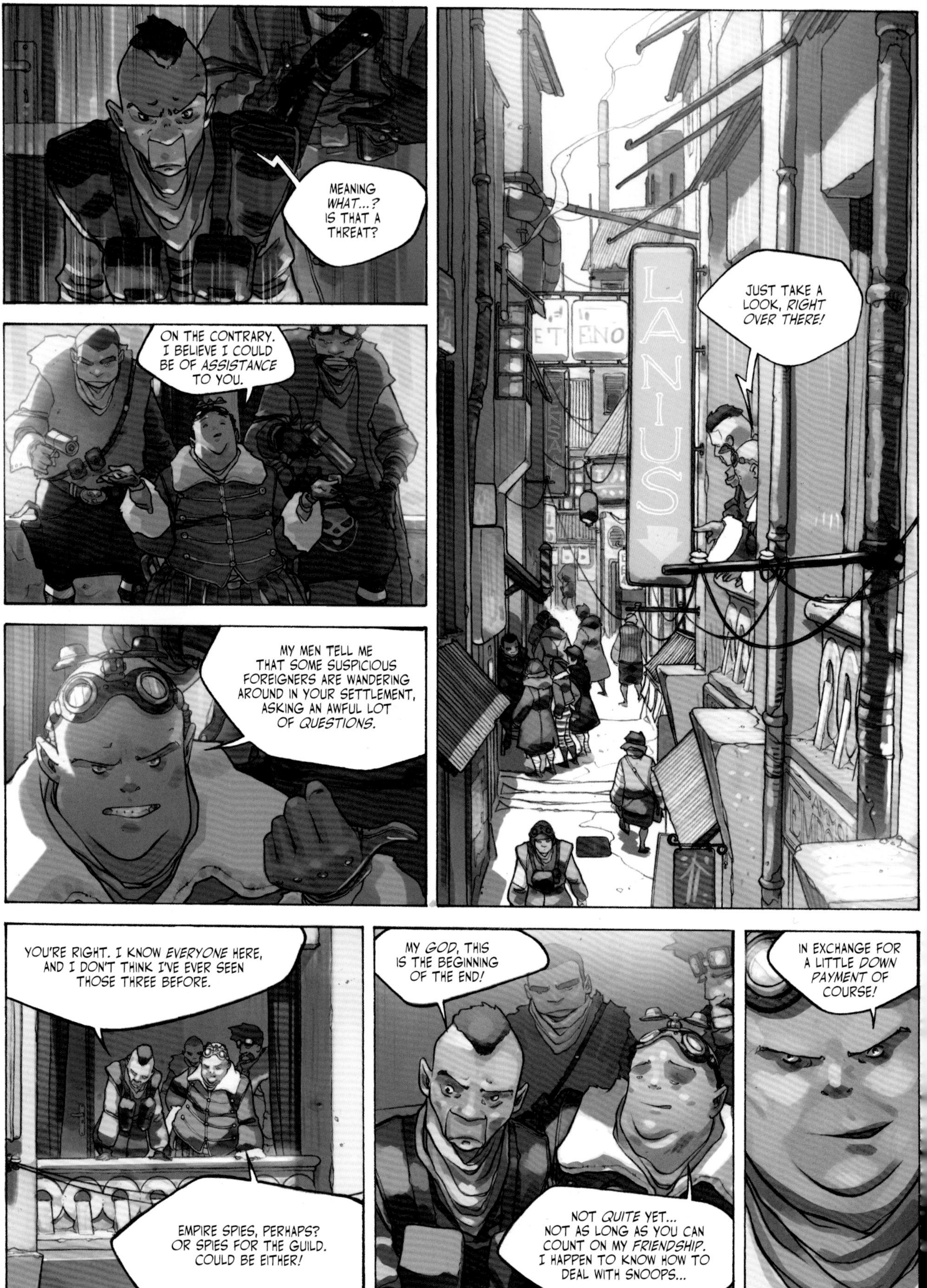
MEANING WHAT...? IS THAT A THREAT?
ON THE CONTRARY. I BELIEVE I COULD BE OF ASSISTANCE TO YOU.
MY MEN TELL ME THAT SOME SUSPICIOUS FOREIGNERS ARE WANDERING AROUND IN YOUR SETTLEMENT, ASKING AN AWFUL LOT OF QUESTIONS.
JUST TAKE A LOOK, RIGHT OVER THERE!
LANIUS
YOU'RE RIGHT. I KNOW EVERYONE HERE, AND I DON'T THINK I'VE EVER SEEN THOSE THREE BEFORE.
EMPIRE SPIES, PERHAPS? OR SPIES FOR THE GUILD. COULD BE EITHER!
MY GOD, THIS IS THE BEGINNING OF THE END!
NOT QUITE YET... NOT AS LONG AS YOU CAN COUNT ON MY FRIENDSHIP. I HAPPEN TO KNOW HOW TO DEAL WITH SNOOPS...
IN EXCHANGE FOR A LITTLE DOWN PAYMENT OF COURSE!

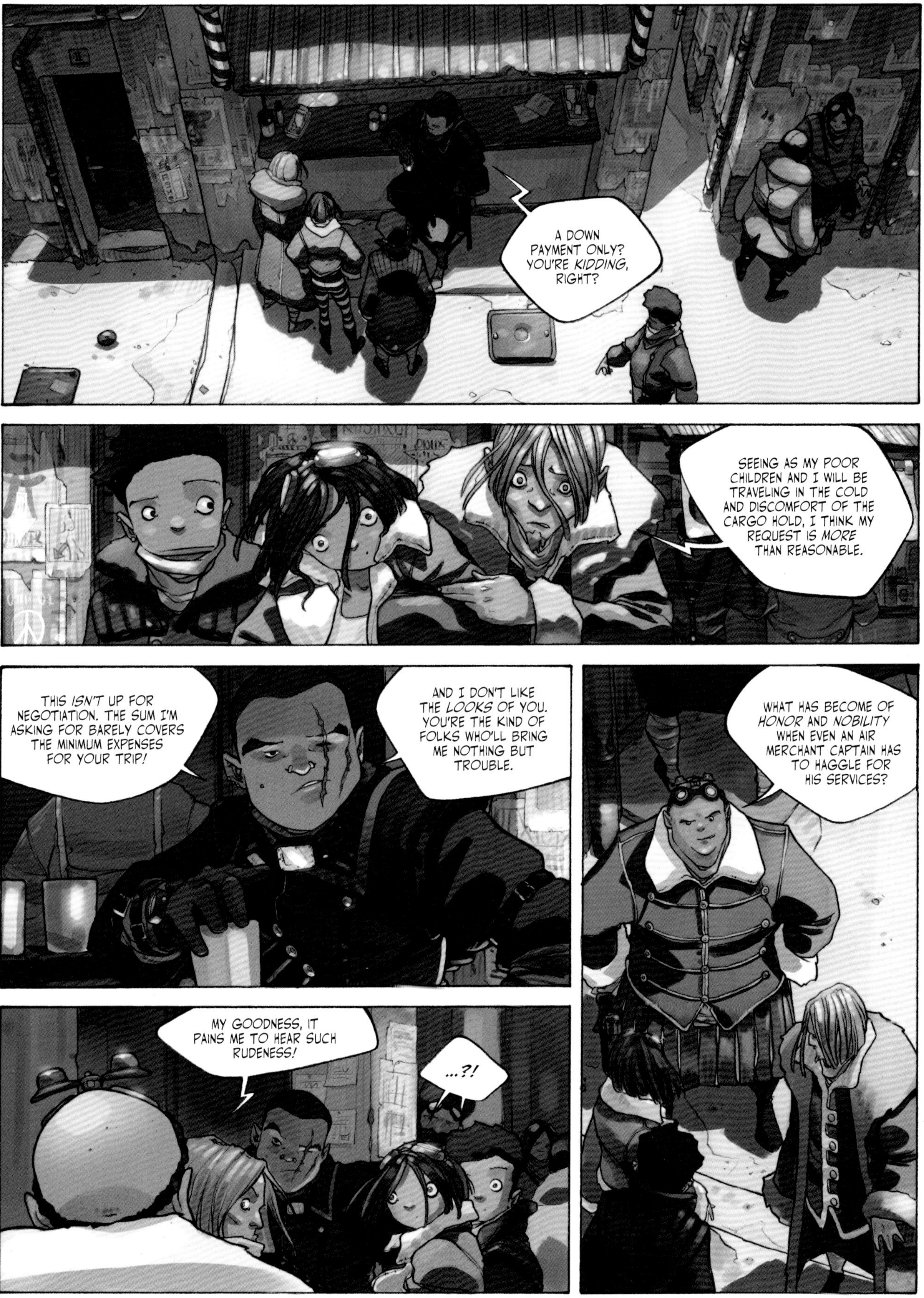
A DOWN PAYMENT ONLY? YOU'RE *KIDDING*, RIGHT?
SEEING AS MY POOR CHILDREN AND I WILL BE TRAVELING IN THE COLD AND DISCOMFORT OF THE CARGO HOLD, I THINK MY REQUEST IS *MORE* THAN REASONABLE.
THIS *ISN'T* UP FOR NEGOTIATION. THE SUM I'M ASKING FOR BARELY COVERS THE MINIMUM EXPENSES FOR YOUR TRIP!
AND I DON'T LIKE THE *LOOKS* OF YOU. YOU'RE THE KIND OF FOLKS WHO'LL BRING ME NOTHING BUT TROUBLE.
MY GOODNESS, IT PAINS ME TO HEAR SUCH RUDENESS!
...?!
WHAT HAS BECOME OF *HONOR* AND *NOBILITY* WHEN EVEN AN AIR MERCHANT CAPTAIN HAS TO HAGGLE FOR HIS SERVICES?

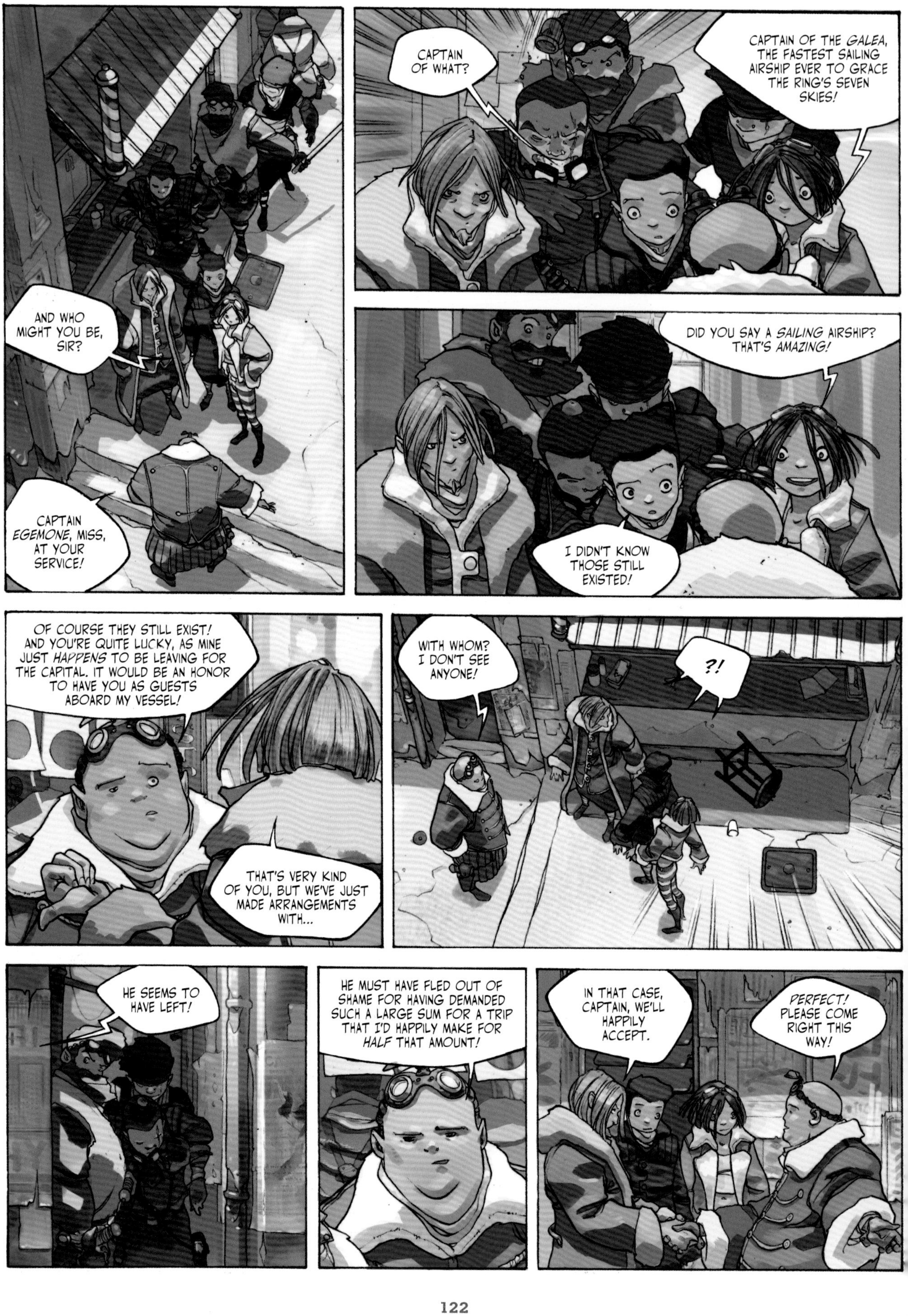

AND WHO MIGHT YOU BE, SIR?
CAPTAIN EGEMONE, MISS, AT YOUR SERVICE!
CAPTAIN OF WHAT?
CAPTAIN OF THE *GALEA*, THE FASTEST SAILING AIRSHIP EVER TO GRACE THE RING'S SEVEN SKIES!
DID YOU SAY A *SAILING* AIRSHIP? THAT'S *AMAZING!*
I DIDN'T KNOW THOSE STILL EXISTED!
OF COURSE THEY STILL EXIST! AND YOU'RE QUITE LUCKY, AS MINE JUST *HAPPENS* TO BE LEAVING FOR THE CAPITAL. IT WOULD BE AN HONOR TO HAVE YOU AS GUESTS ABOARD MY VESSEL!
THAT'S VERY KIND OF YOU, BUT WE'VE JUST MADE ARRANGEMENTS WITH...
WITH WHOM? I DON'T SEE ANYONE!
?!
HE SEEMS TO HAVE LEFT!
HE MUST HAVE FLED OUT OF SHAME FOR HAVING DEMANDED SUCH A LARGE SUM FOR A TRIP THAT I'D HAPPILY MAKE FOR *HALF* THAT AMOUNT!
IN THAT CASE, CAPTAIN, WE'LL HAPPILY ACCEPT.
PERFECT! PLEASE COME RIGHT THIS WAY!

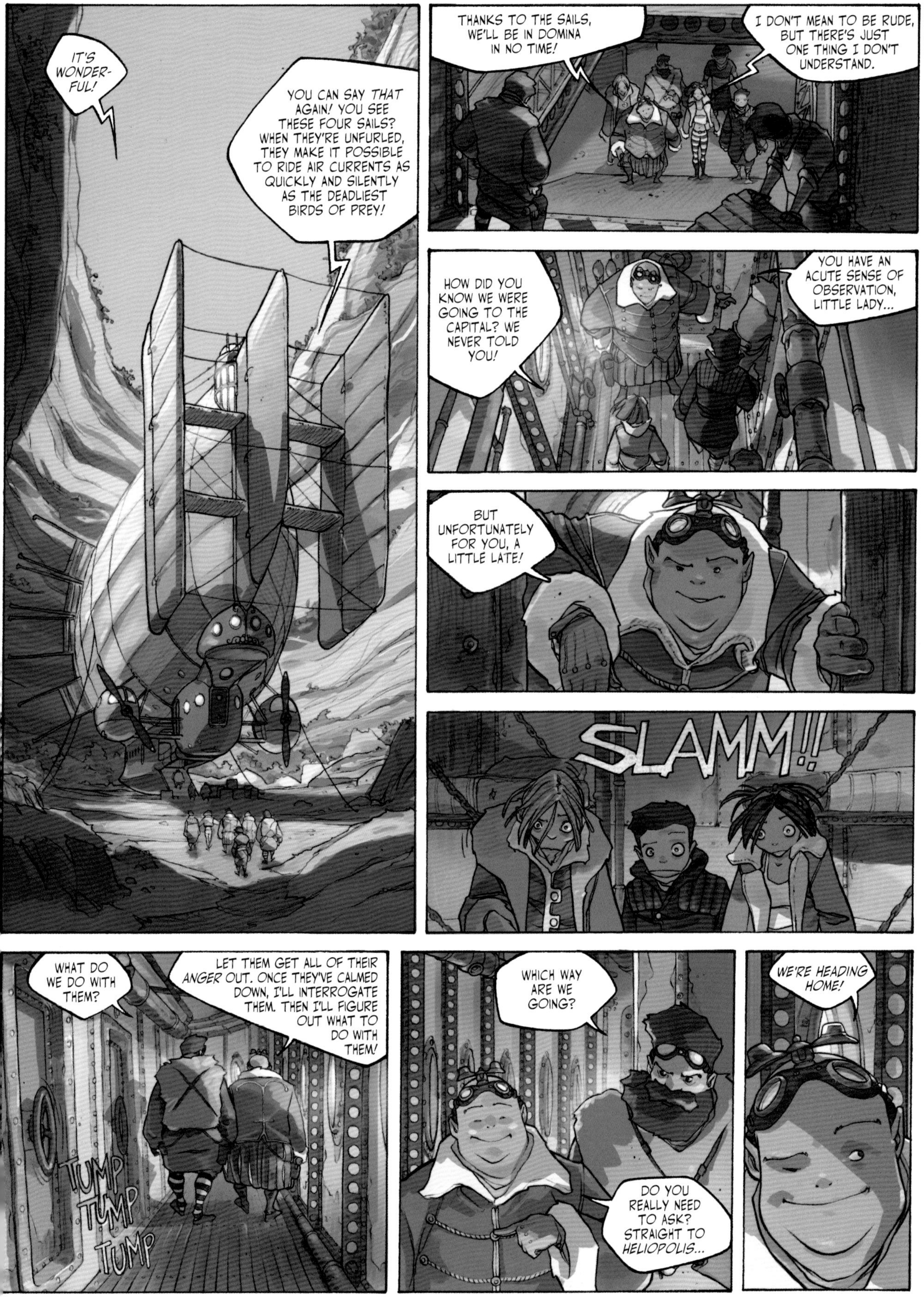
IT'S WONDER-FUL!
YOU CAN SAY *THAT* AGAIN! YOU SEE THESE FOUR SAILS? WHEN THEY'RE UNFURLED, THEY MAKE IT POSSIBLE TO RIDE AIR CURRENTS AS QUICKLY AND SILENTLY AS THE DEADLIEST BIRDS OF PREY!
THANKS TO THE SAILS, WE'LL BE IN DOMINA IN NO TIME!
I DON'T MEAN TO BE RUDE, BUT THERE'S JUST ONE THING I DON'T UNDERSTAND.
HOW DID YOU KNOW WE WERE GOING TO THE CAPITAL? WE NEVER TOLD YOU!
YOU HAVE AN ACUTE SENSE OF OBSERVATION, LITTLE LADY...
BUT UNFORTUNATELY FOR YOU, A LITTLE LATE!
SLAMM!!
WHAT DO WE DO WITH THEM?
LET THEM GET ALL OF THEIR *ANGER* OUT. ONCE THEY'VE CALMED DOWN, I'LL INTERROGATE THEM. THEN I'LL FIGURE OUT WHAT TO DO WITH THEM!
TUMP TUMP TUMP
WHICH WAY ARE WE GOING?
DO YOU REALLY NEED TO ASK? STRAIGHT TO *HELIOPOLIS*...
WE'RE HEADING HOME!

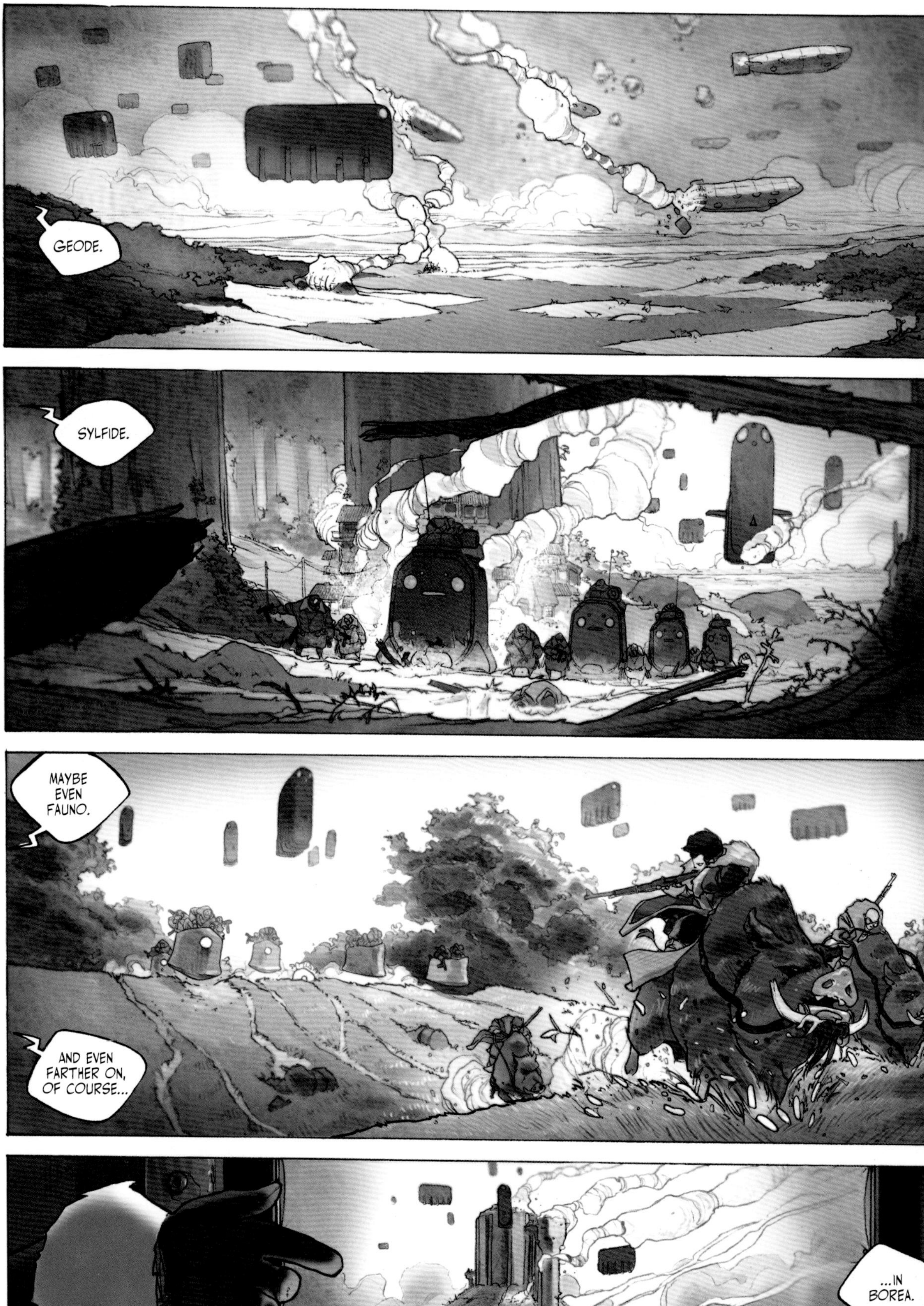
GEODE.
SYLFIDE.
MAYBE EVEN FAUNO.
AND EVEN FARTHER ON, OF COURSE...
...IN BOREA.

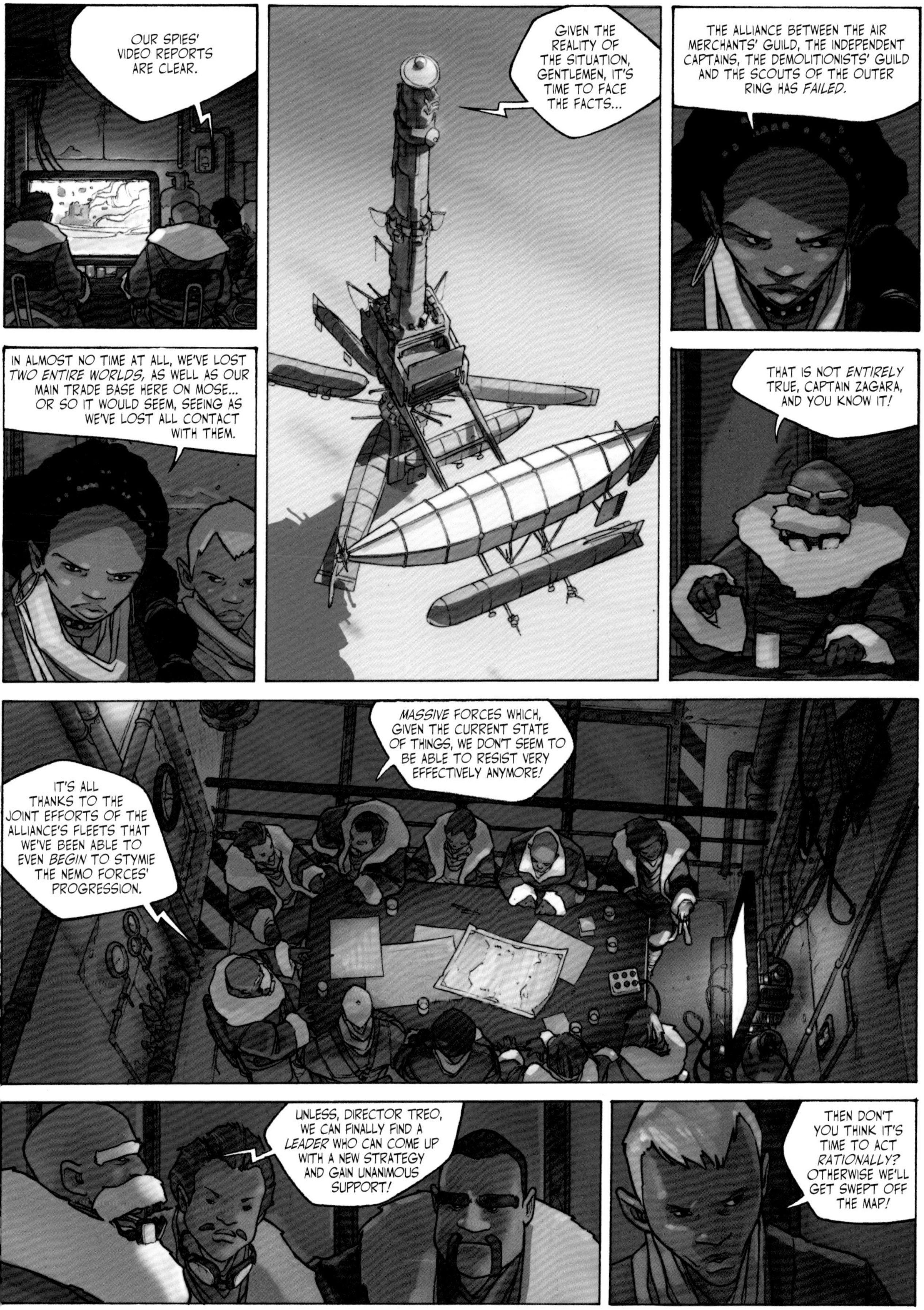
OUR SPIES' VIDEO REPORTS ARE CLEAR.
GIVEN THE REALITY OF THE SITUATION, GENTLEMEN, IT'S TIME TO FACE THE FACTS...
THE ALLIANCE BETWEEN THE AIR MERCHANTS' GUILD, THE INDEPENDENT CAPTAINS, THE DEMOLITIONISTS' GUILD AND THE SCOUTS OF THE OUTER RING HAS *FAILED.*
IN ALMOST NO TIME AT ALL, WE'VE LOST *TWO ENTIRE WORLDS,* AS WELL AS OUR MAIN TRADE BASE HERE ON MOSE... OR SO IT WOULD SEEM, SEEING AS WE'VE LOST ALL CONTACT WITH THEM.
THAT IS NOT *ENTIRELY* TRUE, CAPTAIN ZAGARA, AND YOU KNOW IT!
IT'S ALL THANKS TO THE JOINT EFFORTS OF THE ALLIANCE'S FLEETS THAT WE'VE BEEN ABLE TO EVEN *BEGIN* TO STYMIE THE NEMO FORCES' PROGRESSION.
MASSIVE FORCES WHICH, GIVEN THE CURRENT STATE OF THINGS, WE DON'T SEEM TO BE ABLE TO RESIST VERY EFFECTIVELY ANYMORE!
UNLESS, DIRECTOR TREO, WE CAN FINALLY FIND A *LEADER* WHO CAN COME UP WITH A NEW STRATEGY AND GAIN UNANIMOUS SUPPORT!
THEN DON'T YOU THINK IT'S TIME TO ACT *RATIONALLY?* OTHERWISE WE'LL GET SWEPT OFF THE MAP!

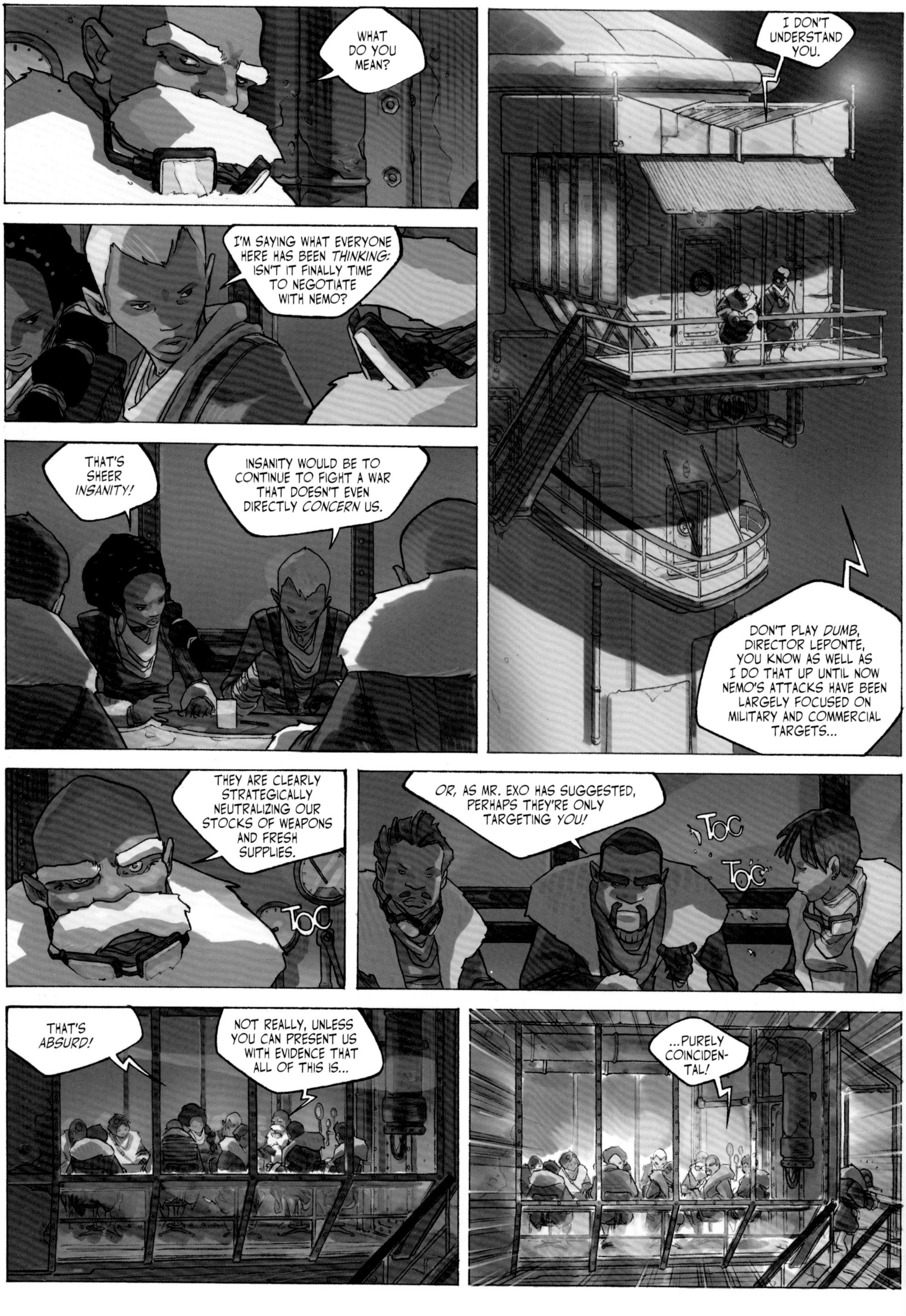
WHAT DO YOU MEAN?
I'M SAYING WHAT EVERYONE HERE HAS BEEN *THINKING:* ISN'T IT FINALLY TIME TO NEGOTIATE WITH NEMO?
THAT'S SHEER *INSANITY!*
INSANITY WOULD BE TO CONTINUE TO FIGHT A WAR THAT DOESN'T EVEN DIRECTLY *CONCERN* US.
I DON'T UNDERSTAND YOU.
DON'T PLAY *DUMB,* DIRECTOR LEPONTE, YOU KNOW AS WELL AS I DO THAT UP UNTIL NOW NEMO'S ATTACKS HAVE BEEN LARGELY FOCUSED ON MILITARY AND COMMERCIAL TARGETS...
THEY ARE CLEARLY STRATEGICALLY NEUTRALIZING OUR STOCKS OF WEAPONS AND FRESH SUPPLIES.
TOC
OR, AS MR. EXO HAS SUGGESTED, PERHAPS THEY'RE ONLY TARGETING YOU!
TOC
TOC
THAT'S *ABSURD!*
NOT REALLY, UNLESS YOU CAN PRESENT US WITH EVIDENCE THAT ALL OF THIS IS...
...PURELY COINCIDEN-TAL!

CRAAAAAAASHH!!!

CRAAAAAASHH!!!

WÓOOOOOOOOOOOOOOSHHH

AHHH!!

WHAT ON EARTH...?!

THEY'RE *CLOWN SWALLOWS* AND *SANDER HAWKS!*

IMPOSSIBLE! SWALLOWS AND HAWKS DON'T MIGRATE TOGETHER, AND *CERTAINLY* NOT AT THIS TIME OF YEAR!

THEY'RE NOT MIGRATING — THEY'RE *FLEEING!*

YOU WANT *PROOF?* THESE SWALLOWS ARE FROM *TRELICE* AND THOSE FALCONS ARE FROM *ACRE.*

THOSE ARE *YOUR* CITIES. THEY'RE *ALL* UNDER ATTACK!

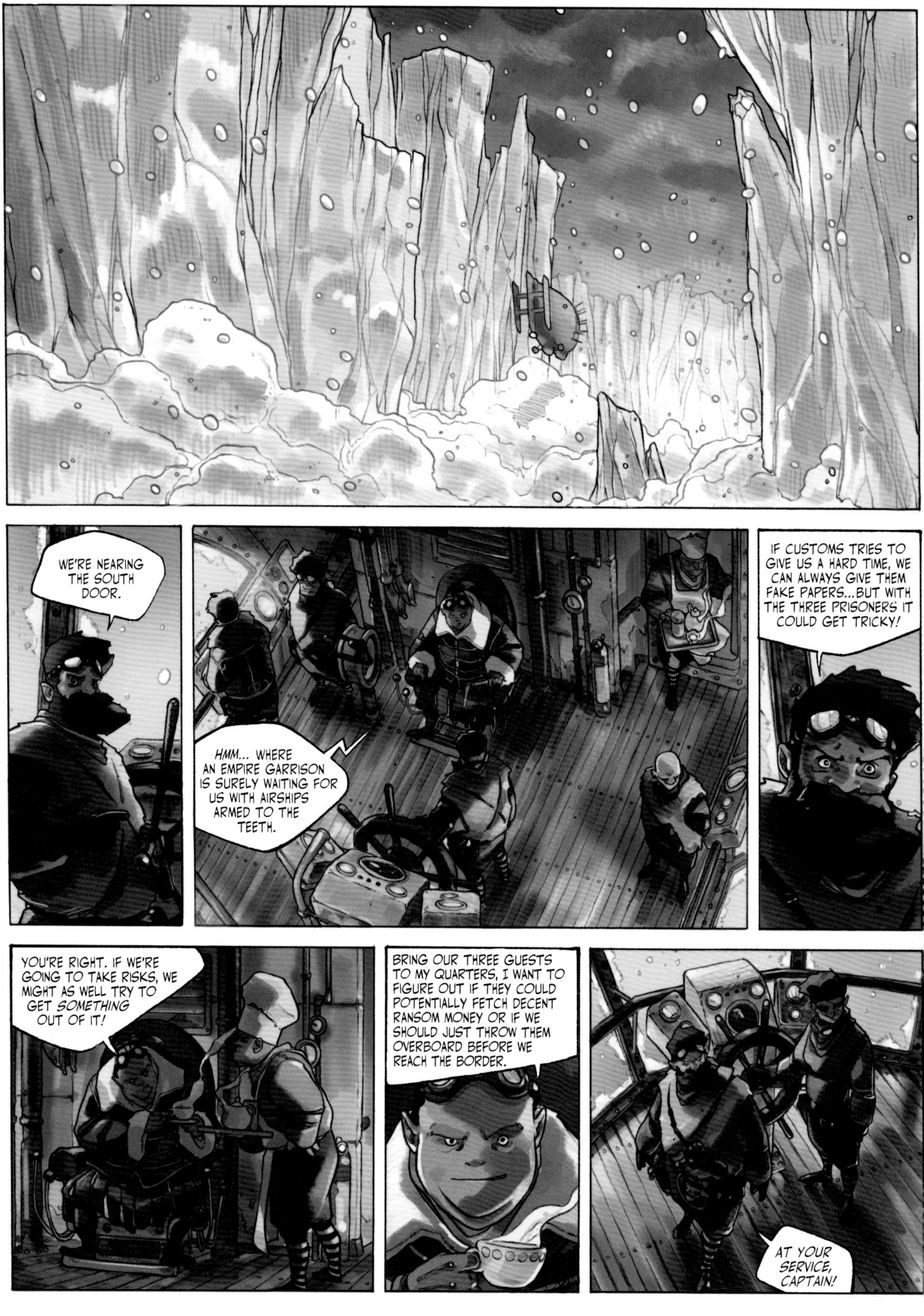
WE'RE NEARING THE SOUTH DOOR.
HMM... WHERE AN EMPIRE GARRISON IS SURELY WAITING FOR US WITH AIRSHIPS ARMED TO THE TEETH.
IF CUSTOMS TRIES TO GIVE US A HARD TIME, WE CAN ALWAYS GIVE THEM FAKE PAPERS...BUT WITH THE THREE PRISONERS IT COULD GET TRICKY!
YOU'RE RIGHT. IF WE'RE GOING TO TAKE RISKS, WE MIGHT AS WELL TRY TO GET *SOMETHING* OUT OF IT!
BRING OUR THREE GUESTS TO MY QUARTERS, I WANT TO FIGURE OUT IF THEY COULD POTENTIALLY FETCH DECENT RANSOM MONEY OR IF WE SHOULD JUST THROW THEM OVERBOARD BEFORE WE REACH THE BORDER.
AT YOUR SERVICE, CAPTAIN!

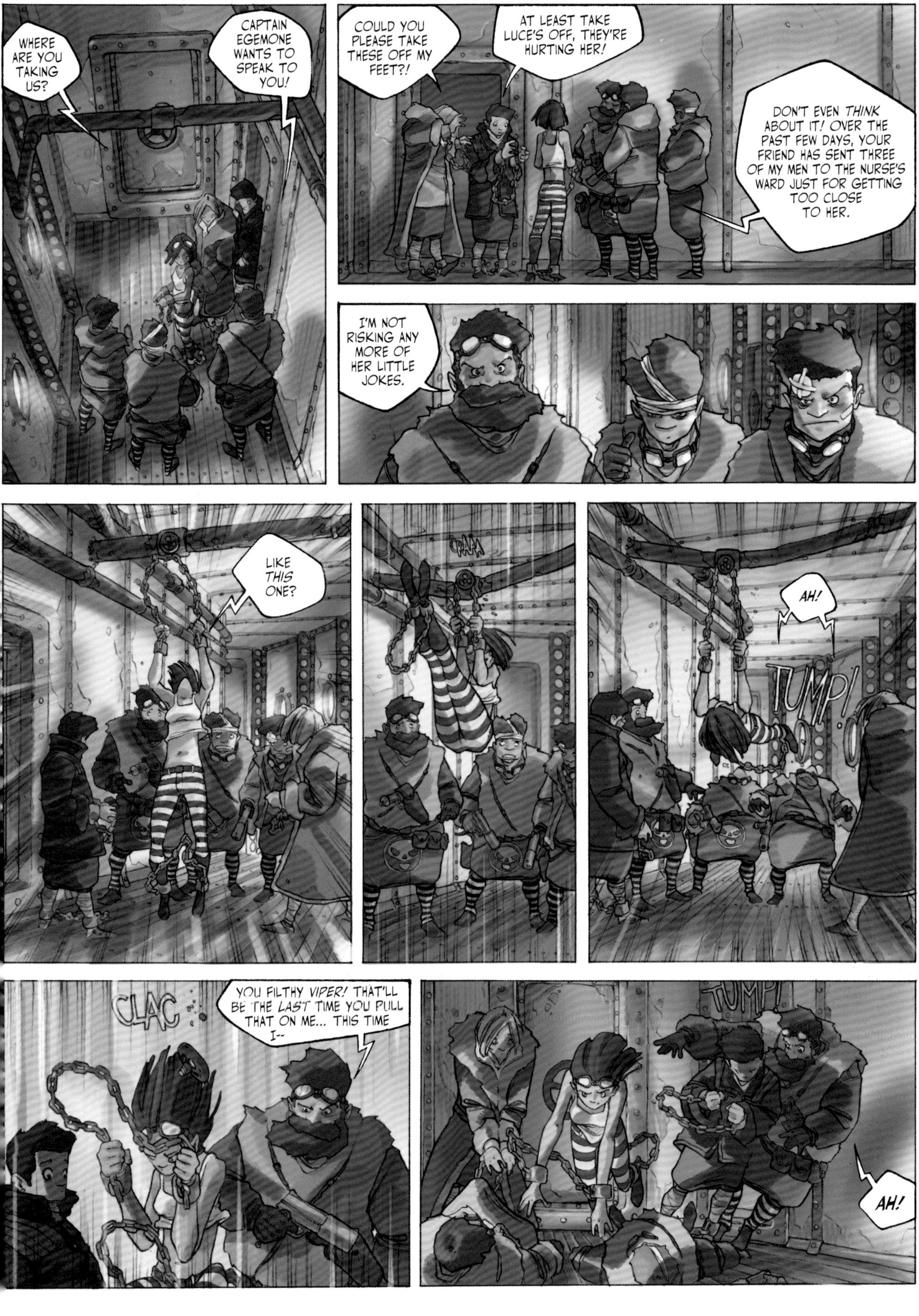
WHERE ARE YOU TAKING US?
CAPTAIN EGEMONE WANTS TO SPEAK TO YOU!
COULD YOU PLEASE TAKE THESE OFF MY FEET?!
AT LEAST TAKE LUCE'S OFF, THEY'RE HURTING HER!
DON'T EVEN THINK ABOUT IT! OVER THE PAST FEW DAYS, YOUR FRIEND HAS SENT THREE OF MY MEN TO THE NURSE'S WARD JUST FOR GETTING TOO CLOSE TO HER.
I'M NOT RISKING ANY MORE OF HER LITTLE JOKES.
LIKE THIS ONE?
CRAAA
AH!
TUMP!
CLAC
YOU FILTHY VIPER! THAT'LL BE THE LAST TIME YOU PULL THAT ON ME... THIS TIME I--
TUMP!
AH!

SHOOT! TAKE HER DOWN!

RUN, LUCE, RUN!

LET GO OF ME!

YOUR TIME HAS COME, YOU LITTLE WRETCH!

ZING ZING

CLANG!

LIKE THE CIRCUS, TIMO! REMEMBER THE FIRST NIGHT WE MET!

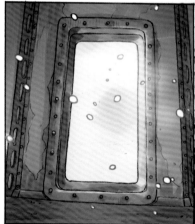

NOOO!!

SHE'S LOST HER MIND!

WHAT A FOOL! FROM THIS ALTITUDE SHE'LL BASH HER SKULL WIDE OPEN!

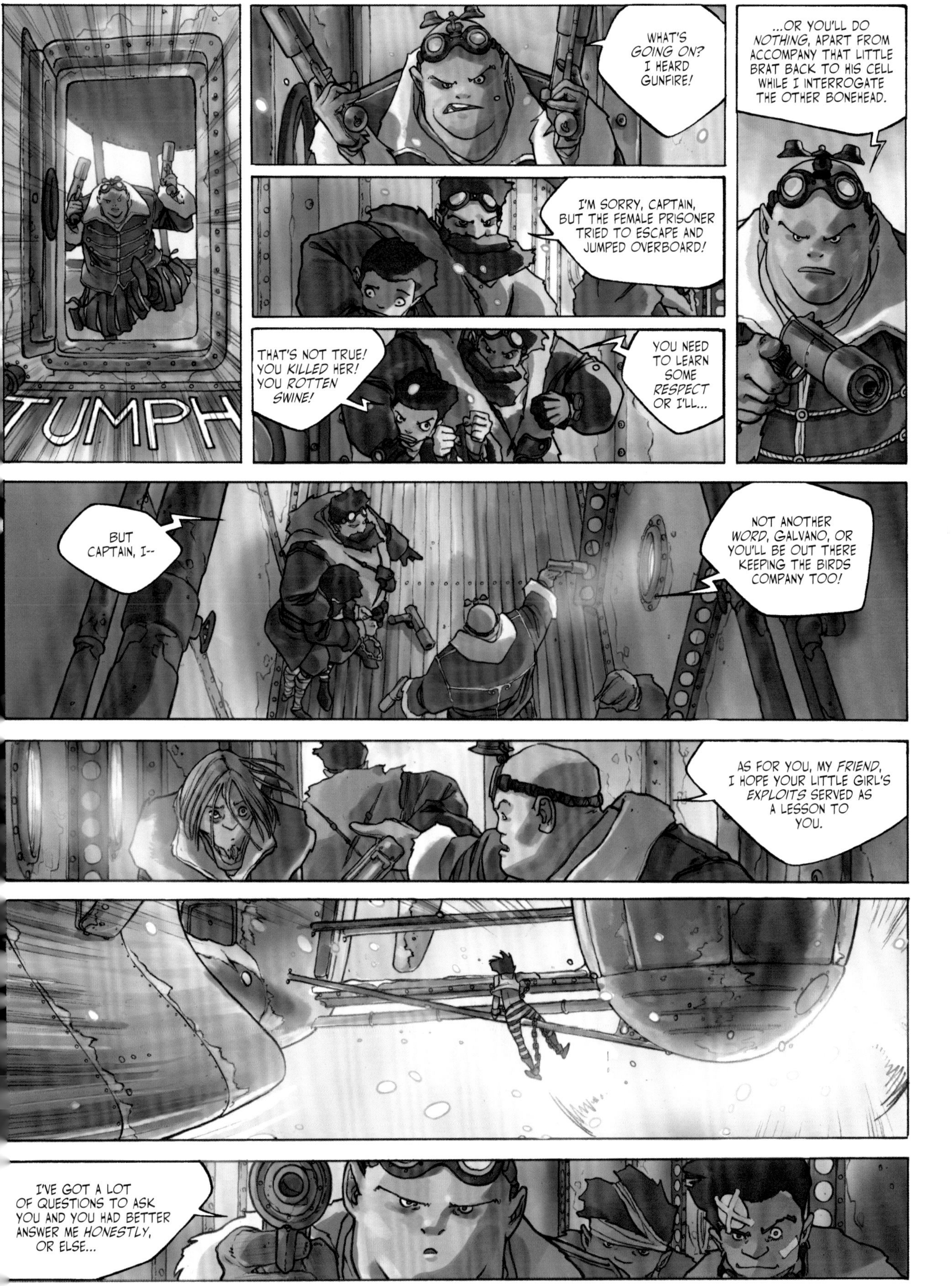
TUMPH
WHAT'S GOING ON? I HEARD GUNFIRE!
I'M SORRY, CAPTAIN, BUT THE FEMALE PRISONER TRIED TO ESCAPE AND JUMPED OVERBOARD!
THAT'S NOT TRUE! YOU *KILLED* HER! YOU *ROTTEN* SWINE!
YOU NEED TO LEARN SOME *RESPECT* OR I'LL...
...OR YOU'LL DO *NOTHING*, APART FROM ACCOMPANY THAT LITTLE BRAT BACK TO HIS CELL WHILE I INTERROGATE THE OTHER BONEHEAD.
BUT CAPTAIN, I--
NOT ANOTHER *WORD*, GALVANO, OR YOU'LL BE OUT THERE KEEPING THE BIRDS COMPANY TOO!
AS FOR YOU, MY *FRIEND*, I HOPE YOUR LITTLE GIRL'S *EXPLOITS* SERVED AS A LESSON TO YOU.
I'VE GOT A LOT OF QUESTIONS TO ASK YOU AND YOU HAD BETTER ANSWER ME *HONESTLY*, OR ELSE...

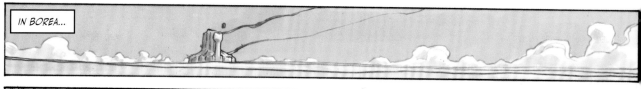

IN BOREA...

PLEASE, HAVE MERCY! THEY'RE ONLY *CHILDREN*!

LEAVE THEM BE, THEY DIDN'T DO ANY-THING!

THE CROWD'S BECOMING MORE THREATENING... HOW DO WE HANDLE IT?

YOU HEARD GOVERNOR FERAXIS' ORDERS, DIDN'T YOU? IF THE RESISTANCE LEADERS DON'T TURN THEMSELVES IN BEFORE NOON, WE PROCEED WITH THE *EXECUTIONS*!

WE'RE NEARLY THERE. THE SUN IS AT ITS *ZENITH*!

IT'S TIME! GIVE THE ORDER.

I BEG YOU TO *RECONSIDER*, GOVERNOR FERAXIS.

I UNDERSTAND YOUR DESIRE FOR REVENGE, BUT IN DOING SO WE WOULD MERELY BE FANNING THE FLAMES OF THE RESISTANCE!

ALLOW ME TO REMIND YOU THAT THE FLEET IS FAR OFF AND WE DON'T HAVE ENOUGH MEN TO CONTAIN THE CROWDS. IF ADMIRAL NYKTOS KNEW WHAT--

ENOUGH!

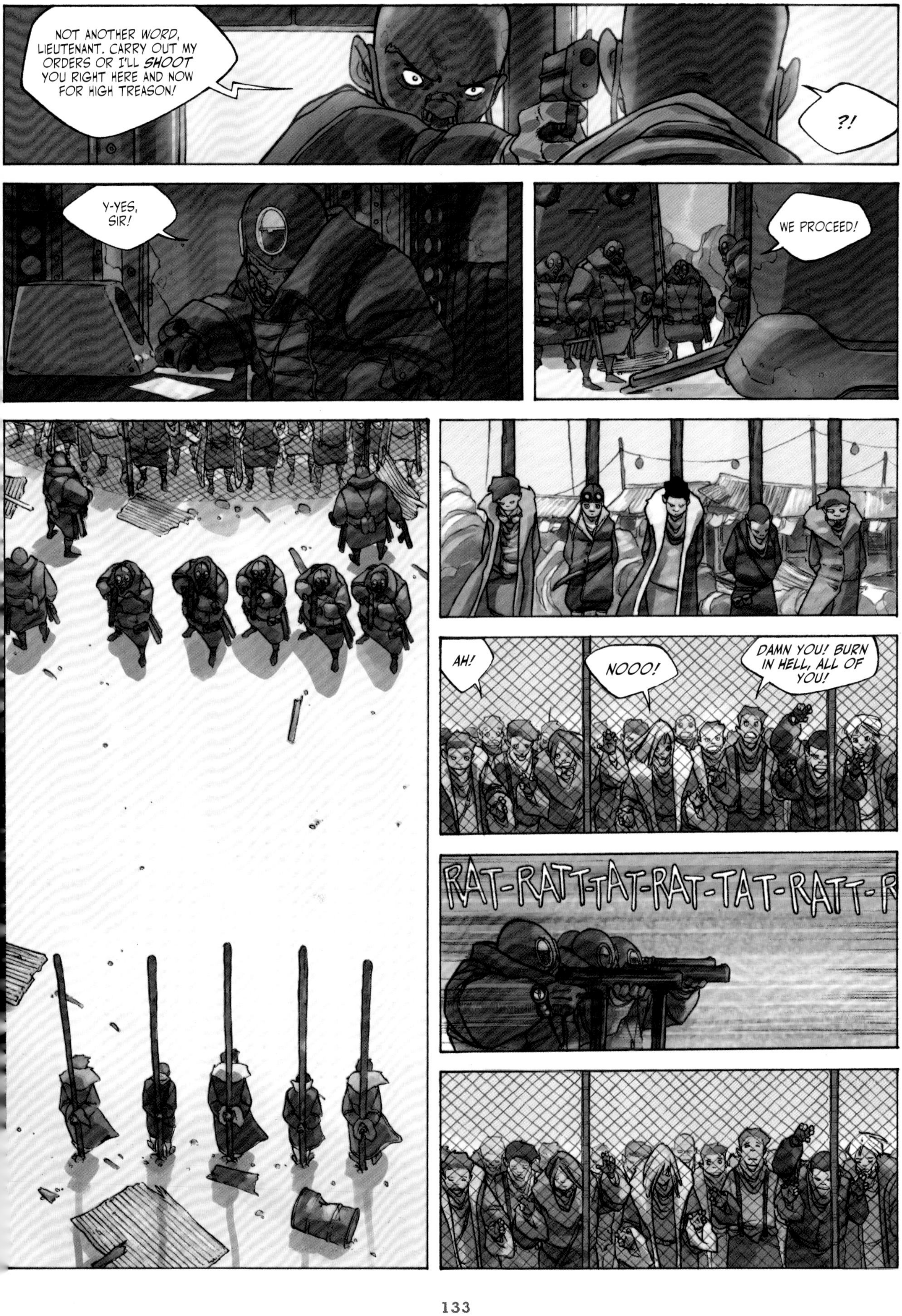

NOT ANOTHER WORD, LIEUTENANT. CARRY OUT MY ORDERS OR I'LL SHOOT YOU RIGHT HERE AND NOW FOR HIGH TREASON!
?!
Y-YES, SIR!
WE PROCEED!
AH!
NOOO!
DAMN YOU! BURN IN HELL, ALL OF YOU!
RAT-RATT-TAT-RAT-TAT-RATT-R

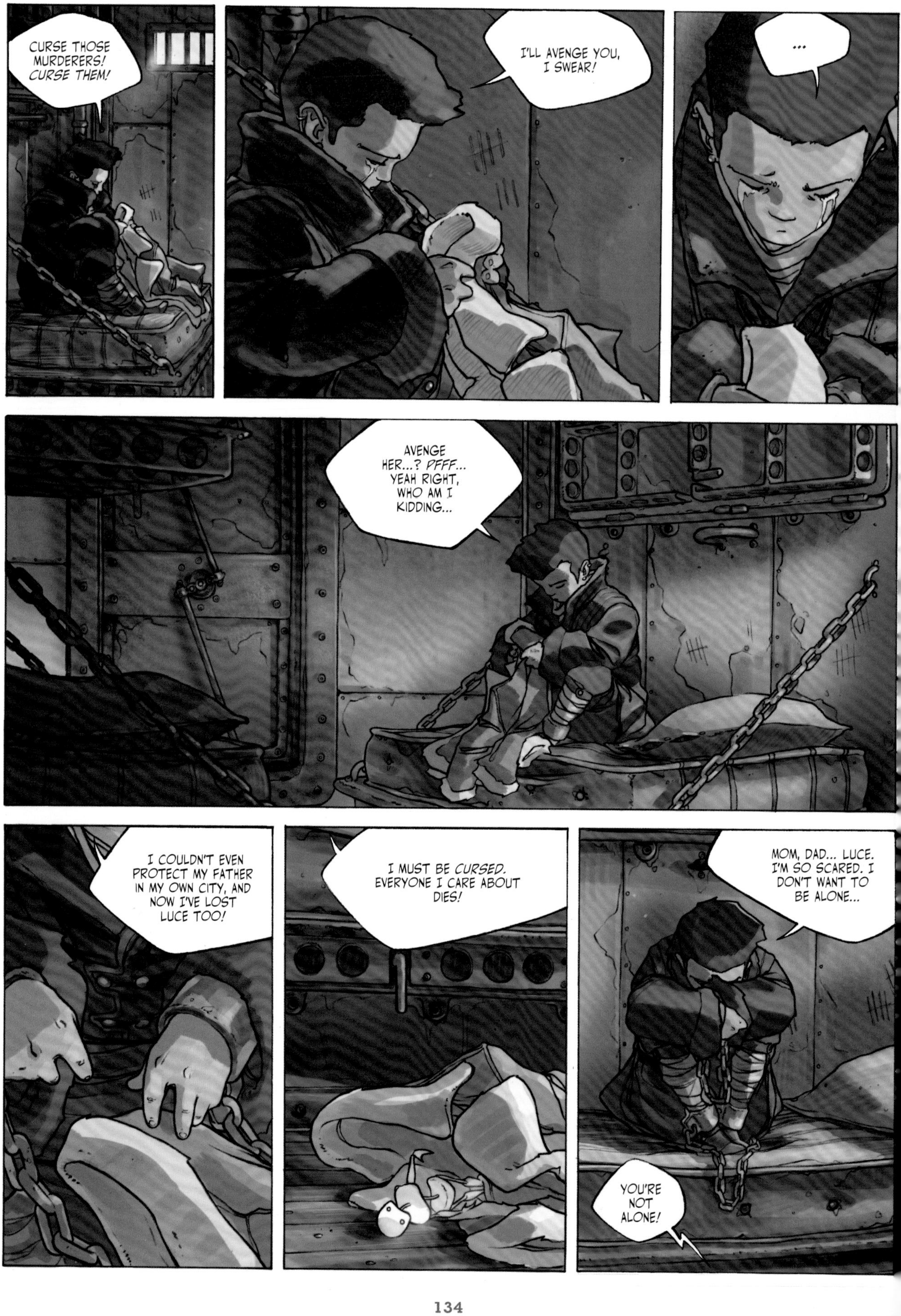
CURSE THOSE MURDERERS! CURSE THEM!
I'LL AVENGE YOU, I SWEAR!
...
AVENGE HER...? PFFF... YEAH RIGHT, WHO AM I KIDDING...
I COULDN'T EVEN PROTECT MY FATHER IN MY OWN CITY, AND NOW I'VE LOST LUCE TOO!
I MUST BE CURSED. EVERYONE I CARE ABOUT DIES!
MOM, DAD... LUCE. I'M SO SCARED. I DON'T WANT TO BE ALONE...
YOU'RE NOT ALONE!

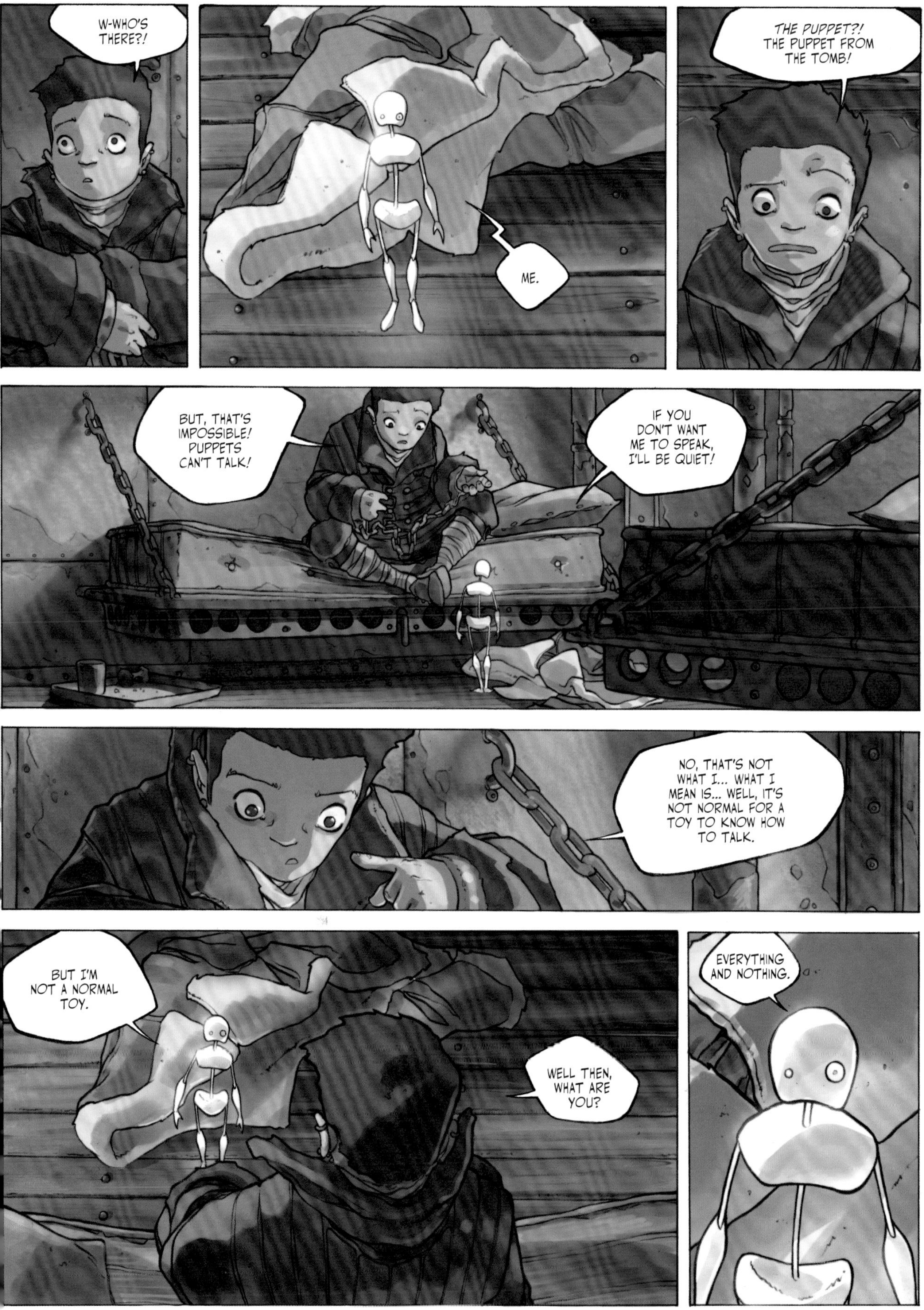
W-WHO'S THERE?!
ME.
THE PUPPET?! THE PUPPET FROM THE TOMB!
BUT, THAT'S IMPOSSIBLE! PUPPETS CAN'T TALK!
IF YOU DON'T WANT ME TO SPEAK, I'LL BE QUIET!
NO, THAT'S NOT WHAT I... WHAT I MEAN IS... WELL, IT'S NOT NORMAL FOR A TOY TO KNOW HOW TO TALK.
BUT I'M NOT A NORMAL TOY.
WELL THEN, WHAT ARE YOU?
EVERYTHING AND NOTHING.

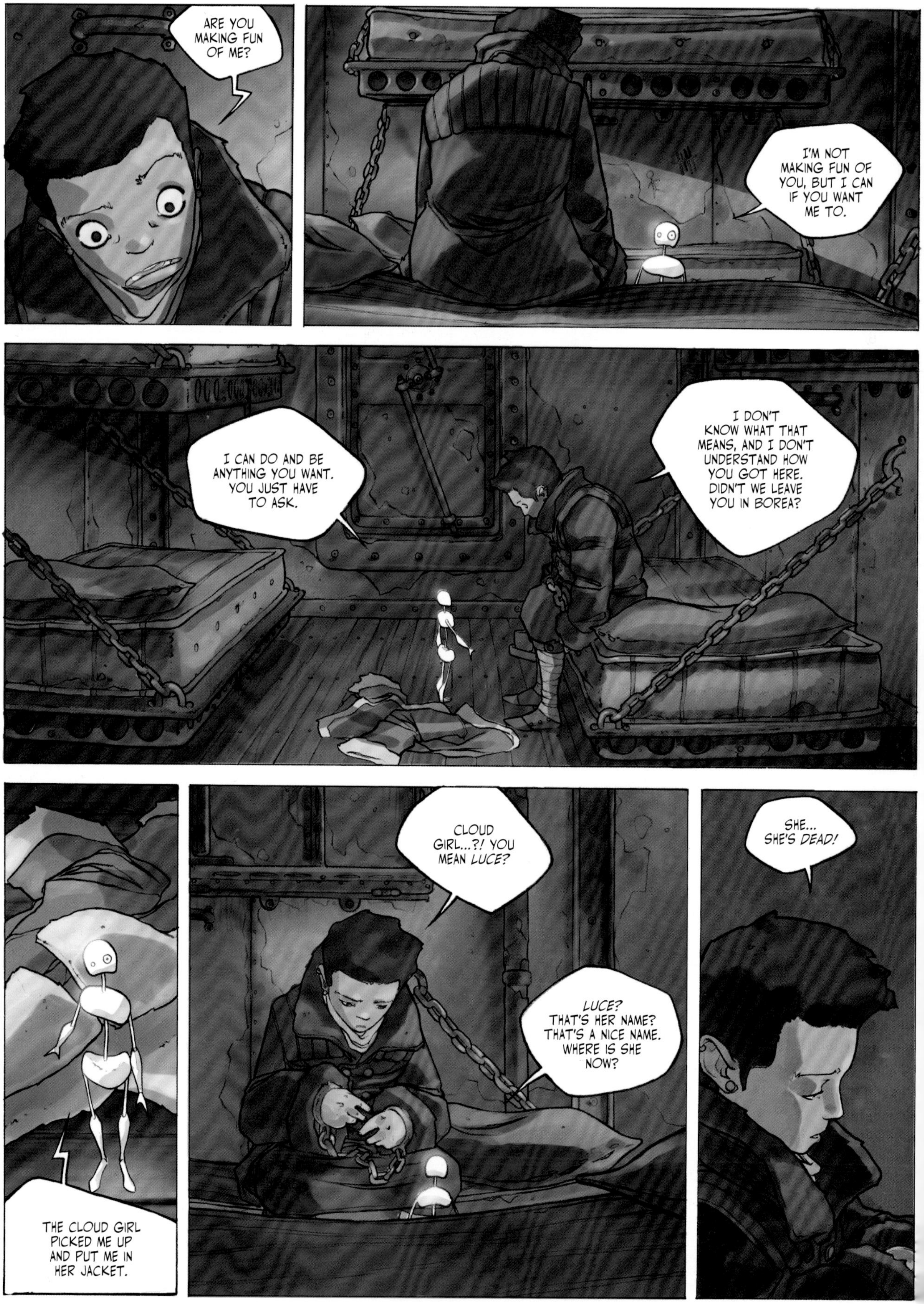

ARE YOU MAKING FUN OF ME?
I'M NOT MAKING FUN OF YOU, BUT I CAN IF YOU WANT ME TO.
I CAN DO AND BE ANYTHING YOU WANT. YOU JUST HAVE TO ASK.
I DON'T KNOW WHAT THAT MEANS, AND I DON'T UNDERSTAND HOW YOU GOT HERE. DIDN'T WE LEAVE YOU IN BOREA?
THE CLOUD GIRL PICKED ME UP AND PUT ME IN HER JACKET.
CLOUD GIRL...?! YOU MEAN LUCE?
LUCE? THAT'S HER NAME? THAT'S A NICE NAME. WHERE IS SHE NOW?
SHE... SHE'S DEAD!

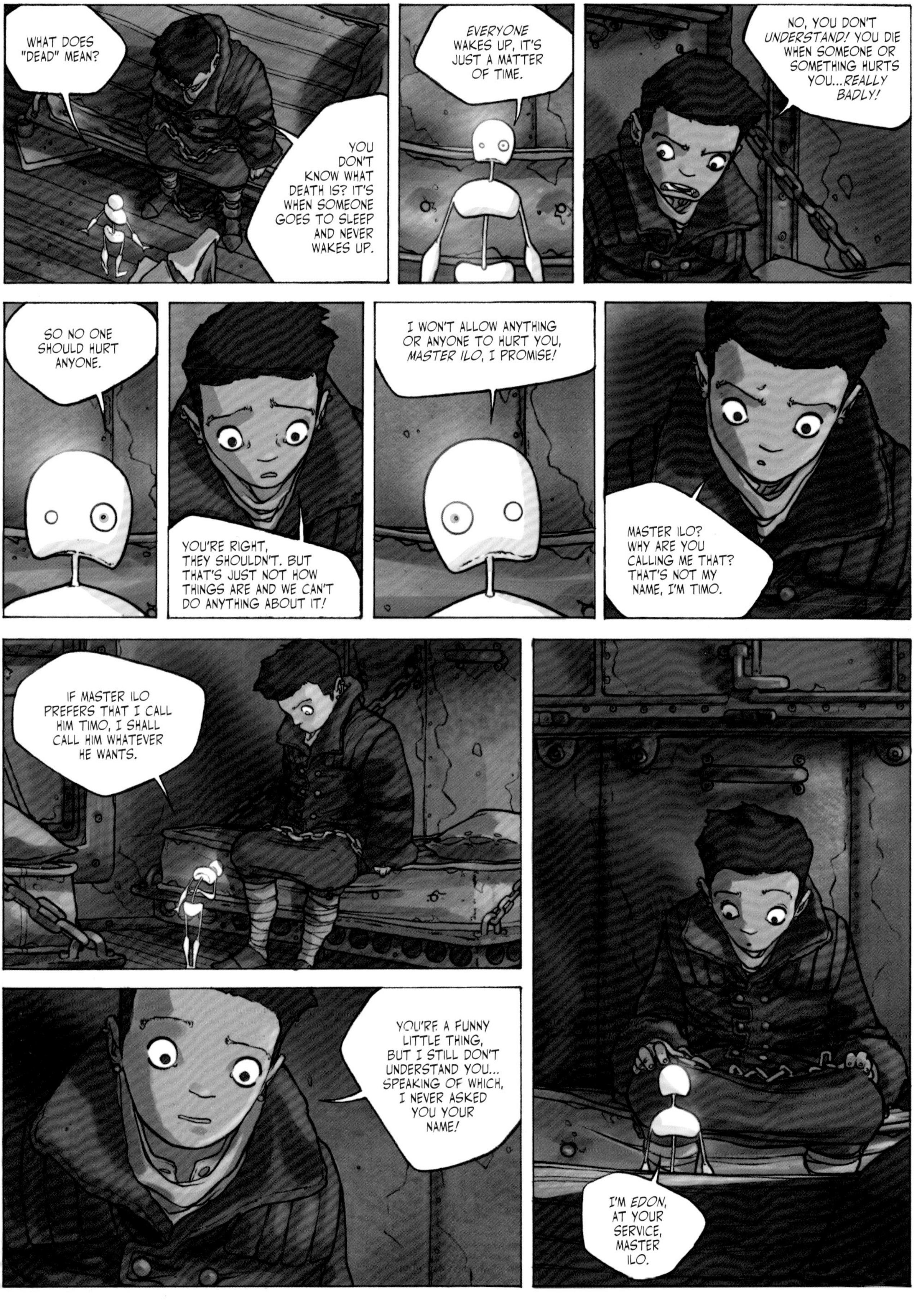
WHAT DOES "DEAD" MEAN?
YOU DON'T KNOW WHAT DEATH IS? IT'S WHEN SOMEONE GOES TO SLEEP AND NEVER WAKES UP.
EVERYONE WAKES UP, IT'S JUST A MATTER OF TIME.
NO, YOU DON'T UNDERSTAND! YOU DIE WHEN SOMEONE OR SOMETHING HURTS YOU...REALLY BADLY!
SO NO ONE SHOULD HURT ANYONE.
YOU'RE RIGHT, THEY SHOULDN'T. BUT THAT'S JUST NOT HOW THINGS ARE AND WE CAN'T DO ANYTHING ABOUT IT!
I WON'T ALLOW ANYTHING OR ANYONE TO HURT YOU, MASTER ILO, I PROMISE!
MASTER ILO? WHY ARE YOU CALLING ME THAT? THAT'S NOT MY NAME, I'M TIMO.
IF MASTER ILO PREFERS THAT I CALL HIM TIMO, I SHALL CALL HIM WHATEVER HE WANTS.
YOU'RE A FUNNY LITTLE THING, BUT I STILL DON'T UNDERSTAND YOU... SPEAKING OF WHICH, I NEVER ASKED YOU YOUR NAME!
I'M EDON, AT YOUR SERVICE, MASTER ILO.

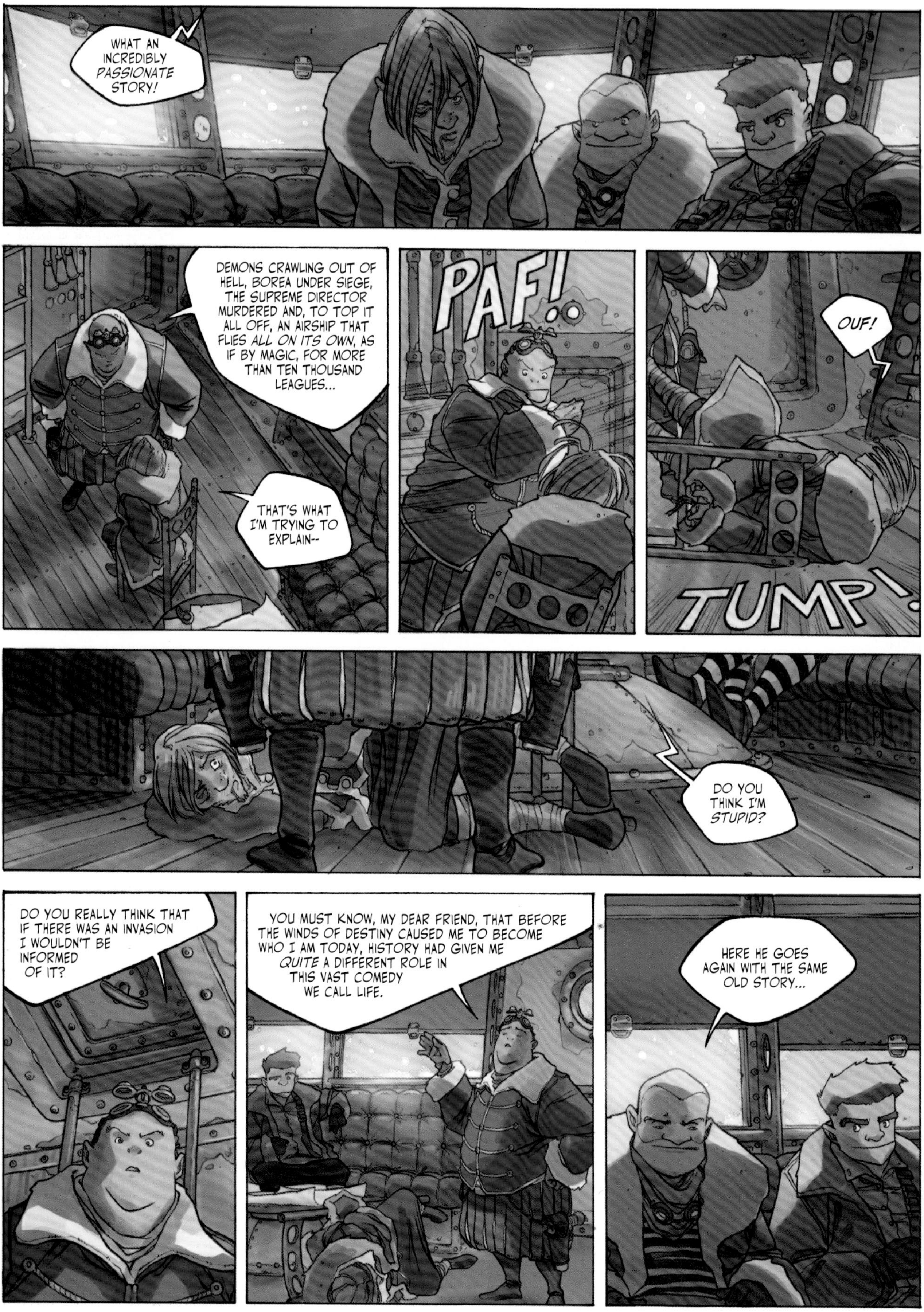
WHAT AN INCREDIBLY *PASSIONATE* STORY!
DEMONS CRAWLING OUT OF HELL, BOREA UNDER SIEGE, THE SUPREME DIRECTOR MURDERED AND, TO TOP IT ALL OFF, AN AIRSHIP THAT FLIES *ALL ON ITS OWN*, AS IF BY MAGIC, FOR MORE THAN TEN THOUSAND LEAGUES...
THAT'S WHAT I'M TRYING TO EXPLAIN--
PAF!
OUF!
TUMP!
DO YOU THINK I'M *STUPID?*
DO YOU REALLY THINK THAT IF THERE WAS AN INVASION I WOULDN'T BE INFORMED OF IT?
YOU MUST KNOW, MY DEAR FRIEND, THAT BEFORE THE WINDS OF DESTINY CAUSED ME TO BECOME WHO I AM TODAY, HISTORY HAD GIVEN ME *QUITE* A DIFFERENT ROLE IN THIS VAST COMEDY WE CALL LIFE.
HERE HE GOES AGAIN WITH THE SAME OLD STORY...

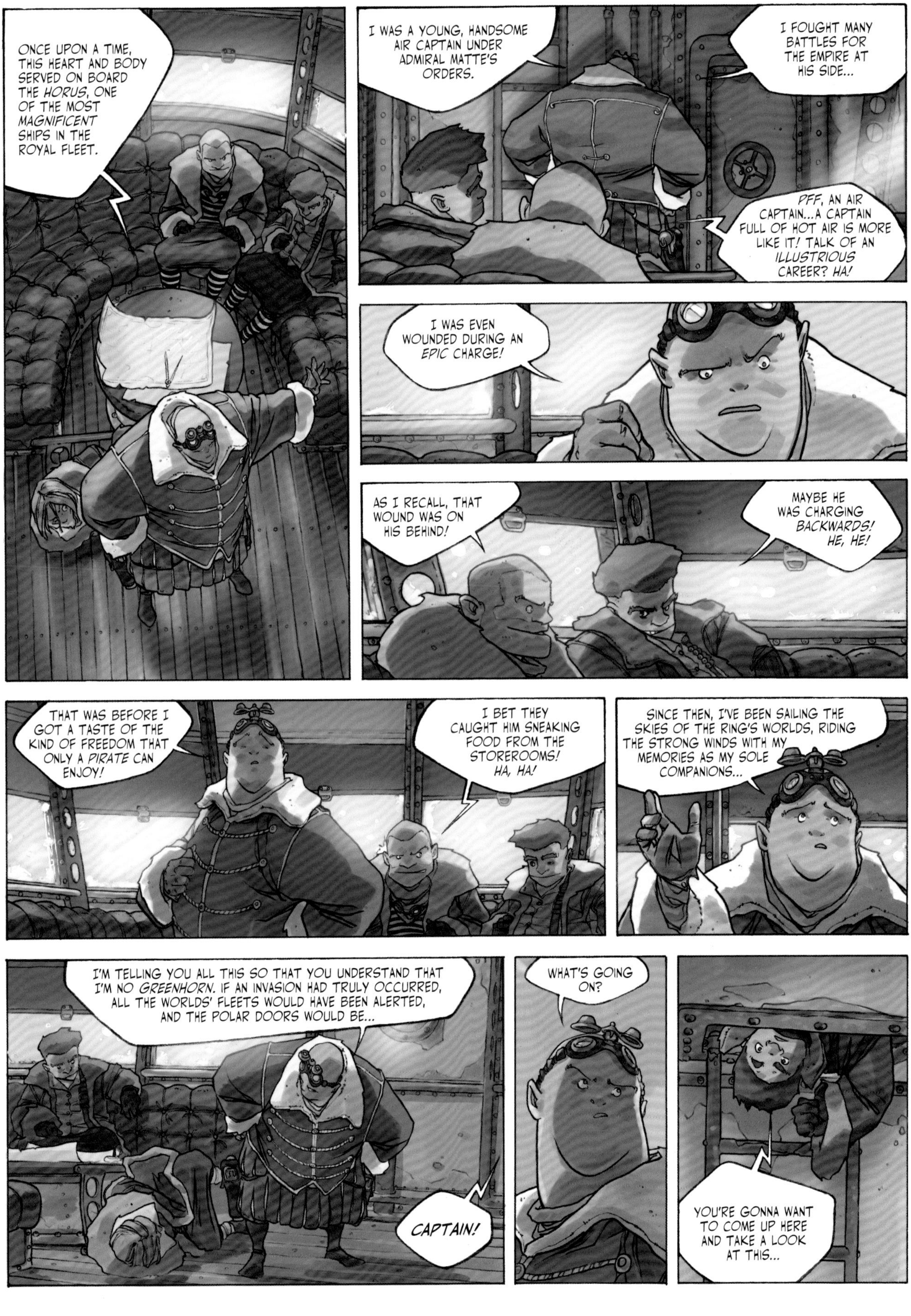

ONCE UPON A TIME, THIS HEART AND BODY SERVED ON BOARD THE *HORUS*, ONE OF THE MOST *MAGNIFICENT* SHIPS IN THE ROYAL FLEET.
I WAS A YOUNG, HANDSOME AIR CAPTAIN UNDER ADMIRAL MATTE'S ORDERS.
I FOUGHT MANY BATTLES FOR THE EMPIRE AT HIS SIDE...
PFF, AN AIR CAPTAIN...A CAPTAIN FULL OF HOT AIR IS MORE LIKE IT! TALK OF AN *ILLUSTRIOUS* CAREER? HA!
I WAS EVEN WOUNDED DURING AN *EPIC CHARGE!*
AS I RECALL, THAT WOUND WAS ON HIS BEHIND!
MAYBE HE WAS CHARGING *BACKWARDS!* HE, HE!
THAT WAS BEFORE I GOT A TASTE OF THE KIND OF FREEDOM THAT ONLY A *PIRATE* CAN ENJOY!
I BET THEY CAUGHT HIM SNEAKING FOOD FROM THE STOREROOMS! HA, HA!
SINCE THEN, I'VE BEEN SAILING THE SKIES OF THE RING'S WORLDS, RIDING THE STRONG WINDS WITH MY MEMORIES AS MY SOLE COMPANIONS...
I'M TELLING YOU ALL THIS SO THAT YOU UNDERSTAND THAT I'M NO *GREENHORN*. IF AN INVASION HAD TRULY OCCURRED, ALL THE WORLDS' FLEETS WOULD HAVE BEEN ALERTED, AND THE POLAR DOORS WOULD BE...
CAPTAIN!
WHAT'S GOING ON?
YOU'RE GONNA WANT TO COME UP HERE AND TAKE A LOOK AT THIS...

AN AERIAL TRAFFIC JAM? WHAT ON *EARTH* ARE YOU TALKING ABOUT?!

I'M NOT TALKING ABOUT ANYTHING, CAPTAIN, I'M JUST READING THE CONTROL TOWER'S SIGNALS.

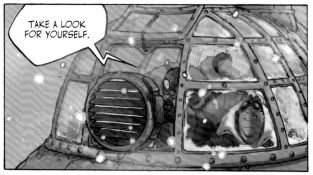

TAKE A LOOK FOR YOURSELF.

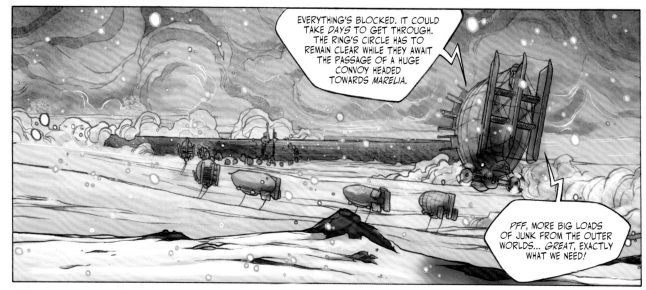

EVERYTHING'S BLOCKED. IT COULD TAKE *DAYS* TO GET THROUGH. THE RING'S CIRCLE HAS TO REMAIN CLEAR WHILE THEY AWAIT THE PASSAGE OF A HUGE CONVOY HEADED TOWARDS *MARELIA*.

PFF, MORE BIG LOADS OF JUNK FROM THE OUTER WORLDS... *GREAT,* EXACTLY WHAT WE NEED!

WELL, LET'S PROCEED SLOWLY, AND COME TO A STOP IN FRONT OF...

AH!!

RRRRRRRRRR

WHAT THE *HELL* ARE YOU DOING DOWN THERE? I TOLD YOU TO GO SLOWLY, NOT JAM ON THE ACCELERATOR!

WE'VE BEEN TAKEN BY SURPRISE!

SHE'S A DEVIL, HELP!

WHAT ARE YOU SAYING? WHAT THE *HELL* ARE YOU TALKING ABOUT?

ARE YOU STILL THERE? ANSWER ME, YOU *IDIOTS,* OR I'LL COME DOWN THERE AND...

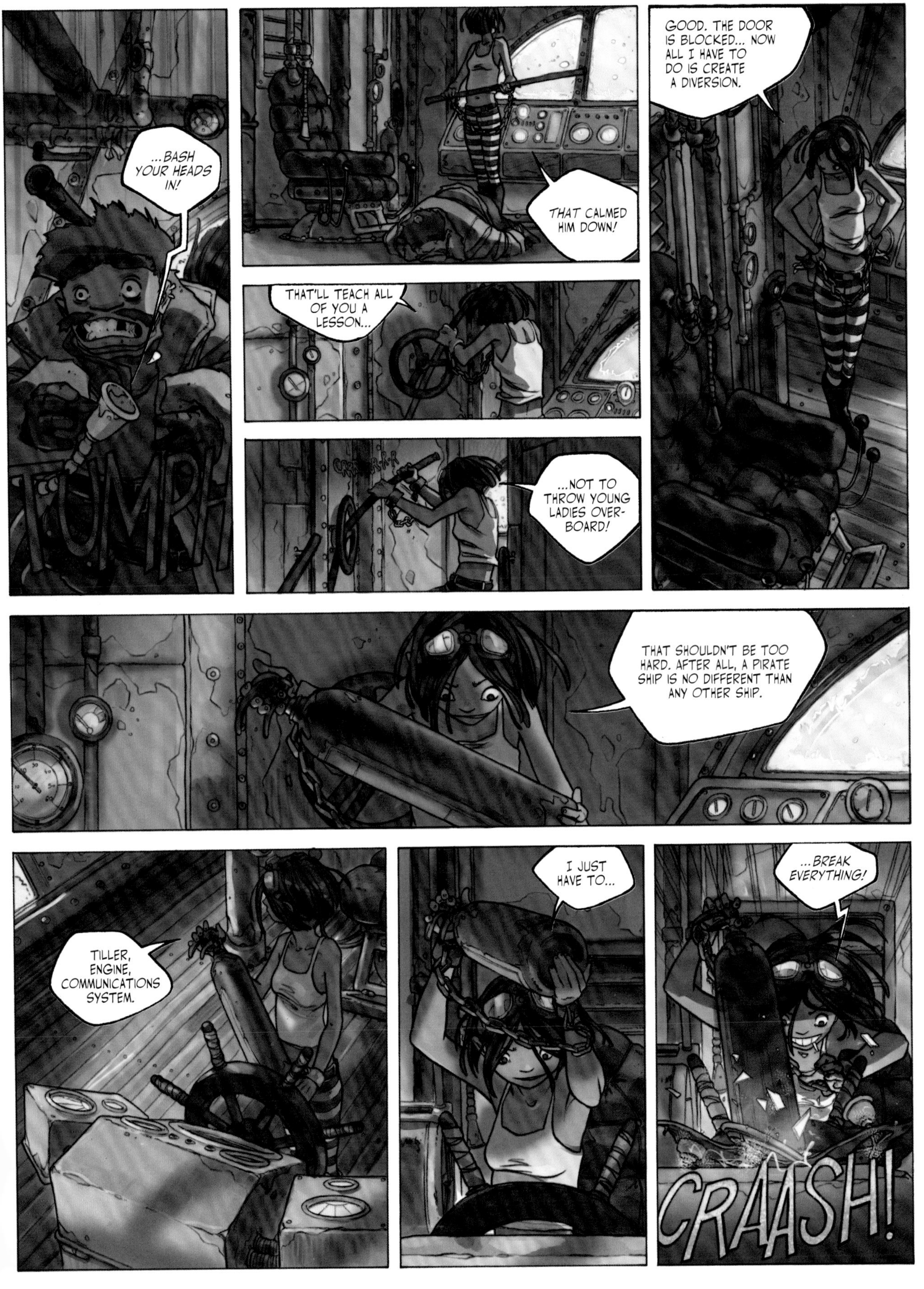
...BASH YOUR HEADS IN!
TUMP!
THAT CALMED HIM DOWN!
THAT'LL TEACH ALL OF YOU A LESSON...
...NOT TO THROW YOUNG LADIES OVER-BOARD!
GOOD. THE DOOR IS BLOCKED... NOW ALL I HAVE TO DO IS CREATE A DIVERSION.
THAT SHOULDN'T BE TOO HARD. AFTER ALL, A PIRATE SHIP IS NO DIFFERENT THAN ANY OTHER SHIP.
TILLER, ENGINE, COMMUNICATIONS SYSTEM.
I JUST HAVE TO...
...BREAK EVERYTHING!
CRAASH!

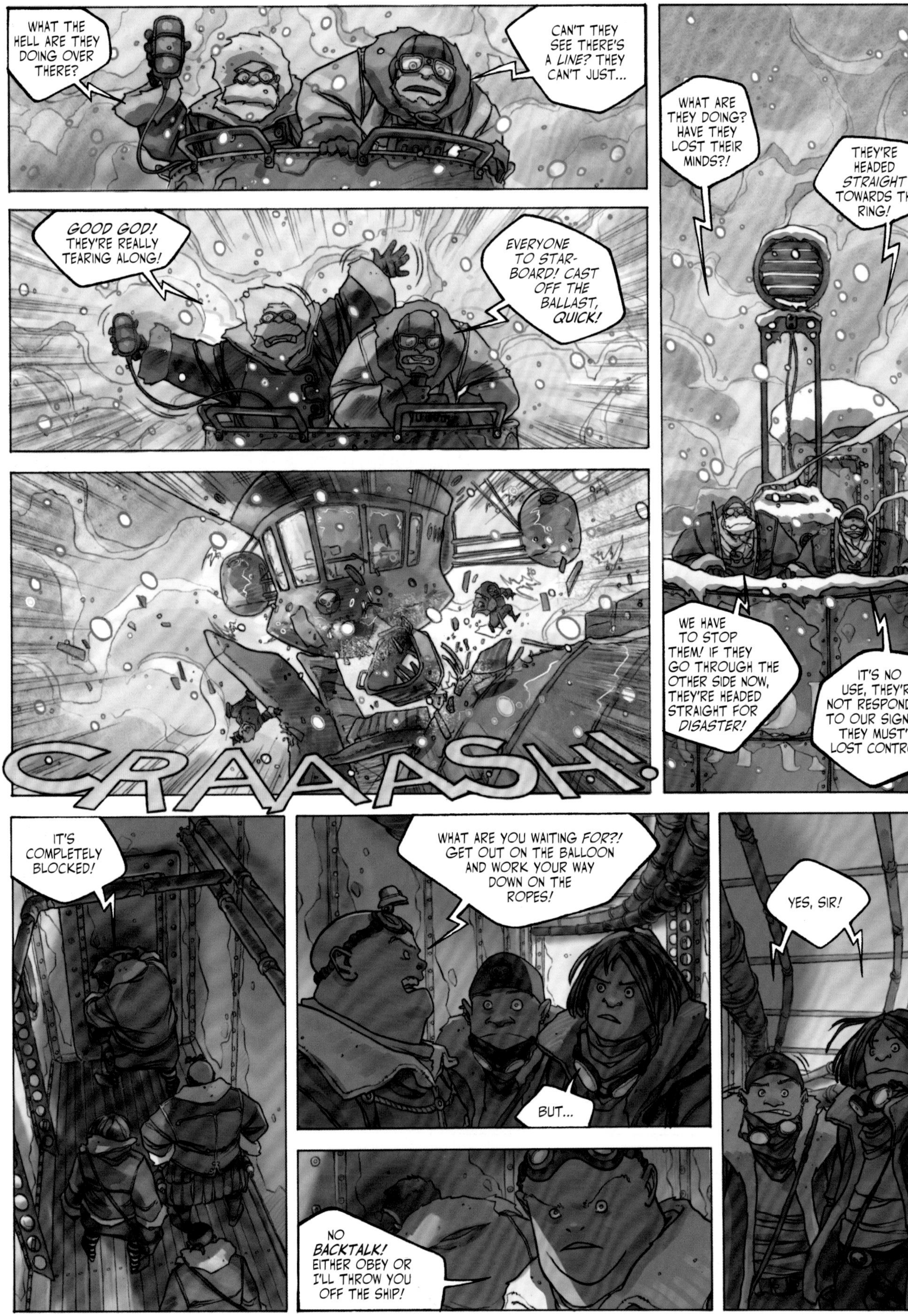
WHAT THE HELL ARE THEY DOING OVER THERE?
CAN'T THEY SEE THERE'S A *LINE?* THEY CAN'T JUST...
WHAT ARE THEY DOING? HAVE THEY LOST THEIR MINDS?!
THEY'RE HEADED *STRAIGHT* TOWARDS THE RING!
GOOD GOD! THEY'RE REALLY TEARING ALONG!
EVERYONE TO STAR-BOARD! CAST OFF THE BALLAST, **QUICK!**
CRAAASH!
WE HAVE TO STOP THEM! IF THEY GO THROUGH THE OTHER SIDE NOW, THEY'RE HEADED STRAIGHT FOR *DISASTER!*
IT'S NO USE, THEY'RE NOT RESPONDING TO OUR SIGNALS. THEY MUST'VE LOST CONTROL!
IT'S COMPLETELY BLOCKED!
WHAT ARE YOU WAITING *FOR?!* GET OUT ON THE BALLOON AND WORK YOUR WAY DOWN ON THE ROPES!
BUT...
NO *BACKTALK!* EITHER OBEY OR I'LL THROW YOU OFF THE SHIP!
YES, SIR!

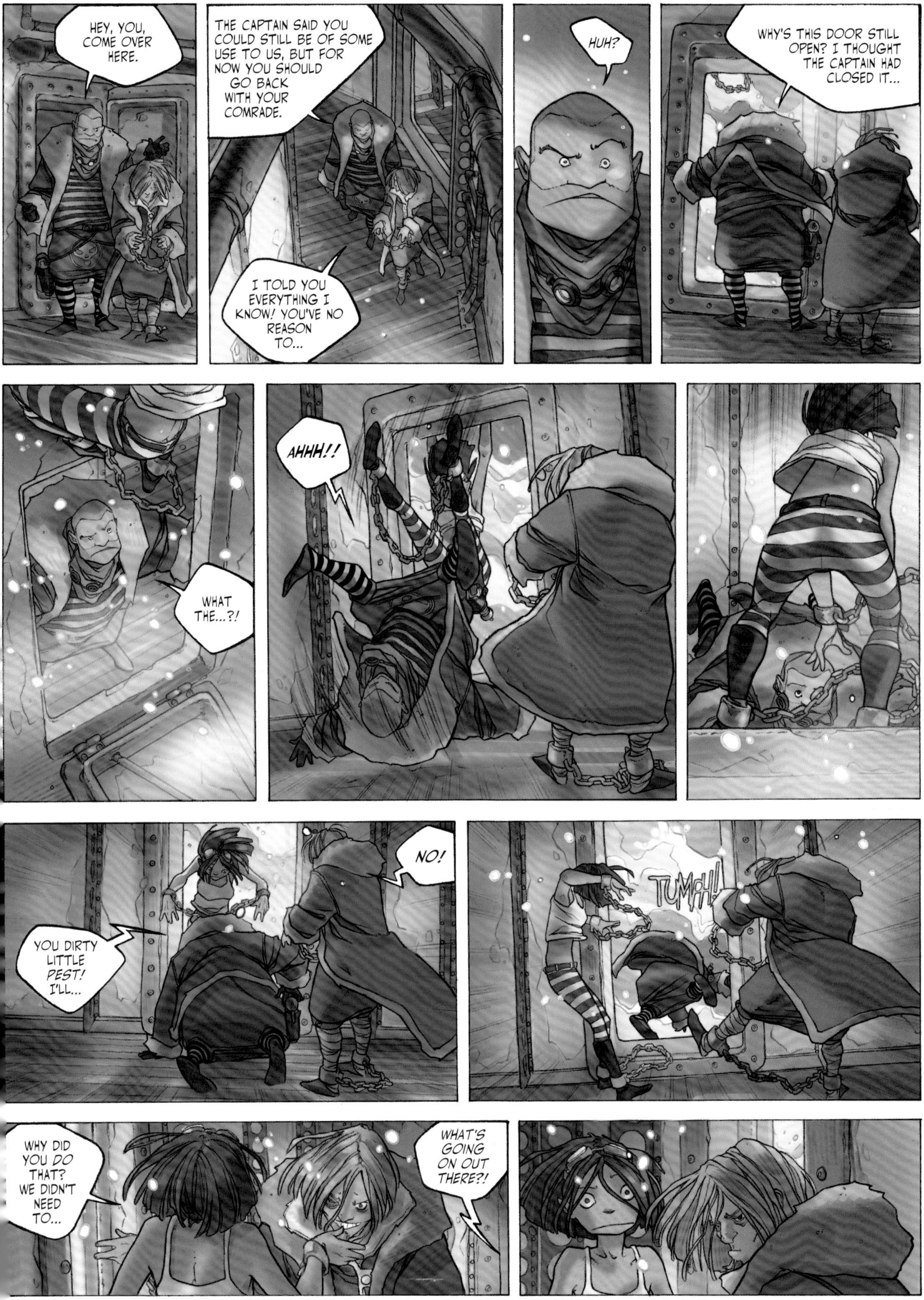
HEY, YOU, COME OVER HERE.
THE CAPTAIN SAID YOU COULD STILL BE OF SOME USE TO US, BUT FOR NOW YOU SHOULD GO BACK WITH YOUR COMRADE.
I TOLD YOU EVERYTHING I KNOW! YOU'VE NO REASON TO...
HUH?
WHY'S THIS DOOR STILL OPEN? I THOUGHT THE CAPTAIN HAD CLOSED IT...
WHAT THE...?!
AHHH!!
NO!
YOU DIRTY LITTLE PEST! I'LL...
TUMPH!
WHY DID YOU DO THAT? WE DIDN'T NEED TO...
WHAT'S GOING ON OUT THERE?!

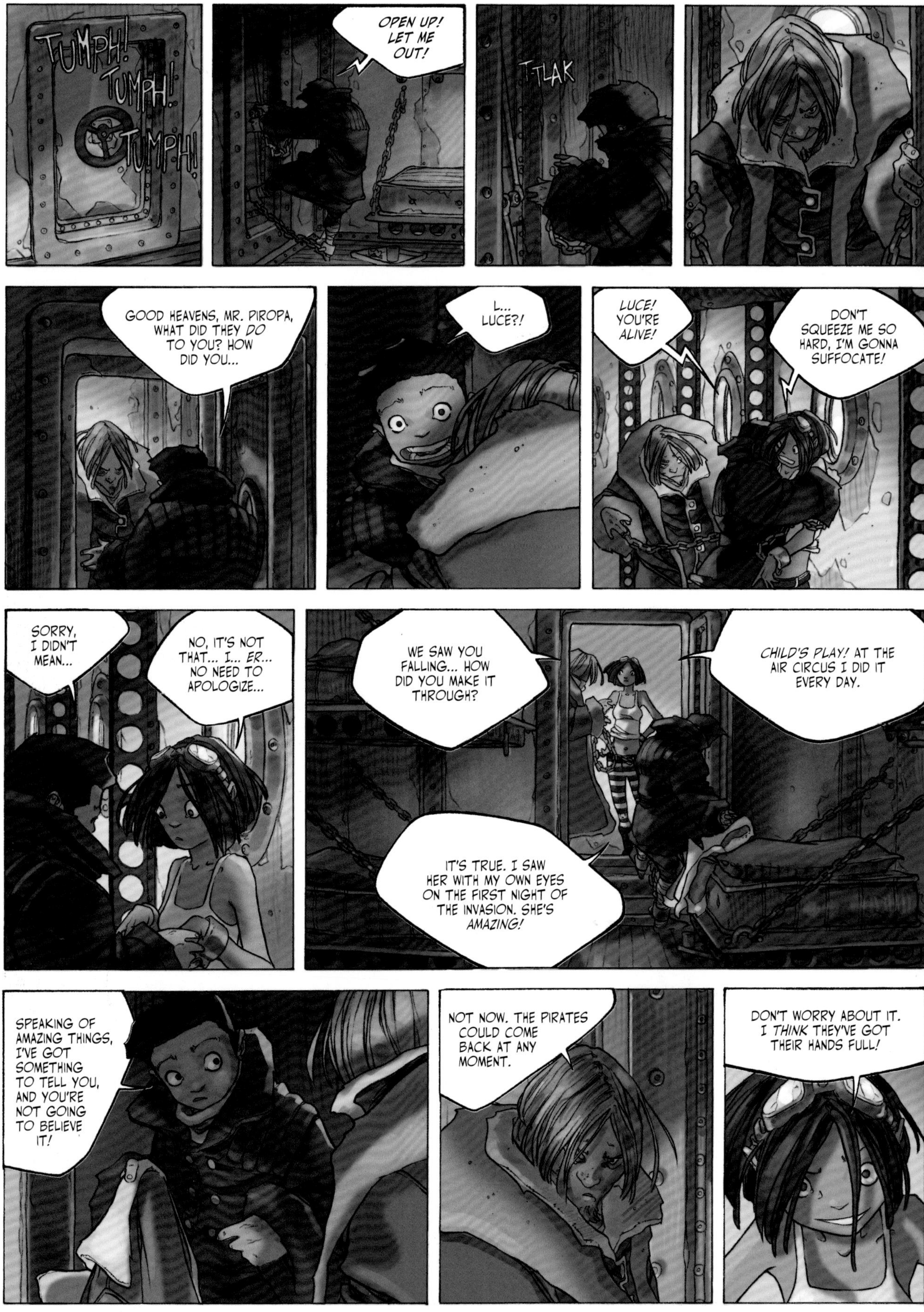
TUMPH! TUMPH! TUMPH!
OPEN UP! LET ME OUT!
T-TLAK
GOOD HEAVENS, MR. PIROPA, WHAT DID THEY *DO* TO YOU? HOW DID YOU...
L... LUCE?!
LUCE! YOU'RE ALIVE!
DON'T SQUEEZE ME SO HARD, I'M GONNA SUFFOCATE!
SORRY, I DIDN'T MEAN...
NO, IT'S NOT THAT... I... *ER*... NO NEED TO APOLOGIZE...
WE SAW YOU FALLING... HOW DID YOU MAKE IT THROUGH?
CHILD'S PLAY! AT THE AIR CIRCUS I DID IT EVERY DAY.
IT'S TRUE. I SAW HER WITH MY OWN EYES ON THE FIRST NIGHT OF THE INVASION. SHE'S *AMAZING!*
SPEAKING OF AMAZING THINGS, I'VE GOT SOMETHING TO TELL YOU, AND YOU'RE NOT GOING TO BELIEVE IT!
NOT NOW. THE PIRATES COULD COME BACK AT ANY MOMENT.
DON'T WORRY ABOUT IT. I *THINK* THEY'VE GOT THEIR HANDS FULL!

WE'RE OUT OF OPTIONS. THE HELM'S BROKEN, THE COMPASS IS SMASHED, AND THE ALTIMETERS LINKED TO THE BALLAST ARE RUINED.

EVEN BY MANUALLY TURNING OFF THE MOTORS, WE STILL COULDN'T CHANGE OUR ROUTE IN TIME.

WE'RE GOING TO BE SWALLOWED UP BY THE RING BEFORE WE EVEN REALIZE IT AND WITHOUT ANY IDEA OF WHAT AWAITS US AFTER THE JUMP.

AND ALL THIS BECAUSE OF THAT *STUPID CLOUD GIRL!!*

I SWEAR THAT IF WE MAKE IT THROUGH TO THE OTHER SIDE ALIVE...

...I'LL KILL THEM!

EVERY LAST ONE OF THEM!

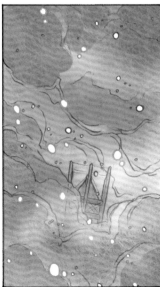

WE NEVER WOULD'VE BEEN ABLE TO GET TO *TRELICE* IN TIME, BUT BY FOCUSING OUR EFFORTS ON *EREMOVENTOSO*, HOPEFULLY WE'LL BE ABLE TO KEEP THE CITY FROM FALLING.

THAT WAY WE'LL PIERCE THE ENEMY'S FLANK AS THEY MAKE THEIR WAY TOWARDS THE CAPITAL. IT'LL BE A GATEWAY TO BOREA.

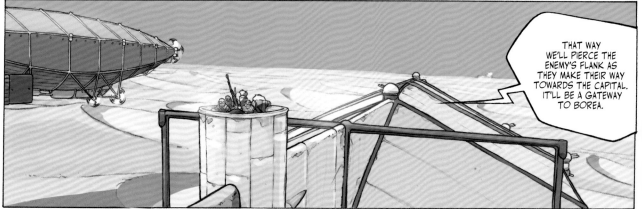

EXACTLY. PROVIDED THAT WE ARRIVE *BEFORE* THE GROUND INVASION BEGINS AND OUR ATTACK STRATEGY GOES ACCORDING TO PLAN!

TRUST ME, LEPONTE, I KNOW THE WINDS THAT WHIP EREMOVENTOSO LIKE THE KEEL OF MY OWN SHIP. IF THE REST OF THE FLEET CAN CARRY OUT THEIR COMMANDS DOWN TO THE LETTER, THEN THIS'LL BE A DAY THAT NEMO WILL *NEVER FORGET!*

WE'RE HERE.

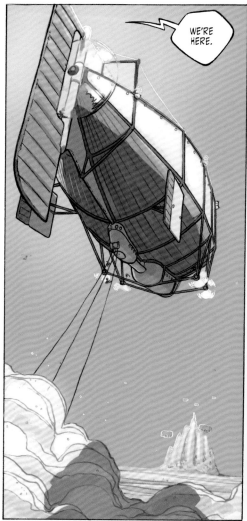

I HOPE SO, CAPTAIN ARDESIA, I REALLY DO... BECAUSE OTHERWISE, IT'LL BE THE END OF US.

ANYWAY, WE'LL KNOW SOON ENOUGH.

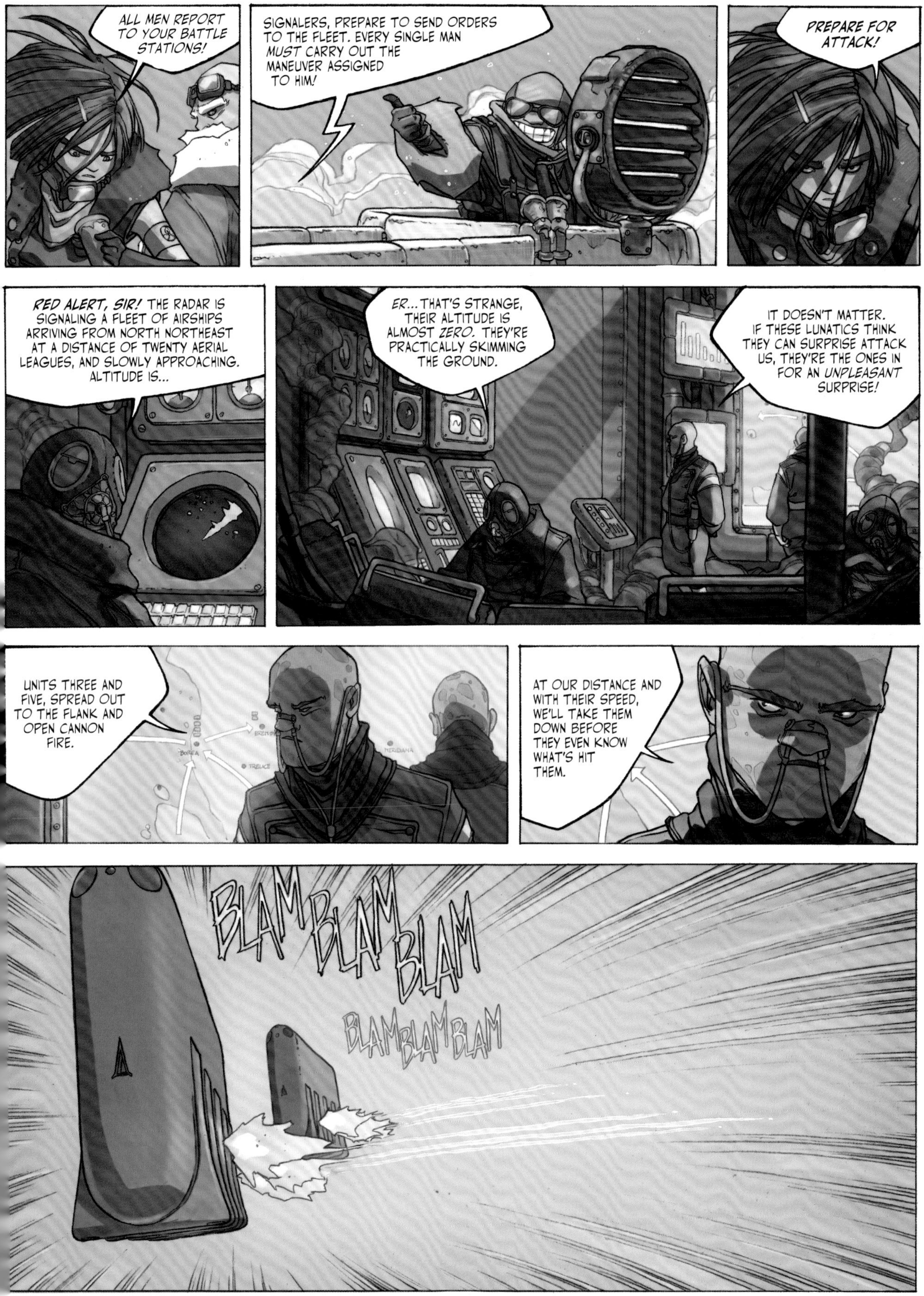
ALL MEN REPORT TO YOUR BATTLE STATIONS!
SIGNALERS, PREPARE TO SEND ORDERS TO THE FLEET. EVERY SINGLE MAN *MUST* CARRY OUT THE MANEUVER ASSIGNED TO HIM!
PREPARE FOR ATTACK!
RED ALERT, SIR! THE RADAR IS SIGNALING A FLEET OF AIRSHIPS ARRIVING FROM NORTH NORTHEAST AT A DISTANCE OF TWENTY AERIAL LEAGUES, AND SLOWLY APPROACHING. ALTITUDE IS...
ER... THAT'S STRANGE, THEIR ALTITUDE IS ALMOST *ZERO.* THEY'RE PRACTICALLY SKIMMING THE GROUND.
IT DOESN'T MATTER. IF THESE LUNATICS THINK THEY CAN SURPRISE ATTACK US, THEY'RE THE ONES IN FOR AN *UNPLEASANT* SURPRISE!
UNITS THREE AND FIVE, SPREAD OUT TO THE FLANK AND OPEN CANNON FIRE.
AT OUR DISTANCE AND WITH THEIR SPEED, WE'LL TAKE THEM DOWN BEFORE THEY EVEN KNOW WHAT'S HIT THEM.
BLAM BLAM BLAM BLAM
BLAM BLAM BLAM

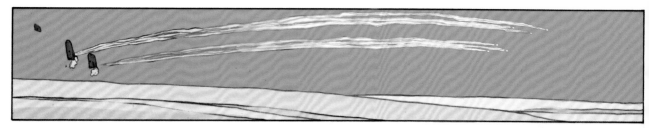

THEY'RE COMING. STAND AT THE READY!

NOW!

CAST OFF THE BALLAST!

ZAK!
ZAK!

EVERYONE FORWARD!

SSSSS S S S S
SSSSS SS S S
SSSSS S S S

WRAAM
WRAAM
WRAAM

WHAT HAPPENED?!

UNITS THREE AND FIVE, CAN YOU CONFIRM THE DESTRUCTION OF ENEMY SHIPS?

NEGATIVE. THE DUST CAUSED BY THE EXPLOSIONS IS MAKING IT DIFFICULT TO SEE CLEARLY. BUT IT'S IMPOSSIBLE THAT THEY WENT UNHARMED AFTER SUCH AN...

WHAT?! IT CAN'T BE!!

GOOD GOD, WHAT HAPPENED?

THEY'RE HERE! THE ENEMY HAS CROSSED OUR LINES OF DEFENSE!

IT WORKED! AFTER OUR SLOW SPEED, WEIGHED DOWN BY THE BALLAST, THAT SUDDEN LEAP FORWARD WHEN WE LET OFF THE EXTRA WEIGHT BOOSTED US PAST THEIR LINE OF FIRE!

AND NOW IT'S OUR TURN TO ATTACK!

SIGNALERS, COMMAND THE TAIL UNIT TO FIRE THEIR HARPOONS!

... AND IF THEY MISS SUCH A HUGE TARGET AT THIS DISTANCE, I'LL THROW THEM OVERBOARD MYSELF!

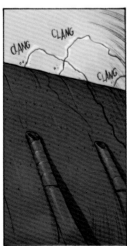

CLANG
CLANG
CLANG

WE'VE BEEN HIT!!

DECOMPRESSION ON ALL DECKS! WE'RE LOSING OUR VITAL ASSISTANCE.

ALERT! FIRE IN THE AMMUNITION HOLD! EVACUATE QUICKLY BEFORE--

BOOOOOOOOOMM

WHAT HAPPENED?

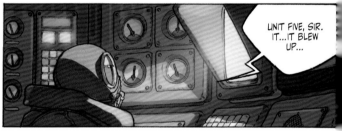

UNIT FIVE, SIR. IT...IT BLEW UP...

...AND WE'RE ABOUT TO COLLIDE WITH UNIT THREE!

BOOOOOOOM

IT'S A LITTLE EARLY TO BE SHOUTING VICTORY. WE JUST GOT LUCKY BECAUSE WE ACCIDENTALLY STRUCK ONE OF THEIR VITAL DECKS.

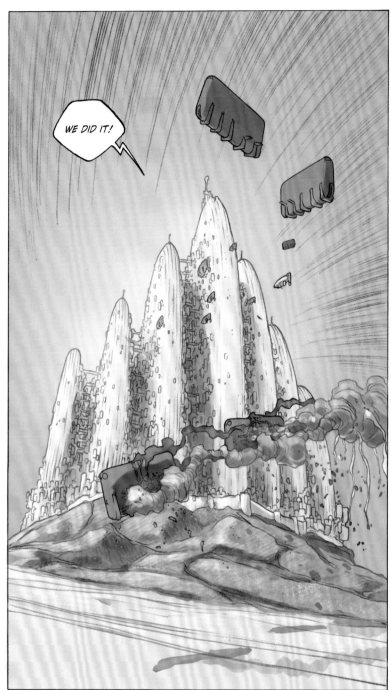

WE DID IT!

WE NOW HAVE TO BE MORE CLEVER THAN THEM.

TWO SHIPS! WE'VE LOST *TWO* SHIPS! HOW THE *HELL* COULD THIS HAVE HAPPENED?!

CAPTAIN, YOUR ORDERS PLEASE.

UNITS TWO AND FOUR WILL CHASE THEM. WE'LL CHANGE ALTITUDE AND REPOSITION OURSELVES ABOVE THE CITY TO COORDINATE OUR ATTACK.

BUT SIR, WHAT ABOUT THE INVASION? WE HAVE TO UNLEASH OUR GROUND TROOPS.

NEGATIVE. I WANT TO SEE THESE ENEMY SHIPS BURN FIRST! *BEGIN OUR ASCENT!*

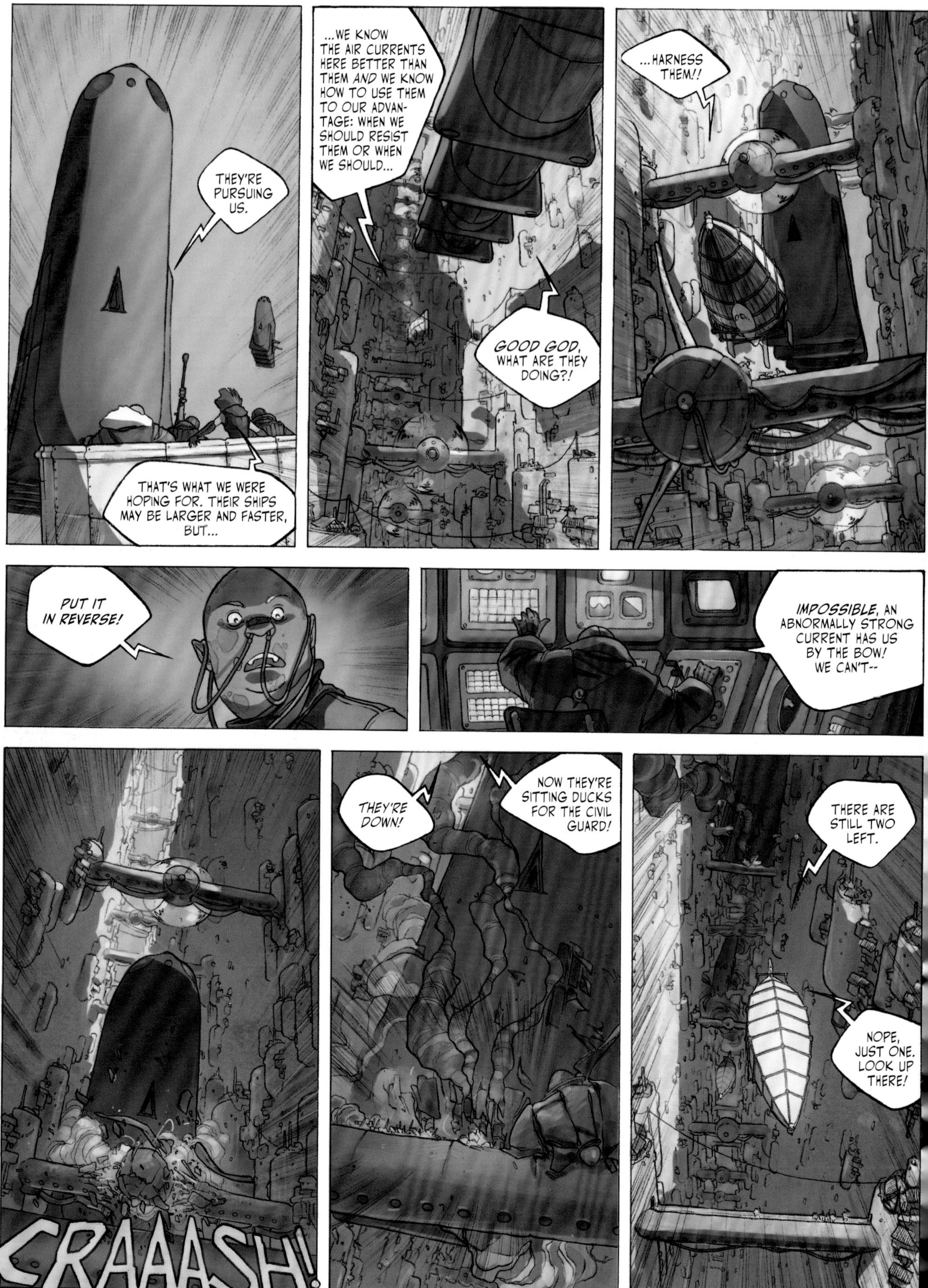
THEY'RE PURSUING US.
THAT'S WHAT WE WERE HOPING FOR. THEIR SHIPS MAY BE LARGER AND FASTER, BUT...
...WE KNOW THE AIR CURRENTS HERE BETTER THAN THEM *AND* WE KNOW HOW TO USE THEM TO OUR ADVANTAGE: WHEN WE SHOULD RESIST THEM OR WHEN WE SHOULD...
GOOD GOD, WHAT ARE THEY DOING?!
...HARNESS THEM!!
PUT IT IN REVERSE!
IMPOSSIBLE, AN ABNORMALLY STRONG CURRENT HAS US BY THE BOW! WE CAN'T--
CRAAASH!
THEY'RE DOWN!
NOW THEY'RE SITTING DUCKS FOR THE CIVIL GUARD!
THERE ARE STILL TWO LEFT.
NOPE, JUST ONE. LOOK UP THERE!

WE'VE LOST ALL CONTACT WITH UNIT FOUR. AND UNIT TWO JUST SIGNALED THAT IT'S BEEN TAKEN DOWN, SIR.

WE HAVE TO GO DOWN AND HELP THEM!

NEGATIVE. WE HAVE TO GET TO THE STRATOSPHERE, WE'LL BE SAFE THERE. WITHOUT A PRESSURIZED SHIP LIKE OURS, THEY WON'T BE ABLE TO FOLLOW US!

IMPOSSIBLE. WE'RE TOO *HEAVY* WITH OUR OVERLOADED HOLDS...

ALERT! ENEMY UNITS APPROACHING!

NO, IT CAN'T BE! GET TO YOUR BATTLE POSTS! PREPARE TO--

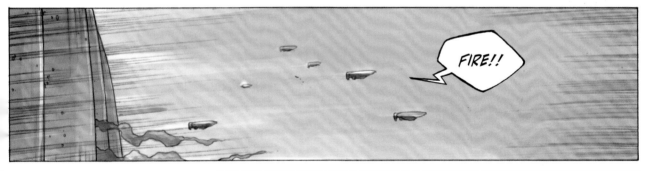

FIRE!!

BLAM! BLAM! BLAM! BLAM! BLAM! BLAM! BLAM! BLAM! BLAM! BLAM! BLAM! BLAM! BLAM!

BRAAAM! BRAAM! BRAAM!

153

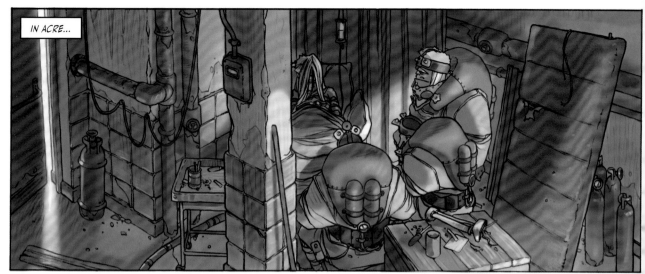

IN ACRE...

AHHHH!!

CALM DOWN, IT'S OK. IT WAS JUST A *DREAM,* A BAD DREAM.

WHERE AM I? WHAT HAPPENED TO ME?

YOU HAD AN ACCIDENT. YOU WERE IN BITS AND PIECES, BUT WE'VE STITCHED YOU BACK UP AND YOU SHOULD BE BACK ON YOUR FEET SOON.

WHAT ACCIDENT? I DON'T...

YOUR AIRSHIP WENT DOWN AND YOU GOT TRAPPED AMONGST SOME SHEET METAL. THAT'S WHY YOUR FRIENDS DIDN'T SEE YOU AND LEFT.

MY FRIENDS?!

THE BOY, THE NASTY LOOKING MAN, AND THE ANGRY, PURPLE-HAIRED GIRL!

NOW I REMEMBER... I JUMPED ONTO THE AIRSHIP WHEN IT TOOK OFF, BUT I WAS WOUNDED AND LOSING A LOT OF BLOOD...

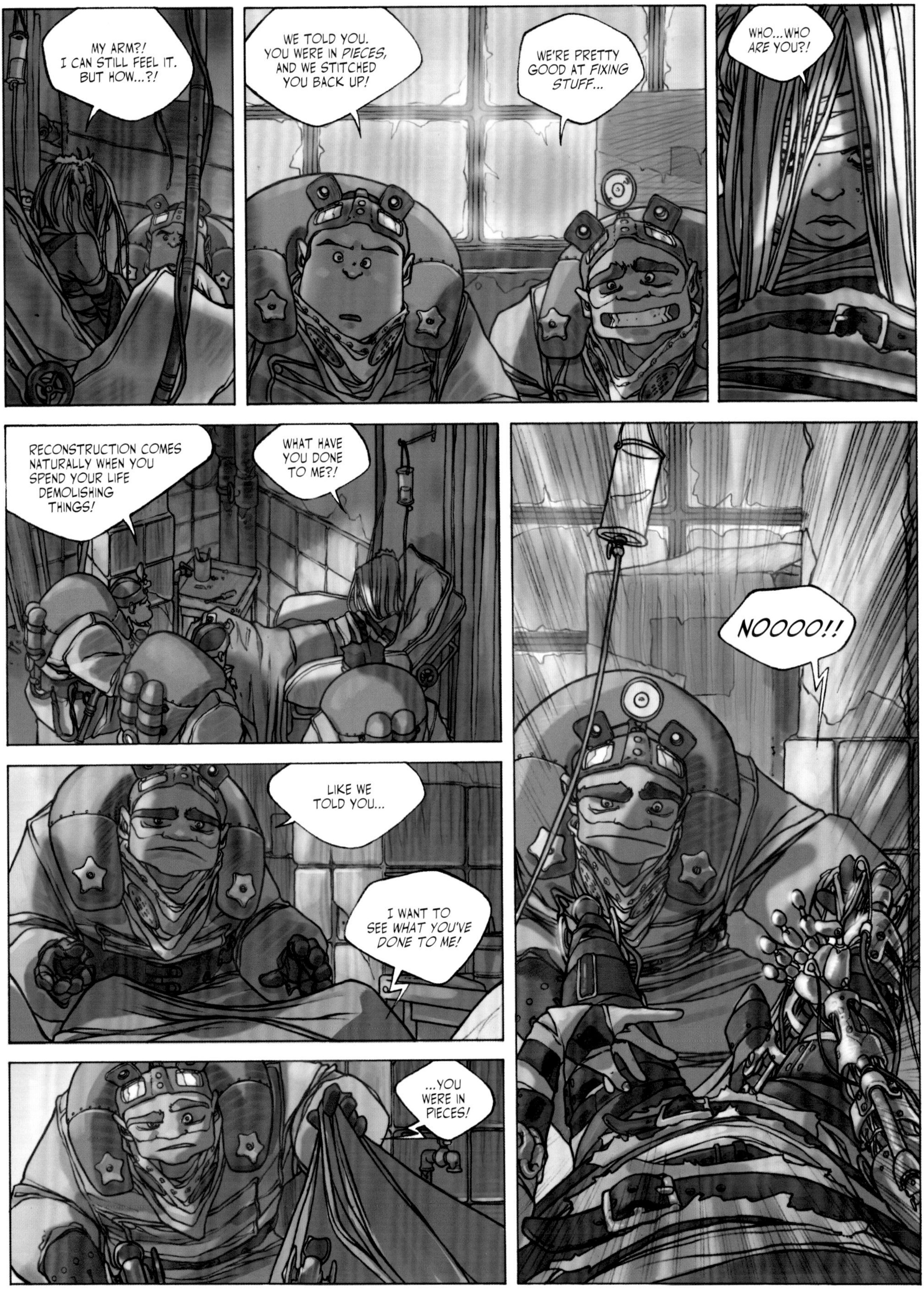
MY ARM?! I CAN STILL FEEL IT. BUT HOW...?!
WE TOLD YOU. YOU WERE IN PIECES, AND WE STITCHED YOU BACK UP!
WE'RE PRETTY GOOD AT FIXING STUFF...
WHO...WHO ARE YOU?!
RECONSTRUCTION COMES NATURALLY WHEN YOU SPEND YOUR LIFE DEMOLISHING THINGS!
WHAT HAVE YOU DONE TO ME?!
LIKE WE TOLD YOU...
I WANT TO SEE WHAT YOU'VE DONE TO ME!
...YOU WERE IN PIECES!
NOOOO!!

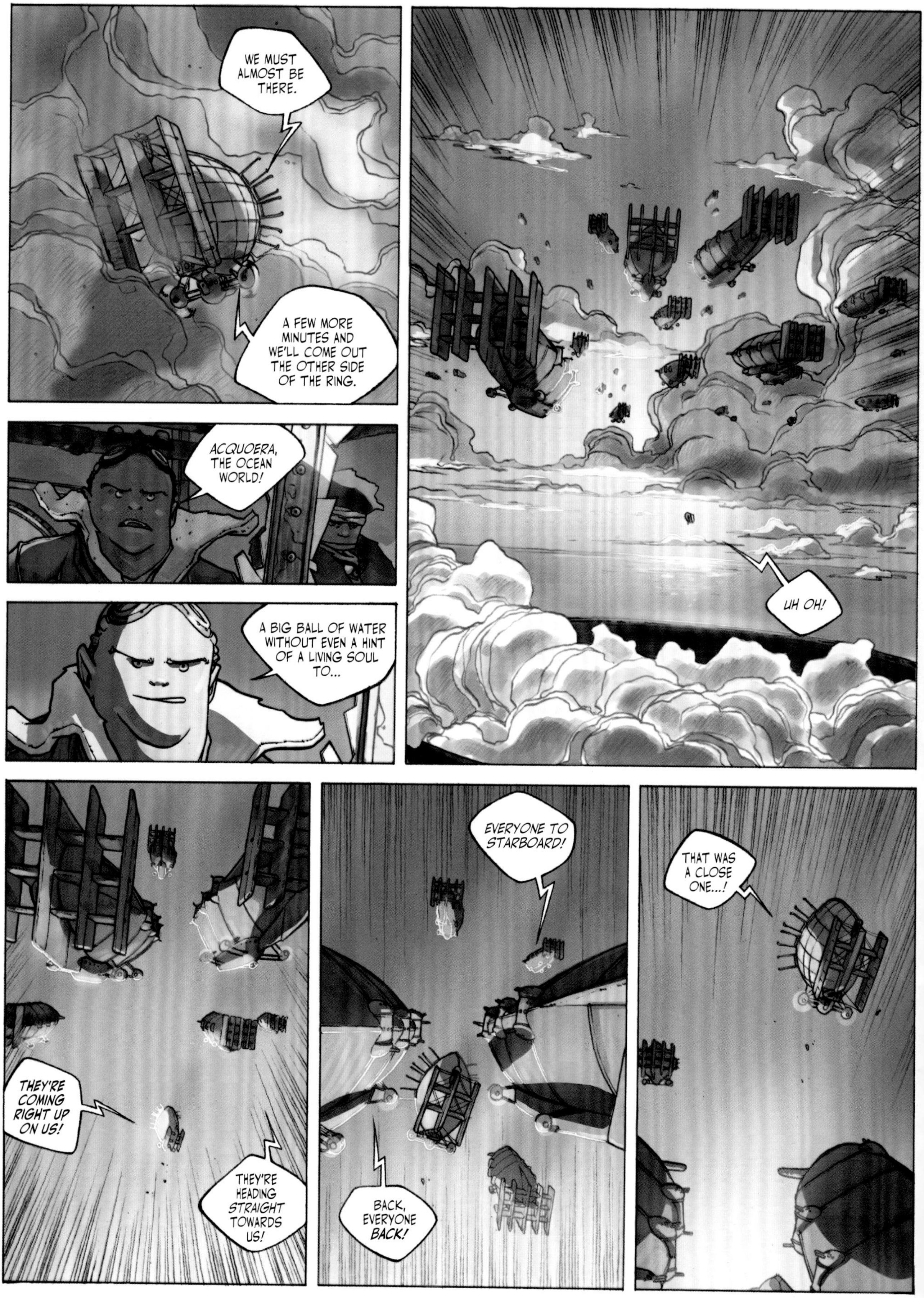
WE MUST ALMOST BE THERE.
A FEW MORE MINUTES AND WE'LL COME OUT THE OTHER SIDE OF THE RING.
ACQUOERA, THE OCEAN WORLD!
A BIG BALL OF WATER WITHOUT EVEN A HINT OF A LIVING SOUL TO...
UH OH!
THEY'RE COMING RIGHT UP ON US!
THEY'RE HEADING STRAIGHT TOWARDS US!
EVERYONE TO STARBOARD!
BACK, EVERYONE BACK!
THAT WAS A CLOSE ONE...!

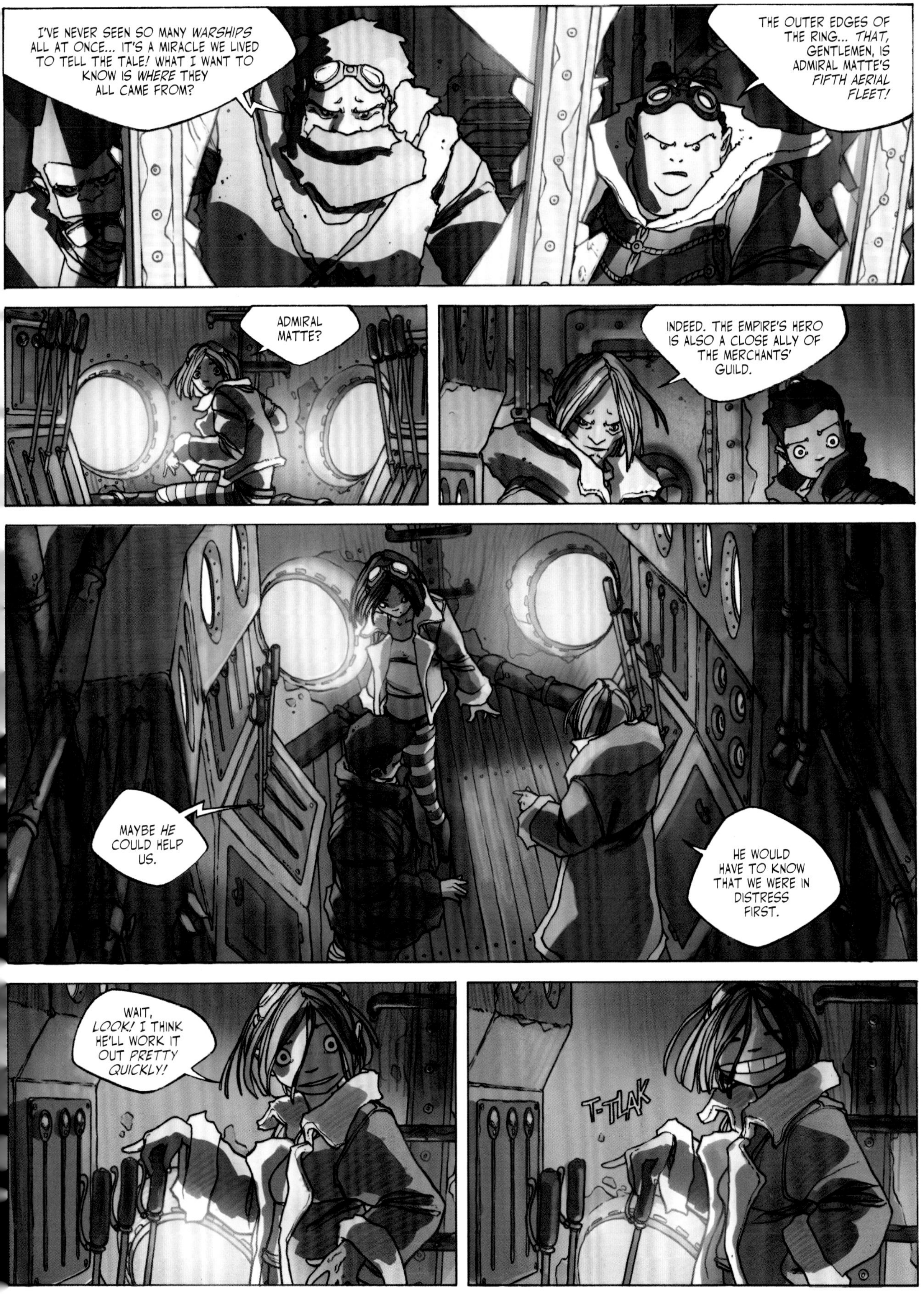
I'VE NEVER SEEN SO MANY WARSHIPS ALL AT ONCE... IT'S A MIRACLE WE LIVED TO TELL THE TALE! WHAT I WANT TO KNOW IS WHERE THEY ALL CAME FROM?
THE OUTER EDGES OF THE RING... THAT, GENTLEMEN, IS ADMIRAL MATTE'S FIFTH AERIAL FLEET!
ADMIRAL MATTE?
INDEED. THE EMPIRE'S HERO IS ALSO A CLOSE ALLY OF THE MERCHANTS' GUILD.
MAYBE HE COULD HELP US.
HE WOULD HAVE TO KNOW THAT WE WERE IN DISTRESS FIRST.
WAIT, LOOK! I THINK HE'LL WORK IT OUT PRETTY QUICKLY!
T-TLAK

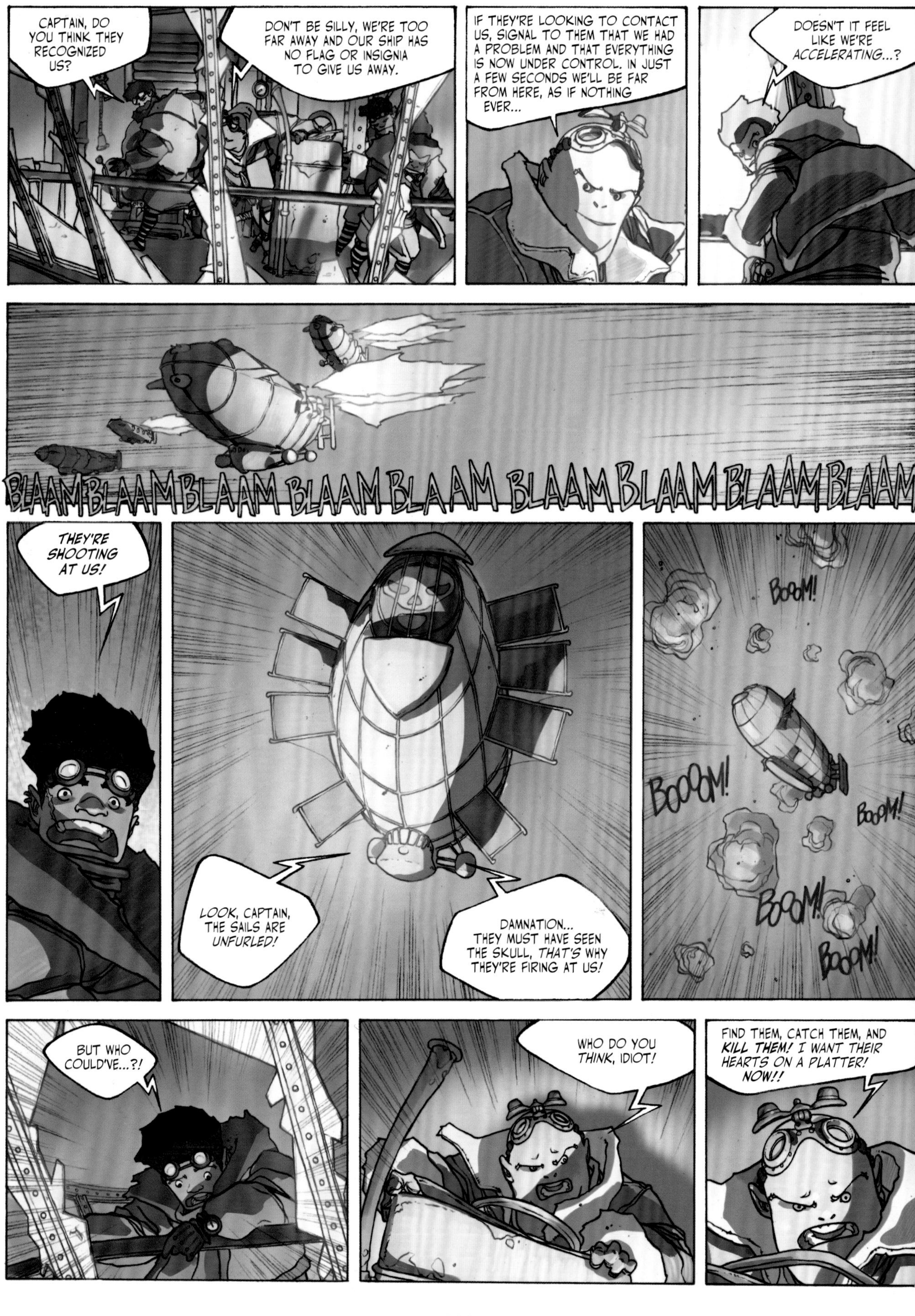
CAPTAIN, DO YOU THINK THEY RECOGNIZED US?
DON'T BE SILLY, WE'RE TOO FAR AWAY AND OUR SHIP HAS NO FLAG OR INSIGNIA TO GIVE US AWAY.
IF THEY'RE LOOKING TO CONTACT US, SIGNAL TO THEM THAT WE HAD A PROBLEM AND THAT EVERYTHING IS NOW UNDER CONTROL. IN JUST A FEW SECONDS WE'LL BE FAR FROM HERE, AS IF NOTHING EVER...
DOESN'T IT FEEL LIKE WE'RE ACCELERATING...?
BLAAM BLAAM BLAAM BLAAM BLAAM BLAAM BLAAM BLAAM BLAAM
THEY'RE SHOOTING AT US!
LOOK, CAPTAIN, THE SAILS ARE UNFURLED!
DAMNATION... THEY MUST HAVE SEEN THE SKULL, THAT'S WHY THEY'RE FIRING AT US!
BOOOM!
BOOOM!
BOOOM!
BOOOM!
BOOOM!
BOOOM!
BUT WHO COULD'VE...?!
WHO DO YOU THINK, IDIOT!
FIND THEM, CATCH THEM, AND KILL THEM! I WANT THEIR HEARTS ON A PLATTER! NOW!!

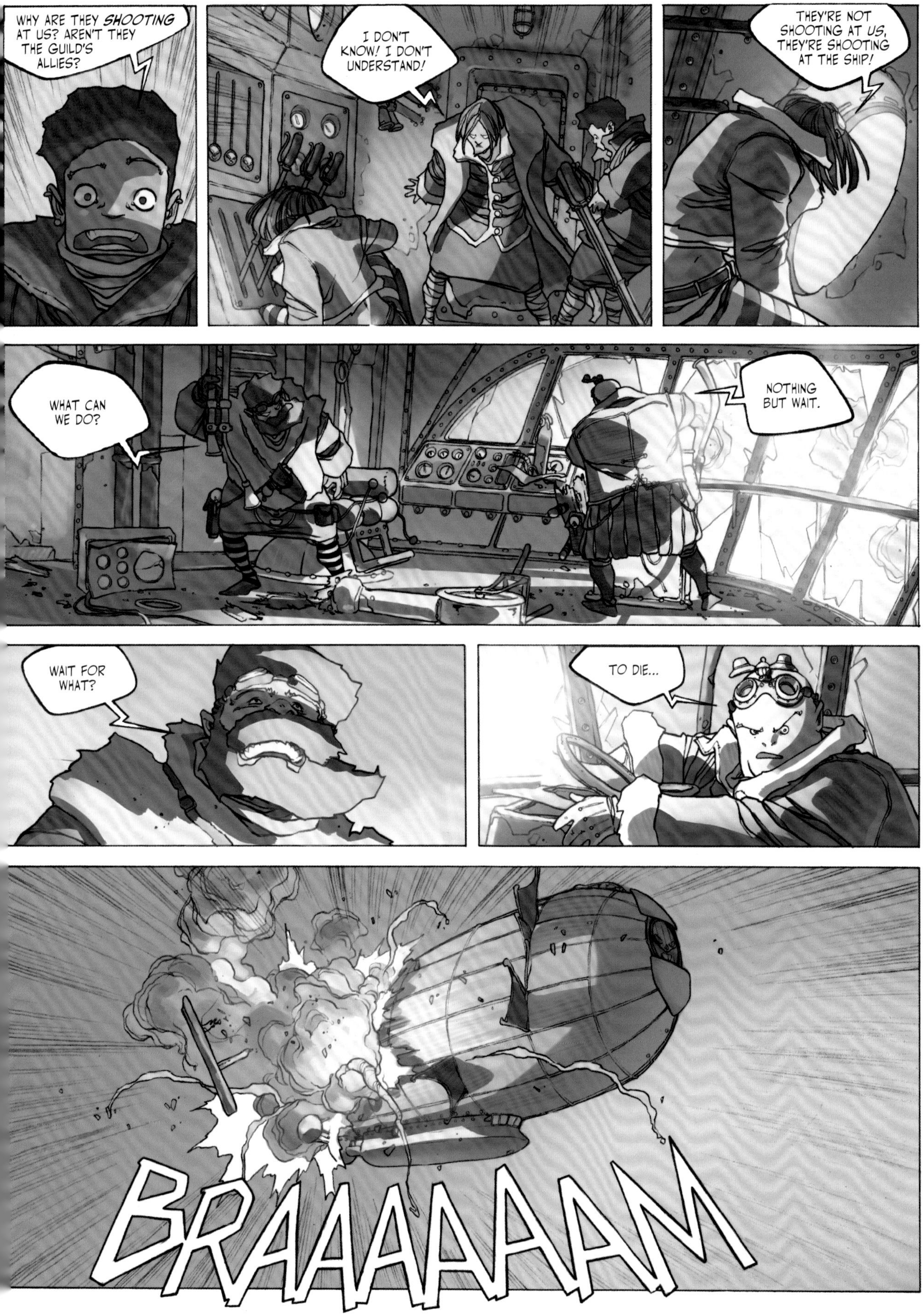
WHY ARE THEY SHOOTING AT US? AREN'T THEY THE GUILD'S ALLIES?
I DON'T KNOW! I DON'T UNDERSTAND!
THEY'RE NOT SHOOTING AT US, THEY'RE SHOOTING AT THE SHIP!
WHAT CAN WE DO?
NOTHING BUT WAIT.
WAIT FOR WHAT?
TO DIE...
BRAAAAAAM

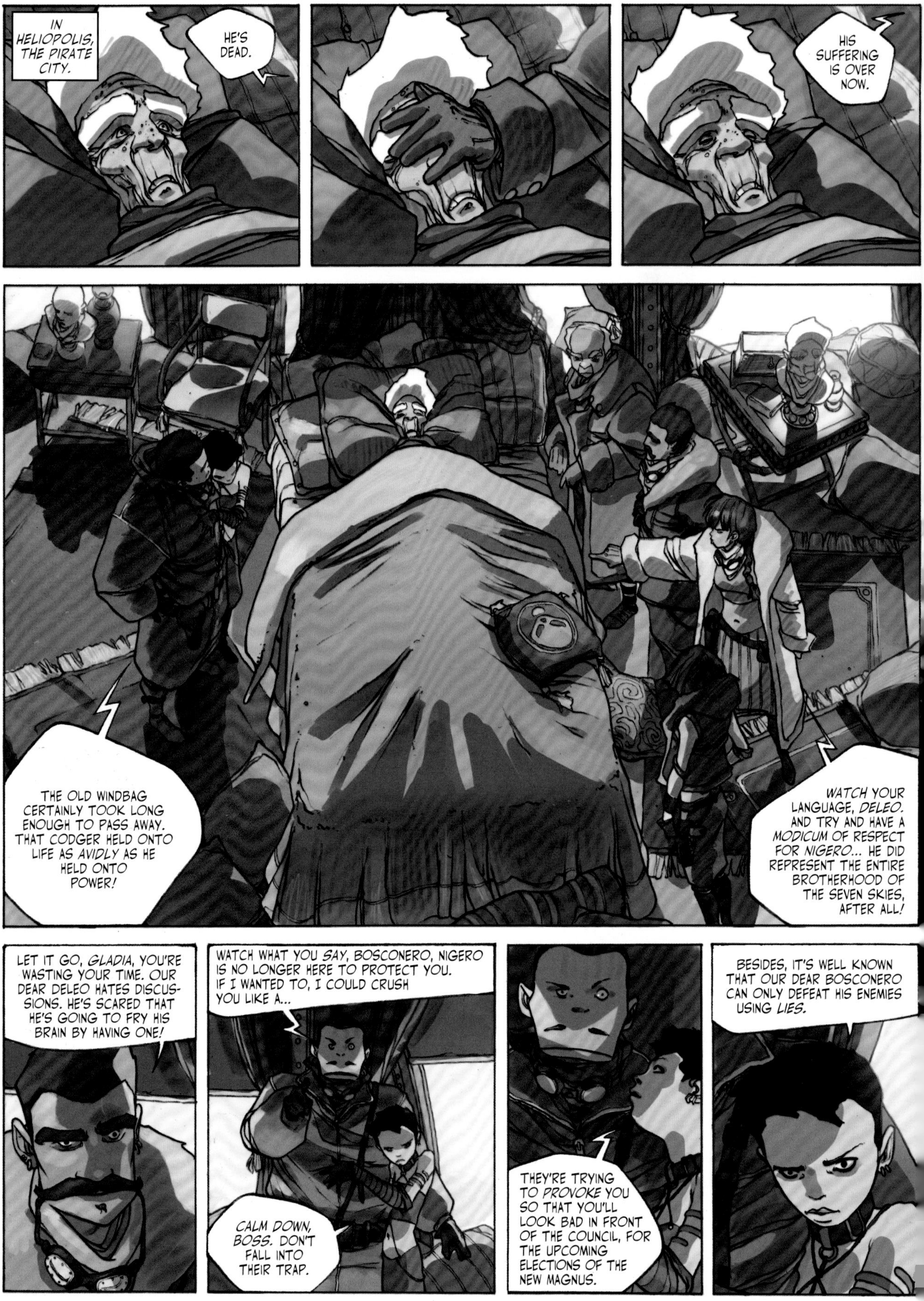
IN HELIOPOLIS, THE PIRATE CITY.
HE'S DEAD.
HIS SUFFERING IS OVER NOW.
THE OLD WINDBAG CERTAINLY TOOK LONG ENOUGH TO PASS AWAY. THAT CODGER HELD ONTO LIFE AS *AVIDLY* AS HE HELD ONTO POWER!
WATCH YOUR LANGUAGE, *DELEO.* AND TRY AND HAVE A *MODICUM* OF RESPECT FOR *NIGERO*... HE DID REPRESENT THE ENTIRE BROTHERHOOD OF THE SEVEN SKIES, AFTER ALL!
LET IT GO, *GLADIA*, YOU'RE WASTING YOUR TIME. OUR DEAR DELEO HATES DISCUS-SIONS. HE'S SCARED THAT HE'S GOING TO FRY HIS BRAIN BY HAVING ONE!
WATCH WHAT YOU *SAY*, BOSCONERO, NIGERO IS NO LONGER HERE TO PROTECT YOU. IF I WANTED TO, I COULD CRUSH YOU LIKE A...
CALM DOWN, BOSS. DON'T FALL INTO THEIR TRAP.
THEY'RE TRYING TO *PROVOKE* YOU SO THAT YOU'LL LOOK BAD IN FRONT OF THE COUNCIL, FOR THE UPCOMING ELECTIONS OF THE NEW MAGNUS.
BESIDES, IT'S WELL KNOWN THAT OUR DEAR BOSCONERO CAN ONLY DEFEAT HIS ENEMIES USING *LIES.*

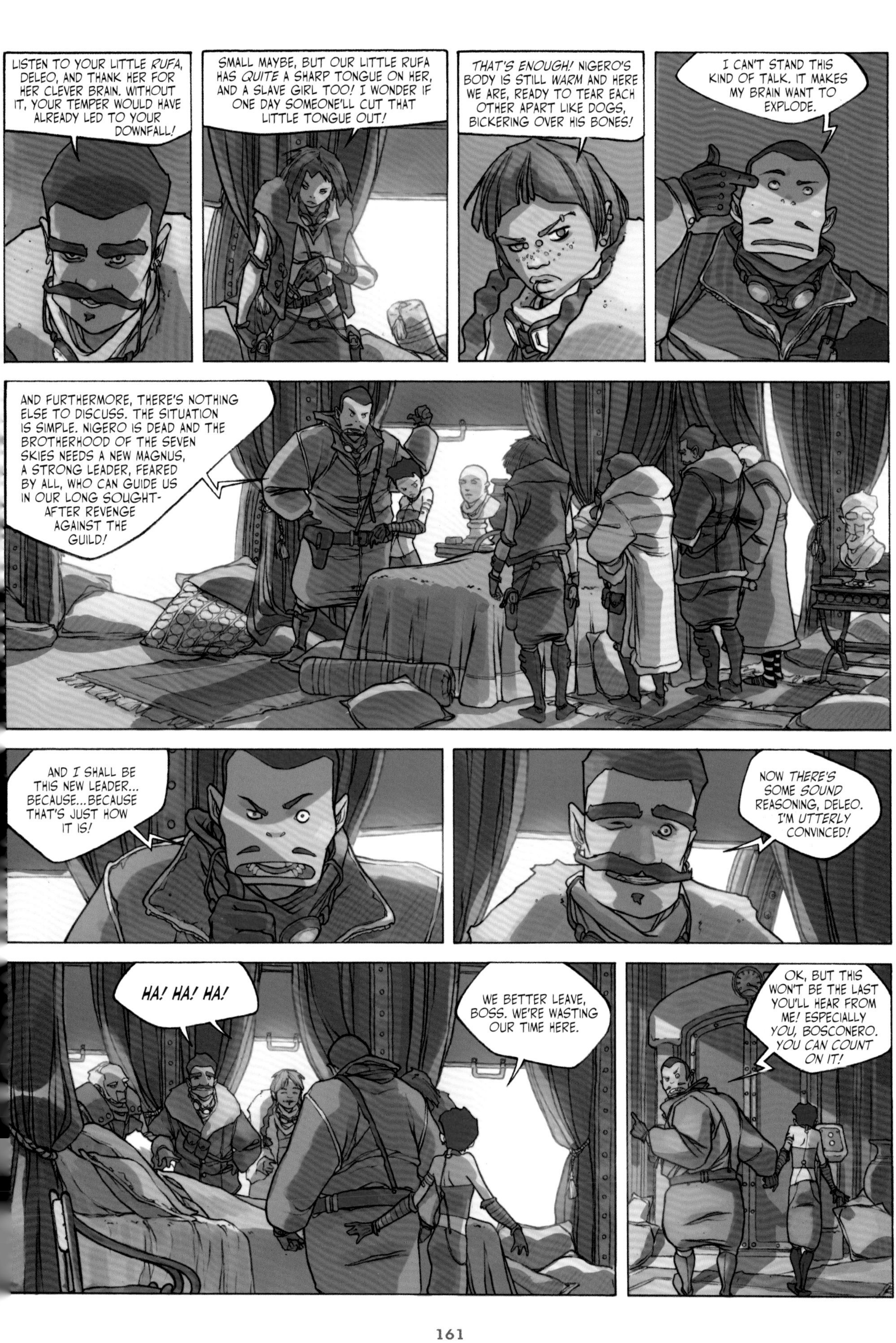

LISTEN TO YOUR LITTLE *RUFA*, DELEO, AND THANK HER FOR HER CLEVER BRAIN. WITHOUT IT, YOUR TEMPER WOULD HAVE ALREADY LED TO YOUR DOWNFALL!
SMALL MAYBE, BUT OUR LITTLE RUFA HAS *QUITE* A SHARP TONGUE ON HER, AND A SLAVE GIRL TOO! I WONDER IF ONE DAY SOMEONE'LL CUT THAT LITTLE TONGUE OUT!
THAT'S ENOUGH! NIGERO'S BODY IS STILL *WARM* AND HERE WE ARE, READY TO TEAR EACH OTHER APART LIKE DOGS, BICKERING OVER HIS BONES!
I CAN'T STAND THIS KIND OF TALK. IT MAKES MY BRAIN WANT TO EXPLODE.
AND FURTHERMORE, THERE'S NOTHING ELSE TO DISCUSS. THE SITUATION IS SIMPLE. NIGERO IS DEAD AND THE BROTHERHOOD OF THE SEVEN SKIES NEEDS A NEW MAGNUS, A STRONG LEADER, FEARED BY ALL, WHO CAN GUIDE US IN OUR LONG SOUGHT-AFTER REVENGE AGAINST THE GUILD!
AND I SHALL BE THIS NEW LEADER... BECAUSE...BECAUSE THAT'S JUST HOW IT IS!
NOW *THERE'S* SOME *SOUND* REASONING, DELEO. I'M *UTTERLY* CONVINCED!
HA! HA! HA!
WE BETTER LEAVE, BOSS. WE'RE WASTING OUR TIME HERE.
OK, BUT THIS WON'T BE THE LAST YOU'LL HEAR FROM ME! ESPECIALLY YOU, BOSCONERO. YOU CAN COUNT ON IT!

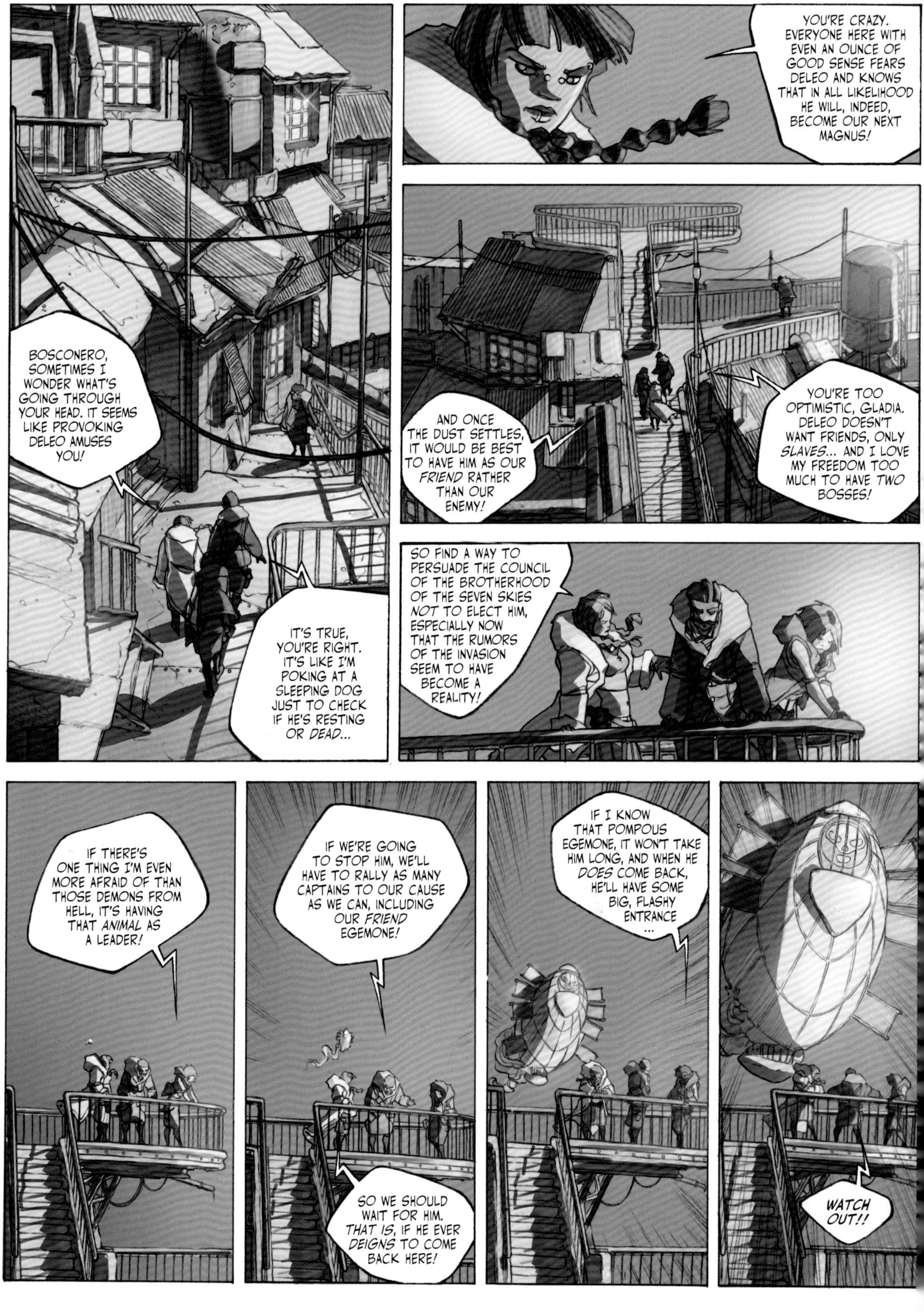

BOSCONERO, SOMETIMES I WONDER WHAT'S GOING THROUGH YOUR HEAD. IT SEEMS LIKE PROVOKING DELEO AMUSES YOU!
IT'S TRUE, YOU'RE RIGHT. IT'S LIKE I'M POKING AT A SLEEPING DOG JUST TO CHECK IF HE'S RESTING OR *DEAD*...
YOU'RE CRAZY. EVERYONE HERE WITH EVEN AN OUNCE OF GOOD SENSE FEARS DELEO AND KNOWS THAT IN ALL LIKELIHOOD HE WILL, INDEED, BECOME OUR NEXT MAGNUS!
AND ONCE THE DUST SETTLES, IT WOULD BE BEST TO HAVE HIM AS OUR *FRIEND* RATHER THAN OUR ENEMY!
YOU'RE TOO OPTIMISTIC, GLADIA. DELEO DOESN'T WANT FRIENDS, ONLY *SLAVES*... AND I LOVE MY FREEDOM TOO MUCH TO HAVE *TWO* BOSSES!
SO FIND A WAY TO PERSUADE THE COUNCIL OF THE BROTHERHOOD OF THE SEVEN SKIES *NOT* TO ELECT HIM, ESPECIALLY NOW THAT THE RUMORS OF THE INVASION SEEM TO HAVE BECOME A REALITY!
IF THERE'S ONE THING I'M EVEN MORE AFRAID OF THAN THOSE DEMONS FROM HELL, IT'S HAVING THAT *ANIMAL* AS A LEADER!
IF WE'RE GOING TO STOP HIM, WE'LL HAVE TO RALLY AS MANY CAPTAINS TO OUR CAUSE AS WE CAN, INCLUDING OUR *FRIEND* EGEMONE!
SO WE SHOULD WAIT FOR HIM. *THAT IS*, IF HE EVER *DEIGNS* TO COME BACK HERE!
IF I KNOW THAT POMPOUS EGEMONE, IT WON'T TAKE HIM LONG, AND WHEN HE *DOES* COME BACK, HE'LL HAVE SOME BIG, FLASHY ENTRANCE ...
WATCH OUT!!

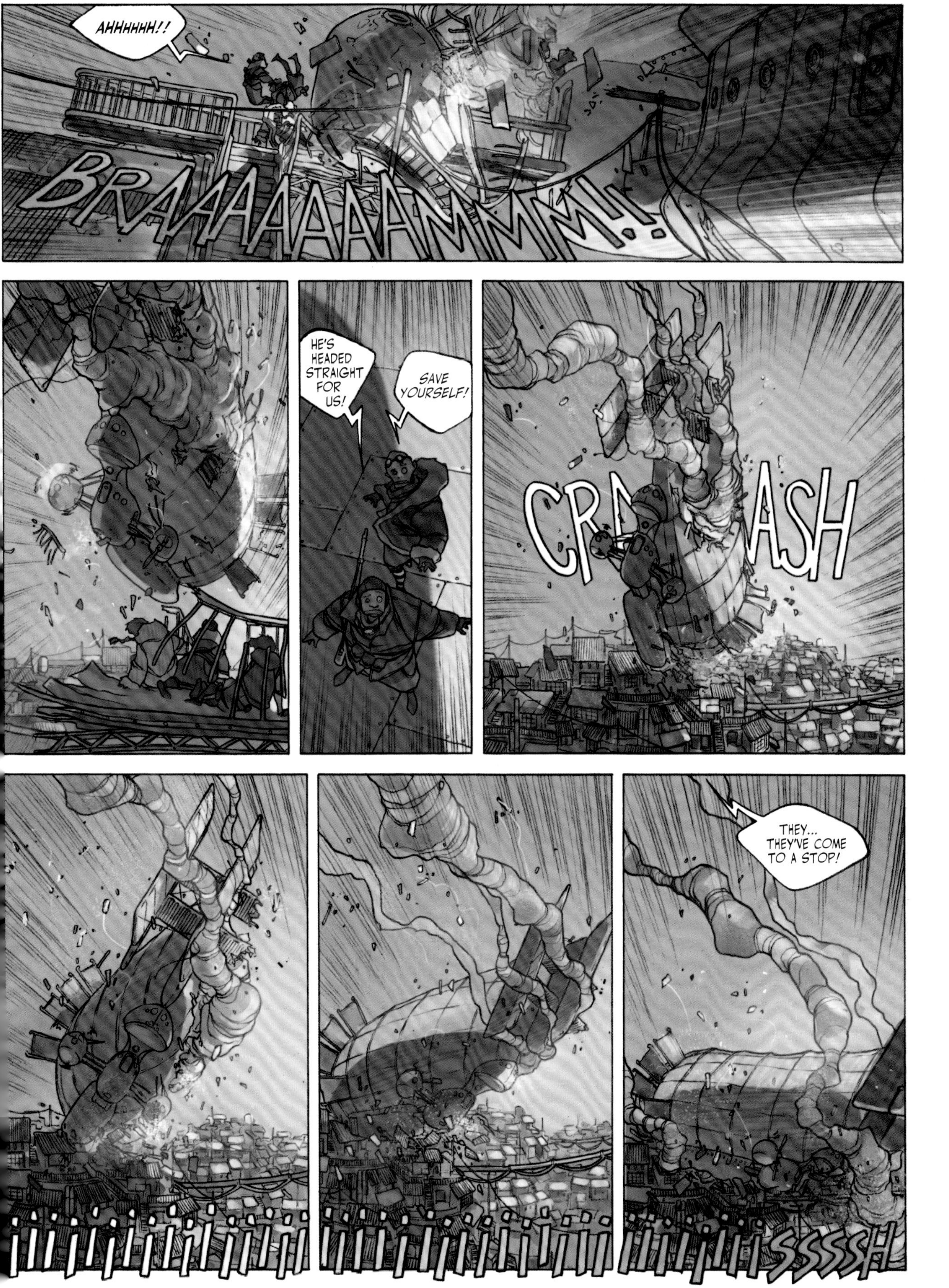
AHHHHHH!!
BRAAAAAAAMMM!!
HE'S HEADED STRAIGHT FOR US!
SAVE YOURSELF!
CRASH
THEY... THEY'VE COME TO A STOP!
SSSSH

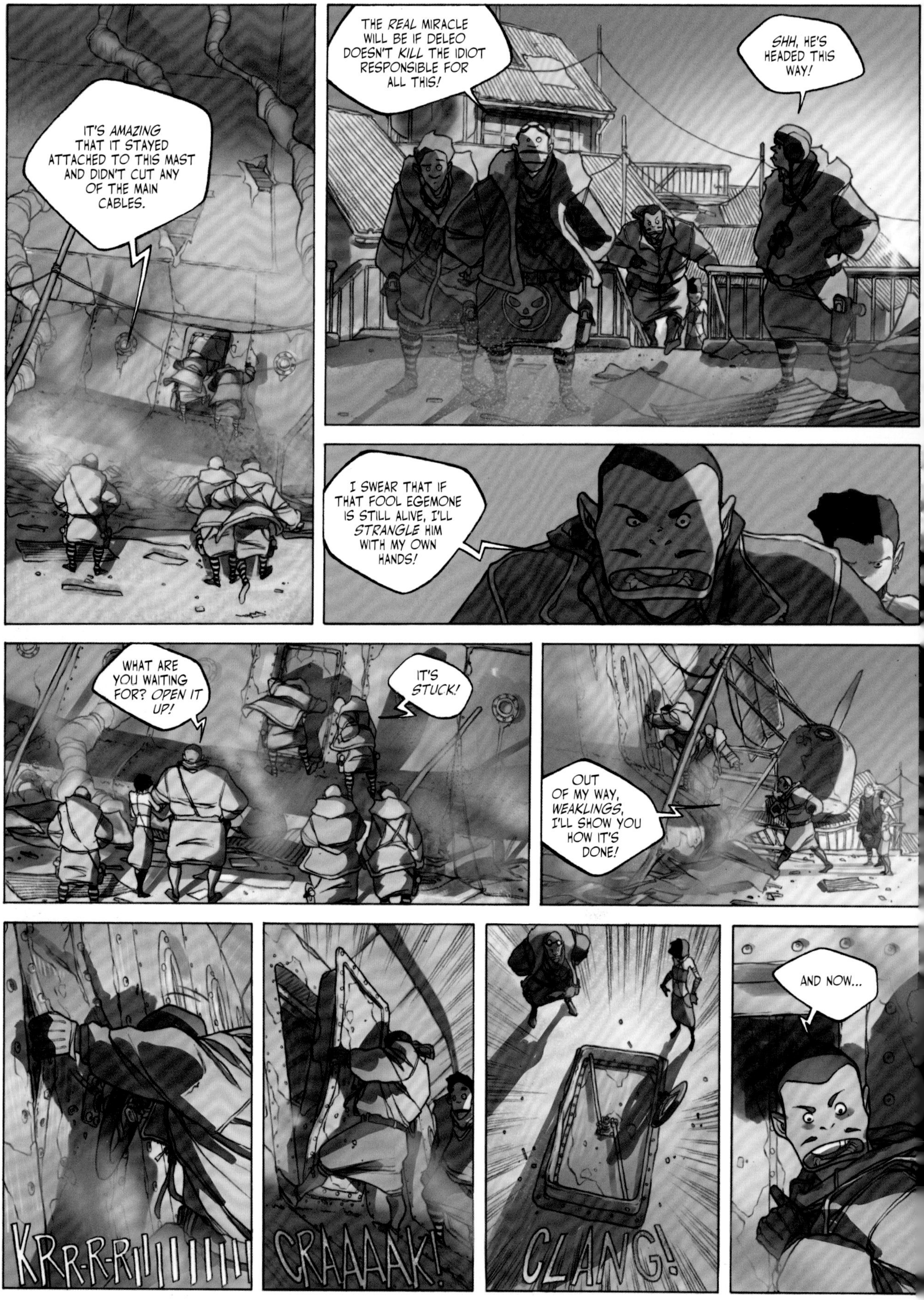
IT'S *AMAZING* THAT IT STAYED ATTACHED TO THIS MAST AND DIDN'T CUT ANY OF THE MAIN CABLES.
THE *REAL* MIRACLE WILL BE IF DELEO DOESN'T *KILL* THE IDIOT RESPONSIBLE FOR ALL THIS!
SHH, HE'S HEADED THIS WAY!
I SWEAR THAT IF THAT FOOL EGEMONE IS STILL ALIVE, I'LL *STRANGLE* HIM WITH MY OWN HANDS!
WHAT ARE YOU WAITING FOR? *OPEN IT UP!*
IT'S *STUCK!*
OUT OF MY WAY, *WEAKLINGS*, I'LL SHOW YOU HOW IT'S DONE!
KRR-R-RIIIIIIIIH
CRAAAAK!
CLANG!
AND NOW...

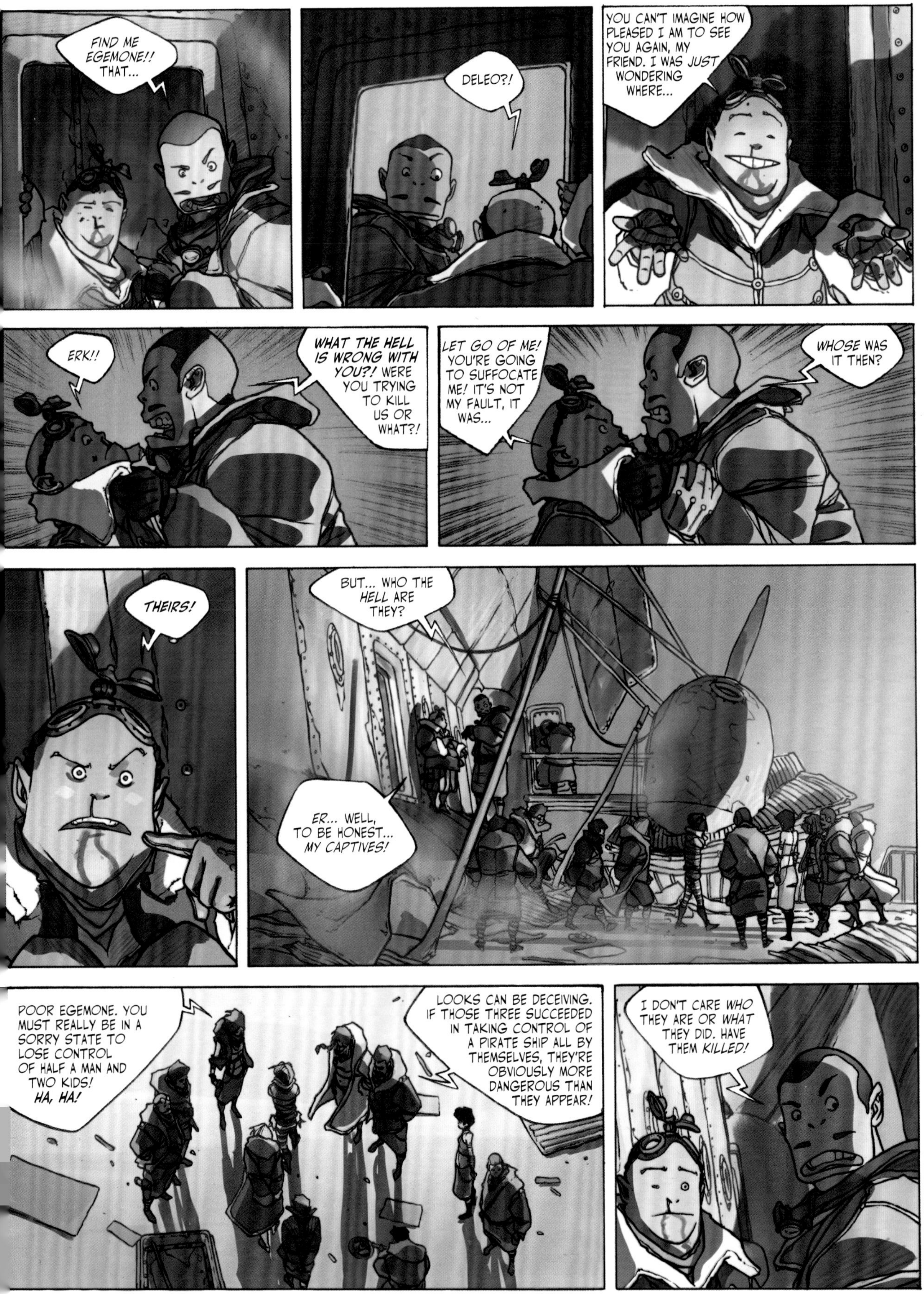

FIND ME EGEMONE!! THAT...
DELEO?!
YOU CAN'T IMAGINE HOW PLEASED I AM TO SEE YOU AGAIN, MY FRIEND. I WAS JUST WONDERING WHERE...
ERK!!
WHAT THE HELL IS WRONG WITH YOU?! WERE YOU TRYING TO KILL US OR WHAT?!
LET GO OF ME! YOU'RE GOING TO SUFFOCATE ME! IT'S NOT MY FAULT, IT WAS...
WHOSE WAS IT THEN?
THEIRS!
BUT... WHO THE HELL ARE THEY?
ER... WELL, TO BE HONEST... MY CAPTIVES!
POOR EGEMONE. YOU MUST REALLY BE IN A SORRY STATE TO LOSE CONTROL OF HALF A MAN AND TWO KIDS! HA, HA!
LOOKS CAN BE DECEIVING. IF THOSE THREE SUCCEEDED IN TAKING CONTROL OF A PIRATE SHIP ALL BY THEMSELVES, THEY'RE OBVIOUSLY MORE DANGEROUS THAN THEY APPEAR!
I DON'T CARE WHO THEY ARE OR WHAT THEY DID. HAVE THEM KILLED!

WHY DO YOU WANT TO HAVE US KILLED? WE DID YOU NO HARM!

HE KIDNAPPED US. WE JUST WANT TO GO HOME!

NOW THAT YOU KNOW HELIOPOLIS'S LOCATION, YOU MUST DIE! IT'S THE LAW!

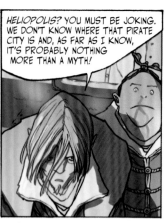

HELIOPOLIS? YOU MUST BE JOKING. WE DON'T KNOW WHERE THAT PIRATE CITY IS AND, AS FAR AS I KNOW, IT'S PROBABLY NOTHING MORE THAN A MYTH!

A MYTH, YOU SAY?

WELL THEN, IN THAT CASE...

...WELCOME TO THE MYTH!

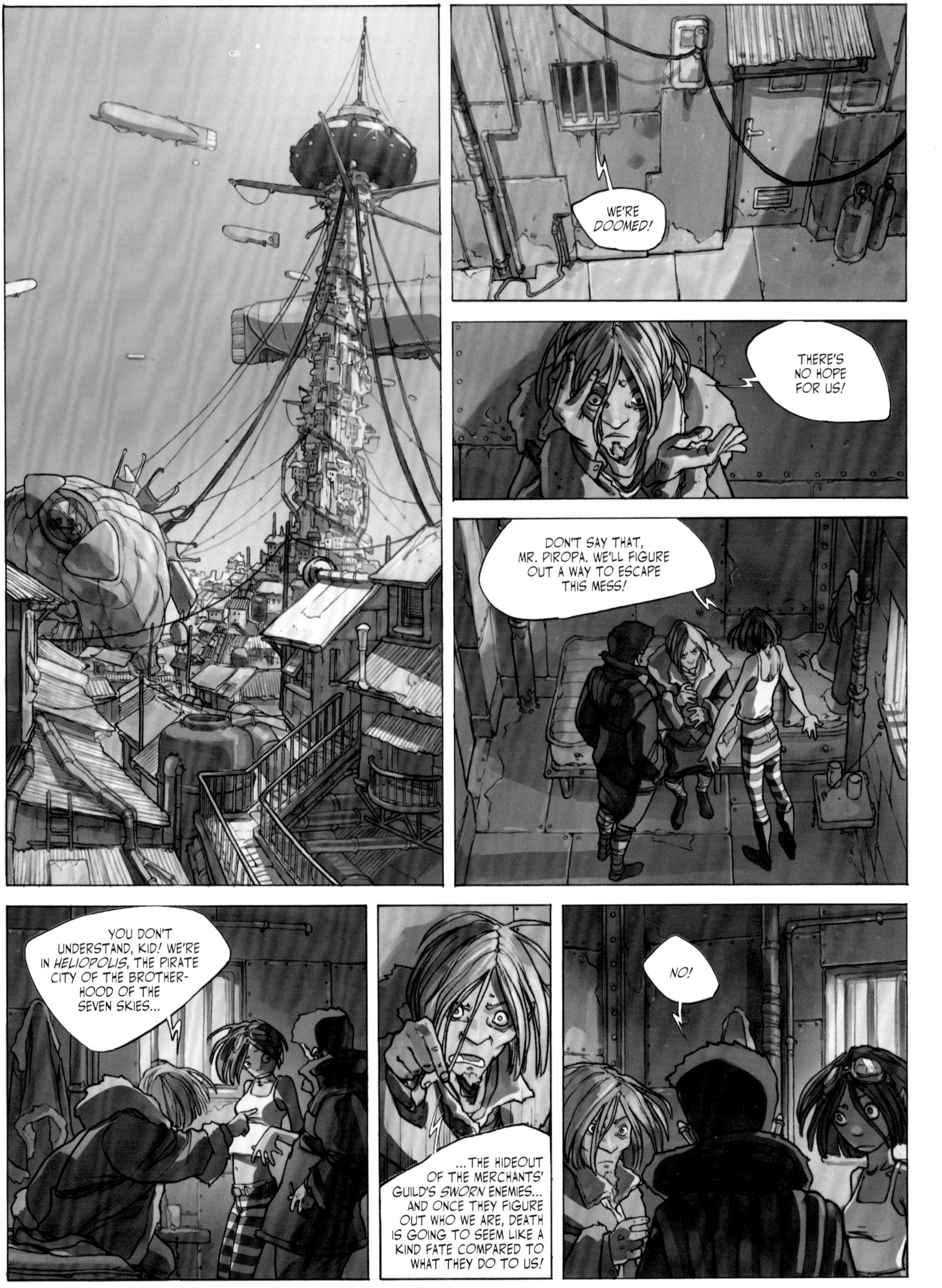
WE'RE *DOOMED!*
THERE'S NO HOPE FOR US!
DON'T SAY THAT, MR. PIROPA. WE'LL FIGURE OUT A WAY TO ESCAPE THIS MESS!
YOU DON'T UNDERSTAND, KID! WE'RE IN *HELIOPOLIS*, THE PIRATE CITY OF THE BROTHER-HOOD OF THE SEVEN SKIES...
...THE HIDEOUT OF THE MERCHANTS' GUILD'S *SWORN* ENEMIES... AND ONCE THEY FIGURE OUT WHO WE ARE, DEATH IS GOING TO SEEM LIKE A KIND FATE COMPARED TO WHAT THEY DO TO US!
NO!

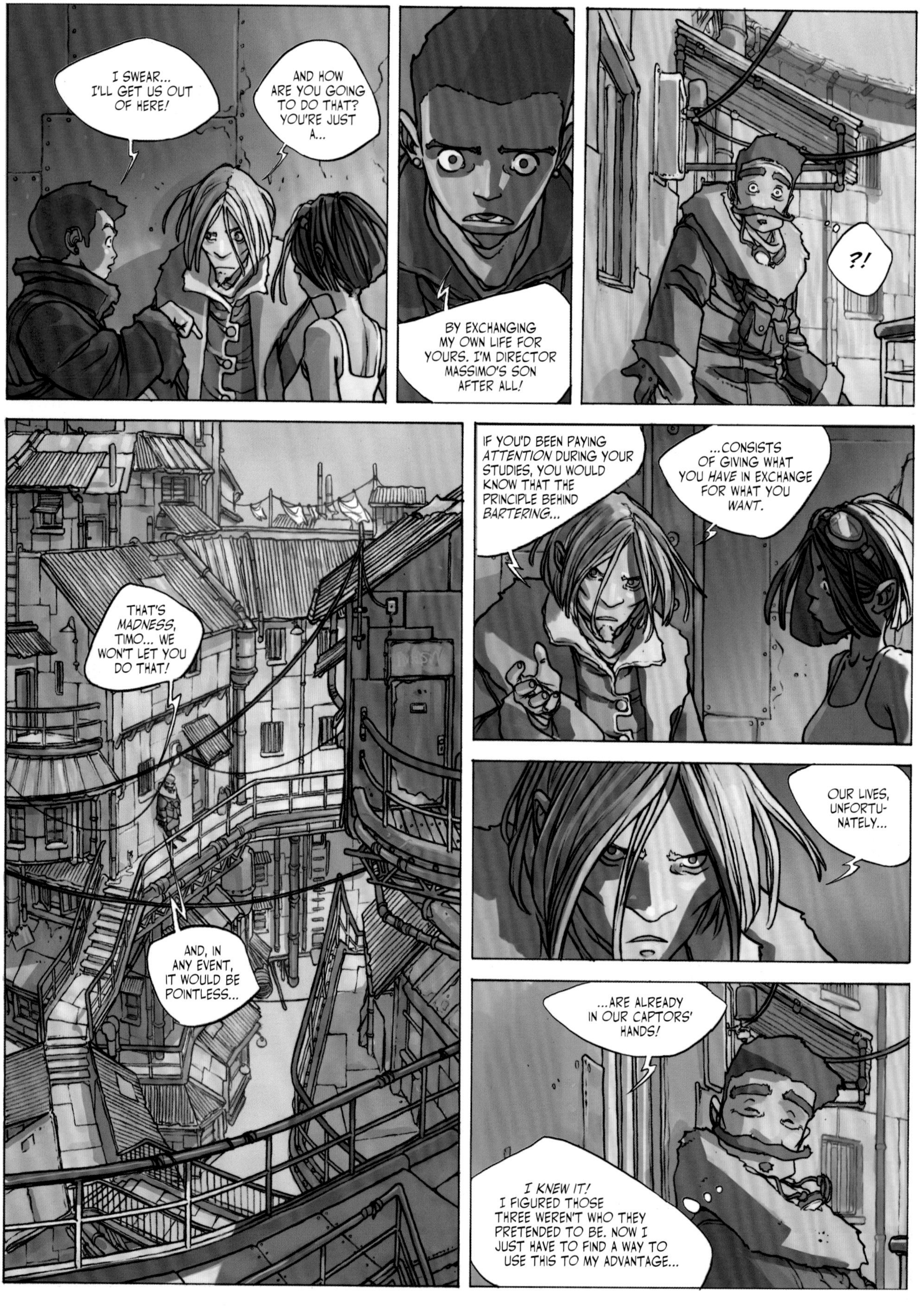
I SWEAR... I'LL GET US OUT OF HERE!
AND HOW ARE YOU GOING TO DO THAT? YOU'RE JUST A...
BY EXCHANGING MY OWN LIFE FOR YOURS. I'M DIRECTOR MASSIMO'S SON AFTER ALL!
?!
THAT'S *MADNESS*, TIMO... WE WON'T LET YOU DO THAT!
AND, IN ANY EVENT, IT WOULD BE POINTLESS...
IF YOU'D BEEN PAYING *ATTENTION* DURING YOUR STUDIES, YOU WOULD KNOW THAT THE PRINCIPLE BEHIND *BARTERING*...
...CONSISTS OF GIVING WHAT YOU *HAVE* IN EXCHANGE FOR WHAT YOU *WANT*.
OUR LIVES, UNFORTU-NATELY...
...ARE ALREADY IN OUR CAPTORS' HANDS!
I KNEW IT! I FIGURED THOSE THREE WEREN'T WHO THEY PRETENDED TO BE. NOW I JUST HAVE TO FIND A WAY TO USE THIS TO MY ADVANTAGE...

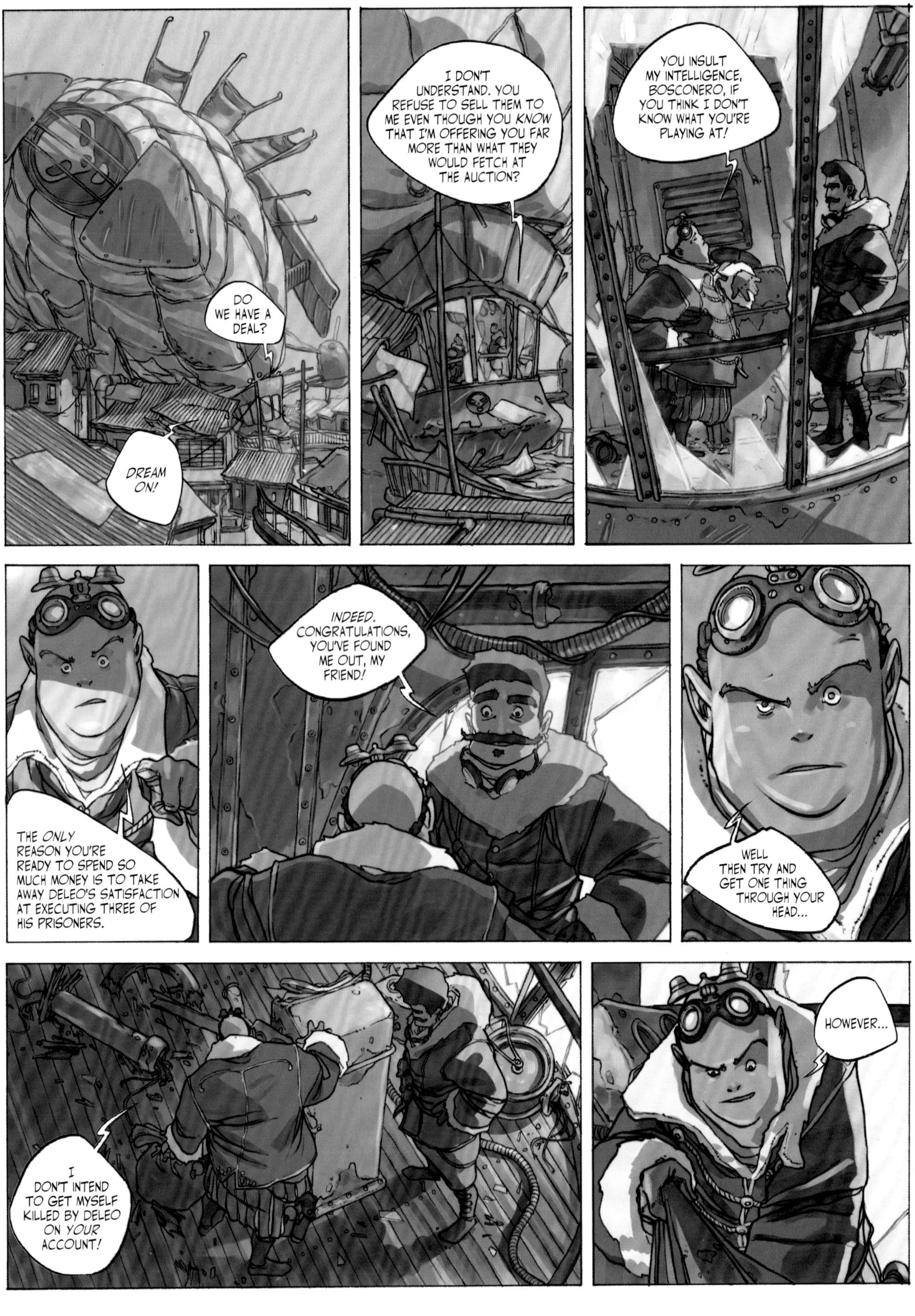

DO WE HAVE A DEAL?
DREAM ON!
I DON'T UNDERSTAND. YOU REFUSE TO SELL THEM TO ME EVEN THOUGH YOU *KNOW* THAT I'M OFFERING YOU FAR MORE THAN WHAT THEY WOULD FETCH AT THE AUCTION?
YOU INSULT MY INTELLIGENCE, BOSCONERO, IF YOU THINK I DON'T KNOW WHAT YOU'RE PLAYING AT!
THE *ONLY* REASON YOU'RE READY TO SPEND SO MUCH MONEY IS TO TAKE AWAY DELEO'S SATISFACTION AT EXECUTING THREE OF HIS PRISONERS.
INDEED. CONGRATULATIONS, YOU'VE FOUND ME OUT, MY FRIEND!
WELL THEN TRY AND GET ONE THING THROUGH YOUR HEAD...
I DON'T INTEND TO GET MYSELF KILLED BY DELEO ON *YOUR* ACCOUNT!
HOWEVER...

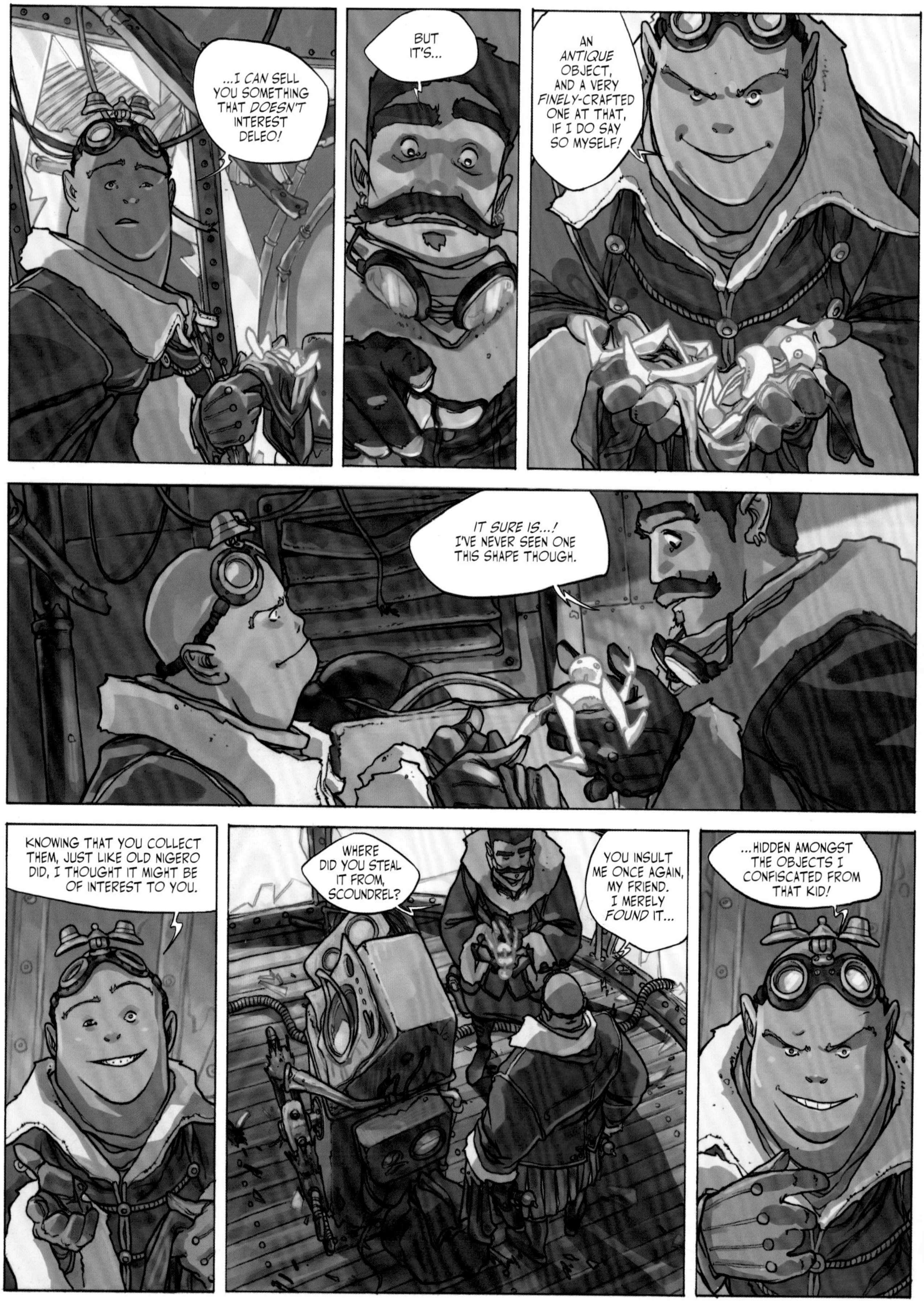
...I CAN SELL YOU SOMETHING THAT DOESN'T INTEREST DELEO!
BUT IT'S...
AN ANTIQUE OBJECT, AND A VERY FINELY-CRAFTED ONE AT THAT, IF I DO SAY SO MYSELF!
IT SURE IS...! I'VE NEVER SEEN ONE THIS SHAPE THOUGH.
KNOWING THAT YOU COLLECT THEM, JUST LIKE OLD NIGERO DID, I THOUGHT IT MIGHT BE OF INTEREST TO YOU.
WHERE DID YOU STEAL IT FROM, SCOUNDREL?
YOU INSULT ME ONCE AGAIN, MY FRIEND. I MERELY FOUND IT...
...HIDDEN AMONGST THE OBJECTS I CONFISCATED FROM THAT KID!

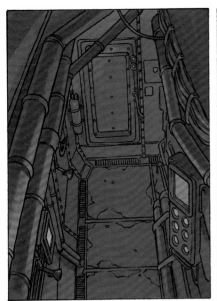

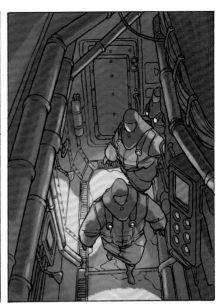

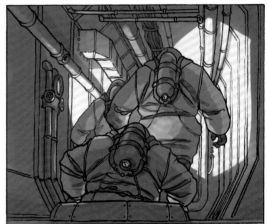

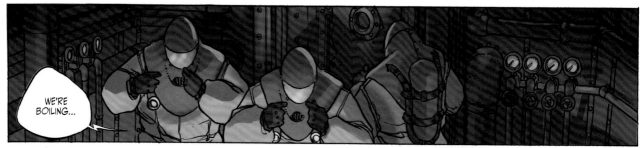

WE'RE BOILING...

...IN HERE!

IT'S EVEN WORSE WITHOUT THE PROTECTIVE SUIT. WHY KEEP A FURNACE LIKE THIS RUNNING INSIDE THE SHIP?

TO REPLICATE NEMO'S *CLIMATE*, NO DOUBT. THE SAME GOES FOR THIS STRANGE, REDDISH GAS THROUGHOUT THE SHIP, WHICH WE BELIEVE HELPS THEM BREATHE.

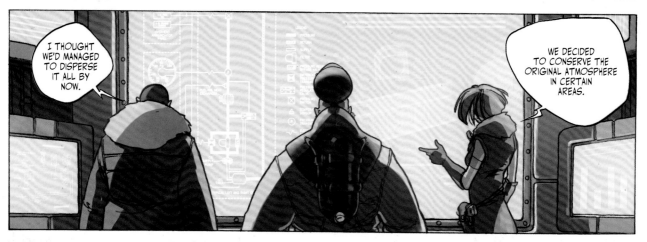

I THOUGHT WE'D MANAGED TO DISPERSE IT ALL BY NOW.

WE DECIDED TO CONSERVE THE ORIGINAL ATMOSPHERE IN CERTAIN AREAS.

THERE WERE ALSO A FEW POCKETS OF GAS THAT WE COULDN'T SEEM TO GET RID OF.

A COMPOUND WHICH, AS IT TURNS OUT, IS *TOXIC* BUT *NOT DEADLY*. JUST LIKE OUR ATMOSPHERE FOR THEM, ACCORDING TO OUR RESEARCH!

I MERELY ASKED YOU TO WEAR THE GAS PROTECTION SUIT AS A *PRECAUTIONARY* MEASURE, LEPONTE.

OF COURSE, DIRECTOR TREO. YOUR SPECULATIONS WERE QUITE WELL-FOUNDED.

OUR TECHNOLOGY DOESN'T SEEM TO BE *TOO* DIFFERENT FROM THAT OF THESE SUPPOSED DEMONS!

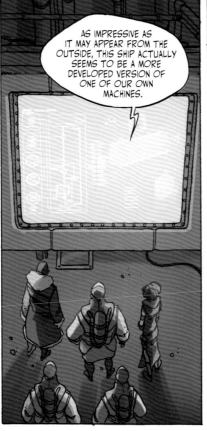

AS IMPRESSIVE AS IT MAY APPEAR FROM THE OUTSIDE, THIS SHIP ACTUALLY SEEMS TO BE A MORE DEVELOPED VERSION OF ONE OF OUR OWN MACHINES.

PROPULSION, PILOTING INSTRUMENTS, BALLAST SYSTEM... IT'S ALL QUITE SIMILAR TO OUR OWN, THOUGH SOME OTHER CHARACTERISTICS REMAIN MYSTERIOUS TO US.

FOR INSTANCE, THIS INSTRUMENT WHICH ALLOWS THE USER TO DETECT THE ECHO OF OBJECTS TOO DISTANT TO BE PERCEIVED BY THE NAKED EYE ALONE.

WE ALSO HAVE A THEORY FOR HOW THE VESSEL REMAINS IN THE AIR. IT APPEARS THAT THERE IS A NEW *CHEMICAL ELEMENT*, WHICH COMES FROM NEMO BUT DOESN'T EXIST IN OUR EMPIRE.

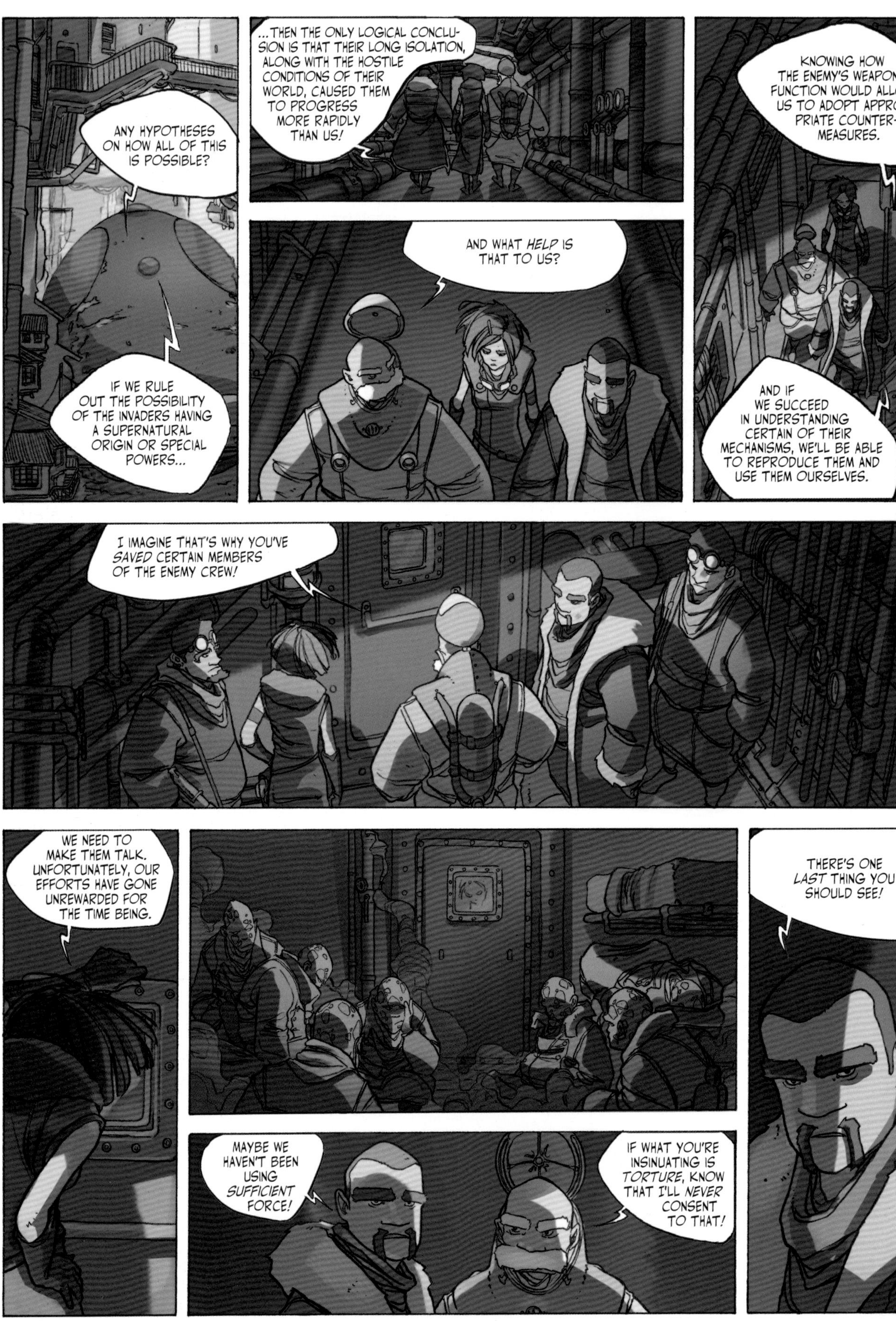
ANY HYPOTHESES ON HOW ALL OF THIS IS POSSIBLE?
IF WE RULE OUT THE POSSIBILITY OF THE INVADERS HAVING A SUPERNATURAL ORIGIN OR SPECIAL POWERS...
...THEN THE ONLY LOGICAL CONCLUSION IS THAT THEIR LONG ISOLATION, ALONG WITH THE HOSTILE CONDITIONS OF THEIR WORLD, CAUSED THEM TO PROGRESS MORE RAPIDLY THAN US!
AND WHAT HELP IS THAT TO US?
KNOWING HOW THE ENEMY'S WEAPONS FUNCTION WOULD ALLOW US TO ADOPT APPROPRIATE COUNTER-MEASURES.
AND IF WE SUCCEED IN UNDERSTANDING CERTAIN OF THEIR MECHANISMS, WE'LL BE ABLE TO REPRODUCE THEM AND USE THEM OURSELVES.
I IMAGINE THAT'S WHY YOU'VE SAVED CERTAIN MEMBERS OF THE ENEMY CREW!
WE NEED TO MAKE THEM TALK. UNFORTUNATELY, OUR EFFORTS HAVE GONE UNREWARDED FOR THE TIME BEING.
MAYBE WE HAVEN'T BEEN USING SUFFICIENT FORCE!
IF WHAT YOU'RE INSINUATING IS TORTURE, KNOW THAT I'LL NEVER CONSENT TO THAT!
THERE'S ONE LAST THING YOU SHOULD SEE!

WE DISCOVERED IT BY ACCIDENT, VERY CAREFULLY SEALED, AS IF IT WERE SOME KIND OF TREASURE!

HEAVENS! WHAT ON EARTH...?!

IT'S AN *ATMOSPHERIC DISTILLER*. IT CONTAMINATES OXYGEN WITH A CERTAIN SUBSTANCE AND TURNS IT INTO THE RED GAS.

BUT IF YOU LOOK A LITTLE CLOSER...

...THERE ARE TWO HALVES OF A KIND OF SHELL...

THE POSITIONING OF WHICH MEANS THE DISTILLER CAN TRANSFORM THE GAS INTO...

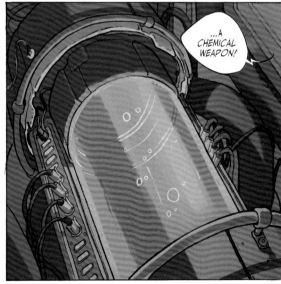

...A *CHEMICAL WEAPON!*

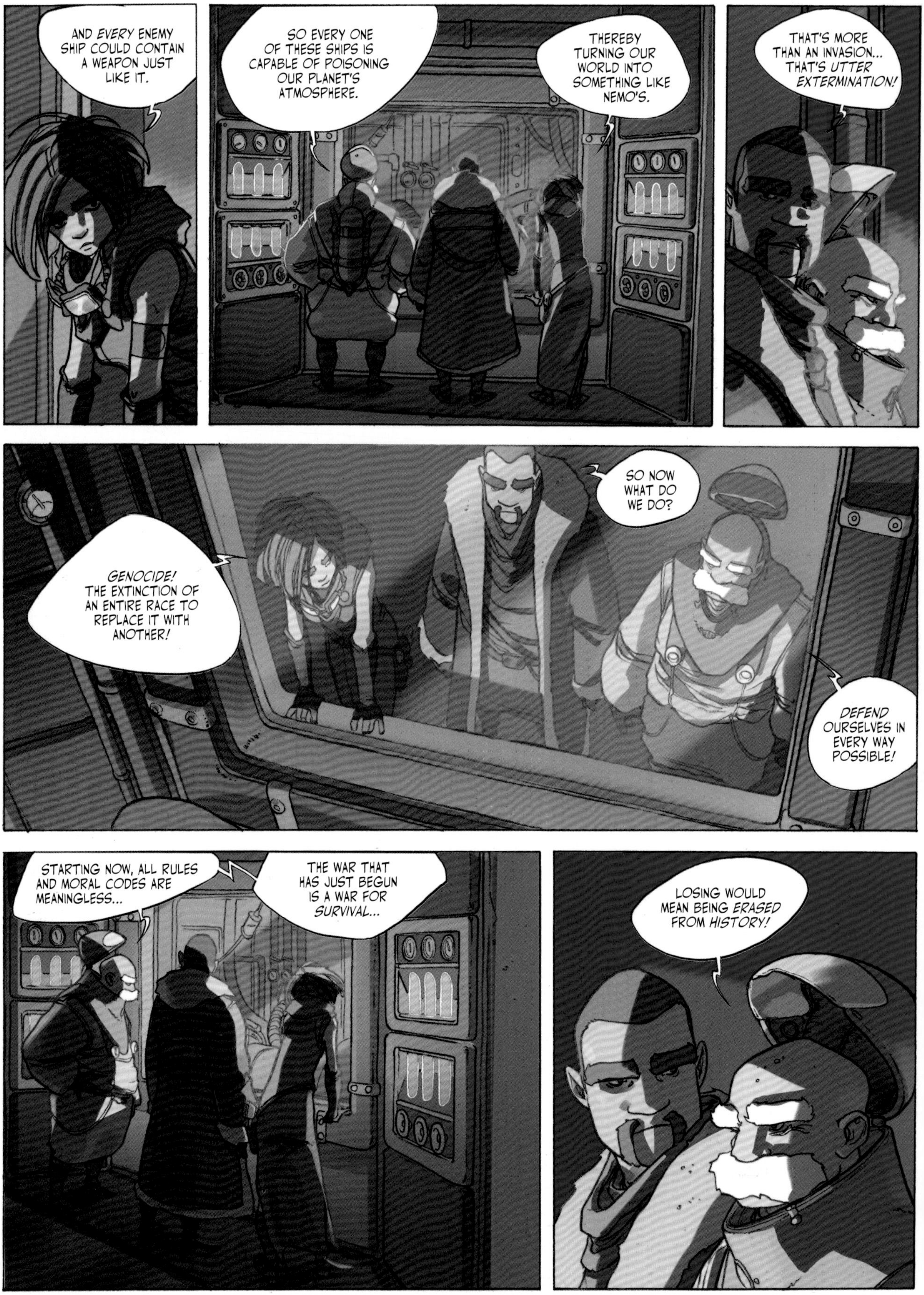
AND *EVERY* ENEMY SHIP COULD CONTAIN A WEAPON JUST LIKE IT.
SO EVERY ONE OF THESE SHIPS IS CAPABLE OF POISONING OUR PLANET'S ATMOSPHERE.
THEREBY TURNING OUR WORLD INTO SOMETHING LIKE NEMO'S.
THAT'S MORE THAN AN INVASION... THAT'S *UTTER EXTERMINATION!*
SO NOW WHAT DO WE DO?
GENOCIDE! THE EXTINCTION OF AN ENTIRE RACE TO REPLACE IT WITH ANOTHER!
DEFEND OURSELVES IN EVERY WAY POSSIBLE!
STARTING NOW, ALL RULES AND MORAL CODES ARE MEANINGLESS...
THE WAR THAT HAS JUST BEGUN IS A WAR FOR *SURVIVAL*...
LOSING WOULD MEAN BEING *ERASED* FROM *HISTORY!*

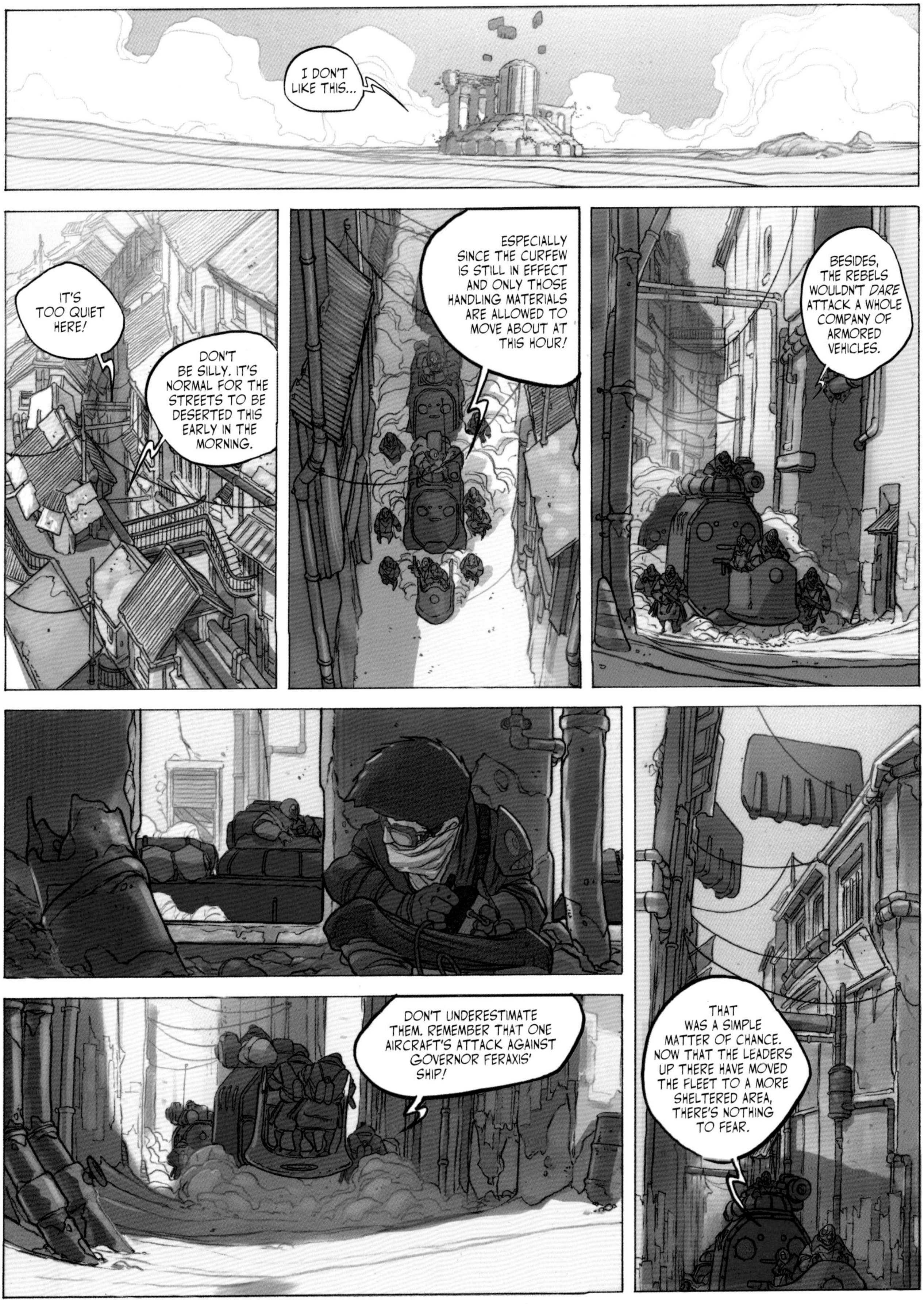
I DON'T LIKE THIS...
IT'S TOO QUIET HERE!
DON'T BE SILLY. IT'S NORMAL FOR THE STREETS TO BE DESERTED THIS EARLY IN THE MORNING.
ESPECIALLY SINCE THE CURFEW IS STILL IN EFFECT AND ONLY THOSE HANDLING MATERIALS ARE ALLOWED TO MOVE ABOUT AT THIS HOUR!
BESIDES, THE REBELS WOULDN'T *DARE* ATTACK A WHOLE COMPANY OF ARMORED VEHICLES.
DON'T UNDERESTIMATE THEM. REMEMBER THAT ONE AIRCRAFT'S ATTACK AGAINST GOVERNOR FERAXIS' SHIP!
THAT WAS A SIMPLE MATTER OF CHANCE. NOW THAT THE LEADERS UP THERE HAVE MOVED THE FLEET TO A MORE SHELTERED AREA, THERE'S NOTHING TO FEAR.

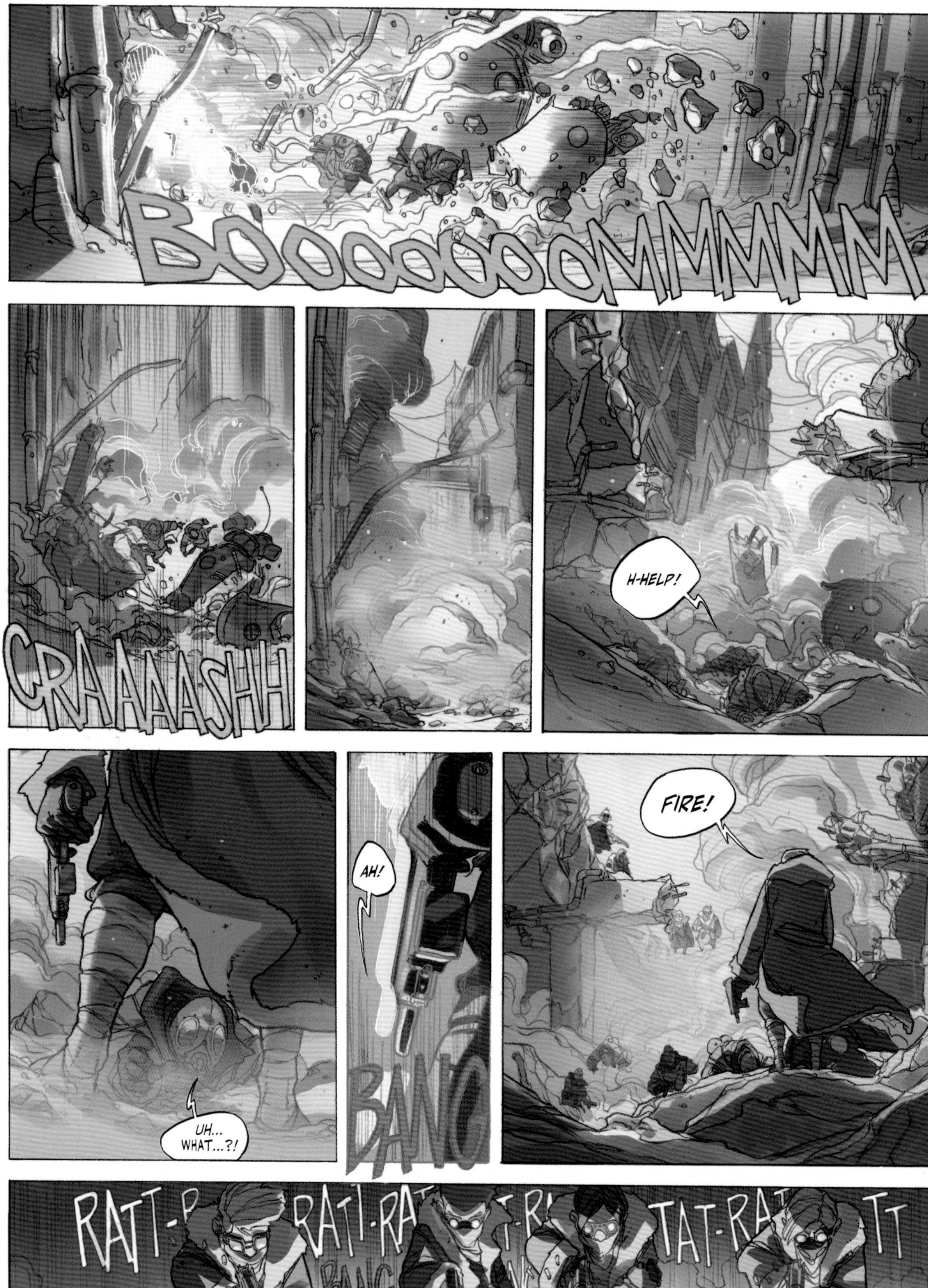
BOOOOOOOMMMMMM
CRAAAASHH
H-HELP!
UH... WHAT...?!
AH!
BANG
FIRE!
RATT-R
RATT-RAT
T-R
TAT-RAT
TT
BANG

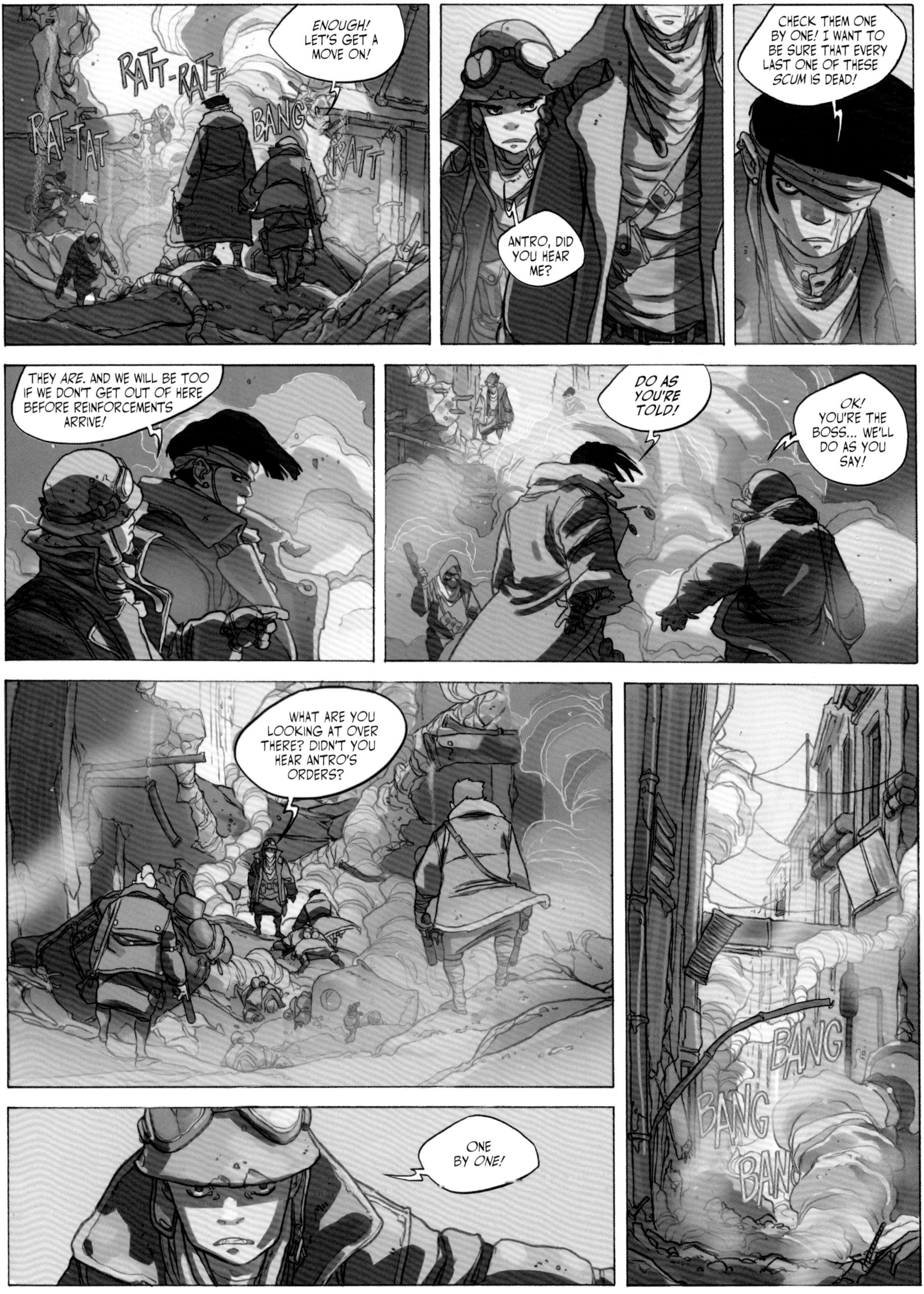
RATT-RATT
RAT-TAT
BANG
RATT
ENOUGH! LET'S GET A MOVE ON!
ANTRO, DID YOU HEAR ME?
CHECK THEM ONE BY ONE! I WANT TO BE SURE THAT EVERY LAST ONE OF THESE SCUM IS DEAD!
THEY ARE. AND WE WILL BE TOO IF WE DON'T GET OUT OF HERE BEFORE REINFORCEMENTS ARRIVE!
DO AS YOU'RE TOLD!
OK! YOU'RE THE BOSS... WE'LL DO AS YOU SAY!
WHAT ARE YOU LOOKING AT OVER THERE? DIDN'T YOU HEAR ANTRO'S ORDERS?
ONE BY ONE!
BANG
BANG

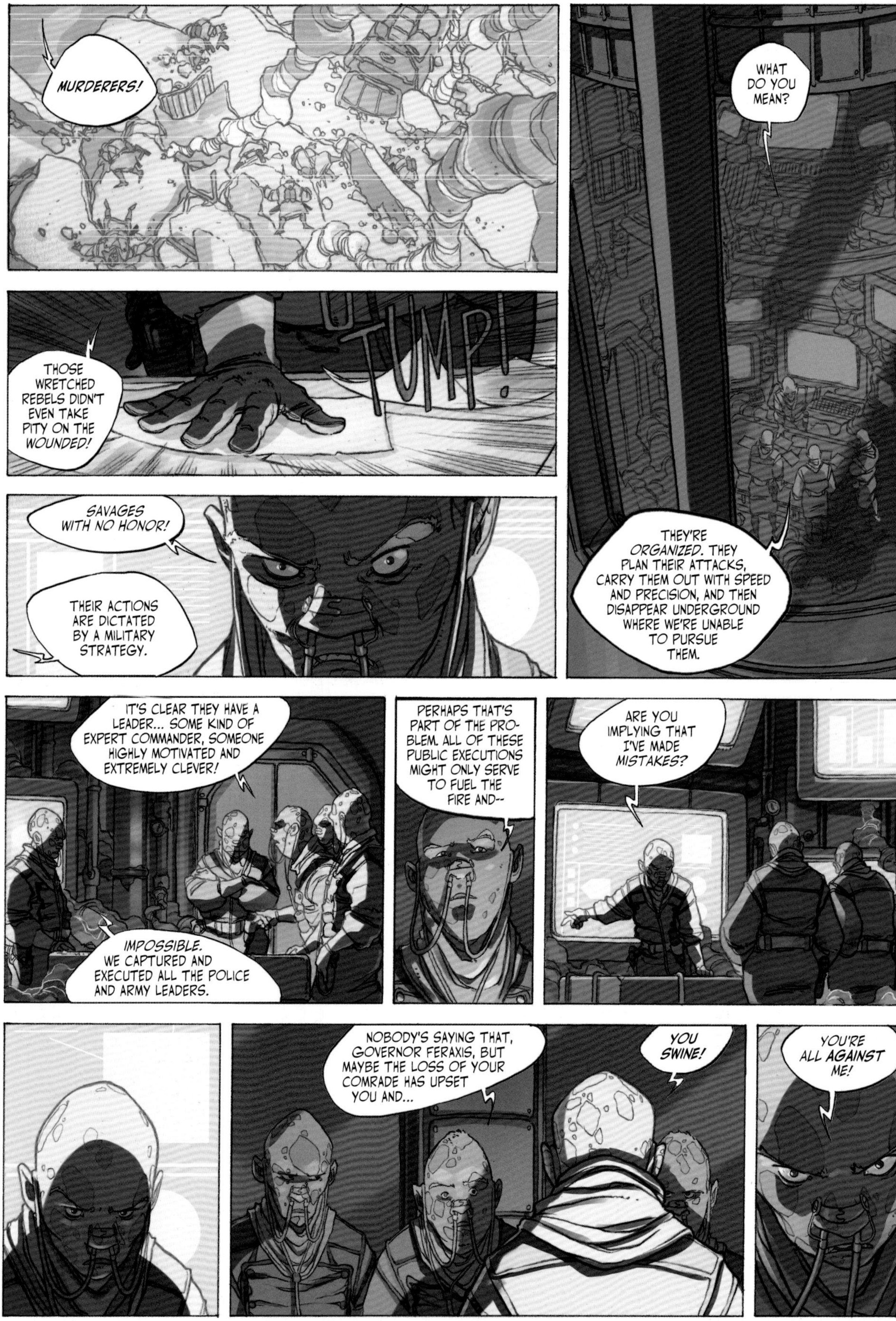

MURDERERS!
THOSE WRETCHED REBELS DIDN'T EVEN TAKE PITY ON THE WOUNDED!
TUMP!
SAVAGES WITH NO HONOR!
THEIR ACTIONS ARE DICTATED BY A MILITARY STRATEGY.
WHAT DO YOU MEAN?
THEY'RE ORGANIZED. THEY PLAN THEIR ATTACKS, CARRY THEM OUT WITH SPEED AND PRECISION, AND THEN DISAPPEAR UNDERGROUND WHERE WE'RE UNABLE TO PURSUE THEM.
IT'S CLEAR THEY HAVE A LEADER... SOME KIND OF EXPERT COMMANDER, SOMEONE HIGHLY MOTIVATED AND EXTREMELY CLEVER!
IMPOSSIBLE. WE CAPTURED AND EXECUTED ALL THE POLICE AND ARMY LEADERS.
PERHAPS THAT'S PART OF THE PRO-BLEM. ALL OF THESE PUBLIC EXECUTIONS MIGHT ONLY SERVE TO FUEL THE FIRE AND--
ARE YOU IMPLYING THAT I'VE MADE MISTAKES?
NOBODY'S SAYING THAT, GOVERNOR FERAXIS, BUT MAYBE THE LOSS OF YOUR COMRADE HAS UPSET YOU AND...
YOU SWINE!
YOU'RE ALL AGAINST ME!

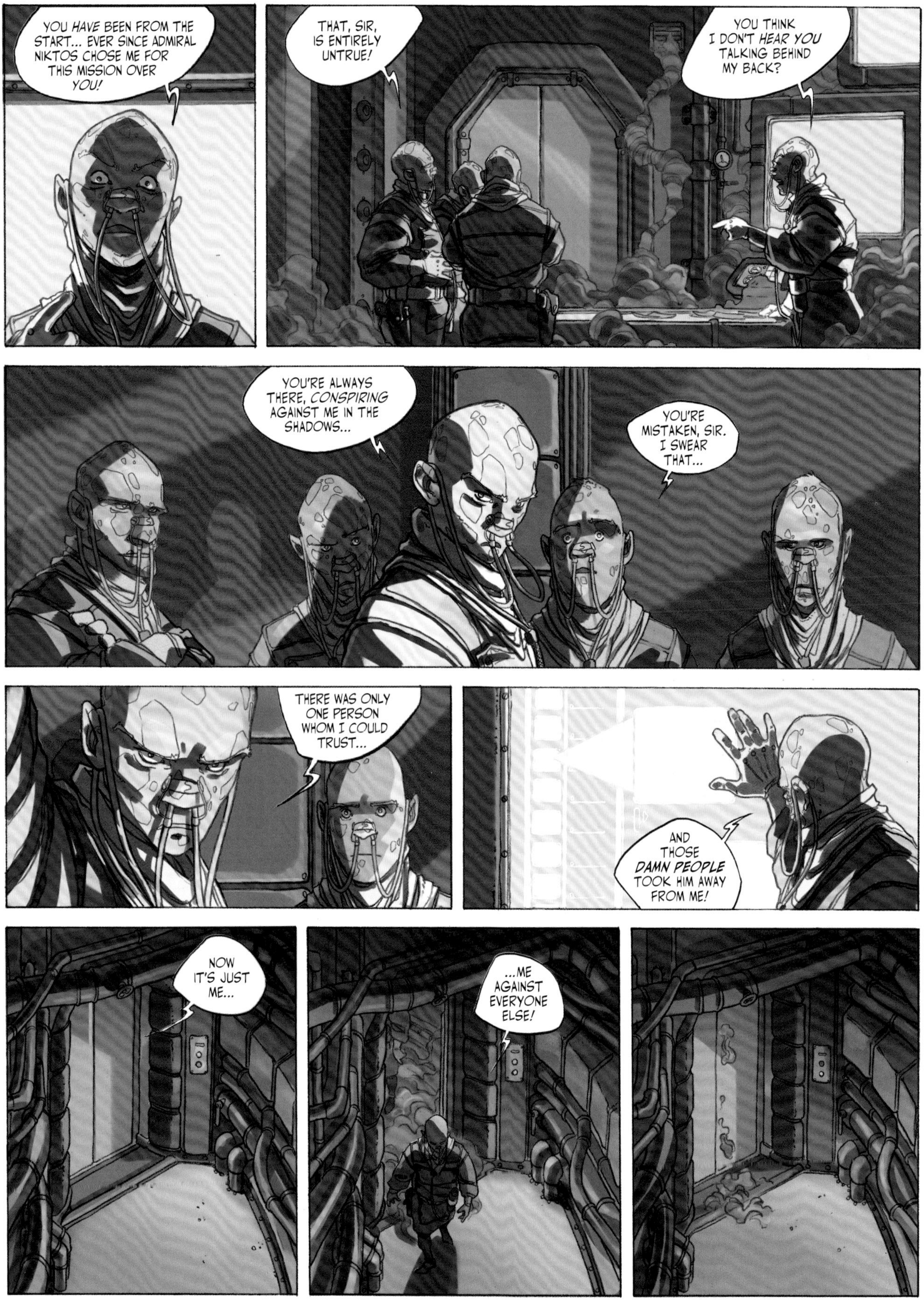

YOU *HAVE* BEEN FROM THE START... EVER SINCE ADMIRAL NIKTOS CHOSE ME FOR THIS MISSION OVER *YOU!*
THAT, SIR, IS ENTIRELY UNTRUE!
YOU THINK I DON'T *HEAR YOU* TALKING BEHIND MY BACK?
YOU'RE ALWAYS THERE, *CONSPIRING* AGAINST ME IN THE SHADOWS...
YOU'RE MISTAKEN, SIR. I SWEAR THAT...
THERE WAS ONLY ONE PERSON WHOM I COULD TRUST...
AND THOSE ***DAMN PEOPLE*** TOOK HIM AWAY FROM ME!
NOW IT'S JUST ME...
...ME AGAINST EVERYONE ELSE!

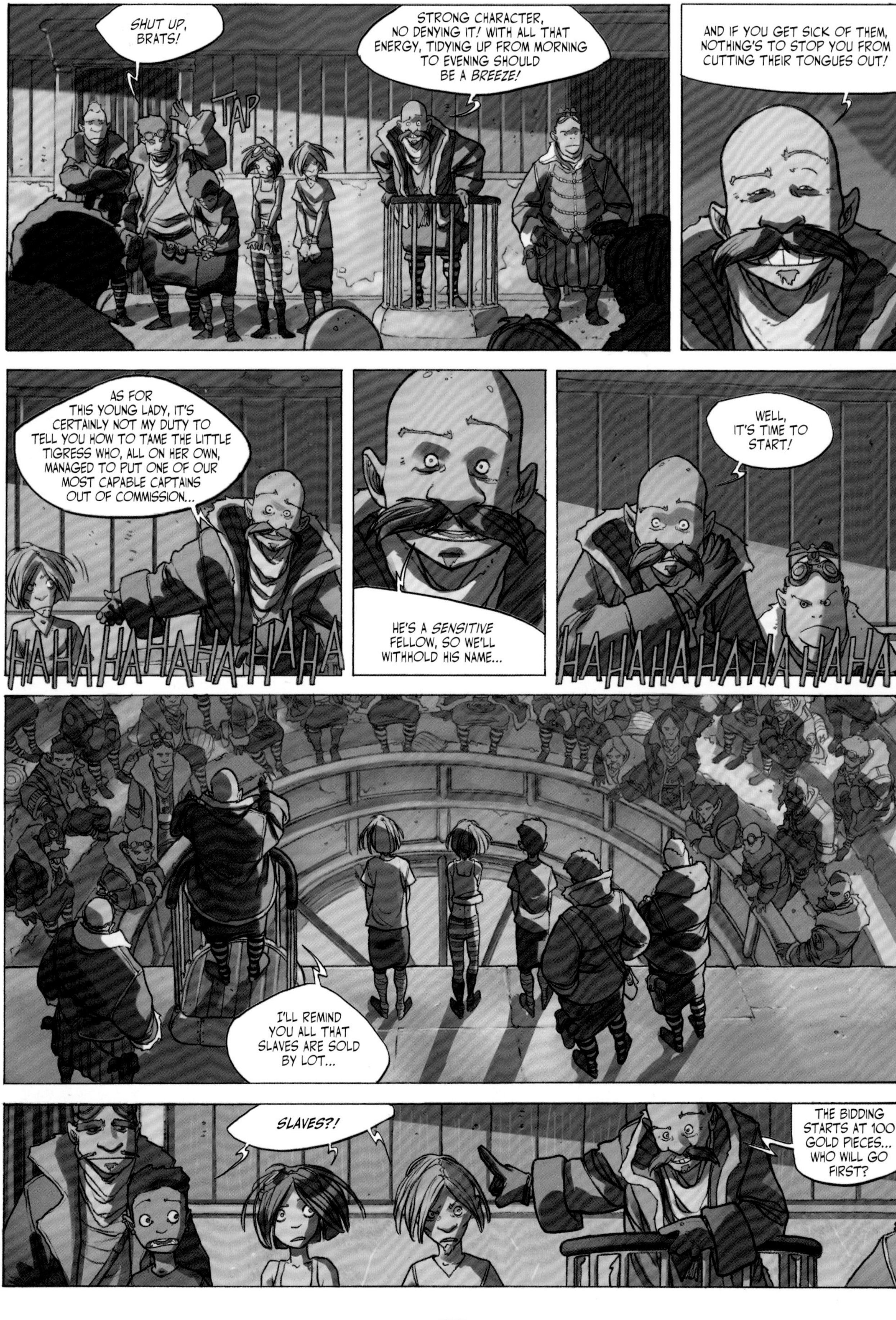
SHUT UP, BRATS!
TAP
STRONG CHARACTER, NO DENYING IT! WITH ALL THAT ENERGY, TIDYING UP FROM MORNING TO EVENING SHOULD BE A BREEZE!
AND IF YOU GET SICK OF THEM, NOTHING'S TO STOP YOU FROM CUTTING THEIR TONGUES OUT!
AS FOR THIS YOUNG LADY, IT'S CERTAINLY NOT MY DUTY TO TELL YOU HOW TO TAME THE LITTLE TIGRESS WHO, ALL ON HER OWN, MANAGED TO PUT ONE OF OUR MOST CAPABLE CAPTAINS OUT OF COMMISSION...
HAHAHAHAHAHAHAHA
HE'S A SENSITIVE FELLOW, SO WE'LL WITHHOLD HIS NAME...
WELL, IT'S TIME TO START!
HAHAHAHAHAHAHAHA
I'LL REMIND YOU ALL THAT SLAVES ARE SOLD BY LOT...
SLAVES?!
THE BIDDING STARTS AT 100 GOLD PIECES... WHO WILL GO FIRST?

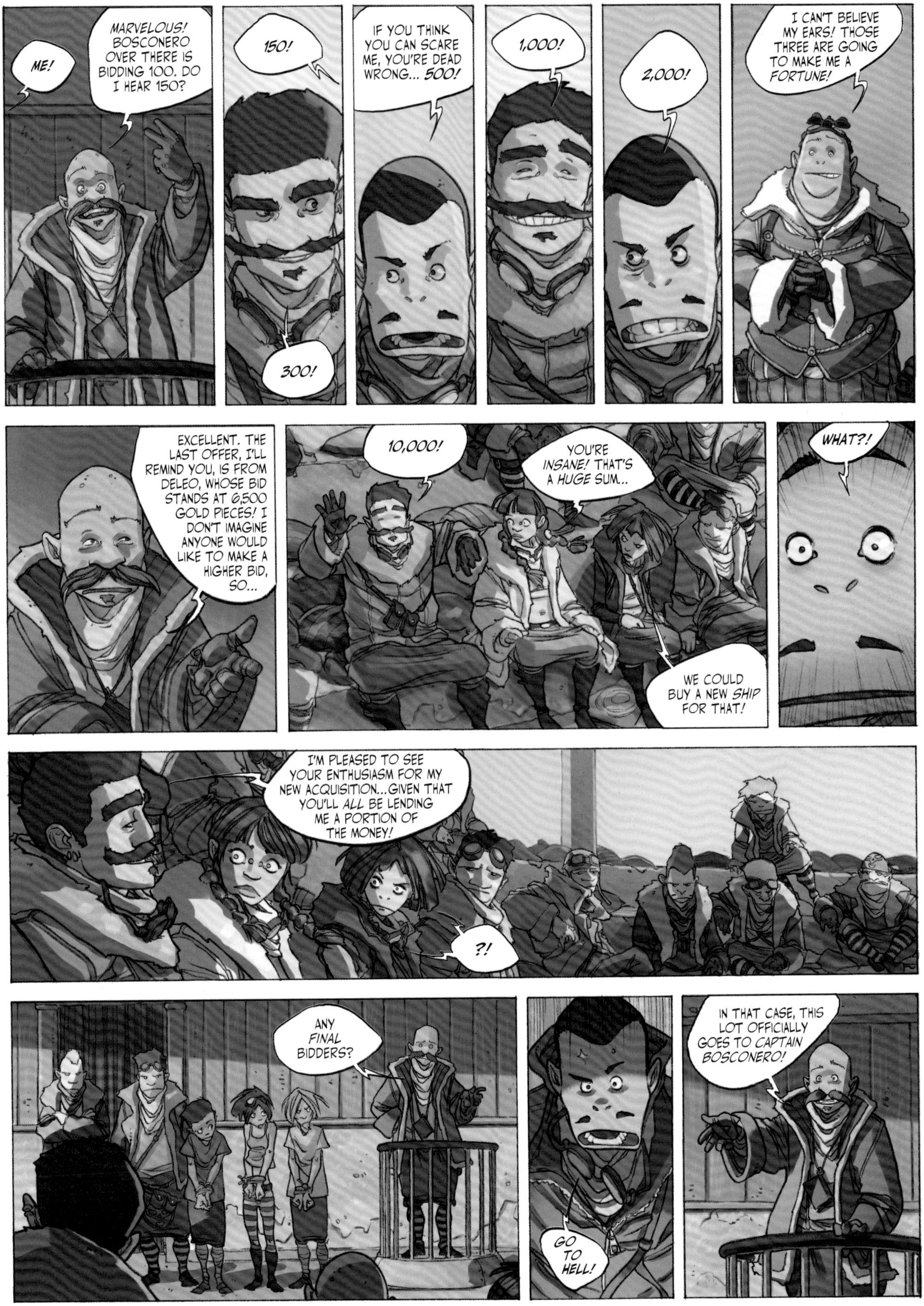
ME!
MARVELOUS! BOSCONERO OVER THERE IS BIDDING 100. DO I HEAR 150?
150!
300!
IF YOU THINK YOU CAN SCARE ME, YOU'RE DEAD WRONG... 500!
1,000!
2,000!
I CAN'T BELIEVE MY EARS! THOSE THREE ARE GOING TO MAKE ME A FORTUNE!
EXCELLENT. THE LAST OFFER, I'LL REMIND YOU, IS FROM DELEO, WHOSE BID STANDS AT 6,500 GOLD PIECES! I DON'T IMAGINE ANYONE WOULD LIKE TO MAKE A HIGHER BID, SO...
10,000!
YOU'RE INSANE! THAT'S A HUGE SUM...
WE COULD BUY A NEW SHIP FOR THAT!
WHAT?!
I'M PLEASED TO SEE YOUR ENTHUSIASM FOR MY NEW ACQUISITION...GIVEN THAT YOU'LL ALL BE LENDING ME A PORTION OF THE MONEY!
?!
ANY FINAL BIDDERS?
GO TO HELL!
IN THAT CASE, THIS LOT OFFICIALLY GOES TO CAPTAIN BOSCONERO!

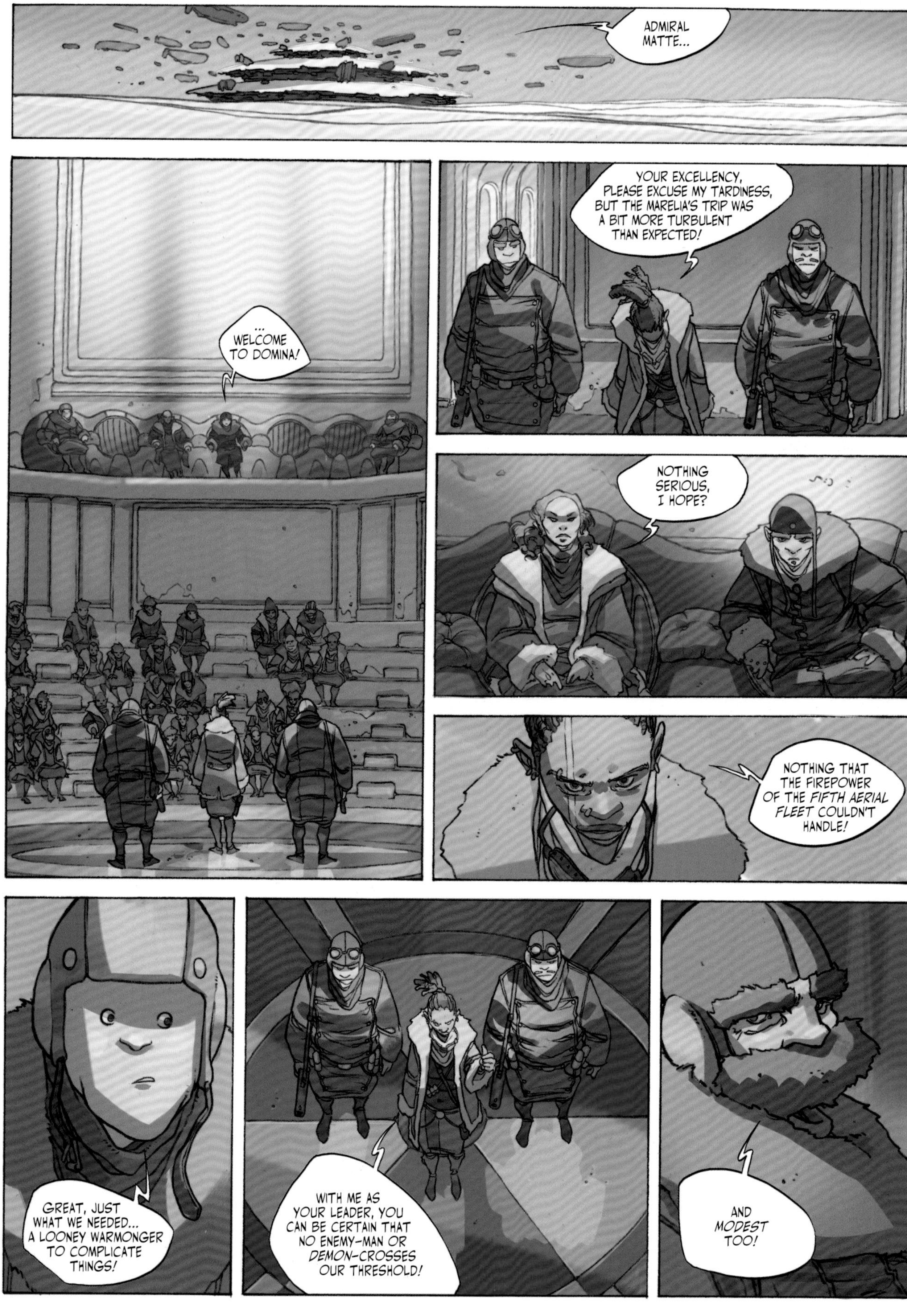
ADMIRAL MATTE...
... WELCOME TO DOMINA!
YOUR EXCELLENCY, PLEASE EXCUSE MY TARDINESS, BUT THE MARELIA'S TRIP WAS A BIT MORE TURBULENT THAN EXPECTED!
NOTHING SERIOUS, I HOPE?
NOTHING THAT THE FIREPOWER OF THE *FIFTH AERIAL FLEET* COULDN'T HANDLE!
GREAT, JUST WHAT WE NEEDED... A LOONEY WARMONGER TO COMPLICATE THINGS!
WITH ME AS YOUR LEADER, YOU CAN BE CERTAIN THAT NO ENEMY—MAN OR *DEMON*—CROSSES OUR THRESHOLD!
AND *MODEST* TOO!

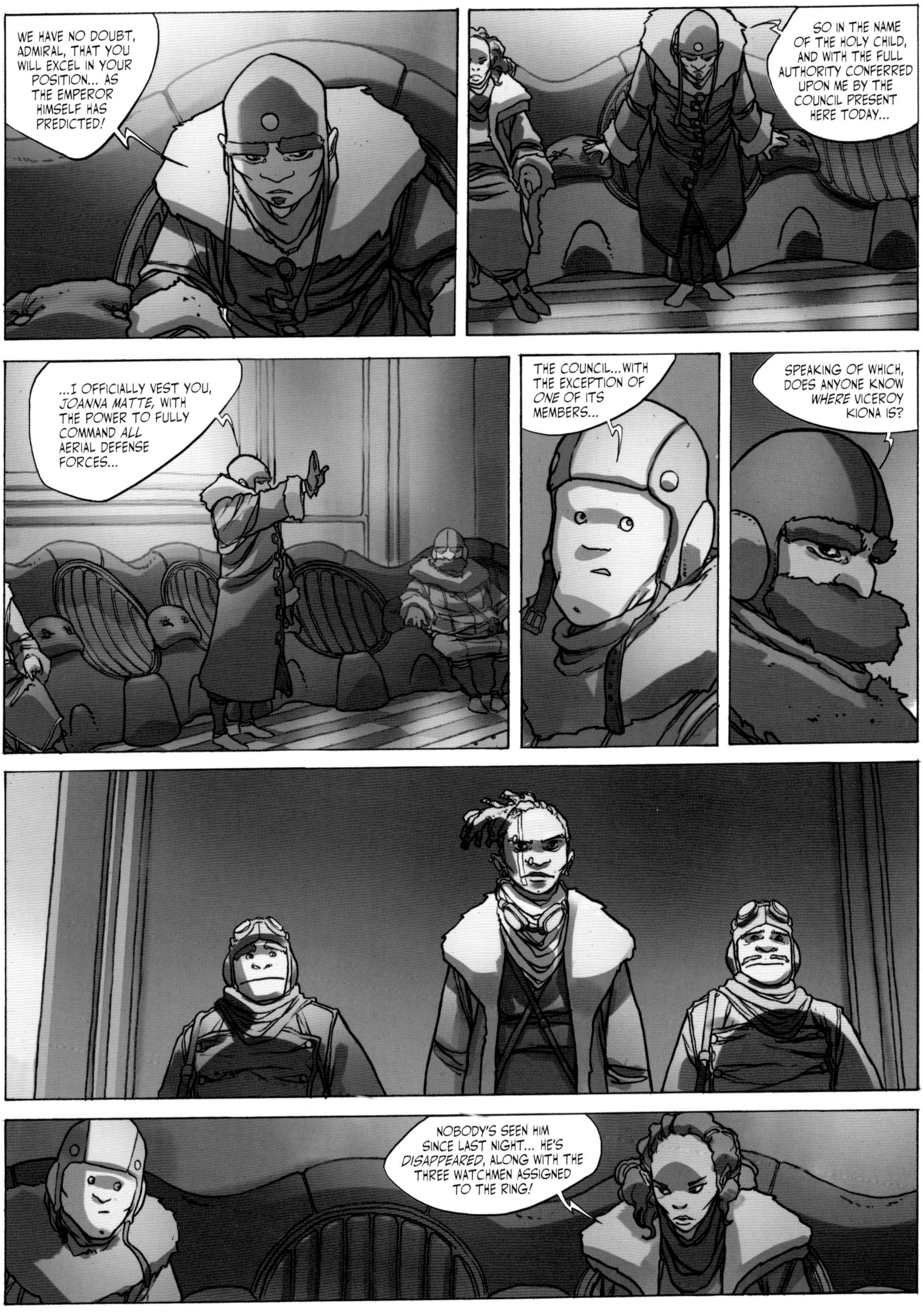
WE HAVE NO DOUBT, ADMIRAL, THAT YOU WILL EXCEL IN YOUR POSITION... AS THE EMPEROR HIMSELF HAS PREDICTED!
SO IN THE NAME OF THE HOLY CHILD, AND WITH THE FULL AUTHORITY CONFERRED UPON ME BY THE COUNCIL PRESENT HERE TODAY...
...I OFFICIALLY VEST YOU, JOANNA MATTE, WITH THE POWER TO FULLY COMMAND ALL AERIAL DEFENSE FORCES...
THE COUNCIL...WITH THE EXCEPTION OF ONE OF ITS MEMBERS...
SPEAKING OF WHICH, DOES ANYONE KNOW WHERE VICEROY KIONA IS?
NOBODY'S SEEN HIM SINCE LAST NIGHT... HE'S DISAPPEARED, ALONG WITH THE THREE WATCHMEN ASSIGNED TO THE RING!

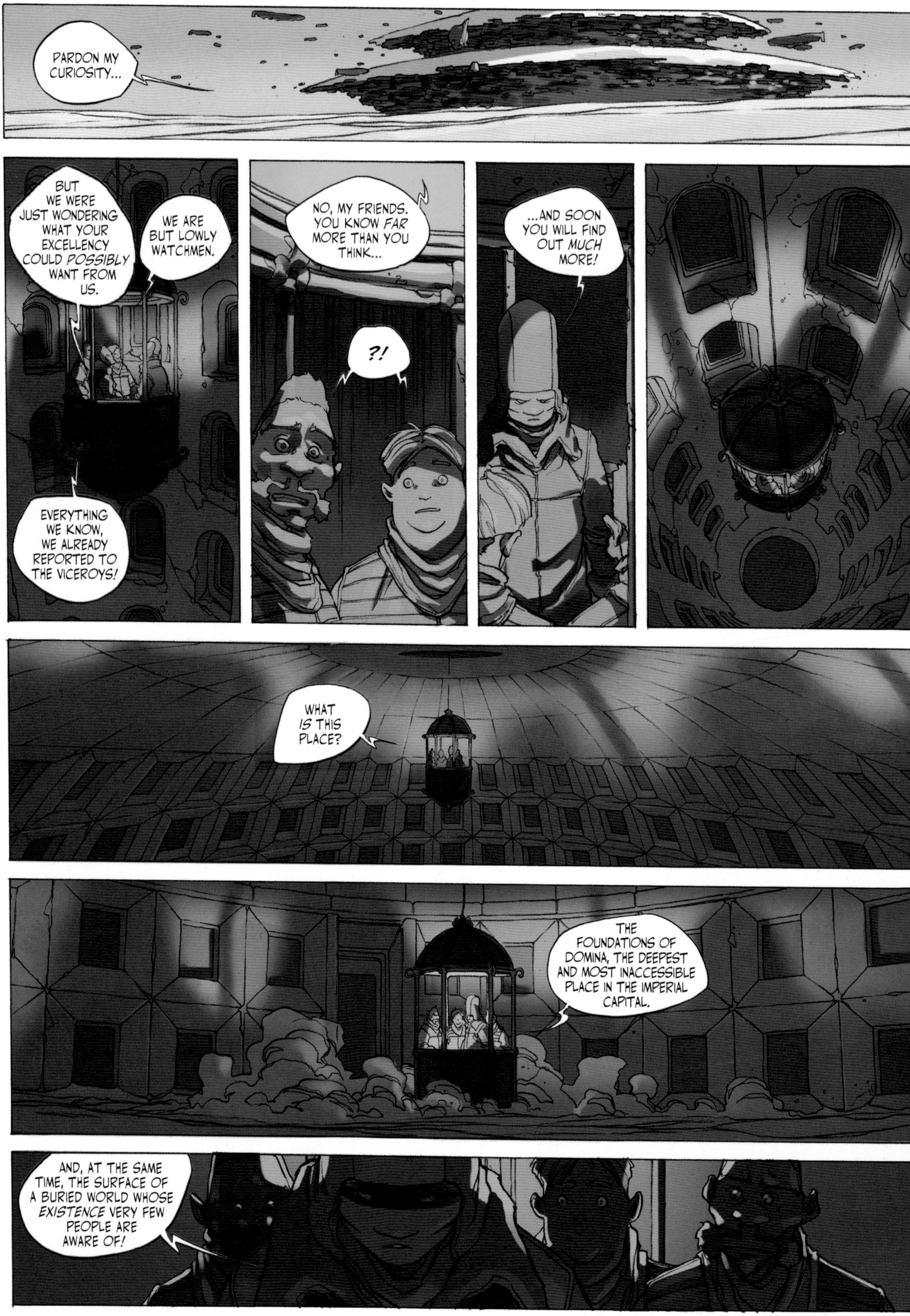
PARDON MY CURIOSITY...
BUT WE WERE JUST WONDERING WHAT YOUR EXCELLENCY COULD *POSSIBLY* WANT FROM US.
WE ARE BUT LOWLY WATCHMEN.
EVERYTHING WE KNOW, WE ALREADY REPORTED TO THE VICEROYS!
NO, MY FRIENDS. YOU KNOW *FAR* MORE THAN YOU THINK...
?!
...AND SOON YOU WILL FIND OUT *MUCH* MORE!
WHAT *IS* THIS PLACE?
THE FOUNDATIONS OF DOMINA, THE DEEPEST AND MOST INACCESSIBLE PLACE IN THE IMPERIAL CAPITAL.
AND, AT THE SAME TIME, THE SURFACE OF A BURIED WORLD WHOSE *EXISTENCE* VERY FEW PEOPLE ARE AWARE OF!

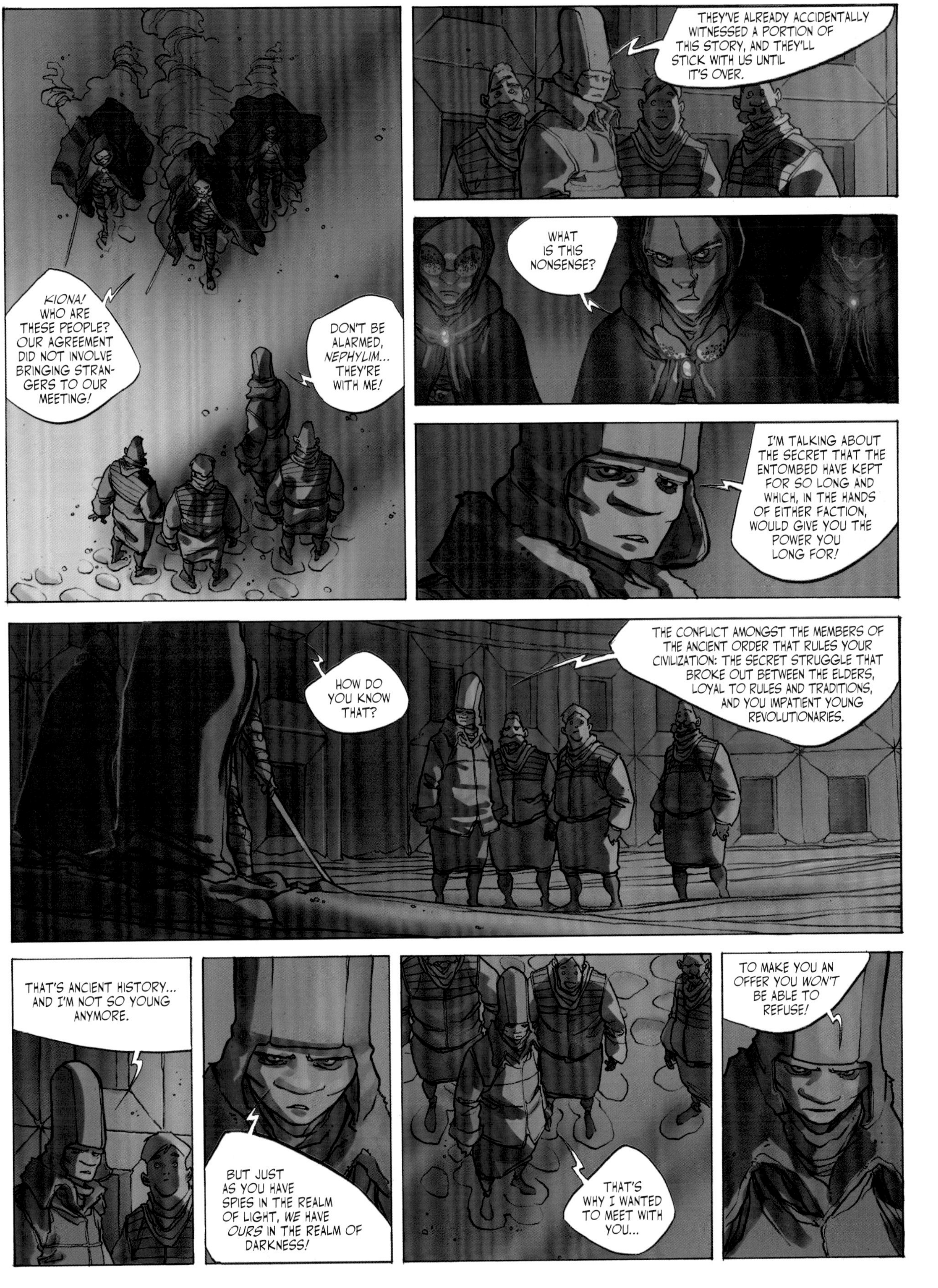
KIONA! WHO ARE THESE PEOPLE? OUR AGREEMENT DID NOT INVOLVE BRINGING STRANGERS TO OUR MEETING!
DON'T BE ALARMED, NEPHYLIM... THEY'RE WITH ME!
THEY'VE ALREADY ACCIDENTALLY WITNESSED A PORTION OF THIS STORY, AND THEY'LL STICK WITH US UNTIL IT'S OVER.
WHAT IS THIS NONSENSE?
I'M TALKING ABOUT THE SECRET THAT THE ENTOMBED HAVE KEPT FOR SO LONG AND WHICH, IN THE HANDS OF EITHER FACTION, WOULD GIVE YOU THE POWER YOU LONG FOR!
HOW DO YOU KNOW THAT?
THE CONFLICT AMONGST THE MEMBERS OF THE ANCIENT ORDER THAT RULES YOUR CIVILIZATION: THE SECRET STRUGGLE THAT BROKE OUT BETWEEN THE ELDERS, LOYAL TO RULES AND TRADITIONS, AND YOU IMPATIENT YOUNG REVOLUTIONARIES.
THAT'S ANCIENT HISTORY... AND I'M NOT SO YOUNG ANYMORE.
BUT JUST AS YOU HAVE SPIES IN THE REALM OF LIGHT, WE HAVE OURS IN THE REALM OF DARKNESS!
THAT'S WHY I WANTED TO MEET WITH YOU...
TO MAKE YOU AN OFFER YOU WON'T BE ABLE TO REFUSE!

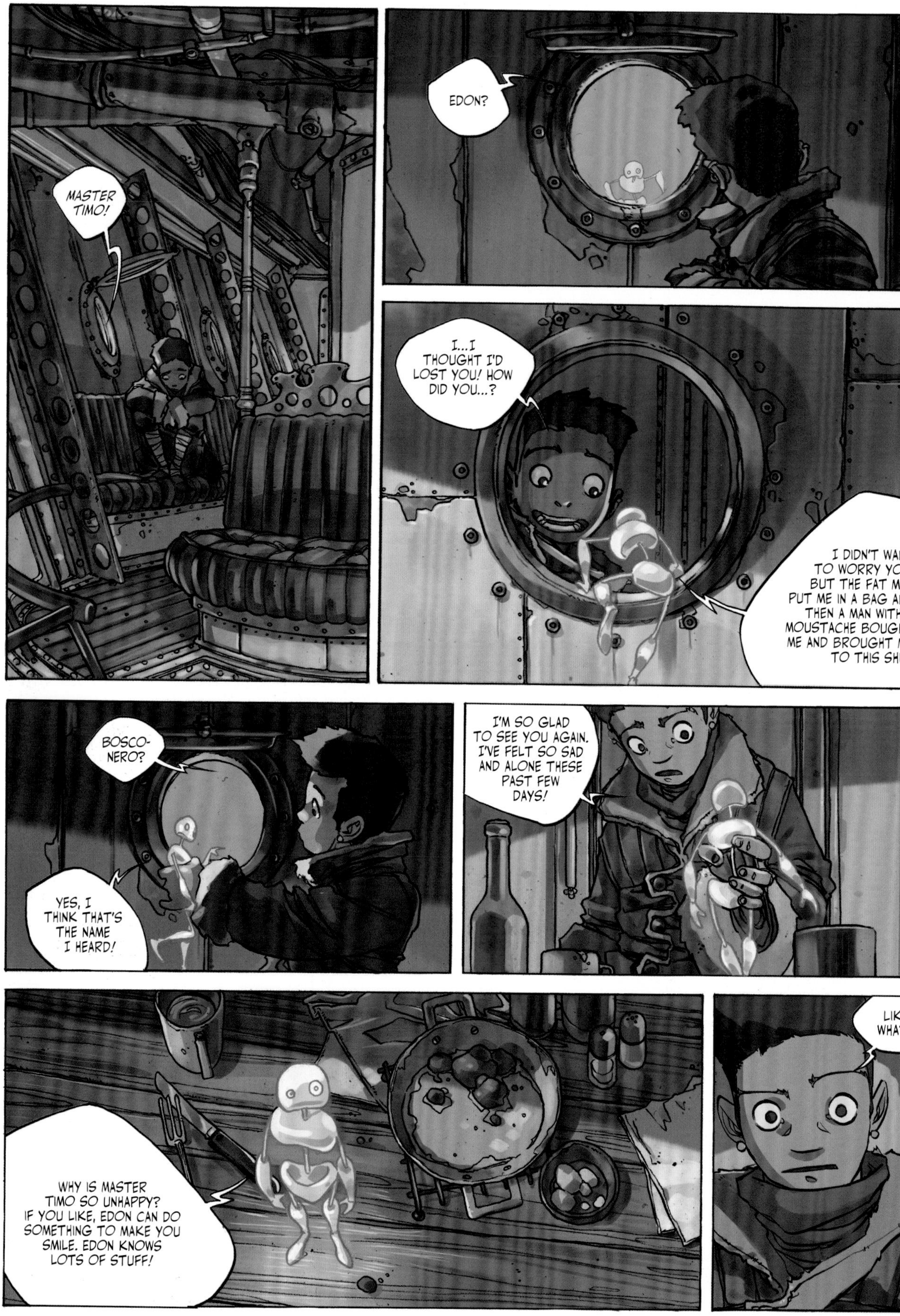
MASTER TIMO!
EDON?
I...I THOUGHT I'D LOST YOU! HOW DID YOU...?
I DIDN'T WANT TO WORRY YOU, BUT THE FAT MAN PUT ME IN A BAG AND THEN A MAN WITH A MOUSTACHE BOUGHT ME AND BROUGHT ME TO THIS SHIP.
BOSCO-NERO?
YES, I THINK THAT'S THE NAME I HEARD!
I'M SO GLAD TO SEE YOU AGAIN. I'VE FELT SO SAD AND ALONE THESE PAST FEW DAYS!
WHY IS MASTER TIMO SO UNHAPPY? IF YOU LIKE, EDON CAN DO SOMETHING TO MAKE YOU SMILE. EDON KNOWS LOTS OF STUFF!
LIKE WHAT?

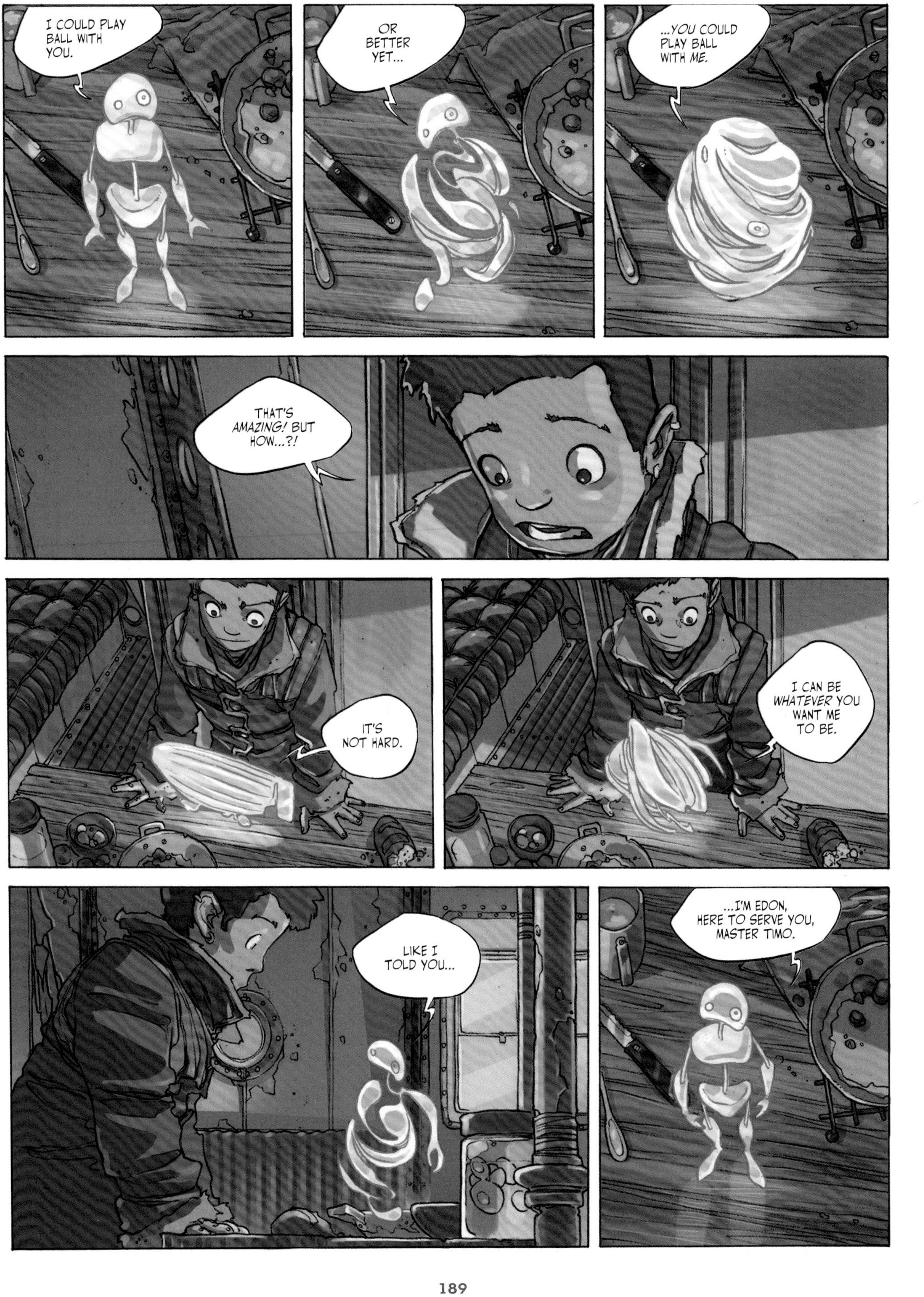
I COULD PLAY BALL WITH YOU.
OR BETTER YET...
...YOU COULD PLAY BALL WITH *ME.*
THAT'S *AMAZING!* BUT HOW...?!
IT'S NOT HARD.
I CAN BE *WHATEVER* YOU WANT ME TO BE.
LIKE I TOLD YOU...
...I'M EDON, HERE TO SERVE YOU, MASTER TIMO.

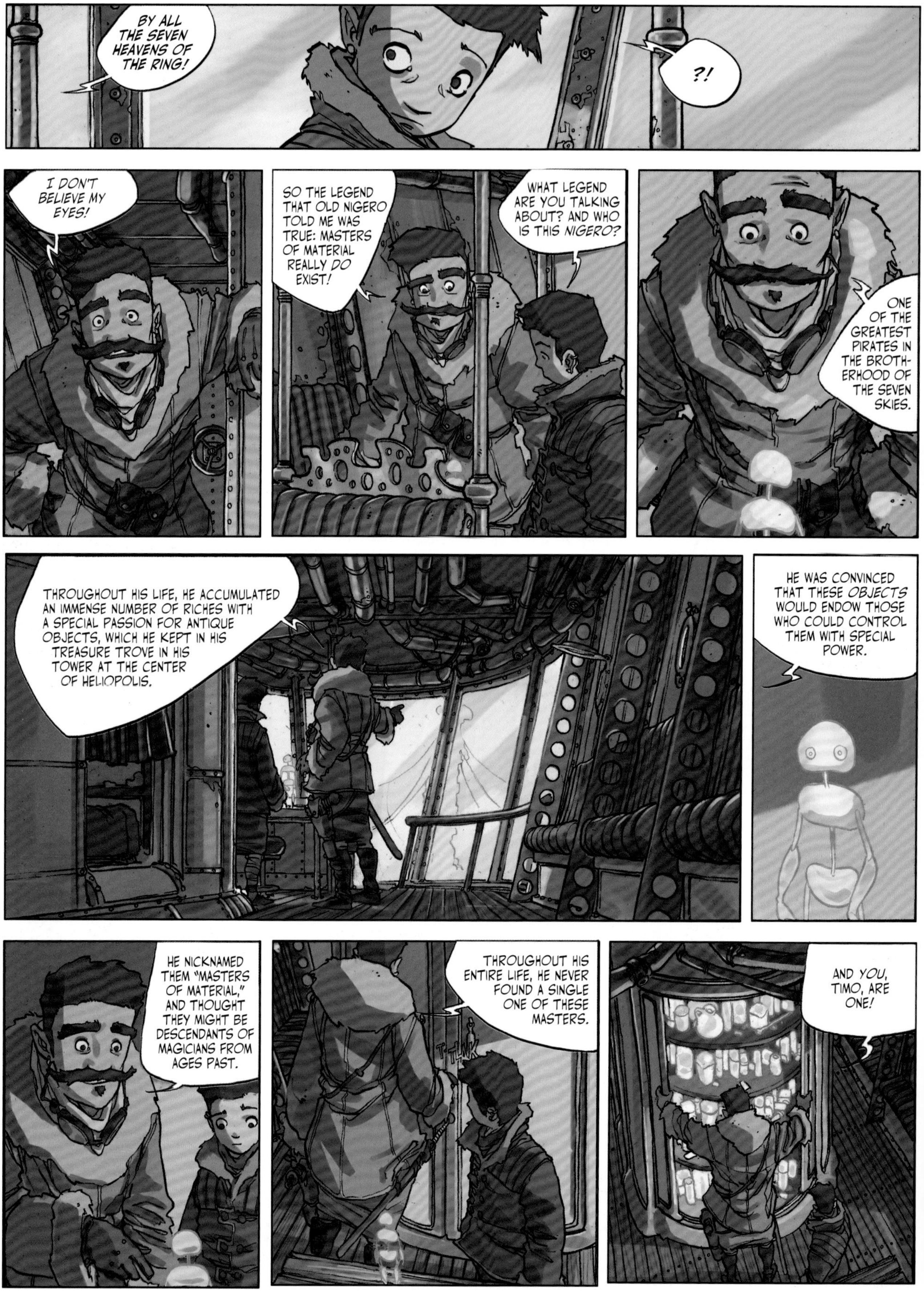

BY ALL THE SEVEN HEAVENS OF THE RING!
?!
I DON'T BELIEVE MY EYES!
SO THE LEGEND THAT OLD NIGERO TOLD ME WAS TRUE: MASTERS OF MATERIAL REALLY *DO* EXIST!
WHAT LEGEND ARE YOU TALKING ABOUT? AND WHO IS THIS *NIGERO*?
ONE OF THE GREATEST PIRATES IN THE BROTHERHOOD OF THE SEVEN SKIES.
THROUGHOUT HIS LIFE, HE ACCUMULATED AN IMMENSE NUMBER OF RICHES WITH A SPECIAL PASSION FOR ANTIQUE OBJECTS, WHICH HE KEPT IN HIS TREASURE TROVE IN HIS TOWER AT THE CENTER OF HELIOPOLIS.
HE WAS CONVINCED THAT THESE *OBJECTS* WOULD ENDOW THOSE WHO COULD CONTROL THEM WITH SPECIAL POWER.
HE NICKNAMED THEM "MASTERS OF MATERIAL," AND THOUGHT THEY MIGHT BE DESCENDANTS OF MAGICIANS FROM AGES PAST.
THROUGHOUT HIS ENTIRE LIFE, HE NEVER FOUND A SINGLE ONE OF THESE MASTERS.
T'TLAK
AND *YOU*, TIMO, ARE ONE!

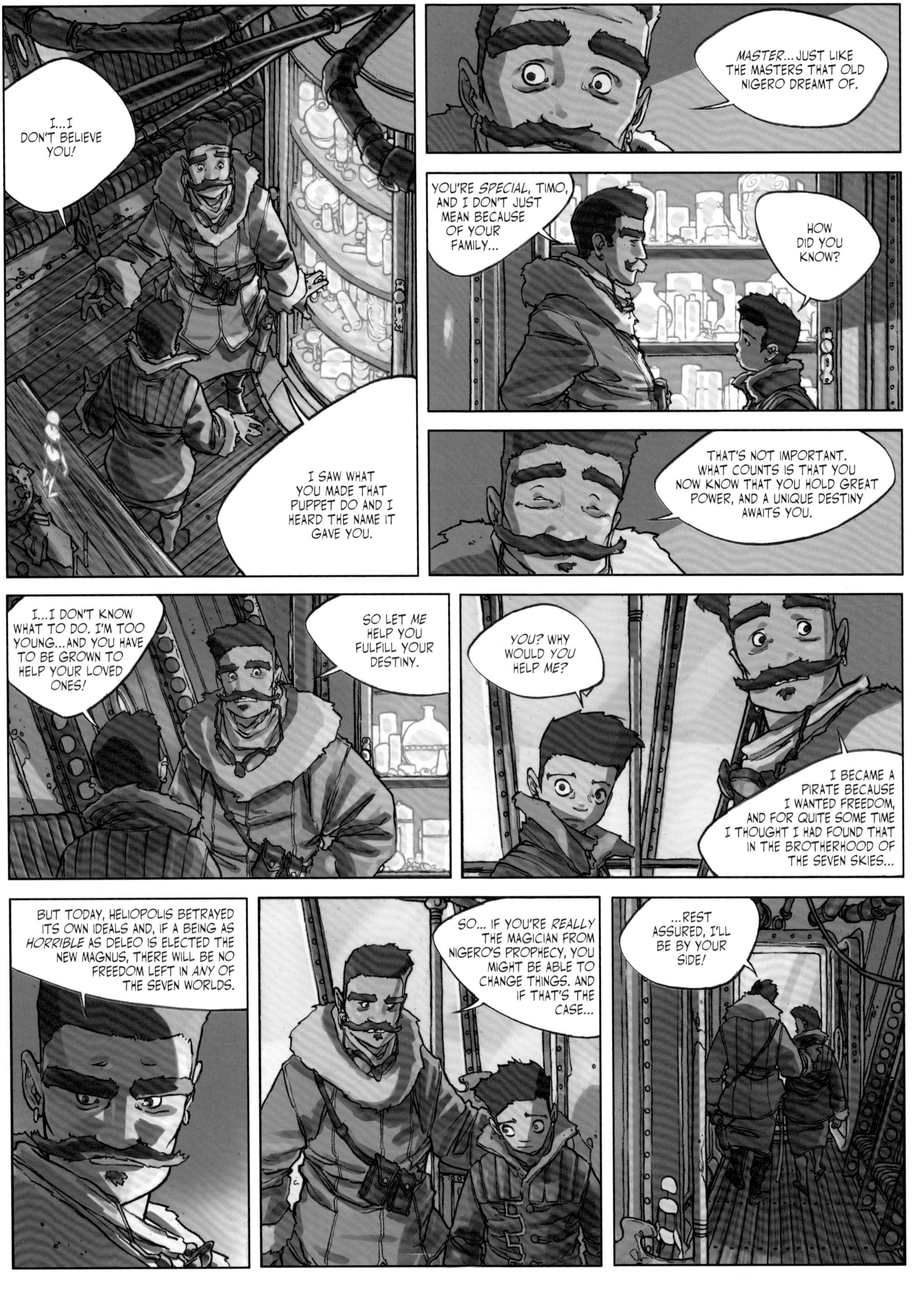
I...I DON'T BELIEVE YOU!
I SAW WHAT YOU MADE THAT PUPPET DO AND I HEARD THE NAME IT GAVE YOU.
MASTER... JUST LIKE THE MASTERS THAT OLD NIGERO DREAMT OF.
YOU'RE *SPECIAL*, TIMO, AND I DON'T JUST MEAN BECAUSE OF YOUR FAMILY...
HOW DID YOU KNOW?
THAT'S NOT IMPORTANT. WHAT COUNTS IS THAT YOU NOW KNOW THAT YOU HOLD GREAT POWER, AND A UNIQUE DESTINY AWAITS YOU.
I...I DON'T KNOW WHAT TO DO. I'M TOO YOUNG...AND YOU HAVE TO BE GROWN TO HELP YOUR LOVED ONES!
SO LET *ME* HELP YOU FULFILL YOUR DESTINY.
YOU? WHY WOULD *YOU* HELP *ME*?
I BECAME A PIRATE BECAUSE I WANTED FREEDOM, AND FOR QUITE SOME TIME I THOUGHT I HAD FOUND THAT IN THE BROTHERHOOD OF THE SEVEN SKIES...
BUT TODAY, HELIOPOLIS BETRAYED ITS OWN IDEALS AND, IF A BEING AS *HORRIBLE* AS DELEO IS ELECTED THE NEW MAGNUS, THERE WILL BE NO FREEDOM LEFT IN *ANY* OF THE SEVEN WORLDS.
SO... IF YOU'RE *REALLY* THE MAGICIAN FROM NIGERO'S PROPHECY, YOU MIGHT BE ABLE TO CHANGE THINGS. AND IF THAT'S THE CASE...
...REST ASSURED, I'LL BE BY YOUR SIDE!

MASTER TIMO IS RIGHT ...

YOU HAVE TO BE GROWN...

...TO HELP YOUR LOVED ONES!

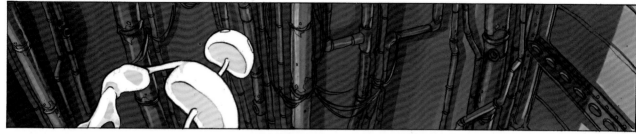

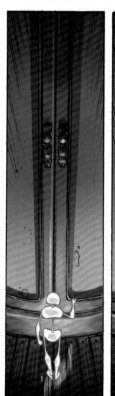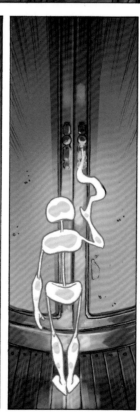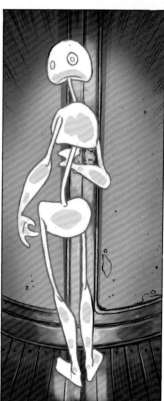

AND OVER THERE I'M GOING TO FIND WHAT I NEED TO BECOME EVEN BIGGER!

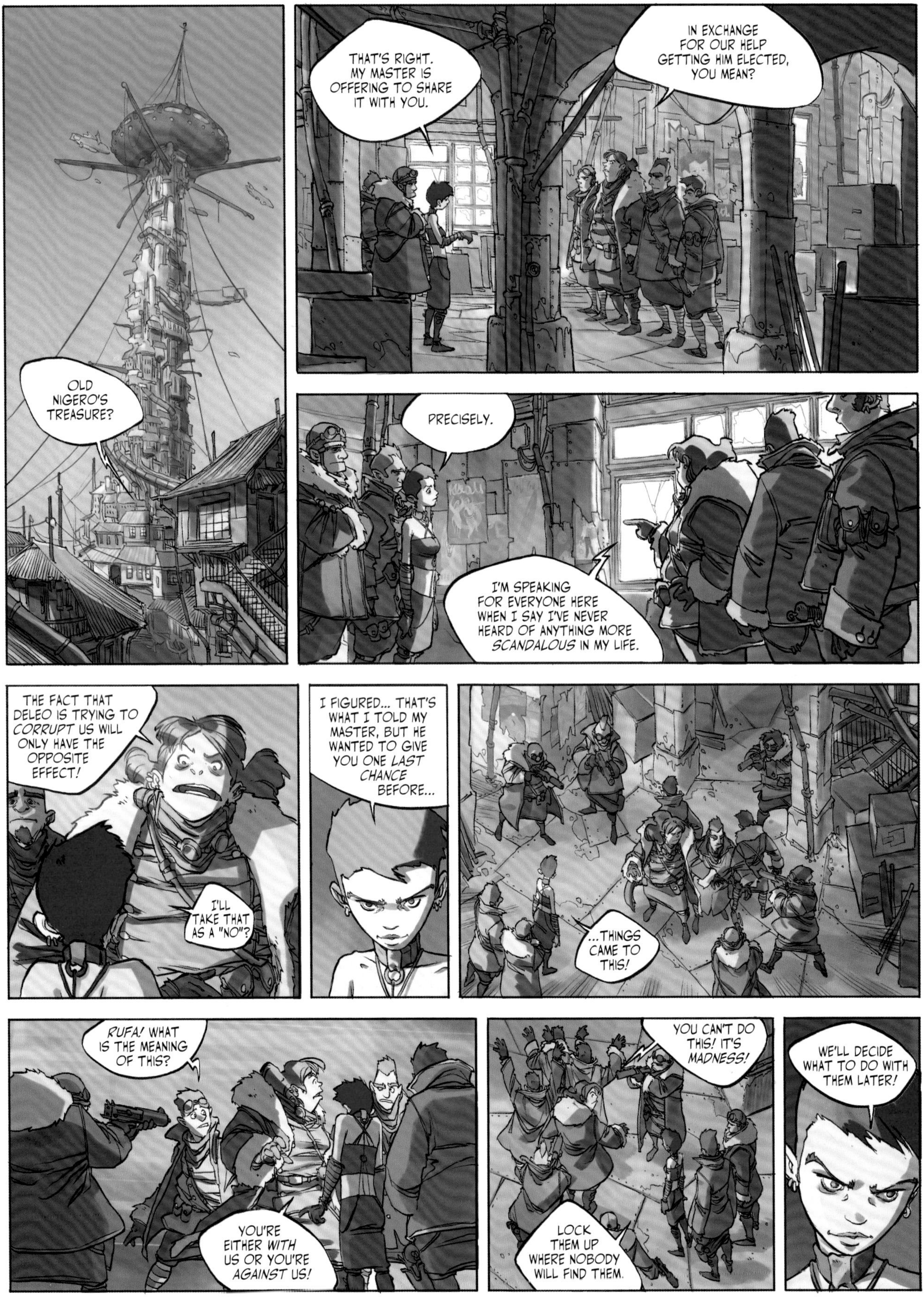
THAT'S RIGHT. MY MASTER IS OFFERING TO SHARE IT WITH YOU.
IN EXCHANGE FOR OUR HELP GETTING HIM ELECTED, YOU MEAN?
OLD NIGERO'S TREASURE?
PRECISELY.
I'M SPEAKING FOR EVERYONE HERE WHEN I SAY I'VE NEVER HEARD OF ANYTHING MORE *SCANDALOUS* IN MY LIFE.
THE FACT THAT DELEO IS TRYING TO *CORRUPT* US WILL ONLY HAVE THE OPPOSITE EFFECT!
I'LL TAKE THAT AS A "NO"?
I FIGURED... THAT'S WHAT I TOLD MY MASTER, BUT HE WANTED TO GIVE YOU ONE *LAST CHANCE* BEFORE...
...THINGS CAME TO THIS!
RUFA! WHAT IS THE MEANING OF THIS?
YOU'RE EITHER *WITH* US OR YOU'RE *AGAINST* US!
YOU CAN'T DO THIS! IT'S *MADNESS!*
LOCK THEM UP WHERE NOBODY WILL FIND THEM.
WE'LL DECIDE WHAT TO DO WITH THEM LATER!

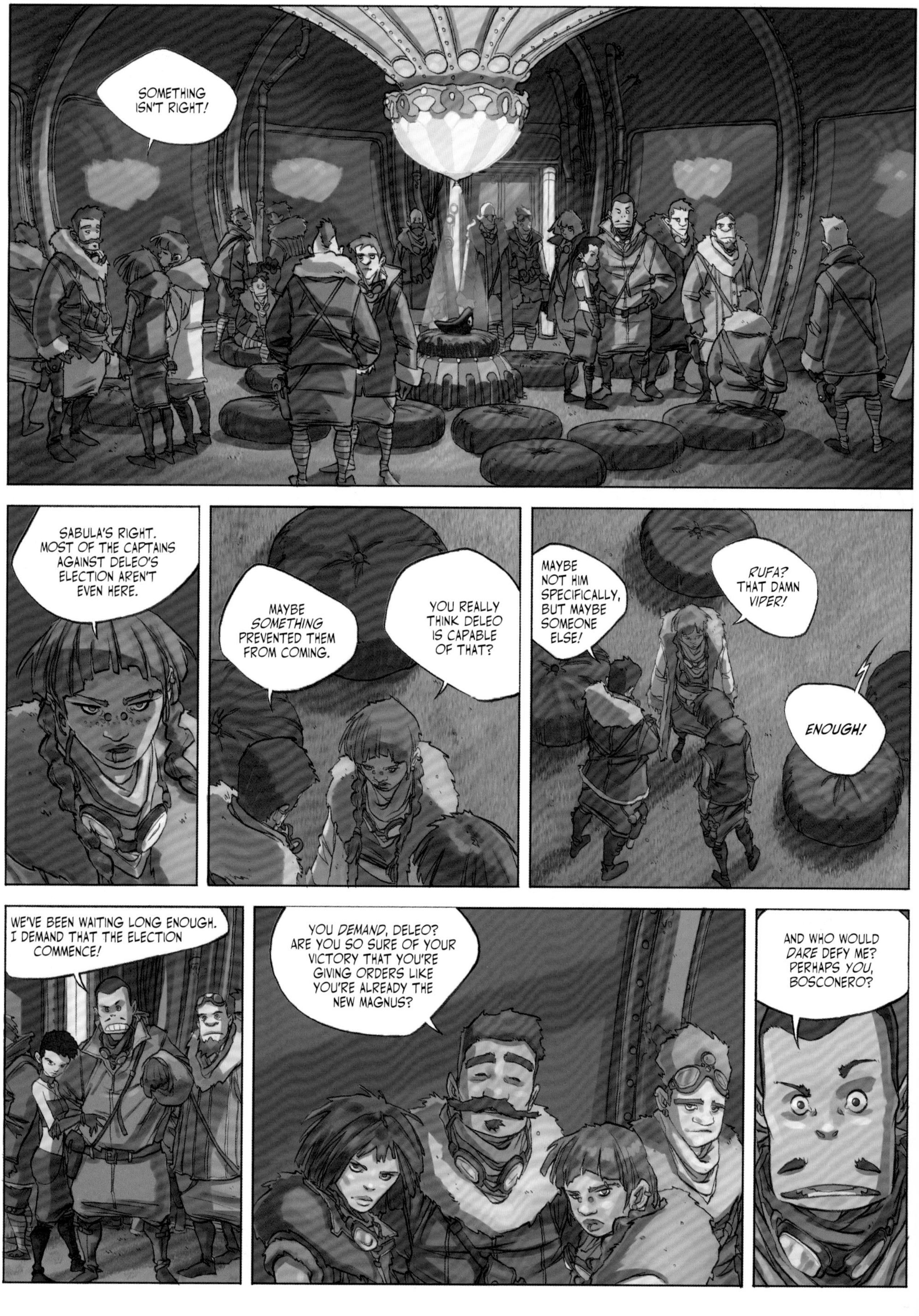
SOMETHING ISN'T RIGHT!
SABULA'S RIGHT. MOST OF THE CAPTAINS AGAINST DELEO'S ELECTION AREN'T EVEN HERE.
MAYBE *SOMETHING* PREVENTED THEM FROM COMING.
YOU REALLY THINK DELEO IS CAPABLE OF THAT?
MAYBE NOT HIM SPECIFICALLY, BUT MAYBE SOMEONE ELSE!
RUFA? THAT DAMN *VIPER!*
ENOUGH!
WE'VE BEEN WAITING LONG ENOUGH. I DEMAND THAT THE ELECTION COMMENCE!
YOU *DEMAND*, DELEO? ARE YOU SO SURE OF YOUR VICTORY THAT YOU'RE GIVING ORDERS LIKE YOU'RE ALREADY THE NEW MAGNUS?
AND WHO WOULD *DARE* DEFY ME? PERHAPS *YOU*, BOSCONERO?

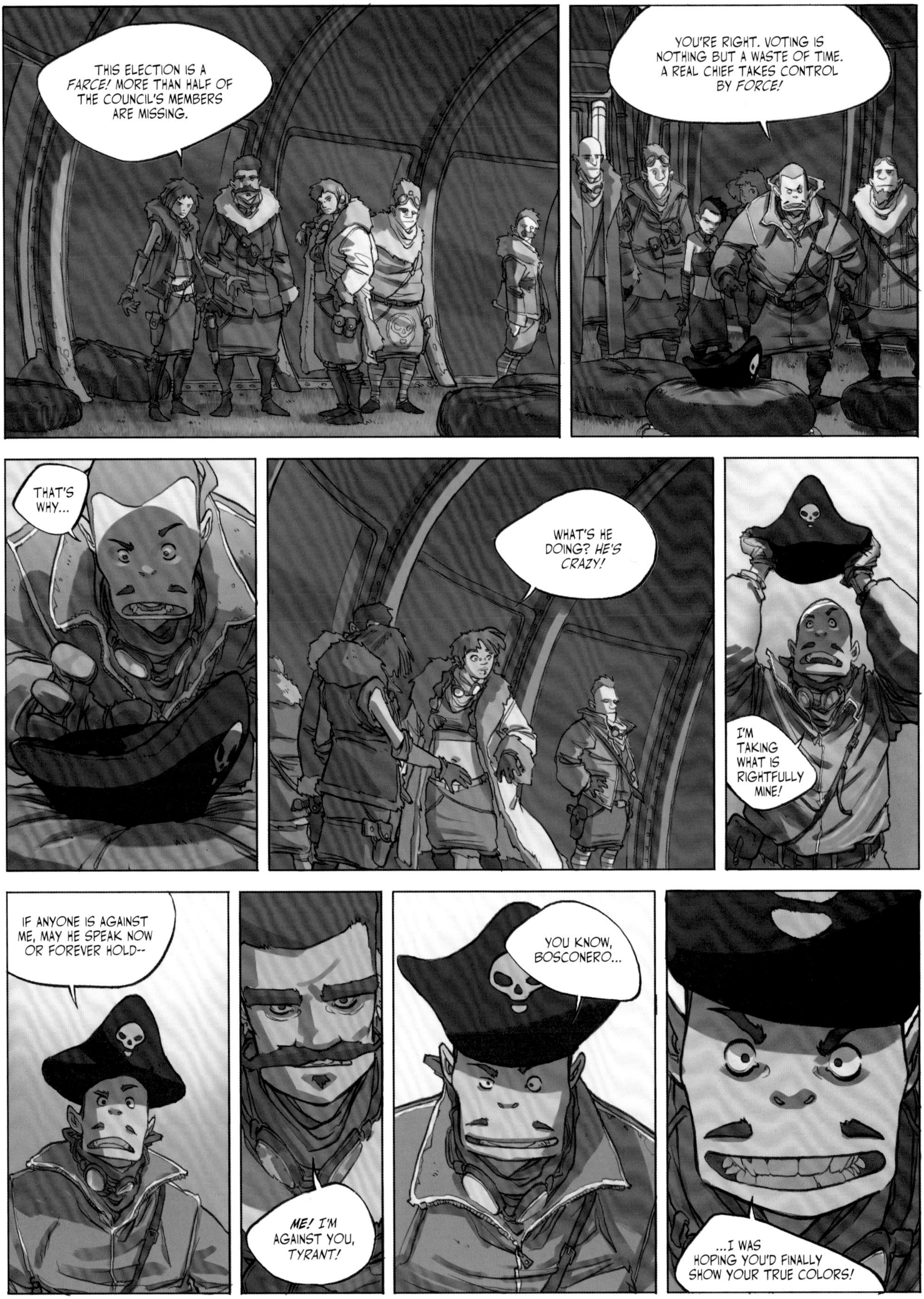
THIS ELECTION IS A FARCE! MORE THAN HALF OF THE COUNCIL'S MEMBERS ARE MISSING.
YOU'RE RIGHT. VOTING IS NOTHING BUT A WASTE OF TIME. A REAL CHIEF TAKES CONTROL BY FORCE!
THAT'S WHY...
WHAT'S HE DOING? HE'S CRAZY!
I'M TAKING WHAT IS RIGHTFULLY MINE!
IF ANYONE IS AGAINST ME, MAY HE SPEAK NOW OR FOREVER HOLD--
ME! I'M AGAINST YOU, TYRANT!
YOU KNOW, BOSCONERO...
...I WAS HOPING YOU'D FINALLY SHOW YOUR TRUE COLORS!

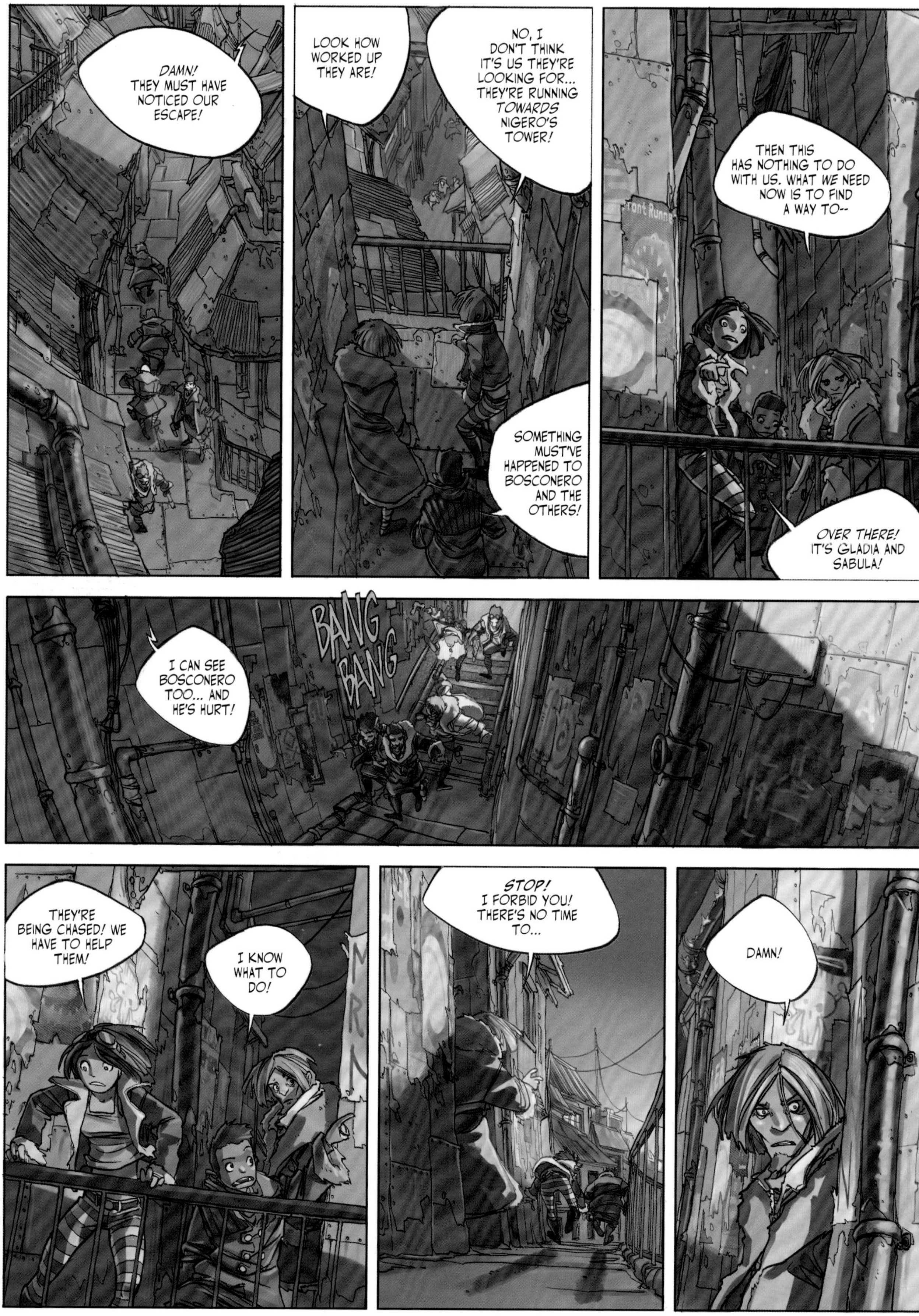
DAMN! THEY MUST HAVE NOTICED OUR ESCAPE!
LOOK HOW WORKED UP THEY ARE!
NO, I DON'T THINK IT'S US THEY'RE LOOKING FOR... THEY'RE RUNNING TOWARDS NIGERO'S TOWER!
SOMETHING MUST'VE HAPPENED TO BOSCONERO AND THE OTHERS!
THEN THIS HAS NOTHING TO DO WITH US. WHAT WE NEED NOW IS TO FIND A WAY TO--
OVER THERE! IT'S GLADIA AND SABULA!
BANG
BANG
I CAN SEE BOSCONERO TOO... AND HE'S HURT!
THEY'RE BEING CHASED! WE HAVE TO HELP THEM!
I KNOW WHAT TO DO!
STOP! I FORBID YOU! THERE'S NO TIME TO...
DAMN!

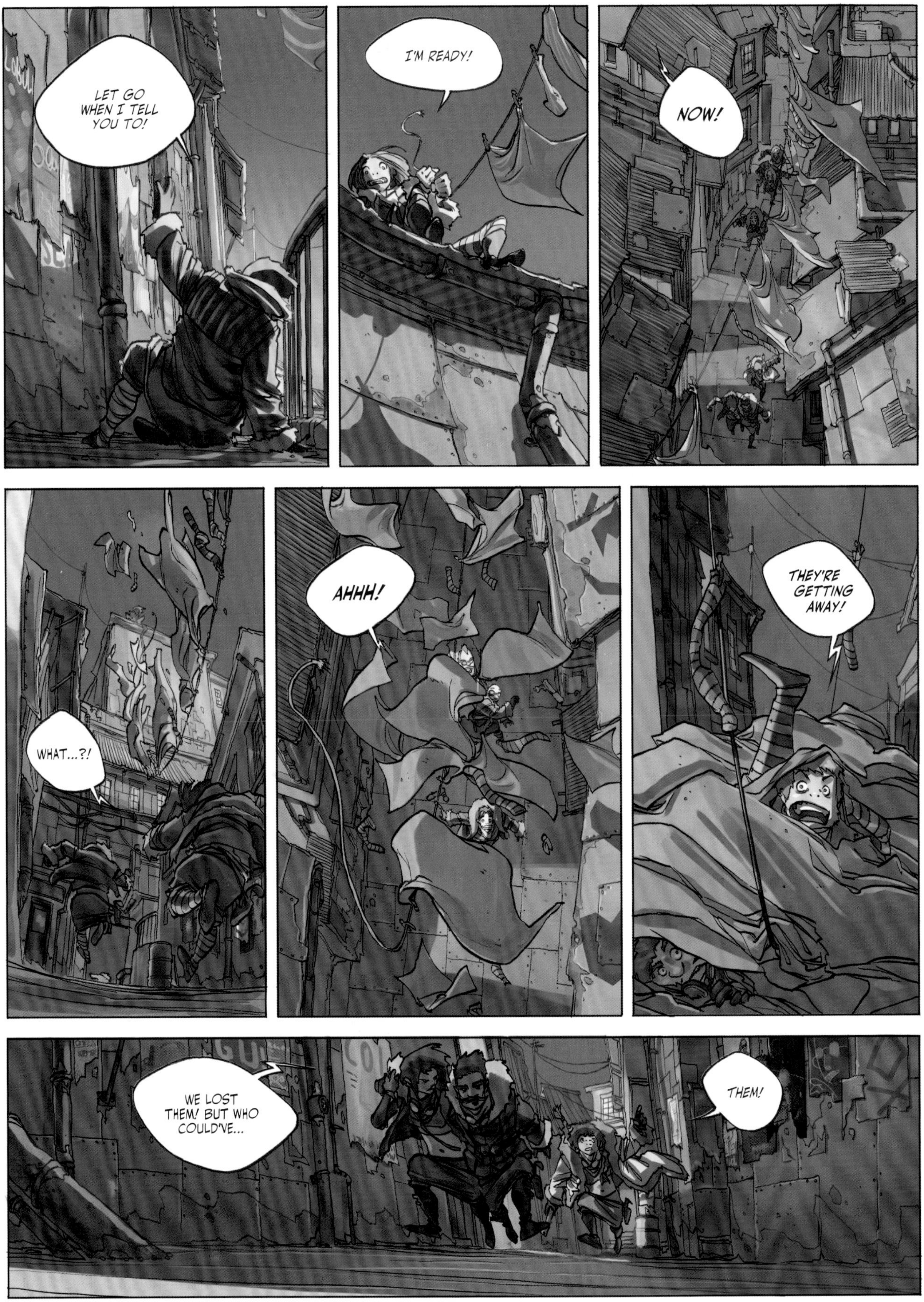
LET GO WHEN I TELL YOU TO!
I'M READY!
NOW!
WHAT...?!
AHHH!
THEY'RE GETTING AWAY!
WE LOST THEM! BUT WHO COULD'VE...
THEM!

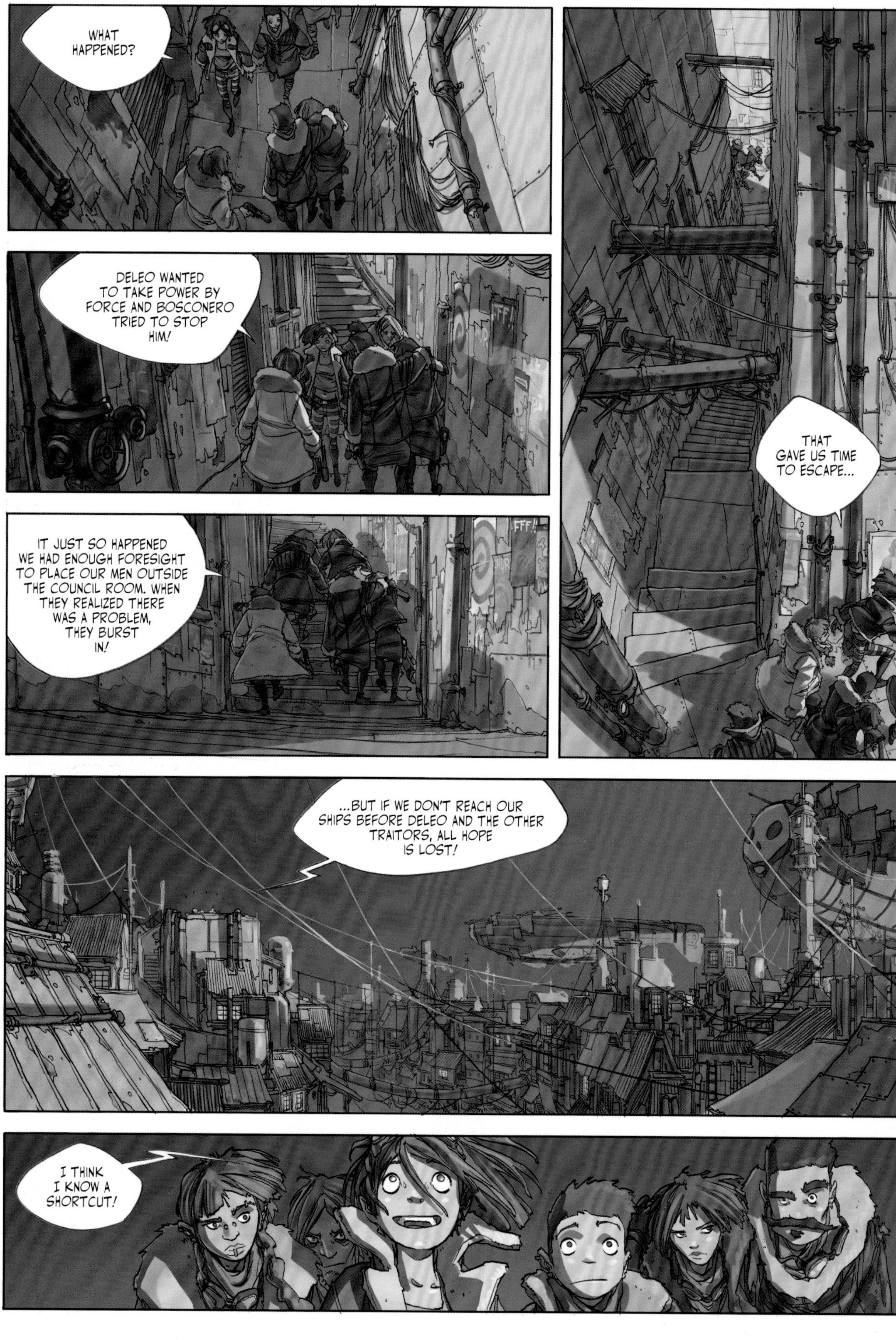
WHAT HAPPENED?
DELEO WANTED TO TAKE POWER BY FORCE AND BOSCONERO TRIED TO STOP HIM!
IT JUST SO HAPPENED WE HAD ENOUGH FORESIGHT TO PLACE OUR MEN OUTSIDE THE COUNCIL ROOM. WHEN THEY REALIZED THERE WAS A PROBLEM, THEY BURST IN!
THAT GAVE US TIME TO ESCAPE...
...BUT IF WE DON'T REACH OUR SHIPS BEFORE DELEO AND THE OTHER TRAITORS, ALL HOPE IS LOST!
I THINK I KNOW A SHORTCUT!

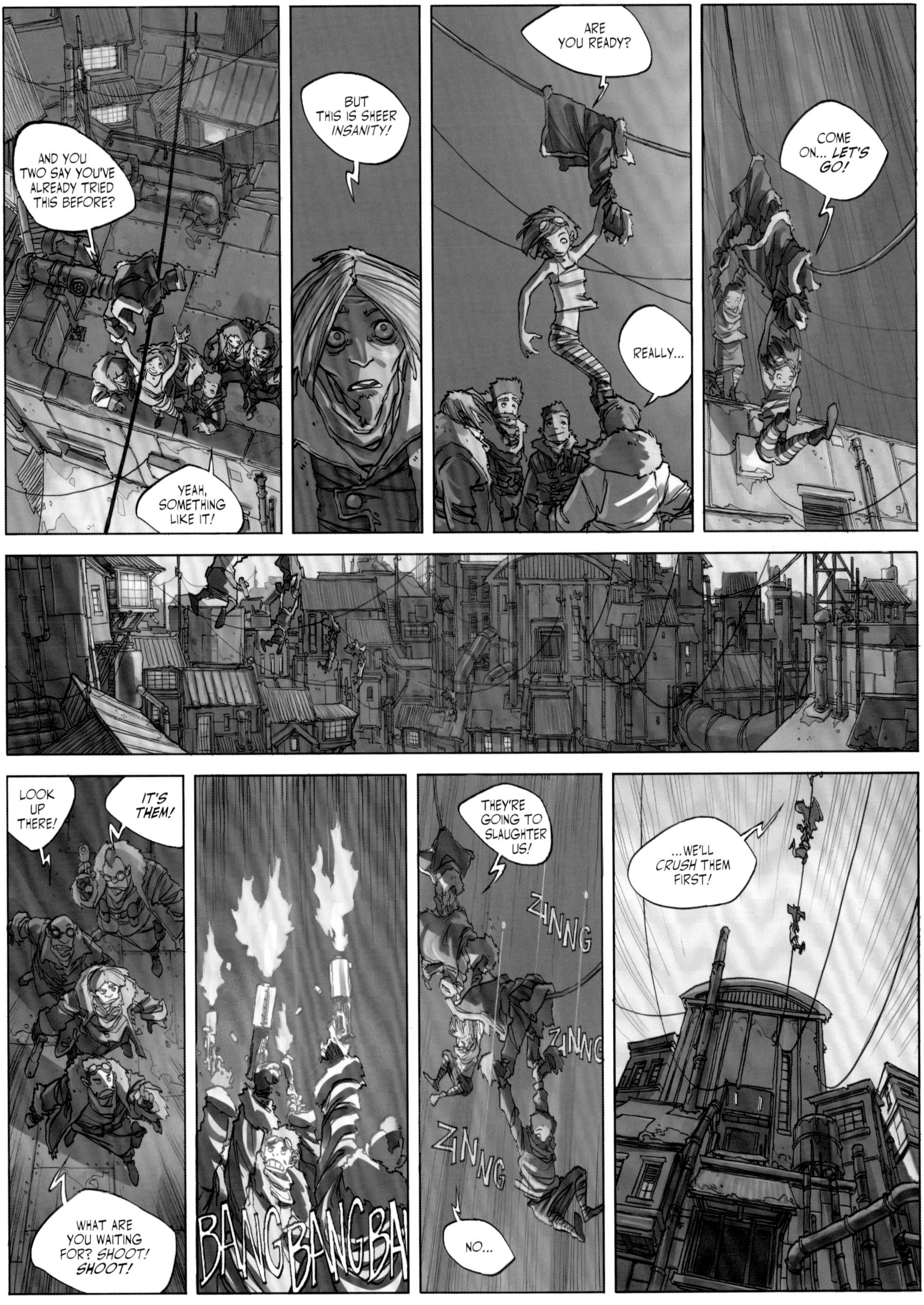
AND YOU TWO SAY YOU'VE ALREADY TRIED THIS BEFORE?
YEAH, SOMETHING LIKE IT!
BUT THIS IS SHEER *INSANITY!*
ARE YOU READY?
REALLY...
COME ON... ***LET'S GO!***
LOOK UP THERE!
IT'S THEM!
WHAT ARE YOU WAITING FOR? *SHOOT!* ***SHOOT!***
BANG BANG BA
THEY'RE GOING TO SLAUGHTER US!
ZINNG
ZINNG
ZINNG
NO...
...WE'LL *CRUSH* THEM FIRST!

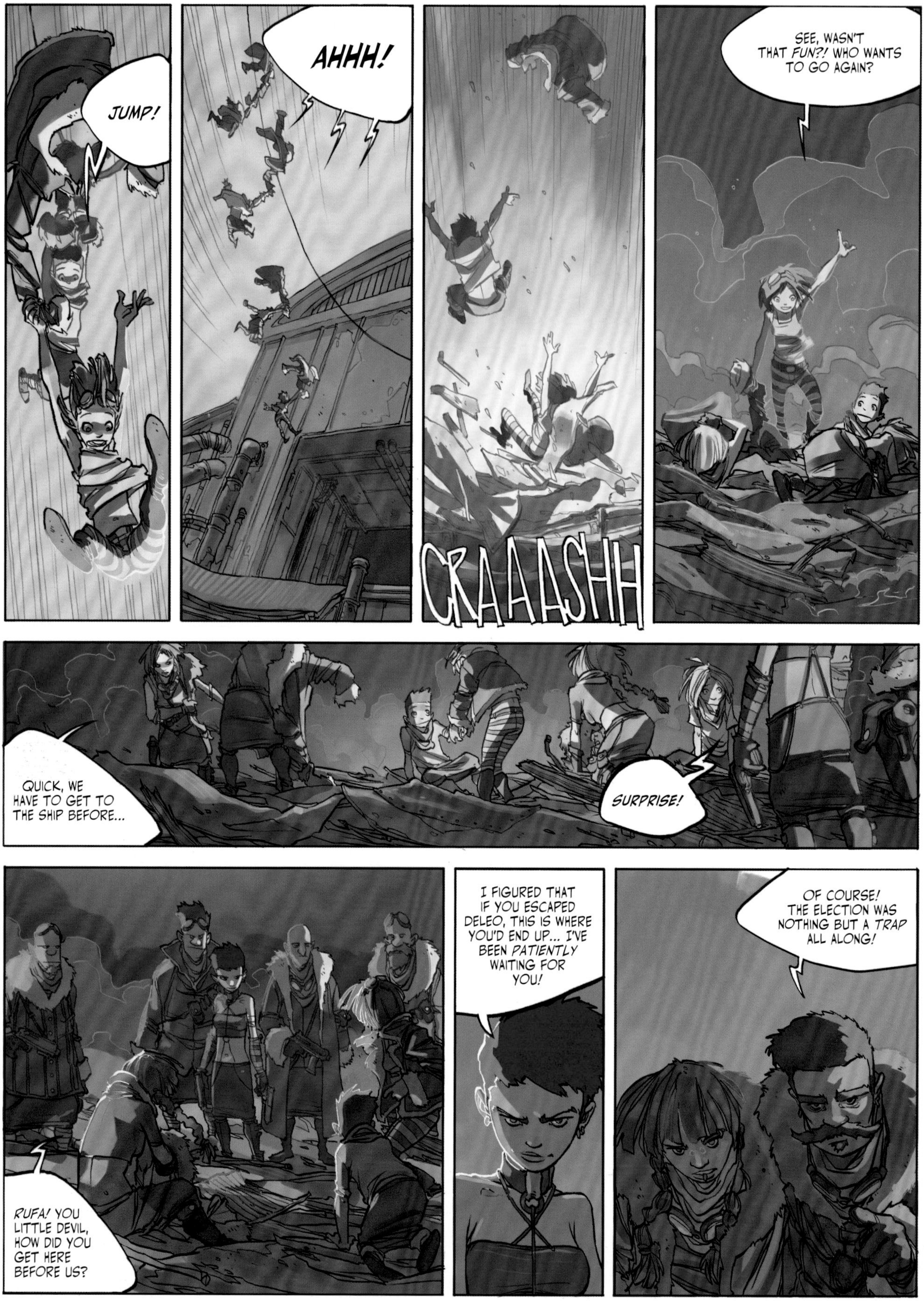
JUMP!
AHHH!
CRAAASHH
SEE, WASN'T THAT FUN?! WHO WANTS TO GO AGAIN?
QUICK, WE HAVE TO GET TO THE SHIP BEFORE...
SURPRISE!
RUFA! YOU LITTLE DEVIL, HOW DID YOU GET HERE BEFORE US?
I FIGURED THAT IF YOU ESCAPED DELEO, THIS IS WHERE YOU'D END UP... I'VE BEEN PATIENTLY WAITING FOR YOU!
OF COURSE! THE ELECTION WAS NOTHING BUT A TRAP ALL ALONG!

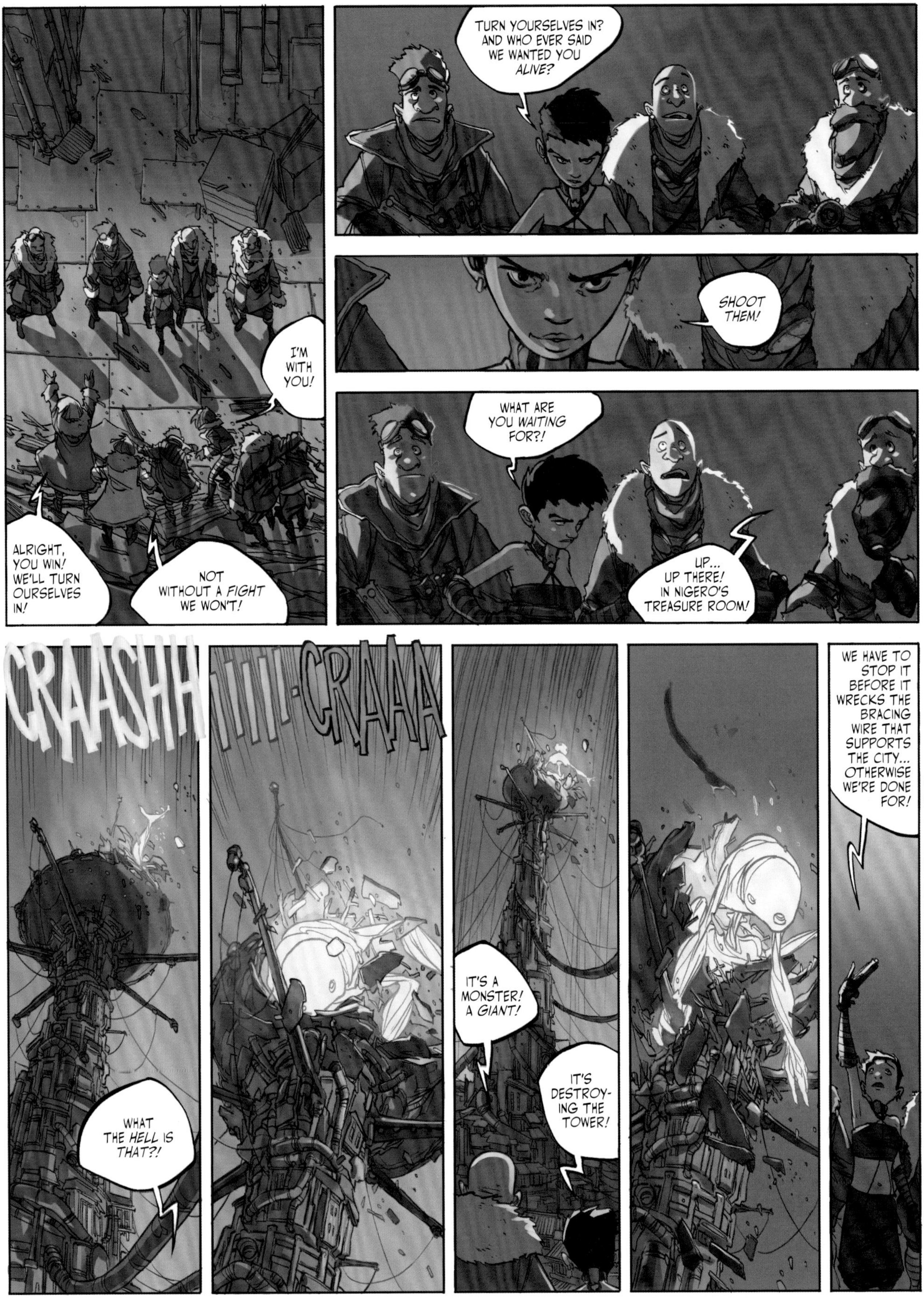
I'M WITH YOU!
ALRIGHT, YOU WIN! WE'LL TURN OURSELVES IN!
NOT WITHOUT A *FIGHT* WE WON'T!
TURN YOURSELVES IN? AND WHO EVER SAID WE WANTED YOU *ALIVE?*
SHOOT THEM!
WHAT ARE YOU WAITING FOR?!
UP... UP THERE! IN NIGERO'S TREASURE ROOM!
CRAASHH
IIIII-CRAAA
WHAT THE *HELL* IS *THAT?!*
IT'S A MONSTER! A *GIANT!*
IT'S DESTROYING THE TOWER!
WE HAVE TO STOP IT BEFORE IT WRECKS THE BRACING WIRE THAT SUPPORTS THE CITY... OTHERWISE WE'RE DONE FOR!

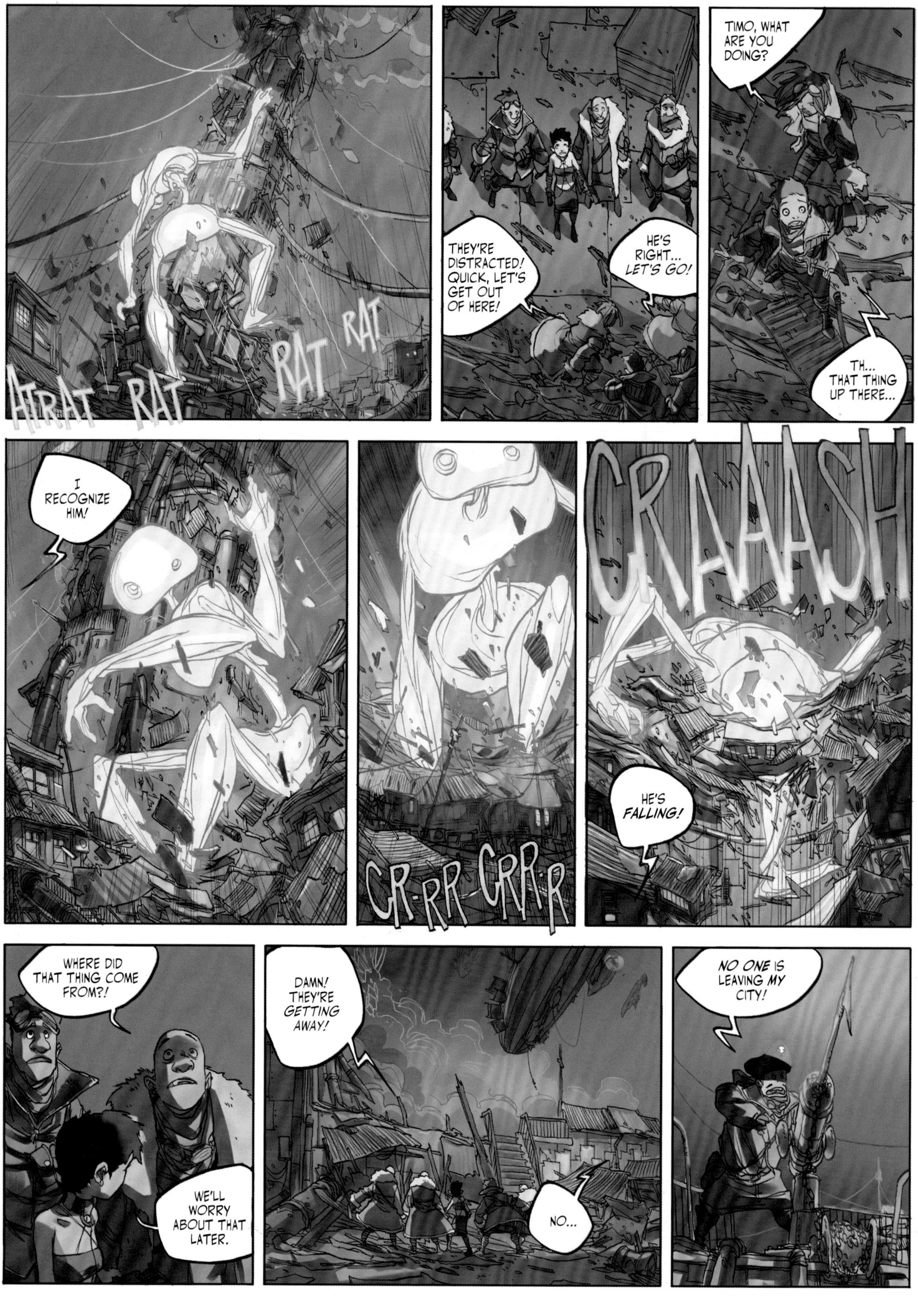
ATRAT RAT RAT RAT
THEY'RE DISTRACTED! QUICK, LET'S GET OUT OF HERE!
HE'S RIGHT... LET'S GO!
TIMO, WHAT ARE YOU DOING?
TH... THAT THING UP THERE...
I RECOGNIZE HIM!
CR-RR CRR-R
CRAAASH
HE'S FALLING!
WHERE DID THAT THING COME FROM?!
WE'LL WORRY ABOUT THAT LATER.
DAMN! THEY'RE GETTING AWAY!
NO...
NO ONE IS LEAVING MY CITY!

LOOK UP THERE! IT'S DELEO!

IF HE HARPOONS US, WE'RE DEAD!

FAREWELL, YOU *SCUM!*

CRRRRRR

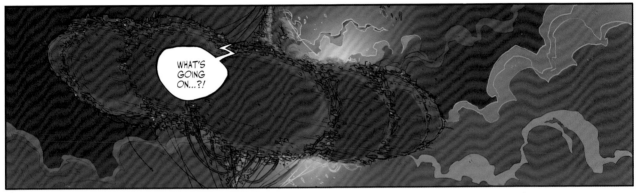

WHAT'S GOING ON...?!

CRASH!

NO!

I DON'T UNDERSTAND. THE MONSTER'S PROTECTING US!

HE'S NOT A MONSTER... HE'S...HE'S A *FRIEND* OF MINE!

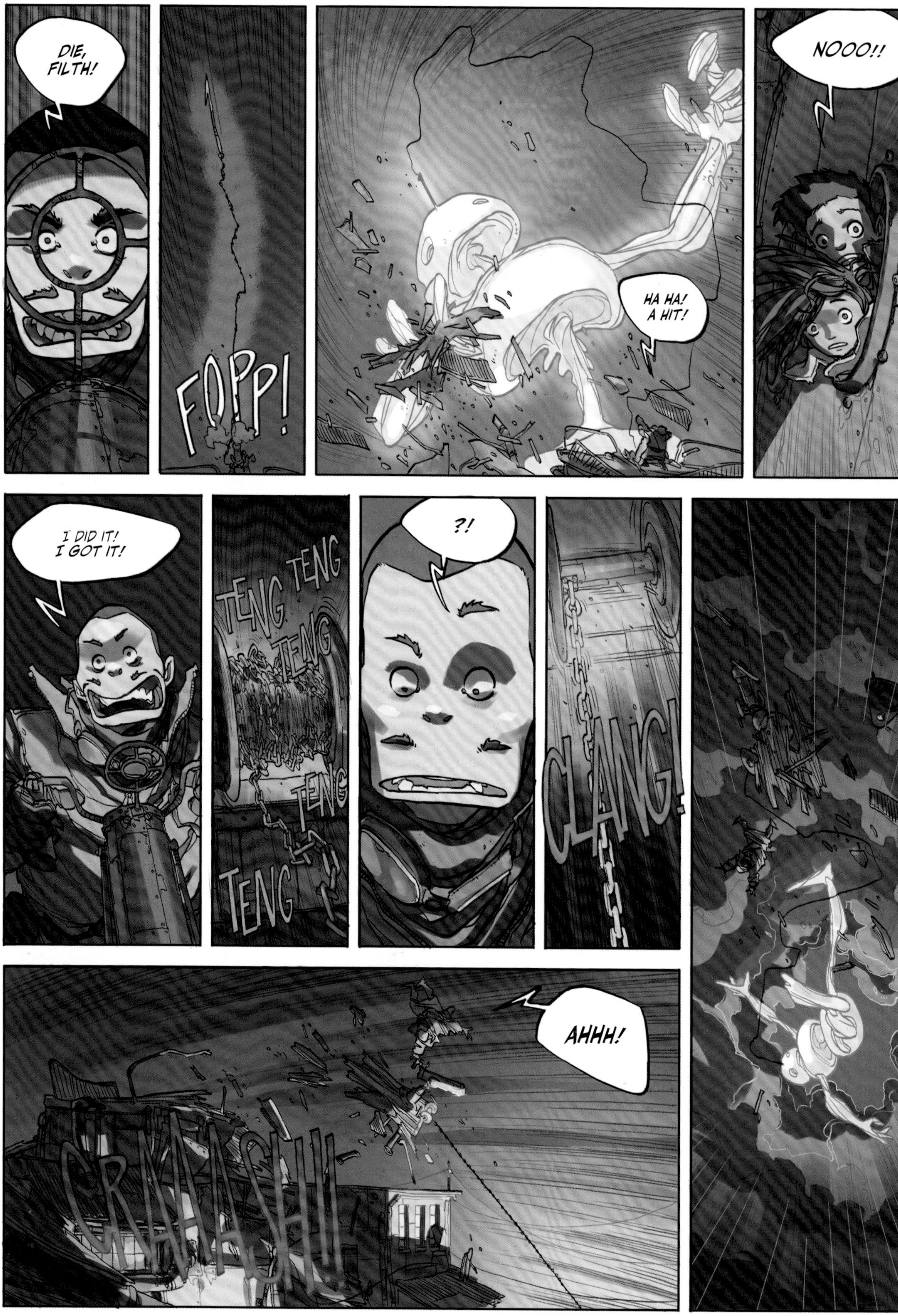
DIE, FILTH!
FOPP!
HA HA! A HIT!
NOOO!!
I DID IT! I GOT IT!
TENG TENG TENG TENG TENG
?!
CLANG!
AHHH!
CRAAASH!

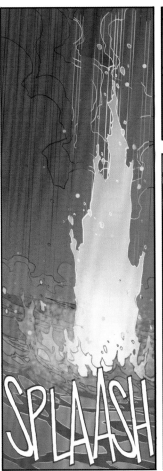

SPLAASH

EDON! NOOO!

I'M SORRY, TIMO... BUT YOU HAVE TO STAY STRONG. UNFORTUNATELY, THERE'S NOTHING WE CAN DO TO HELP YOUR FRIEND.

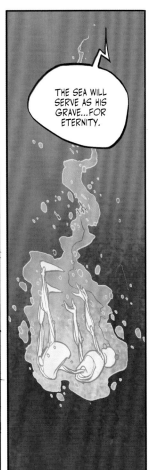

THE SEA WILL SERVE AS HIS GRAVE...FOR ETERNITY.

LOOK UP THERE!

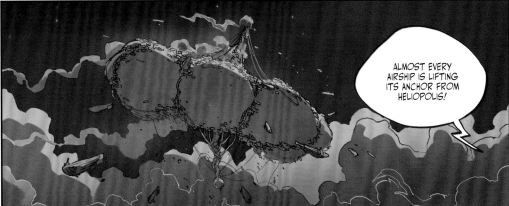

ALMOST EVERY AIRSHIP IS LIFTING ITS ANCHOR FROM HELIOPOLIS!

THEY KNOW ALL IS LOST AND THEY'RE GETTING READY TO ABANDON IT!

DO YOU THINK THEY'LL COME AFTER US?

I DON'T THINK SO. NIGERO IS DEAD AND THE BROTHERHOOD OF THE SEVEN SKIES HAS BEEN DISMANTLED.

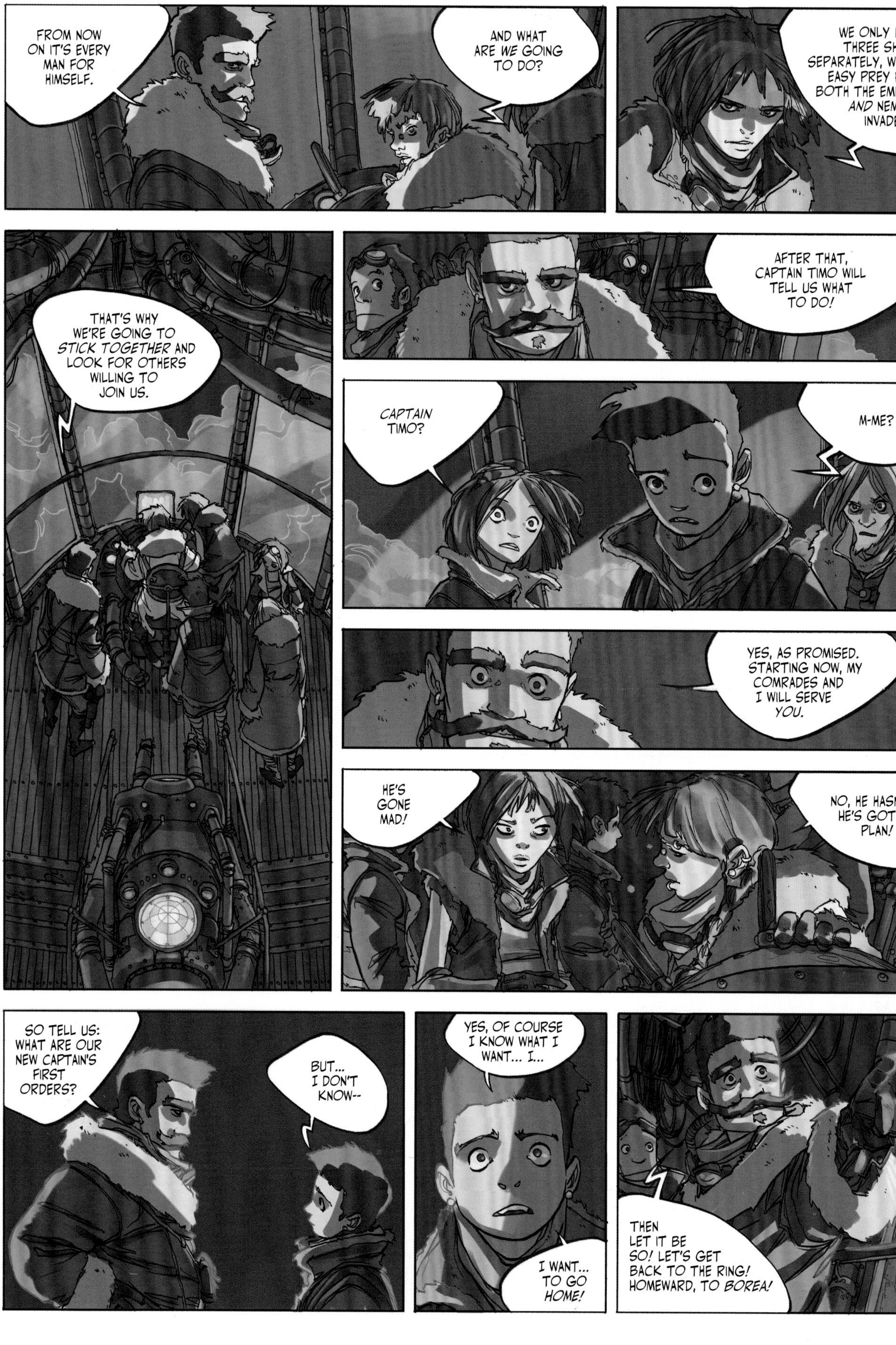
FROM NOW ON IT'S EVERY MAN FOR HIMSELF.
AND WHAT ARE *WE* GOING TO DO?
WE ONLY HAVE THREE SHIPS. SEPARATELY, WE'RE EASY PREY FOR BOTH THE EMPIRE *AND* NEMO'S INVADERS.
THAT'S WHY WE'RE GOING TO *STICK TOGETHER* AND LOOK FOR OTHERS WILLING TO JOIN US.
AFTER THAT, CAPTAIN TIMO WILL TELL US WHAT TO DO!
CAPTAIN TIMO?
M-ME?
YES, AS PROMISED. STARTING NOW, MY COMRADES AND I WILL SERVE *YOU*.
HE'S GONE MAD!
NO, HE HASN'T. HE'S GOT A PLAN!
SO TELL US: WHAT ARE OUR NEW CAPTAIN'S FIRST ORDERS?
BUT... I DON'T KNOW--
YES, OF COURSE I KNOW WHAT I WANT... I...
I WANT... TO GO HOME!
THEN LET IT BE SO! LET'S GET BACK TO THE RING! HOMEWARD, TO *BOREA!*

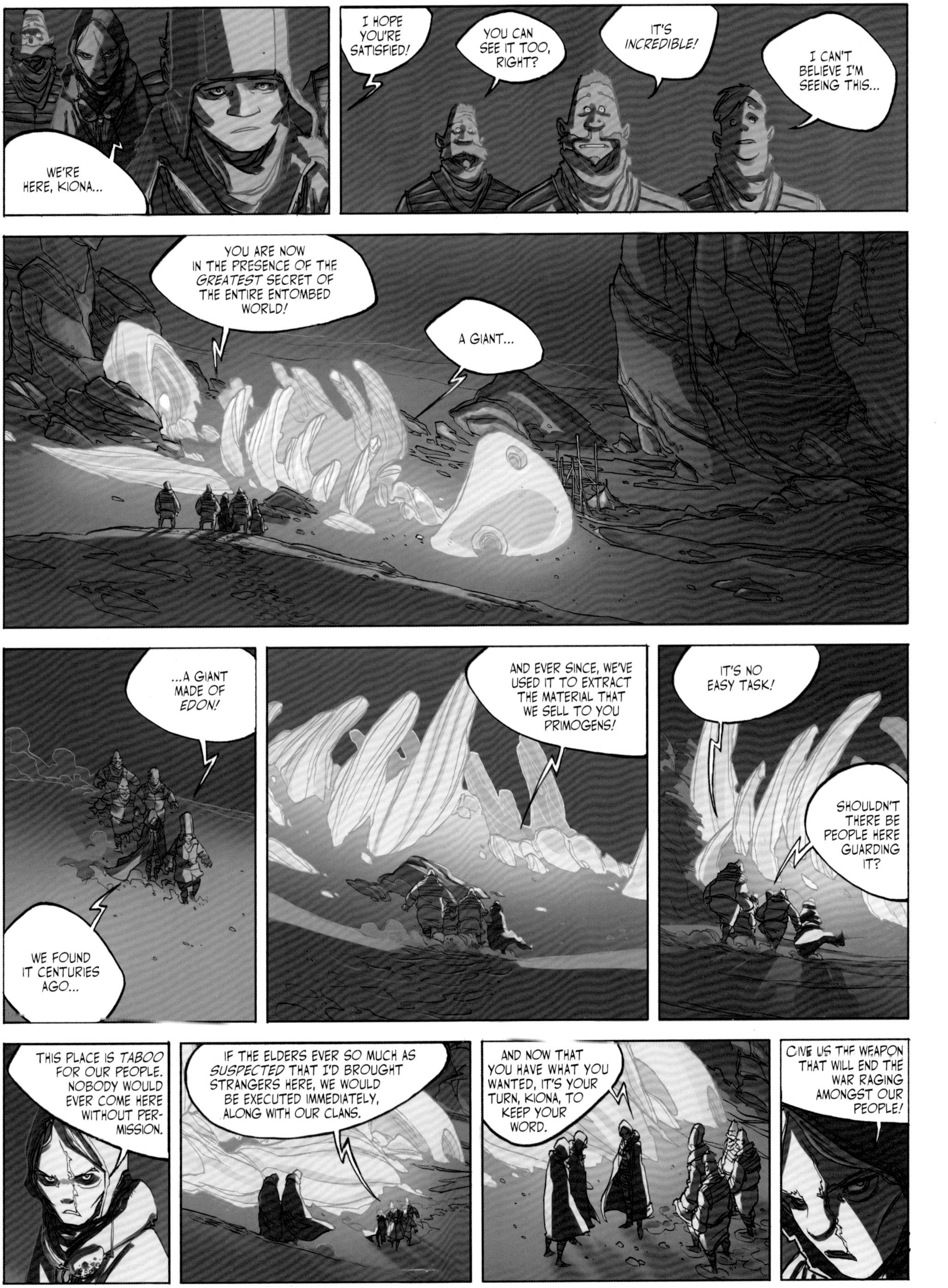
WE'RE HERE, KIONA...
I HOPE YOU'RE SATISFIED!
YOU CAN SEE IT TOO, RIGHT?
IT'S INCREDIBLE!
I CAN'T BELIEVE I'M SEEING THIS...
YOU ARE NOW IN THE PRESENCE OF THE GREATEST SECRET OF THE ENTIRE ENTOMBED WORLD!
A GIANT...
...A GIANT MADE OF EDON!
WE FOUND IT CENTURIES AGO...
AND EVER SINCE, WE'VE USED IT TO EXTRACT THE MATERIAL THAT WE SELL TO YOU PRIMOGENS!
IT'S NO EASY TASK!
SHOULDN'T THERE BE PEOPLE HERE GUARDING IT?
THIS PLACE IS TABOO FOR OUR PEOPLE. NOBODY WOULD EVER COME HERE WITHOUT PERMISSION.
IF THE ELDERS EVER SO MUCH AS SUSPECTED THAT I'D BROUGHT STRANGERS HERE, WE WOULD BE EXECUTED IMMEDIATELY, ALONG WITH OUR CLANS.
AND NOW THAT YOU HAVE WHAT YOU WANTED, IT'S YOUR TURN, KIONA, TO KEEP YOUR WORD.
GIVE US THE WEAPON THAT WILL END THE WAR RAGING AMONGST OUR PEOPLE!

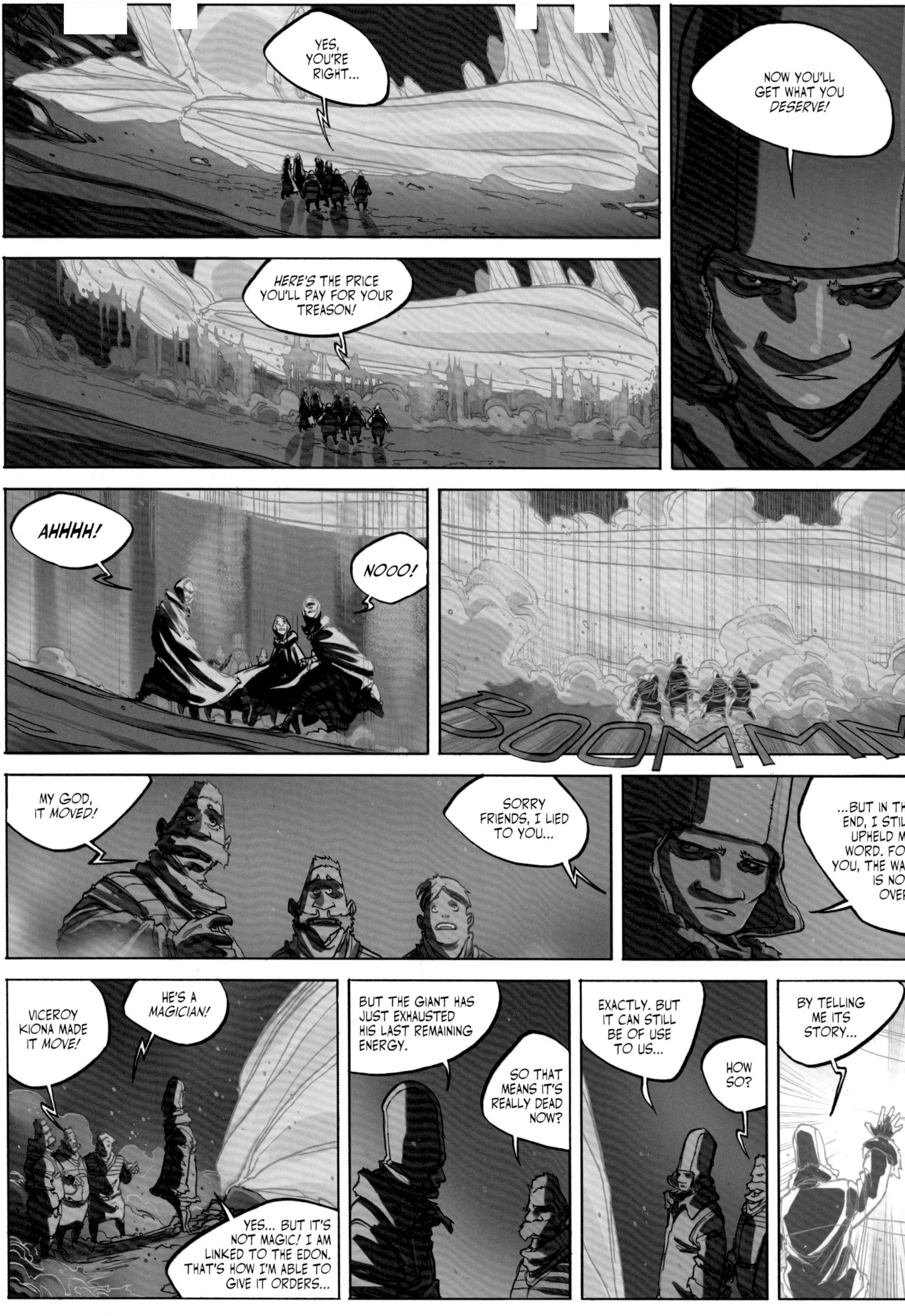

YES, YOU'RE RIGHT...
NOW YOU'LL GET WHAT YOU *DESERVE!*
HERE'S THE PRICE YOU'LL PAY FOR YOUR TREASON!
AHHHH!
NOOO!
BOOMMMM
MY GOD, IT *MOVED!*
SORRY FRIENDS, I LIED TO YOU...
...BUT IN THE END, I STILL UPHELD MY WORD. FOR YOU, THE WAR IS NOW OVER.
VICEROY KIONA MADE IT *MOVE!*
HE'S A *MAGICIAN!*
YES... BUT IT'S NOT MAGIC! I AM LINKED TO THE EDON. THAT'S HOW I'M ABLE TO GIVE IT ORDERS...
BUT THE GIANT HAS JUST EXHAUSTED HIS LAST REMAINING ENERGY.
SO THAT MEANS IT'S REALLY DEAD NOW?
EXACTLY. BUT IT CAN STILL BE OF USE TO US...
HOW SO?
BY TELLING ME ITS STORY...

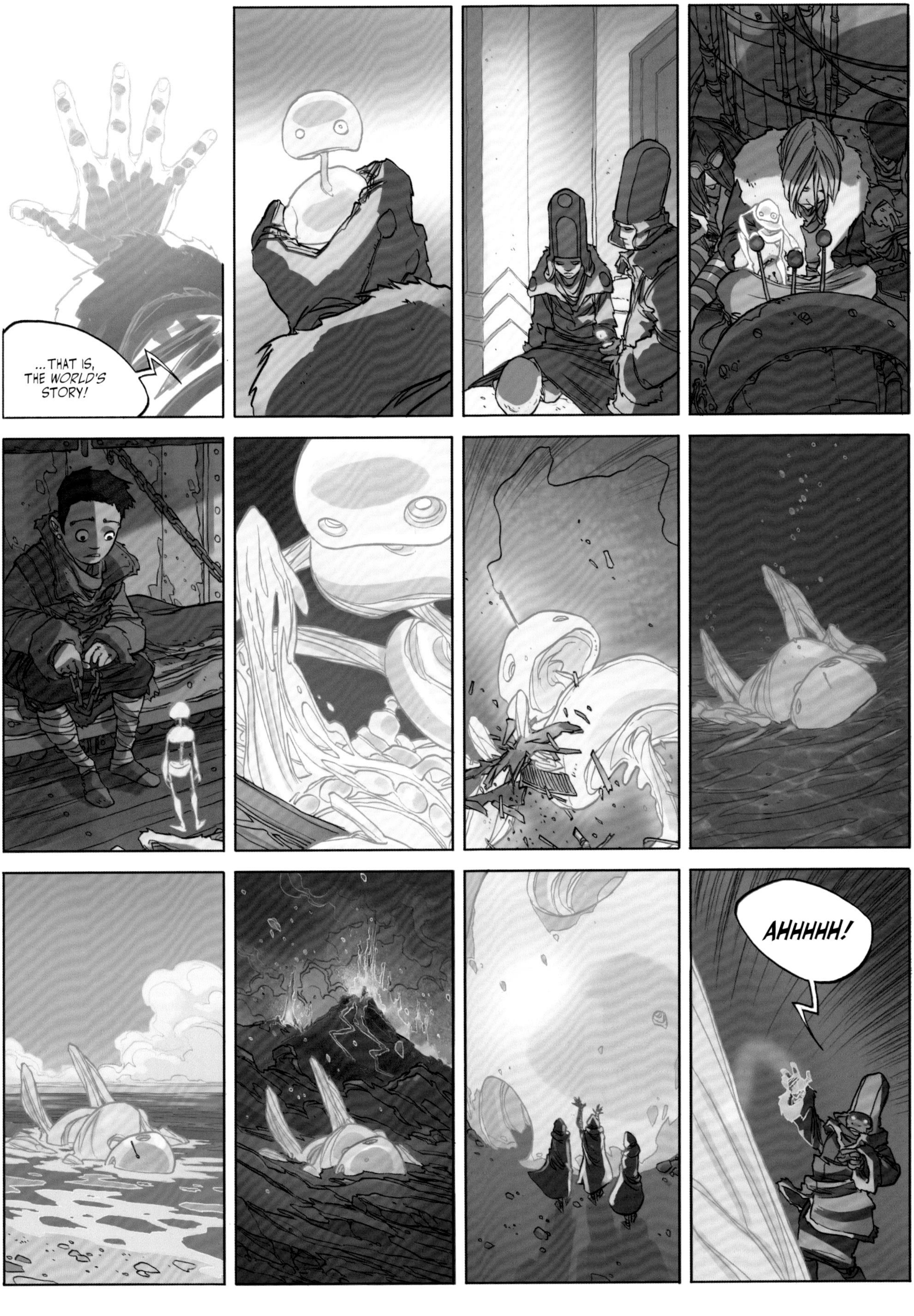
...THAT IS, THE WORLD'S STORY!
AHHHHH!

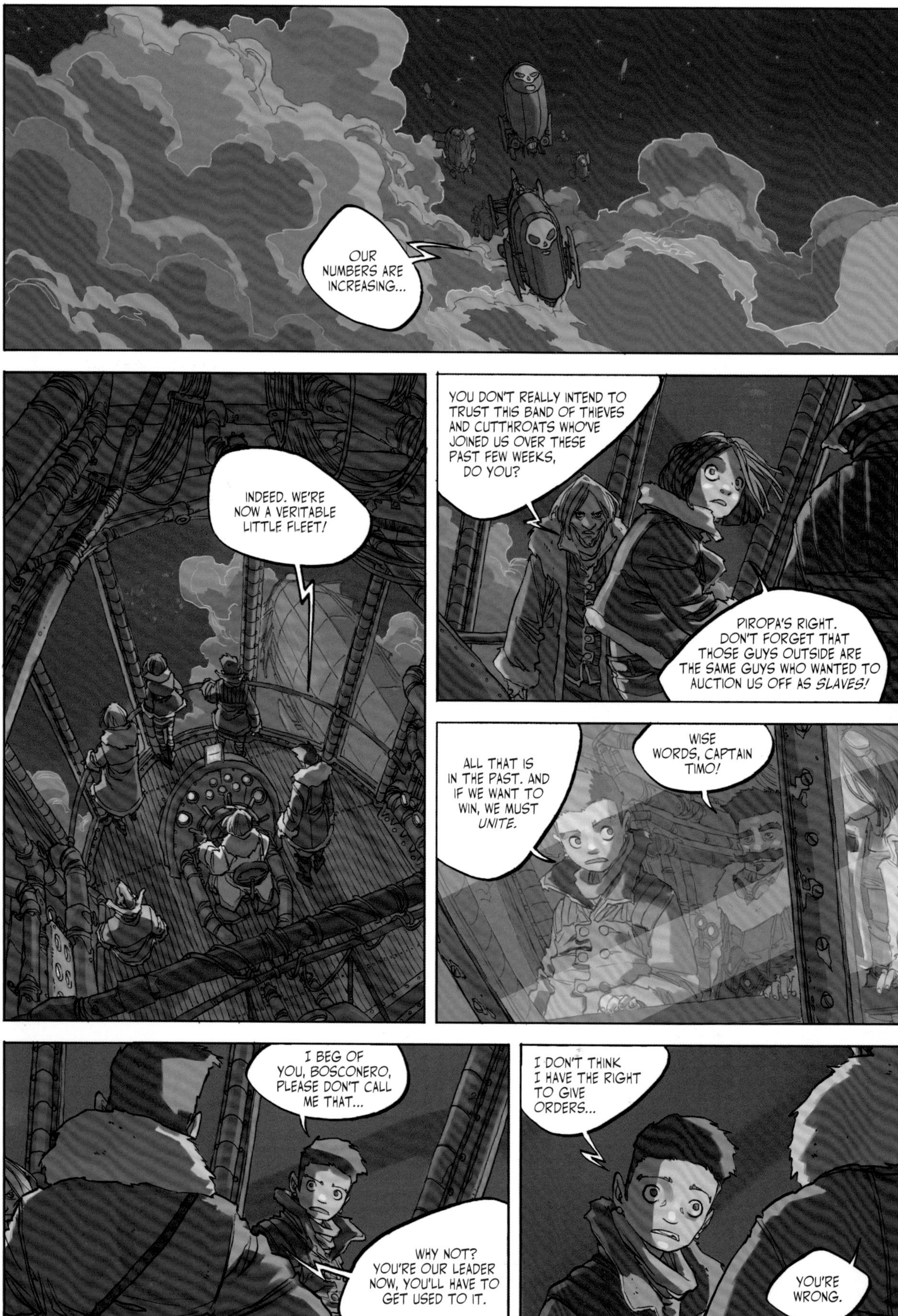
OUR NUMBERS ARE INCREASING...
INDEED. WE'RE NOW A VERITABLE LITTLE FLEET!
YOU DON'T REALLY INTEND TO TRUST THIS BAND OF THIEVES AND CUTTHROATS WHO'VE JOINED US OVER THESE PAST FEW WEEKS, DO YOU?
PIROPA'S RIGHT. DON'T FORGET THAT THOSE GUYS OUTSIDE ARE THE SAME GUYS WHO WANTED TO AUCTION US OFF AS *SLAVES!*
ALL THAT IS IN THE PAST. AND IF WE WANT TO WIN, WE MUST *UNITE.*
WISE WORDS, CAPTAIN TIMO!
I BEG OF YOU, BOSCONERO, PLEASE DON'T CALL ME THAT...
WHY NOT? YOU'RE OUR LEADER NOW, YOU'LL HAVE TO GET USED TO IT.
I DON'T THINK I HAVE THE RIGHT TO GIVE ORDERS...
YOU'RE WRONG.

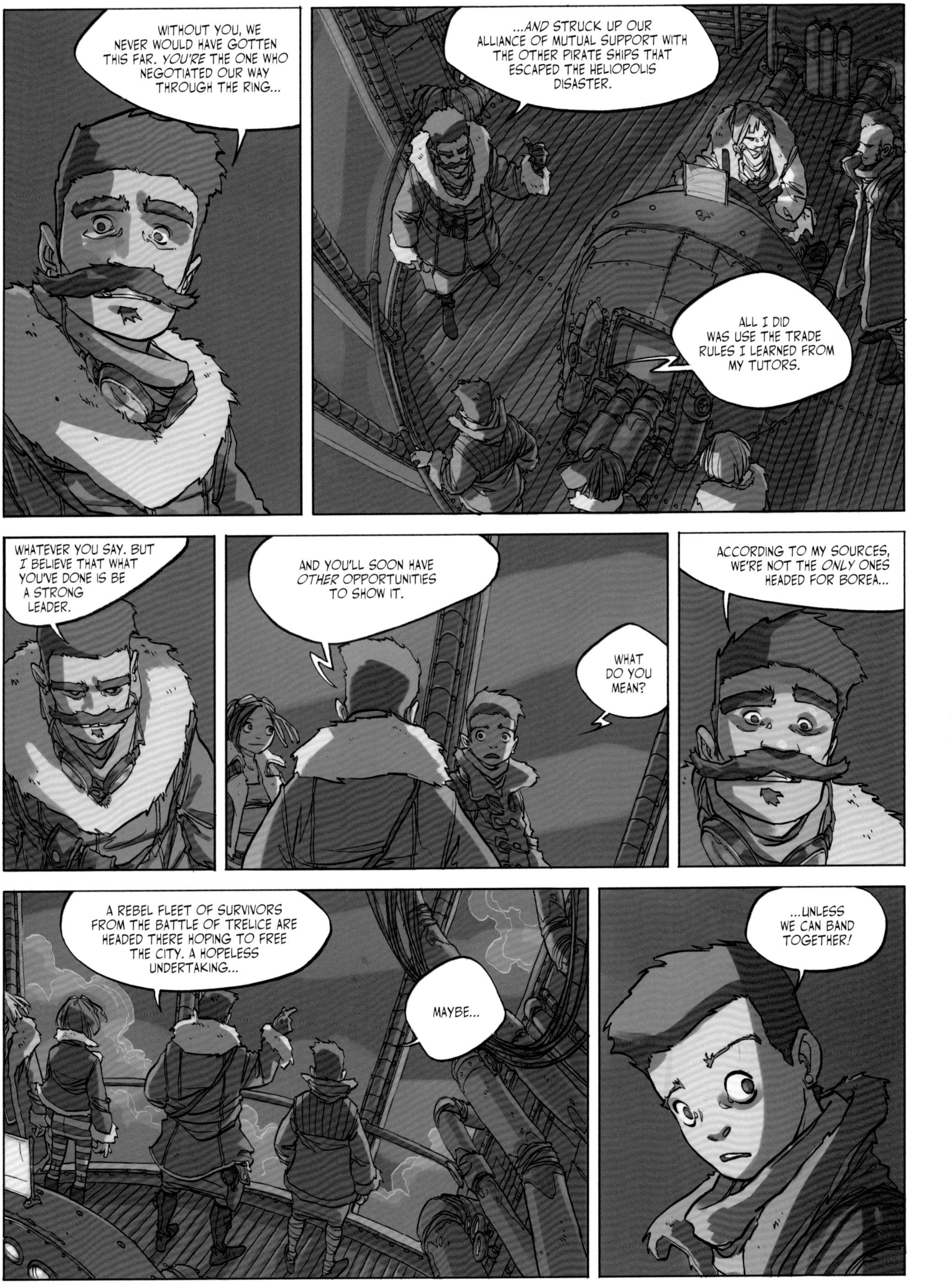
WITHOUT YOU, WE NEVER WOULD HAVE GOTTEN THIS FAR. *YOU'RE* THE ONE WHO NEGOTIATED OUR WAY THROUGH THE RING...
...*AND* STRUCK UP OUR ALLIANCE OF MUTUAL SUPPORT WITH THE OTHER PIRATE SHIPS THAT ESCAPED THE HELIOPOLIS DISASTER.
ALL I DID WAS USE THE TRADE RULES I LEARNED FROM MY TUTORS.
WHATEVER YOU SAY. BUT *I* BELIEVE THAT WHAT YOU'VE DONE IS BE A STRONG LEADER.
AND YOU'LL SOON HAVE *OTHER* OPPORTUNITIES TO SHOW IT.
WHAT DO YOU MEAN?
ACCORDING TO MY SOURCES, WE'RE NOT THE *ONLY* ONES HEADED FOR BOREA...
A REBEL FLEET OF SURVIVORS FROM THE BATTLE OF TRELICE ARE HEADED THERE HOPING TO FREE THE CITY. A HOPELESS UNDERTAKING...
MAYBE...
...UNLESS WE CAN BAND TOGETHER!

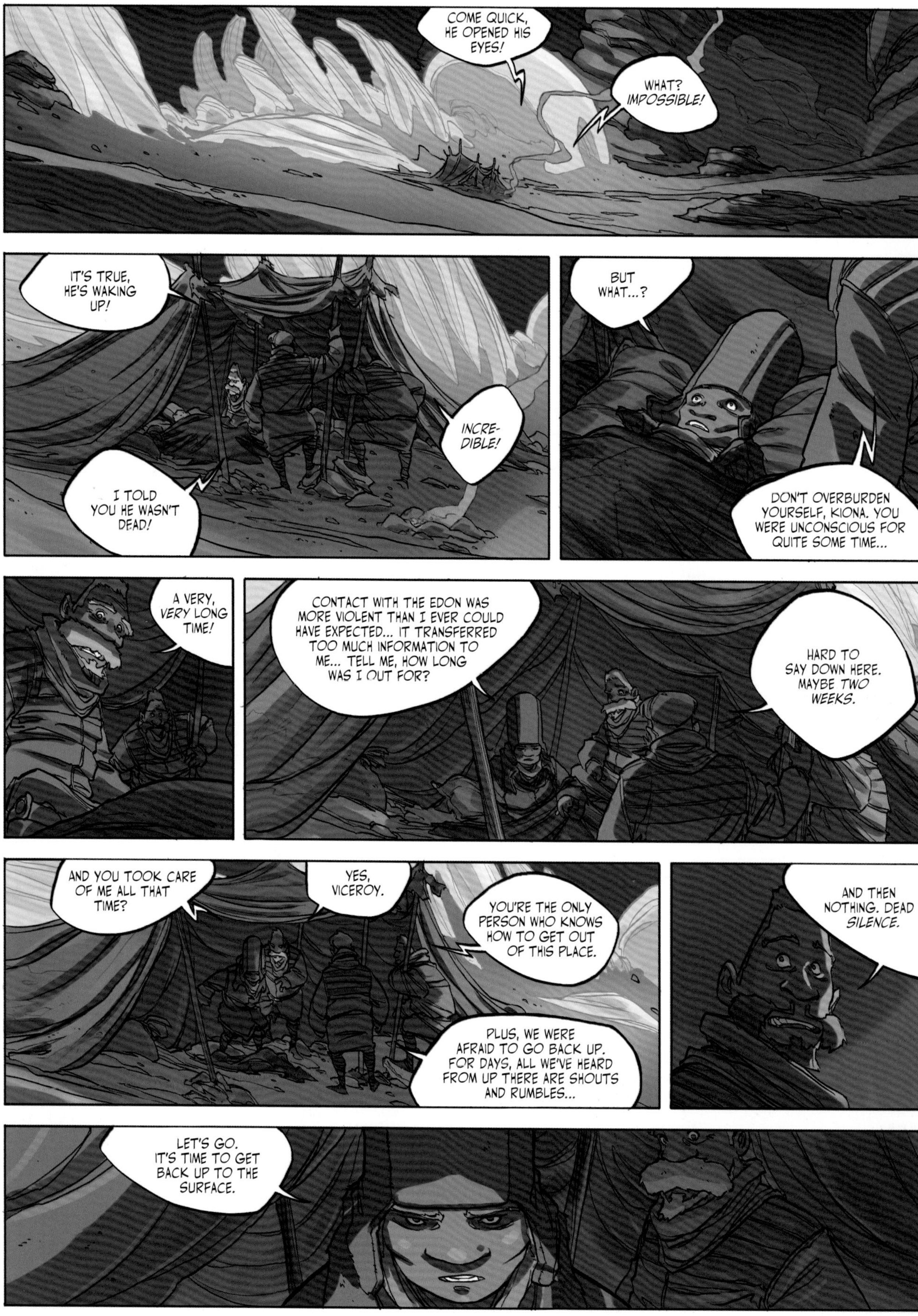
COME QUICK, HE OPENED HIS EYES!
WHAT? IMPOSSIBLE!
IT'S TRUE, HE'S WAKING UP!
INCRE-DIBLE!
I TOLD YOU HE WASN'T DEAD!
BUT WHAT...?
DON'T OVERBURDEN YOURSELF, KIONA. YOU WERE UNCONSCIOUS FOR QUITE SOME TIME...
A VERY, VERY LONG TIME!
CONTACT WITH THE EDON WAS MORE VIOLENT THAN I EVER COULD HAVE EXPECTED... IT TRANSFERRED TOO MUCH INFORMATION TO ME... TELL ME, HOW LONG WAS I OUT FOR?
HARD TO SAY DOWN HERE. MAYBE TWO WEEKS.
AND YOU TOOK CARE OF ME ALL THAT TIME?
YES, VICEROY.
YOU'RE THE ONLY PERSON WHO KNOWS HOW TO GET OUT OF THIS PLACE.
PLUS, WE WERE AFRAID TO GO BACK UP. FOR DAYS, ALL WE'VE HEARD FROM UP THERE ARE SHOUTS AND RUMBLES...
AND THEN NOTHING. DEAD SILENCE.
LET'S GO. IT'S TIME TO GET BACK UP TO THE SURFACE.

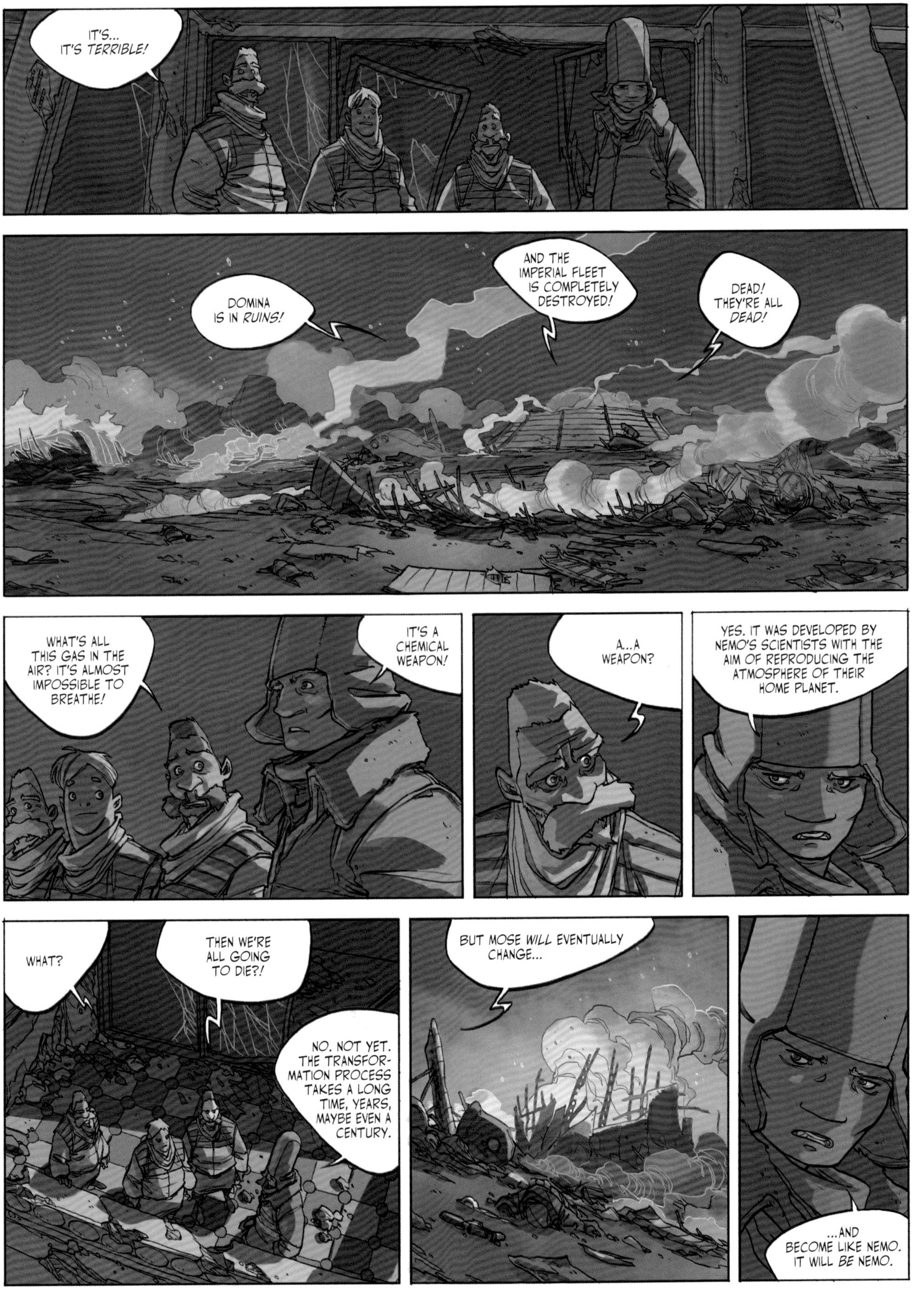
IT'S... IT'S *TERRIBLE!*
DOMINA IS IN *RUINS!*
AND THE IMPERIAL FLEET IS COMPLETELY DESTROYED!
DEAD! THEY'RE ALL *DEAD!*
WHAT'S ALL THIS GAS IN THE AIR? IT'S ALMOST IMPOSSIBLE TO BREATHE!
IT'S A CHEMICAL WEAPON!
A...A WEAPON?
YES. IT WAS DEVELOPED BY NEMO'S SCIENTISTS WITH THE AIM OF REPRODUCING THE ATMOSPHERE OF THEIR HOME PLANET.
WHAT?
THEN WE'RE ALL GOING TO DIE?!
NO. NOT YET. THE TRANSFORMATION PROCESS TAKES A LONG TIME, YEARS, MAYBE EVEN A CENTURY.
BUT MOSE *WILL* EVENTUALLY CHANGE...
...AND BECOME LIKE NEMO. IT WILL *BE* NEMO.

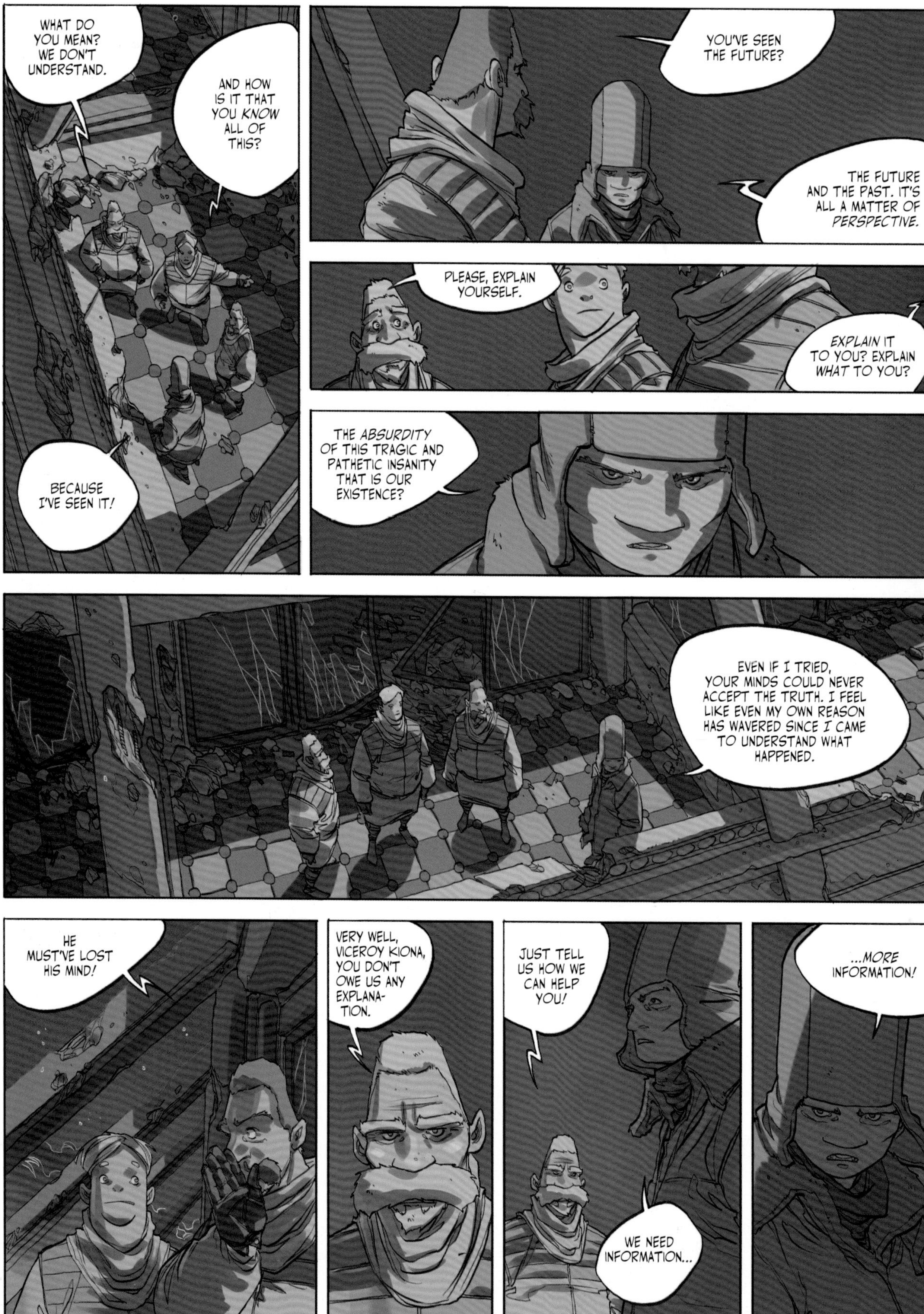
WHAT DO YOU MEAN? WE DON'T UNDERSTAND.
AND HOW IS IT THAT YOU *KNOW* ALL OF THIS?
BECAUSE I'VE SEEN IT!
YOU'VE SEEN THE FUTURE?
THE FUTURE AND THE PAST. IT'S ALL A MATTER OF *PERSPECTIVE.*
PLEASE, EXPLAIN YOURSELF.
EXPLAIN IT TO YOU? EXPLAIN *WHAT* TO YOU?
THE *ABSURDITY* OF THIS TRAGIC AND PATHETIC INSANITY THAT IS OUR EXISTENCE?
EVEN IF I TRIED, YOUR MINDS COULD NEVER ACCEPT THE TRUTH. I FEEL LIKE EVEN MY OWN REASON HAS WAVERED SINCE *I* CAME TO UNDERSTAND WHAT HAPPENED.
HE MUST'VE LOST HIS MIND!
VERY WELL, VICEROY KIONA, YOU DON'T OWE US ANY EXPLANA-TION.
JUST TELL US HOW WE CAN HELP YOU!
WE NEED INFORMATION...
...*MORE* INFORMATION!

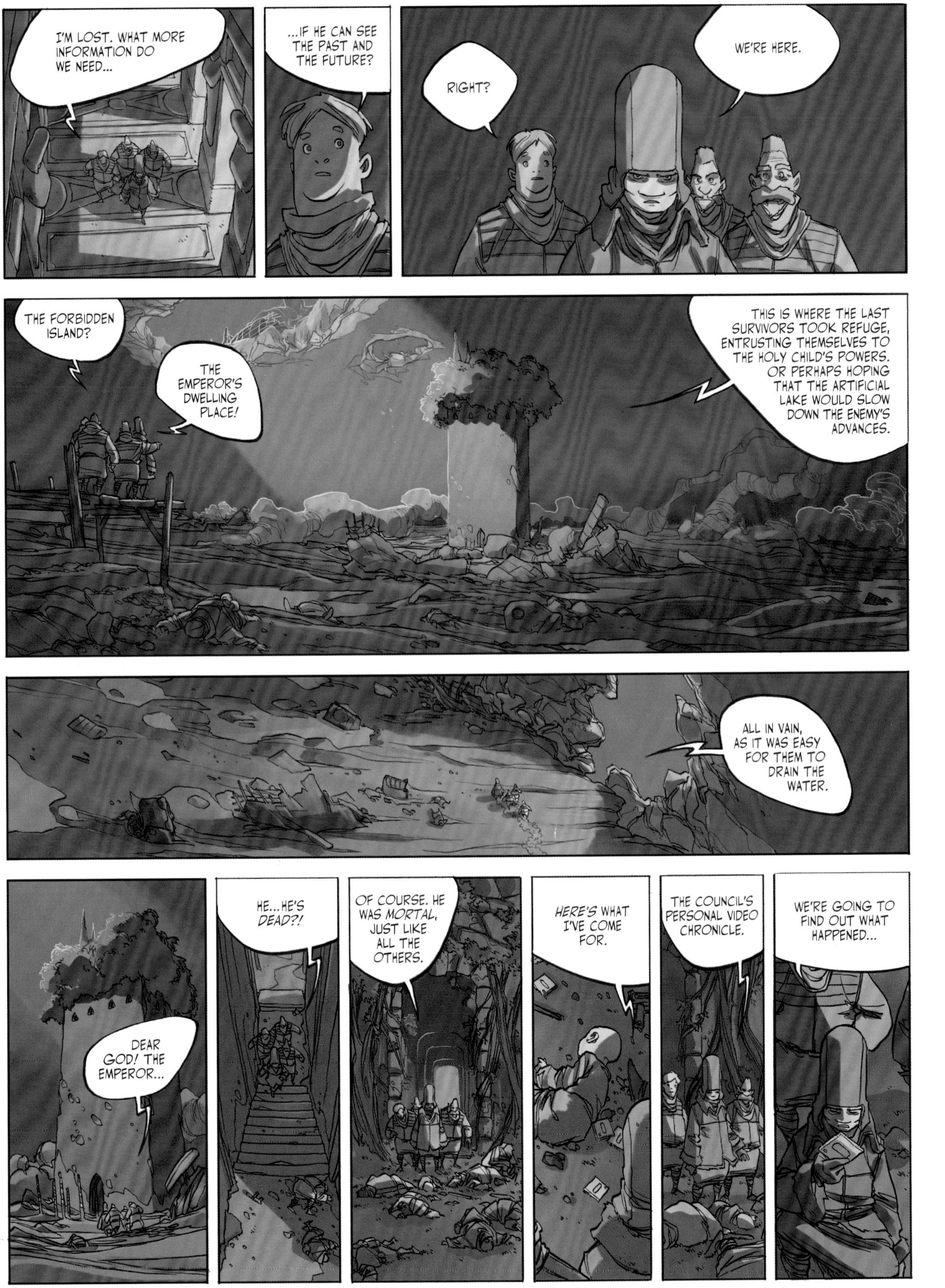
I'M LOST. WHAT MORE INFORMATION DO WE NEED...
...IF HE CAN SEE THE PAST AND THE FUTURE?
WE'RE HERE.
RIGHT?
THE FORBIDDEN ISLAND?
THE EMPEROR'S DWELLING PLACE!
THIS IS WHERE THE LAST SURVIVORS TOOK REFUGE, ENTRUSTING THEMSELVES TO THE HOLY CHILD'S POWERS. OR PERHAPS HOPING THAT THE ARTIFICIAL LAKE WOULD SLOW DOWN THE ENEMY'S ADVANCES.
ALL IN VAIN, AS IT WAS EASY FOR THEM TO DRAIN THE WATER.
DEAR GOD! THE EMPEROR...
HE...HE'S *DEAD?!*
OF COURSE. HE WAS *MORTAL*, JUST LIKE ALL THE OTHERS.
HERE'S WHAT I'VE COME FOR.
THE COUNCIL'S PERSONAL VIDEO CHRONICLE.
WE'RE GOING TO FIND OUT WHAT HAPPENED...

IT ALL STARTED IN BOREA.

IT IS THERE THAT A REBEL FLEET, COMPOSED OF SPACESHIPS FROM ALL OVER THE EMPIRE, ATTACKED THE CITY TO TRY AND FREE IT FROM THE ENEMY OCCUPATION.

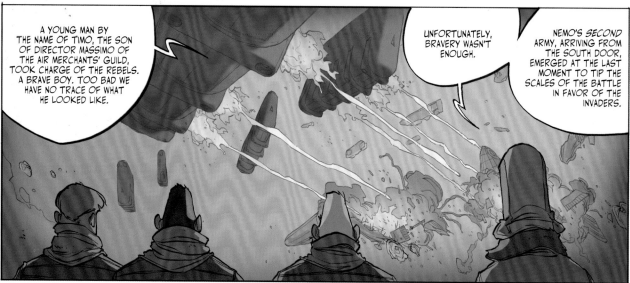

A YOUNG MAN BY THE NAME OF TIMO, THE SON OF DIRECTOR MASSIMO OF THE AIR MERCHANTS' GUILD, TOOK CHARGE OF THE REBELS. A BRAVE BOY. TOO BAD WE HAVE NO TRACE OF WHAT HE LOOKED LIKE.

UNFORTUNATELY, BRAVERY WASN'T ENOUGH.

NEMO'S *SECOND* ARMY, ARRIVING FROM THE SOUTH DOOR, EMERGED AT THE LAST MOMENT TO TIP THE SCALES OF THE BATTLE IN FAVOR OF THE INVADERS.

THEY ULTIMATELY RELEASED A CHEMICAL WEAPON INTO THE ATMOSPHERE TO BEGIN TRANSFORMING THE PLANET'S AIR.

DEAD. EVERY LAST ONE OF THEM...

AND TIMO AND THE OTHER REBELS?

YEAH, WHAT HAPPENED TO THEM?

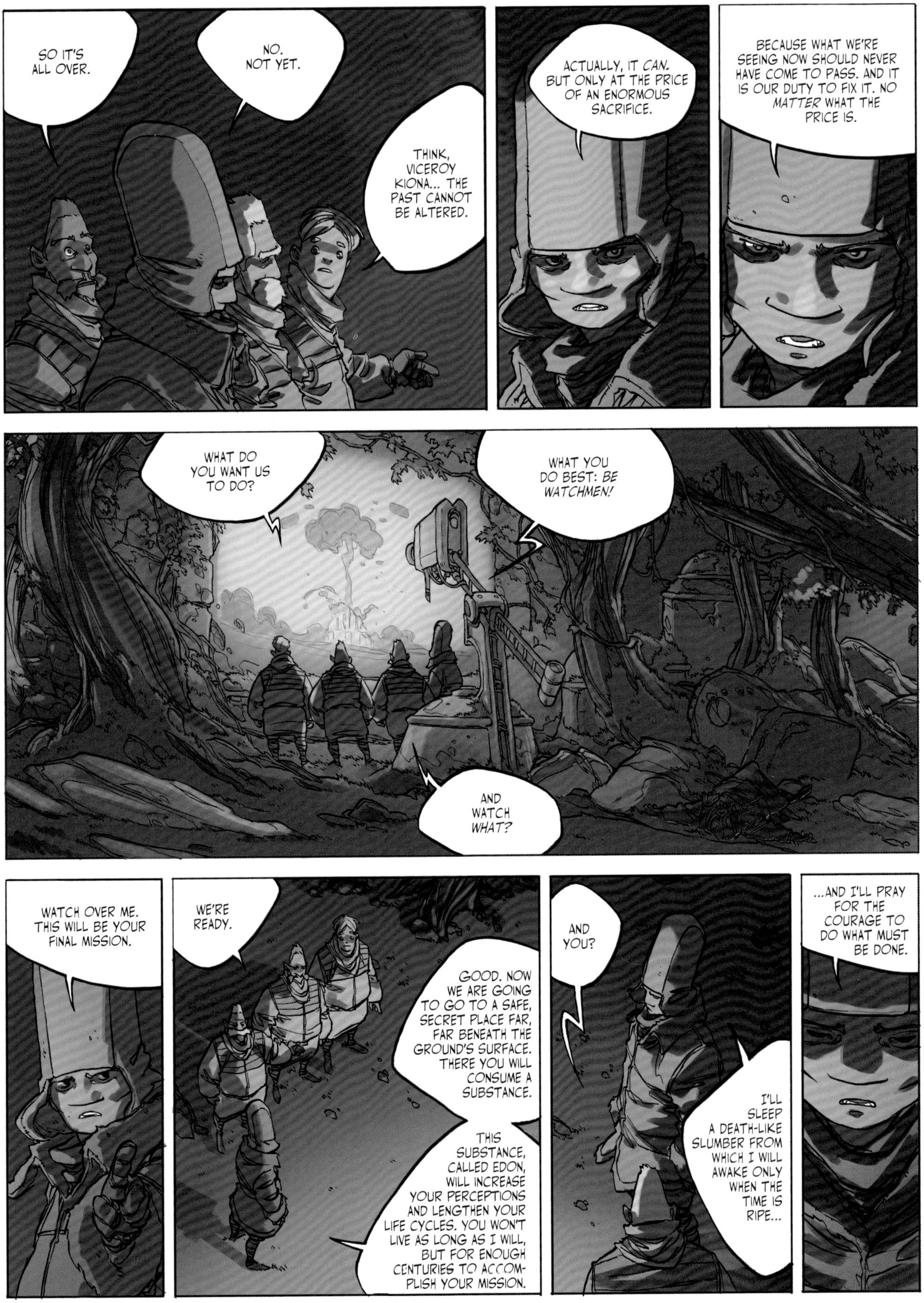
SO IT'S ALL OVER.
NO. NOT YET.
THINK, VICEROY KIONA... THE PAST CANNOT BE ALTERED.
ACTUALLY, IT *CAN*. BUT ONLY AT THE PRICE OF AN ENORMOUS SACRIFICE.
BECAUSE WHAT WE'RE SEEING NOW SHOULD NEVER HAVE COME TO PASS. AND IT IS OUR DUTY TO FIX IT. NO *MATTER* WHAT THE PRICE IS.
WHAT DO YOU WANT US TO DO?
WHAT YOU DO BEST: *BE WATCHMEN!*
AND WATCH *WHAT?*
WATCH OVER ME. THIS WILL BE YOUR FINAL MISSION.
WE'RE READY.
GOOD. NOW WE ARE GOING TO GO TO A SAFE, SECRET PLACE FAR, FAR BENEATH THE GROUND'S SURFACE. THERE YOU WILL CONSUME A SUBSTANCE.
THIS SUBSTANCE, CALLED EDON, WILL INCREASE YOUR PERCEPTIONS AND LENGTHEN YOUR LIFE CYCLES. YOU WON'T LIVE AS LONG AS I WILL, BUT FOR ENOUGH CENTURIES TO ACCOMPLISH YOUR MISSION.
AND YOU?
I'LL SLEEP A DEATH-LIKE SLUMBER FROM WHICH I WILL AWAKE ONLY WHEN THE TIME IS RIPE...
...AND I'LL PRAY FOR THE COURAGE TO DO WHAT MUST BE DONE.

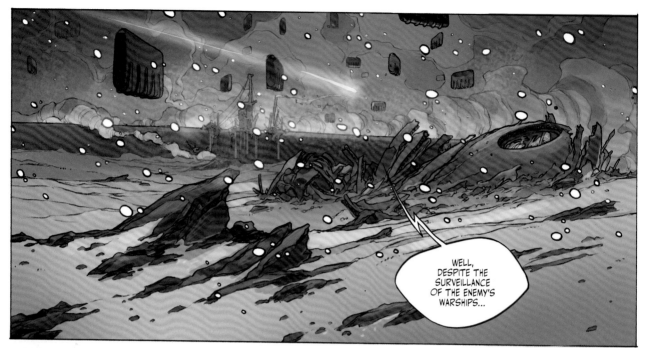

WELL, DESPITE THE SURVEILLANCE OF THE ENEMY'S WARSHIPS...

...GETTING ACROSS THE DOOR AT MOSE'S POLE WAS ACTUALLY QUITE SIMPLE.

IT COULDN'T HAVE BEEN OTHERWISE.

THE EDON DISC TRAVELS AT UNEQUALED SPEEDS AND ALTITUDES AND EXECUTES MANEUVERS THAT NOTHING ELSE CAN.

IT IS CLEAR THAT, ALTHOUGH TECHNO-LOGICALLY SUPERIOR TO THEIR COUSINS IN THE EMPIRE, THE INHABITANTS OF NEMO REMAIN BARBARIANS!

THAT'S GOOD. SUBJUGATING SUCH A PEOPLE SHOULD BE EASIER THAN...

AND THEIR WORLD IS JUST AS BAD. THE DATA COLLECTED BY OUR DEPUTIES DESCRIBE IT AS A HELL OF FIRE AND GAS.

BOOoooooOOMMM

SOMETHING HIT US!

W-WHAT HAPPENED?

THE HALO'S HULL IS INTACT BUT THE FORCE OF THE SHOCK DESTROYED THE CENTRAL SYSTEM.

WE'RE LOSING ALTITUDE FAST!

IT'S NOT POSSIBLE! THIS CAN'T BE!

I'VE LOST CONTROL OF IT!

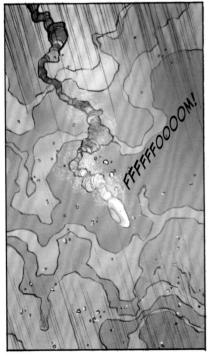

FFFFFFOOOOM!

AHHHHHH!

SPLAAASH!

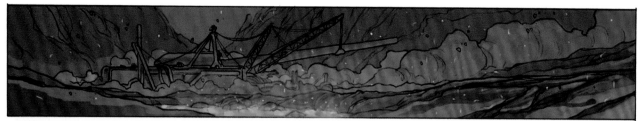

THAT'S IT. IT'S OVER!

EVEN THE LARGE CANNON IS NOW COMPLETELY UNUSABLE. BUT THAT'S UNDERSTANDABLE. IT WAS CONCEIVED OF AS PART OF A *SINGLE* DEADLY ATTACK.

ENTIRE GENERATIONS GAVE THEIR LIVES FOR THIS BRIEF, UNIQUE MOMENT... AND WE'LL NEVER KNOW WHAT – NOR WHOM – WE DESTROYED, WILL WE?

SUCH IS PRINCE GERARCA'S WILL.

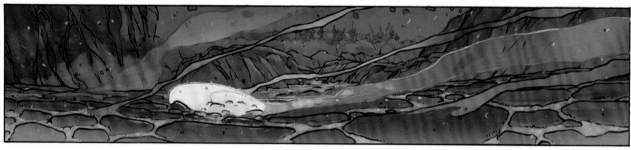

BUT IF IT ADDS ANY MEANING TO YOUR EXISTENCE, KNOW THAT THE MISSION YOU'VE CARRIED OUT WILL SAVE YOU ALL...

...AND WILL CONDEMN ME FOR ETERNITY!

I DON'T UNDERSTAND, COUNCILMAN KIONA!

IT IS OF NO IMPORTANCE. NOTHING HERE IS OF ANY IMPORTANCE ANYMORE.

EXCEPT, OF COURSE, WHAT HAPPENS NEXT.

I DON'T UNDERSTAND WHAT YOU'RE...

BY GOD, LOOK!

NO, IT CAN'T BE!

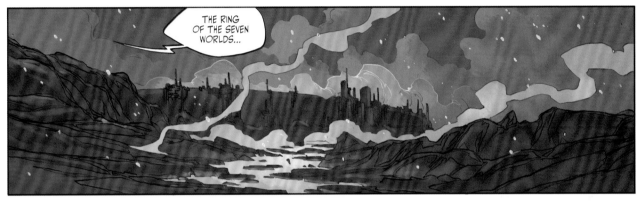

THE RING OF THE SEVEN WORLDS...

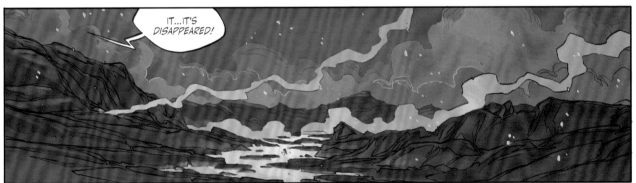

IT...IT'S DISAPPEARED!

BUT HOW?

VICEROY KIONA! WHERE...?

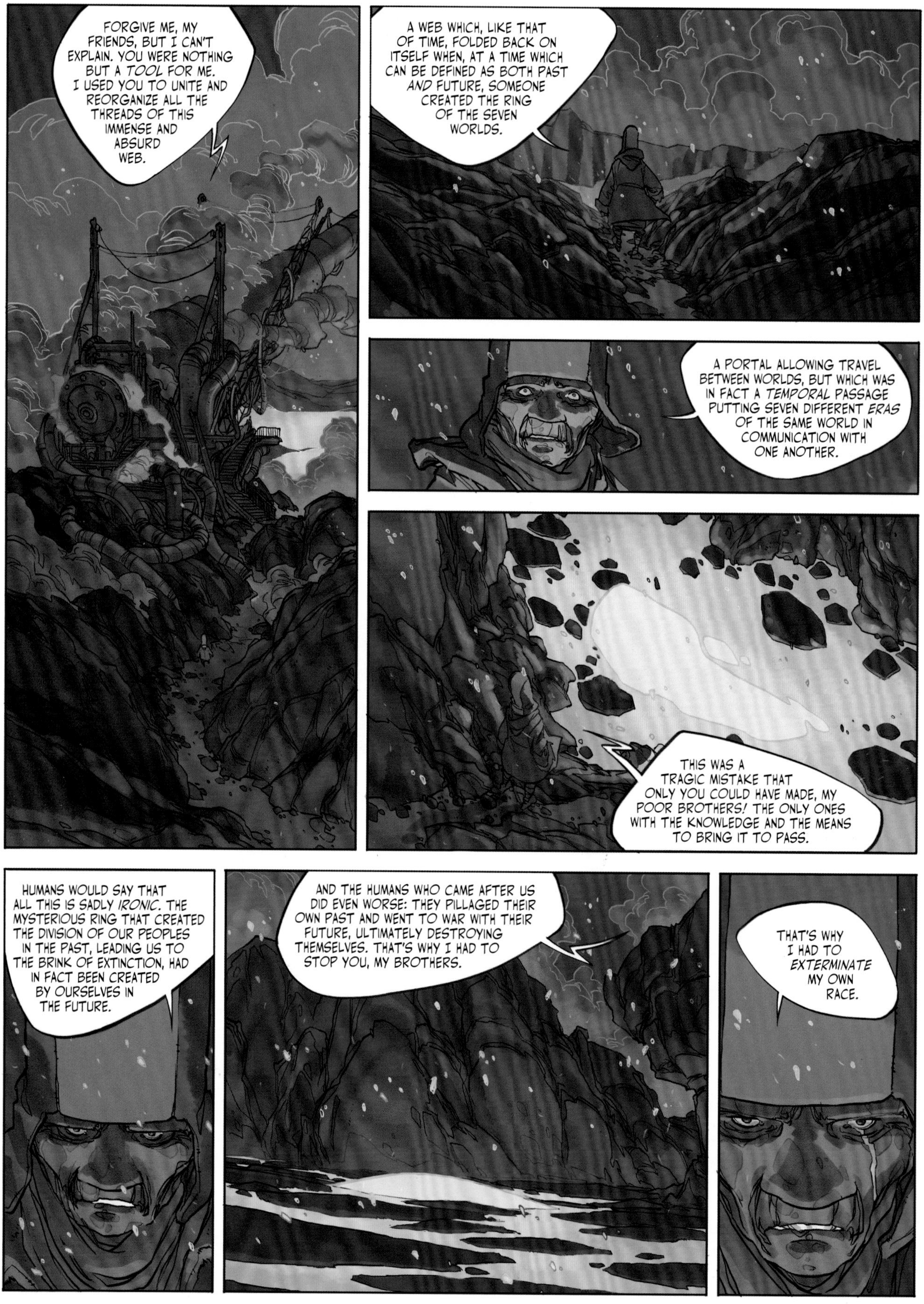
FORGIVE ME, MY FRIENDS, BUT I CAN'T EXPLAIN. YOU WERE NOTHING BUT A *TOOL* FOR ME. I USED YOU TO UNITE AND REORGANIZE ALL THE THREADS OF THIS IMMENSE AND ABSURD WEB.
A WEB WHICH, LIKE THAT OF TIME, FOLDED BACK ON ITSELF WHEN, AT A TIME WHICH CAN BE DEFINED AS BOTH PAST *AND* FUTURE, SOMEONE CREATED THE RING OF THE SEVEN WORLDS.
A PORTAL ALLOWING TRAVEL BETWEEN WORLDS, BUT WHICH WAS IN FACT A *TEMPORAL* PASSAGE PUTTING SEVEN DIFFERENT *ERAS* OF THE SAME WORLD IN COMMUNICATION WITH ONE ANOTHER.
THIS WAS A TRAGIC MISTAKE THAT ONLY YOU COULD HAVE MADE, MY POOR BROTHERS! THE ONLY ONES WITH THE KNOWLEDGE AND THE MEANS TO BRING IT TO PASS.
HUMANS WOULD SAY THAT ALL THIS IS SADLY *IRONIC*. THE MYSTERIOUS RING THAT CREATED THE DIVISION OF OUR PEOPLES IN THE PAST, LEADING US TO THE BRINK OF EXTINCTION, HAD IN FACT BEEN CREATED BY OURSELVES IN THE FUTURE.
AND THE HUMANS WHO CAME AFTER US DID EVEN WORSE: THEY PILLAGED THEIR OWN PAST AND WENT TO WAR WITH THEIR FUTURE, ULTIMATELY DESTROYING THEMSELVES. THAT'S WHY I HAD TO STOP YOU, MY BROTHERS.
THAT'S WHY I HAD TO *EXTERMINATE* MY OWN RACE.

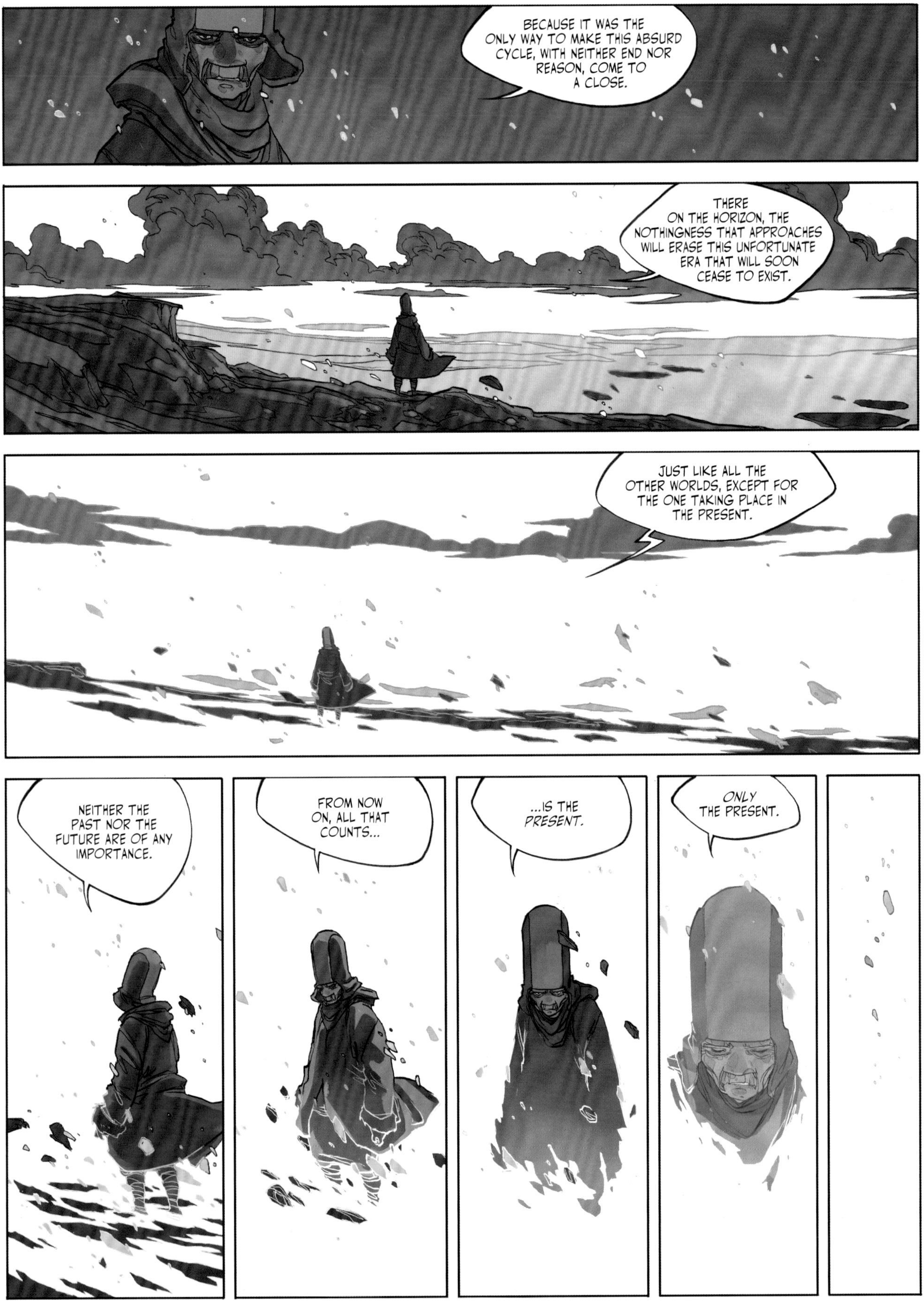
BECAUSE IT WAS THE ONLY WAY TO MAKE THIS ABSURD CYCLE, WITH NEITHER END NOR REASON, COME TO A CLOSE.
THERE ON THE HORIZON, THE NOTHINGNESS THAT APPROACHES WILL ERASE THIS UNFORTUNATE ERA THAT WILL SOON CEASE TO EXIST.
JUST LIKE ALL THE OTHER WORLDS, EXCEPT FOR THE ONE TAKING PLACE IN THE PRESENT.
NEITHER THE PAST NOR THE FUTURE ARE OF ANY IMPORTANCE.
FROM NOW ON, ALL THAT COUNTS...
...IS THE *PRESENT.*
ONLY THE PRESENT.

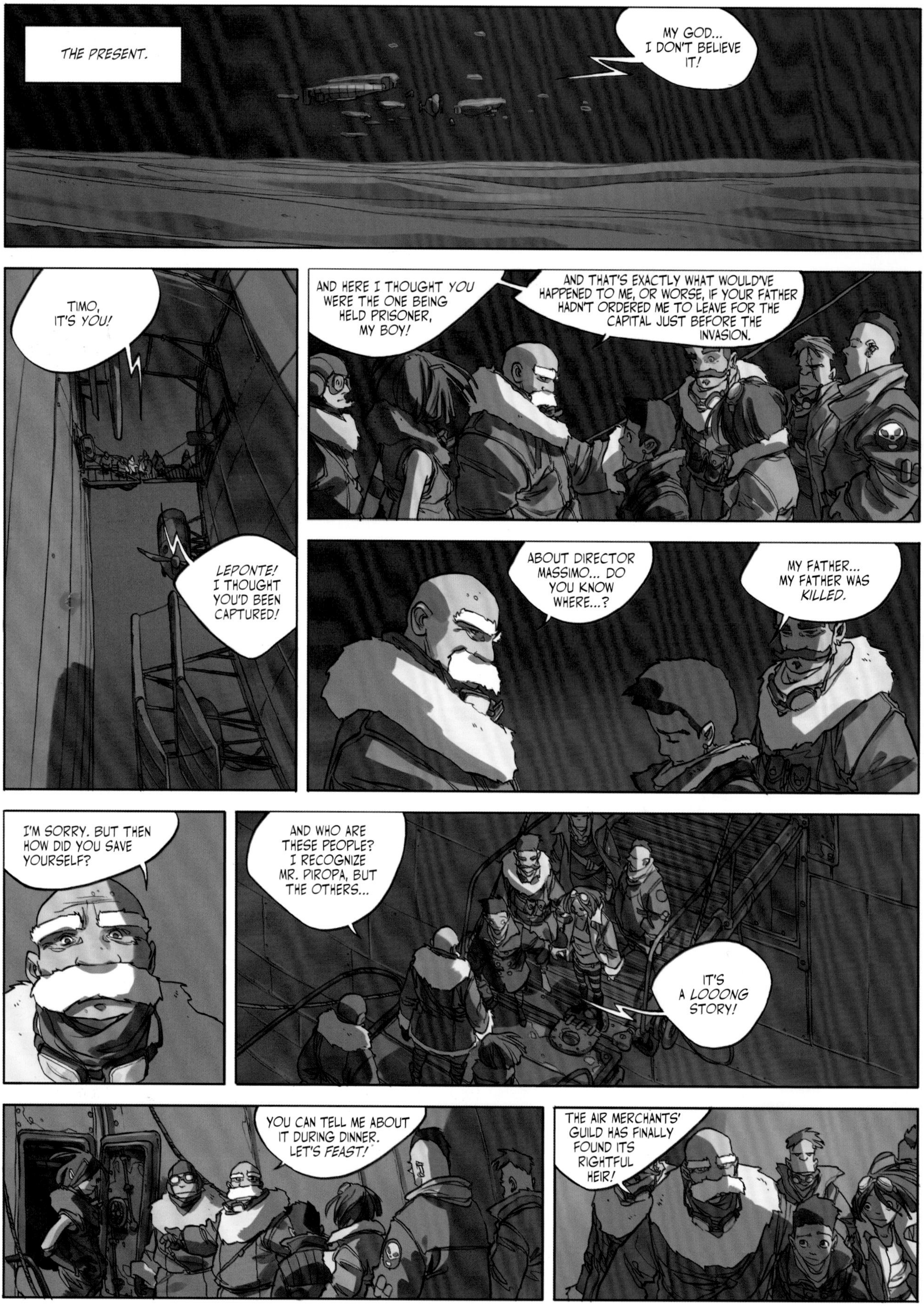
THE PRESENT.
MY GOD... I DON'T BELIEVE IT!
TIMO, IT'S YOU!
LEPONTE! I THOUGHT YOU'D BEEN CAPTURED!
AND HERE I THOUGHT YOU WERE THE ONE BEING HELD PRISONER, MY BOY!
AND THAT'S EXACTLY WHAT WOULD'VE HAPPENED TO ME, OR WORSE, IF YOUR FATHER HADN'T ORDERED ME TO LEAVE FOR THE CAPITAL JUST BEFORE THE INVASION.
ABOUT DIRECTOR MASSIMO... DO YOU KNOW WHERE...?
MY FATHER... MY FATHER WAS KILLED.
I'M SORRY. BUT THEN HOW DID YOU SAVE YOURSELF?
AND WHO ARE THESE PEOPLE? I RECOGNIZE MR. PIROPA, BUT THE OTHERS...
IT'S A LOOONG STORY!
YOU CAN TELL ME ABOUT IT DURING DINNER. LET'S FEAST!
THE AIR MERCHANTS' GUILD HAS FINALLY FOUND ITS RIGHTFUL HEIR!

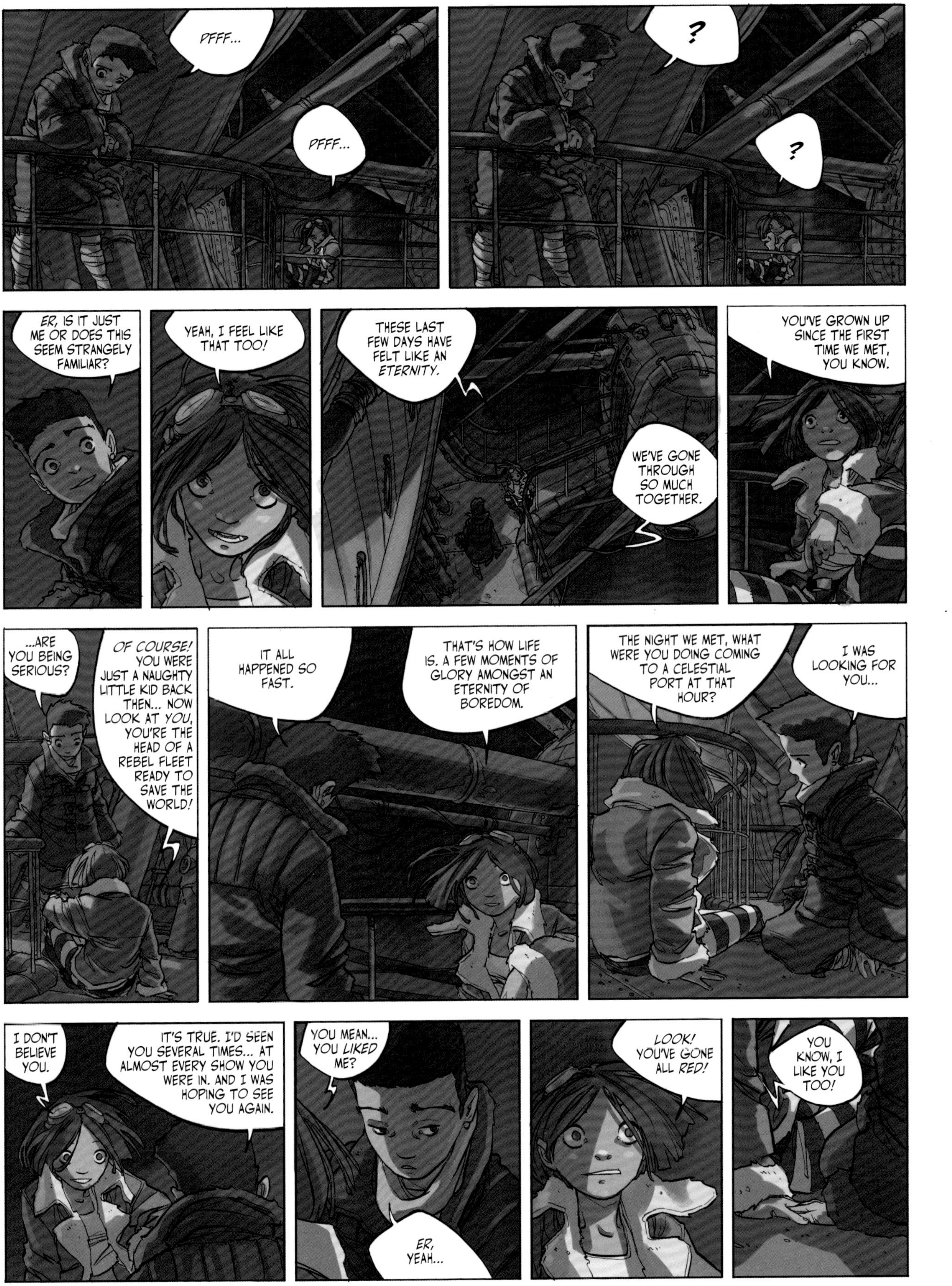

PFFF...
PFFF...
?
?
ER, IS IT JUST ME OR DOES THIS SEEM STRANGELY FAMILIAR?
YEAH, I FEEL LIKE THAT TOO!
THESE LAST FEW DAYS HAVE FELT LIKE AN ETERNITY.
WE'VE GONE THROUGH SO MUCH TOGETHER.
YOU'VE GROWN UP SINCE THE FIRST TIME WE MET, YOU KNOW.
...ARE YOU BEING SERIOUS?
OF COURSE! YOU WERE JUST A NAUGHTY LITTLE KID BACK THEN... NOW LOOK AT YOU, YOU'RE THE HEAD OF A REBEL FLEET READY TO SAVE THE WORLD!
IT ALL HAPPENED SO FAST.
THAT'S HOW LIFE IS. A FEW MOMENTS OF GLORY AMONGST AN ETERNITY OF BOREDOM.
THE NIGHT WE MET, WHAT WERE YOU DOING COMING TO A CELESTIAL PORT AT THAT HOUR?
I WAS LOOKING FOR YOU...
I DON'T BELIEVE YOU.
IT'S TRUE. I'D SEEN YOU SEVERAL TIMES... AT ALMOST EVERY SHOW YOU WERE IN. AND I WAS HOPING TO SEE YOU AGAIN.
YOU MEAN... YOU LIKED ME?
ER, YEAH...
LOOK! YOU'VE GONE ALL RED!
YOU KNOW, I LIKE YOU TOO!

IT'S TOO QUIET!

WHAT ARE YOU SAYING, SIR?

THE CITY IS TOO CALM. IT'S AS IF THEY'RE WAITING FOR SOMETHING.

THEY'LL ATTACK US SOON, I CAN FEEL IT.

THE REBELS FROM THE LOWER CITY?

I'M NOT SURE. BUT I KNOW SOMETHING'S GOING TO HAPPEN TONIGHT. ALERT THE GARRISON.

BUT THERE'S NOTHING ON THE RADARS.

OBEY MY ORDERS!

YES, SIR. EVERYONE, TO YOUR BATTLE STATIONS!

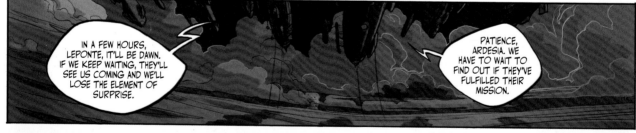

IN A FEW HOURS, LEPONTE, IT'LL BE DAWN. IF WE KEEP WAITING, THEY'LL SEE US COMING AND WE'LL LOSE THE ELEMENT OF SURPRISE.

PATIENCE, ARDESIA. WE HAVE TO WAIT TO FIND OUT IF THEY'VE FULFILLED THEIR MISSION.

THEIR PLAN IS ABSURD. IT'LL NEVER WORK.

PRAY THAT IT DOES. OTHERWISE, OUR ATTACK WILL BE THE SHORTEST IN HISTORY.

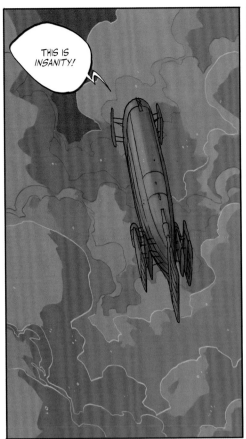

THIS IS *INSANITY!*

IN FACT, IT'S *SUICIDE!* AT THIS HEIGHT, THE WINDS ARE TOO STRONG! THEY'LL RIP THE UPWARD SAILS APART LIKE TISSUE PAPER!

YOU'RE WRONG. IT'S NOT ORDINARY FABRIC, BUT THE SAME MATERIAL USED ON THE WINGS OF MONOHELIXES.

IT WAS *LUCE'S* IDEA AND I'M CONFIDENT IT'S GOING TO WORK.

WELL, DO AS YOU WISH, BUT YOU'RE ALL COMPLETELY INSANE!

IT'S GOING TO WORK, RIGHT?

WE'RE ABOVE THE TARGET. GET READY TO JUMP!

I'M SCARED.

DON'T WORRY, I USED TO DO THIS ALL THE TIME AT THE AIR CIRCUS!

BESIDES, NOW THAT I'VE FOUND YOU...

...I'M NOT GONNA LET YOU *GOOOOOOOO!*

WHY ARE WE GUARDING THE TOP OF A SHIP? IT MUST BE TRUE WHAT THEY SAY: GOVERNOR FERAXIS HAS LOST HIS MARBLES!

WATCH WHAT YOU SAY! IF SOMEONE HEARD YOU, YOU'D BE IN REAL TROUBLE!

AND HOW WOULD THEY HEAR US? UP HERE, WE'RE ALL ALONE!

TUMP!

UH!

HEY, WHAT'S THAT?

AH!

PERFECT, WE'RE EXACTLY WHERE WE SHOULD BE. NOBODY'S SEEN US ARRIVE AND, MORE IMPORTANTLY, NO CASUALTIES.

SADLY, I'M NOT SO SURE ABOUT THAT...

TIMO DIDN'T MAKE IT. A BURST OF WIND SWEPT HIM EAST. I FEAR HE'S--

TIMO'S ALIVE!

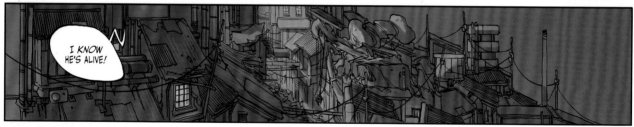
I KNOW HE'S ALIVE!

HE DOESN'T LOOK LIKE ONE OF THEIRS.

NO, BUT HE DOESN'T LOOK LIKE ONE OF OURS EITHER.

WELL, THEN HE MUST DIE!

ONE SECOND...

I...I KNOW HIM!

IT'S TIME!

LET'S GO!

ENEMY SHIPS APPROACHING!

I KNEW IT!

GO ON, WHAT ARE YOU WAITING FOR? ATTACK!

SOMETHING ODD IS HAPPENING...

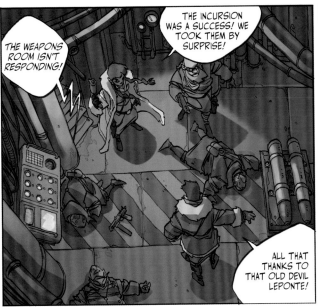

THE WEAPONS ROOM ISN'T RESPONDING!

THE INCURSION WAS A SUCCESS! WE TOOK THEM BY SURPRISE!

ALL THAT THANKS TO THAT OLD DEVIL LEPONTE!

WITHOUT THE INFORMATION HE GOT OUT OF THOSE PRISONERS FROM NEMO, WE NEVER WOULD'VE KNOWN HOW TO RELEASE ALL THAT GAS AND PUT ALL THOSE GUYS OUT OF COMMISSION.

WITH THE FLAGSHIP OUT OF THE WAY, THE OTHER ENEMY VESSELS SHOULD TAKE A WHILE TO GET ORGANIZED. AND THAT'LL GIVE OUR FLEET A DECENT SHOT AT GETTING TO THE CITY!

BUT IT'S ALL UP TO US NOW...

...AND LUCE!

SHE'S GOT THE TOUGHEST MISSION OF ALL!

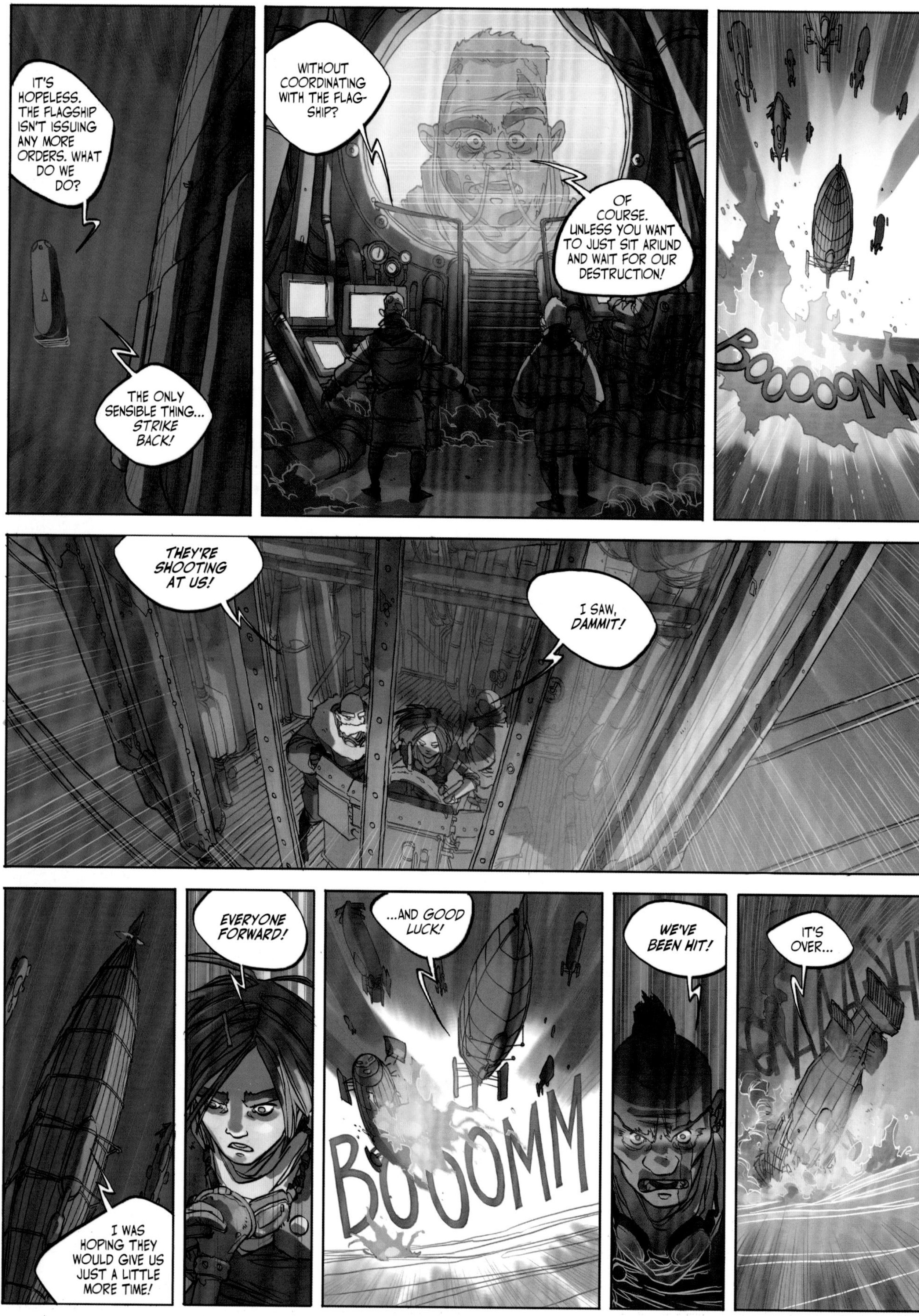
IT'S HOPELESS. THE FLAGSHIP ISN'T ISSUING ANY MORE ORDERS. WHAT DO WE DO?
THE ONLY SENSIBLE THING... STRIKE BACK!
WITHOUT COORDINATING WITH THE FLAG-SHIP?
OF COURSE. UNLESS YOU WANT TO JUST SIT ARIUND AND WAIT FOR OUR DESTRUCTION!
BOOOOOMM
THEY'RE SHOOTING AT US!
I SAW, DAMMIT!
I WAS HOPING THEY WOULD GIVE US JUST A LITTLE MORE TIME!
EVERYONE FORWARD!
...AND GOOD LUCK!
BOOOMM
WE'VE BEEN HIT!
IT'S OVER...

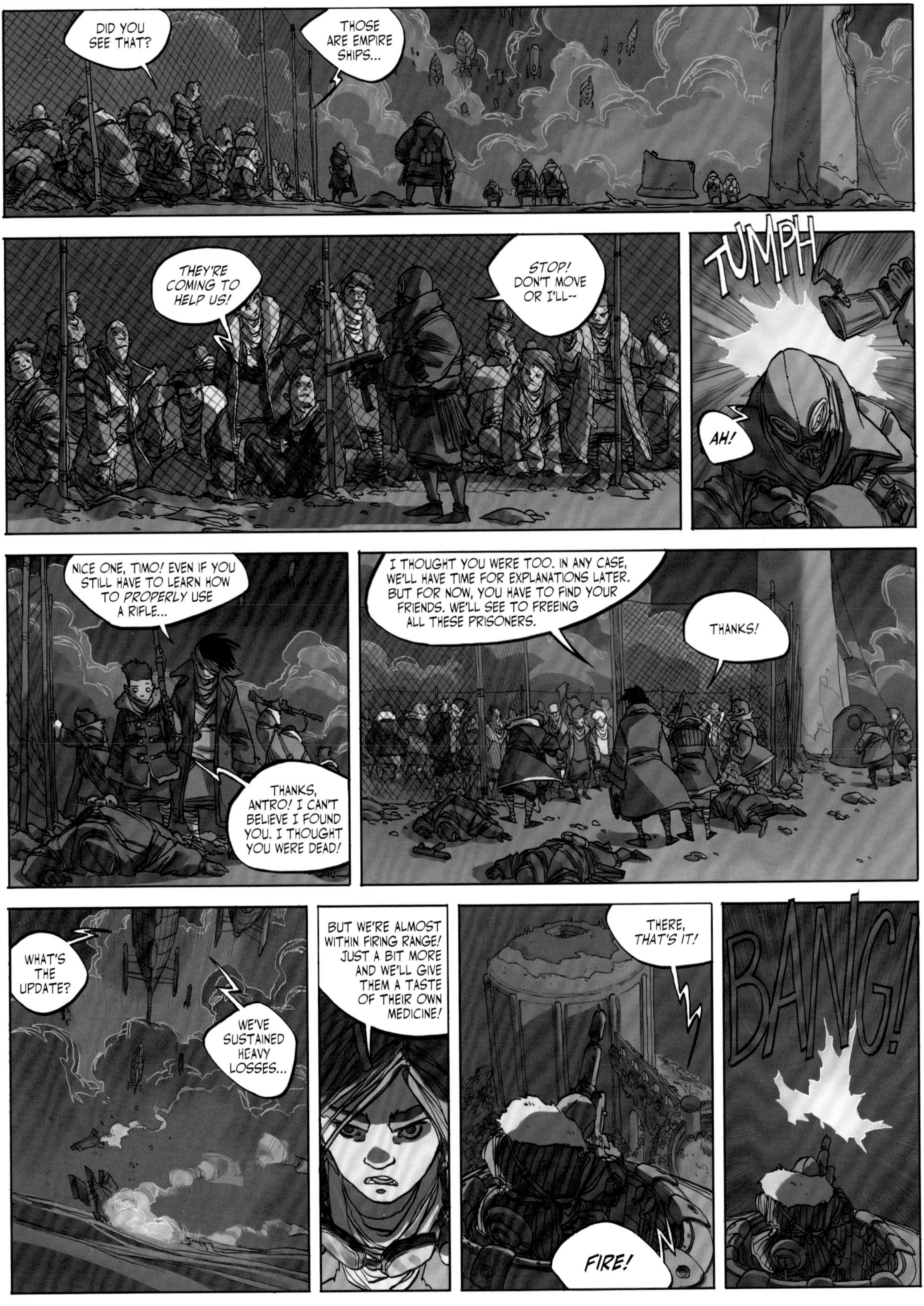
DID YOU SEE THAT?
THOSE ARE EMPIRE SHIPS...
THEY'RE COMING TO HELP US!
STOP! DON'T MOVE OR I'LL--
TUMPH
AH!
NICE ONE, TIMO! EVEN IF YOU STILL HAVE TO LEARN HOW TO PROPERLY USE A RIFLE...
THANKS, ANTRO! I CAN'T BELIEVE I FOUND YOU. I THOUGHT YOU WERE DEAD!
I THOUGHT YOU WERE TOO. IN ANY CASE, WE'LL HAVE TIME FOR EXPLANATIONS LATER. BUT FOR NOW, YOU HAVE TO FIND YOUR FRIENDS. WE'LL SEE TO FREEING ALL THESE PRISONERS.
THANKS!
WHAT'S THE UPDATE?
WE'VE SUSTAINED HEAVY LOSSES...
BUT WE'RE ALMOST WITHIN FIRING RANGE! JUST A BIT MORE AND WE'LL GIVE THEM A TASTE OF THEIR OWN MEDICINE!
THERE, THAT'S IT!
FIRE!
BANG!

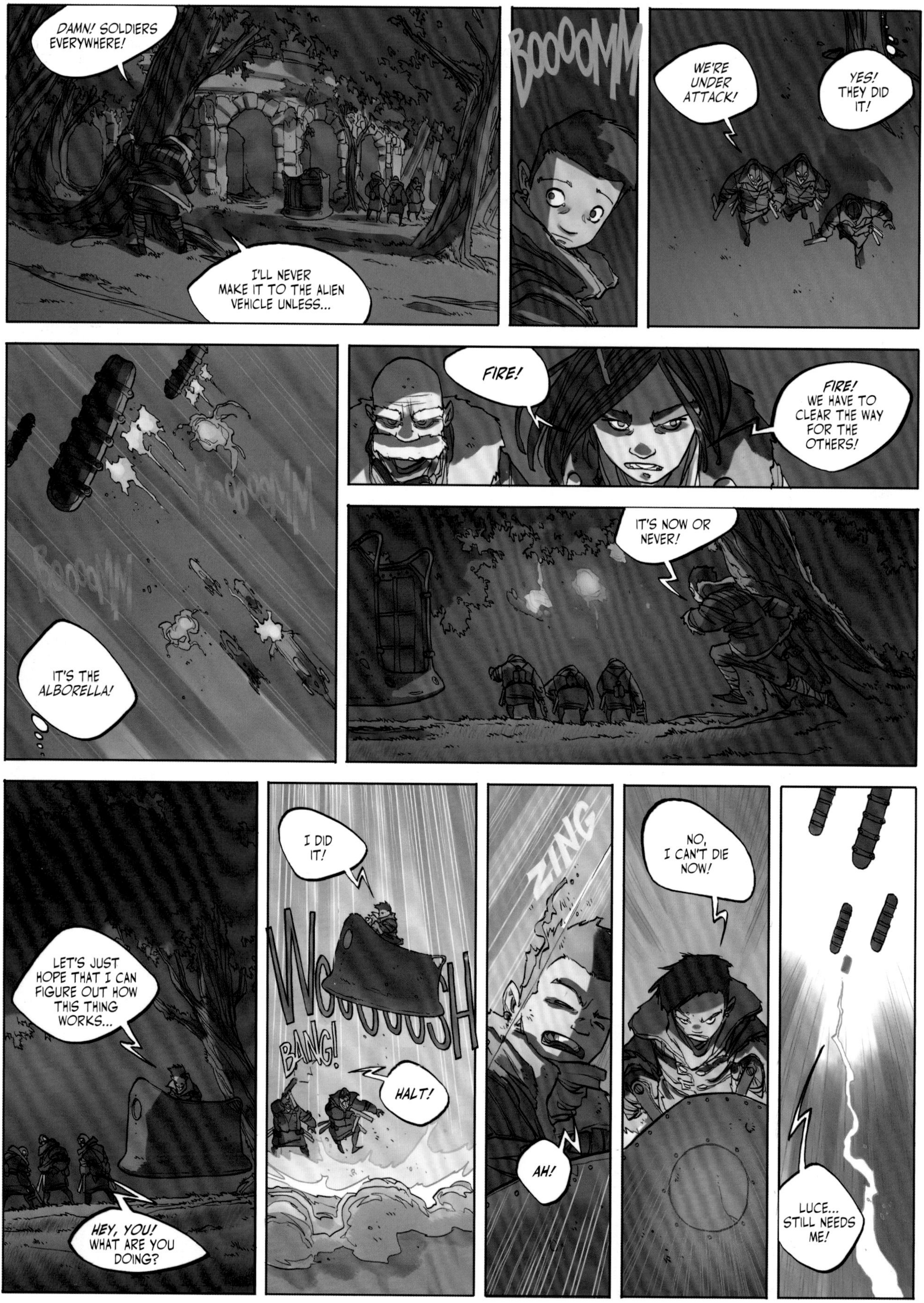
DAMN! SOLDIERS EVERYWHERE!
I'LL NEVER MAKE IT TO THE ALIEN VEHICLE UNLESS...
BOOOOMM
WE'RE UNDER ATTACK!
YES! THEY DID IT!
BOOOOMM
BOOOMM
IT'S THE ALBORELLA!
FIRE!
FIRE! WE HAVE TO CLEAR THE WAY FOR THE OTHERS!
IT'S NOW OR NEVER!
LET'S JUST HOPE THAT I CAN FIGURE OUT HOW THIS THING WORKS...
HEY, YOU! WHAT ARE YOU DOING?
I DID IT!
WOOOOOSH
BANG!
HALT!
ZING
AH!
NO, I CAN'T DIE NOW!
LUCE... STILL NEEDS ME!

BOoo⁰ooMMMM

WE'VE BEEN HIT!

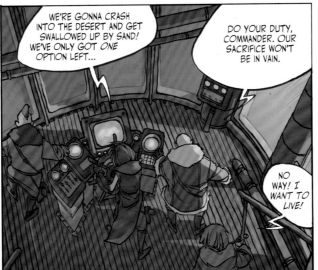

WE'RE GONNA CRASH INTO THE DESERT AND GET SWALLOWED UP BY SAND! WE'VE ONLY GOT ONE OPTION LEFT...

DO YOUR DUTY, COMMANDER. OUR SACRIFICE WON'T BE IN VAIN.

NO WAY! I WANT TO LIVE!

WE'LL DIE ANYWAY. WE'VE ONLY GOT ONE CHOICE LEFT: DIE AS COWARDS...

...OR AS FREE MEN!

WHAT ARE THEY DOING?! ARE THEY CRAZY?!

THEY'RE COMING STRAIGHT FOR US!

SAVE YOUR-SELF!

AHHHHH!

BOooooOMM

CURSES! CURSE THEM ALL!

WE'VE LOST THE BATTLE...

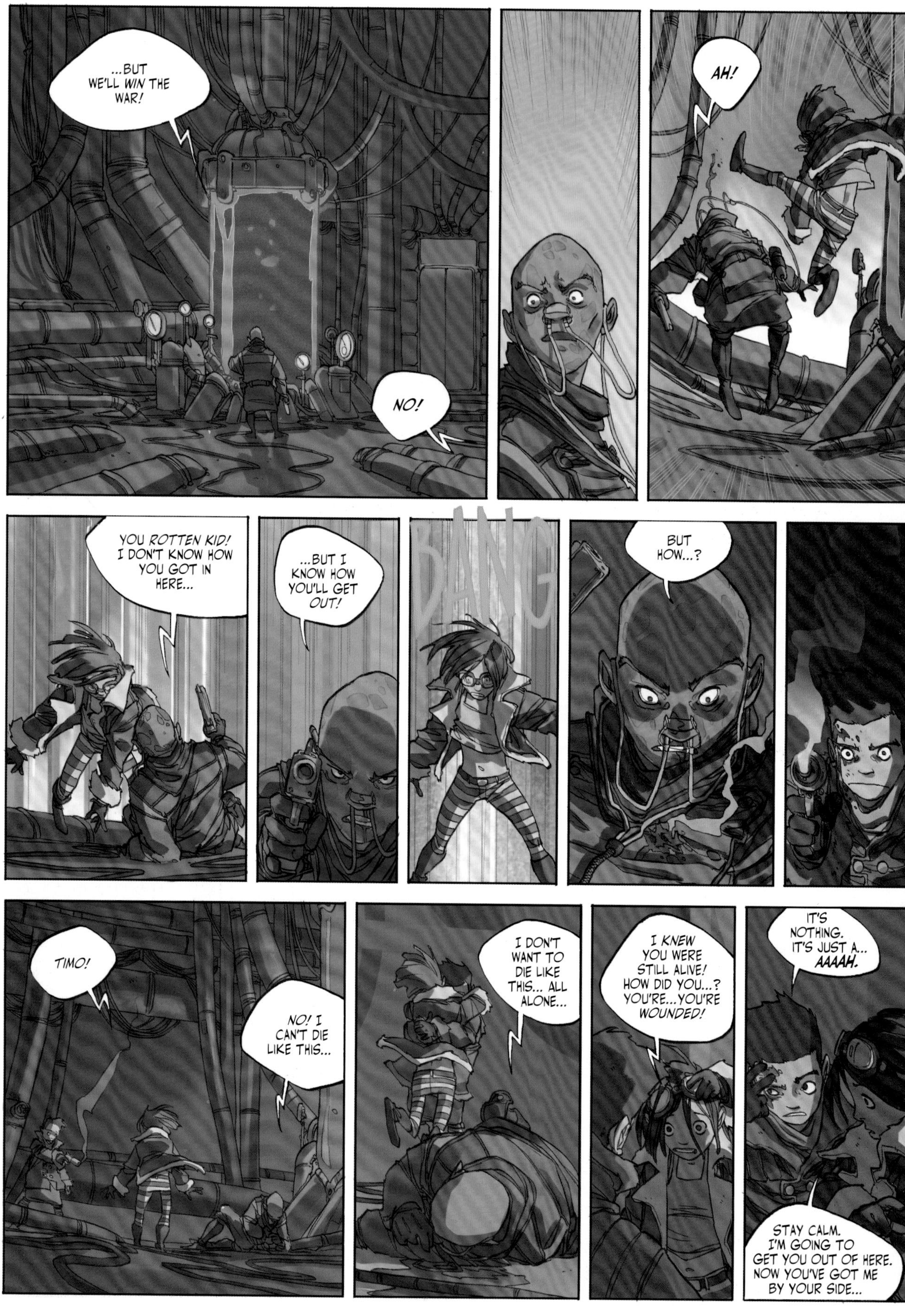
...BUT WE'LL WIN THE WAR!
NO!
AH!
YOU ROTTEN KID! I DON'T KNOW HOW YOU GOT IN HERE...
...BUT I KNOW HOW YOU'LL GET OUT!
BANG
BUT HOW...?
TIMO!
NO! I CAN'T DIE LIKE THIS...
I DON'T WANT TO DIE LIKE THIS... ALL ALONE...
I KNEW YOU WERE STILL ALIVE! HOW DID YOU...? YOU'RE...YOU'RE WOUNDED!
IT'S NOTHING. IT'S JUST A... AAAAH.
STAY CALM. I'M GOING TO GET YOU OUT OF HERE. NOW YOU'VE GOT ME BY YOUR SIDE...

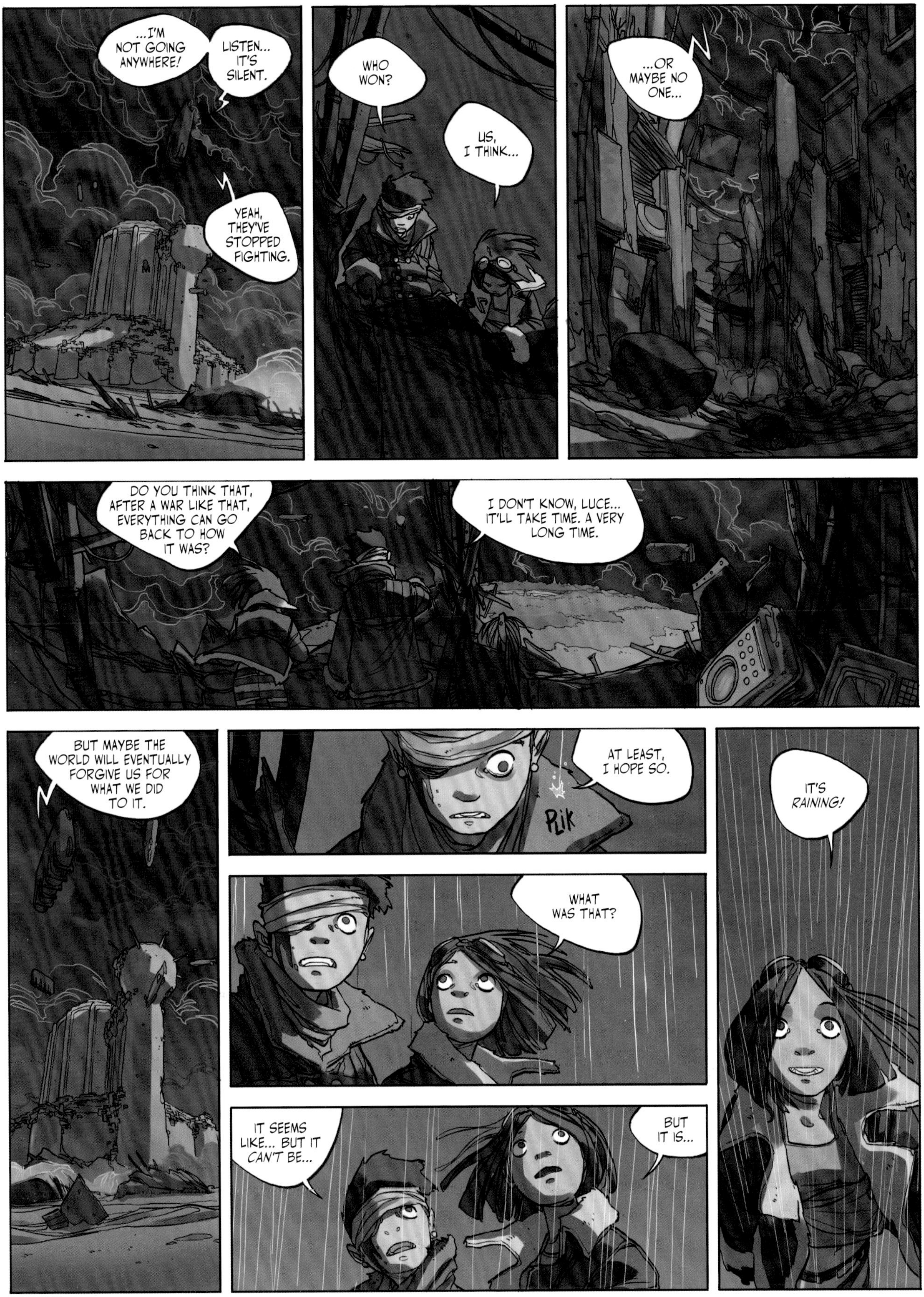
...I'M NOT GOING ANYWHERE!
LISTEN... IT'S SILENT.
YEAH, THEY'VE STOPPED FIGHTING.
WHO WON?
US, I THINK...
...OR MAYBE NO ONE...
DO YOU THINK THAT, AFTER A WAR LIKE THAT, EVERYTHING CAN GO BACK TO HOW IT WAS?
I DON'T KNOW, LUCE... IT'LL TAKE TIME. A VERY LONG TIME.
BUT MAYBE THE WORLD WILL EVENTUALLY FORGIVE US FOR WHAT WE DID TO IT.
AT LEAST, I HOPE SO.
PLIK
WHAT WAS THAT?
IT SEEMS LIKE... BUT IT CAN'T BE...
BUT IT IS...
IT'S RAINING!

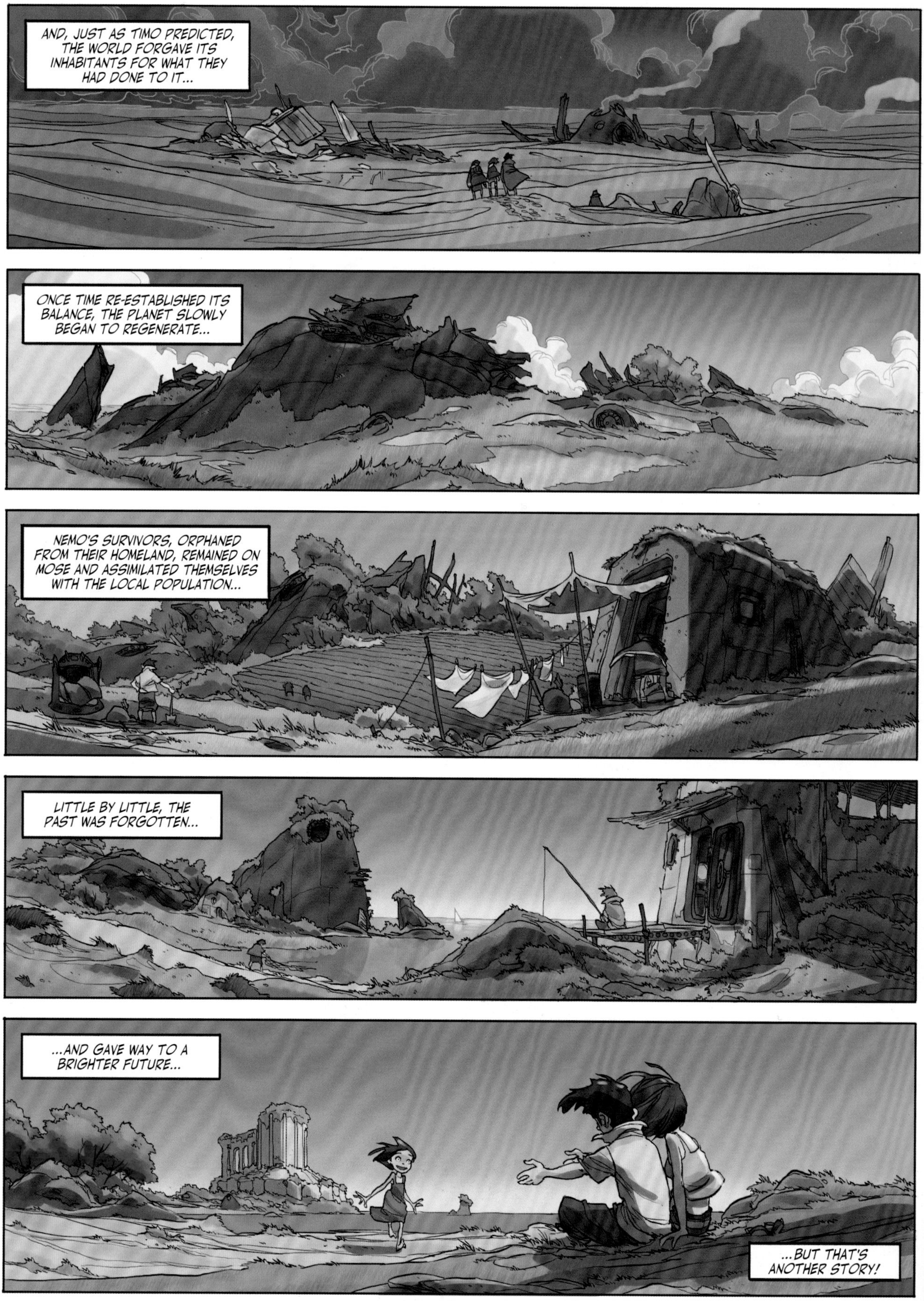
AND, JUST AS TIMO PREDICTED, THE WORLD FORGAVE ITS INHABITANTS FOR WHAT THEY HAD DONE TO IT...
ONCE TIME RE-ESTABLISHED ITS BALANCE, THE PLANET SLOWLY BEGAN TO REGENERATE...
NEMO'S SURVIVORS, ORPHANED FROM THEIR HOMELAND, REMAINED ON MOSE AND ASSIMILATED THEMSELVES WITH THE LOCAL POPULATION...
LITTLE BY LITTLE, THE PAST WAS FORGOTTEN...
...AND GAVE WAY TO A BRIGHTER FUTURE...
...BUT THAT'S ANOTHER STORY!

END.

THE RING OF THE SEVEN WORLDS

ART GALLERY BY MATTEO PIANA

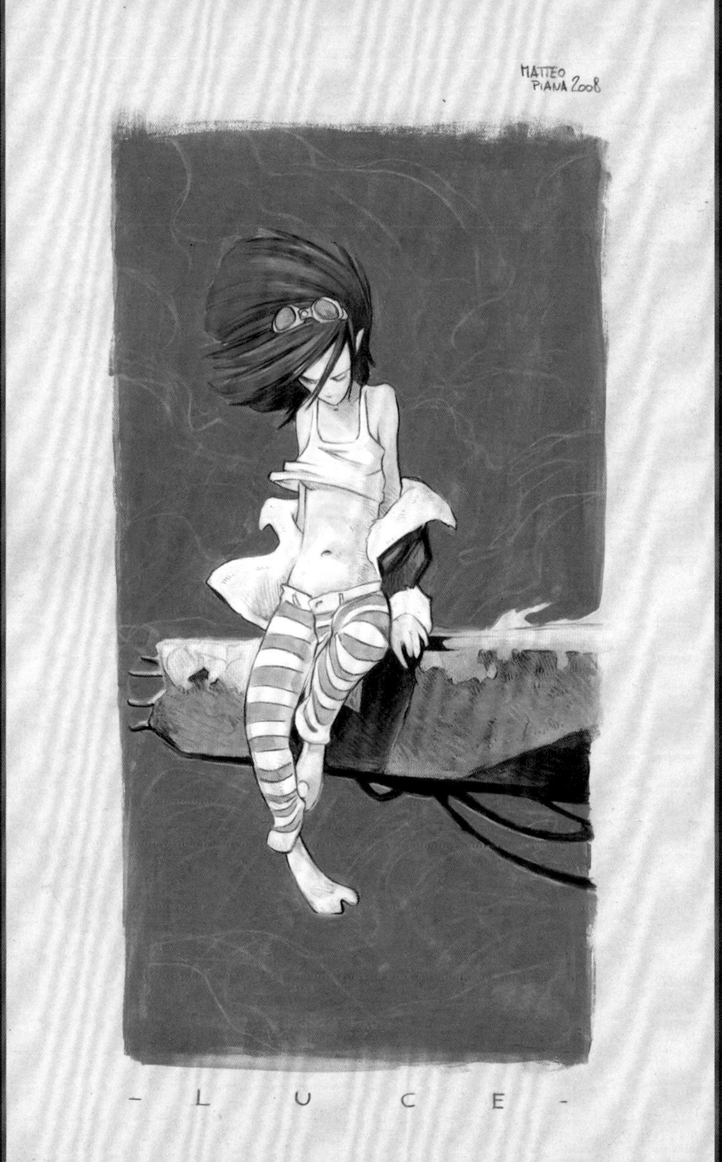
MATTEO PIANA 2008
- L U C E -

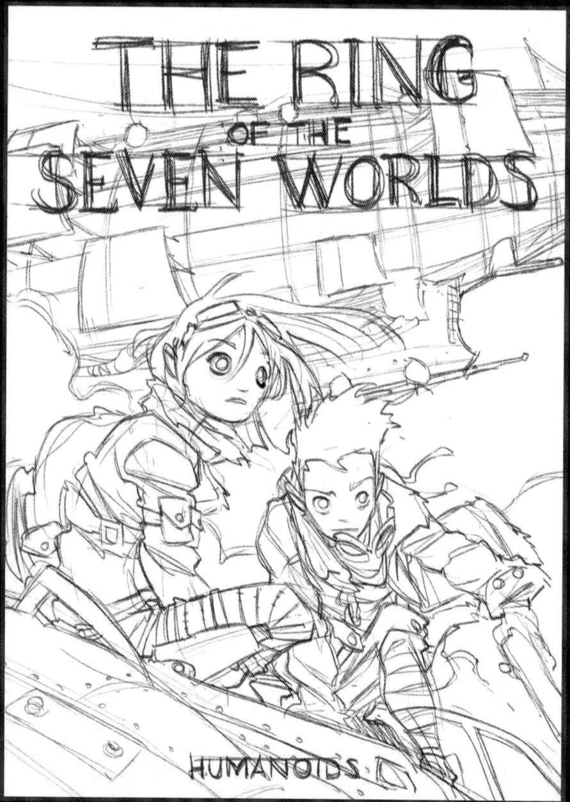
THE RING
OF THE
SEVEN WORLDS
HUMANOIDS
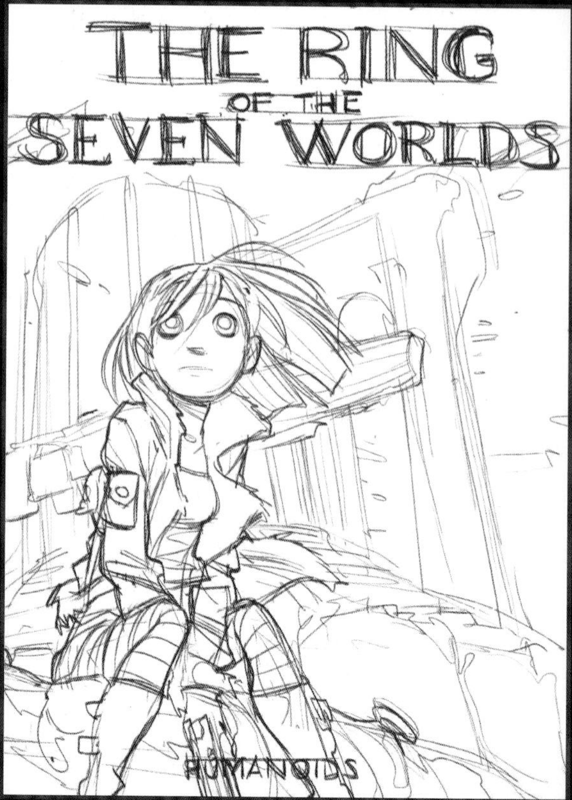
THE RING
OF THE
SEVEN WORLDS
HUMANOIDS
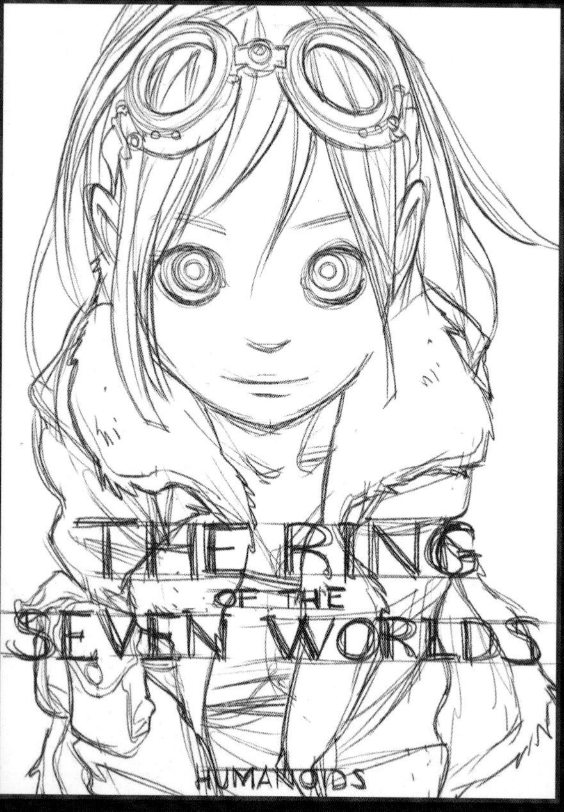
THE RING
OF THE
SEVEN WORLDS
HUMANOIDS
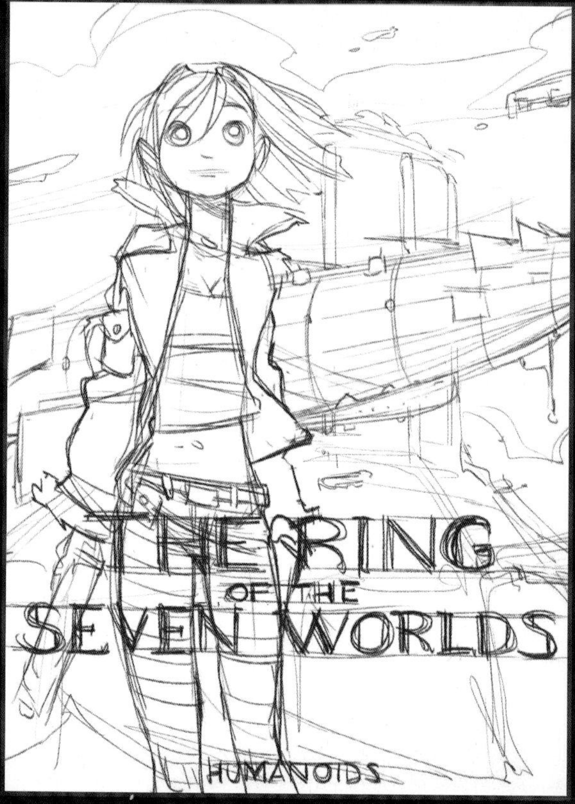
THE RING
OF THE
SEVEN WORLDS
HUMANOIDS

Cover sketches for the 2017 English language edition. The top left version was used.

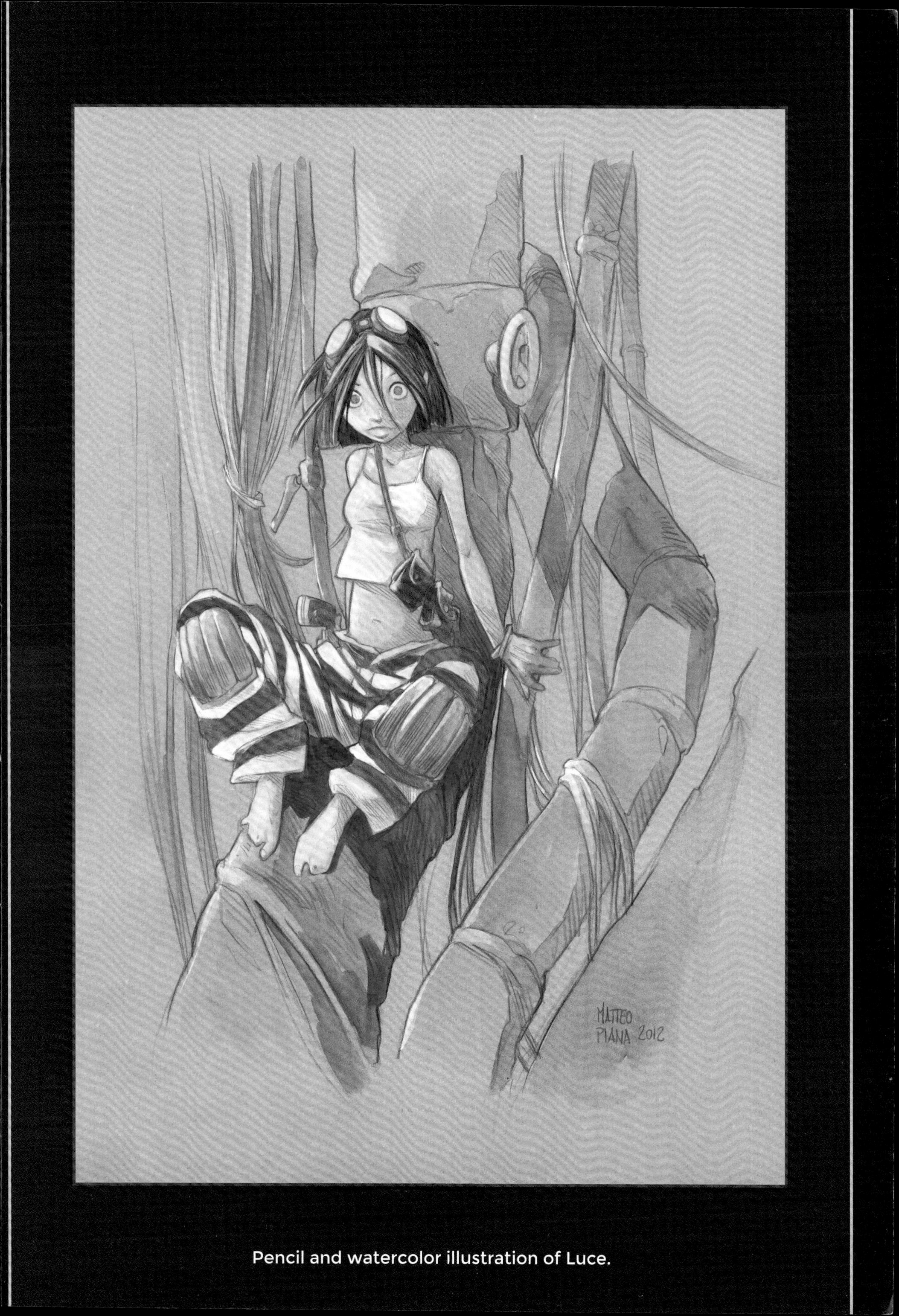
MATTEO
PIANA 2012

Pencil and watercolor illustration of Luce.

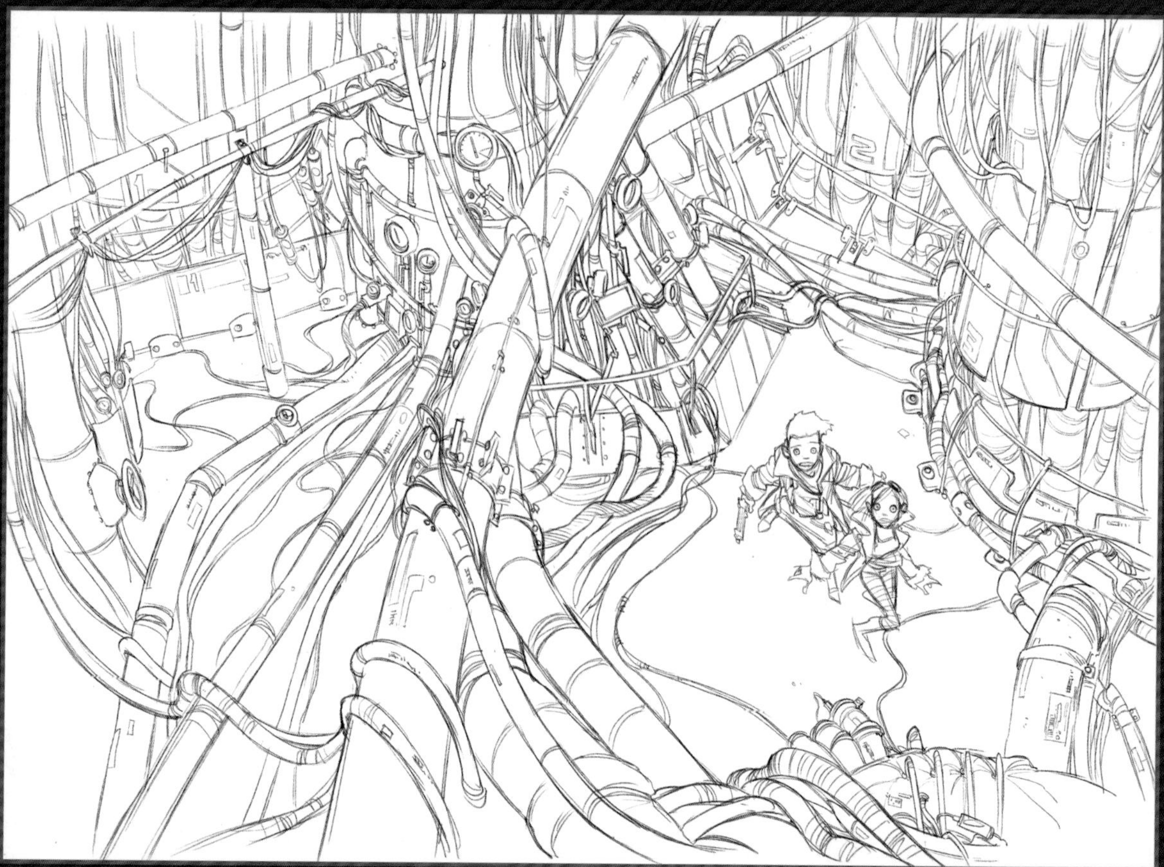

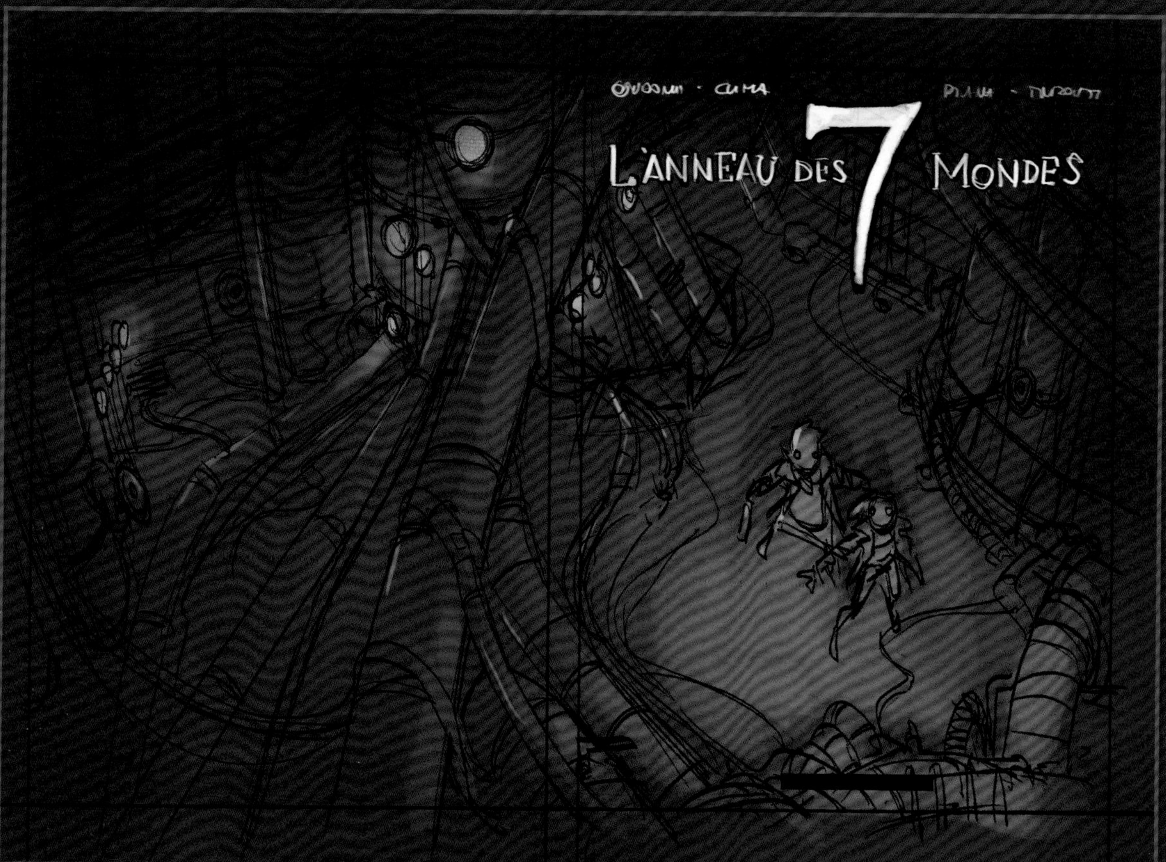
L'ANNEAU DES 7 MONDES

Pencils and color rough for an unused cover of a French omnibus edition.

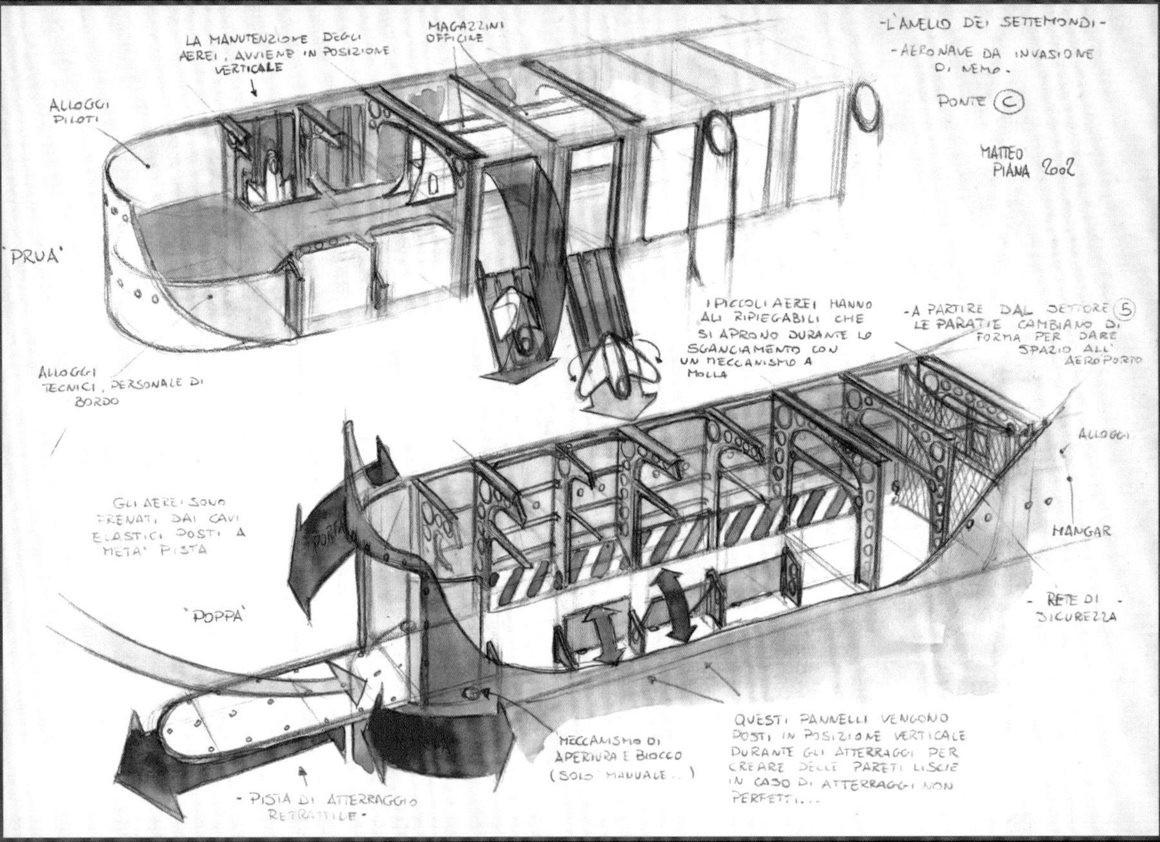
-L'ANELLO DEI SETTEMONDI-
-AERONAVE DA INVASIONE DI NEMO-
PONTE C
MATTEO PIANA 2002
LA MANUTENZIONE DEGLI AEREI, AVVIENE IN POSIZIONE VERTICALE
MAGAZZINI OFFICINE
ALLOGGI PILOTI
"PRUA"
ALLOGGI TECNICI, PERSONALE DI BORDO
I PICCOLI AEREI HANNO ALI RIPIEGABILI CHE SI APRONO DURANTE LO SGANCIAMENTO CON UN MECCANISMO A MOLLA
-A PARTIRE DAL SETTORE 5 LE PARATIE CAMBIANO DI FORMA PER DARE SPAZIO ALL' AEROPORTO
ALLOGGI
HANGAR
GLI AEREI SONO FRENATI DAI CAVI ELASTICI POSTI A META' PISTA
"POPPA"
- RETE DI - SICUREZZA
MECCANISMO DI APERTURA E BLOCCO (SOLO MANUALE...)
QUESTI PANNELLI VENGONO POSTI IN POSIZIONE VERTICALE DURANTE GLI ATTERRAGGI PER CREARE DELLE PARETI LISCIE IN CASO DI ATTERRAGGI NON PERFETTI...
- PISTA DI ATTERRAGGIO RETRATTILE -

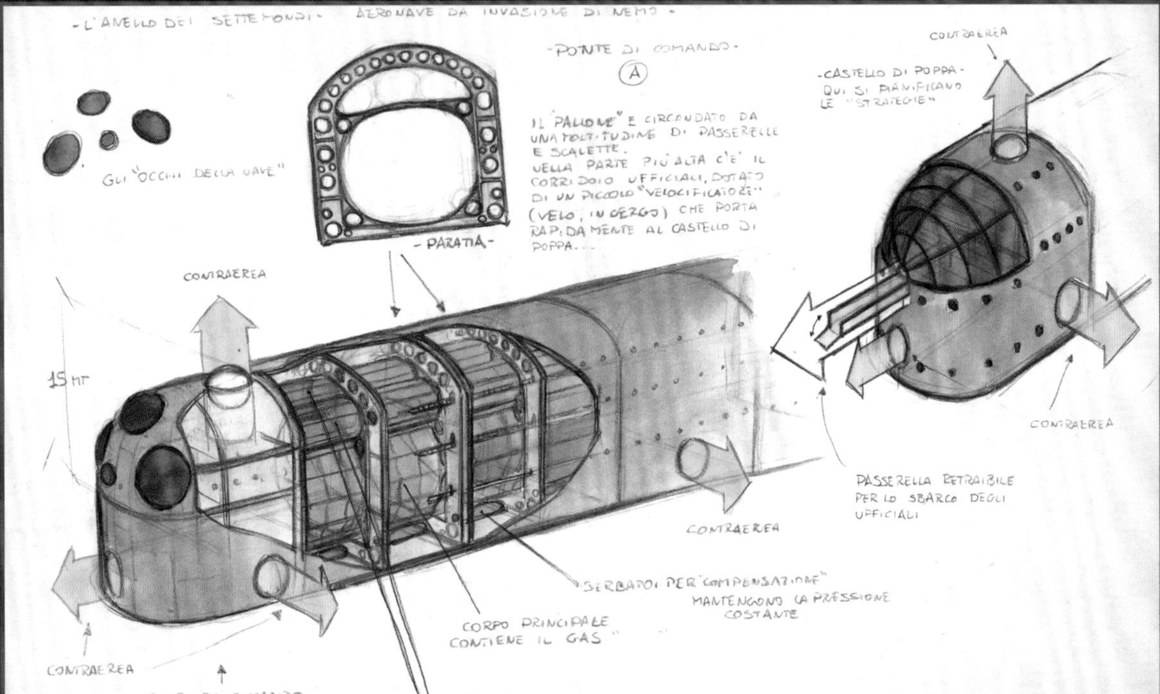
-L'ANELLO DEI SETTEMONDI- AERONAVE DA INVASIONE DI NEMO -
-PONTE DI COMANDO-
A
GLI "OCCHI DELLA NAVE"
- PARATIA -
IL "PALLONE" È CIRCONDATO DA UNA MOLTITUDINE DI PASSERELLE E SCALETTE.
NELLA PARTE PIU' ALTA C'È IL CORRIDOIO UFFICIALI, DOTATO DI UN PICCOLO "VELOCIFICATORE" (VELO, IN GERGO) CHE PORTA RAPIDAMENTE AL CASTELLO DI POPPA...
CONTRAEREA
-CASTELLO DI POPPA- QUI SI PIANIFICANO LE "STRATEGIE"
CONTRAEREA
15 mt
CONTRAEREA
PASSERELLA RETRAIBILE PER LO SBARCO DEGLI UFFICIALI
CONTRAEREA
SERBATOI PER "COMPENSAZIONE" MANTENGONO LA PRESSIONE COSTANTE
CORPO PRINCIPALE CONTIENE IL GAS
CONTRAEREA
IL PONTE DI COMANDO È DIVISO SU PIU' LIVELLI ED È DOTATO DI 4 TORRETTE RETRAIBILI DOTATE DI BATTERIE ANTIAEREE...
CORPI SECONDARI HANNO LA STESSA FUNZIONE
MATTEO PIANA 2002

Schematics for the Nemo attack ships.

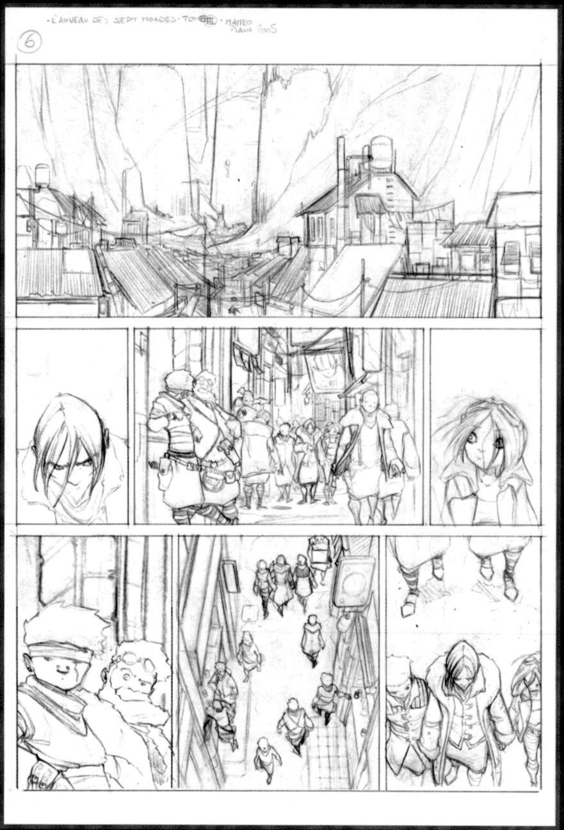
6
L'ANNEAU DES SEPT MONDES - TOME III - MATTEO PIANA 2005
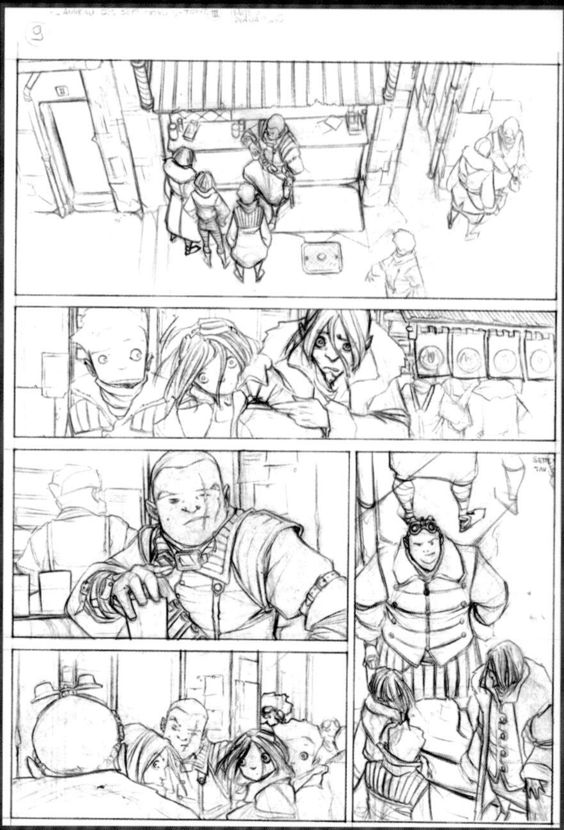
9
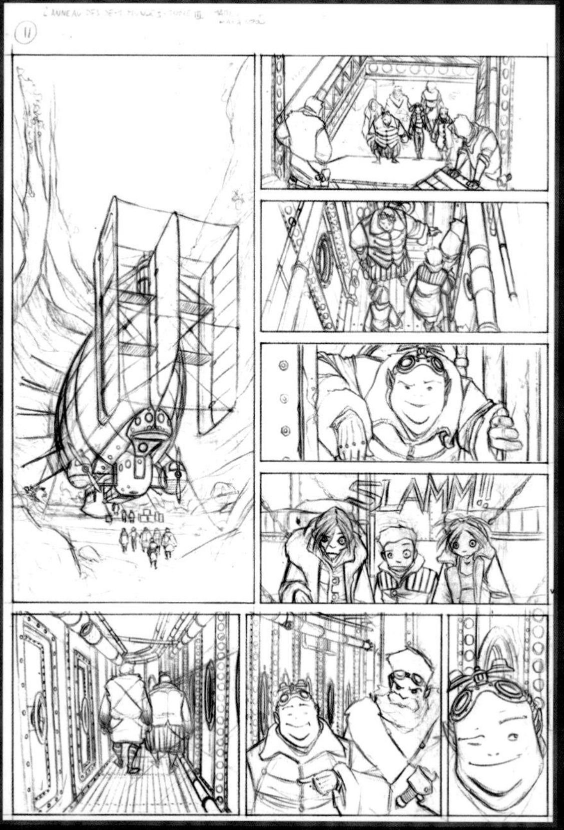
11
SLAMM!!
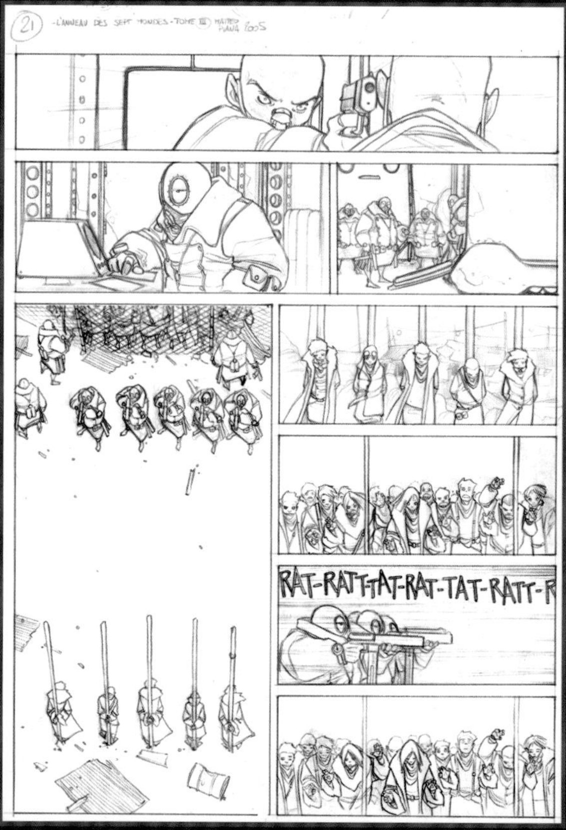
21
RAT-RATT-TAT-RAT-TAT-RATT-R

Pencils for pages 118, 121, 123, and 133.

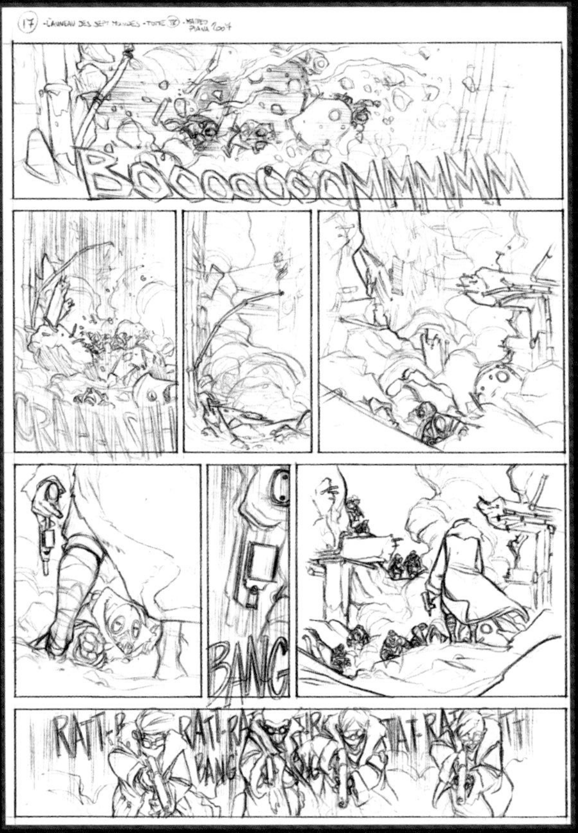
BANG

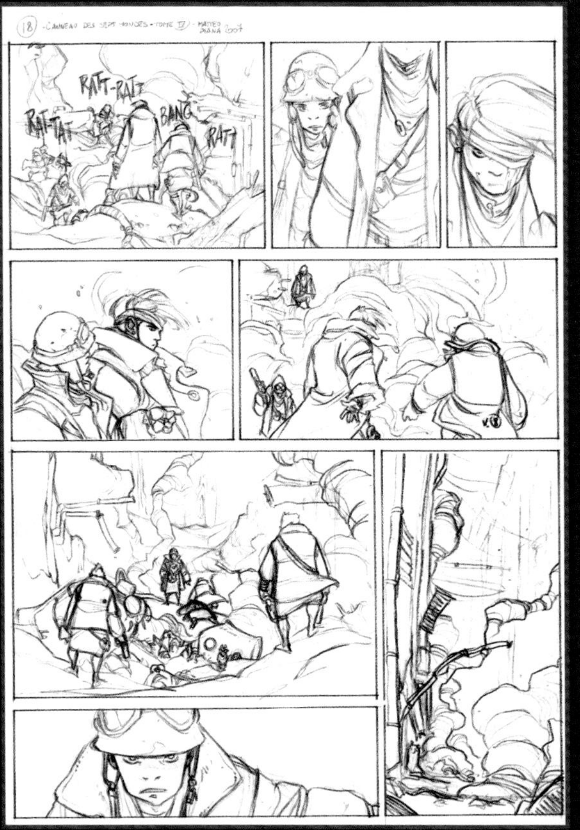
RATT-RATT
RATT-TAT
BANG
RATT

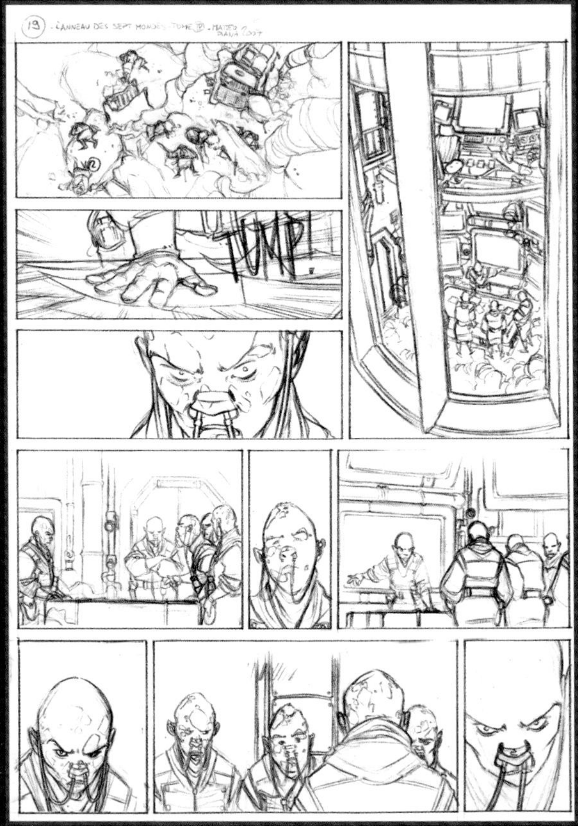
TUMP!

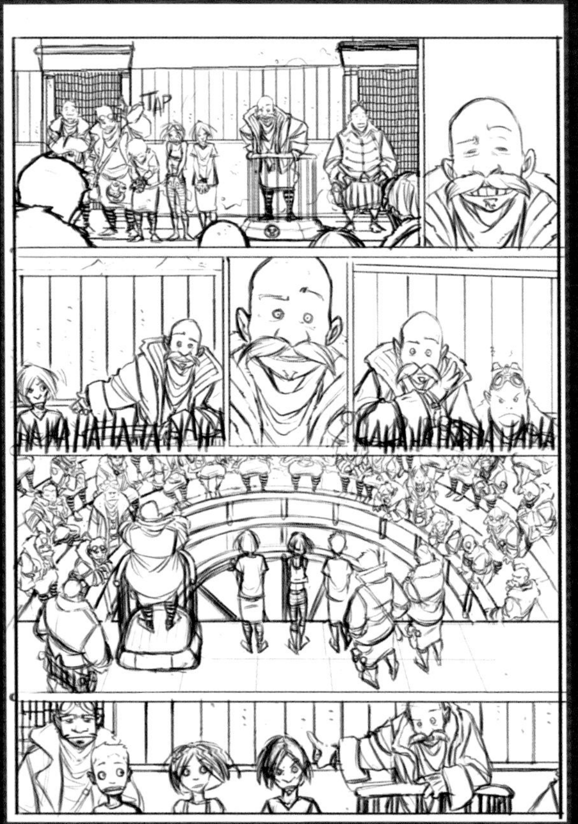
TAP

Pencils for pages 178, 179, 180, and 182.

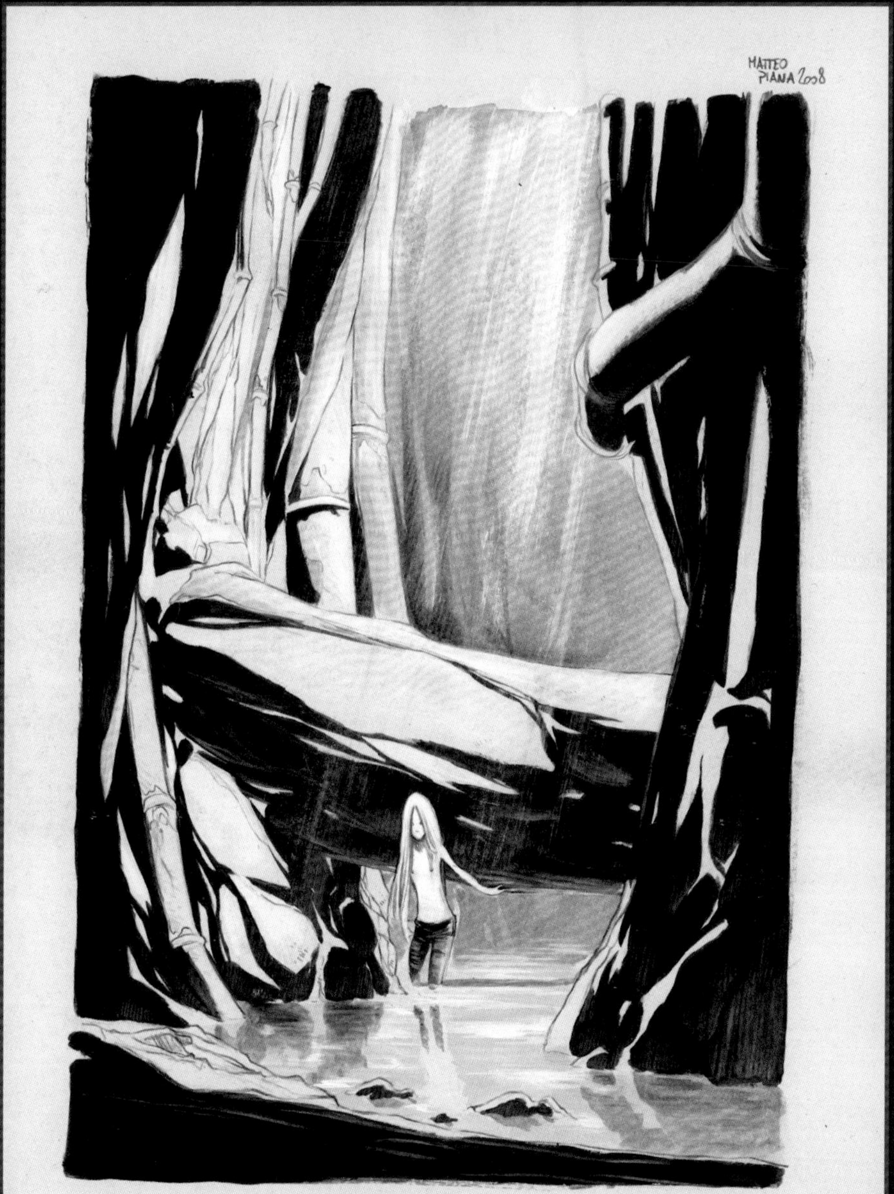
MATTEO PIANA 2008
- L U L E N E -

Pencil and watercolor illustration of Lulene.